EXTINCTION
AND
THE CLOUD

Ray Hammond is a novelist, dramatist and non-fiction author. He is also a futurologist who lectures on future social and business trends for universities, corporations and governments. He lives in London and can be found on the web at www.rayhammond.com.

Also by Ray Hammond

EMERGENCE

EXTINCTION

AND

THE CLOUD

RAY HAMMOND

PAN BOOKS

Extinction first published 2005 by Macmillan
This edition published 2005 by Pan Books
The Cloud first published 2006 by Pan Books

This omnibus first published 2008 by Pan Books
an imprint of Pan Macmillan Ltd
Pan Macmillan, 20 New Wharf Road, London N1 9RR
Basingstoke and Oxford
Associated companies throughout the world
www.panmacmillan.com

ISBN 978-0-330-50792-9

1 3 5 7 9 8 6 4 2

A CIP catalogue record for this book is available from
the British Library.

Typeset by IntypeLibra
Printed in the UK by CPI Mackays, Chatham ME5 8TD

ACKNOWLEDGEMENTS

During my research in Samoa and other islands threatened by the rising seas I was greeted with real warmth and affection by people whose very lives and ways of living are being put at risk by our reckless disregard for this planet, our common home. Their generosity, tolerance and understanding shames those of us who live in a 'developed' society.

For technical input and advice (which I didn't *always* take) I'm grateful to Simon Eccles, Allan W. Eckert (Author of *The Hab Theory* and many other wonderful books) and Dr Bruno Stanek of Astrosoftware. Gillian Redfearn also provided an invaluable service by checking my manuscript for continuity and pushing me to clarify some of my more complex pieces of scientific speculation.

Considerable thanks are also due to my editor Peter Lavery for his patience and encouragement, to my agent Mic Cheetham for her understanding and to her associate Simon Kavanagh for his enthusiasm and *joie de vivre*. I am also very grateful to Nick Austin for his usual meticulous copy editing and script preparation.

Finally, my thanks go, as always, to Liz Hammond for her patient, diligent and intelligent reading of my many drafts.

ONE

May, 2055

A line of ships darkened the horizon. But it wasn't a convoy; they were too close together for that.

As the helicopter approached the floating mass, the pilot pulled on his collective control to gain altitude. The aircraft ascended and now the passengers could see that the ships in the stationary caravan were chained together, bow to stern.

'Go higher,' shouted the sergeant. 'They might open fire.'

The pilot again lifted the collective control and the big United Nations Sikorsky rose another 1,000 feet through the cold air. Now they could see that the line of vessels was merely the edge of a vast floating platform. They already knew it consisted of countless hulks chained, roped and lashed together to form a huge island of rusty metal. Decommissioned oil tankers, bulk carriers and container ships – all streaked with corrosion, some showing evidence of collision or old shell damage – had been linked to each other, creating a hinged carpet of groaning steel floating on the surface of the ocean. Even from their increased altitude of over 2,000 feet it was impossible to make out the vast platform's far edge.

'Jesus, will you look at the size of that thing!' exclaimed Michael Fairfax from his window seat behind the pilot.

'Let's fly a circuit,' suggested the sergeant over the headset intercom, pointing to his left.

The helicopter banked and, careful to remain just out of the potential range of small-arms fire, the pilot began to fly around the eastern edge of this hulk leviathan.

They were almost at the bottom of the world, in the Southern Ocean, 1,500 miles south-east of New Zealand, having been forced to wait in Auckland for six days before a suitable break in the vicious May weather had occurred. This close to the Antarctic the autumn storms could continue for weeks on end and the conditions here did not benefit from any of the climate-management techniques that were now routinely applied to the wealthier regions of the planet.

'It's about thirty miles wide,' said the sergeant, twisting around from the co-pilot's seat to address their only passenger. 'And about the same in length. It'll take us an hour to go all the way round it.'

Michael nodded, then lifted the powerful image-recording binoculars he had brought with him from San Francisco. Adjusting the barrels to fit his eyes, he zoomed in and frowned as the image was electronically stabilized.

The entire visible surface of the giant platform seemed covered in sepia dots – like some old half-tone newspaper image. Then Michael realized that he was looking down at countless brown, cream and yellow faces, crowded together like mushrooms on a dark woodland floor. All of them were upturned towards the beating rotor blades.

Further in, he saw the bright flash of welding arcs as men worked on the old ships and, to his surprise, he saw propeller wakes streaming from a few of the ships at the outer edge of the platform; he had previously understood that none of these hulks retained any engine power. In the far distance, an inner section of the vast hinged platform rose on a giant swell that travelled slowly underneath the whole steel city, lifting twenty or thirty of the huge vessels at a time.

In the front co-pilot's seat, the sergeant – a volunteer seconded to the UN from New Zealand's special forces – kept his own field glasses trained on the scene, scouring the huddled masses for any trace of a shoulder-mounted rocket launcher or other missile-firing system. It was what visitors to these drifting metropolises dreaded most. Even though their passenger today was due to be welcomed by the hulk community's leaders – and despite the Sikorsky's clear UN markings and seven-ton cargo of much-needed food aid and medical supplies – there would still be some who might be tempted to vent their anger and frustration on these representatives of the rich world.

Michael lowered his binoculars from the scene of dispossessed humanity. Despite appearances, the multitudes of environmental refugees on board this hulk city – and the millions more who were forced to live on other, similar, groaning platforms of despair – were the most potentially valuable group of clients that Michael Fairfax's legal firm had ever had the chance to represent. A growing cultural awareness of the immense wrongs that had been inflicted on them by governments and the multinational corporations promised that.

Once again he lifted his field glasses to scan the far edge of *Pacifica One*, as this particular floating refuge had been dubbed by the media.

The day was sullenly overcast and he glimpsed lightning illuminating the interior of grey clouds on the far side of the artificial island. Here and there, light was reflected from golden minarets, crosses, spires and cupolas that the faithful had erected over makeshift mosques, churches, temples and other places of worship. From all across the undulating metal raft, narrow columns of smoke rose into the air; thousands were cooking their midday meals on open fires.

'Task force at ten o'clock,' observed the sergeant. He had now retrained his binoculars in the opposite direction, towards the east. Michael followed his gaze and saw an old-fashioned aircraft carrier and half a dozen grey warships cruising slowly in the far distance. As if on cue, the radio crackled into life. The pilot pressed his transmit button to confirm their aircraft's call sign and flight plan.

'The USS *Vincent* and support vessels from the … Australian … Japanese and … British navies,' the sergeant called out to Michael as he identified the ships' markings one by one. 'They just steam round and round these hulks to make sure they don't try to break out and head across the Pacific – they block any who try.'

'Worst posting in the world,' added the pilot as they left the naval force behind.

Michael turned his attention back to the drifting city and noticed a large, irregularly shaped white mass floating a few hundred yards off the platform's perimeter.

'Looks like an iceberg,' he observed. 'Isn't that a hazard for the outer vessels?'

'They collect them,' explained the sergeant. 'It's their only source of fresh water – other than any rainfall that accidentally comes their way. They set off in tenders to get a line on to one of the smaller bergs, then tow it back and secure it to the main platform.'

Michael nodded and tapped out a brief note to himself on his communicator. He could now see six or seven other icebergs tethered around the hulk city's extensive perimeter. Lashed to one of them was the upturned and disembowelled carcass of a whale; it seemed that the icebergs also served as floating refrigerators.

'There are often skirmishes about fresh water between those who live in the middle of the city and those around the edge who have better access to icebergs,' added the sergeant. 'It can sometimes get very bloody down there.'

Suddenly a loud, clanging alarm filled the cockpit.

'Incoming!' shouted the pilot, banking the aircraft violently to the left. Michael felt a double *whump* as decoy flares and missile-killers were fired from the rear tubes of the chopper's defence system.

The aircraft dropped through the air, as if thrust downwards by a giant hand. Michael saw the pilot wrestling to maintain control as he carried out an emergency descent, and then there was a sudden explosion high overhead as the surface-to-air missile was detonated by one of the defence systems.

Now flying at full power only 200 feet above the waves, the pilot levelled off and scanned his display screens for any further missile signatures.

'Not a very nice welcome,' he said over the intercom, once it became clear that no further SAMs had been fired.

'It's become almost traditional.' The sergeant shook his head. 'That'll be some headstrong kid with an itchy trigger finger.'

They regained altitude and flew on, now two kilometres

further out from the edge of the metal island. Minutes later they noticed a separate and smaller raft, also composed of ship hulks, which was loosely attached to the central mass by scores of ropes and chains. The surface of this platform was quilted with rectangular patches of green, yellow, white and brown.

'That's one of their marine farms,' explained the sergeant. 'They collect topsoil from spots in Antarctica where the ice has melted and then bring it here to grow some crops of their own.'

Michael noticed that four rope bridges had been rigged between the main platform and the floating farmlands; each was lined with tiny figures who had ceased their scurrying to and fro in order to stare skywards

'Why do they keep those farm-ships separate?' he asked.

'So they can untie them and tow them towards any convenient rainfall,' his security escort replied. 'They've got a couple of working tugs which can pull these floating farms hundreds of miles out in search of rain. Judging by the activity down there, it must be harvest time for one of their crops.'

'So they're self-sufficient?'

'Each ship also maintains its own fish farm,' said the sergeant. 'They get by, just about.'

After they had completed a full circumference of the artificial island, they followed the navigational instructions that would supposedly provide them with a safe flight path to land on this metal landscape. Turning inwards, they flew at a level 2,000 feet for fifteen minutes. Michael noticed more welding activity, and more propeller wakes churning deep between the endless rows of lashed-together ships. There seemed to be an air of intense activity everywhere.

Finally they executed a defensive descent – rapid and almost vertical – towards the white-painted deck of an ancient crude-oil mega-tanker situated at the very centre of the ferrous settlement.

It seemed that this particular outsize vessel served as the community's heliport, communications centre, hospital and administrative headquarters, all combined. It extended for a quarter of a mile, had a bridge 200 feet high, and was the only giant carrier in the whole floating platform that was not covered with makeshift dwellings. It also seemed as if the former *Prince*

Sahid was the only ship in its vicinity to have seen a coat of fresh paint recently.

Descending onto its cold, wind-scoured deck, Michael was greeted by the three leaders of the community's ruling council: Rattin Alix, Hoy Soon Juan and Chanda Zia, originally from the Seychelles, the Philippines and Bangladesh respectively – all lands now lost to the risen seas.

Ringed in a distant circle around the perimeter of the flight deck were at least 200 young men, all of them carrying some sort of semi-automatic weapon. Unlike the official greeting party, their attitude did not seem particularly friendly.

'Welcome – *namaste*,' intoned Chanda Zia, pressing his hands together in front of his face, lifting them to his forehead and then bowing deeply. The council leader was wearing a white brimless hat and an old grey Nehru suit.

'*Namaste*,' responded their exotic visitor – a tall white lawyer from the rich world over the horizon, a man who claimed he could provide help to these stateless and status-less unwanted people. Counsellor Michael Fairfax's visit to this hulk city had been set up only through a process of careful and prolonged negotiation by *Médecins Sans Frontières*, the global medical charity, with logistical support provided by the local UN office in Auckland.

The sergeant pulled two large flight cases from a baggage compartment in the helicopter's deep hull as a dozen of the waiting men rushed forward to begin unloading the main cargo of aid and supplies. Then the visitors were quickly escorted to what must have at one time been the captain's stateroom.

'For you,' announced Michael, nodding towards the metal flight cases that the sergeant was placing carefully on an old dining table. The lawyer stepped forward, snapped open the clasps and lifted each lid in turn.

He was presenting the refugee community with a state-of-the-art, solar-powered, global-coverage satellite communications system: all multi-sensory, all ultraband, complete with twenty miniature all-weather cameras linked by a local-area wireless network.

The council members gathered around with interest, lifting

out components of the sophisticated communications network
and turning them over in their hands.

'This technology is essential because I'll need to keep in
touch with you as our case progresses,' explained Michael, as his
hosts examined the rugged communications equipment. 'I will
also need each of you to sign these agreements,' he continued,
unfolding two formal documents and placing them on the well-
used table.

The three men scrutinized the papers carefully. The first was
the crucial document of appointment, a contract giving Michael's
firm exclusive rights to the refugees' compensation case. The
second was a legal writ. With the lawyer's help, Chanda Zia
translated the key passages for the benefit of his colleagues.

'I'll need to apply for special permission to put your claim
before the court,' Michael explained. 'Normally they'll only hear
requests brought by citizens of recognized nation states, but I
intend to argue that your community here deserves to qualify as
a nation. There certainly seem to be enough of you in terms of
numbers.'

Chanda nodded and quickly bent to add his signature to
each document. After a brief discussion, the others also signed
their names painstakingly.

When the sergeant had witnessed the signatures, Michael
refolded the documents and carefully returned them to an inside
pocket. His face remained impassive but he had just secured the
right to represent what was likely to become the largest civil
case for compensation in all legal history.

Michael now had the opportunity to try and improve the
lives of millions of the world's poorest inhabitants – human
detritus referred to by the more fortunate as 'environmental
refugees' – people who had been forced to flee their former
homes because of flood, drought or famine. But the member
states of the United Nations still refused to grant these masses
any rights to asylum, rights from which so-called 'political'
emigrants benefited automatically. These refugees, all victims of
extreme global warming, were the 'unofficials' that no nation
was prepared to welcome onto its shores.

The business transaction now completed, Michael's new

clients led their legal representative out to begin his tour of
inspection.

In blustery wet winds that failed to deliver sufficient rainfall
to be usefully collected, he was led across a succession of slippery
gangplanks and up and down treacherous ladders as they crossed
from one groaning hull to another. Michael's sub-miniature lapel
cameras captured everything he witnessed.

Each huge deck seemed to be crammed with its own ragged
population, their driftwood huts interspersed with pitched tents
between which tattered washing flapped and billowed wildly.
Everywhere mangy goats and chickens ran about amidst this
makeshift accommodation, nibbling and pecking at any available
scraps.

Whole tenements had also been built beneath the main
decks. Inside a former petroleum tanker, Michael bent his lanky
frame, entered a low corridor and emerged into a main hold to
find that layer upon layer of dark and airless accommodation
had been constructed within its cavernous expanse.

Endless rows of cubicles, made from wood, cardboard, fabric
and waste plastic, were strewn with pallets on which lay a
sighing, moaning, coughing mass of bodies that could not or
would not be coaxed up into the topside cold to meet their
important visitor. Michael noticed several television sets dotted
incongruously about, all tuned to satellite channels and all
powered by a single sputtering generator. When Chanda asked
if he would like to penetrate still deeper into this stinking
labyrinth, the lawyer declined politely, forcing himself not to gag
on the stench.

Everywhere he visited, he was struck by the silence of the
hordes who gathered to watch their progress. The men stood,
sullen and mute, some armed with knives or ancient automatic
weapons, just staring at this interloper from the rich civilization
over the horizon. Though simply dressed in navy sweater and
jeans, his thick brown hair covered by an old woollen hat,
Michael was aware that his shining whiteness alone marked him
out as belonging unmistakably to that other world.

At each pause he was announced to them in their own
language as the American attorney who intended to fight for

their rights to official refugee status, for their unhindered rights of passage across the seas in search of better weather conditions, and eventually for the basic entitlements of immigration and resettlement. But, equally importantly, he aimed to win for them all some financial compensation for what they had suffered at the hands of the giant energy corporations.

But after three hours of exhausting progress, he realized that all he was hearing in return were the dreams they harboured of finding sanctuary in his own rich, unflooded, well-fed world. It seemed that these people didn't want to fight global capitalism; they merely wanted to join it.

'United States? We go to United States – America.'

'England, please.'

'Canada, my brother is there.'

'Please, Germany – I have friends to live with. I work hard.'

Only one person, a short, teak-coloured man in early middle age, raised an alternative subject. 'We need rain, proper rainfall,' he insisted. Michael caught the trace of a Western education in his voice.

'I have already arranged some real rainfall,' he announced loudly, 'though not as much as I'd have liked. You can expect to see a Volume Two precipitation here for approximately seventy minutes next Tuesday afternoon, starting at oh-two-hundred GMT. And that comes with the compliments of my law firm – Gravitz, Lee and Kraus, of San Francisco.'

The little man smiled, then turned to translate this news to others. Amid further smiles, a single hand waved an acknowledgement of thanks. The visitor wondered what their religious leaders must make of a world where rain could only be guaranteed to fall in any quantity after prior payment had been made to some invisible extraterrestrial controlling force.

'And we also need that diesel fuel,' said Chanda quietly in Michael's ear. 'For our main generators.'

The lawyer nodded. He had been given a list of his clients' requests over one of their old-fashioned voice-only satellite phones before he came here, but it had proved difficult to find a tanker company willing to deliver fuel to the 'hulk people' of the Southern Ocean.

'It's on schedule, Mr Zia,' he told his client. 'Arriving Friday, as agreed.'

Chanda smiled, then pressed his hands together in thanks and bowed.

Although Michael's tour took over four hours, he estimated that he had visited only twelve or fifteen vessels. But he knew that there were over 900 hulks of varying sizes lashed together in this one floating community alone. And he also knew there were four other similar hulk nations of the environmentally dispossessed scattered across – but tightly corralled within – the angry seas of the unpopulated southern latitudes.

'How many people do you reckon live here altogether?' he asked Chanda Zia.

'We can't be sure, Mr Fairfax,' said his guide, after a short silence. 'We tried to do a proper count last year, but with over sixty languages, a dozen religions, and ships arriving every month...' He tailed off, then hazarded, 'At least three-quarters of a million.'

Financial Times

Tuesday, 23 May 2055

INSURERS DIVERT TYPHOON AWAY FROM JAKARTA

A group of Western insurance companies led by Zurich Indemnity, has contracted directly with the ERGIA Climate Management Corporation to provide atmospheric energy to steer a Category 5 typhoon away from Jakarta. It was forecast that the storm would have made landfall on the outskirts of the capital within the next 72 hours.

The insurers' intervention follows the Indonesian government's refusal last year to pay increased charges for annual climate management and typhoon control.

TWO

Champagne does not fizz in space, so Perdy Curtis shook her ball-valve plastic glass vigorously up and down in the hope of producing some bubbles. But, despite her efforts, when she pushed the spring-loaded ball down into the glass with her little finger, nothing happened. She frowned and shook the glass again.

As a television producer, Perdy was an interloper into what was an otherwise exclusive briefing for almost eighty of the world's most influential stock-market analysts. They were being ferried in four separate shuttles up to the ERGIA Climate Control Space Station where it sat in a permanently maintained deep orbit, 66,000 kilometres above the Earth. The occasion for this visit was the company's announcement of a new natural energy resource and of its plans to float shares in this new service on the world's stock markets.

Despite her respected position within the BBC and the wider broadcasting community, it had been Perdy's first trip into space and when Narinda Damle, her executive producer in London, had arranged for Perdy's participation in this exclusive financiers' junket she had been quietly delighted.

At thirty-two she seemed to have been the only space virgin remaining amongst her many high-flying media friends. And in the year 2055 – the age of so-called 'walk-on, walk-off' space travel – that was not something to boast about.

Their ferry ride into orbit had been short but exhilarating. It had taken the hybrid rocket-plane just eight minutes to escape the Earth's atmosphere and although many of her fellow passengers had exhibited an air of cultivated boredom at the mundane routine of going into space, Perdy had not tried to disguise her own curiosity and sense of wonder.

The analysts and fund managers joining this trip had been invited to visit the largest of the world's weather-control space stations, and Perdy had joined the group to assist her research for a forthcoming documentary, a co-financed BBC-MSN production called 'Nice Weather We're Having – 25 Years of Global Climate Management'. It was scheduled to air worldwide in six months' time, to mark the quarter-century since Mankind first took control of the planet's weather and began to manage away the worst effects of global warming.

As they approached their destination Perdy could not help but exclaim, 'My God! That's quite *something*.'

Framed in the small triple-layered window beside her was a giant silver object that seemed to hang in space. It looked just like a chrome-plated windmill.

'That's the ERGIA space station – where we're headed.' The man seated next to her was an investment banker from Morgan-Stanley New York. 'Those fan blades are directional mirrors reflecting sunlight back down to Earth.'

Perdy thought she had never seen anything more beautiful. The giant fan hung absolutely stationary in the night sky – a shining man-made jewel against the backdrop of a billion stars. She had only ever seen this 'night-sun' from Earth, of course, and from such a distance she had never been able to make out its precise shape.

As their orbital ferry approached the space station, Perdy realized that she had seriously underestimated the size of the ERGIA control centre. She glanced down at the information the investor-relations staff had provided to the guests.

The diameter of the solar reflectors from tip to tip is almost twenty miles, while the central hub of the space station is a triple-skinned titanium sphere over 900 feet wide. It carries a permanent staff of sixty-five, with accommodation for up to 100 visitors. In Earth's gravity, the space station would weigh 245,000 tons.

For the next five minutes the ferry edged its way through the final 300 metres of computer-controlled slow manoeuvring and, as Perdy watched – now glued again to her window – the hub of the space station came to seem like a huge hemispherical building. It was certainly as high as any of the towers in downtown London or Manhattan.

Finally they felt a series of shudders as the space station grasped the ferry and locked it into the main docking hold alongside four other passenger transports. All around them, numerous smaller shuttles and escape craft also sat in the vast docking bay at the base of the space-station hub.

Their one-hour tour of the ERGIA control centre was packed with information. Perdy had already read a lot about the company's climate-management systems, but it was not until she actually witnessed exactly how entire regions of the Earth's weather were controlled and directed that she fully understood just how impressive this achievement was. By reflecting concentrated sunlight onto the upper atmosphere, the ERGIA Corporation and its competitors could change the temperature and altitude of the stratospheric winds. This allowed whole weather systems to be seeded, grown, aborted, directed or dispersed. Perdy recorded everything she was shown with her personal micro-cams.

Each visitor was given a pair of Velcro-soled overshoes to wear throughout their visit, and guides escorted them in separate groups of twenty to visit the living accommodation, the extensive gym and leisure facilities, the canteen, the computer centre and, last but not least, the main weather-control centre and its famous viewing gallery.

'The trick is not to raise one foot until the other is securely grounded again,' their guide reminded them, as the doors to the viewing gallery rose to admit them. 'And please hold firmly onto the handrails at all times.'

As the party carefully foot-sucked its way into the main observation centre, they were confronted by a huge panoramic viewing window, in which their home planet hung suspended like a giant three-dimensional Imax image.

The concave window pane was a one-hundred-feet-high

sheet of thick, armoured cerami-glass which, despite its perfect transparency, was proof against all radiation, space dust and even sizeable particles of stray space debris. The vast expanse of glass stretched from side to side for a distance almost three times its height, making the observation chamber itself seem like a giant floating aquarium.

Behind the visitors, the men and women busy controlling the climate on the planet down below were seated in an amphi-theatre of steeply tiered rows of workstations, so that each one of them had a clear view of the blue and white planet Earth and its beautiful swirling weather patterns. The space station itself, the visitors were informed, was currently positioned precisely above the day–night meridian.

'I've got a bid of eleven million dollars for a one-hour Volume Six rain storm in Marrakesh,' yelled one of the controllers suddenly.

'I've got thirteen million two for that precipitation – if we can send it on to Cairo,' called another.

Another shout announced a further bid from Marrakesh. The next voice asked if anyone had two hours of late-night sunshine available, for a film shoot in Seattle which had overrun on its schedule.

'If you could make your way up to those spare seats above – ' the tour guide pointed ' – we can begin the presentation.'

As she took her seat, Perdy found another glass of cham-pagne at her elbow. She had now got the hang of the ball-valve mechanism. The trick was to just touch the ball with the tip of your nose while sucking the champagne up through the built-in straw.

'May I have your attention, ladies and gentlemen?'

As the room quietened, the cosseted visitors – collectively advisers to funds with over $118 trillion under investment – turned their attention towards the podium positioned in front of the vast viewing window. A sharply suited woman with a short haircut was holding up her hand to gain their attention.

'Well, we have now come to the main purpose of your visit with us today,' she continued. 'Please join me in welcoming the president of the ERGIA Corporation, Mr Nicholas Negromonte.'

The clapping was necessarily subdued because many of the bankers were still holding their glasses of champagne. Others were busy adjusting cameras and personal information systems to record or to relay this event down to ERGIA-approved colleagues on the ground.

The world-famous entrepreneur bounded onto the stage, waving cheerfully. Everybody in this audience felt that they knew him personally, simply because his face appeared so often in the media. Apart from his celebrated business activities, he was a keen pilot of vintage airplanes and spacecraft and in his youth he had pursued a career as a junior tennis champion – until his older brother had been killed in a terrorist incident and Nicholas Negromonte had retrained to take over the family-run business.

'Welcome aboard, everybody,' he said, grinning widely. 'Today it is my pleasure to give you a private preview of the latest and most powerful of our company's climate-management resources. Over the past three years we have been building a new solar-energy resource on the moon that we call LunaSun.'

He paused to underline the significance of this announcement.

'Very soon I hope that you and your colleagues will react with enthusiasm to our first public offering of shares. We plan to bring LunaSun to market at the beginning of October this year.'

Negromonte gazed keenly around the faces of this group of influential banking analysts. Their recommendations would decide the fate of his company's share offer.

'OK. Let's roll the video,' he said, stepping off stage. As the room darkened, the huge viewing window transformed itself into a 3-D screen.

The opening clip revealed the moon as seen from an approaching spacecraft, then the action cut to a massive building site being created on the lunar surface. Using time-elapsed photography, the video then followed the construction of a vast array of solar reflectors that had been installed successively on the moon's barren terrain.

As a reverential voice-over reminded them, the United

Nations had granted the ERGIA Corporation a unique licence to utilize a tract of the Earth-facing lunar surface for solar capture. As a result, 2,600 square miles on either side of the moon's equator had in recent months been covered with over 42,000 high-luminosity, self-cleaning, self-repairing, curved mirrors that could be individually directed and angled towards different sections of the Earth, each by its own set of solar-powered servo motors.

The moon was the latest, and by far the largest, solar-reflector project to be developed by the ERGIA Corporation and, although not yet fully on-line, it had already become the most powerful light source to shine in the night-time sky – a nocturnal sun that would soon quietly adjust atmospheric temperatures, disperse clouds and provide light and heat precisely where it was required, playing its part in the ongoing battle to keep global warming in check while simultaneously providing the world with low-cost, low-intensity energy.

This newly equipped moon still went through its primeval phases, of course – from new moon, to full, to waning crescent – but in each part of the visible lunar cycle it now shone in the sky like a celestial halogen lamp. By day it was like a small sibling of the sun; by night it became the burning centrepiece in a string of fairy-light reflectors that, to the fury of Earth-bound stargazers, now outshone the natural stars in the night sky and made ground-based astronomy almost impossible around heavily populated areas.

Then the presentation switched to a live link. TV cameras were sending signals back from the company's main administration building – a ten-acre extension to Luna City, the international moon colony that had been growing rapidly over the last twenty years.

As the commentator reminded them, focused heat from geostationary reflectors in lunar orbit not only provided a warm environment inside the human settlement but had also melted a small part of the moon's buried polar ice reserves to provide the colonists with a plentiful supply of fresh water.

The finale of the telecast presentation showed off-duty engineers and support staff diving into LunaSun's indoor swimming pool, a facility constructed inside a small impact crater and filled with melted polar ice. Then the video faded to black, and the large screen resumed its function as a viewing window.

The hub of the space station had rotated meanwhile, and now they were suspended over the dark side of their home planet. The moon itself was in view in the distance, shining full.

As they watched, it seemed as though someone had suddenly set fire to that lump of lifeless rock; the visitors were dazzled as all the mirrors on the lunar surface turned in unison to reflect the sun's rays directly towards the space station. Then, just as suddenly, the reflectors were redirected away and, blinking, the audience once again adjusted their eyes to the dim light of the viewing gallery.

Someone then started to clap and necks craned all around as others sought to identify what had prompted this applause. Then, as more joined in, Perdy saw what had caught their attention.

Right in the middle of the dark mass of the Indian Ocean, far below, shone a bright light reflected onto the Earth's night-time surface by the solar mirrors up on the moon. The image it formed was the encircled E of the ERGIA corporate logo.

Very smart, Perdy thought, as she too joined in the applause. She ran her fingers through her short, blonde-highlighted hair as she wondered just how bright and how extensive that image of light on the water must be for them to be able see it from 66,000 kilometres up.

The guide was now ushering the visitors down to stand by the viewing window themselves, for a better vantage point. Though Perdy found herself standing at the back of the throng, she was quite tall and could still see clearly. She marvelled again at the sleeping Earth laid out below her, then gazed up at the moon which once again appeared no brighter than normal.

'I hear you're making a film about us, Perdita?' said a quiet, deep voice at her shoulder.

The BBC producer turned to find Nicholas Negromonte at her side. She was almost as tall as him but she was surprised at how muscular he seemed close up; he seemed to radiate an aura of fitness. His dark, wavy hair almost glowed.

'Most people call me Perdy,' she told him smilingly. 'And thanks for letting me tag along today. It's been very informative.'

'Would you like to visit the moon for yourself, Perdy?' asked Negromonte, glancing back at the lunar surface. 'I have to visit the LunaSun facilities again in a couple of weeks. So if the BBC would like to come along...'

Before she could answer there was a sudden deafening roar. The lights in the viewing gallery flicked out and Perdy felt the floor under her feet begin to move. Like everybody else's, her soles had been stuck to the suction carpet, but she suddenly found herself shaken loose and catapulted up towards the lofty ceiling.

Her head struck metal and she instantly lost consciousness.

THREE

Two days after visiting the hulk community, Michael Fairfax was 3,000 miles further north, thirty degrees of latitude closer to the equator, and in a considerably kinder climate.

He had broken his journey home to stop over in the island republic of Independent Samoa, in the naturally balmy South Pacific.

But he wasn't visiting for rest and recreation; tourists no longer visited these islands. The rising oceans had spared few of the nation's beaches, the formerly idyllic weather had become far too unpredictable, and the local crime rate was now notoriously high.

As he turned his face away from the setting sun, Michael noticed some graffiti daubed in faded green paint across a large boulder embedded in the sand, just where the eroded beach finished and the treeline began.

FUCK CLIMATE CONTROL

He turned to Mautoatasi Otasi, his host, and pointed out the scrawled protest. 'Do many of your people feel like that?'

'Most of them,' acknowledged the elderly prime minister sadly.

Samoa had never been a rich nation but in the late twentieth century this group of islands had evolved into a vacation paradise, favoured by those who preferred natural beauty and unsophisticated living to high-rise hotels, crowded swimming pools and neon-lit casinos.

However, over the last fifty years the terrible effects of global warming had swallowed nearly all of the beaches, and the rising seas had also contaminated most of the islands' scant groundwater reserves. That had been the beginning of the end for the country's short-lived tourist boom, and now this remote nation was almost wholly unvisited and its coastal inhabitants had been driven from their homelands.

'Well, we'd better be getting back,' said the prime minister, heaving a sigh. They had spent much of the afternoon inspecting the denuded coastline where those beautiful beaches had been, where the villages had once thrived. Throughout, Michael had been assiduously recording data and images to substantiate his forthcoming legal case against the world's major energy corporations.

Lost in their own thoughts, the two men threaded their way back through an abandoned village to where a ministerial assistant was waiting for them with the official car – and a well-armed security escort. Neither man seemed to notice that the surrounding woodland was unnaturally, claustrophobically mute, the air heavy as if the island was holding its breath.

By the time they reached the narrow dirt road it was almost dark. On this cloud-free evening the full moon seemed enormous and, to eyes more used to northern latitudes, unbelievably close. The stars had started to create a jewelled canopy that Michael now knew from experience would develop quickly into a vast and startling sweep of stellar luminescence. He thought how much Matthew, his thirteen-year-old son and a keen amateur astronomer, would have enjoyed being here now.

Then the hydrogen-powered limo and its small military escort was on its way back to the capital, returning the Samoan government's important guest to Aggie Gray's Hotel in Āpia, the one fully functioning hostelry remaining on the island.

Once in his room, Michael checked that his system had dealt correctly with all of the day's texts, e-mails, voice calls and other forms of electronic communication. Then he spent fifteen minutes talking to his two sons back home in California. As he closed the connection he was suddenly overcome by a sense of profound loneliness.

He sighed and shrugged off such feelings. In less than twenty-four hours he would be flying home to San Francisco, the city in which he had been born, the city that was still his home and was also home to his ex-wife and two children. He realized he was still missing Lucy.

Picking up a remote control from the bedside table he flicked on the wall-mounted viewing panel.

Instantly filling the screen was an image of what looked like a mangled child's toy, and Michael frowned as he tried to work out what it was. Then a news caption appeared.

ERGIA SPACE STATION EXPLOSION
ECO-TERRORISTS SUSPECTED

'US, European and Chinese rescue craft are now on their way to the ERGIA Space Station to aid survivors of a blast that occurred at seventeen-fifty-four GMT today, Wednesday,' a newsreader's voice announced over the image. 'The explosion damaged the docking bay and outer hull, but so far there are no reports of fatalities. The ERGIA control centre has been blown out of orbital alignment, however, and the station's delicate solar reflectors have been severely damaged.'

Michael could clearly see the damage to the long extensions radiating from the hub of the space station; it now looked like a child's plastic whirligig that had been scrunched up by a giant hand.

'The FBI Space Crime Unit has been called in to investigate, while ERGIA has announced that, as an emergency measure, all climate management has temporarily been switched to the company's back-up control centre in Los Angeles. Some disruption to scheduled weather patterns in North America is expected for the next several weeks. This morning, ERGIA stock has plunged to an annual low of three dollars and nine cents on the NAS-DAQ market.'

Michael flicked off the screen thoughtfully. ERGIA was top of his hit list for legal action, but he had little doubt that the mighty corporation would be fully covered by its insurers. The question was, how could terrorists yet again have smuggled a bomb into a space station? It was the third such attack in as many years, and each time public outcry had been followed by security reviews and a tightening up of procedures.

After pouring himself a Scotch and ice, he went into the bathroom for a leisurely soak and, with the taps running, undressed slowly. Then he eased his weary body gratefully into deep, warm water.

He was about to embark on the largest, longest, most high-profile and most worthwhile case of his legal career. Following decades of environmental, social and economic abuse by corporations in all corners of the planet, the United Nations, the EU and, most surprisingly, the all-powerful United States had finally ratified a joint agreement to set up a new international judiciary to administer corporate justice. The world's newspapers and business magazines had recently been rife with speculation about the various cases being planned against certain multinational corporations.

After eight months of persuading enough world-class experts to testify in court that global warming had been caused by fossil fuel emissions – and that the major energy companies had fully known this, even as they went on peddling their toxic products – he would soon be announcing his first gigantic legal action. His claim for damages was likely to run into trillions of dollars.

Michael's body was suddenly jerked upwards, then he fell back and banged his head hard against the edge of the bath. A strange ripple travelled up the tub towards his head and the surface of the bath water broke up into little cross-hatched wavelets.

As he sat forward quickly and reached for a towel, the room lights flickered and went off. Then the loud wail of an electronic siren filled the hotel. Outside the bathroom window there was a strange orange glow high in the sky.

Leaping from the bath, Michael ran towards the sliding door and stepped out onto the white-painted wooden balcony. The town seemed unusually dark.

He heard an immense, improbably deep double boom and gazing to one side over the low rooftops of Åpia he saw the mountain in the distance. Gouts of flame were now spouting from its distant summit and streams of glowing red were already tracking down the upper slopes. He felt the frame of the balcony flex alarmingly beneath his feet.

Then Michael could only stand watching in awestruck horror as the ancient lava plug of Mount Māriota was blown high into the night sky, propelled upwards on a completely vertical column of fire.

Wall Street Journal

Thursday, 25 May 2055

HUNDREDS FEARED DEAD AS SAMOAN VOLCANO ERUPTS

GEOHAZARD'S SHARES TUMBLE

Shares in Geohazard Laboratories, Inc. (GEHAZ) crashed to an all-time low of $1.65 on NASDAQ last night following the company's failure to warn that Mount Māriota, Independent Samoa's long-dormant volcano, was imminently due to erupt.

With a force equal to a fifteen-gigaton atomic explosion, the volcano erupted yesterday at 19.41 Western Pacific Time, blowing billions of tons of rocks and lava into the atmosphere. Early reports indicate that hundreds of Samoans living nearby died in the aftermath.

Fires that broke out in the surrounding dense rainforests and across the capital city of Āpia were still raging out of control this morning. Over 4,000 people have been made homeless and the entire island of Upolu is without power or running water.

Mount Māriota is the world's fourteenth major volcanic eruption so far this year.

FOUR

All was blackness. Then, deep down in the core, there was a red pinpoint of light, racing upwards towards the surface.

The ground started to shake and a deep roar rose like the sound of the burning sun. Suddenly the fiery magma was halted, held back by some impenetrable barrier, filling the air with acrid, seething smoke.

From her motorized viewing chair suspended high over the deep holo-projection pit, Dr Emilia Knight nodded to herself in satisfaction. Then she called to her assistant, seated at a nearby workstation.

'That's correct, the lava plug held for almost twelve hours – jump forward now.'

Emilia projected a personal laser display and counted down the seconds. 'Five, four, three, two—'

With a deafening double explosion, a fountain of red-hot magma blasted up in front of their eyes, as if they were looking straight into the exhaust flames of an upended rocket engine.

Emilia slammed her chair's joystick to the right, and her seat raced on its rails around the perimeter of the deep holo-projection silo. She wanted to see down into the heart of the eruption, into the few seconds after the planet's molten interior had punched a hole upwards through its thin crust.

Now arrived on the other side of the virtual volcanic crater, she saw streams of giant rocks and liquefied metals shooting up past her eyes. As hydraulic rams shook the floor and walls of the Simulation Theater, she gazed deeply into the chimney of the volcano that had damaged both her personal scientific reputation and her company's corporate image.

It was the third time this morning that they had run the holo-simulation – even though it was only thirty-six hours since the actual real-life eruption had occurred on Samoa.

Recordings had been collected from over 6,000 sensors located in the region. Using this data Emilia and her team of seismologists and lab assistants had recreated Mount Māriota's devastating cataclysm in perfect detail, in order to examine the event over and over again to see why they had failed to detect the build-up of pressure, and why they had failed to give a warning enabling the local authorities to order an evacuation of the Samoan capital. Over 600 people were now believed to have died because of their failure.

As Senior Risk Assessment Seismologist for the Pacific Region, Emilia Knight had personal responsibility for monitoring seismic activity around Samoa itself. She herself had been on duty, here at Geohazard's US headquarters in Oakland, California, when the volcano had blown so unexpectedly. She was furious; it was the first major seismic event that she had failed to predict during her eight years with the company, and it was the company's first public failure in fourteen years.

Twisting the joystick again, she propelled her viewing chair around the perimeter rail for another 180 degrees; all of the data and the computer analyses were now displayed in a fast-running real-time overlay around the image of the eruption:

Magma exit velocity: 1,440 km per hour (Mach 1)
Plume height: 28 km
Thermal energy: $Eth = V \cdot d \cdot T \cdot K$
$\qquad\qquad\qquad$ (joules, volume, temp., heat)
Energy released: 2×10^{18} joules
Nuclear equivalent: 15 gigatons, approx.
$\qquad\qquad\qquad\quad$ (100,000 times that of the Hiroshima atomic
$\qquad\qquad\qquad\quad$ bomb.)

Emilia wanted to drink in every detail of this catastrophe, to create a *mental* model that would allow her to understand why

MārIota had behaved so differently from all the other volcanoes that she had ever studied.

Although the special effects of noise, sound, movement and smoke had been included in the Simulation Theater's design mainly to help educate and entertain visiting schoolchildren and members of the public, Emilia found these accompaniments to visual computer simulations extremely helpful; they stimulated ideas and thoughts in the scientific mind about what *might* have happened deep within the earth's mantle.

The first phase of the main eruption had lasted over thirteen hours, but now Emilia touched a control on her personal laser screen to pause the computer-generated re-enactment. Immediately, the floor and walls of the theatre's simulation area returned to their resting positions, and powerful extractor fans began to remove the non-toxic smoke that helped to make these simulations hyper-realistic. The background lighting returned to its normal level once more and the activity-status lights over the exit doors switched from red to green.

'It must have been a spontaneous sub-eugeosyncline occurrence,' Emilia pronounced to the room in general. 'Not a chance in hell of us detecting it in advance.'

Stefano Bardini, her assistant, turned away from his workstation to face her. 'Bad luck, Em,' he said sympathetically. 'But there's got to be a first time for everybody.'

'Not on my watch,' snapped Dr Knight. The petite seismologist was known for her own volcanic temper and she thrust herself angrily out of her chair. 'Let's go over the ambient data for three days prior to the event. There must be something we missed.'

A door in the opposite wall of the Seismic Simulation Theater opened and a smartly attired woman entered, followed by a tall, gaunt man in a severe charcoal-grey suit.

Emilia finished entering instructions on her laser screen, then turned to face the new arrivals. Steve Bardini rose and came to stand slightly behind her.

The female visitor was Gloria Fernandez, Geohazard's head of human resources.

'This is Mr Taylor Blane, our new CEO,' said the HR executive by way of introduction. 'Mr Blane, this is Dr Emilia Knight.'

Emilia shook the man's large hand and lifted her head to meet his stern gaze. Then she turned to her assistant, intending to present him to their new boss.

'So what the hell happened in Samoa?' demanded Blane, interrupting her introduction in a deep Texan drawl. 'With all these high-tech toys, how in Christ's name did you guys fail to spot it coming?'

Emilia eyed the lean man up and down; she wasn't used to being spoken to in this way. She even considered ordering him out of her Simulation Theater, then thought better of it.

'We're not sure yet,' she said coldly. 'We're running the data now.'

'Have you seen what you've done to our goddam stock price?' asked Blane. The CEO's disapproving scowl shifted from Emilia Knight to her assistant and then back again. 'Well?' he demanded.

'We just don't have the budget to keep sufficient trained staff based out there,' said Emilia at last, her voice icy calm. 'We don't even employ local Samoan people as part-time monitors, not since the last round of cutbacks.'

'There was absolutely no warning when Māriota blew,' broke in Steve Bardini, stepping forward. 'No one could have predicted it, except maybe God Himself.'

'Thank you, Steve,' said Emilia quietly, glancing from her assistant back to the CEO.

She didn't have much to add to her preliminary written report, an account that had been so lacking in hard facts – she had struggled to make it extend to two pages – that its brevity had clearly infuriated the new CEO and had led to this confrontation.

'I'm sorry my initial report was so brief, sir,' said Emilia. 'But now that we've built and run a simulation, I'm convinced that the Mount Māriota eruption was a very rare event, a spontaneous sub-eugeosyncline occurrence that . . .'

Her voice tailed off as she noted her CEO's uncomprehending stare. Then she remembered he was an accountant, not a scientist.

Trying an easier tack, she explained, 'You see, we usually notice a pattern of earthquake swarms – little tremors – in advance. And we listen out for what we call groans. But very occasionally there occurs a large seismic explosion so far down in the earth's crust, thirty kilometres or more, that it doesn't provide us with any of the normal advance warnings. The magma just comes shooting right on up – that's what happened on Samoa.'

Taylor L. Blane regarded the two scientists in front of him with scepticism.

'I'll only accept that once I've seen an independent technical review,' he told them. 'I presume you're going out there to visit the *actual* volcano rather than just remaining here and playing with all these fancy gadgets?'

The two scientists exchanged glances. They had been discussing the same thing just before they'd starting running this morning's simulations. The problem was that Emilia had only recently terminated their furtive office romance and neither of them really wanted to be forced back into close companionship during an arduous overseas trip. Or, at least, Emilia didn't. Steve didn't mind at all. He still thought he could get her to change her mind, and they could get back together again.

'We were planning to leave tomorrow,' said Emilia hastily. 'We're selecting our support team right now.'

'Very good,' rasped the CEO. He fixed the senior Pacific Region geophysicist with his rifle-bore gaze. 'Get up on the *real* mountain, Doctor Knight, and be ready to apologize to the world for our failure. I'll get our press office to fix a couple of network TV crews to meet you there. Then say you're *sorry* that the world's leading seismic prediction contractor was unable to warn the public about that eruption. And, for God's sake, woman, *look like you mean it*!'

**WORLD NEWS . . . 17:00 ET . . . 05/26/55 – MSN NEW YORK
ANCHOR, AURORA TEMPLETON
SCREEN CAPTION: FBI RAIDS TERRORIST HIDEOUT**

AURORA:

The FBI today raided an apartment in Venice, Los Angeles
believed to have been used as a hideout by the Planet First
Organization.

With the cooperation of the LAPD, government agents
entered the apartment building shortly before dawn, seiz-
ing computer systems, files and a small quantity of explosives. A female suspect, said to be in her thirties, was
detained for questioning.

Earlier today the PFO claimed responsibility for the
explosion that damaged the ERGIA Space Station and triggered a multinational rescue effort to save over sixty crew
members and nearly one hundred visitors.

In its statement the PFO added, 'Controlling the world's
weather for the sole benefit of wealthier nations is a
criminal act that will inevitably endanger the planet's long-
term health.'

Now we go live to our reporter, Sandy Pertakis, in
Venice Beach, Los Angeles.

'They're blasting now,' Dr Heinrich Jensen yelled into the microphone, just as the sound of another distant explosion shook the prefabricated communications hut. 'They've blown off the tips of two glaciers, and they're now rigging tow-lines to the largest icebergs. Over.'

The research climatologist released the transmit button on his hand-held microphone, and waited for instructions from his project director in Hamburg.

'Who are they? Say again, who are they?' demanded Professor Karl Politza, Director of Antarctic Research, from his office in Northern Germany. The question arrived faintly at the Heard Island base, the short-wave signal bouncing between two satellites, disrupted by the fierce solar radiation and magnetic fields swirling around the South Pole.

'They're hulk people,' said Jenson. 'I can just make out one of their hulk platforms on the horizon. They landed here at dawn. Over.'

Heard Island lay in the Southern Ocean, seven miles inside the Antarctic Circle. Technically, this small volcanic outcrop was administered as an External Territory by Australia. But in the six years that the University of Hamburg had maintained a research team on the island, the personnel who had rotated through the station had never seen even one Australian visitor, and had never experienced anyone attempting a landing by sea – until now.

Jensen's walkie-talkie lay on the bench beside him and it suddenly crackled into life.

'They've got guns,' reported Akiro Kakehashi, shouting over the noise of the howling Antarctic winds. He was the best linguist on the team and along with five others he had gone down to the small cove to remonstrate with the uninvited visitors. 'They've been shooting the penguins and the seals and now they're demanding food, water and diesel fuel from us.'

Jensen relayed this information to Hamburg and waited for a response.

'Don't resist,' ordered Politza, concerned only for the safety of his distant research team. 'Give them all the supplies you can spare. We'll re-equip you from Auckland as soon as the weather allows.'

After the Director signed off, Heinrich Jensen was in two minds about following Hamburg's advice. As he had been helicoptered down to Heard Island from Auckland four months earlier, his aircraft had skirted two of those vast hulk-platforms. He had realized how many tens of thousands must be living out there on the open seas, and once you started handing out precious supplies of food, water and fuel, there would be no end to it...

Dr Emilia Knight waved goodbye to the two TV crews who had interviewed her and watched as the Samoan police escorted them down from the dangerously hot mountainside. She waited until she could see their vehicles throwing up clouds of lava dust on the narrow road leading back towards Āpia – the islands' still-smoking capital, fifteen kilometres to the east. It was now time for her to unpack some equipment and get on with her real work on this newly reawakened volcano.

She had earlier pointed out to the TV journalists the rivers of drying lava, the smoking stumps of rainforest trees, the many belching magma holes, and had made dutiful excuses for Geohazard's failure to predict the horrific event.

But Emilia knew that she and her team had little to apologize for. It simply wasn't possible to detect every seismic disturbance or volcanic eruption before it happened; in fact, it was something of a miracle that their company could predict any of them.

Precise earthquake prediction was particularly difficult, and only an eclectic mix of orbiting cameras and ultra-sensitive in-ground seismic instruments allowed the company to do better than its government-run predecessors.

Today, Geohazard Laboratories felt sufficiently confident to provide 'event likelihood warnings' on a sliding scale of probability, and the company had predicted accurately four out of the last five earthquakes rated above Magnitude 6. That was just as well; in recent times the annual number of non-climatic hazardous events such as earthquakes and volcanic activity had more than doubled.

After a half-hour climb, Dr Knight stood 430 feet higher up

on Mount Māriota, just 200 feet below the smoking edge of the
volcano's recently enlarged crater.

She had donned a silver heat-resistant protective suit with
integral Teflon-Mylar boots. Her head was encased in a wide-
visored, airtight helmet. Two hours' worth of compressed, oxy-
gen-enriched air was strapped to her back, and four miles of
micro-tubing circulated a sodium-based coolant around the suit's
inner lining.

This close to the mouth of the still-active volcano, the ground
temperature reached ninety degrees Celsius, and the sulphurous
mineral air, corrosive as battery acid, was capable of stripping
the lining from unprotected human lungs.

Emilia got down on all fours, raking gloved hands through
the smoking debris of pyroclastic rocks and cinders.

'I'm still getting ground trembles at about three-point-seven
every four or five minutes,' Steve Bardini announced suddenly in
her ear.

Her assistant, with four technical support staff, was still in
the company's temporary monitoring station that they had
established on the outskirts of Āpia, but within the confines of
Emilia's helmet it felt as if he were sharing the suit with her. She
hastily turned off the image of him projected in front of her eyes
– the better to focus on what she was looking for – but he still
shared her view, could see all that she saw. It was comforting
that he could monitor every measurement recorded inside Emilia's suit, including her respiratory function and other vital signs.

Two remotely controlled miniature helicopters hovered one
hundred feet above: one directly over the mouth of the volcano
itself, watching out for 'hot ballistics' – sudden volleys of lava
shot out of the chimney – and the other directly over Emilia's
own position, its down draught helping to disperse the smoke
around her. They too had cameras feeding images back to the
Āpia control centre. Without a climbing partner physically
beside her, this long-distance support team provided the virtual
equivalent.

'You know it's not stable yet,' Steve warned her once again,
tempted – but not yet ready – to call his boss off the hot
mountainside and back to safety. Emilia had been determined to

undertake a brief preliminary site survey, but had promised to remain no longer than forty-five minutes.

'Look at the colour of these,' Emilia said, almost to herself, weighing two small rocks in her gloved palm. 'They're extremely heavy – do you recognize this material? It looks like it's phreato-magmatic.'

'Looks almost chondritic,' Steve observed. 'That's from *very* deep.' He paused. 'You haven't got long now – check your coolant level.'

Moving slowly, like an early moon explorer, Emilia stood up and dropped her two samples into a large collection net clipped to her belt. She glanced up towards the smoking lip of the crater.

'Emilia, no!' Steve's voice was insistent, but she was already heading higher, searching for any material that would have been vomited up during the very last of the volcanic surge – stuff that would have arrived with least force, material originating from the very bottom of the deep magma chimney.

She was now surrounded by 'vog' – a thick, foul-smelling miasma composed of sulphur dioxide and microparticles of volcanic ash. Visibility was less than ten metres at ground level.

'You've got over twenty-two degrees internal,' Steve's voice warned her unnecessarily as she approached the crater's edge. Her suit's system had already displayed a warning icon on Emilia's visor.

Suddenly a rock that had looked like a firm toehold shot backwards from under her right boot. Emilia fell heavily onto her shoulder, then cried out in pain as the bottom edge of her metal air cylinder dug sharply into her lower back.

'Emilia?' Steve's tone betrayed serious alarm.

She stared up at the small patches of blue sky she could see revealed in the immediate vortex of the spinning helicopter blades. It felt as if her spine had cracked.

'Emilia!' Now he sounded almost frantic.

'OK, I'm OK,' she managed, as she sucked in deep breaths. 'Nothing broken,' she gasped, trying to sound more certain than she felt.

She closed her eyes to focus on the pain. After a few

moments of fighting down bile, she realized that it wasn't as bad as she had feared.

'I'm OK,' she repeated.

'I can't see any signs of suit rupture,' reported Steve inside her helmet. Emilia nodded as if he were speaking to her from across the room.

She heaved herself over onto one side, then, gradually up onto her hands and knees. The worst of the pain was definitely subsiding. Lifting her head, she gazed up the remaining stretch of mountainside, across a terrain of smoking rocks immediately around the crater's rim. Suddenly she spotted a fragment that looked unlike anything she had ever seen before. It was about twelve inches across, with jagged convex surfaces that caught the light and glinted a dull silvery-yellow. It lay on the very lip of the crater.

'Look, Steve!' she urged her former boyfriend, who was still checking his read-outs. The instruments indicated no threat to the integrity of her suit, but the exterior level of background radiation was now rising sharply.

Emilia propelled herself higher still and she was suddenly looking down into the vast smoking crater. She estimated it to be about half a mile across, a central basin filled with swirling columns of high-temperature gasses. For a moment she imagined that tongues of fire could still be seen deep in the abyss.

'Come down now!' ordered Steve, finally asserting his authority as Expedition Controller. The integral Geiger counter in Emilia's belt had started to hum continuously.

She reached out her right hand to pick up the unusual rock, but its slick surface slipped from her fingers. As she tried again, she felt its heat, even through her thick, protective gloves. Once more, the sharp-edged rock sample slipped away.

'It does look unusual,' agreed Steve in her ear, now paying closer attention to her find.

'It's almost glowing,' gasped the senior geophysicist.

'We've got an RA spike!' warned Steve as the Geiger counter's song rose angrily inside Emilia's suit.

Unclipping a pair of large specimen tongs from her belt, she reached out with two hands, extended the calliper arms fully, grasped the rock and lifted. The Geiger's song shot into the treble.

'My God!' she exclaimed. 'This feels heavier than lead.'

Suddenly the rock slipped out of the callipers.

'Come down now,' ordered Steve once more. Her stress indicators and vital signs were approaching dangerously high levels. 'We're getting over sixty rads.'

'Hold on,' grunted Emilia. She knelt carefully and got her arms under the peculiar glinting rock.

'Nearly got it . . .' She forced herself to her feet, the hot sample held tight against her chest. Dropping the rock into the collection sack on her belt, she straightened up carefully and gingerly tested her back.

'Unbelievable!' shouted Steve. 'Do you see what that weighs?'

In the sole of each of her boots were gravity meters, strain gauges and weighing scales. Now they had automatically calculated the weight of the new sample Emilia had added to her load.

'It's over forty pounds!' exclaimed Steve.

'I'm on my way down,' shouted his boss over the shrill scream of her Geiger counter.

FIVE

It was raining heavily in San Francisco. Such precipitation wouldn't have surprised any of the city's residents in years gone by, but the region's weather was now closely managed and this particular Thursday evening was scheduled to have been dry and fine. Consequently, the freak rain was proving to be a source of considerable annoyance.

All over the city and the greater Bay Area, carefully planned sports events, outdoor concerts, barbecues and countless other social pursuits were being spoiled. The networks were jammed with locals complaining to TV stations and government offices. This evening was supposed to have been sunny and hot!

'Damn!' exclaimed Michael Fairfax as his foot shot from under him on a slippery wooden step. He almost dropped the packages he was carrying, the gifts he had brought back from New Zealand for his boys. He grasped the walkway's wooden handrail, only just managing to maintain his balance.

When he had made arrangements with Lucy for this hand-over, the weather schedule had promised a sunny evening. It had seemed the perfect opportunity for an early dinner, especially at a bay-side restaurant with an outdoor deck.

But now the old wooden building and jetty were soaking wet and slippery underfoot. Michael stepped up onto the restaurant's covered walkway and shook out his umbrella.

He heard a car horn. Then the boys were tumbling out of the back of his ex-wife's large utility vehicle and running towards him through the rain.

'Hey, Dad,' called Matthew in a thirteen-year-old voice that in the space of just two words managed to oscillate between a piping treble and an uncertain bass.

'Dad!' shouted Ben, not quite six, as he too scrambled up the wooden steps and out of the rain.

Michael put one arm around Matt's shoulders while he hoisted a squealing Ben under the other.

A hostess appeared in the restaurant doorway and smiled at this family horseplay.

'We have a reservation,' panted Michael, as he finally set Ben down on his feet. 'We were supposed to be out on the deck, but...'

'Don't worry,' said the young woman. 'I'll find you a window seat.'

They were visiting the New Trident restaurant, one of San Francisco's most treasured historic haunts. It sat on the shoreline at Sausolito, a small artistic community across the bay from the main city, where Michael had made his home since the divorce.

The restaurant's interior had been lovingly restored: a late-1960s psychedelic trip with highly polished wood surfaces and floral designs from the original hippie period.

But none of these details mattered to the boys. The reason Michael had suggested this venue was the deck – the outdoor seating area which they all enjoyed but which Ben particularly loved. He liked it because it often provided close-up views of the high-powered offshore speedboats that set off from nearby to race out under the Golden Gate Bridge.

As the hostess promised, they were shown to a window table, but dark clouds covered the whole of the distant San Francisco city skyline and the mist was so thick that only the pulsing flash of the lighthouse indicated where Alcatraz Island lay the middle of the bay.

Michael ordered sodas and snacks for the boys and a beer for himself. Then he scooped the presents up from the floor and into his lap.

'I missed you guys,' he said as he handed over the large packages.

Matthew tore at the giftwrap and extracted his present first.

It was a single roll of wallpaper. The boy frowned, suspecting he'd been given something of mere utility.

'Roll it out on the floor,' suggested his father.

Still puzzled, Matt slid off his chair and unrolled a section of the long sheet.

The dark wallpaper was covered with glowing stars: it was an image of the night sky.

'Hey, Dad, thanks!' grunted Matthew, not yet fully appreciating all the features his gift had to offer. 'That's part of Cygnus,' he added, pointing to a star formation on the paper sheet.

Michael grinned at his astronomy-mad elder son. 'That's just part of your present, Matt,' he explained. 'There's another ten rolls that will be delivered to your home tomorrow. They're all electronic, and when they're put together you can create the whole night sky in your bedroom. The stars glow and move, like the real universe.'

Ben had temporarily stopped pulling at the metallic gold paper wrapped around his own gift to see what it was his brother had received.

'Turn it around,' suggested Michael. 'It won't tear.'

Matthew pulled at the long sheet of electronic paper, Ben jumping down from the table to help him, and the boys turned the sheet around to face the other way along the wooden floor. As they did so, the star patterns rotated. Matt realized what was happening.

'Is it magnetic, Dad? The stars are changing their position.'

'There's a tiny cellular GPS receiver in each roll,' explained Michael, delighted by Matthew's obvious pleasure. 'It always knows where it is. It just changes the display to fit.'

'*Carpe Diem!*' exclaimed Matthew softly.

'I've already talked to your Mom about it,' added Michael. 'And we've arranged for decorators to come in and repaper your room – as soon as you like.'

Matt pushed himself up from the restaurant floor and seemed about to embrace his father. But he suddenly became self-conscious and merely raised two thumbs in thanks and mute approval. Then he bent and carefully rerolled the electronic wallpaper.

Both boys returned to sit at the table just as their drinks and snacks arrived.

'And what have *you* got?' asked Michael, putting an arm around his younger son's shoulders.

Ben took a first slurp of his pink, sugar-free milk-shake and quickly pulled at the wrapping paper on his gift. As the inner layer fell away, the boy saw the flying-saucer frisbee inside its box.

'It's solar-powered,' explained his father. 'When the sun's shining, it will stay in the air for ever.'

'*Lightspeed*,' said the awed Ben, borrowing one of his big brother's many superlatives.

'And it's remote-controlled,' added Michael.

'Hey, Dad,' announced Matt with a grin. 'Did you hear that a restaurant full of lawyers was held hostage?'

'Noooo,' Michael said, shaking his head exaggeratedly, as if he were a wet dog emerging from the sea. 'OK, tell me what happened?'

'The bad guys threatened that until all their demands were met they would release one lawyer unharmed every hour.'

Despite himself, Michael couldn't help laughing, and Ben, although he had clearly endured many rehearsals of the joke, laughed so hard he almost fell off his chair.

'So, tell us about the volcano, Dad?' asked Matthew. He still held the sheet of celestial wallpaper partly unrolled in his lap.

'Nothing to tell, really,' said Michael, smiling. 'I just saw the volcano erupt from my hotel balcony. The hot stuff didn't come anywhere near me.'

'Look,' said Ben, pointing his small forefinger across the restaurant towards the empty bar area. 'The wolcano!'

There was a large screen mounted behind the bar and Michael recognized an image that was all too familiar to him.

'Come on, Dad,' said Matthew, heading towards the bar.

Michael walked across the restaurant with his two sons – both still carrying their gifts – and the bartender turned up the volume.

The screen showed a short, attractive woman in a protective hard hat standing on the slopes of a smoking volcano.

'... And this unanticipated eruption is continuing to spew

lava and ash high into the atmosphere over Samoa. Specially directed winds are now dispersing the airborne debris harmlessly over the Southern Ocean and Antarctica.'

'That's where you were, Dad,' said Ben excitedly.

'That's where the hulk people are forced to live,' Michael reminded his privileged sons.

'It's impossible to calculate the economic and social impact of the volcano's eruption on the people of these islands,' continued the female presenter in a surprisingly sensual voice. Then a caption appeared at the bottom of the screen.

> *Dr Emilia Knight*
> *Earth scientist, Geohazard Labs*

'This was the moment of explosion, caught by our permanent monitoring camera four days ago,' said the presenter, now gracing her viewers with a mischievous smile.

Suddenly the screen was filled with an image that was already burned into Michael's memory. It was shown here from another angle, but he would never forget the awful slowness, the immense scale of the energy released, as the volcano blew its ancient lava cap high into the night sky.

The scientist-presenter came back on the screen and, with a rueful grin, apologized for her company not having been able to warn about the eruption in advance – *A very attractive woman*, thought Michael, *very attractive indeed*.

Then the image changed to reveal a news presenter in a studio.

'Come on, guys,' said Michael, turning away. 'The weather's clearing. Perhaps we can go out on the deck after all.'

Dr Emilia Knight leaned her forehead against the tiled wall of the shower cubicle and allowed the powerful jets of hot water to course all over her body.

She was back at Aggie Gray's Hotel in the Samoan capital, and she had lost count of the number of showers to which she had already subjected her body.

Once again, she worked up a rich lather with the hotel's perfumed soap and carefully washed every inch of her body. She used a wet towel to reach the small of her back, where she knew a small graze had been made when she had fallen on her oxygen cylinder.

Could radioactivity just be washed away? That was what the manual said, anyway. Logically, she knew that her biohazard suit should have prevented radioactive material reaching her skin, but she felt an overwhelming desire to scrub herself repeatedly.

Emilia turned the mixer tap off again, dried herself and stepped out of the cubicle.

Picking up one of the hand-held Geiger counters supplied by Geohazard, she placed it on her stomach, her chest, her neck and her pelvic region. She was testing how much radiation exposure she had suffered from her foolhardy handling of the strange rock sample up on Mount Māriota.

From each site on her body the reading said, 'Borderline-Dangerous.'

She put her arm behind her back and held the sensor to her spine: 2.767. Where her skin was broken the reading was above borderline. Emilia didn't know enough about radiation sickness to know whether that meant her blood had been affected.

With a shake of her dark, wet curls, she stepped back into the shower cubicle and turned on the water once again.

As the ship carefully maintained its position, six and a half miles above the seabed of the North-East Pacific Basin, at the third deepest spot in the whole Pacific Ocean, Chief Oceanographer Valerie Cummings triggered a very loud noise, the first in what would be a series of such acoustic explosions.

At its source, the sound was so deafening that it exceeded the decibel level of a sonic boom. But neither Val Cummings, nor any of the other thirty-four crew members on board the US Navy Research Vessel *Orlando*, heard a thing. The noise was emitted from huge concrete-cased underwater loudspeakers positioned on the seabed 231 miles to the north.

The system clock had been reset to zero, as always when such an acoustic test was triggered, and the underwater microphones now waited, ready for the sound waves from the first test in the series to arrive.

The US *Orlando* was in the North Central Pacific, at 22.5N, 147.2W, 430 miles north-east of Hawaii. Below the ship lay a sufficient depth of water to cover the peak of a submerged Mount Everest and still leave a half-mile clearance.

The research vessel was one of a fleet operated by the San Diego Naval Academy of Oceanography, and Valerie Cummings was creating an accurate and up-to-date deep-water temperature map of the water strata covering the floor of the Central Pacific ocean.

A muted roar over the speakers in the floating lab told her that the sound she had triggered had reached the microphones. The system would verify its data, then calculate the speed at which the sound had travelled through the water. The technique was known as Acoustic Thermometry of Ocean Climate – ATOC – and had proved to be a cost-effective and reliable way of measuring deep-sea temperatures. Sound travels faster through warm water than it does through cold, and a simple calculation would provide an accurate measurement.

Jesus, that couldn't be right. She scanned the data display on her main screen, then replayed the entire experiment from start to finish. The temperature seemed to have risen by 1.3721 degrees Celsius since the last check was made! Impossible.

Valerie filed the data, reset the system, then repeated the experiment. Now the increase was shown as 1.8911 degrees C! The temperature of the water at the bottom of the world's deepest ocean appeared to have soared by almost two degrees in a single year. If that was correct, the ocean's entire heat budget would be wrecked.

She instructed her system to continue the planned series of ATOC measurements, moved to her communications keyboard, and started to write a short emergency report to the Oceanography Academy in San Diego. Just before she was about to transmit it, she recalled the recent eruption on Samoa and she

added a second recipient to the circulation list – *Stefano Bardini,
Geohazard Laboratories, Inc., Pacific Region, Oakland, California* –
before hitting 'Send'.

Then she used her personal communicator to send a private,
unauthorized and highly encrypted message to certain recipients
in San Diego and Berkeley, California.

'How do you feel, Em?' asked Steve Bardini anxiously. It seemed
like the hundredth time he had asked her the same question in
the past three hours.

'I'm OK, OK – for the *last* time,' snapped Emilia Knight
irritably. During this trip she had made it quite clear that she
had no intention of resuming their romantic relationship, but his
over-solicitousness now left her feeling both annoyed and guilty.
Then she suddenly wondered whether her current bad temper
might itself be a symptom of radiation sickness.

'Sorry, Steve,' she added, 'I'm just tired. I didn't sleep very
well.'

They were in a passenger jet flying 28,000 feet above the
Pacific, and once again Emilia saw her assistant surreptitiously
slide the thin silver cylinder out of his trouser pocket and hold it
tight against the left-hand side of her body.

She heard the treble note rising and increasing in frequency
as it pinged, then Steve pressed a button and raised the Geiger
counter so they could both read its built-in display.

'Two-point-one,' he said. 'Still the same.'

Before leaving the hotel that morning she had taken a dozen
more showers, each time scrubbing herself hard with a stiff-
bristled brush, while taking exceptional care never to scratch or
break the surface of her sore skin.

The team at base camp monitoring her descent from the
mountainside had quickly realized that the unusual rock fragment was far more radioactive than any geological sample they
normally encountered in the field. Steve had even urged her to
abandon the hot rock, to leave it behind on the mountainside,
but Emilia had argued the importance of carrying out a proper
analysis in the lab.

'This suit is radiation-resistant,' she had reminded them as she placed the rock into one of the shielded sample cases in the back of her four-wheel-drive vehicle. 'Don't worry so much.'

Now Emilia Knight took the small radiation gauge from her assistant and quickly scanned the supplementary data that it had captured.

They had already called ahead, had warned their colleagues in Geohazard that they were bringing home an unusually radio-active sample that needed urgent analysis – the sample that was now inside a double-shielded flight case in the aircraft's hold. They had also informed Human Resources that Emilia herself would need to see a doctor.

The Geiger counter's read-out still suggested that she was borderline OK. She felt no physical symptoms of discomfort although she had once or twice imagined she could feel a burning deep inside her, near where the heavy rock had slapped against her waist and thigh. As a geologist she knew of only one natural element that was both radioactive and heavier than lead and she didn't at all like the idea that she might have been close to it, still worse that she'd actually picked it up.

'Emilia!' cried Steve suddenly, staring now at the screen of his personal communicator. 'Vesuvius is getting ready to blow again! Look at these long-period events.'

She took the unit from him and scanned the seismic data he had just received from Geohazard's European HQ in Athens.

'You're right,' she exclaimed, all worries about her own health suddenly banished. 'And it's going to be big. I'm going to fly straight on to Italy.'

London Times

Tuesday, 6 June 2055

VESUVIUS ERUPTS
Third Time this Century

Naples:

Mount Vesuvius erupted again last night for the third time this century. The main crater was reopened at 10.37p.m. local time by a blast of magma which propelled debris over 30 kilometres into the atmosphere.

Villages at the foot of the mountain had remained uninhabited since the last eruption in 2039, so there is thought to have been little or no loss of life.

In Naples, residents were urged to stay inside with doors and windows shut. In the streets many citizens are choosing to wear smog masks to protect themselves from ash particles.

All air traffic is being routed away from southern Italy.

SIX

Perdita Curtis remembered nothing of her rescue from the damaged ERGIA Space Station, nor of her subsequent return to Earth. She had woken to find herself in a hospital bed in Florida.

'You're very lucky,' the doctor explained as he showed her the scans. 'You were quite severely concussed, but there's no internal bleeding and no lesions. Rest and observation for another three days. Then, if everything is well, you can go home.'

The headache had lasted a week, a headache whose severity forced Perdy to reclassify as rapture all headaches she had suffered previously.

The BBC's insurers had paid for her repatriation to the UK in a supersonic business-class jet, and, eight days later than she had originally planned, she had rescued her marmalade cat from her neighbour and resumed her bachelor girl's life in Shepherds Bush, West London.

Perdy returned to work at BBC Network Headquarters on the following Monday morning to be greeted as a heroine by everybody she met as she made her way to her office. There were flowers from her boss waiting for her, and a large and expensively gift-wrapped box had been placed precisely in the centre of her glass-topped desk.

First she admired the flowers, then she undid the ribbon-bow on the box and folded back its spangled giftwrap. Inside she saw a plasti-glass cube, about half a metre square.

In the centre of this transparent case, seemingly suspended within it and turning slowly, was a perfect scale model of the Earth, complete with floating clouds and swirling weather patterns.

Ringed all around the tilted planet was a network of solar-reflecting satellites, some orbiting, some stationary, and a large space station. Powered by some unseen source, they were beaming light down onto the slowly revolving planet.

Perdy bent and examined the model through the glass. How did it all remain in place? She could see no wires or supports. The degree of the tilt at which the planet revolved surprised her; she presumed it to be accurate, but very few of the ubiquitous TV or video images of the globe made the tilt *this* apparent – and you certainly didn't notice it from space either!

'Hi, Perdy, how are you feeling . . . ?'

Narinda Damle, her executive producer, had arrived in the doorway but the greeting died in his mouth as he noticed the model that sat on her desk. He too bent over and stared through the glass.

'How wonderful! It's a sort of orrery,' he observed. 'A moving model of the Earth and its satellites.'

Perdy slit open the ivory-white envelope that had been placed beside the box.

FROM THE DESK OF NICHOLAS NEGROMONTE

Dear Perdy,

On behalf of us all at the ERGIA Corporation, please accept my apologies for the injuries you suffered during your visit to our Control Center. I understand that the FBI have already detained one suspect in the case and that further arrests are expected in the near future.

I will be in England myself for the next couple of weeks and if it would be of help for your documentary I would be pleased to welcome you to Langland Park, my residence in Lincolnshire. I would also like the opportunity to apologize in person for the injury and shock you experienced when we last met.

Sincerely,
Nicholas Negromonte

Perdy smiled ruefully as she finished reading the handwritten invitation. Then she handed it to Damle.

'They all think they can buy us, don't they?' he said, snorting indignantly as he finished reading. 'As if we've never been invited to a stately home before.'

'Well, I haven't,' said Perdy, shrugging. 'And I think I ought to go anyway. If I can persuade Negromonte to talk on camera, we'll get a prime-time transmission slot.'

'I want to go straight for the jugular,' Michael Fairfax announced to his executive board. 'Slapping a writ on Nick Negromonte will make a big splash in the media.'

'Wouldn't be worth the paper it's written on,' grunted Saul Levinson, the firm's senior partner, dismissively. 'How many lawyers do you think ERGIA keeps on permanent retainer?'

Why was Levinson suddenly being so negative? Like the rest of the board, he'd known about this case for months. But Michael just happened to know the precise answer for his colleague.

'Eight hundred and eleven Bar-recognized attorneys, Saul,' he conceded. 'And that's just in the USA. They use outside law firms throughout the rest of the world.'

'And we would be taking on one of the world's richest corporations in what is, after all, a new and wholly untested legal jurisdiction,' observed Marjory Hinterscoombe gloomily. She was the senior finance partner of Gravitz, Lee and Kraus. It was her job to keep speculative litigation within manageable bounds.

'Come on, Marjory,' said Michael disbelievingly. 'You're not getting last-minute jitters, are you?'

The lawyer was on his feet, facing his partners in the main boardroom on the sixty-second floor of the recently completed Embarcadero Space Needle in downtown San Francisco. He had just spent an hour outlining the case he wanted to launch against the world's major energy companies.

'If you go for the jugular, as you put it,' said Saul Levinson, 'are you really ready for the weight that's going to descend on you – on all of us? It won't be just legal opposition. They'll do anything to stop us, to delay this action, to discredit you, to prevent you hurting their share price. It could get very nasty – and very personal.'

Michael glanced from face to face, weighing up the remaining level of commitment among the firm's senior partners.

'Public opinion will be the final jury in this matter,' he told them. 'It was public opinion that forced the politicians to set up the new civil justice court to try such cases. The question is, are we now going to fail to bring these offending corporations to justice? Are we going to leave it to some other law firm that is braver than we are?'

'Your hulk people are already seriously upsetting public opinion,' snapped Levinson. 'Look at their recent attack on that Antarctic research colony – all the scientists' supplies were stolen.'

'I'm assured that my own clients weren't responsible for that. I've warned them not to do anything rash, no matter how desperate they feel.'

The partners exchanged glances, and then everyone was gazing towards Saul Levinson. Finally, with a sigh, the senior partner shook his oppugnant head.

'I'm sorry, Michael,' he said, 'this is just too big. If you want to pick off a small part of your claim and make it into a stand-alone case, I'll support you. Otherwise I must say no to a full-scale class action. You'd be risking the very future of this firm – a practice that's taken over a century to build up.'

'I have to agree with Saul,' added Marjory Hinterscoombe – too quickly, as if rehearsed. 'The financial risk would be far too great for us.'

Now Michael felt a distinct sense of alarm. This was not how partners' meetings normally went. Any contentious issue was usually resolved well ahead of time, in pre-emptive discussions held prior to the official meetings, in corridor canvassing, in private deals made beside water-coolers, or in discreet nego-tiations conducted in quiet restaurants. He had thought that approval for his case was a done deal.

'I'm not prepared to walk away from this,' Michael heard himself saying. 'And I'm not prepared to scale it down into a minor case that will achieve nothing effective for most of those people who have lost their homes and their livelihoods.'

Levinson's dark gaze bored into the younger lawyer's as if he wished to silence him completely. 'I'm truly sorry, Michael,' he growled, as if that were his last word. 'It's just too soon to know how this new international court will interpret the law. We should wait a while until it resolves a few cases.' He closed the lid of his textpad with determined finality.

Michael picked up the remote control that he had been using earlier for his presentation and aimed it again at the large 3-D screen.

The lights in the boardroom dimmed and the display was once more filled with views of the hulk platform, images which Michael himself had captured during his research trip. The partners watched the vast mass of rusty metal floating on the ocean, then the picture cut to show hundreds of silent, rag-swathed people standing in a wind-lashed silence on the heaving deck of an elderly oil tanker.

Michael allowed the video to continue running until the camera went below decks, into the darkness of the hulk's interior. He froze the image on the rows of bodies lying below deck, then he brought the room lights back on.

'This injustice is not something that I'm prepared to give up on easily,' he said quietly. 'If I have to, I'll take my case to Beauchamp, Seifert and Co.'

As he spoke he knew that he was potentially delivering his resignation, something he had never anticipated having to do. The Brussels-based legal firm he had just mentioned was the largest of all litigators in the environmental and ecological field, and it had already filed three major cases to be heard before the newly established court.

'I don't think *they* would be frightened of it,' he added, hearing the words leaving his mouth but wholly unable to take them back.

'You may resign if you so choose,' said Levinson angrily. 'But the case stays here. The intellectual property belongs to our firm.'

'We are absolutely *surrounded*, sir,' insisted Louise Waller. The Chairwoman of the Pitcairn Island Council clutched her nightgown tighter around her throat as she gazed out of her open bedroom window, the telephone clamped to her ear.

'Surrounded?' barked Sir Hugo Poole, Britain's High Commissioner to New Zealand.

Although it was seven-fifteen a.m. with a winter dawn just breaking in the South Central Pacific, the day was four hours younger in Auckland and the HC had been woken up by the night duty officer to take this urgent call.

'How the devil can you be *surrounded*?'

'I'm looking out of my window now, sir,' replied Miss Waller, who doubled as the mayor of Adamstown, the tiny island's only village. 'The ships have formed a circle that stretches all round the coast, as far as I can see.'

'How many damn ships?' demanded the High Commissioner testily.

Miss Waller had completed a rapid count while she had been waiting for him to be roused.

'I can see twenty-eight at least, but the convoy runs around the island on both sides. And they're big ships too, old oil tankers and freighters, although some of them have what look like guns or missile systems mounted on deck.'

'What are they actually doing at present?' demanded Poole.

She raised her binoculars and focused on the activity at the island's extensive oil storage depot.

'One of the tankers has moored beside the oiling jetty. I think they intend to take on fuel.'

Miss Waller moved her binoculars back to focus on the ships in the bay.

'Now they've launched two inflatables,' she reported. 'There's a party coming ashore, and it looks as if they're well armed.'

'Right, I'll get on to London. You go down and talk to them,' ordered Poole. 'Don't take any unnecessary risks, you hear me?'

'Yes, sir,' agreed the spokeswoman of one of the world's most remote communities.

Michael Fairfax was still in a state of shock when he arrived back at his office on the sixty-third floor of the Embarcadero

Space Needle. His executive assistant, Serena Jones, was waiting for him in the doorway with an air of anticipation. He knew she was expecting to hear when their massive legal action would be launched.

But he didn't want to discuss the case with her. He hadn't yet worked out why he had been ambushed in the partners' meeting. He didn't yet know whether he was going to swallow his pride and stay on with the firm, or whether he had already gone too far in talking himself out of his lucrative partnership. Either way, he knew that he would soon have to call his new clients in the Southern Ocean and advise them that their case was temporarily on hold. *After everything he had promised them.*

'Just give me a little while, Serena, would you?' he asked absently.

He was about to close his office door when she said, 'There's a call on line two, Mike. A woman – says she must speak with you very urgently.'

'I'm not taking any calls this afternoon,' said Michael, giving a firm shake of his head. 'Just say I'm in conference.'

'The caller is the woman the FBI picked up in Los Angeles – the alleged member of the PFO cell who bombed the ERGIA space station. She's calling from a state penitentiary.'

The attorney stared at his assistant as if she had gone mad. After three years of working for him, it now seemed as if she had learned nothing.

'You know I don't do any criminal work,' he snapped. 'Put it through to Alison Zeffirelli or Mitch Tonks in Public Justice – they'll handle it.'

He moved again to close his door, but Serena stretched out a hand to stop him. She glanced over her shoulder to check if they were being observed by any staff in the outer office, then stepped inside.

'She claims she's an ex-girlfriend of yours and you're the only lawyer she can trust,' Serena hissed in a semi-whisper. 'Apparently you were at college together. Her name is Carole Gonzaga.'

Michael felt rooted to the spot: Carole Gonzaga, the first major love of his adult life; the wild-child arts student who had helped him break away from his archly conservative upbringing;

the woman he had once loved with a burning youthful passion but who had eventually broken his heart.

But how could Carole Gonzaga be caught up with eco-terrorists?

'Well?' asked Serena, as her boss stood silently staring into space. When he didn't respond, she insisted, 'Mike, will you take this call or not?'

'Put it through,' he said, nodding curtly.

SEVEN

They hadn't even allowed Dr Emilia Knight to visit her own home, let alone catch a connecting flight on to Italy, where an army of volcanologists was already gathering on the flanks of Mount Vesuvius.

As soon as she had cleared Immigration at San Francisco airport, Emilia was met by Gloria Fernandez, Geohazard's head of human resources. The brusque HR woman handed her details for a reservation on a domestic flight leaving ninety minutes later, and Emilia had suddenly found herself bound for San Diego, 500 miles further south.

On arrival she was collected by a female naval ensign and driven directly to the US Navy Medical Center.

Internal radiation sickness cannot be treated: there is no cure for damaged bone marrow, lymph glands or blood cells. Emilia had made herself an instant expert on this condition, long before she arrived at one of the few American medical facilities equipped to diagnose and treat the effects of human exposure to radioactivity.

For two days, as the hospital's lone civilian patient, she was subjected to a series of painful and intrusive tests that forced her to acknowledge parts of her body that she had hardly known existed before. Tissue samples were taken from her skin, muscles, liver, spleen, kidneys, and even bone marrow.

In brief respites between these repeated physical invasions she lay in her private room fielding hundreds of work-related and personal e-mails, while privately testing her body and her moods against the short checklist of key symptoms that she had memorized.

'I've got no radiation sores, and I don't feel any unusual weakness,' Emilia informed the doctors with more assurance than she actually felt. 'I haven't vomited and I've still got my appetite.'

The naval medics nodded, said little, then annotated their electronic charts before arranging for yet further tests.

Three days after she had first been admitted to the hospital an older male doctor whom she hadn't encountered before came to visit her.

'Miss Knight,' he began, 'I'm Dr Bowman. I'm the consultant in charge of this unit.'

Emilia stiffened and sat more upright in her hospital day-chair.

'You've put my decontamination team through a very useful drill, but I'm pleased to say that we don't think you have suffered any serious long-term damage from your radiation exposure.'

Emilia let out a sigh that could have propelled a racing yacht.

'Whatever it was you picked up on that mountainside was certainly very nasty, but your suit stopped most of the rads from getting into your body. You've had what we call a Grade Five Exposure.'

Something in his tone started her worrying again. 'Grade Five?' she asked.

'Light occupational,' the consultant said. 'The sort of exposure we see in nuclear workers when there's been a small leak. Nothing to worry about, really.'

'So there will be no ill effects?' asked Emilia.

The doctor started a grimace, which turned into a smile. 'We can't *quite* say that, Miss Knight,' he admitted. 'We need to monitor over a longer period the samples of your bone marrow that we've taken. But you're fit enough to get back to work – providing you don't start collecting any more radioactive rocks.'

'So what *would* be the effects?' persisted Emilia.

'Exposure to radioactivity usually damages blood-forming tissue to some extent,' Bowman explained. 'There is a corresponding reduction in the supply of blood cells and platelets, and this increases the tendency to bleed – something you might notice, for example, if you suffered some other injury. It also reduces the body's defence against infection.'

'You mean I'm more likely to catch things?' asked Emilia.

The doctor twisted his neck as if his shirt collar was too tight. 'Not to any noticeable degree,' he said. 'But we'll need to do regular follow-up checks – say every three months.'

In the true spirit of artistic altruism, Capability Brown created grand English gardens, parks and vistas that he knew he himself would never live to see revealed in their mature glory.

Perdita Curtis stood on the balustraded south terrace of Langland Park in Lincolnshire and gazed out with pleasure along a central avenue of mature elms that had been planted almost 300 years before she was born.

In the foreground lay a formal Victorian water garden complete with rectangular ponds, classical fountains, topiary hedges, gravel paths and so many pale statues it looked like a well-kept cemetery. In the far distance, perhaps two miles away at the end of the broad avenue of trees, Perdy could just make out the glint of a lake.

It was a warm and sunny morning in early June, a perfect English summer's day, with just a few puffball white clouds decorating a Wedgwood-blue sky.

Perdy wasn't particularly awed by her gracious surroundings – she was a confident woman, at home no matter how high the ceiling or how exalted the company – but she *was* intensely curious. If she could get permission to film Negromonte in this palatial setting, it would give her documentary some much-needed attractive imagery to offset the many space shots and computer-generated graphics that would be required to show her audience how climate management actually worked. It would also guarantee that her documentary reached the largest possible audience.

'Miss Curtis?'

Perdy turned to see Bob Johnson, her ERGIA public relations escort for the day, emerging from the interior of the great

Georgian house. Earlier he had accompanied her up from London in one of the company's helicopters.

'Mr Negromonte is out flying,' he apologized, 'but he left a message asking me to . . .'

The PR man's words tailed off as he shielded his eyes against the sun and pointed into the distance. 'I think that's him now.'

Perdy turned, following Johnson's gaze out along the avenue of elms. At first she couldn't see what he was indicating. Then she noticed a black speck low down on the skyline.

As it rapidly grew bigger, she could see that it was an antique warplane – a single-wing, propeller-driven fighter – that was being flown towards them between the avenue of trees, as if it were intending to attack the house.

'Spitfire Mark Four,' explained Johnson in her ear. 'Over one hundred years old. It's his new toy.'

With a bellowing roar Negromonte increased the aircraft's power and headed straight for them as they stood on the terrace. At the last moment he lifted the aircraft's nose and, in a slowly executed victory roll, shot over their heads and up over the multiple roofs of the great house.

Perdy flinched under a powerful down draught of warm air. She heard all the casements rattle in the façade behind her as the throbbing note of the Spitfire engine pounded at them, then began to recede.

She turned to see the PR man's reaction. He simply shrugged, as if to say, *What can you do with him?*

The roaring tsunami reared even higher as it came within a hundred metres of the shoreline. It was impossible to make out either end of the giant wave.

As it hit the beach, the wall of water rose still higher, then rushed on inland, the ground shaking under its massive weight as it engulfed the low sea wall, rolled across a dual carriageway and smashed broadside into a densely populated commercial district.

In every street people were milling about wildly, some seeking refuge in buildings, some running away from buildings, some lying face down in terror, others crouching behind walls. But the torrent of water washed them all away with an earth-shaking roar that seemed to continue for a cruelly long time after the limbs of its human victims had ceased to thrash helplessly.

Dr Emilia Knight propelled her viewing chair around the holo-pit, to take up a position right behind the seething mass of water she had created. Pausing the simulation, she gazed down on the wreckage that the tsunami had caused along her virtual model of the Hawaiian coastline, then shook her head sadly. 'What if we gave the population a twenty-minute warning instead?' she asked Steve Bardini.

He tapped the figures into his workstation, and the revised data was instantly displayed on the information overlay in front of the now-frozen image in the holo-pit. *1,627 fatalities, 6,300 homeless. Damage estimated at $14.67 billion.*

'A bit better, but still awful,' Emilia murmured. 'Let's go back and run the underwater quake again – this time make it Magnitude Four.'

They were modelling the deep-sea data that Valerie Cummings had forwarded from the US Navy Research Vessel *Orlando*. Her ocean-temperature readings had suggested fresh seismic activity beneath the Pacific seabed, prompting Emilia and Steve to spend the whole morning gathering additional ambient data from Geohazard's deep-sea pressure detectors, coastal tide gauges, and tsunameters.

It was Dr Knight's first day back at work after her hospital-ization, and she was now feeling fully recovered. But this new data from the Pacific floor was truly alarming. The simulation they had created showed that a major undersea quake might allow the Hawaiians only a three-hour warning of an approach-ing tsunami. If the event was Magnitude Five or above, their model suggested that over 20,000 people would lose their lives, and the island would be plunged underwater for a distance of up to three miles inland from the northern coast.

'Shouldn't we at least be issuing a preliminary alert?' Steve asked as he keyed the new instructions into their modelling system.

Emilia sat back in her viewing chair and considered carefully.

Exactly when to issue alerts was always a tricky decision. If you warned a community too early before an event, or when nothing actually happened, they would cease to believe in warnings altogether – which always proved disastrous in the long run. If you delayed issuing a warning too long, the population living in the danger zone didn't have sufficient time to get themselves clear.

'OK, hold up on running that new model,' she agreed. 'Let's send a Level Three warning to our liaison contact in the Pacific Disaster Center on Hawaii – and copy it to the Governor's office. Make clear it's just a precaution, with no imminent threat of earthquake or tsunami at the moment.'

Steve nodded and swivelled back to his keyboard.

Emilia extended a personal laser screen, cleared the simulation from the holo-pit, and brought all the theatre's screens back to their normal pan-global views as they monitored the restless planet.

She zoomed in on a large screen that provided an orbital view of Vesuvius. The old girl was still belching vast clouds of smoke over all of the eastern Mediterranean, although good advance warning meant that at least she hadn't killed anyone this time – yet.

Then Emilia spotted a seismic alert in a very unusual latitude. She pulled up a geographical overlay and saw that seismic pressure was building up in the middle of England. That was unusual: there had been no major earthquakes in Britain since the seventeenth century. But she was relieved to note that Geohazard in Athens was already monitoring the build-up in seismic activity. *Nowhere's safe these days*, she thought.

Her personal communicator pinged. 'Glad you're working in the building today, Doctor Knight,' said Taylor Blane, the CEO. 'Would you come up to my office?'

Chanda Zia was standing on the old dining table in the stateroom of the *Prince Sahid*. For over an hour he had been addressing the full ruling council of *Pacifica One* as well as many other hulk residents who had insisted on thronging into the room to attend this emergency meeting.

'No, no,' he repeated, 'our lawyer says that we MUST wait until he can successfully bring our case to court – he claims there will only be a short delay. If we try to break away from this region, we'll automatically lose public support in all the rich countries.'

There was hubbub again amongst those who understood English – the only semi-common language within this wildly heterogeneous community – and to this din was added the babble of interpreters relaying Chanda's words to others.

Rifles and automatic weapons were brandished excitedly and Chanda knew that if they'd been outside in the cold winds the young men would already have been firing angry shots into the sky.

'We must wait,' he repeated, waving his arms to try and cool down these hotheads. 'We've waited years for this chance, and we must wait just a little longer to see how the new international court works.'

But the council leader knew that patience was finally running out. After three decades of being harried from ocean to ocean, the younger men were no longer prepared to be constantly pushed away from the richer parts of the world, treated like rubbish deposited at sea and forgotten. For months they had been repairing those old ships that were still serviceable, getting their engines working again, while new vessels had been arriving with spares, fuel and even, some said, weapons.

Thirty years before, when Chanda himself and his extended family had first been forced to flee their flooded homelands in Bangladesh, they had taken over one of the laid-up oil tankers in the Chittagong ships' graveyard. Others had followed suit, and soon the abandoned hulks had provided weatherproof homes for thousands of displaced families from the lower-lying lands of the equatorial belt. Then millions more had followed, from flooded, desertified or drought-ridden areas of Africa, the Philippines, Cambodia, Thailand and Egypt – and from China's coastal plains.

Some of these redundant ships had originally possessed working engines, others relied on tows, but somehow they managed to move and eventually every rich nation had been intimidated by these hordes of homeless, status-less people roaming the oceans in old, unseaworthy hulks. They had sent out their navies to harass and corral the hulk people further and further away from their shores, pushing them finally into the vast empty seas of the southern latitudes.

Ultimately, unable to secure fuel or even spare parts for their engines, these environmental refugees had been forced to chain their old ships together to survive the howling storms of the Antarctic seas. Not one single nation was prepared to open its borders to these refugees, people who were regarded as voluntary, unofficial migrants. Thus the hulk platform communities had been created.

'Sixty of our ships already have engine power,' bellowed a darkly bearded young man Chanda knew to be John Gogotya, one of the more aggressive of the young African-born community leaders. 'Another hundred will be able to sail as soon as they have diesel fuel. Now is the time for us to go and find new homes!'

Scores of voices roared their support. Chanda knew that many of the recently repaired ships had already been slipping away at night, using the cover of bad weather to cloak them from the radar of the circling naval escort, then returning a few nights later. The rumours were that these expeditions had gone in search of new sources of food, water and, most importantly, diesel fuel.

'No!' shouted Chanda, over the din. 'No! Our only hope is to stick together. Let's just give our lawyer a few weeks more to get his case going.'

There was a sudden loud report, deafening in the enclosed space. Then all went quiet.

'We will wait no longer,' pronounced John Gogotya, as he lowered his automatic rifle. 'We have no land, no water, no sunshine, no rain. And now we have no legal case. We are leaving here to find a new home.'

There were whoops and shouts of support from all round.

Then most of the young men were jumping up and down, chanting.

'Then do what you must,' said Chanda with his head bowed. But no one heard him over the din.

Lunch had been set up for Perdy and her host in a colonnaded gazebo on the west lawn where a table had been laid with white linen and glittering silver cutlery. Two chairs were placed in readiness. A butler in a grey tunic and dark striped trousers was waiting to greet Perdy. He was uncorking a bottle of Cristal champagne.

Nicholas Negromonte arrived ten minutes later, driven across the verdant lawn in a balloon-tyred golf cart.

'Welcome to Langland Park, Perdy' he said, bounding into the gazebo. 'How did you like my Spitfire?'

So American, thought Perdy. *No hesitation in talking immediately about himself and his expensive toys.* She knew that his father had been a Greek shipping tycoon who had taken US citizenship only shortly before his first son had been born, but this Negromonte seemed wholly American in his unashamed love of money and technology.

'Must be expensive to keep such an important antique flying,' she said, offering him a wry smile.

Negromonte glanced at her quickly, trying to assess whether she was being ironic or merely stating the obvious. It wasn't easy to know with these Brits.

'One of the last three still flying,' he said, as he accepted a glass of champagne from the butler's silver tray and sat down beside her. 'To you,' said Negromonte, raising his glass.

'To this glorious day,' said Perdy. 'It's beautiful here. You're very lucky.'

She'd meant her statement to be a little provocative. Did he think of himself as lucky, or as clever, or as merely entitled?

'I am very lucky indeed,' he agreed smoothly. 'Especially to have you here for … how long can you stay with us? I was hoping you could stay for dinner this evening, at least.'

As he spoke, Perdy noticed the table in front of her starting to sway. Instinctively, she reached out to steady it, thinking that it had been caught by a gust of wind. Then she felt her chair flex beneath her and she saw a crack suddenly snake down one of the gazebo's white Doric columns.

Negromonte leaped to his feet. 'Outside,' he yelled, grabbing Perdy's arm and yanking her from her chair. 'We must get away from the building.'

Twelve miles to the north of the Langland Park estate, the Reverend Nigel Phillips, rector of the little parish of Dale Deep, Lincolnshire, was alone in the little thirteenth-century church of St Michael's when the first tremor hit.

The vicar was a devout man and, as was his weekday afternoon custom, he had locked himself inside his church for privacy and was now on his knees in the front pew. He was praying for the recovery of a seriously injured girl who had been knocked down and run over in the village High Street the week before.

At first, Reverend Phillips thought he must have been taken ill. His eyes snapped open and he hung onto the pew for support. It seemed as if his balance had been suddenly impaired.

Then he noticed that the old brass chandelier above the altar was swinging wildly from side to side. He frowned in confusion, then suddenly guessed what must be happening. Almost 300 years earlier, Lincolnshire had suffered England's worst earthquake on record.

The vicar realized what he should do. He jumped to his feet and ran along the flagstoned aisle towards the pair of high-arched doors at the far end of the nave. He knew that he had to get outside immediately, away from the old stone church.

As he reached the doors, he felt the worn slabs beneath his feet begin to heave. Then he saw a crack starting to open up between the massive wall and the floor.

Swaying from side to side in an attempt to remain upright, he tried to insert the old key in the large escutcheon lock of the ancient door. As he missed the keyhole, he heard a sudden loud crash from above, then a booming bell-toll. He looked up as the master bell, Brother James, plunged through the floor of the belfry, smashed onto the top of an interior stone buttress, then ricocheted outwards and tumbled down on top of him.

Crushed under twelve and a half tons of fifteenth-century Belgian-cast bronze, the vicar died instantly. He was to be one of the three human casualties of the Lincolnshire earthquake of 2055, Britain's worst-ever seismic shock. It lasted almost two minutes and registered 4.8 on the Richter Scale.

'Dr Knight – Emilia? Do come in,' said Taylor Blane cordially as she put her head round her boss's office door. Emilia noted that Gloria Fernandez, Blane and three other men were already gathered around his meeting table.

'Coffee?' asked the CEO smiling. His attitude was now very different to what it had been at their first meeting.

Emilia declined and took a seat beside Gloria Fernandez.

'This is Colonel Greene from the US Defense Nuclear Agency,' said Blane, as he introduced a sallow man in late middle age.

'Doctor Bowman you already know...' She realized it was the medical consultant who had recently treated her, from the Radiation Unit in the San Diego Naval Hospital. As she returned his smile she felt a sense of alarm – what was *he* doing here?

'And this gentleman is from a government agency in Washington...' said Blane. Emilia waited for his name and department details, but her boss didn't provide them.

'Now, how are you feeling after your adventure on Mount Māriota?' asked the CEO, almost solicitously.

'I'm fine, absolutely fine,' said Emilia, frowning slightly. She couldn't imagine what this meeting was about.

'It turns out you have done your country a great service,' Blane continued, looking down at a DigiPad on the desktop in front of him. 'But before we can share any more information with you, we need you to sign this. Mrs Fernandez will witness your signature.'

He turned the DigiPad towards her and pushed it across the table. Emilia read the heading.

UNITED STATES OF AMERICA
NATIONAL SECRECY AGREEMENT

'It's the standard agreement for government contractor employees,' explained Gloria. 'I've already signed one – it's really just a technicality.'

'Except that we put you in prison if you ever repeat what you are about to be told,' said the unnamed man from the unidentified government agency.

'Then I'd rather not know at all!' snapped Emilia, rising from the table.

She was about to leave the room when Taylor Blane stood up quickly and intercepted her. He placed a kindly hand on her shoulder and led her back to the table.

'I think we rather got off on the wrong foot, Emilia.' He smiled, motioning her back to her chair. 'You have done something of very great value and I'd like to tell you about it, but we *do* need you to sign this agreement...'

Shrugging reluctantly, she lifted the DigiPad and read through the chapter headings.

'It just means that you can't divulge information that's of crucial importance to our country,' said Gloria Fernandez. 'That's not unreasonable, is it?'

Emilia considered, then gave another shrug, unclipped the stylus and added her signature in the space indicated. She then passed the electronic reader to the HR executive.

'Very good,' said Colonel Greene, the man from the Defense Nuclear Agency, as Gloria witnessed the document. 'We have since analysed the radioactive rock sample you brought back from Samoa. Any idea what it is?'

'Well, from its weight, and from the dosage of radiation I picked up, I thought it might contain some traces of uranium.'

'Dead right,' said Greene. 'But in fact it is something more special than that. It is thirty-five per cent nickel, twenty-eight per cent iron, and thirty-one-point-six per cent *pure* uranium.'

Emilia immediately thought back to the size of the sample she had collected – almost a third of that had been pure uranium!

She'd never read about uranium ore being found before in such concentration.

Then she completed the calculation. 'And what about the other five-point-four per cent?' she asked.

'That's why we're all here,' said the unnamed agent. 'That was plutonium.'

There was a silence as Emilia digested this additional information. Geology had been her foundation subject at university and she remembered that plutonium was normally found only in trace amounts. The super-heavy metal used for making atomic weapons was produced in quantity only within nuclear reactors.

'Are you sure?' she asked, stunned.

'Not only was it plutonium, it was isotope two-three-nine,' said the colonel from the Defense Nuclear Agency. 'Fissile material, almost weapons grade.'

'I don't understand,' said Emilia. 'How could it possibly be plutonium?'

'That's what we intend to find out,' said the colonel. 'We're going to dig down into that volcano as soon as the present eruption subsides. We'd be grateful for a copy of the simulations you've created, and we're going to have to impound all the video material and data that you and your assistants captured on site . . .'

Emilia was no longer absorbing much of what was being said around the table. Her mind was racing; she knew that fissile plutonium could only be produced by neutron irradiation, by the sort of atomic bombardment that takes place during nuclear reactions.

If that sample had been brought up from deep inside the Earth, did it mean that there was nuclear activity occurring within the core? Some maverick scientists had suggested such a thing in the past – had suggested that the Earth was a mini-sun, that only continuing fission at the core could produce the swirling magnetic fields that protect the planet from cosmic radiation.

And if plutonium was now breaking away and travelling up through the previously impervious mantle to be ejected by a volcano, what must be happening at the core?

'Dr Knight . . . Emilia?'

She realized that they were trying to regain her attention. It was Dr Bowman who was speaking to her now.

'Once I learned that you'd been handling pure plutonium, I thought I should come up and see you myself,' said the doctor. 'The half-life is so long that we're going to have to keep a much closer eye on you.'

'You mean I've got to go back into hospital?' asked Emilia, alarmed.

'No, but I think you ought to be transferred to light duties for the moment,' said Bowman. 'Until we establish the rate of decay in the bone marrow samples we've taken.'

'I'm arranging for you to take on a local PR role for Geohazard,' said Gloria Fernandez. 'Go round the schools, talk to the children about earthquakes, that sort of thing.'

'But what about monitoring the Pacific Region?' asked Emilia.

'We're bringing Carlos Robredo up from Mexico City,' said Blane, firmly. 'He's arriving this afternoon.'

Under spreading cedar trees that were already ancient when King Henry VIII had hunted across these rolling pastures, Nick Negromonte and Perdy Curtis strolled together in a companionable silence. It was late evening and they had not long finished dinner.

The afternoon's earth tremors had subsided quickly, and her host had soon gathered status reports from his staff all around the estate. There was the crack in the gazebo column, but there had been no obvious damage to the venerable old house itself, nor to any of its many outbuildings, gatehouses or estate cottages.

'Quite a surprise,' Negromonte had said as they were driven back in the golf cart across the lawns. 'Not the sort of thing you expect in England.'

Then he had given Perdy a personal tour of the house. She learned that it had been extended and refashioned by the sixth Lord Langland between 1763 and 1786, and that this tract of the English wold had been graced with Robert Adam's Palladian genius and Capability Brown's green artistry to celebrate the noble lord's success in the Virginia cotton plantations.

'What a fantastic art collection!' Perdy enthused, gazing at seemingly endless walls of pictures, including paintings by Canaletto, Tintoretto and Rubens.

'Most of them came with the house,' Negromonte admitted. 'The last owner didn't want to split them up – and your government didn't want them to leave the country.'

'So do you ever open this place to the public?' she asked, staring up at a large painting of a woman captioned *Portrait of an Unknown Woman; From the Studio of Michelangelo.*

'For a few months a year, when I have to be elsewhere.'

The tour had taken almost two hours and even then Perdy realized that she had seen only part of the mansion. As she passed some open doors she was aware of a quiet buzz of activity, and she realized that the ERGIA Corporation maintained a sizeable staff at Langland.

'Will you allow us to film here?' she asked. 'I'd very much like to interview you in this setting.'

'Let's talk about that over dinner,' Negromonte had proposed. 'I presume you'll be able to stay over. If not, the helicopter can fly you back to London in an hour. '

In the mirrored dining room they had dined on wild salmon and venison from the estate's own deer park. As they ate, Negromonte asked Perdy about the other weather-management companies she intended to cover in her documentary, questioning her about her own attitude to climate control. Then he asked if his public relations people could have sight of her film before it was broadcast.

'Absolutely not,' said Perdy firmly. 'That's not BBC policy.'

Now, as they strolled under the ancient cedar trees, Perdy returned to the request she had made earlier.

'I really would like to film you here, against this backdrop.' She turned to wave towards the grand house behind them. 'It would be an elegant counterpoint to all the high-tech space imagery.'

It was a perfectly clear night, the stars ablaze in the country sky, while the moon, three-quarters full, gallantly added its own natural reflection to their soft glow.

'I'm not sure that would be a good idea,' said her host at last, turning to gaze down into her eyes. 'I'll have to talk to my media people. They just might think all this is a little over the top for your programme.'

Perdy heard a ping and Negromonte lifted a communicator to his ear.

He listened carefully, then said, 'Excellent, well done. Give me two minutes at level two, then rejoin the main network.'

He flipped the communicator shut and returned it to his pocket. There was a pre-emptive smile hovering around his lips, as if he was about to tell her a joke.

Perdy waited to see what he was going to say, then he lifted his right hand and snapped his thumb and forefinger together.

Suddenly the entire park was bathed in bright sunlight. Perdy instinctively shut her eyes tight against the glare, but gradually reopened them, looking about her, as they adjusted to an eerie nocturnal daylight.

'Our space station repairs are now finished and we're back on line,' said Negromonte. 'This is their way of letting me know.'

From nearby, Perdy heard a bird start to sing in the treetops. Then it was joined by another, and suddenly all of the birds nesting in the great trees around them woke to the false dawn.

As suddenly as it had arrived, the sunlight was switched off again. Now it seemed even darker than it had before.

Perdy felt her host moving closer. 'You're not cold?' he asked.

She shook her head, then felt Negromonte's arms slip round her shoulders. He was bending his head as if for a kiss.

'No!' said Perdy firmly, turning away. 'Let's keep our relationship on a strictly professional footing.'

EIGHT

As no airline offered direct flights between San Francisco and the Santa Barbara peninsula, Michael Fairfax chose to drive the 300 miles south to Lompoc. He was on his way to visit the state penitentiary in which the Los Angeles Police Department was holding his one-time girlfriend – a woman now accused of belonging to a PFO terrorist cell.

When he had taken her call he had wondered at first if this might be a hoax, but as soon as he heard her throaty voice he was left in no doubt. He hadn't seen Carole Gonzaga for over fifteen years, not since they had been students together on the same UCLA campus, but her vibrant personality had reached out to him once again over the networks, instantly familiar.

'I need your help, Mike,' she told him huskily. 'Not as a lawyer, but as a friend – if you can still think of me in that way.'

He explained that what she needed above all else was a criminal-law attorney to represent her, but during this one permitted phone call she had begged him to visit her. 'I have no one else I can trust and there's something *very* important I have to tell you.'

Because this trip was not directly connected with the firm's business, Michael had taken two days of his annual vacation entitlement to drive down Route One – the old scenic highway that wound its way sinuously along the Pacific coastline.

He was pleased to have an excuse to get out of the office; informing the hulk community that there was going to be a delay in bringing their case before the international court had been both difficult and humiliating. When he had originally secured their agreement of representation, he had promised his clients an initial hearing within three months of his appointment. He felt instinctively that their simmering anger could not be contained for much longer.

Michael drove on through Big Sur, Monterey, Carmel and Grover Beach – all in beautiful late-spring sunshine just as scheduled, now that the local weather-management services were back on line – and then on through the agricultural flower fields of Lompoc, thousands of acres that, thanks to climate control, were now filled year round with magnificent outdoor blooms.

Skirting the Brandenburg US Air Force base, he soon identified the ugly state penitentiary fences as they loomed over the surrounding flower fields.

Shortly before four-thirty p.m. he was shown into a shabby interview room in the outer ring of low buildings. Almost as a matter of routine he laid a DigiPad on the small table as if about to record an interview with a client.

The door opened and two overweight female prison guards entered, escorting a woman prisoner, manacled at her hands and feet, between them. She was wearing an orange all-in-one prison-issue suit.

As Carole lifted her head, Michael found it hard to conceal his surprise. He doubted that he would now have recognized her if they'd passed on the street. Her dark hair was close-cropped and her large-featured, theatrical face that had once captivated him now looked deeply shadowed and haunted. She looked so much older than he remembered.

He nodded to her – the usual curt greeting of a lawyer to a client in restraints – then asked the warders to remove her manacles for the duration of the interview.

Without replying, one of the guards removed Carole's wrist cuffs, but pointedly left her leg irons in place.

'It's OK, Mike,' said Carole. That throaty voice again – the only thing about her that seemed unchanged.

The female guards stepped back to stand either side of the door, and Carole shot him an urgent look of request.

'Outside, please,' he told them.

They glanced at each other and then reluctantly turned and left the room. Michael saw that one of them remained stationed on the other side of the door, watching them through the wire-reinforced observation window.

Carole Gonzaga stooped and began peering under the table top. Then she picked up a metal-framed chair and examined it.

'What are you looking for?' asked Michael.

'I'm a terrorist,' she hissed, as she continued her searching. 'Don't you understand, they listen in wherever I go.'

'But anything they recorded covertly between us would be totally inadmissible as evidence,' protested Michael. 'They couldn't use any of it.'

'That's not what I'm worried about.'

He had wondered how she would be, what he could say to her after all these years: *Hi, Carole, great to see you again. How are things?*

But he hadn't expected to find the haunted, anxious creature who was now shuffling along each wall in turn, apparently expecting to find hidden microphones.

Michael sat down at the interview table and pointedly turned off the recording function in his DigiPad.

'What can I do for you?' he asked firmly.

Carole was now by the door, examining the architrave. For a moment he wondered if she was mentally ill. Then she shuffled back to her chair, sat down and leaned her head fully forward, across the table. Instinctively, Michael did the same.

'Put some music on, loud,' she said, nodding at his DigiPad.

As a busy lawyer, he didn't usually bother to carry much music around with him, but he located something that he thought might be sufficiently loud, touched *Play* and turned the volume up. The beat filled the room.

'OK,' Carole said quietly, still leaning forward over the table so that their heads were almost touching. 'You'll have to remember everything I'm going to tell you. You must get in contact with Professor Robert Fivetrees at Berkeley – Department of Planetary Geophysics. He's discovered there's something seriously damaging the Earth's magnetic field, but our wonderful government has slapped an NSO – a National Secrecy Order –

on his work. He can't publish his findings or even talk about them.'

Michael was listening carefully, though what she was saying sounded like wild eco-activist paranoia – or something worse. He stared intently at her, their eyes only inches apart. But he detected no madness there, only a steely determination.

'He gave us the information secretly,' hissed the prisoner. 'Fivetrees says climate management is seriously disrupting the magnetic poles. We tried to get the media interested, but they think we're just freaky extremists. The professor needs to find a legal way to get his research published – maybe somewhere abroad. Will you meet him – see if you can help him? He's really nervous now – because of his connection with us. But he'll talk to *you* if you tell him I sent you – if you tell him about our time together.'

Michael straightened up and his former lover slowly did the same. Her wide dark-eyed gaze held his, seeming all the more intense because of her cropped hair. She nodded once, as if to reinforce her request.

'And that's it?' he asked in a normal voice.

'That's it,' Carole confirmed.

'But you will still need a criminal lawyer to prepare your case – to see if you can get bail.'

'I don't want bail,' she told him, 'and I'll be representing myself. I intend to make a statement from the witness box and tell the world in open court – where they can't stop me – what our government is covering up.'

'Commander on the bridge!'

'Commander on the bridge!' repeated the watch lieutenant, coming to attention. Then he staggered forwards and fell hard into the commander's arms, just as the senior officer stepped into the ship's high-tech control centre. All of the other six members of the watch were now clinging to pieces of equipment or grabbing at handles to stop themselves being thrown across the sloping floor.

Lt Commander Buckler R. Jarvis, captain of the USS *Vincent*, already knew he currently had the worst naval posting of all – not just the worst posting in the US Navy, but the worst posting in *any* of the world's navies. Steaming in circles in an attempt to corral the hulk platforms and their millions of environmental refugees within these wild Antarctic seas was a humiliating duty just on its own, but the uncontrolled weather of these extreme latitudes made the task so miserable that each ship spent only three months on 'hulk station duties' before being relieved.

'Well, what is it?' Jarvis demanded as he heaved the young watch lieutenant back onto his feet and fought his way over to the captain's chair. It was three-twenty a.m. local time and he had been summoned out of a deep sleep by his Executive Officer.

As Jarvis had hurriedly pulled on his uniform he had wondered if this bad weather was causing problems for the rest of the fleet; although the nuclear-powered *Vincent* could ride out almost any storm, the Force Nine gale that they were currently experiencing could cause serious problems for the smaller escorts.

Even the mighty aircraft carrier now reared like a frightened horse as she crested a giant wave and, not for the first time, the commander understood the wisdom of the hulk people in lashing their many ships together to form a single platform. It was a raft so large that it could float across the giant undulations of the oceans like a leaf on the surface of a flood.

'We're getting strange radar signals, sir,' yelled the Exec over the noise of the howling gale outside. 'From the far side of the hulk platform. It looks like some of their ships are coming adrift.'

Lt Commander Jarvis nodded for the signal to be fed to his own screen, then gazed at the jagged image which shimmered in front of him.

'We're also getting a lot of false images and interference from the bigger waves,' shouted the Exec. 'Some of those blips might just be water.'

The commander studied the picture again. It did seem as if scores of ships had broken away from the main platform, but it was impossible to be sure.

The carrier rose up once more, and everybody on the bridge braced themselves for the mighty crash that would follow. It was a wicked night for anybody to be out on the open seas.

'Satellite imagery?' asked the commander.

The Exec shook his head. 'Total cloud cover, sir.'

'Can we put up a recon drone?' he asked, already guessing the answer.

'Can't launch in this, sir. We'll have to wait until it gets below Force Three.'

The commander nodded. The ship was therefore almost blind. He leaned forward to examine the radar image again. The far side of the hulk platform was over sixty nautical miles south of the task force's current position. In this weather it would take them ten or eleven hours to steam all the way round the platform to see precisely what was going on.

'It looks like part of the platform is breaking up,' Jarvis said to his Executive Officer. 'Those breakaway blips are far too big to be single ships.'

'Unless they're very big wave series,' observed the Exec.

'What's the met forecast?'

The Exec had a printout ready. 'This is expected to last for another forty-eight hours at least, sir.'

The commander nodded. With another two days and nights of this pounding, and if the hulk platform was really breaking up, there wouldn't be much left of any ships caught on their own without engine power.

'Send a signal to Pearl Harbor,' ordered the commander: '"Ships appear to be separating from hulk platform." Send them a copy of our radar data files – perhaps they'll be able to get more out of them.'

'Sir, message coming in from HMS *Portsmouth*,' shouted the watch lieutenant. 'One of her engines is overheating and they'll have to shut it down for repairs.'

That settled it. The *Vincent* would now have to nursemaid the little British destroyer through the rest of this storm, maintaining station close enough to evacuate her crew if she got into further trouble. The hulk people would just have to look out for themselves.

'Send to *Portsmouth*, "Coming to your assistance immediately."' The commander glanced at his Exec, who had already tapped the new heading into the navigation system.

'Fifteen minutes, sir,' he said.

'And: "Be with you oh-four-twenty-five,"' said the commander, finishing his dictation.

'Ready on the new heading, twenty-one degrees south-southeast,' said the Exec. 'Shall I inform the other captains, then come about and proceed at three-quarters speed?'

'Make it so,' said the commander, stepping down from his chair. 'You have the helm.'

Emilia Knight lived alone in an isolated house on a high bluff overlooking an inlet called Muir Beach. The small bay was on Marin County's Pacific coast, fifteen miles north of San Francisco's Golden Gate Bridge, and she rented the property from her predecessor at Geohazard, an older male colleague who had accepted a two-year posting to the company's seismic monitoring centre in Tokyo.

The 'beach' below her house was small and shingly, set back deep inside the cove. Despite year-round weather management the Pacific could still be quite wild on this exposed coast. But Emilia loved the location and she appreciated the fact that before buying the house her Geohazard co-worker had made a thorough check of the building's earthquake-resistant foundations.

The redwood dwelling was on two levels, with a small garden to the south, while to the west – the ocean side – there was a large 'sunset deck' and the obligatory Californian hot tub.

Three days after she'd learned that she'd inadvertently been handling virtually pure plutonium, Emilia lounged on her deck on a Saturday evening, watching the sun go down. It had turned the sky into a vast sheet of ruby and gold carnival glass.

She had taken to carrying a pocket Geiger counter wherever she went, but although she checked the level of radioactivity on her body at least twice a day, the readings were now close to normal.

'Hello? Em?' The man's voice sounded behind her, from

within the house, and she started before realizing that it was only Steve Bardini. 'Anyone at home?'

'Here,' she called and after a few moments her assistant and former boyfriend stepped out onto the deck.

'I did ring the doorbell,' he explained apologetically, and she realized that he still retained her access and entry codes. She would have to reprogram her locks and security system.

But she was pleased to see him this evening. They had not met nor had a chance to talk since she had been so abruptly reassigned. Emilia had set all of her communications systems to just take messages while she absorbed the news and weighed up what she had been told.

'Hi, Steve. Grab a beer,' she greeted him, shielding her eyes against the low sun.

He fetched a bottle from the kitchen and came to sit beside her. Outside of the office there was still a slight awkwardness about their recently recategorized relationship.

'How've you been?' he asked.

'Two-point-one,' said Emilia, smiling. 'And falling.'

'Oh, great. I was worried because I heard you'd been transferred out of Risk Assessment.'

She wondered how much she could tell him.

'They're transferring *me* to night shifts for a while,' Steve added sheepishly. 'I guess it's because we screwed up on Mount Māriota.'

Emilia merely nodded and stared into the sunset.

'And they made me sign a goddam National Secrecy Agreement! Said that in the future I couldn't tell anyone about our trip to Samoa.'

'Did they tell you why?' she asked.

He shook his head. Then she realized: if Steve had also signed an NSA, she could tell him what she knew.

An hour later and it was almost dark, only the faintest red line on the horizon indicating the sun's passing. Emilia picked up a remote control and lit the deck lamps and anti-bug zappers. In the last sixty minutes she and Steve had allowed their scientific imaginations to run wild, hypothesizing about what sort of phenomenon could produce practically pure plutonium deep underground, and how it could be propelled to the Earth's surface. Both wanted to go back over the data collected before the Samoan eruption to see if there was any buried clue. They agreed that they would do so in their spare time, over the coming week.

Steve rose to get himself another beer. As he passed Emilia's lounger he squatted down beside her, reached out a hand and caressed her cheek.

'And what about us, Em?' he asked. 'I'm really worried about you now.'

Emilia smiled in the gloom and caught his hand in hers. She lifted it away from her face.

'I'm grateful for your concern, Steve,' she said. 'But I've already told you. It *really* is over as far as I am concerned.'

New York Times

Monday, 16 June 2055

U.S. AGREES LONG-TERM AID PACKAGE FOR INDEPENDENT SAMOA

The U.S. State Department today announced an aid package for Independent Samoa worth $48 billion over the next decade.

'It is inequitable that standards of living in American Samoa and its independent near neighbour should be so different,' said State Department Official Gyro Mandible. 'Our package of aid will enable Independent Samoa to join the ASEAN-Pacific Climate Management Consortium to regulate local weather patterns. This will provide a much-needed boost to tourism in the region.'

Filbert Steps had been one of San Francisco's most exclusive
residential addresses for over a century. Perched on the eastern
side of Telegraph Hill, the wooden stairs provided access to a
score of old wood-frame Victorian cottages and villas. The
incline was so steep that residents had to carry their shopping,
bicycles and leisure gear up and down the treacherous steps by
hand. It was an alpine lane suited for people who enjoyed the
spectacular views that the hill provided, rather than for those
who favoured their own personal comfort.

Michael Fairfax and his bride Lucy had chosen this rarefied
location for their family home shortly before they'd got married.
They knew that on their own they couldn't have afforded a
house in such an exclusive area of the city, but Lucy's father had
helped with the large down-payment.

Telegraph Hill, on which Filbert Steps itself was only one of
a handful of picturesque streets and residential, bougainvillea-
draped stairways, was a small but sheer phallic pinnacle – geo-
logically 'a sandstone tor' – thrust up by the San Andreas fault
system on the very edge of San Francisco's wide, semi-landlocked
bay: the largest and most beautiful harbour in the world.

Michael walked carefully down the wooden steps and
entered the small front yard of 'Jersey Villa', the finest Victorian
house on the hill, remembering to close the low picket gate
behind him. It was his first scheduled return to the family home
since his divorce. Lucy had agreed that he could visit to see how
Matthew's electronic wallpaper looked now that it was installed
in his bedroom.

Matt opened the front door and minutes later Michael was
up in a darkened bedroom on the fourth floor of the house,
staring around him at a glowing night sky.

'It's absolutely fantastic, Dad!' exclaimed Matthew. 'When I
go to sleep the stars are in one position and when I wake up
they've moved to exactly where they should be.'

'It's not keeping you awake?' asked Michael.

'Sometimes I just lie here watching the sky move very slowly
around me, and it's as if I can feel the whole planet turning. Ask
Mom if you can stay over – you should try it yourself!'

The divorcé sensed privately that it was a little too early for him to request such a privilege, but Michael was delighted that his gift had proved so successful. He merely smiled and nodded.

'Hey, Dad,' said Matthew suddenly, in a stagy voice. 'Why does the Bar Association prohibit sexual relations between a lawyer and his client?'

Michael was already smiling; his older son never stopped teasing him about his much-derided profession. 'I don't know. Why *do* they prohibit lawyers having sex with their clients?'

'So they don't bill their clients twice for the same service.'

Michael's guffaw was totally unforced. He'd usually heard Matt's lawyer jokes before, but he always delighted in the pleasure his son derived from teasing him. This gag, he realized, represented a testing of the taste boundaries as his son entered adolescence. He wondered whether he was expected to disapprove slightly.

'But there's just one problem about the wallpaper, Dad,' said Matthew, serious again. 'The alignment is a fraction of a degree out.'

The boy pulled aside a curtain screening a pair of glass doors, opened them outwards and stepped out onto the wooden deck outside his attic bedroom. His father followed.

Arranged on the timber platform outside were three old-fashioned optical telescopes, all of them linked to image grabbers and computer cables snaking back into the boy's bedroom.

'You must be the only guy in the country still bothering with opticals,' marvelled Matthew's father. He knew that almost all other amateur astronomers now took their visual feeds from the Galileo IX or from one of the many other space telescopes in orbit around the Earth or Mars. The advent of solar-reflective climate management had produced so much light pollution in the night sky that only the brightest of stars remained visible over heavily populated regions.

'But the wallpaper isn't quite accurate,' Matthew insisted. 'I've got my telescopes trained on the Pole Star, Orion and Arcturus, and they just don't quite line up with the stars in my room. Either they're one parsec out or Telegraph Hill is subsiding.'

Michael stepped back into his son's bedroom and gazed up at the simulated night sky again. He had bought this expensive electronic wallpaper in a department store in Auckland, and he had been very specific about the need for both realism and accuracy. With a son as star-mad and knowledgeable as Matthew, it wouldn't do to present him with anything of less than professional standard.

'One hundred per cent accurate, sir,' the well-informed shop assistant had assured him. 'The eighth-generation cellular-GPS networks are sub-millimetre precise.'

This gave Michael an idea for a father-and-son outing. 'How about packing up your telescopes and us driving out into the mountains one night?' he suggested. 'We could do some real stargazing away from the city lights.'

'Great,' said Matthew. 'But I'll have to check with Mom first.'

NINE

'Santa Maria, it's an Armada!' shouted Squadron Leader Julio Velasquez over the intercom. He had just seen the radar image on his head-up display.

In the rear seat of the long-outdated Peruvian Air Force fighter jet, Flight Sergeant Ricardo Garcia punched buttons that would calculate the number of individual ship signatures that were being picked up by the aircraft's imaging system.

'There's over two hundred vessels out there,' the navigator advised his pilot.

Flying in formation behind the forty-year-old twin-engined Eurofighter Typhoon, one of the last manned warplanes ever built, were seventeen similar jets. All were armed with laser-guided bombs and air-to-ground missiles. They had been scrambled from their bases at Chimbote and Callao on Peru's Pacific coast after a commercial jet pilot had reported seeing a large number of unidentified cargo vessels approaching the nation's territorial waters.

Suddenly the squadron leader made visual contact with his target. The ships were spread out line abreast on the horizon, in a rank so wide that it was impossible to make out either end. There were old mega-tankers, crude-oil carriers, container ships and freighters. Velasquez realized that they must be hulk-people ships, but now they were all steaming under their own power.

Velasquez's orders were clear. He issued an instruction for the large squadron to break into three groups, two to overfly the approaching ships from opposite directions, at 2,000 feet, one group to descend to 300 feet to pass low over the old vessels, to enable themselves be clearly seen – and heard.

'This is Squadron Leader Velasquez of the Peruvian Air Force, calling the captains of ships approaching Peruvian national waters,' he radioed in English over Channel Nine, the international frequency for all emergency broadcasts.

He waited, then repeated his call. There was no response.

'Transmit on all frequencies,' Velasquez instructed his navigator. Then he repeated his message twice more, once in Spanish.

'They've lit up a missile range-finder,' shouted Garcia. Until this point there had been no suggestion that any of the old vessels might be armed.

'We've got incoming.' The shout came from one of the aircraft flying down at sea level. Velasquez banked his plane sharply to the left, and peered down to try and get a visual fix.

'It's an old Chinese SAM,' reported Garcia as his radar identified the weapon. 'No problem – I have a lock on their launcher.'

Almost immediately there was a flash of light far away to the south. Then they heard a shout in their headsets: 'We got it!'

'Missile kill confirmed,' said Garcia from the Typhoon's back seat. 'Shall I take out their launcher?'

'Negative,' said Velasquez, levelling his jet out again. He opened his transmission to include all aircraft. 'Do not return fire,' he ordered his squadron. 'I repeat, do not fire. Delta wing return to zero-two-zero and resume formation.'

He tried again to make radio contact with the vessels below, this time adding a warning that any further missile launches would be met with immediate lethal retaliation. Once again he ordered the ships to change their heading immediately to a direction that would take them away from Peruvian waters.

There was no response to any of his communications.

The squadron had now been circling the ships for over thirty minutes and fuel limitations meant that they would soon have to turn and head back to base.

Julio Velasquez issued curt orders to his wingman and two

other pilots in the squadron. Then he led them down to sea level.

The four jets began their bombing run at a height of 300 feet, coming out of the east. Each of their laser-guided bombs was set to detonate 600 yards ahead of the targets they selected.

'Bomb away,' shouted Garcia, and Velasquez watched on his head-up video display as the 200-pound bomb detonated right in the path of one massive oil tanker. A huge plume of water shot high into the air and the shock of the explosion sent a giant wave radiating outwards.

The four attack jets lifted their noses to climb to their recon altitude. Five minutes later, as they smoothly rejoined formation, Velasquez heard one of the other navigators call out, 'Ships are turning, ships are turning.'

He glanced down and saw that several of the antiquated vessels were indeed starting a long, slow turn to starboard, as if choreographed. Then the remaining ships also began to slow and turn in the same direction.

After ten minutes of flying the length of the scattering convoy, to ensure that all of the ships continued along their slow semicircles, Squadron Leader Velasquez ordered the rest of his flight to return to base. He remained on station for a further fifteen minutes, pushing his own emergency fuel limit to the maximum. He wanted to ensure that none of the skippers on the ships below had second thoughts about trying to sneak back to anchor at any point along the long and sparsely populated Peruvian coastline.

'On behalf of the people of Samoa, I wish to express my government's gratitude for your interest in our cause and for all the help you have given us so far. But, I repeat, we must withdraw from participation in the legal case you are pursuing.'

Michael Fairfax had been surprised to hear again from Mautoatasi Otasi, prime minister of Independent Samoa, so soon after he had been forced to tell his clients that there would be a delay in getting their case before the international court. In the meantime he had been intrigued to read of America's decision to grant the tiny nation a generous aid package, something he himself hadn't even known was in the offing.

'I don't understand, Prime Minster,' he said. 'Your case for compensation remains excellent, and the current delay in bringing it to court is purely temporary.'

'There's a whole new future for Samoa now,' said Otasi, 'thanks to the generosity of your government. My cabinet colleagues and I feel that it would be wholly inappropriate to continue with a legal action – especially as so many of the corporations concerned have a large number of American shareholders.'

Michael nodded, even though Otasi could not see him. Neither man had chosen to select 'visual' for this conversation.

'I understand. Thank you, Prime Minister,' said Michael and he returned his phone to its cradle.

He sat for a while in his office on the sixty-third floor, just staring out of the window. From here, he could see all the way to the snow-capped summits of the Diablo Mountains, fifty miles to the north-east.

The recently constructed Embarcadero Space Needle had already become the city's most famous landmark. Over three-quarters of a kilometre tall, it had been built right on the shoreline of the San Francisco Bay, on a site formerly occupied by the old Hyatt Regency hotel and the Embarcadero shopping centre.

Despite being constructed on reclaimed land only 500 yards from the water's edge, mid-twenty-first-century civil engineering techniques and materials had allowed the builders to erect the world's highest commercial, residential and retail building – a total of 181 floors topped off with a rotating viewing gallery – in a high-risk earthquake zone, whilst proclaiming with full confidence that the Needle could withstand any degree of shaking that the ever-parturient San Andreas Fault could deliver.

The tower's construction continued down below ground level for a depth equivalent to twenty storeys, where its massive base sat on huge metal rollers which were themselves laid on a vast concrete platform. The theory was that even in the most severe shaking, the building above would merely glide back and forth on its rolling foundations, while the nanotube and carbon-fibre upright girders would allow the tall building to flex and sway like a blade of grass in the wind.

Michael turned his gaze to the sprawling city of Berkeley, on the other side of the bay. It was a clear day, as scheduled, and picking up the binoculars he kept on his desk, he rose to his feet and focused them on a well-known Berkeley landmark.

His meeting with his former girlfriend inside Lompoc Penitentiary had unsettled him. On his long drive back north he had taken Highway 101, the more direct, non-scenic route, and once he had handed the driving over to computer-guided cruise control he had allowed his mind to wander again over what she had told him.

The more Michael thought about it, the more ridiculous Carole's request seemed. He didn't want to get tangled up with her again, or have anything to do with Planet First extremists or eco-terrorists. He believed that, for all its faults and delays, the law was the right way to deal with all forms of injustice and environmental abuse.

Through his powerful binoculars the Berkeley University campus looked neat and well-kept.

With a sigh he returned to his desk and slumped in his chair. Neither Saul Levinson nor any of his other partners had mentioned the hulk-people case to him again – and none of his colleagues had referred again to his threat to leave the firm. It seemed as if, having made their decision, they were now expecting him to simply pick up the threads and get on with alternative litigation.

But he had spent almost two years preparing his case against the giant energy companies. By now, he had expected to have a team of thirty or forty lawyers working for him, and a date set down for a preliminary hearing at the new Court of International Civil Justice in The Hague over in the Netherlands.

Michael stared at his desk, now clear of everything except his pictures of Matthew and Ben, then turned to his info screen. Ignoring the scores of e-mails and messages competing for his attention, he touched the number his inquiry produced and waited for the call to be put through.

'Professor Fivetrees's office,' said a female voice.

He picked up the phone. 'This is Michael Fairfax, I'm an attorney. I'd like to speak with Professor Fivetrees.' He hesitated, then added, 'Please tell him I'm an old friend of Carole Gonzaga.'

'Who knows how *old* Planet Earth is?'

Dr Emilia Knight glanced around the class of thirteen-year-olds and waited. Some of their faces were turned towards her but many students were making notes, doodling or affecting lack of interest. Yet, after an unsure start, she was starting to enjoy these local speaking engagements.

This afternoon's visit to the Robert Louis Stevenson High School in San Francisco's Sunset district was her third such experience within a fortnight. She had given the class her usual talk about how to be prepared for earthquakes in the Bay Area, and now she was moving on to more general geoscience.

'Ten million years,' said a pretty African-American girl with a bob haircut and acne.

'A bit longer,' said Emilia, glancing across at the strained-looking class teacher – a pinched man in his late forties.

'A hundred million years,' suggested an Asian girl with lime-green hair.

'Even longer – quite a bit longer,' Emilia prompted. She knew that these kids would have done basic earth sciences back in sixth grade, but it seemed as though they hadn't retained much.

Turning to the large screen on the wall, she picked up the electronic stylus and started to write in capital letters: THE EARTH IS . . .

Roger Mantle, the form teacher, cleared his throat pointedly. Emilia glanced across at him and then turned to follow his gaze. A slim boy with a thick tangle of brown hair, seated at the back of the room, had his hand half raised, at head height.

'Yes?' prompted Emilia.

'Ah, it's kinda between five-point-eight and six-point-two billion years old,' offered the boy. 'But it, ah, seems like that date is being pushed back every year. Ten years ago they thought it was only four and a half billion years old.'

'Absolutely right,' Emilia told him. Then she wondered if it would be good teaching practice to push this knowledgeable student a little harder. She followed her instinct. 'And do you know why the date has been changing?'

'We keep discovering that the universe is older than we thought,' said the boy, now slightly uncomfortable, glancing quickly to his right and left, trying to ascertain how his fellow students were reacting to his performance. 'And we can't rely on testing rocks on the earth – they seem to be younger than they are because of crustal recycling. They have to do isochron age tests on lead traces to measure uranium decay.'

The visiting scientist glanced at the teacher and saw that he now wore a smile of pride.

'Do we have a budding geophysicist here?' asked Emilia, talking half to the boy who had answered, half to his teacher. There was no response from either and Emilia's instinct now told her to move on. The boy had hung his head, biting at a hangnail, not wanting to make further eye contact.

'Excellent. That's quite right. We're still in the process of learning how old both the Earth and the universe really are.'

She turned and wrote quickly on the wall screen: THE EARTH IS BETWEEN FIVE AND SIX BILLION YEARS OLD.

Then she told the class bluntly just how little scientists really knew about the interior of the planet – something she herself had been forcibly reminded of in recent weeks.

Emilia explained that, in relative terms, the Earth's crust is thinner than the shell of an egg, and inside this delicate casing vast blobs of molten viscous rock wallow and balloon slowly, like globules in a giant lava lamp.

Projecting some of Geohazard's stock computer graphics onto the screen, she showed the class that inside their planet was a solid inner core – about 500 miles in diameter, slightly smaller than the moon – which seemed to float at the centre of an outer core of molten metals.

She described how there was also some evidence that the hard inner core was rotating around its own axis at a different speed and direction to the rest of the planet. It was the independent motion of this inner core that produced the powerful magnetic field that ballooned out around the planet, protecting it and its inhabitants from the sun's fierce magnetic wind.

'So, in fact, we know very little for certain about the inside of our own planet,' Emilia concluded. 'And none of us can really prove that Jules Verne wasn't right all along.'

The class laughed at this. A new movie version of *Journey to the Centre of the Earth* had recently been released, this time with full 3-D imagery and MegaSense effects.

Roger Mantle stepped back in front of his class, and thanked Dr Knight of Geohazard Laboratories for providing her stimulating talk. Emilia acknowledged the small ripple of applause. Then a loud buzzing sounded from outside in the corridor.

The students rose noisily from their desks and soon the only people left in the classroom were Emilia, Roger Mantle and the tousle-haired boy who had answered her question.

'This is Matthew Fairfax,' said the teacher.

Emilia shook the tall teenager's hand and gazed up into his green eyes.

'So you're really interested in geology?' Emilia asked.

'Matt's our star pupil in the sciences,' said Mantle proudly.

There was an awkward silence and Emilia wondered if the lad had a question for her about one of the recent volcanic eruptions.

'I live on Telegraph Hill, near the piers,' said the boy. 'Do you know the area?'

'Of course,' agreed Emilia. 'Great location – you're a lucky guy.'

'Have there been any earth tremors recorded in that area recently, Dr Knight?'

Emilia stared up at the intense young questioner and smiled. 'Maybe twenty or thirty every day. The ground beneath San Francisco is always moving. But you won't notice anything, usually. Most tremors are very mild.'

'But they're strong enough to move Telegraph Hill?'

Emilia laughed out loud. 'Oh no, absolutely not. There's been nothing under the city that humans could feel for over two years. And I don't think Telegraph Hill itself would be shaken, even if there was. You only really get that reaction with soft earth – sedimentary soils, landfills, that sort of thing. Like down in Mission or in the Marina district.'

'Well, the hill must be sinking then,' said Matt. 'My dad says it's made of bedrock, but . . .' He hesitated and then gazed directly at the pretty geologist. 'I do computer-aided optical astronomy. I did a star declination last night, and found that the whole sky seemed to have moved south-east by eight MAS. I checked my alignments – the hill *has* to be moving.'

Emilia shook her head doubtfully. Before her transfer to Geohazard she'd been the local Bay Area earthquake monitor. She knew every danger zone in and around the Bay Area cities; had walked most of them, sneakers in one hand, water bottle in the other.

She always wondered why humans with sufficient money to live anywhere in the world would choose one of its most dangerous locations. But she knew it was the vigorous subterranean activity that made the region's landscape so appealing; it was so beautiful that even she lived within the area, although she could at least claim some professional justification.

'*This must be your standard outfit,*' the earthquake monitor had regularly warned all those who lived or worked in such dangerous areas. '*In this area, always wear comfortable shoes and carry water. You're going to have to walk out one day.*' She knew *all* the local seismic hotspots.

'Your father's right,' said Emilia. 'It *is* bedrock – Massive Sandstone from the Cretaceous period. That's why there's an old quarry on Green Street. All the land around you may move, but the whole city would have to fall into the sea before Telegraph Hill itself shifted.'

Matthew glanced at his teacher, then back at the guest lecturer. 'That's what I thought too, but I've checked it over and over again. I'm sure it's moving.'

Undoing the fasteners of his school bag – she sensed an air almost of desperation in his movements – the boy produced a sheaf of papers and gridded photographs. Emilia took them from him and rippled through the pages. They were star maps, and all of them were timed and dated; the apparent anomalous movement that he had mentioned was highlighted and measured to the astronomical 'MAS' or milliarcsecond, an angle equal to one thousandth of an astronomical arc second.

'Could we stay on in here for a few minutes?' Emilia asked the form teacher.

'There's about ten minutes left of this break,' explained Mantle. 'I'm off to get a coffee. It's all yours.'

Emilia smiled her thanks, walked to the front row of desks, and laid out the data sheets that the boy had given her.

'Why don't you take me through these chronologically?' she suggested.

It seemed as if no time at all had passed before Roger Mantle reappeared. 'You've got to be in the music room in one minute,' the teacher reminded Matthew.

The boy hurriedly gathered his printouts together. Dr Knight had already admitted how it did seem from his data that the point of observation had moved by a minute amount, but she was also thinking of the many errors that could account for the aberrant readings. Measuring space and the relative motions of many stellar bodies thousands or millions of light years apart could be a very tricky business.

'Would your parents let you come visit the Geohazard Observatory at Mount Tamalpais?' Emilia asked him. 'We don't use it much these days. Maybe we could do a star declination there and also check out your equipment.'

TEN

On a clear Thursday evening in mid-June, Michael Fairfax left his office at seven p.m., collected his hydrogen-powered BMW sports saloon from the garage beneath the Embarcadero Space Needle, and drove out of the city across the lower deck of the Bay Bridge.

Skirting Oakland, he passed through the satellite cities of Concord and Stockton and continued up into the foothills of the Sierra Nevada on the old and almost deserted Highway 49, the original panhandlers' trail into the mountains.

It was shortly before ten p.m. when the car's navigation system told him that he had completed 154 miles and should now slow down in preparation for arrival at his destination.

He spotted the truck stop set back beside the westbound carriageway and, crossing over the oncoming lane, swung into its large parking space. The lot was filled with big 32-wheel truck rigs, pick-ups, motorbikes and off-road utilities, but at the end of one ragged row of vehicles he noticed a classic car that seemed totally out of place in this setting. It was a green turn-of-the-century sports Jaguar that appeared to be in immaculate condition.

Michael removed his tie and opened the collar of his white shirt. He had intended to go home for a change of clothing before driving out of town for this unusual rendezvous, but he had been delayed by a monthly caseload meeting that had overrun. He was now being regularly assigned to handle his legal partners' overspill litigation.

Engaging maximum-security defences on his own vehicle,

the attorney strode across the cinder-strewn car park towards the truck stop's bar. From inside came a sound of heavy retro-rock that made the walls and windows vibrate. As Michael pushed open the swing door, he was hit by a wall of amplified sound. A rock group was playing at the far end of the low room, slamming out the sort of heavy beat that was still played by specialist radio stations up and down the length of California. Odours of tobacco smoke, beer, bourbon, cheap perfume and testosterone-laden sweat washed over him.

Couples were dancing in a small area in front of the low stage – large, tattooed men in denims and leather-clad women with big hair – strutting and bobbing with stiff shoulders and straight backs.

The elegantly suited lawyer felt more than a little out of place and, as he pushed through the crowd, he became aware that some of the redneck customers were casting him suspicious, even threatening glances; at least his contact shouldn't have any difficulty in identifying him.

As he mimed an order for a beer, a huge figure loomed out of the crowd to stand close beside him at the bar. Michael pointedly refrained from looking sideways at the stranger, but then he felt a large hand descend on his shoulder.

The man had to be almost seven feet tall and he had long, greying hair swept back and bunched into a ponytail that fell to the middle of his broad shoulder blades. His weather-beaten face looked as hard as an anvil and his annealed cheeks were concave, like the bows of a warship.

'I am Fivetrees,' said the man, bending his head close to Michael's ear. 'Stay close.'

Throwing some dollars onto the bar counter, Michael picked up his beer bottle and followed the large man towards an empty booth to one side of the stage. As he slid onto the ripped plastic of the banquette, he realized why this booth had remained unoccupied. It was positioned right in front of one of the group's PA system loudspeakers. Michael could feel his chest bone vibrate with each beat. It would be impossible to talk.

The huge man – of Native American extraction, Michael guessed – slid into the seat opposite and handed him a small white cordless earpiece, indicating for him to insert it in his ear. Then he reached forward and stuck a Velcro-backed miniature microphone onto Michael's jacket lapel.

'Now' – the man's voice sounded clearly in his inner ear – 'can you hear me?'

Michael nodded.

'This is a privacy gizmo that one of my Berkeley colleagues developed. It's a comms system that filters out all sound but the users' own voices.'

Ten minutes later, Michael and Professor Robert Fivetrees were deep in a wholly private discussion. They had swapped and checked each other's digital identifications, and the professor had shown Michael how to train his system to recognize his own voice, even over the high-decibel din of the rock music.

Robert Fivetrees had been one of Carole Gonzaga's more recent lovers, Michael now learned.

'She told me about you when we were still together,' Fivetrees told him. 'That was before she got mixed up with these Planet First people.'

The professor started to explain what his work in planetary geophysics entailed, and as he ranged across subjects such as kinematic dynamo theory, magnetosphere anomalies, global paleointensities and solar pressures on the geomagnetic force field, Michael quickly recognized the immense intellect and depth of learning camouflaged beneath the long hair, red check shirt and cowboy boots. He also learned that Fivetrees was one of the few remaining descendants of a tribe of Yokuts Indians who had once lived in the San Joaquin Valley, in the Sierra Nevada. Eventually he steered the man around to their reason for meeting.

'The government served me with an emergency secrecy order three months ago,' complained Fivetrees, dropping his voice still further, despite their private communications system. 'As soon as I submitted a paper to the *US Geophysical Review*, agents were all over me. They called it a matter of national security.'

'What's so threatening about your work?' asked Michael.

The professor held up one finger, thrust a hand into his jeans pocket and extracted a slim silver container that looked like an old-fashioned cigarette case. Then he plucked two folding menus from their holder at the end of the table and stood them upright, to form an enclosed and shielded area on the table top.

Flipping open the lid of the silver case, Fivetrees placed the unit within the screened area. Suddenly a miniature holo-image of the Earth appeared in the makeshift mini-theatre.

'Another prototype from the Berkeley consumer electronics department,' explained the planetary geophysicist.

As he watched, Michael saw bright purple rings crackling out from the small-scale planet in scores of different directions, like electricity radiating outwards from an electrostatic generator.

'This is our planet's normal magnetosphere – the magnetic field,' said Fivetrees, glancing around to check if any of the gyrating dancers were paying undue attention.

'But *this* is starting to happen...'

Huge whorls in the magnetic force fields appeared near both poles, and then the electric rings swung laterally around the sphere, reversing themselves through 180 degrees before snapping upright again. The effect was quite beautiful.

'I've detected a serious weakening in the Earth's magnetic field,' said Fivetrees. 'It looks as if its polarity is getting ready to flip.'

'Flip?' queried the lawyer, astonished by such an idea.

The scientist shrugged. 'Over geological time it's been natural for the magnetic poles to reverse – to flip – every quarter of a million years or so; it's happened hundreds of times. But we're now way overdue. It's been half a million years since the last time the magnetic north pole swung down and became the south pole – and vice versa.'

'But you think it's started to happen now?' asked Michael.

'Well, the flip usually occurs when the Earth's magnetic field loses intensity, when it weakens,' explained the professor. 'In the past we think this has been down to changes in the Earth's dynamo speed – the rate at which the core and the mantle revolve relative to each other. But this time I think it's due to something else.'

Even though the band's music was still pounding out so

loudly that Michael could feel it through the floor, and despite having their own private form of electronic communication, the geophysicist leaned even closer across the table.

'There has been no internal change in the way the core and mantle are behaving. Something else is weakening the magnetosphere and causing this oscillation.' Fivetrees glanced around again carefully. 'I'm certain it is being caused by the new climate-management technologies. The orbiting reflectors are directing the solar wind back towards the Earth and weakening its polarity bias. This wind is filled with trillions of charged particles that all interact with the geomagnetic fields around the planet – in the ionosphere. In turn, their magnetic repulsion induces eddies of magnetic currents deep within the Earth. One result of this technology is that the climate changes, a second is that we screw up our planet's main protective shield, and a third is that we mess with the magnetic forces deep in the Earth's mantle and, perhaps, even in its core.'

'What makes you think so?' asked Michael, uncertainly.

The professor turned and snapped the miniature holo-projector shut, then leaned back over the table towards him.

'I've spent the last eleven years deciphering and digitizing hand-written observations of the weather and records of seismic events that were kept by Jesuit monks over the last four centuries. His intense dark-eyed gaze was focused fixedly on Michael's face. 'In three hundred different monasteries scattered over every region of the world, these monks recorded the daily weather, and any seismic activity, as part of their daily routine. My analysis proves that there is a direct link between electrical activity in the magnetosphere, the planet's climate, and the degree of seismic unrest. Stronger magnetic fields in the ionosphere directly weaken the magnetic fields produced by the dynamo of the Earth's molten core – the two are *totally* interdependent – and when you start artificially changing the climate around the planet, you weaken the magnetic fields being produced *inside* the Earth. The result is that the mantle flows are disrupted and you get a sudden increase of seismic events in the Earth's crust.'

The scientist sat back and gazed at his audience of one to

judge how this information was being received. Michael wasn't sure how to react, so he gave a single brief nod.

'I've also measured joule output and plasma-particle dispersion from the solar reflectors. The periods of peak output for weather modification are invariably followed a few days later by seismic disturbances – I've created formulae and algorithms that prove this circumstantial link. But in addition I've built a model that predicts the actual magnetic disruption in the mantle and the seismic activity that invariably follows. It is clear that climate management is the reason why the world is suffering so much volcanic activity and so many earthquakes.'

Michael had no idea if this man was a crank or whether there might be something to his claims. He had checked the professor out on Berkeley's website and he certainly appeared to be eminently qualified in his field. But the lawyer's own training and experience had taught him to be sceptical of any claim until he had verified it for himself. But he also realized that he wouldn't be able to check out this wild theory without some high-level expert help.

'I'm worried that there may be an abrupt and permanent reversal of the magnetic poles if we continue to interfere with the Earth's natural feedback loops,' added Fivetrees, his forefinger hammering home his concerns on the table top.

'And what would that mean in real terms?' asked Michael.

'Nobody knows for sure, but pole reversal seems to be part of the planet's regular renewal process. There would be an abrupt loss of magnetosphere protection which would allow a lot more radiation to hit our atmosphere. That alone can be fatal to life forms – if it goes on for very long. There would also be some huge gee-gees and then—'

'Gee-gees?'

'Global-scale geophysical events,' explained Fivetrees. 'Like a super-volcano erupting, or a mega-tsunami. Then there would be a very rapid melting of the polar ice – perhaps a monstrous rising of the oceans. Like I said, it's been half a million years since the last time the magnetic poles reversed, and nobody was then able to record what happened. Certainly it would be totally catastrophic, something that would qualify as what biologists call an "extinction event" – the loss of a whole species, or even multiple species, like when the dinosaurs died out.'

'But why on earth would our government want to suppress such information, and to shut you up?' asked the lawyer.

'They just think I'm a troublesome crank.' Fivetrees shook his head. 'They've accused me of being unnecessarily alarmist because I want all forms of climate management banned immediately.'

'But if there's even a remote chance that you're right ... ?' protested Michael.

'It's a *politically* unacceptable theory,' Fivetrees spat out, stressing the world 'politically' as if it were a venereal disease.

The band finished a number. Both men glanced up and turned round in their seats to join in the applause. Then, almost immediately, the remorseless beat struck up once more.

'Politicians are now too scared to relinquish climate management,' continued Fivetrees, as the ambient sound level rose again. 'All of the developed economies in the world have become totally dependent on tightly scheduled weather patterns – energy consumption and production is now wholly geared to it. If governments suddenly banned climate control, industries like tourism, agriculture, insurance and energy would be set back by decades, with colossal losses. Worldwide recession would follow – and no politician holding office is going to risk that.'

That much was obvious: Michael nodded. 'What do you want me to do?' he asked.

The professor picked up his miniature holo-projector from the table top.

'Take this,' he said, handing the unit to the lawyer. 'As well as my models of the magnetic poles and the seismic disturbance in the mantle, it contains all my analysis of those monastery records, and also a copy of the government's emergency secrecy order. Take a look at my legal position to see whether I really can't publish here. Let me know if there's any way I can get this information out – I don't know, maybe to the media or to some publication abroad. Maybe it should even go to the UN.'

*

There are many theories about why ancient civilizations venerated and celebrated the planet's solstice days. But the most convincing reason proposed for humankind's almost universal celebration of midwinter is that the prehistoric people of the high European latitudes could never feel wholly sure that the declining sun was going to return again.

The prehistoric British temple of Stonehenge, on the other hand, appears to have been built to celebrate the summer solstice, the point at which the Earth's acute axial tilt brings maximum sunshine to the northern hemisphere.

Each June, Senior Lecturer Jean Landsman invited a group of her Cultural Anthropology students from Bath University to forgo their sleep on Midsummer Eve in order to board a midnight coach for the thirty-mile drive to the spot where Stonehenge sat disconnected from both its time and its culture on the bleak open spaces of Salisbury Plain.

She organized this annual end-of-term trip partly because her undergraduates were mostly young and liked slightly crazy adventures and partly because the modern Druids, New Age Romantics and other neo-hippie types who also turned up to witness and worship the solstice themselves provided plenty of material for the enquiring anthropological mind.

It was also true that, in the thirteen years she had been organizing these field trips, Jean herself had never failed to be thrilled by the occasion. Each midsummer she had stood there, gazing towards the two great rings of sarsen stones through the massive triple uprights and out towards the east, to see the morning sun rise in precise alignment, throwing its first blinding rays over the Heel Stone, through the centre 'window' of the great lintelled quadriform, and out along a line so precisely predicted and delineated by the prehistoric temple's builders. Jean always felt a profound sense of awe then, a closer connection with some of the very earliest people to have lived, worshipped and died in her native land.

The advent of weather-management services also meant that solstice enthusiasts could now rely on enjoying cloud-free midsummer nights followed by perfectly clear sunrises; the British government understood how important Stonehenge and its sun worshippers were to its tourist trade.

On this particular solstice, fourteen of Jean's students had agreed to make the trip with her. She had advised them to bring folding chairs, small stepladders or boxes to stand on, as the area around Stonehenge now got so crowded that it was sometimes impossible to see the sunrise over other people's heads.

By three minutes to five a.m., British Summer Time, the sky in the east had been brightening steadily for a quarter of an hour.

'Thirty seconds,' Jean called out to her small flock as they stood around her, perched on their steps and chairs. This midsummer's dawn the expectant crowd at the ancient monument seemed larger than ever.

Suddenly a ray of light shot upwards into the sky, and it seemed as if a million light bulbs had been switched on all along the horizon.

There were cries of 'Oooo' and 'Ahhh' from the crowds all around, some worshippers immediately falling to their knees in prayer. But after a few seconds it seemed as if this crowd's response was more muted than usual.

'Excuse me, Miss Landsman?' asked Mimi Ikutaro politely. She was one of Jean's younger Japanese students, and was balancing on a small set of aluminium steps beside her lecturer, video camera at the ready. 'Shouldn't the sun shine through – I mean, in *between* those stones?'

The vast crowd fell silent as realization spread that on this particular solstice the sunrise had missed the Heel Stone and was instead completely obscured by one of the outer circle's huge upright monoliths.

The *Global Haven*, the largest ocean-going passenger ship ever built, was steaming at twenty-six knots some 430 miles northeast of Hawaii, almost at the Tropic of Cancer, when the radar blip first appeared on her screens.

As the world's most exclusive marine residence for the international hyper-wealthy – 6,160 people who lived their lives permanently offshore, in a floating, self-governing, tax-free maritime state – the *Global Haven* sailed by strict rules and regulations that prohibited unscheduled stops or interchange with other vessels on the high seas.

But even when they are in control of the world's richest ship – a vessel containing some of the most expensive condominiums, flats, apartments and duplexes ever built – sailors remain seamen at heart, so the sight of another vessel in distress prompts atavistic impulses to provide assistance.

'She's steaming very slowly, sir,' observed Thomas Johansson, the ship's First Officer, as he watched the radar blip. 'Making almost no headway at all.'

Captain James Monroe, an upright, bearded Scot who looked as though Central Casting had been approached for 'a traditional ship's master', straightened up from the screen and said simply, 'Maintain present heading and speed.'

Almost two kilometres long and two-thirds of a kilometre wide, the *Global Haven* displaced over two million tons. This vast white flat-topped ziggurat-pyramid of the sea sat catamaran-style astride her two elongated multi-compartment hulls, each four times longer than an old super-tanker.

The vessel's incredible size had been made possible only by the development of new plasti-ceramic materials that, while being both flexible and light, possessed a tensile strength greater than steel or carbon fibre.

In terms of volume, the mega-vessel provided as much interior space as six large conventional cruise liners. But although 3,700 domestic attendants lived on board to service the lives of their rich employers, the giant ship herself was heavily computerized and required only thirty officers and eighty seafaring crew members to pilot her around the world's more amenable oceans.

The *Global Haven* was heading for Los Angeles. This route was one leg of a carefully planned year-round cycle which took the residents to the Mediterranean in spring (Cannes Film Festival, Monaco Grand Prix, side trip to Wimbledon), then on to Australia and New Zealand (Round-the-World yacht race, Melbourne Gold Cup, and so on) before a two-week stopover in Hawaii, which had been the ship's most recent port of call.

During the northern hemisphere's winter months, the *Global*

Haven could be seen cruising off the coasts of Argentina (polo), Brazil (partridge shooting) and Mexico (shopping). During all stages of her annual voyage, the vessel would take advantage of the pre-published climate-management schedules to ensure that (other than when she was steaming at high speed on the open seas) each stopover was blessed by fine weather for shore excursions.

But each year fewer and fewer of the *Global Haven*'s residents chose to leave the ship for longer than a few hours at a time. When she had been launched six years earlier, it had been thought that most of the wealthy leaseholders would spend almost as much time ashore as they did on board, but it was now clear that the protected and luxurious environment provided within the ship removed much of their incentive to return to dry land.

Inside its ultra-wide superstructure, four main atria reached up through twenty deck levels, each enclosing gardens, trees, ornamental pools and fountains. Two dozen smaller courtyards, with interconnecting lanes, created a network of quaint and leafy environments for shopping malls, sports facilities, restaurants, bars, clubs and cafés. A pair of separate monorail loops provided transport for residents at upper and lower levels, while 262 elevators and forty-eight escalators provided vertical connection between the twenty-four residential decks.

The long, flat top deck of the ship served as the community's airport and provided a main runway for medium and small jets, six helicopter landing pads, and an elevator that took aircraft to a large lower-deck apron which provided parking and maintenance facilities.

At the vessel's stern, the starboard hull opened inwards in a wide horseshoe-shaped curve to provide a large, fully enclosed marina. Powerful hydraulically powered sea gates and a solid harbour bottom turned the ship's private port into a wet-dock enclosure, allowing the moored vessels within to travel with the mother vessel while she was under way. An ingenious lock even allowed attendant craft to arrive and leave the giant ship while she was still in motion.

Captain James Monroe made visual contact with the unidentified radar blip shortly before four p.m. She was ahead, thirty degrees off the port bow, also steaming in the direction of Southern California. An old freighter, she was riding low in the water, laden with scores of huge metal containers piled high on her decks and, most alarmingly of all to seafaring eyes, a thick column of black smoke was rising into the still air from somewhere in the centre of the ship. Fire at sea remained the worst nightmare for any sailor.

First Officer Thomas Johansson attempted to make radio contact with this container ship on Channel 9, then on all the other available frequencies, but there was no response.

As they came up rapidly on the limping freighter, Captain Monroe ordered an unmanned drone aircraft to be launched from the flight deck, and within ten minutes he and his officers were gazing at close-up video pictures of a few semi-naked crewmen using ancient hoses to frantically fight a fire within one of the holds.

'Liberian markings,' observed Johansson. 'The *Java Trader*, out of Manila – I'd say about twenty thousand tons. There won't be more than fifteen or twenty crew aboard.'

He tapped the details into a computer and, seconds later, said, 'Well, she's not on the Lloyd's Register. Perhaps she's changed her name recently.'

The bridge of the *Global Haven* was wholly state of the art. When the ship's developers had been busy marketing her 2,568 spacious residential units (many with their own private pools, elevators and deck gardens), they had been keen to stress the ship's numerous safety features, her inbuilt anti-terrorist protection systems, and the strict rules of engagement that would always bind the captain and the crew. Most important of these was that the ship would never make an unscheduled or unauthorized stop at sea except when the captain considered it necessary for the safety of the *Global Haven* herself, or for any of her residents – and then only after the ship's heavily armed defence helicopter had been launched to circle the mother ship as a precautionary measure.

'Reduce speed to one-eighth,' ordered the captain. 'Take us to within one thousand yards.'

Johansson glanced sideways at his skipper, but received no acknowledgement that his look of enquiry had even been noted.

'One-eighth speed it is, sir,' he responded, nodding to the helmsman to punch in the instructions. 'Head one-forty north-east.'

The massive twin-hulled cruise ship seemed to rest slowly back on her haunches as the power was reduced.

'Shall I order the chopper up, sir?' asked the lieutenant.

'We're not stopping, Mister Johansson,' said Monroe sharply. 'Prepare to launch *Global Support One*. Order her crew to their stations immediately.'

'Aye aye, sir,' said Johansson and he relayed his captain's orders.

Monroe ran the ship as if he were still a frigate commander in the Royal Navy. The ship's developers had reasoned that old-fashioned British naval values would appeal to potential residents – and they had been right. Monroe was universally popular among the wealthy residents and was regarded as one of the ship's greatest commercial assets. There was now a waiting list of six years for apartments in the mighty vessel.

Messages were barked into telephones, and preparations were put in hand to launch the large fire-fighting tug that *Global Haven* transported within her floating dock.

'Their orders are to provide all assistance and, if necessary, to take the crew off that freighter,' Monroe told his first lieutenant. 'Tell them to radio us once the emergency is over and we'll circle back and collect them.'

Fifteen minutes later, the *Global Haven* was almost abreast of the old container ship. From a distance of just over 1,000 yards the *Java Trader* was totally dwarfed by the towering white leviathan.

'Slow to five knots and launch *Global Support One* when ready,' ordered Monroe.

The captain, his first lieutenant, the helmsman and the four other crew members on bridge duty all watched on their monitor screens as the hydraulic pumps raised the water level in the stern dock around the support tug and pumped in an artificial current.

For a safe launch, the water within the wet dock had to be moving at almost the same speed as the ocean itself was moving relative to the mother ship.

Then the end boom of the dock lowered, and the ocean-going tug slipped effortlessly away and out to sea.

'Sir?' Johansson now had his binoculars trained again on the stricken container ship. 'SIR!'

All heads snapped round to follow his gaze. The outside walls of three of the large containers on the antiquated ship had fallen into the sea. Then the tops and remaining sides of these containers were suddenly yanked away as if they were made of no more than cardboard.

'For God's sake, no,' shouted Monroe, snatching the glasses from his lieutenant.

But the pair of deck-mounted multi-tube missile launchers were now plain to see, even with the naked eye. As the officers of the *Global Haven* watched in horror, one of the launchers swivelled and tracked towards the huge vessel. Moments later two laser-guided missiles were fired in quick succession.

The rockets streaked over the bridge and, with enormous blasts, exploded far above them on the flight deck. From their video monitors the officers could see their defence helicopter and a business jet explode in balls of flame.

Monroe flipped up a metal lid on the control panel and hit the master alarm. A loud wailing filled the bridge, as it was simultaneously filling every other space within the vast ship. Almost instantly metal shutters began lowering inside all windows and portholes, other than on the bridge itself.

Suddenly the radio crackled to life, on Channel 9.

'Skipper of *Global Haven*,' shouted a male voice in heavily accented English. 'Stop your engines. Repeat, stop your engines. I have live missiles locked on to your bridge, communications centre and residential areas. I will fire again unless you stop your engines immediately.'

The captain lifted his binoculars and gazed intently at the treacherous cargo ship once more. Now he realized that all of the containers were fake – wood or cardboard decoys built and painted simply to trap him. Six men were gathered around each of the missile launchers, and there were at least a dozen missiles remaining in their tubes, aimed directly at his ship and ready to be fired.

'Stop all engines,' Captain James Monroe ordered.

London Times

Monday, 24 June 2055

DRUIDS DAMAGE STONEHENGE: SOLSTICE SUNRISE 'OUT OF LINE'

Police arrested sixty-two members of a modern-day Druid cult early yesterday morning following a riot at Stonehenge, the famous 5,000-year-old stone circle in Wiltshire.

Druid leaders claimed that the sun had failed to rise in its usual alignment over the ancient monument.

Astronomer Royal Kevin Jones said yesterday: 'There are frequent anomalies in the Earth's orbit around the sun. Our calculations show that a variation of point one of a degree in the planet's orientation was responsible for this phenomenon. Over long periods, such variations are normal, and are to be expected.'

The old freighter had suddenly burst into life. No sooner had the engines of the *Global Haven* come to a halt than hordes of armed men appeared on the decks of the *Java Trader*. At first it seemed as if they numbered in their scores, then Captain Monroe and his officers realized that there had to be many hundreds of them.

While the container ship's laser-guided missiles remained firmly trained on their target, a dozen inflatables were launched from jury-rigged derricks mounted along the side of the freighter. Waves of heavily armed men swarmed down ropes into the boats and headed for the mega-cruiser's stern dock.

Ten minutes later a dozen members of the boarding party were standing on the bridge, levelling ancient automatic weapons at the captain himself and his officers.

In the meantime, Monroe had reported the ambush to the ship's owners in Zurich. He had explained how his defence helicopter had been destroyed and stressed that laser-guided missiles were now aimed directly at his vessel. He quickly dumped all data and video evidence to Switzerland by private satellite link.

After a short delay he received his instructions: above all, he must do nothing that would put any of his ship's residents' lives at risk. Monroe guessed that the *Global Haven*'s insurers were already calculating the incredible size of the claim they would now be facing for the loss of the vast amounts of art treasures, jewellery, cash and other negotiables that were carried on board. He also knew just how enormous these claims would become if any of the billionaire and trillionaire residents were harmed.

The Swiss proprietors then told him that they were already alerting the police, coastguard and navy in both Hawaii and Los Angeles.

Finally Monroe had issued his orders over the ship's master PA system even as scores of raiders were still clambering up the side of the ship's floating dock.

'All residents, crew and staff, this is the captain speaking. We are being boarded by a force of unknown origin. Do not offer resistance. Repeat, do not offer resistance. The authorities in Hawaii and Los Angeles have been informed.'

Monroe turned and stared defiantly at the dozen armed men who had arrived on his bridge.

'What exactly is it you want?' he asked the bearded youth who seemed to be their leader. 'Money, I suppose?'

'Your ship, captain,' replied John Gogotya. 'We will provide you all with alternative transport.' He turned and pointed to the western horizon.

Monroe squinted into the sun, but could see nothing there. He picked up his binoculars and, as he focused, he made out scores of black hulls coming over the horizon, heading straight towards the *Global Haven*.

ELEVEN

'So how does it feel to be one step ahead of the professionals?' asked Emilia Knight. 'You did some very good work, Matthew.'

The geophysicist straightened up from the boy's computer screens, put her hands on her hips, arched her body backwards to banish the dull ache in her lower spine, and stared up at the implausible richness of stars in the glittering canopy overhead.

As scheduled, the night was clear, and from this altitude there was visibility for forty miles in all directions. She breathed deeply for a few moments, caught in mystic wonder, as always, then glanced over at Matthew's father who was hovering a few yards away. They had met for the first time only three hours earlier.

'You should be very proud of your son, Mr Fairfax,' she told him. 'NASA has only just announced that there is indeed an axial variation in the Earth's orbit – but Matthew realized ten days ago that something strange was going on.'

They were in a small paved parking area beside the Geohazard Observatory, near the summit of Mount Tamalpais, some sixteen miles north of the Golden Gate Bridge. The mountain was 2,400 feet high and to the south and far below them the distant lights of San Francisco and its satellite cities glowed small as scattered dimes. The air was noticeably thinner and colder at the top of the mountain.

After meeting Dr Knight at his high school, Matthew had asked his father if the two of them could take up the scientist's invitation to visit the observatory.

Michael had cleared the trip with Lucy, promised Ben a

special outing to the aquarium to make up for his not being included on their evening jaunt, and had then phoned the woman herself at Geohazard Laboratories.

They had agreed to meet in the car park beside the old observatory, and as Emilia had shown father and son round the now largely disused but still intact facility, Michael felt increasingly sure that he had met this attractive geophysicist somewhere before. He finally realized what had prompted that notion as he was helping his son to set up his telescopes and computers.

'Didn't I see you recently on TV, doing a broadcast from the side of that Samoan volcano?' he asked as Emilia arrived back with a light plastic table she had borrowed from a security hut.

No sooner had she confessed to the television appearance than Matt blurted, 'Dad was actually there in Samoa, the night the volcano erupted!'

This tenuous connection seemed to put the whole outing on another footing and Emilia proceeded to ask a string of questions about the actual sequence of the eruption and what it had felt like being so close. After they had exhausted that topic, Matthew had proudly revealed the process he had used to calculate the tiny misalignment between the Earth and the surrounding night sky.

Now it was time to pack up. Michael helped his son dismantle his portable computers and telescopes and load them into the BMW. The Geohazard scientist returned the table and various other borrowed items to the security cabin.

'Thanks a lot, Dr Knight,' said Matthew, shaking their host's hand.

'It's been great,' added Michael, as he too shook hands.

'You're welcome.' Emilia gave them both a smile.

Father and son turned towards their car, but as he reached his door the lawyer hesitated. He turned and walked back to where the geophysicist was still standing.

'Dr Knight,' he said quietly. 'May I call you sometime?'

Humans do not thrive in space. In fact, zero-gravity conditions will quickly kill all Earth-evolved animals. This is the main limiting factor to human aspirations for the manned conquest of space.

Men and women will not be venturing to the stars – at least, not the sort of humankind currently bred on Earth.

Nicholas Negromonte was more aware of this than most; he would spend at least four months of every year in Earth orbit or on the moon, and he knew from experience the immense physical effort required to cope with such hostile environments.

'Twenty-five kilometres,' announced the cycling machine.

Negromonte blew out his cheeks, exhaled deeply, and raised his sweating torso from the handlebars. His personal trainer arrived beside him instantly, proffering a warm flannel and a towel.

They were currently in the large, fully equipped gym on board the recently repaired ERGIA Space Station. In each twenty-four-hour cycle, Negromonte and all other resident staff members were obliged to undergo at least two hours of vigorous workout simply to maintain the same muscle tone that would be achieved by a normal day's activity on the planet down below them. Such schedules meant that meetings had to be conducted under unusual conditions.

The CEO dismounted and nodded a greeting to the two men and one woman who had been hovering in anticipation of him finishing his stationary bike ride.

He was about to receive his daily executive briefing on corporate developments. He foot-sucked his way carefully across to a running machine, set the speed to 'Fast Walk', and began to stride out as his executive committee gathered round.

'The class action due to be brought against us on behalf of the hulk people and others at the court in The Hague has now been shelved indefinitely,' said Consuela Ponting, ERGIA's chief corporate attorney. 'The senior partner at the law firm involved intends retiring next year, and he's hoping to run for the Senate. We've donated fifteen million US to his campaign fund.'

'Very good,' approved Negromonte with a slight inclination of the head. 'Next?'

'We've tested public opinion on your proposed solo re-enactment voyage to the moon,' said Hanoch Biran. 'We have an over eighty per cent approval rating in all focus groups within our target markets.'

'Excellent.' The CEO smiled broadly, stepping up his walking speed by two miles an hour.

To launch ERGIA's new lunar energy resource, LunaSun, Nick Negromonte had come up with his most audacious extreme-sports stunt yet. He intended to fly single-handedly a refurbished Apollo 11-type spacecraft from Earth-orbit to the moon. The combination four-piece craft had been a spare back-up vehicle from the Apollo programme that Negromonte had purchased from a failing private aerospace museum in Colorado.

Although the refurbished Apollo had been given modern-day engines, safety systems and navigation aids, he intended to pilot the lunar module down to the moon's surface manually, just as Neil Armstrong and Buzz Aldrin had done eighty-six years earlier. Negromonte had already spent many hours in a simulator, learning how to fly such an old-fashioned spacecraft.

'We're go for you to leave Earth orbit on October sixteenth,' added Biran, the director of corporate communications, unconsciously parodying Houston-speak. 'You'll land at Tranquillity Base on October nineteen, just two weeks ahead of our IPO. We've sold exclusive world-wide TV broadcast rights to MSN.'

Negromonte flicked the walking machine's speed still faster. 'Excellent,' he said, beaming. He genuinely loved the adventure in such stunts, and this one would additionally guarantee massive publicity for his LunaSun share flotation.

'Also, we've just had a tentative approach from the BBC. As you know, they're producing a documentary on climate management due to go out shortly before our IPO, and they've asked if you will participate in a live studio debate?'

'Conducted where?'

'New York or London, I would think,' said Biran.

Negromonte flicked the control three notches faster, till he was suddenly jogging.

'How about our hosting the debate live from our LunaSun building on the moon?' he gasped between heavy breaths. 'That would give them a first.'

*

Ensconced in the captain's stateroom on board the *Global Haven*, John Gogotya used a remote control to turn up the volume on one of the three large entertainment screens. He wanted to catch the latest news.

'And now, the Ten O'Clock News, live from MSN Headquarters in New York.'

'Good evening, I'm Aurora Templeton.

'Over five thousand former residents and crew of the residential luxury ship *Global Haven* arrived in Honolulu harbour this morning on board a decommissioned oil tanker.

'These wealthy tax exiles reported that pirates had boarded the *Global Haven* when she was four hundred and fifty miles north-east of Hawaii, and forced them at gunpoint to transfer to the former crude-oil carrier. There are no reports of any injuries or fatalities among either residents or crew.

'Many well-known people own homes on board the *Global Haven*, and opera star Ormanston Dunne announced that he and many other residents were furious that the US authorities failed to come to the ship's rescue. The estimated cost of the loss of both the ship and its contents is over five hundred billion dollars.

'We cross now to Congresswoman Marla Mendola, who heads the Congressional subcommittee on international terrorism.

'Miss Mendola, why did the US Navy fail to protect so many US citizens believed to have been the victims of this act of terrorism on the high seas?'

'Aurora, as far as we understand it, this was not an act of terrorism – nobody was hurt and no demands have yet been made. It has to be considered an act of common piracy, and one conducted outside US territorial waters.

'Further, the *Global Haven* is not in fact a US-registered vessel, nor is the US Navy responsible for the personal safety or protection of property of those who choose to live outside all national boundaries. These people pay no taxes

in the United States, nor taxes in any nation with a
reciprocal taxation agreement. If they evade their taxes in
this way and do not contribute to maintain our military
and law-enforcement agencies, they can expect no
protection from us. It's very straightforward.'

John Gogotya smiled, muted the sound and refilled his
brandy glass. He was sampling Captain Monroe's private stock
of *Très Vieux*, a Premier Cru Grande Champagne-Cognac that,
prior to bottling, had been matured in black-oak casks for over
sixty years.

The decorative lights of the double-decked Bay Bridge soared
out towards Oakland, almost within touching distance of the
lofty window beside the couple – or so it seemed.

Michael Fairfax was out on a date, his first such social
engagement since he had split up with Lucy – in fact, his first
proper date in over fifteen years. At thirty-eight years of age, and
as an international litigation attorney, he felt himself a little too
old and much too worldly-wise to be feeling so nervous.

He and Emilia Knight were seated together at a window
table in Julius's Castle, a small French restaurant that had
perched, eyrie-like, high up on a rocky ledge on the northern
side of Telegraph Hill for over a century.

Below them, dusk was falling across the bay and lights were
coming on at points all around their sweeping 270-degree view,
turning the darkness into a glittering fairyland.

Michael had been direct when he had called Emilia, employ-
ing a brusque lawyerly manner to mask his nervousness. He had
explained rapidly about his own divorced status and, perhaps
too eagerly, had added that he would like to get to know her
better. 'If that isn't an inappropriate request,' he had added.

She too had been forthright, almost mocking his businesslike
approach. 'It isn't at all inappropriate,' she said, laughingly. 'And
I too would like to see you again.'

They had met at this restaurant at eight-thirty: the tall man
with thick brown hair and a careful manner, the dark-haired,

vivacious woman – only a little over five feet four tall – with the bright amber eyes and attractive, ever-mobile face.

Michael had earlier dropped in on the way to see his boys on the Filbert Steps, only slightly lower down the hill; it was a relief that Lucy no longer demanded advance notice for his visits.

'Matthew's just getting to that difficult age,' Michael explained to Emilia. 'He's now thirteen and everything he mentions these days seems to relate to sex – when it isn't about astronomy.'

'He's very bright,' observed his dinner partner.

'I suppose he's pushing the boundaries. I think he actually wants me to discuss sex with him.'

'Are you two close enough to talk about that stuff?'

Michael shrugged. 'It's been difficult since the divorce. I didn't see much of the boys in the first year or so. Lucy was still very sore at me.' Then, sensing the need for a change of subject: 'So what's it like being a risk-assessment seismologist?'

Emilia laughed. 'Well, up until the last year or so I would have described it as long periods of boredom mixed with short periods of terror. But now it seems as if the periods of boredom are getting shorter.'

'What does this axial anomaly actually mean, this new tilt in the Earth's axis?'

She shook her head. 'I'm not a planetary geophysicist, just a humble seismologist, but after NASA confirmed that what your son had spotted was actually occurring, I logged into all the geophys chat rooms to listen to what the experts were saying...'

She tailed off, realigning the cutlery in front of her.

'And?' prompted Michael.

'Well, nobody really knows what it is,' admitted Emilia. 'It seems that the angle of the planet's tilt varies naturally over time, over very *long* periods of time. But this is the first occasion a deviation has ever been directly observable – at least since we started being able to measure such things, which isn't very long, of course. I would guess it's probably nothing to worry about.'

During the main course, as their conversation drifted back to Samoa, Michael noticed his guest becoming evasive as she explained how an injury sustained on the slopes of the volcano had led her to being transferred to lighter duties.

Something in Emilia's sudden reticence prompted the lawyer in him to probe further, inquiring exactly what sort of injury she'd sustained. He was taken aback when she suddenly snapped at him, 'Look, I can't really talk about it, OK? They've slapped an NSA on me – I presume you know what that is?'

For a moment Michael wondered whether she mistook him for some ambulance chaser, the sort of opportunistic attorney who sought to represent people who suffered injury at work. He hadn't told her much about his own career – his disappointment over the postponed hulk people litigation was still too keen.

'I'm sorry, forgive me,' he apologized quickly. 'I didn't mean to pry. It's just my goddamn lawyer's habit.' Then he frowned. This was the second application of a statutory instrument of national secrecy he had heard of in just two weeks – and in a similar field of science.

'No, I'm the one who should say sorry,' said Emilia. She reached across the table and gave his hand a quick squeeze. 'It's just that I caught something ... rather, I was exposed to something dangerous while I was up that mountain. I've become a bit over-sensitive about it.'

Michael felt in his jacket pocket, then glanced around the restaurant. It was a Tuesday evening, and only three other tables were occupied, all at some distance away from theirs.

'Have you ever heard of a Professor Robert Fivetrees?' he asked as he withdrew the prototype miniature holo-projector from his jacket. 'He works in the Department of Planetary Geophysics at Berkeley.'

'Of course I have,' said Emilia. 'He's one of this country's leading geo-scientists. But I've never actually met him.'

'Watch this,' urged Michael as he flipped open the holo-projector, and initiated the simulation the professor had shown him in the truck-stop bar.

'That's amazing,' exclaimed Emilia as she watched. 'It's showing the magnetic fields around the Earth, isn't it? But they're oscillating strangely. Now they're reversing...'

She gazed up into his eyes and frowned. 'Where did you get this thing?'

'From Robert Fivetrees – he's a new client of mine. The

Pentagon has issued a blanket secrecy order on all his work, and he's asking me to try and find a way round it – to find a way to get this stuff published. He seems convinced that the planet's magnetic poles are about to reverse suddenly, which would be very dangerous for ... well, for all of us.'

Michael glanced at Emilia to see if this was making sense. 'Not that I'm qualified to know, of course. This might all be just so much nonsense, and ...'

'Not if Bob Fivetrees himself believes it.' Emilia sat back pensively in her chair. 'But how could he tell you anything, or even give you this, if they've imposed a secrecy order on him?' She frowned at the now-quiescent holo-projector lying on the white table cloth.

'I agreed to be his legal counsel. That means the law enables him to tell me anything. It's covered by attorney-client privilege.'

'You mean that if I asked you to be *my* counsel, I could then tell you things covered by a National Secrecy Agreement?' she asked.

'Absolutely,' agreed Michael. 'You have a full legal right to discuss any issues with an attorney of your choosing.'

'OK. How much do you know about plutonium?'

Emilia lay naked in the dark, limply starfished on top of her bedcovers. Despite the lateness of the hour it was still hot in her bedroom and the house timbers were ticking intermittently, like insects signalling to each other. She usually chose not to run the air-conditioning at night but was now debating whether to touch a button and summon up a soothing breath of manufactured cool air to waft across her skin.

Moving her arm, she found the remote control and, as a compromise, rolled up the motorized blackout blind that covered the window. The top sash was still open and she gratefully felt a slight breeze. Now she smelled the sea – the low roar of the surf down below was her constant and welcome companion – then eucalyptus, and then a wave of competing siren scents, almost sexual in their intensity. Outside in her garden the foxgloves, lupines, columbines, lavender and a forest of peonies were all in bloom – or rebloom – thanks to the benefits of climate management.

Emilia turned her head, noticed that it was 2.42 a.m., then directed her gaze towards the window. On this clear night, stars were strewn in indigo, like diamonds glittering on a jeweller's velvet cloth. A late flight was gliding southwards, towards the airport, like a shooting star falling in slow motion.

Michael's face appeared in her mind yet again. Since she had left the restaurant, his image had kept on returning, despite her efforts to think of other things.

When asked what it would take for her to appoint him her legal counsel, he had explained, 'All you have to do is say the words. That's sufficient.' So she *had* said the words. And then she had said a lot more.

She told him all about her find on Mount Māriota, and about Washington's intention to mine the volcano once its eruption had fully subsided.

After warning Emilia that everything he now told her would also be subject to the same secrecy agreement, Michael had then described Professor Fivetrees's diligent analysis of Jesuit monastery records, and his belief in a demonstrable link between climatic behaviour and the degree of seismic unrest exhibited by the planet itself.

The lawyer had then asked her to take the miniature holo-projector and to examine its data for herself, to see if she agreed with the professor's startling conclusions. She had already decided that that would be her first priority, if she could find some time in the Simulation Theater tomorrow.

Then Michael had told Emilia about his own plans to sue the major energy corporations. 'It's the same old fossil-fuel energy companies who are now controlling the weather,' he fumed. 'It's as if, after causing global warming in the first place, they're now charging the whole world millions of dollars every day for managing away its worst effects.'

Before parting outside the restaurant Michael had asked if he might see her again. When he'd kissed her cheek, his lips had lingered tantalizingly close to her mouth.

Emilia yawned. Already three o'clock had tiptoed by. She

flipped her pillow over to its cool side again, in the vain hope
that sleep would seep up from it, and stared up into the darkness.
She considered again Professor Robert Fivetrees's theory, trying
to recall what she herself knew about planetary motion.

As she lay on her bed, Emilia knew that her feet faced north.
She also knew that, as the Earth spun, her body was hurtling
eastwards, rotating towards the dawn at 1,000 miles an hour. A
snippet of information surfaced from her distant memory: artil-
lerymen firing giant guns always needed to allow for the direction and speed of the Earth's rotation – left in the Northern
Hemisphere, right in southern latitudes.

She imagined the sun now beneath her, on the opposite side
of the world. Then she tried to imagine the spinning, tilted earth
itself – 'like a pool ball that's been given plenty of screw', to
quote one of her old college lecturers – flying sideways through
space at 64,000 miles per hour, also eastwards in its annual circumnavigation of the sun.

The insomniac starfish fastened her gaze on the square of
stars visible through the window, relishing the lick of cool air on
her bare stomach. *1,000 miles per hour plus 64,000 miles per hour.*
As she gazed at the heavens she allowed her body to relax,
feeling everything draining out towards the five points of her
body. She imagined she could even feel the spin powering
herself, the house, the land, the sea – everything – eastwards
through time. *But is there any 'east' out there?*

Then, of course, the Milky Way too was rushing headlong
through space. She tried to extend her thoughts to encompass
that. But she was a child of the Earth and the only model for
the tilted, spinning, orbiting, rushing planet that her exhausted
mind could summon up was of a a Waltzer ride in a long-ago
funfair of her childhood.

Her communicator pinged. Emilia woke and glanced at the
clock: 3.45 a.m.

'Em, it's Steve. I'm at work. There's a huge swarm of tremors
going on right under us. We're just about to issue a highest-level
alert.'

She swung her legs out of the bed. 'Have you found its
centre?'

'Not yet. We're just seeing swarms racing along our section of the San Andreas Fault – all the way from Monterey to Mendocino.'

Over 400 miles.

'Jesus!' she exclaimed. 'How strong?'

'Two rising three. But it's going to be much bigger when it goes.'

'I'm on my way in,' Emilia said.

TWELVE

Viewed from directly above, the contour map of San Francisco and the surrounding Bay Area resembled a giant's thumbprint.

Swirls of tightly compressed lines clearly indicated where the sharp rises and falls in the land surface had occurred as massive tectonic heavings and shudderings had lifted and depressed rocks countless times since the North American and Pacific continental plates first abutted.

These giant segments of crust, floating on the molten surface of the planet's mantle, bumped and crushed each other without respite, like two fat schoolboys jammed into the back seat of a compact car.

At 6.02 on the morning of Wednesday, 2 July 2055, Northern California experienced 'The Big One' that everybody had been expecting since the earthquake of 1906, which had killed over 700 people. At that time the population of the Bay Area had been around 500,000. Now it was almost ten million.

But unlike the old mining-supply and harbour town of the early twentieth century, the modern cities in the San Francisco region had been built using earthquake-resistant techniques. Buildings were purposefully constructed to be flexible. Many were seated on top of huge rollers that would allow high-rise office blocks to glide backwards and forwards as the ground beneath them heaved. In addition, the highly trained staff of Geohazard Labs was on hand to warn the region's inhabitants of any impending quake.

It is difficult, however, to alert a large community to danger in the small hours of the morning. Emilia Knight, Steve Bardini and the rest of Geohazard's hastily summoned emergency-response team withdrew to the earthquake-proof seismic monitoring and command centre in the company's Oakland basement. By 5.40 a.m. they had got their urgent warnings out to every emergency service, every radio, TV and press outlet, and to all branches of local government. But the Geohazard team could only watch their monitors with mounting anxiety as the strain gauges broke, the movement meters shattered, and the Bay Area population slumbered peacefully on.

In a video conference with the police chiefs of the region's nine counties, they debated sounding all the old air-raid sirens that still remained dotted around the cities of San Francisco, Oakland, Berkeley and the outlying areas. But they agreed that the sound of these would only reach a tiny proportion of the total population.

They reasoned that, being a weekday, by 6.30 a.m. many of the region's inhabitants would be awake and tuning in to the radio and TV stations that were already broadcasting a continuous stream of emergency warnings. So they decided against triggering the sirens and, as the police, firefighters and hospitals began to put their emergency disaster plans into practice, the Geohazard seismologists waited and watched anxiously while pre-quake symptoms accumulated all along the Hayward branch of the San Andreas Fault.

But the earthquake itself would not wait; *it* woke the millions of Bay Area residents just after six a.m. Its epicentre was at Glossfield, on the eastern edge of the San Francisco Bay, and its magnitude was later measured by Geohazard's field instruments as 9.132 – by far the largest and most powerful earthquake ever measured by modern science.

The downtown area of the City of San Francisco was located at the very tip of a thin, finger-like peninsula that separated the Pacific from the wide inland bay. In one gigantic heave and resettlement, the ground level at the southern end of this isthmus, from Daly City down to SFO International Airport, dropped by over thirty feet. The Pacific then surged hungrily inland and San Francisco's city centre immediately became a new island off the coast of California.

That morning all the world's civil engineers, designers, architects and builders were forcefully reminded that 'earthquake-resistant' does not mean 'earthquake-*proof*', as few structures, old or new, escaped the damage wrought by a three-minute shaking of over Magnitude 9.0.

As its designers had predicted, the Embarcadero Space Needle withstood this buffeting throughout, but the massive concrete platform on which the building was supported rapidly sank into a tectonic-plate fissure at an angle of almost forty-five degrees, tipping the 182-storey tower sideways into the San Francisco Bay.

The exclusive oceanside communities of Sea Cliff, Baker Beach and Land's End, on the north-western edge of the peninsula, became detached from the main raft of the newly formed island, like a crust being snapped off a hard piece of stale bread. They sank immediately beneath the encroaching waves.

All areas around the bay that were built on reclaimed marsh and landfill – Marina, Mission, Presideo, Embarcadero, the Oakland shores, the Alameda oil refineries, the airports – found their buildings, roads, pipes and bridges shaken to rubble, the soil beneath them adopting the consistency of oil, so violently was it vibrated.

Despite being an outcrop of igneous sandstone bedrock, the shaking of Telegraph Hill levelled every building, new and old, on its flanks during the massive quake. The same elegant French restaurant at which Emilia Knight and Michael Fairfax had dined the previous evening was hurled from its lofty perch to plunge down into Stockton Street, 600 feet below.

Every home on the Filbert Steps was destroyed. Inside Jersey Villa, Lucy Fairfax and her younger son Ben were killed outright when all three floors of the Victorian timber building collapsed at once. Up on the top floor, Matthew Fairfax's legs were crushed by a falling roof beam, leaving him trapped alive inside the rubble.

Both the Golden Gate and the Bay Bridge collapsed almost immediately. In the Bay Area over half a million people were to die during the first day following the initial shock.

Two stacks of aircraft, patiently waiting their turns to land at

Oakland and SFO airports, suddenly lost all contact with their air-traffic controllers while signals from the airport-landing beacons also disappeared. Although the flight crews had already received notification of Geohazard's warnings, highly alarmed pilots were all trying at once to contact the Regional Air Traffic Control Center at Sacramento to report the outages and request instructions.

Gerry Castlemain, captain of an American Airlines widebody flight returning home from Sydney, which was at the front of the long landing queue for SFO, suddenly saw the runway on which his plane was scheduled to set down disappear beneath the foaming Pacific Ocean. So did most of his passengers with starboard window seats. Many other passengers elsewhere in the aircraft were still struggling with their personal communications systems as they tried to restore lost contact with the ground.

Captain Castlemain switched to manual control, boosted engine power, lifted the nose of his plane, retracted the undercarriage, turned right, and began a climb back towards 2,000 feet. His path took him west, out over the churning ocean, before he turned right once more to fly up what had recently formed the coastline of the San Francisco peninsula.

The plane arrived over the island that had lately been the city's downtown area, and the captain slowed his aircraft to 200 knots, just above stall speed. Then, in the clear dawn light, the crew and the passengers on the starboard side of the plane could see that all three spans of the Golden Gate Bridge were missing. Beyond it, massive columns of black smoke were starting to rise from the hills of the city centre.

Gerry Castlemain double-checked that the passengers' seatbelt sign was still illuminated. He knew that if panic broke out and the 600 passengers without a starboard window rushed to the right-hand side of the plane in an attempt to see the devastation for themselves many of them might be injured.

But the captain did not find himself able to press his microphone button and speak to the passengers personally – he didn't trust his own voice. His wife and four children lived down there in the sea-level waterfront district near the Palace of Fine Arts, two miles east of the now wrecked suspension bridge, and he was fighting an overwhelming urge to break every FAA rule and dive his huge jet down to wavetop level in order to fly past his home to check on the damage.

Castlemain did turn right once again, over the top of the ruined Golden Gate Bridge and on into the rising sun. He reached for his sunglasses, checked his immediate airspace for other aircraft, and flew eastwards across the bay and towards his native city's new and wholly unfamiliar skyline. Then he banked the plane to the right – at a sharper angle than was authorized by either his airline or the aviation authorities – and gazed down on his own home area.

Everything in the Marina district looked fuzzy, as if it were out of focus, and he could not even make out a distinct shoreline. It was no longer clearly defined by the broad sea walls, and the green on which he jogged and often picnicked with his wife and children was under water; the famous bay had seeped inland. He could not make out his own house, nor locate any of the ruler-straight avenues that had run up from the waterside to broad Lombard Street. Most of the houses seemed to have collapsed, and vast accumulations of wreckage were already floating on the flecked and foaming seas. He levelled out his aircraft once again.

Castlemain's co-pilot and close friend, First Officer Anne Mackowski, held out her open communicator for him to see: *No Signal.* He flipped open his own: *No Signal.*

Anne reached across the cockpit and squeezed his forearm hard. Then she touched the flight-control computer and summoned the new heading that would take them on to Sacramento, ninety miles to the east and two hours back by road.

But the bridges were out and there was now no overland route to the city from the south.

The captain returned flight control to the computer and as they started to climb he noticed that Telegraph Hill had shaken the Coit Tower from its summit – a monument that had been erected in tribute to the firemen of the 1906 earthquake. Beyond, he saw the mighty Embarcadero Space Needle now lying completely on its side in the bay, stretching almost out to Treasure Island.

On the other side of the bay, enormous columns of black

smoke mushroomed upwards from the naval dockyard and the oil refinery and storage depots.

The devastation seemed total.

'He's agreed!' announced Hanoch Biran triumphantly. 'It will be the first time a serving US president has visited the moon.'

Everyone seated around the elegant mahogany table nodded enthusiastically: it was a *coup*. President James T. Underwood had agreed to officiate at the formal opening of ERGIA's LunaSun moon energy facility. The endorsement for ERGIA could not be more significant. All it had taken to secure this honour was the largest single donation ever made to a political re-election campaign.

'The White House wants to take over a moon ferry completely, of course, for security reasons, and they want extra security features added. But they're prepared to meet the cost of conversion themselves.'

'Or have the American taxpayer meet the cost,' observed Nick Negromonte. But he was smiling at his team from his position at the head of the table.

'Looks like we've got ourselves a great launch party,' he added. 'You've done well, Hanoch.'

The perception-management team handling the initial public offering of shares in LunaSun was meeting with the ERGIA boss at his English stately home. Most members had visited Langland Park before, and they were used to conducting business beneath glittering chandeliers and under the glazed gaze of long-dead Florentine worthies.

'We've been having a think about how best to neutralize this forthcoming BBC documentary on climate control,' continued Biran, ERGIA's Israeli-born director of corporate communications. 'The BBC can be very difficult, and very independent. Our recommendation is that we should embrace them entirely, overwhelm them with cooperation and input. In fact, I even recommend that you give Miss Curtis the exclusive interview she wants and let them film here at Langland Park. The more help we give them, the harder it will be for them to criticize.'

Negromonte smiled to himself. He'd already reached the same conclusion. 'Where does their broadcast fit into our schedule?'

Biran scrolled up a page on his DigiPad. 'You land on the moon in Apollo Eleven on October nineteen, the president arrives on the twentieth, and carries out the official opening the next day. The BBC and MSN have scheduled their documentary to be broadcast immediately after the opening dedication – to be followed by a live studio debate on the ethics of climate control. Our LunaSun IPO comes to market two weeks later.'

'Perfect,' said Negromonte. 'Did you offer them our invitation to hold the debate in the LunaSun facilities?'

Biran nodded. 'The BBC is worried about the cost – they say nothing has ever been broadcast from the moon on that scale before. They'd have to lift twenty or thirty people up to LunaSun, just to run the technical side. Then there's the question of how all the guests would get there.'

'Tell them we might be able to get the President of the United States to be the keynote speaker for their debate,' said Negromonte, smiling. 'That'll make them rethink their ratings forecasts – and their budgets.'

'Sir?' It was Bob Johnson, one of the team's assistants. He had been working at a small side table while the main meeting was in progress.

Heads turned, and the junior executive rose to his feet. 'I'm sorry to interrupt, but there's been a major earthquake, something huge, in San Francisco,' he said. Then he held his communicator up. 'You can even see it from space – the city has just become an island.'

All heads turned back to the table, and to their own personal communications systems. Quickly, Hanoch Biran patched his feed to a large wall-screen. The views coming in were relayed from a helicopter belonging to Channel 9 News, a local San Franciscan TV station.

They watched in silence as the chopper flew over the smoking undulations of the city, its hillsides covered with flattened debris, the slopes naked as if they had been suddenly deforested. Then they could see the Embarcadero Space Needle lying on its side, semi-submerged in the bay.

The US President declared a state of national emergency, dispatching 20,000 troops to the Bay Area. He also ordered the US Navy to sea, sending all available ships from their home port in San Diego to serve as emergency ferries in order to link the new island of San Francisco with the mainland.

From all over the state of California, volunteer medics, paramedics, search-and-rescue teams, digging parties and blood donors rushed to provide their services. Earth-moving equipment and heavy lifting gear was flown into Sacramento by the army, and then driven westwards to the disaster area. Specialist listening equipment and specially trained sniffer dogs needed to locate trapped victims were airlifted in from all over the USA, Europe, Russia and the Middle East.

Self-propelled satellites were repositioned and retasked to hover in geostationary orbit above the disaster area, bringing their long-focus, high-definition zoom lenses to bear on the devastation at all wavelengths, visible and non-visible. At the President's personal request, the ERGIA Corporation liaised with the military authorities in charge of search-and-rescue to subdue and re-route Pacific onshore winds that might have fanned the flames of the myriad fires now raging all over the Bay Area. It was agreed that using spot rain to subdue the fires would only hinder the search-and-rescue effort.

In Geohazard's headquarters in Oakland the scientists worked back-to-back shifts without sleep, continually warning the public about multiple aftershocks, checking all of the local fault lines for new movement, providing specialist advice about building structures, and dealing with endless official enquiries.

Emilia Knight didn't leave the risk-monitoring centre for four days. She snatched what sleep she could in disused offices, showered in the company's facilities, changed into company-issue field clothing and begged repeatedly to be allowed to go out and physically help with the rescue efforts that were going on all around them. Each time her colleagues told her that her specialist knowledge was far more valuable to the population than her muscle power. But they too felt the urge to rush outside and simply dig.

Michael Fairfax suffered eighteen hours of almost unendurable anxiety. He had been woken by the first shock, half thrown out of his bed as his single-level house shook on its foundations. It stood on the bedrock of the Sausolito hills and although its roof was completely separated from its supports the thick brick walls had withstood the repeated convulsions.

He'd grabbed a dressing gown, run into his front yard and thrown himself flat on the lawn. The heaving seemed to go on and on, loud reports coming from all around as tree trunks snapped, walls cracked and power lines came down.

As Michael lay with his face pressed into the grass, all he could think about was his sons – and Lucy. He knew that Telegraph Hill was also bedrock, generally considered by insurers to be at lower risk than other parts of the city, but the house itself was old. It even pre-dated the 1906 earthquake. That thought gave him heart; if it had withstood that disaster, it would also withstand this one.

When the ground's heaving finally relented, he pushed himself to his feet. But he found it hard to comprehend what he was seeing. From his front yard he had a view right across the bay to the downtown city skyline and the Bay Bridge.

It was a clear morning but the sun was still low, and at first he thought it must be some trick of the light. There was no Embarcadero Space Needle. His office building, the dominant landmark of the city, had simply disappeared. Then he realized that he could see all the way to Alameda, on the far-distant opposite shore. There was no Bay Bridge either.

Michael started to shake uncontrollably. From somewhere nearby a dog began to bark, and he saw his elderly neighbours cautiously stepping out of the opening in which their front door had formerly hung. Now it lay flat on their veranda.

He ran inside for the binoculars he always kept by the front window. There was broken glass all over the floor where his pictures had been hurled off the walls and smashed.

Stepping carefully, he found the optics and returned to the

front lawn. His hands were shaking so violently that he had to depress the electronic image-stabilizing button to make anything out.

As the microchip compensated for his physical tremors, everything suddenly appeared sharp and crystal clear. His gaze swept past Telegraph Hill twice before he recognized it. Coit Tower had gone, as had all of the buildings on the hill's western flank. He panned left, to where the Bay Bridge had been, and saw the giant Space Needle now lying in pieces across the bay.

Michael rushed inside for his communicator – a satellite model whose operation should be unaffected by local network problems – and he tried all of the numbers he had for his ex-wife and sons and their home. But even the satellite phone he had given Matthew on his birthday went unanswered.

Less than fifteen minutes later, he was powering his BMW rapidly up the sloping road that led out of Sausolito, intending to join the south-bound Highway 101 near where it approached the Golden Gate Bridge.

Cresting a ridge he shot a glance to his left, as he so often did, to estimate the traffic flow on the bridge itself. It was part of his normal morning commuting routine. What he saw caused him to brake hard and bring his car to a stop. He switched off the engine and got out of the vehicle.

Although its two giant ochre-red uprights were still intact, all three connecting spans of the Golden Gate Bridge were missing.

Fifteen minutes later Michael was down in the marina at Sausolito trying to find a boat that hadn't been damaged. The quake had been so strong that many of them had been thrown up onto the quayside and smashed.

Eventually he found a place on a regular Sausolito–San Francisco passenger ferry crammed with others also anxious about their families and friends in the city. But it was another two hours before he reached the Filbert Steps, and the heaped wreckage of Jersey Villa.

There was nobody around to help him as he tore at the large mound of tiles, stones and broken timbers. As he had run and walked up here through the littered wreckage of the city, voices had constantly cried out to him for assistance. Everywhere people were digging at rubble, pleading with him to stop and help them find their loved ones. Everywhere, retrieved corpses were being laid out in neat rows. There seemed to be no emergency services working yet in the city, but Michael realized that all access roads were probably blocked.

As a native San Franciscan, educated about earthquake threat since childhood, he had brought along with him a flashlight, water bottles, ropes and basic tools and he was thankful that there was no fire blazing at his house or in the wreckage of the houses on either side. Probably this was because there was no gas supply to the Steps, he thought as he worked – they couldn't pump it up this high. Many of the houses he had passed lower down the hill had been burning.

He found Matthew in less than fifteen minutes. The boy was unmistakably dead but not yet completely cold. He was surrounded by his smashed computer equipment and telescopes, the stars on the room's shredded wallpaper still glowing. From the enormous amount of blood that had soaked into the wreckage around his pulped legs, Michael guessed that his elder son had bled to death.

The father could not allow himself time to grieve and, after forty minutes of hard sawing through a fallen beam, he carefully removed Matthew's body and laid him out on the lawn. He immediately returned to continue sawing and tugging at the old redwood timbers that had once been his family home.

It was dark by the time he finally found Lucy and Ben. They had died together in the same bed – perhaps the five-year-old had had a bad dream and his mother had taken him in to sleep with her. They had been killed instantly, crushed by a massive ceiling beam and the weight of the floors above.

Michael left them where they were and went to sit beside Matthew. The moon was full, and by its bright light he saw that his hands were covered in blood; he had been sawing, hammering and clawing at the rubble for seven hours. He had lost most of his fingernails and there was no surface skin left on his fingers or on the palms of his hands.

THIRTEEN

The audacious commandeering of the *Global Haven* by the hulk people achieved for them in just a few weeks what years of diligent campaigning by charities, social campaigners and the more responsible member states of the United Nations had failed to achieve in decades.

All over the world, the media's lead news story was the great San Francisco earthquake and its aftermath. But the second item in most bulletins was the roaming convoy of hulk people – now with the *Global Haven* as its new flagship – that was cruising the international waters of the Pacific Ocean, not least because so many famous and wealthy people who had lost their homes and their possessions in the hijacking were complaining loudly on the airwaves.

Of special interest was the new and ambivalent position towards the hulk flotilla being taken by the law-enforcement agencies of the world's leading democracies.

After half a century during which tens of thousands of super-rich individuals had fled their nation states to live aboard luxury ships that cruised outside all national boundaries (thus escaping taxes and other communal responsibilities), it almost seemed as if the societies they had deserted were now gleefully rounding on *them*. Receptive to the opinion of their voters, all governments claimed that this act of piracy fell outside their own jurisdictions, while issuing public assurances that they would act firmly if the hulk ships ever entered their own territorial waters. Not one member state was prepared to raise the issue at the United Nations.

And the fact that the pirates had not injured a single one of the thousands of individuals whom they had so unceremoniously unloaded onto an ancient French oil-tanker also played strongly in the hulk people's favour.

The newspapers had created computer graphics showing what the luxury interior of the *Global Haven* might look like now that its luxury apartments, ballrooms, swimming pools, atria and gymnasiums had been taken over by as many as 50,000 of the world's poorest people.

The vessel's insurers were naturally furious. But, after decades of fearful rejection, public sentiment began to swing inexorably in favour of the hordes of status-less, homeless human beings who were forced to live out on the open seas, rather than towards sympathy for those who did so solely for purposes of tax avoidance.

'We can certainly use the hulk people's story as an angle to open our film,' Perdita Curtis explained to her executive producer as, with six other team members, they marched through one of the transparent aerial walkways that provided the main architectural feature of the BBC's new West London headquarters.

Narinda Damle and his production staff were heading for a meeting with the corporation's head of news and current affairs. This was a conference in which their request for a massive increase in budget – sufficient to stage and transmit a live debate from the moon – would be considered. MSN New York, their co-production partners, had authorized their own increased share of the budget, as soon as the American President's participation in this debate had been confirmed.

'And there's something else, Narinda – something *important*!' Perdy stopped dead in the corridor, forcing her boss and the rest of the team to pause in their headlong rush to their meeting.

Glancing at his watch, Narinda Damle turned to face her. 'We're due in six minutes,' he reminded her anxiously.

'I know, but I've only just found this out,' Perdy apologized. 'Guess what Negromonte is going to do with the billions raised by the LunaSun IPO? He'll use it to begin climate modification on Mars. They're going to melt polar ice and stimulate oxygen production by planting GM crops specially designed for Martian conditions. ERGIA's *long-term* aim is to sell Martian real estate.'

The little group was stunned.

'My God!' exclaimed Damle. 'That's a wonderful story, but how can we include it? We've only got a fifty-minute slot.'

'That's the trouble, we *can't* include it,' Perdy informed her colleagues. 'I learned about this under embargoed non-disclosure – because of Wall Street regulations over the Luna-Sun share flotation. We can't even talk about it on air until we get to the live debate – which is *after* our documentary goes out.'

'Then we'll certainly use it *in* the debate,' said Damle as he resumed marching through the walkway. 'Come on, the boss is going to love this. Perhaps we can get some Planet First people to join the discussion. Think how they'll react to the idea that humanity is just about to start modifying the climate on yet *another* planet.'

Six weeks after his sons and former wife had died in the Great San Francisco Earthquake of 2055, Michael Fairfax was back working again. He was on his feet addressing over 300 members of the global news media who had gathered in the ballroom of the Intercontinental Hotel in Brussels.

'This is the largest claim for compensation ever made in a court of law,' he informed the attentive journalists. He had just shown them the video of the hulk people which he had shot inside the Antarctic Circle. 'It's larger in real terms than the tobacco settlements of the twentieth century, and the alcohol, cellphone and antidepressant awards of more recent times. Over eleven million people have lost their homes because of global warming, a phenomenon directly caused by the energy companies who once marketed oil, gas and coal.'

He listened carefully to his own voice as it was amplified around the room. It sounded OK: strong, no hint of a waver. He was doing fine; he had been right to plunge back in. Work was always the best antidote.

As he had suspected – and as he had once threatened his over-cautious partners in a meeting that now seemed to have taken place in another lifetime – the Brussels-based law firm

Beauchamp, Seifert and Co had been delighted to pick up his hulk-people litigation.

Saul Levinson, the senior partner who had originally blocked Michael's pursuit of this case, was now dead. So were three more of the equity-holding partners, as well as sixty-one other attorneys and staff members – all killed by the earthquake itself or in its aftermath. The firm's former offices in the Embarcadero Space Needle now lay under the waters of the San Francisco Bay. Like so much else in that area, the legal practice once known as Gravitz, Lee and Kraus was no longer functioning.

Despite having had almost a century and a half since 1906 to get ready for another large earthquake, the Bay Area authorities had turned out to be woefully under-prepared for the scale of the seismic calamity when it finally came.

The city authorities had no temporary morgues and no processing procedures capable of dealing with 500,916 fatalities in a single day, nor the 136,879 deaths that followed in the ensuing forty-eight hours. Power was out across the entire area, and there were no crematoria or cemeteries able to cope with such vast numbers of deceased. The military took charge.

Lucy Fairfax and her two sons were buried at sea, from the deck of a large US Navy cargo ship. Almost 14,000 others were committed during the same ceremony, the dead far outnumbering those few mourners who, like Michael, stood on the deck as pallet after pallet of white, weighted bundles were brought up from refrigerated holds and slid down into the ocean.

None of the other Fairfax relatives or in-laws were able to attend this hastily arranged committal. Lucy's own parents were in Los Angeles and Michael's parents lived in Lake Tahoe, but no commercial flights were yet landing in the Bay Area. In any case, there was still no civilian access to the city. It was estimated that it would be at least a year before any new airport facilities could be built. Replacement bridges to link downtown San Francisco to the mainland were expected to take even longer, and many were already questioning the wisdom of rebuilding in such a high-risk zone.

The day after his sons and ex-wife were committed to the Pacific, Michael gathered up the paperwork and data dumps he kept at his damaged home, packed two large suitcases, and drove the 250 miles to Reno, Nevada. There he boarded a flight to Chicago and travelled on overnight to Brussels.

Within thirty-six hours of his arrival in Europe, he was making a presentation to the managing partners of Beauchamp, Seifert and Co, the world's leading environmental and human-rights law practice. Being a prudent man, Michael had kept back-ups of every piece of paper and every scrap of data intended for his hulk-people case at his own home.

The partners agreed unanimously to fund Michael's case, to appoint him an associate partner of the European firm, and to retain in escrow a proportion of any compensation won for the benefit of Gravitz, Lee and Kraus of San Francisco – if and when that stricken firm was able to resume its own practice or appoint liquidators.

'I will now take any questions,' Michael told his audience. A forest of arms shot up and he pointed his latex-gloved hand towards a man in the front row. One of the presentation assistants handed a microphone to the first questioner.

'Chris Van Assche, NTL,' announced a tall balding man. 'Despite the very large sums that you are claiming from the energy companies, you have not told us exactly how you will proceed with this case. What will be your first step?'

Michael nodded, pleased by the question. He had deliberately kept his formal statement to a minimum, with the intention of supplying the more important detail during Q & A. That made journalists feel they had wheedled the information out for themselves.

'We have this morning applied to the Court of International Civil Justice in The Hague for two injunctions – the first naming Mr Nicholas Negromonte, the second his ERGIA Corporation – to order them to shut down all extraterrestrial solar reflectors, refractors, lenses and focusing devices and to cease providing climate-management services throughout the world.'

There was an immediate hubbub, exactly as Michael had hoped for. Flashlights flared and a loud hum of conversation filled the large room, while twenty questions were shouted at once, all without the benefit of a microphone and all wholly unintelligible.

'Tomorrow we will seek similar injunctions against all the other companies who offer climate-modification services,' added Michael, over the din. 'Climate management must henceforth be completely shut down.'

'Tune in to CNN now,' said Narinda Damle as he burst into Perdy's office. 'Your pal Negromonte's being sued.'

She pressed a button on a remote, and the wall-screen came to life.

They saw a tall, dark-haired man addressing a press conference. Beneath the picture, a screen caption read:

World's Largest-Ever Lawsuit
Launched Against Major Energy Companies

'Record,' Perdy told her system. Then she punched the buttons necessary to patch the TV feed through to the workstations used by the rest of her production team.

They saw a balding journalist rise to his feet. 'What are your grounds for seeking these injunctions, Mr Fairfax? What will you be telling the court in The Hague?'

'I now have evidence that weather-management technologies are seriously disrupting this planet's magnetic fields,' the lawyer said. The TV director in Brussels cut away to show the audience reaction. There was now absolute silence. Many of the attendant journalists were recording, some taking notes. 'And this is now affecting materials way beneath our feet – at the planet's very core. In fact, I have scientific evidence about climate management which proves that by reflecting so much additional solar radiation towards the Earth the massive increase in electrically charged particles is warping the magnetosphere, the Earth's magnetic shield. In turn, these new forces are pulling at the magnetic fields deep in the planet's mantle and this is the direct cause of the devastating volcanic eruptions and earthquakes we have been suffering lately.'

'You've got to get *him* for our film,' said Damle. 'Find out how long he's going to be in Europe.'

Perdy reached for her phone. 'I've got a friend at CNN,' she told her boss. 'She'll be able to find out his immediate movements.'

Michael Fairfax pressed a button on his remote control and turned to the large 3-D presentation screen. The house lights dimmed, and the audience watched Professor Fivetrees's shimmering hologram of the Earth and its force fields. Michael allowed the demonstration to run without comment. When it was finished and the room lights had come back up, he picked up a wireless microphone and walked to the front of the stage.

'What you have just seen is a model of the Earth's magnetic poles reversing,' he told them. 'It was created by one of the world's leading experts in geoscience but he has been officially gagged by an American government secrecy order. However, in view of the devastating San Francisco earthquake he now considers this issue so important that he is prepared to give evidence personally to the international court in The Hague.'

As Michael paused, scores of hands shot up. He held up a white-gloved palm. 'But there is even more direct evidence of serious disturbance inside the earth. In the days following the eruption of Mount Māriota on Samoa, an American seismologist recovered large pieces of radioactive heavy metals from its slopes. According to this expert such a find is unique and suggests that material is now being forced to the earth's surface from a very deep source indeed.'

This time when he paused no hands shot up. They were struggling to understand the implications of this startling information.

'These radioactive samples are now in the hands of the US military, and yet again the US government has imposed a National Secrecy Order to prevent the seismologist who made the find from publicizing or talking about this remarkable discovery. However, following the disaster in San Francisco, the scientist concerned is now also prepared to give personal evidence to the Hague court.'

Los Angeles Times

Wednesday, 16 August 2055

PFO RENOUNCES VIOLENCE

In a statement e-mailed to the *LA Times*, the Executive Committee of the Planet First Organization claims to have renounced all forms of violent protest following the San Francisco earthquake. The statement was accompanied by recognized code words which have previously been used by the PFO. The statement reads:

From today, the Planet First Organization will no longer use any form of direct or violent action to draw attention to the perilous state of this planet's health. The world has already been given the clearest possible demonstration of the catastrophes awaiting us if we do not abandon climate management and other technologies that are being used to mask the true effects of global heating.

'Hey, Nick, how's tricks?'

'Good morning, Mr President. Fine, thank you, fine. And yourself?'

'I'm good, Nick, but I'm also a little worried about you guys floating around up there.'

Nicholas Negromonte, CEO of the ERGIA Corporation, was speaking from his private quarters aboard the company's main space station. He propelled himself over to his window and craned his neck to locate the eastern seaboard of the United States. Then he ran his eyes down to the Delaware peninsula: Washington DC should be just to the west – *there*.

'In what way, sir?' They hadn't selected visual.

'This lawsuit, Nick – it's getting a hell of a lot of coverage.'

'Better now than later,' said Negromonte. 'It will all have blown over before we welcome you to the moon.'

'I've been thinking about that too, Nick. Don't you think it might be wise to delay things for a while?'

'Absolutely not,' said Negromonte firmly, aware that if the date slipped the forthcoming election year would make it almost impossible for the American President to reschedule a visit. 'No need at all.'

'So there's nothing to this idea of a link between climate management and earthquakes?' asked James Underwood. 'What about San Francisco?'

'Sir, that just proves how hysterical all this is. We've known for over a century that a major quake was due in California. The whole state sits on one gigantic fault line. To claim that a little reflected sunshine caused that is ridiculous.'

There was a brief silence.

'In fact, what we most need is the extra output that the moon facility is going to provide,' the ERGIA boss pressed on. 'There are almost twenty nations waiting for climate management, and over the next three years we estimate that will add an extra six per cent to GDP in those regions.'

'That brings me to another point, Nick,' said the President. 'I might just need to beg a little of that additional output from you.'

*

'You can't believe how these people are forced to live!' said Michael Fairfax vehemently, jabbing a forefinger at the image of the hulk people now frozen on the wall screen. 'They have no official status as refugees, so that means they have *less* than nothing. They're even denied natural weather!'

In person, the good-looking American attorney that Perdy Curtis had seen on television looked haggard and drawn. There was a burning intensity in his eyes which seemed at odds with his pallor and his anxiously twitching white-gloved hands. He was pacing as he talked, as if he was constantly on edge.

Their meeting was taking place in his suite at the Brussels Intercontinental and he had just shown Perdy his own footage of the hulk platform adrift in the southern seas.

'But they've now turned pirate,' objected the TV producer, deliberately playing devil's advocate. She had already come to the conclusion that this attorney could make a very powerful contribution to her upcoming film and perhaps to the live debate to be broadcast from the moon. 'What about the *Global Haven?*'

'That doesn't affect their historical claim,' Michael said forcefully, 'and it's only a small minority of the refugees who are on the move. Most of their ships are still trapped inside the Antarctic Circle.'

He walked over to the window and stared down into the busy Avenue Louise far below.

'How bad a blow was it for you when the court refused your request for injunctions?' asked Perdy, changing tack. 'You must have been very disappointed.'

He swung round on his heel to face her. 'On the contrary, on the contrary, it achieved everything I had hoped for. It made headlines all round the world. For the first time people have begun questioning whether climate management is such a good thing. That was only the first round. The real case will start when I call in my expert witnesses.'

'I was wondering . . .' she said pensively. 'Would the scientists you mentioned be prepared to talk on camera? This professor who claims the poles are reversing – and the scientist who found these radioactive rocks? Could we invite them to join the moon debate?'

Michael stopped his pacing and came to sit opposite her, on one of the ruby-red sofas placed at either side of a low coffee table.

'I don't know,' he admitted. 'At first both of them felt very bound by the US secrecy agreements. But after the earthquake ... they're both based in the San Francisco area, you see.'

'Can you give me their names?' she asked.

'Off the record?'

Perdy nodded and paused her recording.

'Professor Robert Fivetrees lectures at Berkeley. He's one of the world's leading planetary geophysicists. Dr Emilia Knight – the seismologist who found the radioactive rock – is at Geohazard Labs in Oakland. They both feel that the truth should come out now, and I'm going to ask the court in The Hague to issue them with a writ of witness protection. It's a legal device which should go some way to help if the US government prosecutes them.'

Perdy had a sudden flash of intuition. 'Are you from San Francisco yourself?' she enquired.

The reaction she saw on Michael's drawn face provided her answer.

'I'm sorry,' she said. 'I hope you didn't lose anyone close.'

He shook his head as if to dismiss the subject. Then she watched as he gathered his courage.

'I lost my two sons,' he said quietly, almost as if to himself. 'And my ex-wife. Matthew was thirteen. Ben was five. All of them were crushed to death in their beds.' He lifted his hands as he spoke, displaying his white surgical gloves. 'I dug them out of the wreckage myself.'

Perdy saw that the lawyer was forcing himself to say the words, to get used to saying something that he would have to repeat over and over again for the rest of his life.

She stared at him in dismay, the awfulness of his tragedy brought directly into this hotel room by the evidence of his damaged hands. Tears suddenly welled in his eyes and rolled down both cheeks. He made no attempt to turn his head away from her, to hide his grief.

Perdy didn't know what to do. But she rose, leaned forward and put a hand on his shoulder. Now Michael was sobbing uncontrollably, resting his forehead on the heels of his palms. She sat beside him as he shook his head in mute apology for his display. Then she put an arm around his shoulders and, acting purely on instinct, drew him closer towards her.

The immense expanse of the central Pacific easily swallowed up the *Global Haven* and the 142 decrepit commercial vessels that now steamed in loose formation around her. Staying well away from all territorial waters, this strange flotilla cruised in slow, wide circles as its crew took stock of what they had gained with their monumental prize – and argued heatedly about what their next step should be.

Their windfall proved to be on an almost unimaginable scale – and wholly unexpected. The super-cruiser's former commander, Captain James Monroe, had already been notified by his employers that he would need to appear before a disciplinary hearing and he was already the target of nearly 1,000 private lawsuits from furious ex-residents. More were expected to follow.

But had the captain and his accusers only realized it, this break-away faction of hulk people had not set out deliberately to snare the *Global Haven* herself. They had set up their decoy to catch *any* modern vessel that happened to be passing. Two months after leaving their deprived but self-sufficient home community in the Southern Ocean, the convoy had started running short of drinking water, food and fuel. After being bombed as they approached the Peruvian coastline, they had subsequently been unable to secure supplies from anywhere else. Their hijacking had been an act of desperation.

But now they had fresh supplies – and in enormous quantities. In her eighty-two main or reserve tanks, housed in each of the double-skinned catamaran hulls, the *Global Haven* carried enough diesel fuel, aviation kerosene and jet fuel to supply her tenders and aircraft for six years of normal operations. Huge tanks of fresh water were topped up by three desalinization plants, while the ship's four main hydrogen-plasma engines had enough fuel pellets for sixty round-the-world trips.

The freezer-holds of the luxury ship held over 100,000 sides of beef, lamb and pork, and copious quantities of frozen and freeze-dried vegetables. Spices, oils, pulses and every conceivable ingredient required for creating the world's cuisines bulged from over 200 dry stores dotted around the vessel and her wine cellars contained over three million bottles of the world's most valuable vintages. The pirates showered, swam, feasted, sunbathed and lazed, each separate hulk-ship community taking it in turns to enjoy twenty-four sybaritic hours aboard the luxury vessel.

The shops in the atria malls held huge stocks of leisurewear, jewellery, designer clothes, sports equipment, fur coats and perfumes from every continent. Fourteen banks carried currency in every important denomination, a TV studio lay ready to record or broadcast and one large retail outlet was filled with nothing but electronic keyboards and self-playing grand pianos.

The ship's main hospital, fourteen operating theatres and six health clinics boasted every sort of drug and the latest and most expensive scanning, diagnostic aid and technological therapies. These were immediately put to work treating hundreds of chronically ill and malnourished refugees who were carefully transferred from the surrounding vessels.

Up on the flight deck the pirates found themselves in possession of twenty-six private helicopters, one long-range air-sea rescue chopper and two dozen business jets, all of them carefully hangared and bolted down for the duration of the trans-ocean passage. But though many of the hulk people were seamen and navigators, none were pilots; in the early days it had been redundant sailors who had helped them commandeer the abandoned tankers that had since become their homes – but not one of them knew how to fly.

Rows started breaking out between the community leaders as they gradually discovered the treasures contained in the vast ship's 3,011 private apartments. Safe after safe was cut open to disgorge jewellery, gemstones, gold – and share certificates worth billions of dollars.

Numerous staterooms were filled with the obsessions of the super-rich, the collections of rare things that gave purpose to the lives of individuals who could buy almost anything: porcelain, *objets d'art*, fine antiques, early musical instruments – clavichords, spinets, virginals, violins, lutes and guitars. One apartment was filled with Renaissance bronzes, another with French armour of the sixteenth century, a third was graced by magnificent Rouen and Nevers *faïence*. One collector kept three cabinets of Classical-era Greek and Roman coins, another only the rarest statuary from ancient Greece.

The apartment walls were covered with thousands of fine paintings – Rembrandts, Van Goghs, Picassos, Titians, El Grecos, Canalettos – many of them individually valuable enough to buy a vast country estate in one of the world's richest nations. But none of these assets represented any value to a group of people unable to set foot in the developed world.

'We should contact the insurers,' John Gogotya urged his lieutenants as they met in one of the ship's grand ballrooms. 'They will pay us well – enough for everyone amongst us to buy a passport.'

'Maybe an Eritrean passport,' sneered Muhammad Sitta, Gogotya's Number Two. 'Or an Angolan one. I say we should trade this ship for the right to live in America – or Europe!'

'He's right,' said one of the older men in the group. 'This is the best asset we have to bargain with. I say we take it to America – to Los Angeles.'

'To Los Angeles!' enthused Muhammad Sitta.

'To Los Angeles!' shouted the others.

Eight weeks after the great Californian earthquake, Dr Emilia Knight lounged on her sunset deck, wondering whether she should ring Michael Fairfax. But she wasn't sure of his current whereabouts. Although she had spoken to him by phone immediately after the catastrophe – even seen him on television announcing his massive legal case – he had not called her since or sent a message.

It was a warm Tuesday evening and Emilia decided that she would light the deck lamps and turn on the electric bug-zapper before making the call. Rising to her feet, she leaned on the deck rail, gazing down at the twinkling lights of other homes dotted around the dark inlet. Most of the properties in the Muir Beach area had withstood the massive quake. Cascading boulders and landslides had changed the curves of the small bay somewhat, but that was the only local evidence of the recent upheaval.

Emilia Knight's rented home had also proved to be a credit to its builders. The stainless-steel bolts that secured its metal underframe to the cliff itself had stoutly withstood the vigorous buffeting and, after five days of almost non-stop duty at Geo-hazard HQ, Emilia had finally returned home to discover little damage other than a freezer full of spoiled food and a few minor breakages.

She had swept up the broken glass and china from the floor, still marvelling that she herself had escaped so lightly. After three days and nights working within the company's emergency command bunker, the US Navy had taken Emilia, Steve Bardini and two Geohazard colleagues across the bay to see for themselves some of the damage downtown. They were scheduled to meet with government building engineers who had to decide which of the shattered buildings should be pulled down, and which were thought able to withstand further shocks.

Their visit had been like walking through a city that had just suffered a direct hit from a nuclear bomb. Only occasionally could Emilia pick out any familiar landmark – a view towards the bay that seemed still unaltered, or a single wall that remained standing, a tattered advertisement on its flank.

Almost alone among her work colleagues, Emilia herself had not lost any close friends or family in the disaster. She was from Boston originally and almost all of her West Coast friends lived fairly near her on the Marin coastline or in other locations well away from the quake's epicentre.

But walking amongst the ruins of the once-great city had affected her profoundly. As an earth scientist, she was used to visiting earthquake sites and areas that had suffered volcanic eruptions. She had witnessed the urban devastation of Kyoto, Madras and Beijing – but she had never before seen destruction on quite this scale. Up until this point she had felt that her geological training and ten-year career in predictive seismology had provided her with a pretty accurate mental model of how fragile the Earth's crust was, and just how easily the shrug of a tectonic plate could cause widespread havoc. But this forced her to rethink, to rescale her mental model of the forces pent up beneath the Earth's surface.

Even as Emilia laid her plans for recalibrating the Geohazard Simulation Theater so as to allow much larger quakes to be replicated, she knew that she was merely operating on autopilot. It was the sheer stillness of the dead San Francisco that had shocked her most. There was almost no noise within the city, just an occasional crash as one of the wreckage-clearing parties managed to free a beam, or the barking of a stray dog scavenging among the debris.

At the end of a two-hour tour through what had been the Marina District and Haight Ashbury, she had been forced to turn her back on her male colleagues to hide her tears. But when Steve Bardini's arm crept round her shoulders and she had recovered sufficiently to turn back to face her companions, she saw that they too were fighting back powerful emotions.

On her return to Geohazard Labs from the city's devastated downtown area, Emilia found an unoccupied office, closed the door, and dialled the satellite-phone number that Michael Fairfax had given her.

He answered on the second ring. The details of the personal loss he then recounted caused her tears to well again, this time uncontrollably. She had never before had to face such a degree of personal involvement in the disasters that she attempted to predict and ameliorate.

For several minutes Michael spoke as if to console *her*. Then, as he described his own family's burial at sea only the day before, she realized that his seeming ice-cold strength was one of denial, a symptom of deep shock.

Then the lawyer abruptly announced that he was about to fly to Europe – to try to lodge his hulk-people case with the International Court of Civil Justice in The Hague.

'Robert Fivetrees has now agreed to give evidence in Holland about his data analysis,' he went on. 'He considers that the earthquake we've just suffered is the final proof. He seems desperately concerned for the safety of cities worldwide if the energy companies keep on interfering with the planet's magnetic force fields.'

'He might well be right...' Emilia was still mentally groping for words to deal with this bereft man. In the aftermath of the earthquake she hadn't had a chance to even look at the professor's data.

'Would you now consider telling the Hague court what you found in Samoa?' the lawyer urged. 'The judges could offer you some degree of protection, but you might still be open to prosecution from our own government here.'

She thought about the devastation she had just walked through. If there was the remotest chance that Professor Fivetrees was right in his theories, it had to be safer to shut down weather-management services until the effects could be studied further.

'But I'm not sure if there is any link,' Emilia told the lawyer. 'We have no real idea why uranium and plutonium were propelled to the surface. Just that it's never happened before, as far as we know.'

'But would you at least be prepared to testify to what you found there?' Michael pressed her.

She thought about it for less than ten seconds – everything had changed now. 'Yes, of course, if you think it will help.'

The next time Emilia saw the attorney he had been appearing on the national news, referring to her find and announcing the start of what might become the world's largest-ever legal case.

Emilia pushed herself away from the deck rail to light the lamps. She finally switched on the electric bug-zapper, then lifted her phone and summoned Michael's number.

Just as she was about to place the call, her front doorbell chimed. She sighed and snapped her communicator shut. Perhaps it was a neighbour dropping by – everybody locally seemed so much more friendly and helpful since the earthquake.

Emilia hoped above all that it wouldn't be Steve Bardini again. After the emotional shock of the earthquake he had redoubled his attempts to restart their affair, until she had been forced to tell him in the clearest possible terms to keep his distance. But despite this, she knew that he was still hanging around her home in the evenings, often walking along the beach down below just in the hope of bumping into her. It was like having a stalker.

'Good evening, Dr Knight, how are you feeling now?'

The visitor was her doctor from the San Diego Naval Hospital. Behind him stood two paramedics in full biohazard safety suits. 'May we come in?'

Wholly bemused, she stepped aside to let them enter.

'What is it, Doctor Bowman?' she began. 'Is something wrong?'

Then she noticed that the paramedics had also donned safety helmets. With Geiger counters in their hands, they advanced across her living room as if checking for radiation.

'Your bone-marrow decay tests...' began the doctor, putting down his black bag. 'Well, I'm afraid the rate is far too high. You didn't keep any small samples of those rocks for yourself, did you?'

'I'm not *mad*,' Emilia snapped angrily. The paramedics had now invaded her bedroom. 'You don't really think I'd bring radioactive samples home with me, do you?'

'And you haven't suffered any blackouts, or fainting spells?' continued the doctor, as if she hadn't spoken. He suddenly reached out for her wrist and checked her pulse between his middle finger and thumb while gazing at his watch.

Emilia glanced round to see what the paramedics were now doing. One of them was in the kitchen, running his Geiger counter over her counter top.

'Would you mind sitting down?' asked Bowman, leading her to an armchair. He then snapped open his bag and extracted a stethoscope, a miniature Geiger counter, and small air-jet hypodermic.

Emilia suddenly felt alarmed. 'Look, what *is* this?' she demanded. 'Why have you suddenly turned up here uninvited? Why didn't you just ask me to come in to the hospital?'

'You're right. I'm sorry,' said the doctor, with a kindly smile on his face as he held his Geiger counter to her abdomen. 'I did try to call you, but you know how bad communications in this area have been recently.'

He glanced at the meter's read-out, then pocketed it without comment. Since the earthquake, Emilia's own mild exposure to radioactivity had seemed of little consequence and she had since given up regularly measuring the levels in her body.

'I just need to take a little blood now,' Dr Bowman said, tearing open an antiseptic sachet. He swabbed a patch of skin inside her elbow, then pressed the hypodermic against it.

Within seconds Emilia seemed to enter a dark tunnel. Then, as she turned her head to ask the doctor what he was doing, her eyes closed abruptly and her chin slumped to her chest.

Bowman took her pulse again, lifted one of her eyelids to check her response to light, then stood upright. He called out to the two men still searching elsewhere in the house.

Ten minutes later, Steve Bardini finished the long climb up from the beach, just in time to see a stretcher being loaded into the rear of a white US Navy ambulance. Catching a glimpse of the patient's face, he realized it was Emilia.

His instinct was to step out of the trees and confront these paramedics, to demand to know what had happened to his boss and former girlfriend. But he knew she would be furious if he interfered in her personal business, if he made any public claim on her.

Remaining within the shadow of the pine trees, Steve watched as the three men finished loading their patient into the vehicle. There was nothing urgent or alarmed about their movements, he noticed.

Then he heard a communicator chirrup, and one of their party answered it.

'Yes, all done,' the man in a dark suit informed the caller, his words drifting clearly through the warm night air. 'We'll have her back in San Diego by two a.m latest.'

Highway 1, California's oldest and most scenic coastal road, had become blocked at seventeen different locations during the earthquake.

Even in times of seismic passivity, this narrow, winding two-lane highway was frequently closed because of landslides and rockfalls, so most busy Californians who needed to get anywhere in a hurry chose to use the newer dual-carriageway Highway 101 that ran further inland.

But the old winding highway was much loved by tourists for its magnificent ocean views, and by motoring enthusiasts who delighted in the hairpin bends, adverse cambers, sheer-drop ravines and alpine passes that characterized its 400-mile run between Fort Bragg in the north and San Simeon to the south.

Shortly after 6.30 a.m. on the first Sunday morning since the California Highway Authority had announced that all stretches of Highway 1 had now been cleared and reopened, Professor Robert Fivetrees gunned his beloved petrol-driven, manual-shift, racing green Jaguar XKS V-8 – a car constructed in England in the year of his birth – around a tight, rising bend that led southwards out of the surfers' resort known as Stinson Beach.

To his right, and far below, stretched the vast Pacific, a deep green-blue in the clear early-morning light. Ahead lay only winding open road. The professor had the roof down, his long hair was tied back, and a driving hard-rock track was blaring from the car's stereo. It was a great way to start the day.

He changed down into second gear for a hard left-hander and then floored the accelerator again for the long straight run up towards the cliff-top ahead, above which he could just see the sun's rays appearing.

Fivetrees had spent the night with Anne Rossiter, his current girlfriend and a former student, at her home in Stinson Beach and, as he often did on a Sunday, he had risen early with the intention of enjoying the thrills that the deserted early-morning clifftop road could offer a passionate driver. Later, he would creep back into the house before she was even awake and begin the task of preparing Canadian bacon, waffles and scrambled eggs for their breakfast on the beachside deck. Then they could spend the rest of the day surfing.

He was doing almost seventy when he had to brake hard again to take the hairpin bend known locally as Jute's Dive. Then he was out of the chicane he knew so well and climbing towards the lip of the cliff.

'I have him in visual,' radioed the helicopter pilot who was flying 300 feet above and 600 feet behind him. 'He's entering the zone ... now.'

Fivetrees changed up into third and crested the cliffside ridge at eighty. Now he could see for miles out to sea, a sheer fall immediately to his right, the red cliff face flashing by on his left. It was a truly beautiful morning.

'Five, four, three ...' the helicopter pilot counted down into his radio, as the Jaguar approached a sharp left-hand bend.

The big truck shot rear-first out of a concealed cliff-side lay-by.

Robert Fivetrees slammed on his brakes, but he was doing almost sixty miles an hour and the slab-sided farm truck was sideways on, blocking the entire road, and was now only twenty feet away. To his left was a sheer wall of rock, to his right a vertical drop.

At the last moment before impact, Fivetrees flicked his walnut-rimmed steering wheel to the right and sailed out into space, the aerodynamic shape of the car holding it steady in the air for the first few moments before the weight of its engine caused it to plummet nose-first towards the rocks and the foaming surf below.

The chopper pilot watched the car fall, and lowered his stick to follow it down. The old Jaguar hit a group of black, foam-washed rocks, and a moment later there was an enormous explosion which made the pilot instinctively veer away, back out to sea.

He circled round, increasing his altitude to 600 feet. Then he visually swept the highway for half a mile to the south, then to the north. There was no other early-morning traffic on the road, no potential witnesses. A thick column of black smoke was now rising from where the Jaguar's wreckage burned amongst the rocks.

'X-Ray One to Zulu,' he reported over the radio. 'It's a home run.'

FOURTEEN

Ben Fairfax's blue eyes widened as he stared down at the selection of hot toast and freshly sliced fruit that the flight attendant had placed on his tray table.

He lifted his wondering gaze from the food and the elegant place-setting, grinned at his father and slowly opened and closed his small fingers as if they were already sticky. Then he dipped his hand into the bread basket.

'Oh man!' he said with a huge grin. 'Ciwomen toast!'

For some reason the whole family was flying first-class.

'Don't go too far inside the volcano, boys,' said Lucy cheerily. She and Matthew were seated on the other side of the aisle.

'Sir? Sir?' A flight attendant was shaking him by the shoulder. Michael Fairfax struggled back to wakefulness, and with a wave of inner anguish realized that he had been dreaming yet again about his lost family.

'We'll be landing in Sacramento in ten minutes,' she said. 'Could you please straighten your seat?'

Michael was returning home to California, intending first to visit his elderly parents in Lake Tahoe for a few days. They were also grieving and he knew it would make them feel happier if they could fuss over him for even a short while. He now felt strong enough to be strong for them.

Then he planned to summon up his courage and drive back to the Bay Area, to take stock of local conditions and to test his own feelings about the stricken region. It had been his home for all his life, but now he wasn't sure how he would react. Still, at least there would be practical chores to occupy him.

Before leaving, Michael had done his best to make his house secure from looters, but he suspected it might have suffered a break-in. While he had been preparing to fly to Europe, the local authorities had kept advising all residents to stay close to their homes, damaged or not, because the scourge of looting had escalated into such a problem that the army was permitted to stun-gun looters on sight. Michael had taken most of his portable valuables round to his elderly neighbours who, horrified by his bereavement, were only too willing to help.

On his arrival, he decided that his first task must be to find out from the authorities how long it would take before his house could be properly checked for structural damage. Then, if it was worth repairing at all, it would have to be re-roofed. He supposed that he could probably manage to camp out in one of the damaged rooms for a couple of nights.

He was also planning to contact – if possible visit – both Professor Robert Fivetrees and Dr Emilia Knight, to discuss with them when they could schedule some time to appear in The Hague as just two of his many expert witnesses.

Michael had now taken possession of a new office in Brussels, although he sometimes worried whether, in the aftermath of the world's worst-ever recorded seismic catastrophe, others might think he was acting with unseemly haste. But to himself he justified the speed of his actions by the urgent need to bring the potential dangers of climate management to international attention. This flurry of activity had allowed him little time to brood about Ben, Matthew and Lucy, but he was surprised at just how deeply his ex-wife's death had affected him – he felt it just as keenly as if they had never been through a painful divorce.

His new European base could not have been more different to the ultra-modern premises occupied by his old firm in the Embarcadero Space Needle. The third-floor corner office in Brussels city centre overlooked the Chaussée de Charleroi and boasted three large curved windows of intricate leaded and stained-glass design. These were considered an important architectural feature of the elaborate Art Nouveau building, which the firm of Beauchamp, Seifert and Co had occupied since it had first opened in 1902.

Fine antiques filled Michael's new working environment and he already had a legal assistant, three full-time European litigation lawyers and a dozen paralegals all working on the preparations for the first round of his landmark case. EU Immigration officials had issued their approval for him to work as an 'alien professional' within Europe for two years, though he anticipated that he would now have to split his time equally between the two continents.

The plane landed smoothly and, after what seemed like an interminable time as it waited for a gate, Michael finally reached the arrivals hall, only to find it hopelessly mobbed. He realized that it would be a long time before he cleared Immigration and, perhaps, an even longer time before his baggage arrived on one of the many overcrowded carousels. With a mental groan he tagged onto the end of a long line shuffling towards a row of passport-inspection counters.

Since the earthquake, Sacramento International Airport had been attempting to operate at six times its normal capacity. Following the loss of both San Francisco and Oakland International airports, it had become the only terminus in Northern California capable of handling international flights, and the only remaining hub for the endless number of military and government planes which flew people and resources in and out of the disaster area.

Temporary dispensation had been given by the FAA for flights to continue arriving and departing throughout the night hours, and many civilian flights had also been suspended. But these measures proved to be of only marginal assistance. The main problems were lack of apron space for aircraft parking, lack of terminal facilities to handle such large numbers of passengers, a shortage of trained Immigration staff to process international arrivals, and a serious shortfall in baggage-handling facilities.

'Mr Michael Benjamin Fairfax?'

The lawyer turned from his place in the shuffling queue to see a pale, bespectacled young man in a creased brown suit, beside whom stood an airport cop with his thumbs hooked in his gun belt.

'Yes?'

The young man flashed a badge. 'US Immigration. Would you please follow me, sir?'

'My bags,' protested Michael, pointing towards the distant bank of carousels. People in the line were now staring at him as if he were an illegal immigrant – or a terrorist.

'We'll have them collected for you, sir,' said the immigration officer. 'This shouldn't take long.'

Puzzled, Michael followed his guide from the arrivals hall, heading through a security door and into a harshly lit labyrinth of interior corridors. The cop plodded along close behind them.

Eventually the immigration official halted and punched a combination of numbers into a wall panel. Michael was ushered into a windowless interview room containing a rectangular white table, six chairs, a wall-screen, and a pair of surveillance video cameras suspended from the ceiling.

Three suited men rose from positions around the table.

'Mr Fairfax,' said the nearest man. He was very tall, teak-black, completely bald, and dressed in a silver-threaded grey suit. 'Please take a seat.' He indicated a vacant chair at one end of the table.

'Is there some problem?' asked Michael.

'My name is John Defoe,' said the tall man. He held out a badge. 'National Security Agency. This is Mr Reynolds, from the Defense Nuclear Agency and this gentleman' – he pointed to the third man at the other end of the table – 'is also a government employee. Mr White is attached to the Pentagon.'

'What *is* this?' asked the lawyer, his voice growing firm. He had now guessed precisely what this was about, but he didn't like these men's tactics nor their body language.

'Please sit down,' said the NSA agent who had provided the brief introductions.

As Michael did so, the others resumed their places and waited while the immigration officer and the cop both left the room.

'Mr Fairfax, it has come to our attention that you have revealed a number of US state secrets on international television, and you have done so knowing them to be the subject of National Secrecy Orders,' said Agent Defoe.

The lawyer felt adrenalin rush into his brain, dispelling the weariness of his journey. This encounter was happening far sooner than he had anticipated – but he was ready for it.

'Then I suggest that you prosecute me,' he said, careful not to smile, nor to show any hint of arrogance or impertinence. He knew the video recording of this interview might become evidence to be used against him. But he also knew that the last thing they would want to do would be to prosecute him, not now that he was an associate partner in the highest-profile human-rights law firm in the world. And not unless they wanted the information he had to be repeated in gory detail during a televised US court hearing.

'Who told you about the nature of the rock samples found on the Samoan volcano?' asked Reynolds, the man from the Defense Nuclear Agency.

'I'm afraid I can't tell you that,' said Michael, once again carefully keeping his face impassive.

'Why not?' his questioner asked, equally unemotionally.

'That would be a breach of attorney-client privilege.'

'Very well,' said the Nuclear Agency man. 'What further details do you yourself know about these rock samples?'

'I'm afraid I can't tell you that, either,' said Michael.

'For what reason?'

'That too would be a breach of attorney-client privilege.'

'And under what jurisdiction would such privilege be protected?'

'Under both Californian and Federal law. As you must know.'

'But we're not in the USA at the moment. Legally we're still in extra-national territory.'

'Nothing is outside the law when it comes to attorney-client privilege – as you must surely well know,' the lawyer said gently.

'Except when it comes to plutonium, uranium and materials that can be used to construct nuclear weapons,' snapped the man from the Pentagon, speaking for the first time. 'The Patriot Act of 2002 specifically gives authorized agents of the US government the right to detain any individual, whether US citizen or alien, both within the United States and in overseas territories that have reciprocal extradition treaties, if that individual is suspected of being involved with terrorist organizations.'

He paused, drumming his fingertips on the table top. 'I can

detain you in a US military facility indefinitely, Mr Fairfax, and there is no leave to appeal, no right to a hearing. I don't even need to *prosecute* you.'

Michael struggled not to show his alarm at such extreme threats. 'But why would you think I am involved with terrorists? You must know my record as a civil-law attorney?'

'Are you, or have you ever been, a member of the Planet First Organization?' continued the man originally introduced as Mr White.

'I am not and never have been,' said Michael clearly.

'Why, then, did you visit Carole Gonzaga at Lompoc State Penitentiary?' asked Defoe.

'Because I am a lawyer and she asked me to,' Michael told him. Then he added, 'I'm sure you already know that she was a friend from my university days, so I also felt personally obliged to go and see her. Unfortunately I don't do criminal work so I recommended Mr Mitchell Tonks from my firm – from my previous firm – to handle her case.'

'I presume that the planetary geophysicist you mentioned in your press conference is Robert Fivetrees?' probed the man from the Defense Nuclear Agency.

'I'm afraid that information too is covered by attorney-client privilege,' stated Michael, his tone more defiant than he now actually felt.

'Fivetrees is another known PFO terrorist sympathizer,' said Defoe, a man so shiningly bald that the sutures of his skull could be clearly made out.

The representative of the Pentagon rose to his feet and walked around the table. He stood with one hand on the back of a vacant chair, staring down at the interviewee. Then he pulled the chair out from the table and sat heavily in it, shoving his face forward until it was no more than a foot from Michael's own.

'Did Dr Knight keep any of that plutonium back for herself?' he asked quietly.

Michael stared back at him, appalled. He now understood what this was about. They'd put two and two together and made five.

'I don't know,' he admitted. 'I would think that very unlikely.'

'Mr Fairfax, have you yourself passed weapons-grade pluto-nium on to the PFO?'

Michael stared at his questioner in shock. 'Of course not,' he protested. 'I wouldn't—'

'Have you set up a supply route of plutonium for them?'

'Look, I have no connection with either the PFO or pluto-nium,' snapped Michael. 'I'm merely here to prepare my legal case against the energy companies.'

All three interrogators stared at him for a few seconds.

'If that's true,' said Defoe, 'I warn you strongly to have no more contact with Fivetrees or Gonzaga. We now intend to take the PFO down, one way or the other.'

The NSA agent allowed his words to hang in the air for a while, to give Michael the time to understand fully the nature of the threat they contained. Then White spoke again.

'Mr Fairfax,' he began. 'Many people do have sympathy for your clients on the hulk ships. But don't allow that particular case to get tangled up with matters of national security. If you ignore this warning, and attempt to produce evidence in the court at The Hague that is the subject of a US National Security Order, you will be immediately stripped of your licence to practise law in the state of California.'

'You know you can't do that,' Michael told him, holding his gaze. 'The State Bar of California would never—'

'Yes, we can,' insisted the Pentagon man. 'Your licence will be revoked by Federal order, under the Patriot Act. Then, if you persist in using this evidence, your arrest will be sought no matter where you are in the world and, under that same Act, you will be repatriated to a US facility here or abroad, where you will be detained indefinitely as an enemy of the state. There is no appeal.'

The man's dark stare seemed to bore into Michael's brain. 'Do I make myself clear?'

By the middle of the twenty-first century, successive administrations had excavated beneath the White House grounds to extend the executive offices as far south as the Washington Needle. Unbeknown to the millions of tourists who each year tramped along the grassy Mall, the world's most powerful nation conducted much of its business directly beneath their feet.

The most recent facility to be added to this large subterranean complex was the Situation Theater, the President's enhanced personal command centre, from which he or she could conduct wars, manage crises, organize coups, and ponder how best to lead a bitterly divided world. Capable of holding up to 300 advisers, military staff and executives, the 'ST' was reached by a new underground shuttle that ran from a small terminus beneath the Oval Office directly into the Theater itself. The journey took just three minutes.

'So what have you got for me this evening?' asked President James T. Underwood as he stepped from the shuttle and headed up into the centre of the ST.

An aide extended a laser panel, touched a holo button, and the Theater's circular viewing area was filled with a large 3-D image of a sun-swept ocean. The air filled with the smell of ozone, while hidden loudspeakers added an audio simulation of the sea itself.

'This comes live from one of our own satellites, sir,' said General Thomas P. Crouch, chief of the Pentagon Liaison Staff, as the President eased himself into his command chair. 'We're now looking at a point in the Pacific Ocean midway between Hawaii and California.'

The cameras zoomed in to reveal a large convoy of ships, too many to be quickly counted. Then the lenses tightened on a huge white vessel at the centre of the flotilla that dwarfed all of the other ships around her.

'That's the *Global Haven*, sir,' said the general. 'The hulk people are now heading towards our own territorial waters.'

'Do we know what they want?' asked the President.

'We received a message at eleven hundred hours Eastern Time. They're offering to dock and surrender the *Global Haven* at Long Beach – in exchange for receiving US residency rights for all the people currently on those ships.'

The President shot a disbelieving glance at the general, and then at the small group of White House aides who were hovering behind him.

'How many people, exactly?' asked Underwood.

'They claim they only have a rough headcount, sir. But approximately two hundred thousand.'

'Two hundred thousand!' repeated Underwood, alarmed. 'How long before they enter our waters?'

'They're steaming very slowly,' said the general, 'because they're having to tow some of their vessels that have broken down. At their present rate, we estimate about three and a half days.'

Mirza Fehimovic, the president's assistant press secretary, stepped forward to speak, quietly directing his remarks only at his boss. 'Sir, imagine that picture appearing on the front page of the *Washington Post*, or the *New York Times*. It looks like an invasion force.'

James Underwood nodded. It did indeed look like an invasion force. 'We'd better head them off,' he decided. 'What can you send out from San Diego?'

The general had prepared fully for this meeting. 'Almost nothing, sir. We've got just one carrier group in harbour at present, but they're on R-and-R. Almost everything else has gone north to San Francisco to assist in the clean-up.'

'Pearl Harbor?' asked the President.

'The Pacific Fleet is at readiness, sir. Admiral Millington is standing by for your orders.'

'What if we decided to retake the *Global Haven*?'

'We have two fully equipped SEAL platoons training in Hawaii, sir. They could sail with the fleet.'

'Put them to sea, General,' said Underwood. 'This has gone far enough. I want the *Global Haven* retaken and those ships turned back – *before* I read about them in the *Washington Post*.'

Michael Fairfax arrived home in Sausolito to find that looters had left his damaged house untouched. Neither had they violated any of the other properties in his street, since the residents had organized themselves into a neighbourhood watch and had taken it in turns to stand armed guard at both ends of the road during the worst of the post-earthquake looting.

Eight weeks after the cataclysm there seemed to be almost an air of normality about the area. Michael found rain damage to his living room and his spare bedroom, but the rest of the house was still relatively intact. Power, gas and water supplies had been restored, and he had now spent two days rigging up canvas sheeting to keep out any further water ingress. He had not yet found the courage to board one of the many extra ferries laid on by the navy to shuttle people to and from the devastated downtown area.

His interview with the government agents at Sacramento Airport had lasted almost three hours. Then he had been escorted back through Immigration to the baggage hall only to discover that, while he had been detained, US Customs had ripped open and searched through every one of his bags. They had then left his clothes and toilet articles in a heap for him to repack. They had also managed to crack the glass in the silver frame containing a photograph of Lucy, Matthew and Ben.

During the days he had spent at home with his parents, Michael had pondered the real significance of the warnings he had been given. He had checked the statutes and discovered that the US government did indeed still have laws that gave it rights of detention without trial – extreme and inhuman statutes that dated from the early part of the century, when the American people had suffered their first ever major terrorist atrocity on home soil. Outrage, hurt pride and jingoistic nationalism had been exploited by the neo-conservative administration of the time to slip though laws so draconian that even the Spanish Inquisition would have thought twice before using them.

'The Court of Justice in The Hague might be able to help you,' one of his new Brussels-based partners reminded him. 'They're very alert to nation states trying to interfere with testimony. We could ask them for a writ of witness protection – one that would include you.'

For the moment, however, Michael knew that he must be completely frank with his two scientific witnesses. He would tell both Robert Fivetrees and Emilia Knight of the government's mistaken assumptions about them and the stern warnings he had been given. As their attorney, he would have to counsel them that further legal investigation was going to be necessary before they could consider giving evidence on any topic covered by National Secrecy Agreements.

From his parents' home he rang Professor Fivetrees's personal number and left a message suggesting that they should meet up again when he got back to the Bay Area. He said he would call the professor on his arrival, to make further arrangements.

But the lawyer discovered that he had a strong and urgent desire to speak to Emilia Knight in person. He left two messages on Emilia's personal phone, but she did not return either call. He then tried the number she had given him for her house, but that too went unanswered.

Two days after arriving back in Sausolito he rang Geohazard Laboratories. On his first call he got only Emilia's voicemail, then again on his second and third attempt.

Eventually he rang the company switchboard. When he had explained his problem, the woman operator put him through to the Seismic Risk Assessment Centre.

'She's out of the office,' another female voice informed him. Michael explained that he was Dr Knight's attorney, that he had already tried her personal numbers, and that he needed to speak with his client urgently.

'All we've been told is that she is away for reasons of ill health,' said the woman.

As Felicity Campion, one of Geohazard's student interns, put down the phone on Michael Fairfax, a light, shrilling alarm began to sound in the Oakland monitoring centre. It was quickly muted and Carlos Robredo, Geohazard's duty officer of the day, rapidly began retasking the Pacific satellites and sea-level sensors to gather more data.

'Steve, there's a build-up of tremors on the sea floor a thousand miles north-east of Hawaii,' he said into a phone as he worked.

Three minutes later, Steve Bardini entered the monitoring

centre. He had now been appointed to stand in as Risk Assessment Officer for Dr Knight, while she was on sick leave.

He glanced up at the monitors and the spinning numerals that were constantly refreshing the data as new information arrived from under-water sensors and seabed strain gauges.

'It's a very big build-up – and over a long distance,' he mused, partly to himself and partly to the others on the shift. 'Over six hundred miles.'

Steve stepped forward to one of the control positions, pulled out a chair, and began extracting and transferring historical data that he intended to run in the Simulation Theater.

'I'm going to run this as a sim and see what we get,' he told Carlos Robredo. 'In the meantime, we'd better put out a general alert now. Make it a two-thousand-mile radius – all shipping, all islands.'

Although he was now back at his home in Sausalito, Michael Fairfax was still not having much luck in reaching anybody with whom he needed to talk. Until very recently, such mundane matters as reaching clients on the phone had been handled by his executive assistant Serena Jones.

That thought made him shake his head, and he put his phone back down on the kitchen table. Serena was yet another of the dead – another one whose face and manner remained still painfully fresh in his memory. To suddenly lose a score or more of people with whom you have shared your life was an extreme wrench, one so severe that barely an hour went past without Michael having to stop whatever he was doing and rest his mind for a few minutes, just to recover his composure.

He had continued trying to reach Robert Fivetrees at Berkeley. Once again he was getting only voicemail and message services. Unlike Geohazard Laboratories, the university seemed to have no humans prepared to pick up a phone and answer a straight inquiry. But then, Michael rationalized to himself, who could know how many staff members the university had lost? Nothing was normal any longer in this part of the world – and nor would it be so for a very long time to come.

Rising from his makeshift desk, he walked through the house and out into the front yard. On either side he could hear the sound of householders and their families working busily to bring their properties back up to fully habitable level. Even though two months had now passed since the quake, there were still no professional builders or household tradesmen available anywhere in the entire bay region. They were all employed on priority local-government projects, getting hospitals, schools and other public services working again.

Michael gazed across the bay towards the city once again – he had taken to sitting here regularly in the evenings, watching the ferries busily commuting all around San Francisco Island, as the old downtown area was now being called.

He wondered if Bob Fivetrees too might have received a heavy-handed visit from government agents. That might explain the scientist's silence, and his apparent absence from his university department.

Then Michael was struck by a tremendous sense of guilt; he certainly wasn't functioning properly. He had completely forgotten about Carol Gonzaga. Even though she had insisted that she intended to represent herself in court, Michael had urged the appointment of an attorney to advise her. So, in the end, she had agreed to his suggestion that his colleague Mitch Tonks, a criminal attorney with Gravitz, Lee and Kraus, should take on her case.

The next day, when Michael had arrived back at his office in the Embarcadero Space Needle, the first thing he had done was to drop by Mitch's office.

'Yes!' The young attorney had punched his fist into the air when Michael had mock-innocently asked whether he might care to represent one of the notorious PFO members accused of bombing the ERGIA Space Station.

'*Yes!*' Mitch had relished the opportunity, knowing that, whatever its outcome, the public exposure during such a high-profile trial would catapult him up the unofficial rankings of State-Appointed Defenders.

Only Mitch Tonks was now yet another of the dead. He had been in his car crossing the southbound upper carriageway of the Bay Bridge when that entire section had dropped 400 feet into the water below.

Were it not for a fluke, the circumstances of his death would not yet have been known – he would merely be one of the many thousands still missing following the earthquake. It was believed that over 300 cars had been crossing the Bay Bridge at the time of its collapse, and the Navy had not so far begun diving to clear the wreckage and recover bodies. As a consequence, the bay was now so polluted with rotting corpses that its water had been declared a health hazard.

But Mitch had been talking to his wife at exactly 6.02 a.m. that day. Being a conscientious young criminal attorney, he had got into the habit of rising quietly at 5.15 a.m. on weekday mornings so he could arrive at his office an hour later. It was his habit to ring his wife at six a.m., acting as her alarm clock, to tell her that he loved her and to wish her well in her day's work restoring valuable old paintings for an Oakland art gallery.

'THE BRIDGE IS GOING!' he had yelled to her over the phone that morning. Then she had heard only his screams.

Michael had so far failed to let Carole Gonzaga know what had happened to her defence attorney. And, he realized, no one else from Gravitz, Lee and Kraus could have done so either. He returned to his kitchen, found the number and dialled Lompoc State Penitentiary.

'Can you bring Carole Gonzaga to the telephone, please – that's inmate number Y5091621?' he requested, after he had been transferred to the maximum-security wing. 'This is a call from her attorney's office.'

The female guard who answered the phone had kept him waiting for several minutes.

'Who are you, again?' she asked when she came back on the line.

'Counsellor Michael Fairfax,' he told her, 'from Gravitz, Lee and Kraus, her representative attorneys. Would you like digital authentication?'

He glanced at his communicator and thumbed up his digital ident ready for transmission.

'You should already have been told,' grumbled the prison

guard. 'Gonzaga committed suicide last week. She hanged herself in her cell.'

Steve Bardini was slouched in the motorized viewing chair that circled the holo-pit in the Simulation Theater. He was sunk in very deep thought. He had run six different simulations based on data from the Central Pacific seabed, but even his least ferocious set of parameters still unleashed a tsunami that would have devastating effects on the Hawaiian Islands.

The information coming in from sea-floor sensors clearly indicated that a major seismic event would soon occur just north of the Hawaiian Ridge, a 1,500-mile-long underwater mountain chain to the north-east of the main island group. Steve had run back through the last three months of data, and had matched the new seismic tremors with measurements transmitted to Geohazard by Valerie Cummings from the oceanographic Navy vessel RV *Orlando* three months previously.

Now all that he and the Geohazard team needed to decide was whether the underwater event building up near Hawaii would produce an earthquake or an eruption, then what magnitude it was likely to be, and when it was most likely to occur.

Steve had watched his former girlfriend carry out this type of calculation a hundred times before, and he only wished that Emilia were here now to do it once again.

The day after he had witnessed her being stretchered from her home, he had made enquiries in the Human Resources office about the whereabouts of his boss. He had been at pains to keep his enquiry casual – the last thing he wanted to admit was that he had been hanging around her house yet again.

'Doctor Knight's gone back into hospital,' Gloria Fernandez had told him breezily. 'It's just a routine follow-up – after the dangerous stuff she was handling on that mountain.'

Eight out of the last ten seismic events in the Hawaiian Ridge area had been volcanic, but this one had the look and feel of a quake. There were no long period events, the seismic swarms were shudders not bumps and, although no tectonic plates abutted in the Central Pacific, Steve knew that the instability was rooted in the old crustal fault-line that had first thrown up the underwater ridge over half a billion years ago.

He thrust himself out of his chair, his decision made. The San Francisco earthquake had made all Geohazard staff less caring about the risk of false alarms. He would issue a Grade Three earthquake alert *and* a tsunami warning. His best calculations were that the heave would come late afternoon tomorrow, local time, and that it would measure between six and seven-point-five.

As he arrived back in the Risk Assessment control centre, Steve found Carlos Robredo and Felicity Campion standing and staring up at a wall-screen. The MSN news channel showed an image of a large convoy of ships. Steve studied the screen caption.

HULK-PEOPLE CONVOY
HEADS FOR CALIFORNIA

'Whereabouts are those ships?' Steve demanded.

Robredo merely shrugged.

'They're halfway between Hawaii and Los Angeles,' Felicity informed Steve.

He gazed up at the screen. Despite their large size, some of the old vessels seemed to be riding very low in the water – others were even being towed.

'We're going to issue a Level Three earthquake and tsunami warning to the Hawaiian region,' Steve announced, lowering himself into the duty officer's command chair.

Carlos Robredo and the intern noted the seriousness in his voice, and they quickly took up their own positions at the command console.

Steve Bardini dictated the warning that he had decided upon, including a likely timing for the quake and its probable range of severity. Then he considered various possibilities for a few additional moments. He knew that out in the open sea a tsunami posed little threat to shipping – it merely passed under any ship's hull like an enormous ripple. It was only as it approached land that the wave was forced higher by the upwardly shelving seabed, causing it to rear up to become the towering monster so beloved of disaster-film makers. That was what the word 'tsunami' literally meant – 'harbour wave'.

But those old tankers and freighters looked very low in the water and therefore very vulnerable.

'Broadcast a warning to all shipping in the central and northeastern Pacific,' Steve told Robredo. 'Use all commercial and emergency frequencies, and repeat every hour on the hour until we have more information.'

Michael Fairfax sat at his kitchen table, trying to make sense of the events of the last few days. He was becoming a deeply worried man.

After three days of attempting to phone, e-mail and text Professor Robert Fivetrees, he had still received no response, no acknowledgement, no word from the man's departmental colleagues. But now he knew why.

Shortly after lunchtime, Michael had decided to drive over to the Berkeley Campus and find the Department of Planetary Geophysics and Bob Fivetrees for himself. He suspected that the professor had entertained second thoughts about testifying, either because he too had received a tough warning from government agents or because the emotional shock of the earthquake was now receding.

Gas had proved to be the lawyer's first problem. Car fuel was still rationed all around the Bay Area and Michael waited in line for almost an hour before being allowed to buy just six litres of hydrogen from the little filling station at Sausalito Marina. Even then it had cost twice the normal price.

He didn't arrive on the Berkeley Campus until after five p.m. and, having some knowledge of academic lifestyles, he was concerned that Fivetrees and his staff might already have left for the day.

Campus security directed him towards the low glass building housing the various disciplines grouped under 'Geophysics'. After parking in an almost empty lot, he walked into an atrium filled with rock samples mounted in glass display cases.

A man at the reception desk asked him whom he had come to visit, then paused and scratched his head.

'Look,' he said, pointing, 'the Planetary people are all at the far end of that corridor. Go ask down there.'

Michael did as he was directed and found a room in which a middle-aged woman was packing books into a cardboard box.

'This Professor Fivetrees's office?'

'Well, it was. Who wants to know?'

Twenty minutes later Michael was back in his car and heading home to Sausalito. As people tend to do when they have just learned about a fatal road accident, he was driving more carefully than usual.

The professor had been killed while driving his Jaguar early last Sunday morning. 'No, nobody else was involved,' Fivetrees's former secretary had told him, once Michael had satisfied her that he had been her boss's legal adviser. 'He was a bit of a madcap – he loved to drive that old car of his as fast as it would go. They say he just ran out of road – but he died instantly, the officer told me. He wouldn't have known anything about it.'

Now Michael checked the time by his old kitchen clock: 8.50 p.m. He reached across the kitchen table, picked up his phone and tried Emilia Knight's home number again. If she really was on sick leave, why wasn't she answering? Once more, he got only her message system.

It took him just over twenty minutes to drive westwards across Marin County, braking hard as Highway 1 made its sharp right turn out of Green Gulch Valley and entered Muir Woods. It was now dark, and in his headlights Michael picked out the Pelican Pub where it stood beside the left-hand turnoff to Muir Beach. He knew the inlet well – he had often brought girlfriends here during his courting days. There was a nature reserve just to the south of the little bay, with a quiet parking area overlooking the surf.

Michael drove carefully along the gently rising, tree-lined dirt road that led out onto the wooded promontory. At the very end of the track he saw a turning circle, and a gate displaying the numeral 9. That must be it.

The house was in darkness and Michael glanced at his watch:

9.42 p.m. Not too late to be calling – unless Emilia was so unwell that she was already in bed asleep.

He rang the door chimes and waited. He rang again and then, on instinct, he tried the handle. The door opened. He stepped inside, into the gloom.

He was about to call out, then realized that if Emilia was sleeping he might wake her. He turned to reach for a light switch.

Suddenly Michael was knocked to the floor from behind. As his head was yanked upwards by his hair, he was aware of a forearm, hard as an iron bar, being rammed against his Adam's apple.

Panicked, he rolled sideways, kicking out hard with his legs. He heard a cry, then a fist smashed into the side of his head. Adrenalin took him over completely, and he rolled once more before tensing into a crouch.

Just as he was straightening up, a dark figure ran into him, head down, knocking him flat on his back. As a fist cracked into his jawbone, Michael jabbed his damaged fingers up hard into one of his assailant's eyes. He heard a screech of pain and the figure lurched backwards. With a heave, the lawyer staggered to his feet.

Michael made out a table lamp silhouetted against a window. Flicking on the switch, he saw that his attacker – a man of about thirty, casually dressed, but smart – was down on one knee with both hands clamped over his left eye.

'I'm a lawyer,' shouted Michael, still gasping for breath, one hand stretched out defensively in front of him. 'I'm here to visit Doctor Knight.'

An instant transformation seemed to come over his adversary. His shoulders dropped and he shook his head. After a few seconds he slowly stood upright. He removed his hands from his injured eye and blinked experimentally.

Michael's shoulders heaved as he gulped down lungfuls of oxygen.

'Shit, I'm sorry,' said his attacker. 'Those gloves – I thought you were another looter . . .' He tailed off. 'Are you the one Emilia told me about? The lawyer who was asking her to give evidence over in Europe?'

Michael was filled with relief, then, suddenly, with extreme weariness.

'Yes, that's me,' he said. He sank down into a nearby armchair. 'And you are?'

Their initial exchange and verification of personal information took only a few minutes, Michael explaining that his gloves were protection for injuries he had sustained during the earthquake.

'So what are *you* doing here and how did you get in?' asked the lawyer.

Even before Steve Bardini spoke, Michael noted embarrassment in the younger man's face.

'Emilia and I were friends – quite close at one time. I used to drop by regularly in the evenings.'

Eventually, Steve admitted what he had witnessed a few nights earlier, when Emilia had been removed by a US Navy ambulance.

'Why the hell didn't you ask them what was wrong with her?' demanded Michael, his alarm growing till his words came out more forcefully than he'd intended.

Emilia's colleague shrugged, then bit his lower lip. 'Em had told me to stop coming by. She and I ... well, we used to go out together. She'd have been furious if she'd have known I was here.'

Michael suddenly understood; the ex-boyfriend hanging around Emilia's home like a lovesick hound – ordered to stay away but unable to obey. Then he realized that he was meeting his immediate predecessor in the quest for Emilia Knight's affections. He shook that thought away – first Emilia herself had to be found.

'Do you have any idea why the Navy was involved?'

Steve nodded. 'She was admitted straight to the naval hospital in San Diego once we got back from Samoa. They've got the only radioactivity treatment centre on the West Coast. I presumed that she'd suffered some sort of relapse. That was the word at work, anyway.'

'Do you know what she actually found on Samoa?' asked the lawyer.

Steve considered, then nodded. 'I saw you discussing your

case on the TV news. I knew who you were referring to when you mentioned the find of radioactive rocks.'

'And she seemed to be becoming ill again?' prompted Michael.

'Not as far as I knew,' insisted Steve. 'She worked almost non-stop for five days following the quake, and she still seemed to have a lot of energy. I was just...'

'What?' demanded Michael as the younger man tailed off.

Emilia's assistant slipped his hand into his trouser pocket and withdrew a slim stainless steel tube. 'I was just checking background radiation with this when I saw your car pull up. I've checked out her bedroom, the kitchen, these armchairs. There's no trace of radioactivity at all. But at first, everything she even touched started to sing.'

Michael pushed himself out of the low armchair, crossed Emilia's glowing redwood-strip floor, and stood gazing out of the ocean-facing window. Outside, all was blackness.

After a few moments he turned back to face Steve.

'I'm very suspicious about all this,' he said. 'I'm losing witnesses so fast it's unnatural. Have you ever heard of Professor Robert Fivetrees?'

Steve nodded. 'Em told me about him,' he said. 'She wanted to run one of his computer models in the Simulation Theater, but we were then too busy after the earthquake.'

'He was killed earlier this week in a car accident – just up the coast,' said Michael. 'No witnesses, no other vehicle involved. Six-thirty on a Sunday morning, and an experienced driver allowed his car to just suddenly sail off the cliff road and out into space.'

He sat down again, on the edge of the armchair. 'And the woman who put me on to him, she's also dead. She was accused of being a member of the PFO unit that bombed the ERGIA space station. They claim she committed suicide in her prison cell, last week.'

Steve Bardini now looked horror-struck. 'You don't think...?'

'I don't know what to think,' said Michael. 'But I certainly think I'd better go and see my client immediately, wherever she is.'

'Emilia told me the Naval Hospital is right inside a secure military base,' said Steve, also rising. 'You won't get in there easily.'

'I will with a court order,' Michael told him grimly. 'And I know one or two friendly judges.'

He turned, as if about to leave, then stopped as a thought struck him. 'But I don't know how I'm going to get down to San Diego. I've got no gas and most of the regular air shuttles have been suspended.'

'I can get you some gas,' said Steve. 'As a Geohazard employee I've got a priority card. I can get as much gas as I want.'

The two men standing in Emilia Knight's living room stared at each other. As so often happens between males who have fought each other physically, an immediate bond had formed.

'I'm coming with you,' announced Steve Bardini.

FIFTEEN

Reporter Floyd Merryweather, camera operator Jim McGill and pilot Jenny Reibber, all of Channel 7 TV News Honolulu, got their Bell Long Ranger helicopter into the air just as dawn was breaking.

With mains electricity out on all of the Hawaiian Islands, and unsure whether their news centre would be able to continue to run successfully on generator power alone, they grabbed two SatVid uplink units and took on as much fuel as the four-seater could carry. They expected to be in the air for some hours.

As Geohazard Labs in Oakland had warned, a major earth-quake had occurred in the Pacific seabed seventy miles north-east of the Hawaiiain island chain. But the quake occurred twelve hours earlier than had been predicted and the resultant tsunami ripped into the northern coastlines of the islands shortly before midnight. The news team was on an assignment to provide the world with the first daylight pictures of the damage.

'Your feed's being taken by MSN, CNN and even BBC World,' said Rob Richos, their producer in Honolulu, over the radio link. 'Make it a good one, guys. Going live: three ... two ... one ...'

'This is Floyd Merryweather of Channel 7 News in Hawaii,' announced the reporter into his close-fitting mouth microphone. Beside him, in the other rear seat, Jim McGill was using the remote controls to sweep the helicopter's underbelly camera along the coastline of the main island. The sun had now cleared the starboard horizon.

'A tsunami, sometimes called a tidal wave, came ashore on

the Hawaiian Islands in the Central Pacific at eleven fifty-two last night. Eyewitnesses reported it to be over forty feet high, and emergency services say there has been significant loss of life and serious damage on all the islands.'

McGill's camera was now getting pictures of a blasted land-scape that seemed to run inland for miles. Trees were flattened, buildings washed away, and debris covered the entire surface of the now placid sea.

Merryweather was an experienced reporter and for the next thirty seconds he allowed the awful images to do the talking for him.

'An evacuation order for the northern coasts of these islands was issued by the Governor shortly before seven yesterday evening, but it is thought that many families may still have chosen to remain in their homes overnight.'

Merryweather flicked off his microphone and pulled it away from his mouth. 'Not that they've got any homes left now,' he muttered over the chopper's intercom as he gazed along the coast.

McGill said nothing. He just kept the camera trained down-wards, poking out of its specially designed plasti-glass filming pod, capturing the stumps of ruined trees, the cars piled on top of each other, and the now roofless bungalows.

'Turning right,' warned Jenny Reibber suddenly over the intercom and, after a few more seconds of level flight to allow the camera operator time to zoom out, she banked the helicopter hard to the right and turned out to sea. Merryweather and McGill lifted their heads and shot puzzled glances at the pilot's back. Wordlessly, she pointed towards the horizon.

Then they saw what had attracted her attention. Jim McGill hastily panned the camera away from the coast, telescoping its long lens to maximum range. On one of the monitors positioned at his feet, Floyd Merryweather watched the images now being captured.

'There's a whole line of capsized ships out to sea ... very large ships.' He realized that he was shouting.

Without turning her body, the pilot reached behind her and thrust a map into the reporter's hands. Then, still with her head turned away, she jabbed a forefinger down onto the map. Merryweather read the contours and understood what she was telling him.

'It would seem that these ships have run aground,' he told his global audience, the excitement pushing his voice up half an octave. 'The seabed to the north of Hawaii shelves very gently, and at a mile or so off the coast the depth is only sixty feet.'

Then the images became clearer and seconds later they were circling over the line of stricken vessels.

'It looks like part of the US Navy's Pacific Fleet,' said Merryweather, his voice rising almost to a treble as he lifted binoculars to his eyes. 'Yes ... yes, I can see ... A United States aircraft carrier is lying on her side. I repeat, a US Navy aircraft carrier has capsized! She's ... the USS *John F. Kennedy*. I can see her name and number clearly now. She appears to have no planes whatsoever on her flight deck. I can make out the entire underside of her hull – it looks as if she's been swept inshore by the tsunami, and has breached in shallow water.'

Using his joystick controls, Jim McGill panned the camera slowly from right to left along the huge carrier, and then swept the lens forward to the next grounded vessel.

'That ship is the USS *Lincoln* ... she looks like a guided-missile carrier. I can see Navy tugs with lines attached to her side ...'

They flew on for another thirty seconds. 'Now I can see the USS *Navaho*. She too is lying completely over on her side.'

'Hold up, Floyd,' said Rob Richos, in Merryweather's right ear. 'This might be sensitive stuff. You're just telling the world that our navy's out of action.'

Floyd pressed his broadcast-mute button and spoke to his producer in Honolulu. 'Too late, Rob – they can see for themselves. It's like another Pearl Harbor attack down there. I can see at least a dozen more capsized ships.'

'I'm going to cut away for the moment,' said the producer. 'I've just got a fill-in satellite feed.'

Floyd Merryweather and Jim McGill relaxed involuntarily as they went off air. Then they turned their attention to the broadcast monitor positioned between the helicopter's two front seats.

They saw an image of a vast number of old cargo vessels clustered tightly around a gleaming white cruise liner, a leviathan which dwarfed all the other ships in the pack. Then a screen caption appeared:

HULK CONVOY SURVIVES PACIFIC TSUNAMI

*

The ERGIA Corporation had spent ten days fine-tuning the weather schedule over central England so that Perdita Curtis and her film crew would enjoy precisely the climatic conditions they had requested for their shoot at Langland Park: sunny, warm, but with a few powder-puff white clouds in the azure September sky. This was a change to the previously published programme; originally each morning had been scheduled to get rainfall.

When climate-management services had first been introduced into Europe in 2031, each population had naturally cast their electronic referendum votes in favour of night-time precipitation and daytime sunshine – other than for the much-demanded, and by now obligatory, white Christmas. But after two years of this agreeable weather pattern, it was discovered that the ecology was suffering, since some species of flora and fauna needed to receive their rain during daylight hours.

As a result, ERGIA and other weather-management service providers started to design more natural weather cycles, even though these improved weather patterns were also delivered according to carefully worked-out schedules laid down three years in advance.

Now, after decades of local climate improvement, Britain had once more developed flourishing resort communities on the southern and eastern coasts. Many domestic and international tourists flocked to the UK's sun-drenched 'Rivieras', more worthy of the name these days than they'd been during the previous century.

The science of weather manipulation was highly complex, but Perdy Curtis had swotted hard to improve her understanding of the techniques involved. She needed to make informed decisions about how much detail to provide to her TV-documentary audience.

Most laypeople understood that the solar energy companies used orbiting space mirrors to reflect focused sunshine down onto the top of cloud formations. Over long periods of time, this energy could disperse warm clouds to prevent rain, or could heat up cold clouds to produce precipitation.

The informed public also knew that incredibly large, self-repairing nano-polymer sunblinds had been placed in deep-space orbits between the Earth and the sun, positioned to provide adjustable areas of shade over both polar ice caps and other areas of the globe that were at risk from overheating. Then, in deep solar-stationary orbits, there were the giant Fresnel lenses, which could focus sunlight into such narrow beams that they delivered microwave energy bursts directly to ground-based receivers.

The amount of previously wasted solar power available for tapping was enormous. Each day the Earth's surface received naturally solar energy equivalent to 160 *trillion* tons of TNT, sufficient in seismic terms to split the planet in two. And many million times as much energy streamed straight past the Earth, only to be dispersed in the cold depths of outer space – until ERGIA and others captured some of it, diverting this surplus power back to the planet for the benefit of grateful customers.

The BBC's Virtual Realization Unit had already created 3-D models and graphics of these technologies and various data titbits for use in Perdy's film. She intended to mix actual footage of the space mirrors, blinds and lenses along with the VR material, to demonstrate how they worked.

What Perdy was still unsure about was how much she needed to explain the more advanced climate-manipulation techniques such as atmospheric inversion, wind steering, tornado nudging, cloud seeding and slow-ocean warming.

'You could get too bogged down in the detail and miss the real story,' she told Torrance Olds, her unit director, as they crossed a manicured lawn in front of the house's imposing Palladian facade. 'The interview we're about to do will provide the real meat of this section.'

Nicholas Negromonte had given the BBC crew the run of his English stately home. Everybody on the team remarked on the outstanding level of cooperation that the ERGIA Corporation was providing. No only were all fourteen members of the film unit being put up in the house's fine bedroom suites during filming, Negromonte had ordered ERGIA staff to provide them with transport around the extensive grounds, full catering facilities, and even the exclusive use of one of the company's helicopters.

Olds had been unable to resist this last temptation. He had spent the first day of the shoot getting aerial shots of the house and its surrounding parkland, even though Perdy had warned him that she would be unlikely to be able to use more than thirty seconds' worth of such establishing footage before the big interview with Mr Negromonte himself.

Then they had shot petabytes of video of the house and its interior, and then of the lake and the Doric temple on its island. Negromonte had even provided them with a flying display in his historic fighter plane.

Now, as Perdy and Torrance Olds climbed the flaring stone steps and walked through the entrance portico under grand Corinthian pillars, they were preparing themselves for the big interview with the ERGIA CEO.

'I could get used to this,' chuckled Olds as a footman, anticipating their arrival, opened the large double doors to admit them into the gilded entrance hall.

They had spent the morning in the mirrored dining room, getting its set-up and lighting perfect. A grip had sat in for the ERGIA boss while they found the best camera angles and played with reflections in the large bevelled mirrors that covered much of the walls. They had placed a baronial armchair beside a marble fireplace and positioned Perdy, his interviewer, directly opposite it.

Five cameras had been located carefully; two to record constant close-ups of both interviewer and interviewee, one for a two-shot, one for a long-shot from the other end of the dining room, and a roving Steadicam to provide movement footage for the cutaways.

To her surprise, Perdy now saw that Negromonte was already in position in the large wing chair, a make-up woman applying powder to his forehead. Behind him, two men whom Perdy knew to be from ERGIA's perception-management consultants stood whispering together.

'Can we get started, Perdy?' Negromonte asked, as soon as he saw her. 'I've got to run to a meeting as soon as we're done.'

She nodded and quickly directed the rest of the crew to get ready. Taking the wing chair opposite Negromonte, she lifted her face for a second make-up artist to add a light layer of shine-killing powder. Perdy wasn't intending to use much footage of herself in the final film; most of her questions would be heard in voice-over.

All five cameras confirmed that they were recording. Then the floor manager silently counted down with his fingers.

Perdy's first questions were anodyne, gently leading. She wouldn't use much of this stuff in the final programme. The early exchanges were intended to warm Negromonte up, to put him at his ease. *Not that he needs much warming up*, Perdy thought to herself as she listened to him explaining how he had entered the family business.

'When my father took over Negromonte Oil from my grand-father, all the company possessed was a fleet of tankers and three oil refineries. Thirty years later, when I was still in my teens, Dad had transformed the business into a publicly quoted conglomerate that included aerospace, energy and energy-distribution interests. He'd also moved our family to the United States.'

'But you had never originally intended to enter the business yourself?' prompted Perdy.

'No, my elder brother Chris had been groomed for that role. He was ten years older than me and when my father and mother split up he went to live with Dad whilst I remained with my mother.'

'So you decided to become a tennis player?' Perdy had already selected the Wimbledon Junior Championships footage she would insert at this point.

Her subject gave one of his famous self-deprecating smiles and waved a dismissive hand in the air. 'That was all I seemed any good at when I was at school. My mother moved with me when I went to a tennis academy in Los Angeles and while I spent most of my time hitting balls, she returned to her film-acting career.'

Perdy then got Negromonte to tell how his elder brother had been assassinated by eco-terrorists during a space trip – there would be more archive footage available to insert at this point – and how he, Nicholas, had subsequently given up his professional tennis ambitions to study for an MBA at Harvard, before joining his father in the ERGIA Corporation. Then Negromonte explained how his corporation had bought up a raft of smaller companies that had pioneered solar reflection and climate management, and how ERGIA had become the world's dominant service supplier of managed weather.

Choosing her moment, Perdy pushed herself upright in her chair and began to probe seriously: 'Many ecological experts claim that, far from solving the problems of global warming, climate management merely masks them, and thus delays the point at which humankind must deal properly with the problem.'

Negromonte seemed totally unruffled by her change of direction. 'Well, there's little doubt that the climate has been getting warmer for several centuries. The choice is whether we control things to prevent the worst effects of this warming, or whether we just stand by and allow Mother Nature to flood yet more of our cities and coastlines.'

'How do you react to claims that there is a causal link between climate management and the terrible seismic unrest that the world is suffering – such as the recent events in San Francisco and Hawaii?'

Here Perdy planned to insert footage from Michael Fairfax's press conference in Brussels.

Now Negromonte did visibly stiffen, but Perdy saw his media training kick in as he produced yet another smile.

'Well, I'm limited on what I can say about that – for legal reasons,' he told her. 'But there are thousands of wild theories being produced about climate management every year. The fact is that we are harnessing the most natural resource in our solar system, the sun itself, for the good of all.'

Perdy was tempted to challenge him on this statement, to suggest that there were many communities – such as the abandoned hulk people – who gained no such benefit. But she didn't want to get diverted from her main point.

'So you would say there's no truth to the claim that climate management is interfering with the Earth's magnetic field – that your manipulation of the solar energy swirling around this planet is inducing a weakness that could make the magnetic poles flip?'

Negromonte's smile disappeared for a moment. Then he forced the corners of his lips upwards in a rictal grin from which his eyes totally distanced themselves.

'Absolutely not. Once again, that wild and ridiculous scare story is the subject of legal action, so I can't comment on it directly. But we *are* certain that climate management improves the quality of life for hundreds of millions of people every single day. And it has boosted the global economy into an unprecedented and sustained period of growth – as the OECD has confirmed in its most recent report.'

'But don't you think it unwise to be now turning the moon into a gigantic solar-energy reflector, when there is still so much uncertainty about the whole concept of climate management?'

This interview wasn't going exactly how Negromonte had hoped.

'This *uncertainty*, as you call it, is entirely a media concoction,' he snapped. 'It's just a fantasy dreamed up by those who see large corporations as easy targets for vexatious and frivolous litigation. What we need is more – not less – solar energy to turn this world of ours into a safer and more predictable place.'

Nicholas Negromonte paused, then forced himself to smile again. Now was the time to change tack, to deliver the publicity coup that he and his perception consultants had planned for this interview.

'And I'm pleased to use this opportunity to announce that the ERGIA Corporation is going to provide thirteen per cent of LunaSun's output free of charge for distribution by the United Nations. Hundreds of millions of the world's poorest people will now be able to benefit from ERGIA Climate Management Services, with our compliments.' His smile broadened still further and he sat back in his chair.

'Thank you, Mr Negromonte,' said Perdy. She held her gaze on her subject for a few extra moments, then turned her head. 'And cut,' she said, looking at Torrance Olds.

'Cut,' Olds repeated to his floor manager.

'Cut,' shouted the floor manager to the crew.

'That was a bit of a grilling, Perdy,' said Negromonte, his smile now less forced. He sat forward in his chair as a soundman stepped in to retrieve the pair of sub-miniature wireless mikes that he had attached to the interviewee's shirt front.

'Are you having second thoughts about that live debate on the moon?' Perdy asked, as she plucked the mikes from her own jacket.

'No problem,' Negromonte told her. 'I was just getting warmed up.'

'You are not authorized to turn left at the next junction,' the BMW's navigation system told Michael Fairfax. 'No public access is allowed.'

The lawyer flipped the navigation system off, then muted all of the car's other interactive features.

'There it is.' Steve Bardini pointed to a slip road 300 yards ahead. A sign at the bottom of the exit ramp read NO ENTRY: U.S. NAVY VEHICLES AND AUTHOR-IZED TRAFFIC ONLY.

Their journey south from the devastated Bay Area to San Diego had taken almost two days. Michael had phoned Judge Sybilla Burns at eight o'clock on the morning following his unexpected skirmish at Emilia Knight's house.

Sybilla Burns had been a senior partner at Gravitz, Lee and Kraus when Michael had first joined the firm, and she had subsequently become something of a legal mother-figure to him, guiding him through both the political minefield of office politics and the intricacies of the Californian judicial system. When she had been made a judge, Michael had been delighted for her – but sad to lose a good and trusted friend from his workplace.

At nine a.m. he was sitting in her spacious living room in the Marin County town of Hillsdown, sipping a cup of coffee and recounting how the government agents had threatened him with use of the old Patriot Act.

Judge Burns sucked air in over her lower teeth as she listened to that part, then silently shook her head in disgust.

Michael then explained about the death of Professor Robert Fivetrees, the apparent suicide of Carol Gonzaga and, most recently, the mysterious disappearance of his other key witness.

'I have good reason to believe that Doctor Knight is now being detained against her will in a US naval hospital, either to interrogate her about supposed supplies of plutonium, or to prevent her from giving testimony,' he concluded.

Judge Burns immediately issued a court order providing him with unconditional access to his client. Two hours later Michael had picked up Steve Bardini and his all-important priority gas card outside Geohazard's seismic monitoring centre in Oakland.

Normally, a non-stop drive from the Bay Area down to San Diego would have taken twelve hours. But, after filling up with hydrogen gas, it took them over six hours just to travel the sixty-five miles to San Jose, using the long route around the east of the bay. As most civilian air traffic in and out of the Bay Area was suspended, the highways were jammed with cars, and almost every road seemed reduced to a single lane as construction crews busily repaired underground utilities that had fractured during the earthquake.

By nine p.m. the two travellers realized they would get no further than San Miguel that day, so they found a motel for the night. They were on the road again at six a.m. and although they had expected to be in San Diego before noon, further heavy traffic meant that it was almost four p.m. before Michael ignored the NO ENTRY warning and took the restricted turn-off from Highway 5. They had stopped on the road for more gas – not rationed in the Los Angeles area, Michael realized – and Steve had bought a bunch of flowers for the patient they were travelling to see.

At the top of the highway exit ramp they followed the sign to US Navy Camp Marshall and a quarter of a mile later they saw the turn-off for the naval base itself. There was no commercial or residential building in this part of the city – everything was military.

They swung into the heavily fortified approach road leading to the base and were immediately slowed by concrete bollards and chicanes designed to prevent potential suicide bombers' vehicles approaching the guard post at high speed.

Signs warned drivers to slow down to five m.p.h., but Michael's low-slung BMW was already having trouble negotiating the rutted surface. Two armed US marines were at stand-easy outside the guardhouse.

As his car approached the first of them, Michael lowered his window and brought the vehicle to a stop.

'Are you lost, sir?' barked the young marine, his M-24 gripped purposefully in both hands.

'I'm here to visit a patient in the Naval Hospital,' said Michael.

'Do you have an appointment or a pass, sir?' shouted the marine.

Michael shook his head. 'I'm a lawyer.' He produced his Bar Association ident and offered it through the window for inspection. 'I'm here to visit a client who's currently in your Naval Hospital.'

The marine studied the card with its ID chip, biometric sampler and photograph. Then he nodded sharply.

'Pull over there, sir, for a vehicle inspection.'

More marines now spilled from the guardhouse. Michael and Steve got out of the car as the soldiers lifted the hood, the trunk lid, examined every interior cavity and inspected the underside of the vehicle with robot video cameras. The two visitors were asked to step through a multiple-weapons detector while their electronic idents were being authenticated inside the guardhouse.

After ten minutes, the first marine returned Michael's ident and ignition key and told him to take the perimeter road to the right, for a mile, before turning left into the centre of the camp.

'There's a signpost, sir,' he shouted as Michael rolled up his window and drove onto the base.

Michael and Steve arrived at the hospital building itself shortly before five p.m. It wasn't hard to find – it seemed to be the only high-rise building on the base. About sixteen floors, the lawyer estimated, as he and his companion – Emilia's former lover, carrying a bunch of flowers for her – strode from the parking lot towards the hospital's ground-floor reception area.

Two more armed marines were on duty beside the main doors, but they allowed the visitors to enter without further challenge. Inside, Michael and his companion scanned a departmental guide on the wall.

Radioactivity Exposure Clinic, 14th Floor

A female receptionist and an older male clerk were seated behind a central desk in the foyer.

'I believe you have Emilia Knight as one of your patients,' Michael said. 'She'll be on the fourteenth floor, I think. We're here to visit her.'

The woman tapped at a keyboard, frowned, then produced an apologetic smile. 'I'm sorry, sir, we have no patient by that name.'

The lawyer had half anticipated, half dreaded this response. He knew that the navy was likely to have a dozen different medical facilities dotted around San Diego; it was the US Navy's home town, after all. Which one might they have taken her to instead?

'Are there any other radioactivity clinics in San Diego?' he asked.

'Oh no, sir,' said the receptionist, smiling. 'This is the centre for the whole of the West Coast.'

'Then would you mind checking again?' asked Michael. He

was aware of Steve Bardini scowling behind him 'The patient's name is Knight – that's K.N.I.G.H.T,' he said, spelling it out.

The woman jabbed at her keyboard again and then shrugged. 'Nobody of that name. I'm sorry.'

'Doctor Bowman *does* work here, right?' Steve spoke up suddenly, with real aggression in his tone.

At this point, the male clerk rolled himself along the counter on his wheeled chair to join his colleague.

'She just said we have no patient by the name of Knight,' he repeated emphatically.

Michael heard the glass doors leading into the reception area open behind him. He turned to see one of the marines step inside and take up position halfway between the door and the desk. The male clerk must have triggered some sort of alert.

'Does Dr Bowman work in this hospital?' insisted Steve.

'You didn't hear me, son,' said the male clerk loudly. 'We have no patient named Knight.' He paused, then glanced at the guard. 'Now I have to ask you to leave.'

Michael reached into his jacket pocket and produced the document signed and sealed by Judge Sybilla Burns, along with a copy of it that he had made when they'd stopped for the night at the motel.

'This is an order issued by the High Court of California in Sacramento.' He unfolded the original document and displayed its seal to them. Then he produced his California Bar Association ident and slapped it down hard on the reception counter top.

'I am Counsellor Michael Fairfax, Emilia Knight's personal attorney, and this court order demands any person, organization, state, federal or *military* institution with knowledge of, custody of, care of, or responsibility for Emilia Patricia Knight to grant me immediate, private and unhindered access to her on production of this document. Failure to do so, or obstruction of the court's due process, are offences punishable by fine, imprisonment or both.'

Michael delivered his speech slowly, carefully and distinctly, holding the gazes of both the receptionist and the clerk in turn as he spoke. They stared back at him, now visibly alarmed, and

Michael came to the conclusion that these two, at least, were not hiding anything.

'Does a Doctor Bowman work here?' he asked, repeating Steve Bardini's earlier question.

'Yes, in the REC – the radioactivity exposure clinic,' said the male clerk.

'Is he here now?' asked Michael.

The woman receptionist touched her screen and nodded. 'He's on the fourteenth floor,' she said.

Michael unfolded the copy of his court order and smoothed it out on the counter top. Then he removed one of his card-idents from his wallet and handed the two documents to the female receptionist.

'Would you be kind enough to have these taken up to Doctor Bowman?' he asked. 'We'll wait here.'

As Michael Fairfax and Steve Bardini took their seats in the ground-floor waiting area at the San Diego Naval Hospital, on the other side of the continent James T. Underwood, fifty-sixth President of the United States, and only the nation's second African-American leader, strolled through the wooded grounds of Camp David. With him was a special guest – one of the Democratic Party's most generous supporters, Nicholas Negromonte.

The world-famous businessman was visiting during the President's late-summer vacation. But as James Underwood neither owned a ranch nor a holiday home in Cape Cod nor in any other Brahmin resort, he frequently chose to mix a little business with the pleasure he took here in this retreat's countrified but ultra-secure surroundings.

Negromonte's two-day stay at Camp David was unofficial. There would be no announcement that it was taking place, no press calls and no statements issued. These two men had private business to discuss.

'My thanks for agreeing to open LunaSun,' said Negromonte as he bent to pat the President's golden retriever, Sandy. 'It will mean a lot to all of us.'

It was shortly after eight p.m. and they were walking through a grove of pine trees leading down to the lakeside.

The President stopped in his tracks, slightly lower down the slope. 'It's a privilege, Nick.' He glanced up at his guest. 'I consider your efforts in harnessing the moon to control our weather on Earth as signifying one of this century's greatest technological achievements. And I intend to say just that in my speech.'

'Very kind, sir,' said Negromonte, throwing the dog's ball towards the lake.

'And I'm particularly proud that this is an achievement of an American corporation,' continued Underwood as they fell into step again. 'Or aren't I supposed to mention that fact?'

'Better not,' agreed Negromonte, smiling. 'We're also ferrying up officials from the EU and the East Asian countries. I think the Japanese prime minister is coming too – and the Australian PM. As well as a few African leaders. We want everyone to think this is something beneficial for the whole world.'

'And not another example of American capitalistic colonialism?' Underwood articulated Negromonte's unspoken thought for him. 'I understand. Still, it makes *me* proud.'

Sandy returned with his ball, shaking his wet coat all over their trouser legs, with no obvious regard for rank. Negromonte bent down for the ball and threw it again, this time far out into the lake.

'How much of the globe will you be able to provide for when the moon's fully on-line?' asked Underwood.

'Well, together with our competitors, about seventy per cent of the main land masses.'

There was a sudden sharp movement in the trees over to their left, then one of the normally invisible Secret Service agents stepped out and waved an apologetic arm, identifying himself to other watchers all around. It looked as if the agent had accidentally revealed his position by tripping over something, or stumbling into a rabbit hole.

'And you're absolutely sure that there's nothing significant in this idea of weather management triggering unexpected earthquakes?' asked Underwood, coming to a halt again.

Negromonte met the older man's gaze full on. 'We've grilled our own scientists, sir – they come from the world's most prestigious universities. None of them can see any link whatsoever. That was just a crackpot idea – although I gather the poor man who dreamt it up is now dead – killed in a car accident.'

The President nodded. 'None of my own people think there's any link either, otherwise I'd have to shut you all down.'

Negromonte knew this threat was merely bravado – there wasn't a serving government on Earth that would risk depriving the electorate of its managed weather. Not only would voters hate reverting to an uncontrolled climate, the world economy would be plunged into chaos.

There was a hollow bark from somewhere behind them. This time Sandy's return from the water was more of a nuisance – the dog was soaked from nose to tail. He circled the two men, barking furiously.

President and business leader both backed away as the dog vociferously threatened first this one, then that. Finally he settled on his owner, and shook a huge spray of water all over the President's immaculately pressed brown trousers.

'Get away, Sandy,' shouted Underwood, as he turned and twisted. Then the President picked up the ball and hurled it back into the dark water of the lake.

'I need a favour from you, Nick,' said Underwood, as they resumed their pre-dinner stroll. 'These hulk people out in the Pacific are still on a heading that will bring them into our territorial waters during the next day or so. Can you give me a little of your new moon output for them? If I could guarantee them one reliable session of rain each week, I could probably persuade them to head back down south.'

Emilia Knight seemed either asleep or unconscious inside what looked like a biohazard tent. Her skin was pale, and Michael and Steve could see large red blotches glowing on her face and lower arms. Both men were now wearing white biohazard suits, and had pulled plastic covers on over their shoes.

'All this protection is for her, not you,' explained the young bio-suited doctor who had escorted them to Emilia's private ward. 'Exposure to radioactivity impairs the immune system, so we're just making sure that she doesn't pick up any infection while she's here with us. That's why you couldn't bring your flowers into her room.'

The visitors had been kept waiting downstairs for over two hours, at the end of which time Michael had returned to the main reception desk and threatened to return with the police. As he'd jabbed a finger on the counter top to underline his point, a male nurse had suddenly appeared to escort them to the fourteenth floor.

Michael stared down at the unmoving form of Emilia Patricia Knight, a woman he hardly knew yet who already seemed to occupy a central role in his thoughts. He glanced at his companion and saw the anxiety in Steve's dark eyes.

'She's just been undergoing a bone-marrow biopsy,' explained the doctor. 'I'm afraid she'll be out now for some hours.'

'I'd like to see Doctor Bowman,' said Michael, feeling faintly ridiculous as he turned his entire visored head to talk to the medic.

'I'm afraid Doctor Bowman is currently in theatre.'

'Will you find out for me how long he is going to be there?' asked the lawyer forcefully. He was getting sick of all these obfuscations and delays, although he did have to admit that his unconscious witness seemed to be suffering from something very unpleasant.

The doctor nodded briefly, turned away awkwardly in his clumsy suit and left the room.

Steve Bardini suddenly lifted the side of the tent suspended over Emilia. Michael reached forward to grab the man's arm, not sure what he was intending, and then he noticed the stainless-steel Geiger counter in the seismologist's hand. Steve pressed a button and slowly ran the instrument across the patient's face, down her blistered arm, then across the sheets covering her chest and stomach and down over her legs.

He had only just dropped the tent flap when the young doctor lumbered back into the room.

'I'm afraid it looks as if he's going to be in surgery all night,

Counsellor Fairfax,' he explained. 'He's assisting at a thyroid transplant – for a Chinese submariner who tried to shut down an overheating nuclear core.'

'How long do you expect to keep Emilia in here?' asked Steve.

The doctor glanced at his DigiPad. 'She's still showing over thirty rads superficial,' he said. 'Normally, it should have dissipated by now. But she suffered a slight back injury at the same time as her exposure, and I'm afraid we think her blood became contaminated. We'll know more once we've got the bone-marrow analysis back.'

'So how long?' repeated her former boyfriend.

'Six, perhaps eight weeks,' said the doctor.

SIXTEEN

The breakaway hulk-people convoy had survived the Hawaiian tsunami simply by adopting the tried and tested method they had used for decades to ride out the hideous storms of the Antarctic. They had chained their vessels loosely together.

A wall of water over forty miles long had swept right underneath the old ships, lifting each of them in turn like logs in a giant raft.

The US Pacific Fleet that had been dispatched to turn back the convoy and to retake the *Global Haven* from its pirate captors had instead been ordered to return to the safety of sheltered Pearl Harbor as soon as Geohazard Laboratories had issued its definitive tsunami alert. But the underwater earthquake had struck twelve hours earlier than predicted. Thirteen ships of the fleet had been caught in shallow water as they raced back to port and were either capsized or run aground.

But the American military authorities had quickly regrouped and, now that the hulk-people convoy – its component ships steaming separately once again – was less than twenty-four hours away from entering US territorial waters, the deterrent had been upped significantly.

A total of twenty-two US warships now circled the hulk convoy at high speed. The surviving ships of the Pacific Fleet had been ordered back to sea; the President had declared all navy leave cancelled, and had ordered every available ship in San Diego to lend assistance. Eight missile-carrying catamaran-frigates had even steamed down from devastated San Francisco in a single night's high-speed dash.

It seemed as if a whole squadron of unmanned reconnaissance planes swooped and circled overhead, transmitting back a stream of images and data concerning the fleet of old vessels and their gleaming flagship.

Most worryingly for the breakaway group of hulk people, a number of the latest Red Eagle MMM cruise missiles were circling the convoy – stubby-winged projectiles that were programed to identify a pre-designated target and then remain circling it while their remote mission controllers thousands of miles away chose their moment to strike. The MMM or Triple-M (for Multi-Mission Missile) was the US government's most effective weapon of extreme-force blackmail. Not only did it have a very long range and substantial slow-speed endurance, it also had the ability to depart the target area and return to base – landing on its own retractable undercarriage – for use on another occasion.

On the bridge of the *Global Haven*, John Gogotya shook his head in despair as the recorded image of the US President froze once again and the screen turned dark.

'It doesn't get any better, no matter how many times you play it,' sneered Muhammad Sitta. 'You promised us we would all be American citizens by tomorrow.'

As if it had heard these words spoken, a Red Eagle Triple-M swept across the bow of the giant cruise ship and circled round behind it.

'See *that*?' screamed Gogotya, pointing at the missile trail. 'That thing's got a tactical gamma-ray payload. It could kill every single person on this ship yet leave the boat itself wholly intact – still steaming on towards Los Angeles but filled only with corpses. Is that what you want?'

In his recent message to the breakaway convoy of hulk people, the President of the United States had been very clear about the nature of the weaponry he had sent against this mass of asylum seekers. He had been unsure how much, or how little, these poorly armed, poorly educated, unofficial refugees would know about modern armaments.

'We can kill you all without damaging your ships,' he had warned them. 'Or we can sink every one of your vessels, if you do not turn back.'

Then the President had extended his olive branch. 'Your future must be decided by the United Nations. Every country in the world must play its part in providing you with immigration opportunities. The United States is prepared to sponsor a resolution granting you all official refugee status, so long as you will, for now, return and rejoin the main body of your ships in the Southern Ocean. If you do not turn and follow a course south by eight p.m. Pacific Time tonight, we will have no choice but to strike against all your vessels.'

Then, as if he were a car salesman throwing in an extra luxury accessory to close the deal, the President added: 'I understand your plight and I have arranged for each community of ship dwellers in the Southern Ocean to receive Level Two rainfall for eight hours once a week, for every week until the United Nations and its member states take responsibility for your welfare.'

'Look,' shouted Muhammad Sitta, as he stared up at another screen on the bridge display panel. 'We're on American TV again.'

John Gogotya went to stand beside his contrary lieutenant. A Los Angeles station was indeed showing a live feed from some satellite far overhead. HULK CONVOY NOW ONLY 300 MILES AWAY ran the caption. There was a roar as the Red Eagle missile flashed past the windows of the bridge once again.

'They're never going to let us land,' Gogotya told his followers, the twenty or so young men who had led the breakaway expedition, and who now had come across from the other vessels to attend this crucial meeting.

'They wouldn't bomb us live on TV,' bellowed Sitta. 'That's not the American way.'

'Oh yes, they would,' yelled Gogotya. 'They think we're threatening them in their own homes. They just want to see us blown back to where we came from.'

There was a silence up on the bridge. None of these young men actually had any true concept of what was, or was not, the real American way. Each had only his own fantasy notions of that culture.

'We must start turning back now,' said their leader. 'There's only thirty minutes left before the deadline, and we don't want them to make any mistakes.'

'But we need dry land, homes, work, hospitals, schools, libraries,' snapped Muhammad Sitta. 'We must go on.'

'Well, we don't have the dry land or the work,' said Gogotya, 'But we have luxury homes, hospitals, schools and libraries...' He banged his fist against the *Global Haven*'s control panel. 'We've even got aircraft and maintenance facilities – *and* desalination plants! They haven't demanded back this ship, have they? And if they were going to take her, they'd already have done it. Don't you think we've got enough for the moment?'

The young men glanced at each other, and Gogotya saw nods being exchanged. 'Get back to your own ships quickly,' he said. 'Let's take this ship home so that everyone can benefit from it.'

'Look at this.' Steve Bardini held out the pocket Geiger counter so that the lawyer could see its display. 'There's not a single read-out from her body above one-point-five. That doctor claimed she had over thirty rads.'

Michael Fairfax took the stainless-steel instrument from him and tried to make sense of the data. It was shortly before eight p.m. and they were seated in the lawyer's parked BMW, right outside the Naval Hospital building.

'I'm not familiar with these. What are rads?'

'It's very simple,' said Steve curtly. 'She's no more radioactive than you are. I swept every part of her body that was supposedly affected – nothing showing. Here.' He punched a data-recall button. 'These are the figures I was getting the day after she had handled the hot stuff.'

Michael examined the two sets of data. They certainly seemed very different.

A marine suddenly tapped on Michael's window.

'I'm going to have to ask you to move on, sir. This is a secure area.'

As they drove out of the base, Steve tried to educate Emilia's attorney in the basics of radioactivity and human exposure. As he explained, he himself had researched the subject thoroughly after his boss had first become contaminated.

'Let's find a motel where we can go over this properly,' suggested Michael.

They took two rooms at the Shoreline Motel off Highway 5, bought themselves sandwiches from a small deli counter, and agreed to meet up again in an hour.

Michael wolfed down his roast beef sandwich – he hadn't realized how hungry he was – and then stood under a scalding shower for ten minutes. As the water cascaded over his tired body, he tried to make sense of the conflicting evidence he had heard in the last few hours.

Emilia Knight had looked to be seriously ill. But her former boyfriend insisted that, whatever was wrong with her, it wasn't being caused by exposure to radioactivity.

Then there was her abrupt removal from her home during the night; that hardly seemed part of any normal medical treatment. All of Michael's instincts told him there was something wrong here, something connected with what she had found on Samoa, with the assumptions that the security services had jumped to, and perhaps with her decision to provide testimony to the court in The Hague.

Stepping out of the bathroom, Michael pulled on clean clothes and then automatically reached for his phone. He would speak to the boys before...

A wave of sadness washed over him, and he sank down onto the bed. There was a hard rap on the door.

Steve Bardini, who had also showered and changed, put his finger to his lips as he entered, then stretched out a palm for Michael's inspection.

Cradled in the seismologist's hand were objects that looked like tiny buttons attached to sticky pads. Each had a fine wire trailing from it, like a single hair.

Steve transferred these finds into Michael's cupped hands, put a warning finger to his lips once again, then pulled a circular black pod from his jeans pocket. Positioning himself in the centre of the room, he pressed a button on the pod itself and a thin line of red light appeared across the ceiling and down both walls, like a laser-beam projection.

Slowly, he worked the beam across the ceiling and walls towards the curtained window. Then he stopped and nodded at the light-beam. Michael saw that a section of the red line, just beside a bedside cabinet, had turned green.

Steve pointed urgently and Michael crossed the room, pulling the cabinet away from the wall. Stuck to its back was another of the tiny button-like objects. Michael removed it and added it to the collection in his other hand.

Three more of the miniature radio microphones were found – one near the computer display and fixed phone, one behind the curtain pelmet, and the third behind a cabinet in the bathroom.

When his sweep was complete, Steve indicated for them to maintain their silence, then gathered the listening devices into a plastic laundry bag. Running the bathroom tap, he filled the bag with water, drained it, stamped on the damp contents and then threw the broken mess into the trash bin.

'I don't understand,' said Michael, as soon as Steve had finished his act of destruction. 'How did you know there would be bugs here – and what's that thing?' He pointed to the black scanner that his travelling companion had now placed on top of a drawer unit.

'They weren't meant for us, obviously,' said Steve as he eased himself into one of the two easy chairs in the room. 'Nobody could know we were coming here. But this is a naval town, so they'll have every hotel and motel room in the city cold-wired.'

'Cold-wired?'

'The security services bug every room and meeting space for miles around sensitive locations, using passive mikes with very long-life batteries. Computers listen in to what these bugs are hearing twenty-four-seven. If they pick up a word or a phrase that's in an alert index, they summon a human to listen in. At any one time computers in Washington will probably be listening to twenty or thirty thousand locations in this naval town alone.'

'How do you know all this?' asked Michael. He sensed a more serious, more capable air about the young scientist now.

'That's how your friend Carole Gonzaga was caught. The bomb-maker was in a public washroom in Newport Beach, and he gave the courier her address. They'd filled the bathroom with cold wires – Newport Beach is only twenty miles from Camp Pendleton.'

Michael sat down opposite Steve and stared into the younger man's face.

'How do you know how Carole was caught? How do you know about "cold wires"? And where did you get that thing, anyway?' He pointed again to the bug detector on the drawer unit.

'Can I rely on your confidentiality, counsellor?' asked Steve. 'No matter what I tell you?'

'If you tell me anything in my capacity as a lawyer, yes, you can – if there's a legal aspect to all of this.'

'There's a legal aspect to it, sure enough,' said Steve. 'I'm a scientific adviser to the Planet First Organization.' He laughed grimly as he saw the surprise register on the attorney's face.

Partly to buy himself thinking time, Michael rose from his chair and crossed the room to stare thoughtfully into the large mirror fixed on the wall opposite his king-size bed. Was this the missing link? Were this young man's covert activities the reason why the security agencies seemed to be overreacting so grossly?

'You were over in Samoa with Emilia, weren't you?' He turned back to face the seismologist once more. 'Are you procuring plutonium for the PFO?'

It was now Steve Bardini's turn to look shocked.

'Of course I'm not! I didn't even know what it was she'd discovered until weeks later,' he protested. 'We'd both signed a secrecy order, and she only told me subsequently.'

The attorney weighed up carefully what he was hearing.

'And I don't plant bombs either, counsellor,' Steve added. 'Like I said, I'm just a scientific adviser. Most of the organization is made up of people like me, people who care passionately about the health of this planet. Anyway, since the earthquake, the PFO has announced an end to all terrorist activity. Nature itself has sent the world a far better wake-up call than we could ever have managed.'

Michael now had a straightforward choice. Either he accepted what he was being told at face value, or he had to contact the authorities. But all his instincts, training and long experience with witnesses told him that Robert Fivetrees, Emilia Knight and Steve Bardini were honest, decent people.

'Look, do you think you can handle this, Mike?' demanded Steve, now deadly serious. 'If you can't, let's just forget that we had this conversation. You go back to San-Fran and I'll get Em out of that hospital. One thing I'm certain of, she hasn't got radiation sickness.'

'How do you intend to get her out?' asked Michael.

Wall Street Journal

Monday, 18 September 2055

FIRST PRESIDENTIAL VISIT TO MOON IN OCTOBER

LIVE TV DEBATE TO BE BEAMED FROM LUNAR SURFACE

The White House has announced that President James T. Underwood will become the first serving US President to visit the moon. He will officially open the ERGIA Corporation's new lunar facility on 21 October, following which he will give an address to open a live television debate on the future of climate management.

Other guests at the ceremony will include EU President Hollinger, Japan's Prime Minister Kakehashi and Mr Lu Zen, China's Minister for Extraterrestrial Investment.

Shares in LunaSun Inc., the corporation set up to run and manage the lunar-energy resource, will be offered in a NASDAQ IPO scheduled for 28 October.

An hour after Steve Bardini admitted to his membership of the PFO, there was a soft triple-knock on Michael Fairfax's motel-room door.

'That's them,' said Steve, rising from his chair. 'I'll get it.'

Three fit-looking men in dark clothes entered quickly, followed by a tall woman wearing jeans and a bottle-green T-shirt.

'Tony, Ricky and Doc Cosmo,' said Steve by way of introduction to the men. He nodded towards the woman. 'And this is Doctor Val Cummings of the US Navy's Oceanographic Academy. Her work first alerted us to early signs of the Hawaiian earthquake. And, most importantly, she has top-level security clearance for all areas of the naval station.'

The lawyer shook hands with all four new arrivals. Earlier, Steve had surprised Michael yet again, by producing by a high-security encryption phone and placing two short calls to set up this gathering.

'Cosmo is our medical doctor for the San Diego region,' explained Steve. 'He'll know whether Emilia is really sick or not.'

Then they spent an hour planning how best to extract Emilia Knight from the hospital. Val Cummings projected a map of the naval base onto the room's wall-screen, and marked out what she considered the best routes in and out.

'My lab's on the base and I often have to work during the nights,' she explained. 'The oceans don't observe social hours.'

Shortly before one a.m. Chief Oceanographer Dr Valerie Cummings pulled her large Chevrolet into the vehicle-inspection parking lot beside the guardhouse at the main entrance to the US naval base.

'Hey, Jerome,' she said to the young marine who greeted her. 'What's up?'

'Not much, Doctor Cummings,' he told her through her open window. 'Night shift?'

There were three other soldiers in the guardhouse but none of them were stirring.

'Got some more seismic bumps out in the Pacific,' said Val. 'This here is a colleague from Geohazard Labs.'

Steve Bardini leaned his body across from the passenger seat to hand his ident over, and so that he could be clearly seen. As

Val had predicted, the guardhouse duty had been rotated since his earlier visit.

The marine glanced at the Geohazard identification.

In the roomy trunk of the large car Michael Fairfax and Dr Cosmo Mondadori waited, their bodies rigid in the blackness.

'They never search my car,' Val Cummings had assured them earlier. 'They know me too well.'

'Always a first time,' the man introduced as Ricky had replied during their planning meeting. But it was a risk worth taking, they decided. If Emilia was well enough, they would smuggle her out.

'We'll need to get her out of the country,' said Steve. Yet again he had surprised Michael by extracting Emilia's passport from his jacket pocket and throwing it onto the low table. 'I thought she might need it,' he added by way of explanation. 'And I also brought this – Em had left it in her house.' He placed Professor Fivetrees's miniature holo-theatre on the table top. 'I presume she was intending to work on its data at home.'

The marine handed the identity card back to Steve. 'Thanks, sir.' Then he slapped his hand twice on the roof of the car. 'Have a nice night, Dr Cummings.'

Thirty minutes later the four conspirators were running up the back stairs of the Naval Hospital block. Val Cummings had used her access card to open a rear-entrance door, and Steve Bardini had deployed a data-signal repeater – a PFO-developed wireless device that read and then looped video streams – to render the hospital's network of security cameras ineffective. An alert human monitoring the feeds might realize that something was wrong, as the displays repeated every thirty seconds, but the loop was seamless and there was normally very little movement in the hospital at this time of night.

All four insurgents were panting heavily as they arrived on the fourteenth floor. There were very few lights on as they stepped out of a stairwell door beside the elevator shaft. At the far end of the corridor they could see one lighted window, in what they assumed was a nursing station, but there seemed to be nobody else around.

Emilia Knight herself was still sleeping. Steve Bardini held up a flashlight while Dr Mondadori took the patient's pulse and then started quickly checking her other vital signs.

'What – who?' groaned Emilia.

'Shussh, it's me, Em,' hissed Steve, shining the torch on his own face.

'I don't—'

'Shussh,' repeated Steve. 'This is Doctor Mondadori – a friend. We're going to get you out of here. Just keep quiet!'

Having completed the basic physical checks, Michael and Steve watched as the doctor ran two different scanners along the length of Emilia's body. As soon as he had examined the data read-outs, he stooped and lifted the entire side of the tent away from the patient's bed.

'Well, there's no sign of any radioactivity,' Doc Cosmo hissed. 'And all her vital signs are normal. From her pupils and the way her eyes respond to light, I'd say she's been sedated.'

Emilia's feet hardly touched the floor as Michael and Steve hustled her down fourteen flights of steps. Val Cummings had brought a raincoat for her to wear, and five minutes later Emilia too was crammed into the large trunk of the car, along with Michael Fairfax and Dr Cosmo Mondadori.

SEVENTEEN

'You mean these people aren't really controlling the weather when they're calling out to each other?' asked Perdita Curtis angrily, rounding on her guide.

'No, I'm sorry, they're just for show – for our visitors,' explained Hanoch Biran, ERGIA's director of corporate communications. 'Our perception consultants advised us that tourists don't really want to look at computers, they want to see real people. So we hire actors to play the parts. All weather trades on the daily spot market have been automated for over twenty years.'

The BBC producer had brought her director and a twelve-strong film crew up to the ERGIA Space Station specifically to film the weather brokers shouting and calling out to each other as they traded future rainfall in one part of the planet for a future day's sun in another – just as she herself had witnessed during her first trip into space. She had committed a significant part of her non-moon budget to this part of the shoot and now she felt foolish for not checking out the details of the broking operation more thoroughly in advance.

Perdy, Torrance Olds and the ERGIA publicity executive were standing in the space station's viewing chamber, gazing up at the banked tiers of male and female 'weather controllers', the nearest of whom, having overheard this heated exchange, were now looking distinctly embarrassed.

'I suppose we could just film them going through their routine, without comment,' suggested Olds.

'You mean dupe our viewers by omission,' snapped Perdy.

She felt like swearing out loud. Her TV crew had already spent three hours getting amusing zero-gravity fill-in shots of the off-duty space station crew as well as footage of their living quarters and recreational areas, but what she had really relied on was an exciting segment to show weather trading in action. As these 'climate brokers' shouted out the destinations for the weather patterns on offer, she had intended to cut in real-time shots of the actual regions, allowing viewers to understand how the decisions taken up here on the space station directly affected people on the ground below.

'So what do the computers that really do all of this trading actually look like?' Perdy asked Biran.

He shook his head. 'I'm afraid there's nothing much to see, Miss Curtis – some screens, a few numbers flashing by. Every weather transaction is carried out through one form or other of automated auction. Some systems bid up, some count down. Others use pre-empt. But it's just computers talking to computers, I'm afraid – virtually invisible.'

'And they never break down?' asked Perdita, an idea suddenly occurring to her. Perhaps if they briefly switched the trading to these humans . . .

'No, they never break down,' said Biran. 'If they did, there would be chaos on the planet below. Millions of weather trades are made each hour, so there are back-up systems down on Earth, just in case.'

'What about if we filmed these people doing their thing and called it a dramatized sequence?' suggested Torrance Olds quietly. 'Just by showing a screen caption?'

Perdy glanced up at the now-silent rows of thespian weather-controllers.

'That's brilliant, Torry,' she exclaimed. '"Dramatized on board the ERGIA Weather Control-Space Station." That'll do it.'

Perdy turned back to the corporate communications director. 'Could you ask them to do a run-through again, please?'

Biran glanced up at the men and women sitting in their banked rows. 'From the top, please, people.'

'I've got a bid of eleven million dollars for a one-hour Volume

Six rain storm in Marrakesh,' yelled one of the controllers suddenly.

'I've got thirteen million two for that rain – if we can send it on to Cairo,' called another.

Then there was another shout, followed by a further bid from Marrakesh for the rainfall. Then a voice asked if anyone had two hours of late-night sunshine available for a film shoot in Seattle which had overrun on its schedule.

Perdy nodded and held up her hand to stop them. 'Excellent. Thank you, everybody. If you'd all like to take a break now, we'll get our cameras and lights set up.'

'Giorgio!' exclaimed Emilia Knight with a whoop, as she threw her small body into the arms of the big, curly-haired, dark-bearded, bearlike man and kissed him on both cheeks. Slightly embarrassed by this extravagant display of affection, Michael Fairfax and Steve Bardini hung back a little, hovering at the rear of the European Geohazard Simulation Theater.

'It's been too long, far too long!' Emilia planted yet another kiss on the big man's cheek. 'Come here and meet my very good friend Giorgio,' she told her companions excitedly. 'Giorgio, this is Steve Bardini, he works with me in Oakland. And this is Mike Fairfax, he's my attorney.' But she realized that didn't sound quite right. 'And my friend,' she added.

Doctor Giorgio Zaoskoufis, Geohazard's Senior Risk Assessment Seismologist for the European, Middle East and African regions, shook his visitors' hands warmly.

'Welcome to Athens,' he told them in good if Greek-accented English. 'And also to what we hope will be a quiet night shift.'

It seemed that the resources and tendrils of the Planet First Organization stretched further than either Michael Fairfax or Emilia Knight could have imagined. As soon as she had been extracted safely from the US Navy base, Emilia had been driven to Dr Cosmo Mondadori's home on the outskirts of Lemon Grove, a satellite residential community ten miles east of San Diego.

Here the doctor had submitted the still-woozy geophysicist to two hours of further tests in his home consulting room before returning to make his report to Valerie Cummings and the two male visitors from San Francisco.

By then it was almost five a.m. and the group in the doctor's lounge was staying alert only by swallowing copious quantities of black coffee. While Dr Mondadori had been checking the patient over, Steve Bardini had driven back to the Shoreline Motel and collected the small amount of luggage that he and Michael had left behind. Lanky Val Cummings had used the opportunity to disappear in the hope of finding some clothes that might fit petite Emilia.

'She's perfectly healthy,' announced the doctor. 'Nothing wrong with her blood at all. In fact, she's just getting dressed now.'

'What about her blisters?' asked Steve.

'Some sort of acidic agent rubbed onto her skin to make their story look good, I would think,' said Mondadori. 'It neutralizes instantly with an alkali.'

'So they had sedated her?' asked the lawyer.

'A type of pentothal,' confirmed the doctor, nodding. 'But most of it has now worn off. They obviously wanted very much to keep her out of circulation.'

Or perhaps her condition might have deteriorated, thought Michael. *Perhaps after a few more days of confinement she might have caught an infection, something her impaired immune system would have been unable to resist – and she too would have died, just like Robert Fivetrees and Carole Gonzaga.*

During that long night, Michael had also thought very carefully about what his own next move should be. He now considered himself to be at risk of imminent arrest by US government agents – or possibly something worse. Their murderous overreaction to the PFO and their fears of plutonium being in circulation had shocked him profoundly. Like most American citizens, he had had little idea how ruthless his government's agencies could be when faced with a potential combination of terrorist groups and the components for building nuclear weapons.

For himself, the course became clear. He would return to Brussels and ask the court in The Hague for a Writ of Protection. His European legal colleagues had assured him that despite the threats made against him, such a writ would offer immunity from arrest so long as he remained safely outside the USA. Then he would pursue his case for all he was worth.

But what about Dr Emilia Knight? What would she want?

Two hours later – after Michael had explained to her what he feared were the security agencies' suspicions – Emilia had provided her answer in the clearest way possible. Travelling together in his BMW, Michael Fairfax, Stephano Bardini and Dr Emilia Knight crossed over the US border into Mexico at Tijuana. Nobody tried to stop them.

At the Abelardo L. Rodriguez International Airport they boarded a non-stop Air Mexico flight to Madrid. Once in Spain, they each bought a change of clothing and then caught a connecting flight on to Athens in order to visit Geohazard Laboratories' European HQ. They wanted to run Professor Fivetrees's data in the company's Simulation Theater. Michael had no compunction about paying for all their travel costs out of his case-preparation budget; this seismic data and Emilia's testimony would form a vital part of his evidence.

'Giorgio Zaoskoufis is a wonderful man,' Emilia had told her travelling companions. Only twelve hours after leaving the hospital, the blotches on her face and arms had faded to mere pale pink marks. 'He'll be more than pleased to help us – unofficially, of course.'

Two hours after their midnight arrival at Geohazard Laboratories in the Athens suburb of Piraeus – a facility almost identical to the Oakland complex – Emilia Knight, Steve Bardini and their host Giorgio Zaoskoufis had completed loading all of Professor Fivetrees's data into the Simulation Theater computers, created the necessary interfacing scripts and declared themselves ready to run the first modelling exercise.

'We've linked the data Bob Fivetrees extracted from the Jesuit monasteries to all of our own historical climate data,' explained Steve for Michael's benefit. 'And we've cross-referenced all the available data for climate-management energy output with all recorded seismic events above two-point-oh in the last sixty years. Then, as an overlay, we'll be running Fivetrees's model of the magnetic force fields.'

Michael nodded, but he hadn't the faintest idea of what he was really being told. He wondered if it was his tiredness that was preventing him from understanding fully. He felt both emotionally drained by recent events and sledgehammered by jet lag.

Giorgio ushered Emilia into the holo-pit observation chair and then joined Steve Bardini at one of the control workstations. Michael took a seat in the viewing gallery.

'OK, let's go.' Emilia gunned her chair round to the zero-degree longitude.

The large central holo-pit suddenly lit up and Michael saw a large model of the globe, tilted at an acute angle and turning very slowly. It was covered in swirling white, grey and black cloud patterns.

'Start date and location?' asked Emilia.

The numerals AD 1737 appeared, floating in space on a laser overlay. Then the word PORTUGAL.

Abruptly, huge purple rings and ovals appeared, swirling around the planet.

MAGNETIC FLUX DENSITY 1.0, read a data overlay.

Michael thought how beautiful the image was. The hoops of wavering light oscillated closer and further away from the planet's surface. The rings themselves grew and shrunk as the force field changed in strength.

'Go to ten times actual speed,' ordered Emilia.

A red line of light shot between one outer group of magnetic rings and what looked like the coastline of Western Europe on the globe's surface.

'Hold it,' said Emilia, racing her observation chair around the perimeter of the holo-pit to position herself directly over the point where the beam of red light had struck the Earth.

'That's the great Lisbon earthquake of 1755,' she announced. 'Almost Magnitude Nine. The tsunami that followed killed over sixty thousand people. Run it back.'

The globe reversed so that Michael could see the red line connecting to a huge black weather swirl over the Indian Ocean.

'This is the crucial part of Bob Fivetrees's work,' explained Emilia, swivelling in her motorized chair to face Michael. 'He compared historical climate records with the Jesuit observations, and then related both of them to the seismic logs. Looks like that storm occurred three weeks before the Lisbon quake – his software makes a direct connection.'

After ninety more minutes of simulations of historic data, the researchers had finally caught up to the present day. Each of the main seismic events that had been modelled and matched to weather patterns was now posted on a transparent laser-display board beside the holo-pit, and Emilia finally declared herself ready for a coffee break.

'We're just about to run the magnetic force-fields model with the latest data on climate-management output,' she explained as they stood in the visitor's gallery, sipping sweet Turkish coffee from small china cups.

'Are you going to allow for the new solar output due from the moon?' asked Zaoskoufis. 'I know the resource is not officially open yet, but they're already applying some of its energy.'

Emilia nodded. 'I've modelled it as if the moon is already fully on-line. We've got the published data on their projected output.'

It was just after 4.20 a.m. Athens time when Emilia Knight and her fellow scientists resumed their positions around the Simulation Theater, Michael once more took his seat in the viewing gallery.

Again, he watched with fascination as the bright mauve rings of light representing the planet's magnetic heartbeat spun, skipped and bowed around the globe. Sometimes they flared out into space for three or four times the Earth's own diameter, sometimes they flattened down to creep closely over the surface of the planet itself.

'Let's have it all,' ordered Emilia.

It seemed as if the planet and its force field of magnetic rings had suddenly been hit by a hundred bolts of lightning. Red laser lines shot down from the encompassing flux, connecting to the surface to indicate where the Earth's crust itself was being broken and cracked, as the inner core-dynamo bulged and pushed under the churning magnetic compulsion.

'Stop. *Stop!*' shouted Emilia. Then she extended her own laser-control display and brought the simulation to rest.

There were now too many red lines criss-crossing the planet to count.

'It's started a whole chain reaction of eruptions and earthquakes,' Emilia observed quietly as she gazed at the frozen image. She raised her hands to the side of her face to block out her peripheral sight, to help her think better. 'One global-scale seismic event triggering another, hopping along the same fault line.'

There was a long silence as they all gazed at the model of the Earth. It seemed as if the crust had torn along its seams.

'What's happened?' asked Michael.

Emilia shrugged and projected a data panel onto the simulation overlay. 'We've just witnessed the start of magnetic pole reversal,' she explained, swinging round in her chair. 'The charged particles reflected back towards the Earth by the climate-management mirrors managed to weaken the polarity of the magnetosphere so much that it started to oscillate, north flipping to south, south to north, then back again. Of course, that causes massive disruption to the magnetic currents in the Earth's mantle – which triggers seismic chaos all around the planet.'

Michael had no idea what to say. Eventually he asked, 'How long would it go on for?'

Emilia shook her head. 'We don't really know. Most previous pole reversals on Earth have taken about five thousand years – which is almost instant by geological timescales. But one or two of them seemed to have occurred much faster – there's palaeomagnetic evidence from Steen's Mountain in Oregon that one reversal occurred in just a few weeks. The magnetostratiographic data is very convincing.'

Michael realized that, just like lawyers faced with confusing legalities, Emilia and her scientific colleagues were falling back on the arcane jargon of their discipline to try and impose a structure onto the seemingly chaotic issues now under consideration.

'But what it really means is that many thousands of people will die from earthquakes and volcanic eruptions, right?' he said, deliberately reductionist.

'Well, that might be true, but only *if* Professor Fivetrees was right about this,' agreed Steve Bardini.

Emilia nodded. 'Yes – *if* he was right.'

A high trilling sound filled the Simulation Theater. Giorgio Zaoskoufis reached forward quickly and touched an icon on his workstation to silence it.

'That's a warning coming in from Geohazard Labs in Tokyo,' he said. 'Shall I project it here or go next door to the Risk Monitoring Centre?'

Emilia stepped down from her mobile viewing chair. 'We're done with this, Giorgio. At least for tonight. Let's see what Tokyo wants to tell us.'

The Greek geophysicist killed the display in the holo-pit and patched the Japanese feed onto the large wall-screens. They saw a map of Indonesia appear and the myriad islands of the Java Sea.

'Holy shit,' exclaimed Steve Bardini. 'They've got a Level Five warning out on Papandayan. Zoom in.'

Zaoskoufis obliged and they saw a chain of islands, sixty miles south of Jakarta, one of which was highlighted by a red circle. Inset into this screen display were real-time windows showing seismic sensor readings, magma-flow projections and ash-dispersal zones. Across the bottom of the screen a caption running from right to left estimated the level of strength of anticipated tsunamis.

'Papandayan's a stratovolcano,' Steve explained for Michael's benefit, 'a near neighbour of Krakatoa, in the hottest volcanic belt in the world. It's been dormant since 1942.'

'Not for very much longer, though,' said Zaoskoufis. 'It looks like she's going to blow sky-high in the next forty-eight hours.'

EIGHTEEN

The great Javanese volcano Papandayan, situated on the southern coast of Java at 7.32S – 107.73E, began its latest (and final) venting early on the morning of 26 September 2055.

The first explosion took place at 7.51 a.m. local time, when the lava dome split asunder and ash and boiling water vapour were thrown up into the atmosphere to a height of over eighteen kilometres.

At 11.19 a.m., a second and far larger double explosion occurred when Papandayan's volcanic chimney itself was shot upwards like a plug from a barrel, thrusting an estimated four billion tons of rock, ash and debris over twenty kilometres into the air. The explosion was heard on all 13,000 islands of the Nusantara chain, across all of Indonesia, and as far away as Singapore, Australia, the Philippines and Japan. The total force of the energy released was estimated to be between 500 and 1,000 times greater than the largest hydrogen bomb ever tested.

The previous largest-ever volcanic explosion had been recorded in 1883 when neighbouring Krakatoa erupted, killing more than 36,000 people. Over ninety per cent of those deaths were caused by the mega-tsunamis that swept the coastlines of the Indonesian islands as Krakatoa imploded, causing two-thirds of its underlying volcanic island to fall into the sea.

If volcanoes could ever be thought to be competitive, Papandayan effortlessly topped Krakatoa's paltry efforts. In its great final explosion, Papandayan too ceased to exist, as if making an insensible effort to mimic its former neighbour.

First Papandayan's long-parturient 8,700-foot-high crater was levelled as its superheated pressure-cauldron of magma exploded. The heat and velocity were so great that the spewing lava emerged looking like a pink foam.

Then, as its roaring chimney became more of an obstruction than a vent for the molten rocks below, the mountain itself blew out sideways, like a giant car-bomb stuffed with Semtex. Superheated rocks and gas were ejected over a ninety-mile radius at supersonic speed.

Then the underwater base of the mountain itself imploded.

For the people living on nearby islands day turned to night as the boiling rocks mixed with air in the stratosphere, before cooling and solidifying to descend as light pumice – a debris-fall that lasted for over sixteen hours, forming an obsidian deposit ten metres thick. Unfortunately for animals and for the many humans caught without shelter, this precipitation also included huge quantities of solid rocks falling back towards the ground at a speed of 200 kilometres per hour.

The gloomy, roaring twilight that enveloped all of the south Javanese islands was constantly split by jagged forks of volcanic lightning – an electrical discharge caused by the mid-air collision of volcanic ash and magma.

As Papandayan's abyssal lava chamber emptied, hotter and denser rocks from deep within the mantle rushed up to join the pumice and ash that were now spewing upwards at a rate of 100,000 tons per second.

Even when they *had* found shelter in time, the humans caught within the ninety-kilometre volcanic fallout zone had little chance of survival. Like all stratovolcanos, Papandayan produced a gas that was a mixture of carbon dioxide and hydrogen peroxide, a combination ruinous to mucous membrane and animal tissue. The first inhalation of this gas stripped the linings from human lungs, causing them to fill with fluid. The second breath caused inhaled ash to mix with this fluid to form a cement. The third breath thickened and set that cement. Over 250,000 people suffocated in this horrendous manner.

Other victims nearer to the pyroclastic flow as it burst from the sides of the volcano died instantly of thermal shock – their tissue vaporized, their brains boiled, their bones and teeth crystallizing before being shattered.

Successive waves of mega-tsunamis shot outwards in concentric circles, sweeping over the entire southern coasts of Java and Sumatra, overwhelming the cities of Bengkulu, Padong, Yogyaharta and Kupang.

Of the thousands of separate islands that made up the Indonesian nation, 5,311 were completely stripped of all life forms by successive waves measured by Geohazard's satellites at over fifty metres high.

These multiple mega-tsunamis also radiated north-west for 1,500 miles, completely submerging the Maldives and drowning 800 square miles of southern Sri Lanka.

Just over 600 miles to the south of Papandayan itself, Christmas Island and the Cocos Islands also disappeared beneath the waves, and to the east the successive embankments of water submerged the north-eastern Australian coastline and up to seven miles inland. All the low-lying areas of Darwin were flooded for three days.

Despite the advance warning provided by Geohazard Laboratories in Tokyo, over three million people died in the twenty-four hours following the world's first recorded global-scale geophysical event – mostly those who were unable to escape to high ground.

The skies went dark over all of South-East Asia, and the ash canopy drifted as far east as the Central Pacific. All of the climate-management companies were immediately tasked with the job of directing winds to disperse the ash safely over the remote Southern Oceans.

WORLD'S WORST-EVER VOLCANIC ERUPTION, trumpeted the *Hong Kong Star*. But how did they know? Human beings had a very limited perspective from which to judge the typical geophysical behaviour of their host planet. As a species, *Homo sapiens* had been around for only 0.01 per cent of the Earth's lifetime to date.

*

'Welcome to the BBC,' said Perdita Curtis cheerily, as she ushered Michael Fairfax, Emilia Knight and Steve Bardini into a meeting room on the eleventh floor of the Corporation's new West London headquarters. 'My executive producer will try to join us later, but he's frantically busy preparing for our moon broadcast – as we all are. Only ten days to go!'

The three American visitors sat down around a large smart-table. Automatically, they ran their fingers in rough squares over the glass surface immediately in front of them to set up their own computing, note-taking and communications spaces.

Michael Fairfax now felt both fully rested and back in synch with European circadian rhythms. While Emilia and Steve had remained for two days at Geohazard's European HQ in Piraeus, helping Giorgio Zaoskoufis and other scientific colleagues around the world to cope with the Indonesian disaster, Michael himself had caught up with his sleep in a small Athens hotel before picking up the reins of his case with his Brussels colleagues and discussing what their next move should be.

On the insistence of his new legal partners in Belgium, the firm of Beauchamp, Seifert and Co had formally applied to the International Court of Civil Justice in The Hague for writs of witness protection for *both* Dr Emilia Knight and Counsellor Michael Fairfax. The lawyer had provided live testimony to the court about the threats received from American security agents via a secure video link from Athens. News of the writs' subsequent granting was then supplied to both the California Bar Association and the US State Department.

'If they're still after you, it should at least give them pause for thought,' explained human rights lawyer Anatole Karmin, one of Michael's new associates in Brussels. 'It was only last year that President Underwood went out on a limb to secure US ratification of the new international court. The American security services won't want to be seen to be interfering with witnesses in the first case to involve major American corporations.'

And, with the approval of his new legal colleagues, Michael also made the decision to approach Perdita Curtis and the BBC in London with the latest theories developed by his geophysicist friends.

He himself was unqualified to judge whether there was any validity in the assertion that climate management was triggering worldwide seismic unrest. But he was sure that the claim that it might cause a chain reaction of global-scale geophysical events would not only get the media's attention, it might also bring Nick Negromonte and other such oligarchs of the energy industry rapidly to the negotiating table.

Like his Brussels associates, Michael had little doubt that in the long run the courts would find in favour of the victims of global warming. But he preferred to go for a quick interim settlement, something he could pass on to the hulk people now, to bolster their ongoing belief in what was certain to be a long and very drawn-out process of litigation.

And while he had been waiting in the Athens sunshine, Michael had also found the courage to discard his air-porous latex gloves. After wearing them for over eight weeks, his scarred hands and regrowing nails no longer looked quite so revolting.

'You *are* still available to take part in our debate from Luna City?' Perdy asked him as she pulled her guest list up onto the tabletop. 'I'm relying on you to help make it hard-hitting.'

'Absolutely,' agreed the lawyer. 'I'm looking forward to it. But the reason that I wanted to introduce you to my two colleagues here today is that they have been developing the Berkeley model of the Earth's magnetic fields that I showed you a few weeks ago. They've linked it to climate records – and to climate-management data – and we thought you'd like to see the result.'

Steve Bardini patched the updated, revised and now much-enlarged simulation onto the wall-screen.

'I've speeded it up considerably,' he explained as they sat watching the 3-D image of the Earth as global seismic chaos developed.

As the simulation finished running, Perdy Curtis tapped her fingertips slowly on the glass table top.

'It's certainly very topical – what with that Indonesian volcanic eruption,' she observed. 'Could you speed it up still further?'

Steve nodded. 'It all depends on how much detail you want. You can have anything from thirty seconds to thirty hours.'

'I'd like to use it during my part of the debate,' Michael explained. 'That's if you can find the budget to bring Steve along to run it for me. I'd also like viewers to be able to download the data for themselves, if they're interested.'

'Ah, budget, budget,' sighed Perdy. 'This thing's really getting out of control. It looks like becoming the most expensive live broadcast the BBC has ever done.'

'President Underwood is opening the debate, right?' asked Emilia.

'Everything's gone mad since that announcement,' confirmed Perdy, nodding. She ran her fingers through her short hair. 'It seems as if everybody now wants to come to the moon. Even the Director-General of the BBC says he wants to be part of the audience.'

'And I want you to invite Doctor Knight, too,' said Michael. 'I'd like her to speak immediately after me.'

Perdy sighed and glanced down her lengthy list of names.

'I've got forty-two contributor places available and three hundred and seventeen world-class experts all asking to attend. Plus I've got to find room for some genuine audience.'

'It was Dr Knight who found the plutonium on the Samoan volcano,' explained Michael. 'I'd like to see President Underwood's face when she announces *that* on a live TV broadcast.'

The instant TV ratings polls proved once again that Nicholas Negromonte had an outstanding talent for dreaming up publicity stunts guaranteed to attract world attention. Over two hundred million people had tuned in to watch his blast-off to the moon in the refurbished back-up Apollo 11 spacecraft.

In recent years, every major surge in ERGIA's corporate expansion had been preceded by such a headline-grabbing stunt. Now the forthcoming initial public offering of shares in LunaSun Inc was to be publicized by this historic re-enactment of mankind's first-ever moon landing.

Just as entrepreneurs of previous centuries had broken ballooning records, climbed mountains or raced yachts, Nick Negromonte had continued the tradition of entertaining, amusing and seducing those who might become his shareholders and customers. Many critics and competitors dismissed him as a cynical exploiter of the media. Some said he patronized and despised the public who admired him so much. Others felt that all such acts of self-display were in bad taste.

But the truth was that business and money alone were not sufficiently exciting to fully engage Negromonte's mind. He had been prepared to give up his tennis career after his elder brother died, but he still always wanted more out of life than normal corporate leadership offered. Power and money – for many, drugs in their own way – didn't grip him the way they had seduced his father or his brother. Nick Negromonte also wanted to have fun.

His first such business-related extreme-sports achievement had been to complete an untethered space walk of over thirty kilometres. Using only his backpack's compressed gas for steering and propulsion, he had navigated his way from ERGIA's first-generation climate-control space station to the newly opened Mandarin-Orbital Hotel – a luxury facility built by a Chinese consortium in near-Earth orbit in 2035. On his arrival he had even performed the hotel's opening ceremony, and had become its first VIP guest.

A string of other stunts had followed, many of them involving antique aircraft and space vehicles. But this solo voyage to the moon was his most audacious adventure yet.

Mission Control for the 'new' Apollo 11 launch had been established in the main observation gallery of ERGIA's Space Station. The role-playing weather brokers had been replaced by space technicians moonlighting from jobs at NASA and from the Russian, European and Chinese Space Agencies.

Packed in front of the vast observation window was a crowd of TV correspondents and their crews. A kilometre out in space the Apollo spacecraft now floated in an orbit parallel to that of the ERGIA space station itself. Nicholas Negromonte was not intending to begin his re-enactment mission from *exactly* the same orbit as Armstrong, Aldrin and Collins, but only the most nerdish of space enthusiasts would quibble about that.

The refurbished four-part space vessel had been ferried up to the space station for its final assembly a month before. Externally, the vehicle looked unchanged – except for the ERGIA and LunaSun logos painted on the service module's flanks. Internally, every piece of wiring and every item of plumbing, heating, cooling, sanitary, life-support and systems technology had been brought fully up to the latest standards. Indeed, when Negromonte had originally inspected his purchase he had shuddered and said to his flight director, 'Imagine travelling to the moon in this thing. It's like something Jules Verne dreamed up.'

But no matter how advanced the newly fitted propulsion units, life-support and computer systems were, there remained one obvious problem with the ancient Apollo technology: it provided very little living space. Even though it had been designed to carry three astronauts, its accommodation was still intolerably cramped by modern standards. There had hardly been enough room for the CEO's exercise bicycle.

'We can get you there in less than a day, of course,' the flight director had advised as they had discussed the lack of on-board amenities. Fortunately, modern hydrogen-plasma engines could propel a space vehicle ten times faster than could the unstable chemical fuels used during the early years of space flight.

'No, no, we need the delay to build up tension,' argued Negromonte. 'We'll do it over three days – just like they did back in 1969.'

All was now quiet inside the viewing gallery as the flight controller announced the minus-thirty countdown. Camera lenses that had been focused on the interior of the viewing chamber now swivelled to capture the image of the old spacecraft leaving orbit.

The monitor screens all around the gallery lit with a close-up image of Nick Negromonte strapped into the commander's couch. Realizing that his camera had just gone live, he gave a thumbs-up to all those watching.

'Go for launch,' ordered the flight director, at minus ten seconds.

'Go for launch,' echoed Negromonte. Then, in a departure from the script he added, 'See you on the moon, people.'

'Start engine.'

'Starting engine.' The new Apollo commander leaned forward and touched a button on the main console.

'Five, four, three . . .'

A quarter of a billion TV viewers on Earth witnessed flames spurt from the single large rocket nozzle as the spacecraft blasted out of orbit. What few of them realized was that this rocket plume was merely a visual effect created by specially designed computer-controlled fireworks. As they burned their hydrogen fuel pellets, modern plasma engines emitted only a bright blue column of light that would have been difficult for the television cameras to pick up against the bright blue-and-white background of the Earth.

For over fifty years after first setting foot on the moon, humankind had failed to realize what a vital asset Earth's sole natural satellite presented. It had been the same, perhaps, when the continents of North America and Australia had been discovered. Explorers arrived, identified and named those great empty land masses, and reported back to their own communities, who then did nothing about the new territories for a generation or more. It took time for the collective consciousness to realize how such a significant new asset might be used – and also for economic growth to expand to a point where new opportunities could be properly exploited.

Humanity's first reaction to moon exploration had been one of intense disappointment. After a relay of Americans landed in the late 1960s and early 1970s and reported back that the moon was merely a lifeless lump of barren rock, a dust-covered, crater-scarred, atmosphere-free dead place, no human returned until 2018.

Then, suddenly, the Americans, Russians and Chinese realized, almost simultaneously, that the moon was, in fact, humankind's ideal launch pad for most space exploration. It provided the perfect orbiting base, construction site and maintenance depot for all civilian, industrial and military travel throughout the solar system. Even better, it required no guidance, maintenance, orbital realignment or navigation for itself.

Situated only a quarter of a million miles from the Earth (in terms of the distances of space so close as to be almost touching), the moon provided a stable platform possessing less than one-eighth the gravity of the mother planet as well as ample buried polar ice (providing water and raw hydrogen for rocket fuel) and vast tracts of unclaimed real estate.

With United Nations approval grudgingly extracted, America, Russia and China had invested massive capital sums to create lunar bases, warehouses, vehicle-construction sites and launch pads, all of which were supplied by a never-ending series of unmanned cargo voyages between Earth and its moon. The Europeans had contributed to the moon's development by building three luxury hotels that had become extremely popular with space personnel on extended tours of lunar duty.

Within a decade of this moon-base development beginning in 2024, all maintenance operations for Earth-orbiting satellites, space stations, telescopes and first-generation solar reflectors were being conducted from the lunar surface itself. The cost of lift-off from the moon's low-gravity, zero-atmosphere surface was less than five per cent of the expenditure from hoisting humans and equipment up into orbit from gravity-heavy, atmosphere-dense Earth. For use on the moon, engines could be built that were both small and light.

All voyages to Mars now began and finished on the lunar surface. By the time President James T. Underwood was being ferried up to the moon to open the ERGIA Corporation's vast farm of solar reflectors, over twenty per cent of the Earth-facing side of the satellite was under development.

Michael Fairfax, Emilia Knight and Steve Bardini flew from London to the Jiuquan Space Centre, 1,000 miles west of Beijing, to catch their own ferry ride up to the lunar base. The alternative for them was to re-enter the United States in order to fly from the Kennedy Moon Terminus in Florida, but Michael considered it highly likely that all three of them would be arrested the moment they set foot on US soil.

As for all the other attendees, the BBC had been required to supply their names and identity details to the White House Secret Service for vetting, yet no protest or query had been raised by the presidential security agents. Either their crimes against the state were too minor to register on the White House radar, or the Federal agencies were, as usual, busily embroiled in internecine non-cooperation.

All three travellers had been into space before, the two seismologists having both served tours of duty on Geohazard's orbiting space station while Michael had taken Lucy for a weekend to the StarCenter Earth-orbiting hotel not long after they had been married. Being a cautious man, Michael had put his various affairs in order before he and his companions left for Beijing.

From *Pacifica One*, Council Leader Chanda Zia was able to report that the breakaway convoy of hulk ships had now returned to rejoin the main platform. As he talked, Chanda utilized the camera network that Michael himself had provided to show their legal representative the current conditions within the community.

For all of the massive cruise ship's vast reserves, the food and medicines carried on board the *Global Haven* had not lasted long. But as Zia clicked through the cameras distributed around the luxury vessel, Michael noticed that the *Global Haven* still had electrical power from its hydrogen engines and solar-powered auxiliaries. He also noted that its leisure facilities, swimming pools and gardens were all in constant use, and that the desalination units were all working flat out.

'But the most important thing is that we now have one day of rain guaranteed each week,' said Chanda. As the community leader focused a camera on himself, Michael could see that he was seated in the TV studio aboard the *Global Haven*. 'It means that we can now manage our water supplies properly – or we shall be able to, once the ash from the Indonesian volcano has cleared.'

Michael realized that his client was being too polite to point out that both the scheduled rainfall and their possession of the luxury ship had been gained through the hulk people's direct action rather than by pursuing their legal case.

'We have our first court date set,' he told Chanda. 'March first, next year. We'll need six of you to come to Europe to give evidence in person.'

The small group of Americans arrived in Jiuquan on the evening before their moon ferry was due to depart. They were now easy in each other's company: the tension between the three of them had eased since their hasty escape from the United States a month before.

Without either of them openly declaring their feelings, Michael and Emilia had sought more time alone together. At first they had worried about upsetting Steve but one morning during their stopoff in London the young seismologist had announced, 'I'm going sightseeing now – I know you two would like some time together.' And from that moment on it seemed as if they *had* become a couple.

After the three of them had shared a late supper of superb Szechwan dishes in the Jiuquan Palace, Michael and Emilia took a stroll in the hotel's ornamental gardens. The full moon was in perigee – at its closest point to Earth – vast, gibbous and immediately overhead. It was bathed in a reflected sunlight that revealed in sparkling clarity the mountain ranges and the bruised depressions of its impact craters. Even though the ERGIA resource had not yet been officially opened, its vast farm of solar mirrors was already on-line, shining like a halogen necklace strung around the moon's equator, reflecting enormous quantities of solar energy back down to the Earth.

'Strange to think we'll be up there ourselves tomorrow,' said Emilia softly, as she sat on one of the garden benches. 'It all seems so unreal.'

Michael put his arm around her shoulders. 'I'd like us to visit on our own, one day – sometime when we haven't got such urgent issues on our minds.'

Emilia merely nodded and Michael pulled her closer.

'Isn't it sad, though, that no one's ever going to see the moon in its natural state again?' she observed quietly.

They sat in silence for a few minutes, gazing upwards, each lost in their own thoughts. Then they rose, headed back to the hotel and, exchanging a chaste but warm kiss on the lips, returned to their separate rooms.

NINETEEN

'On behalf of all of the world's peoples, I am proud to rededicate this memorial to the three brave Americans who were the first human beings to land here on the moon.'

In the BBC World television control gallery, executive producer Narinda Damle was himself directing the camera angles to be fed to over 200 partner networks back on Earth.

President James T. Underwood saluted crisply, then stepped forward towards the monument that had been erected inside the Tranquillity Base Visitor Center thirty years earlier. The white, sculpted obelisk had been positioned right beside the highly polished, carefully preserved Lunar Lander that Armstrong and Aldrin had left behind them on the moon's surface in 1969. As he pulled a cord, an engraved gilded plate was revealed, recording this first-ever presidential visit to the moon.

After allowing the main camera to hold this shot for a few seconds, Damle checked the other images he was receiving from external cameras on the moon's surface.

'Camera thirteen,' he instructed the vision mixer.

Against the backdrop of a black, star-studded universe, the rocket exhausts of the refurbished *Eagle*, the Apollo 11's Lunar Module, could clearly be seen. Once again, the flames were cosmetic rather than functional, but the pyrotechnic designers had recreated perfectly the effect of ancient chemical propellants.

Perdy Curtis, seated in the gallery with her boss, had ferried up Magnus Blythe, the BBC's most august world-affairs correspondent, to provide a running commentary for English-speaking audiences around the world. A dozen other anchor people provided voice-overs for viewers in South America, Europe, Asia and Africa. Hardly any of the world's rolling-news networks had declined to pay for this extraterrestrial feed, and it was beginning to seem as if the vast budget allocated for the project by the BBC would self-liquidate even before any repeat fees were taken into account.

Damle cut to an interior close-up of Nick Negromonte's face as he manually controlled the final stages of the *Eagle*'s descent. Sweat had broken out on the pilot's furrowed brow as he struggled with the controls to land in the precise spot dictated by the TV coverage – a manoeuvre proving almost as difficult as the original one undertaken by Neil Armstrong in 1969.

With a final flare of mock retro-rocket fire, Negromonte set the gold-foil-wrapped spacecraft down gently on the lunar surface, only 500 yards from the airlock of the Visitor Center.

'Tranquillity Base here. The *Eagle* has landed,' he radioed.

In Geohazard's seismic monitoring centre in Athens, Dr Giorgio Zaoskoufis gazed up at the wall-screen displaying the events now unfolding on the moon. He knew that Emilia Knight and her friends would be participating later in the live debate and he was keen to see how their warnings would be received.

It was early on a Sunday morning and Giorgio and his two scientific assistants were alone in the facility. Although a seismic monitoring team remained on duty around the clock, Geohazard's admin staff worked normal office hours.

'Excuse me, Doctor Zaoskoufis?' called out Yoyo Kanii, a trainee seismologist on secondment from the Tokyo monitoring centre. She was gazing into a real-time holographic simulation of a deep-sea trench in the eastern Atlantic. 'Should we be seeing this much activity along the edge of the African Plate?'

'I am proud to be here today for the opening of this new LunaSun solar-energy resource.'

James T. Underwood was also very keen to become the first African-American President of the United States to secure a second term in office. His media advisers had assured him that making this trip would enhance the electorate's perception of him as a youthful and daring candidate.

'From today forward the moon will serve all of humankind. The forty-two thousand mirrors on the lunar surface will eliminate the need for street lighting in eighteen of the world's major cities. Applied more creatively, the power captured by LunaSun will bring respite to flooded regions, steer hurricanes and tornadoes away from built-up areas, and bring scheduled rain to those millions of people currently forced to live on floating hulk cities.'

Seated immediately behind the President, Nick Negromonte nodded approvingly.

In the television control gallery, Narinda, Perdy and six technical staff ensured that their live feeds were meeting the needs of all their client broadcasters.

'In a few moments I shall press the button to bring this LunaSun facility officially on-line. But before I do so, I want to say something about those millions of homeless people forced to exist on hulk ships in the southern oceans.'

Damle frowned. This wasn't in the prepared text that he had been given. 'Go to two,' he said. 'And give me a very slow zoom-in on his face.'

'Next week, the United States of America will place a resolution before the United Nations General Assembly calling for all so-called environmental migrants to be reclassified as official environmental *refugees*, with all the same rights to resettlement that political refugees currently enjoy. I shall be asking all the developed countries of the world to play their part in solving what has become our planet's greatest humanitarian problem.'

Nick Negromonte leaped to his feet to initiate the applause, but all around him people were already rising.

In the sixth row of the audience, Michael Fairfax also rose to his feet. As he joined in the clapping, his mind was racing: how would this move affect his case? But, even before the applause died away, he realized that the President had, in fact, offered very little. Bringing a resolution before the UN was no guarantee that its member nations would readily agree to take in the millions who sought resettlement. Judging by all such previous efforts, the initiative would grab headlines at first, then degenerate into an unseemly squabble between nations who would prefer the unfortunate refugees to be accepted anywhere but in their own home territories.

'Ready for the button shot,' Damle alerted, as the President stepped sideways.

'And now, it gives me great pleasure...'

'Coming to you, space station,' said Damle.

'... to declare this LunaSun resource fully operational.'

As the President hit the button, Damle switched broadcast feed to a camera focused on the moon itself from the ERGIA space station, 290,000 kilometres closer to the Earth.

One-point-six billion television viewers watched agog as the moon apparently burst into flame. Thousands of mirrors had turned and flexed in synchronization, reflecting the sun's blazing light back down onto the Earth's night-time surface.

'Los Angeles,' instructed Damle. 'Insert time overlay.'

From the top of the Disney Tower on Wilshire Avenue a camera revealed the dark streets of downtown LA with an overlay caption that read 11.36 p.m. Suddenly the whole scene was bathed in bright white light and there was a faint sound of cheering from the sidewalk down below.

'Honolulu,' said Damle. Then he switched in turn to cameras positioned in Sidney, Tokyo, Singapore and Calcutta.

As ERGIA's perception consultants had organized, hired crowds had gathered in each location to greet the new night sun with what seemed to be outbursts of spontaneous enthusiasm.

It was mid-morning over Morocco and the reaches of the eastern Atlantic as the moon flared into life and, for the first time in its four billion years of existence, became a sibling sun.

But the local populations were not joining in the global celebrations. All along the north-west African littoral, from Casablanca to Dakar, coastal communities were being frantically evacuated. Geohazard Laboratories in Athens had issued a Level 4 tsunami warning – a wave up to three metres high was due to strike the coastline within the next twenty-four hours.

Just under 300 miles out in the Atlantic, the volcano known as Cumbre Vieja, or 'Old Mountain', was beginning an eruption, its first since 1949. Situated on the western flank of Las Palma, the westernmost of the five main islands of the Canaries group, the volcano was likely to pose only a moderate threat to its immediate island neighbours and to the African continent. Any subsequent tsunami would be directed primarily outwards to the west and north, where only the vast expanses of the Atlantic Ocean waited to swallow the mighty wave.

At 11.30 a.m. GMT, Cumbre Vieja erupted explosively, with a force that instantly increased the radius of its main top vent from 200 to 800 metres, ejecting mafic grey pumice at 1.5 million tonnes per second and creating a vertical column of fire that reached twenty-eight kilometres – twice the height of Mount Everest – into the bright morning sky.

The entire western flank of Las Palma island, already weakened by millennia of volcanic activity, collapsed into the Atlantic Ocean, sliding 2,800 metres down the sheer slopes of its underwater mountain. The amount of rock so violently shifted and hurled into the sea was twice the volume of the Isle of Man, or about two-thirds the size of Long Island.

Displaced by this vast landslide, a dome of water 900 metres high and twenty-six kilometres wide reared up and then collapsed, its falling bow creating the first wave in a mighty tsunami train. Travelling at over 500 miles per hour, the eleven-crested mega-tsunami radiated out westwards and northwards, on a never-slowing, non-stop, nine-hour journey to destinations including Cuba, Florida, Virginia, Delaware, New Jersey and New York.

Dr Giorgio Zaoskoufis watched the eruption of Cumbre Vieja in real-time, switching between signals from three different Geohazard satellite cameras as Las Palma's entire western flank collapsed.

Data from sensors on the volcano slopes and the nearby seabed were streaming in by the petabyte to the Athens monitoring centre, all of it confirming what Giorgio already suspected.

Twenty years earlier, he had written his doctoral thesis on mega-tsunamis and the threats that they posed to the world's most densely populated urban communities. He had even modelled a landslide in the Canary Islands as part of his research project.

On the main display screen, every seismic sensor in the eastern Atlantic lit up as the mountain's collapse sent shock waves through the planet's fragile crust. Zaoskoufis shook his head as the introduction to his Ph.D. dissertation came swimming vividly back into his mind: *A tsunami does not behave like a normal wave. To the naked eye, a tsunami moving in deep water is indistinguishable from any other wave. But while normal waves have a length of 150 metres, tsunamis have wavelengths in excess of 100 kilometres. The duration of a normal wave is about ten seconds, while the period of a tsunami is about an hour. Normal waves usually only affect the ocean surface, and are relatively slow. Tsunamis influence the ocean down to its deepest sea floor and can travel at over 700 kilometres per hour – over 420 m.p.h. Unlike normal waves, tsunamis can travel very long distances with almost no diminution of energy.*

But he still found it hard to believe that the rare phenomenon he had once described as part of a dry, academic exercise was now actually happening in real life.

Though seismic activity in the eastern Atlantic fell within the territory monitored by Geohazard Athens, the Caribbean and the east coast of America were the responsibility of the duty officer in Oakland, California. Zaoskoufis realized that every extra minute of warning they could provide to those populations living in the tsunami's path could save thousands of lives.

But he dared not recommend issuing a mega-tsunami warning to the entire eastern seaboard of the United States without being absolutely certain, without having hard data to back up his advice. He would also have to prove his case to his opposite number in Oakland and he – or she – would then have the responsibility for deciding on the timing and the nature of any warning originating from Geohazard.

Leaving his two assistants in charge of the monitoring centre, Zaoskoufis hurried to the Simulation Theater next door, and patched through the data now pouring in from the eastern Atlantic seabed sensors and the 3-D satellite cameras.

Twenty minutes later the geophysicist sat slumped in his holo-pit viewing chair. Frozen in front of him was an image of Manhattan that might have been created by the most maniacal director of disaster movies. The data overlay had predicted a death toll so large that he had paused the simulation and carefully recalculated the core data before running it again and yet again.

There were now just over eight hours until the first crest of the tsunami would reach American soil. He had already alerted Carlos Robredo in California and the Mexican-born seismologist was now busy running a copy of the simulation for himself.

Zaoskoufis opened the connection to Oakland. It was 4.30 a.m. in the Bay Area.

'I woke Taylor Blane up an hour ago,' Robredo informed him. Zaoskoufis understood fully why the local duty officer had felt the need to disturb Geohazard's CEO. 'Blane wanted to inform the President personally, but apparently he's away on the moon, giving some speech. They got the Vice-President out of bed and he's agreed that the White House itself will issue the official warning.'

'What size evacuation zone are you recommending?'

The Greek scientist heard the hesitation in Robredo's voice. 'Twenty miles at sea level. Knock off a mile for every ten yards as the land rises.'

'What about little islands like the Azores, Bermuda or the Bahamas?'

'We can only warn them,' Robredo sighed. 'I know there's not much some of them will be able to do.'

'May God be with them all,' said Zaoskoufis, closing the connection.

He pressed a button providing an intercom link with the main monitoring centre. 'Contact all local Geohazard staff,' he instructed Yoyo Kanii. 'Scientific, support and admin. Inform them about what's happened, tell them that I know it's Sunday afternoon – but they're all needed in here now.'

When he had transmitted his own regional warnings across Europe and dealt with the inevitable follow-up calls of disbelief, Zaoskoufis sprinted back to the monitoring centre. The next twelve hours would be frantic as Geohazard staff all over the world worked together to provide advice and guidance to all the regions affected.

As he came through the door, Zaoskoufis glanced up at one of the overhead screens providing a satellite view of the entire Atlantic ocean. Swirls of white cloud covered its northern part, but a wide central expanse of the ocean was clear.

He stood and stared at the image, reflecting how strange it was that such a vast menace could be travelling through the open sea at 500 miles per hour without leaving any visible trace of its passing.

President Underwood's keynote speech had overrun badly and it was already causing scheduling chaos up in the TV gallery. But nobody had been prepared to cut off the President of the United States in mid-flow.

'This is why I *hate* directing live television,' groaned Narinda Damle as he received a revised set of timings.

Immediately before the debate itself, Perdy's documentary had aired. She had tried to take a balanced approach, explaining the obvious benefits of climate management whilst giving its opponents an opportunity to voice their objections. It was now, in this live debate, that the various protagonists could flesh out their arguments. There was still a huge worldwide audience tuned in.

'Who's up next?' asked Damle, before instructing his camera operators to focus on audience applause at the end of Negromonte's speech.

'Fairfax – the lawyer,' said Perdy. 'But he's furious that we've had to cut out the computer simulation that he had lined up.'

'Too bad,' snapped Damle, sounding delighted that others were suffering too.

'Go to Fairfax in chair eight,' he told camera four.

For the sake of diplomatic protocol, Perdy had allowed the politicians to speak first but, following Underwood's verbose overrun, each had been told to keep their contribution to a minimum. That had proved to be a contradiction too far; politicians and brevity had proved mutually incompatible.

Now the schedule was running fourteen minutes late and Perdy doubted whether she could include either the spokesperson for the Friends of the Earth or the Archbishop of Boston, both of whom were waiting expectantly in their seats.

'There are five main forces governing our universe,' explained Michael as he began delivering his hastily cut-down speech. 'The first is gravity, which holds our planet, our populations and our solar system together. The second and third are the strong and weak nuclear forces which hold the atomic constituents together. The fourth is the electromagnetic force which binds matter itself, and which counter-balances the fifth component: light and all other forms of radiation. These are the fundamental forces of nature, the fabric of our universe, and we tamper with them at our peril.'

'Look at that, Perdy,' said Narinda Damle, pointing to a gallery monitor.

A presidential aide had climbed onto the stage and was scooting along behind the row of chairs in a half-crouch.

'. . . But reflective climate management is now interfering with the magnetic forces that . . .'

'Camera six, go closer in on that running man.' Damle switched the global broadcast feed away from Michael Fairfax and onto the aide now whispering in the President's ear. 'Give me a close-up on the President's face.'

The world watched bemused as President James T. Underwood attempted to digest whatever news was being mouthed into his ear. He was struggling to keep his face impassive, but every viewer realized that whatever he had just been told couldn't be good news. In fact, the President's face wore a look of absolute horror.

By four p.m. Giorgio Zaoskoufis had applied the incoming data from the Atlantic seabed sensors to model and measure the volume of rock that had fallen into the Atlantic, the speed at which the displaced water was now moving westwards, and the overall span of the mega-tsunami. He displayed the results on his main screen.

Current span: 1,861km
Projected crest height at landfall: 50.2m
Volume: 500km³
Speed: 100 m/s⁻¹

Below, the geophysicist had listed the data he would provide to his own clients in London, Dublin, Lisbon and Paris, and to Geohazard in Oakland for distribution onwards to US and Caribbean government agencies. This included the tsunami's estimated arrival times in the Azores, Bermuda, Puerto Rico, the islands of the Greater Antilles, Cuba and the eleven states lining the eastern seaboard of the United States, from Florida up to Maine.

Embedded in all this top-level data were regional timing variations, allowances for local sea conditions, estimates of the extent of coastal ingress, impact force, timings of secondary tsunami landfalls, volumes of water per square kilometre, and a hundred other parameters that would be needed by emergency planners in these projected disaster areas.

'Aircraft leaving the Azores,' announced Yoyo Kanii, switching the long-range satellite image up to the main wall-screen.

A large military transport plane had just taken off, and they could see a score of other large planes taxiing into position on the airfield.

'How many people live on those islands?' asked Yoyo.

'About a quarter of a million – as of last year,' said Zaoskoufis. In the last hour he had refreshed his memory of all population figures in the zones to be affected.

'They won't be able to accommodate them *all* in those planes,' gasped the Japanese trainee, her hand to her mouth.

'There's plenty of high ground on all the Azores islands,' Zaoskoufis reassured her. 'They've had over an hour now to get away from the low-lying areas.' He pulled the Azores data back onto the screen as an overlay.

'Fifteen minutes to landfall,' he announced. 'Let's see if any of the news channels are broadcasting live from there.' He flicked up CNN, but Michael Fairfax's earnest face still filled the screen.

TWENTY

On direct orders from the White House, at 8.13 a.m. EST the Federal Emergency Management Agency issued a mandatory evacuation order for the entire eastern seaboard of the United States. Time was of the essence. The first crest of the mega-tsunami was expected ashore in less than eight hours.

In years gone by, the residents of Florida, Georgia and the Carolinas had been well used to fleeing from Caribbean hurricanes and tropical storms, but climate-management services had been successfully steering such disasters away from American coasts for over twenty years. As a result, few residents in the southern littoral states were prepared for this sudden migration.

But civic evacuation plans were still in place and by nine a.m. highways had been turned into one-way arteries heading westwards and twenty-two million people were now on the move. Thirty miles inland, the army was starting to convert schools, town halls, leisure facilities and shopping malls into temporary reception centres.

In the northern states of Massachusetts, New Hampshire and Maine, as well as in the Canadian territory of Nova Scotia, coastal residents were also able to head inland in long streams of orderly one-way traffic. Helicopters circled overhead on the lookout for breakdowns while police motorcyclists on the ground were ready to deal with any incidents of panic or road rage. Army trucks, Civil Defense units and the National Guard went to hospitals and retirement homes to evacuate those who were unable to move themselves to safety.

The main problems, everyone realized, were going to occur

on Long Island and in New York City itself. Over three and a half million people lived on Long Island, but of the seven bridges serving the island's western tip, only three, in the north, connected directly with the mainland. Another three spanned the East River to Manhattan while one crossed Lower New York Bay to Staten Island.

Six car-ferry services – together operating twenty-two vessels – ran between the island's northern shore and the Connecticut coast, but each one-way journey would take over an hour. Long Island was surrounded by marinas, however, and boat owners on the northern side of the island started to weigh up whether they stood a better chance of getting to safety by sea or by road.

Thirty minutes after the evacuation order was first broadcast, Long Island's six main east-west highways were blocked for a distance of over twenty miles – backed up through Kings County, Queens and Nassau. Police hurried traffic across the bridges to the mainland, but many other fleeing residents were forced to take the tunnel and bridges that led directly *into* Manhattan.

John F. Kennedy International Airport, low-lying and right on the southern coastline of Long Island, was besieged by people hoping to find a seat out on any available plane. Heavily armed police formed cordons around the departure terminals, allowing only ticket-holders through. But the air-traffic control computer systems could not cope with the vastly increased workload as they diverted planes already on final approach, gave clearance to scheduled flights attempting to depart, and tried to cope with the hundreds of business, cargo and private pilots who had scrambled to their planes and were now demanding immediate clearance for take-off.

By default, the computers prioritized runway time and immediate-vicinity air space according to the published schedules. As a result, the departure waiting list grew so long that many of the private pilots sitting waiting with family and friends in warmed-up aircraft were allotted take-off slots falling minutes or even hours after the tsunami was due to strike.

Ten miles to the north, LaGuardia Airport suffered a similar

inundation by would-be evacuees hoping to get off the island.
But the far larger number of private aircraft parked or hangared
at this domestic airport produced chaos on the apron as many
pilots chose to ignore the frantically issued orders from the
control tower and began unauthorized take-offs over the grass.
At one point, private planes were making take-off runs at six
abreast, like successive waves of Second World War fighter
squadrons. Their erratic dispersal into the surrounding skies
brought all scheduled departures to a halt.

Initially, things in Manhattan itself were slightly more
orderly. Unlike some other coastal regions of the United States,
New York City had well-developed plans for civic escape and
evacuation. As the world's most tempting urban target for
terrorist attack, successive mayoral administrations had developed multiple contingency plans to deal with aircraft crashes,
biohazard contamination, radiological attacks, dirty bombs, and
even the explosion of portable nuclear weapons within the
confines of the island city.

Every Manhattan resident was officially issued with a survival
pack and the necessary basic equipment to help them cope in
such a crisis. All around the main island, evacuation zones were
clearly lettered, colour-coded and numbered, the street signs
painted accordingly. Theoretically, there was not one adult living
in the city who did not know where he or she should report to
once an order to leave was given.

But none of these disaster plans, nor the emergency-response
drills staged regularly by police, firefighters and medical teams
could have anticipated that one day the *whole* of Manhattan
would have to be evacuated simultaneously.

At the start of the process, the carefully devised procedures
worked remarkably well. The island's six million residents
quickly began reporting to their designated evacuation areas
wearing warm clothes and sneakers, carrying water, communicators and ready cash. Many carried concealed firearms.

But those on the eastern side quickly realized that their
designated escape routes would only take them closer to the
oncoming threat. First in small groups, then in larger packs, they
began to run the three miles westwards across Manhattan.

On the western flank of the island, tens of thousands were already driving or walking through the Holland and Lincoln tunnels, or to the north, over the George Washington bridge. But only a comparatively small percentage of Manhattanites owned cars. During the first twenty minutes of the evacuation, all 18,000 licensed taxis and 6,000 municipal buses had been commandeered by individuals brandishing either fistfuls of cash or handguns.

All available ferries were packed within minutes. For fear of overloading, some skippers cast off before all the desperately clambering passengers were safely aboard, leaving many still clinging to the boarding rails as the vessels pulled away. As they watched the overladen ferries depart from the Battery terminus and from various quays, jetties and piers along the shoreline of the Hudson River, the crowds still waiting on the island realized that few, if any, of these ships were likely to return.

Meanwhile, skippers of larger boats and commercial vessels prepared to put to sea with the intention of riding out the tsunami in open water, where the wave would do less harm.

Thousands of citizens stuck in midtown's Westside broke down the turnstiles at Pier 86 and streamed up the gangways onto USS *Intrepid*, the Second World War aircraft carrier that had served the city as a floating museum for over half a century. Most of them realized that the old carrier was no longer seaworthy but they hoped such a huge vessel might be able to ride out the onrushing deluge.

From rooftops and landing zones all over the city, hundreds of helicopters rose into the air, carrying those rich enough to possess or command such expensive forms of transport. Seventeen seaplanes managed to take off successfully from the East River Skyport, but six others were sunk by clambering, panicking hordes who fought each other to cling on to the plane's pontoons even while their pilots were trying frantically to get them into the air.

Hundreds of hopelessly overloaded small boats set off from the Manhattan Yacht Club and from the dozen other superexpensive marinas dotted around the island. Some of their skippers headed towards Richmond County or Jersey; others headed out to sea in the hope that they too could ride out the approaching surge.

Below ground, subway stations were so densely packed by people hoping to catch trains leaving the island that those standing on the edges of the platform found themselves remorselessly pressed forward until they fell onto the tracks, like coins on the ledge of a funfair slot machine. Though PA announcements kept repeating the message that all train services had been suspended, these could not be heard above the desperate screaming.

The 30,000 homeless people who lived on the city's streets didn't care much either way. They were simply pleased that there was so much alcohol and food available to them in all the abandoned restaurants, bars, hotels and stores.

'I know climate management has brought many benefits to our planet,' continued Michael Fairfax hurriedly. 'But what I have to say now is of the gravest importance to all of our futures.'

In the gallery, Narinda Damle was watching an off-line image of a group of presidential aides now gathered in a close huddle to one side of the main platform.

'It looks like they're going to have another word with him,' Perdy observed, over his shoulder. 'But go closer in on the lawyer – he's just coming to the important bit.'

Damle nodded to the vision mixer and returned his own attention to the current speaker.

'Some of the most distinguished experts in the world are now concluding that unbridled use of reflected solar energy could disrupt the Earth's magnetic fields. This . . .'

'He *is* coming back,' hissed Damle as the presidential aide jumped back onto the stage. 'Six, follow him.'

The aide ran at a crouch behind the row of speakers' chairs. When he reached his boss, he stopped and spoke in the American leader's ear again.

Though Michael's words were still being broadcast, the viewers were now once more watching Underwood's face as he reacted to what his administrative assistant was saying.

After a moment, the President rose abruptly to his feet and walked quickly off stage.

'Follow him,' Damle shouted to his various camera operators.

'Narinda, we're losing our client networks,' announced production assistant, Liam Burns. 'Eighteen of them have dropped our feed just in the last thirty seconds.'

The Azores had been thrust up in the middle of the Atlantic sometime between the Cretaceous and Cenozoic periods, making them among the most recent outcrops of land to emerge on the surface of the Earth. These nine islands sat precisely on the intersection of the European, African and American tectonic plates, and were home to 260,000 people.

Two hours after the Cumbre Vieja eruption and landslide, Giorgio Zaoskoufis and his entire staff braced themselves to observe the moment of impact as the mega-tsunami raced towards its first landfall at almost 500 miles per hour. Now their instruments and cameras would be able to measure the real force propelling the series of giant waves.

Via their geostationary satellites, the monitoring team in Athens had a clear view of the cloud-free mid-Atlantic. Although no large rift in the surface of the ocean was visible to the naked eye, their computers tracked the eleven crests of the tsunamis in dotted red outline as they advanced on the archipelago.

By now the 24-hour rolling-news channels had got themselves organized, and all were broadcasting live feeds from video cameras dotted around the islands.

'Looks like most of the inhabitants got to high ground,' Zaoskoufis sighed with relief as he gazed up at a monitoring screen. The TV director cut quickly between locations around the stricken islands, before returning to a camera left behind on a beach to record the precise moment of impact.

Suddenly the Geohazard team could see the previously level ocean rear up, as the giant bulge of fast-travelling water hit the undersea flank of Santa Maria – the most easterly island of the Azores. They could clearly hear a low roaring as the giant wave began to break.

'That thing must be at least twenty metres high already,' Zaoskoufis murmured to Yoyo Kanii.

'Twenty-three point six,' she confirmed, monitoring the incoming data flow.

As the first of the multiple tsunamis hit, the CNN director cut quickly between the cameras capturing images of boats being flung ashore, buildings being swept away, and the ocean seeming to change the entire scale of its surroundings – as if viewers were now observing a storm being simulated with models in a movie-studio tank.

'It's now fifty-three metres at its highest point,' announced Yoyo.

Zaoskoufis leaned in to the control panel and turned up the sound as CNN cut to an eyewitness account.

'I think we got almost everybody safely up to higher ground,' an American air-force sergeant shouted into a hand-held mike. In the background could be heard a continuous dull roar, like a stream of supersonic aircraft taking off one after the other. A high wind tugged at the sergeant's uniform as he spoke. 'But most of the town itself seems to have disappeared.'

All along the eastern seaboard of the United States, those residents who were monitoring the news channels understood for the first time the scale of the phenomenon that was now heading for their own shores.

In a small ante-room beside the LunaSun meeting hall, President James Underwood was issuing a direct order to his Vice-President back in Washington.

'Get out of the White House now, Boyne. Fly to Cheyenne Mountain immediately.'

'With respect, sir, I'd like to make sure DC is fully evacuated before I leave myself,' insisted Boyne Leander firmly.

Underwood glanced across at his group of aides; all were busy on communicators speaking to various parts of the Washington administration.

'How long before we've got the population out of DC?' Underwood demanded.

'Another three to four hours, Mister President,' said Carson Jonas, senior home affairs adviser.

'And how long until this giant wave hits?'

'About six hours, sir, allowing for the time it takes to come inland.'

'OK, Boyne,' said the President. 'Stay on for another hour, but get yourself out in good time. We need you in a safe place.'

'It seems as if *you*'re in the safest place, Mister President,' said his deputy.

'Sir?' intervened Carson Jonas as his boss closed the connection with the White House. 'This is Dr Emilia Knight. She's with Geohazard.'

Even under such highly stressful circumstances Underwood still managed to deliver one of his famously warm smiles as he shook her hand.

'I'm sorry we have to meet in this way, Doctor Knight,' he began, 'but I need your help. I have to commandeer that TV set-up outside within the next few minutes and tell the American people what's really going to happen with this tsunami. It's a terrible time for me to be away from my office.'

'Well, I don't know too much myself yet,' Emilia told him. 'But once a tsunami starts rolling the only thing that will stop it is when it comes ashore on dry land.'

'You mean there's no solution to it – I mean, dropping bombs or using energy beams wouldn't slow it down or anything?'

'Not if it's as big as I've just been informed, sir. In itself, it's thousands of times more powerful than any nuclear weapon.'

The President nodded grimly and sank slowly into a chair, the moon's low gravity making his slow movement seem almost balletic. 'How bad is it going to get when it comes ashore?'

'If you can give me just ten minutes, I'll provide you with a full assessment, sir,' Emilia told him. 'I just need to confer with my colleagues down on Earth.'

'Couldn't we slow down this wave by directing high winds against it?' suggested the President.

*

Michael Fairfax was now coming to the end of his cut-down opening statement.

Up in the gallery, an assistant producer was hissing at his boss, 'Narinda ... Narinda.'

Damle turned away from the main monitors. 'What?' he demanded irritably.

'I've got London on the line for you.'

As the AP patched through the call from BBC headquarters, Damle listened intently, shook his head, barked 'When?', then nodded. He slipped off his headphones and stood up slowly.

'We're off the air,' he announced to everybody in the gallery. 'There's some tidal wave crossing the Atlantic. It's so big that nobody wants to take our feed any more.'

Behind him, monitors showed Michael Fairfax still making his closing remarks.

Damle pressed a button on the console that allowed him to talk to all his technical staff. 'We're off the air, people. Another volcanic eruption or something back on Earth. Thank you, everyone.'

One by one the monitors went black.

'Have we still got a broadcast feed from London?' asked Perdy, turning to an assistant.

As all of the screens relit with the signal currently being transmitted from the Earth by BBC World, they saw a view of Manhattan taken from a helicopter. Then the transmission cut to a female reporter on board the chopper.

'This is Aurora Templeton of MSN New York,' the blonde woman shouted into a microphone over the din of the helicopter blades. 'So far it is estimated that over two million people have managed to escape from the city.' A camera beneath the aircraft then zoomed in on the broad spans of the George Washington Bridge, revealing a solid mass of vehicles and pedestrians heading westwards.

As the helicopter circled to head south down the Hudson River, the water seemed strewn with small craft making for the Jersey shore. With a long, slow movement the camera telescoped in on one small speck in the middle of the river. As the image enlarged it was possible to make out three men using planks of wood to paddle a large industrial-waste bin westwards in a crooked line. The camera swept on downriver to focus on a half-filled dumpster that a dozen men were also attempting to propel across the choppy water.

All along the length of the wide river that separated Manhattan from the mainland it seemed that fleeing residents were using bathtubs, doors, packing crates and wooden pallets as makeshift rafts. The camera even found a flotilla of six coffins being paddled hard towards the western bank as the staff from a funeral home desperately made their escape.

'Our pilot is now going to drop me off in Central Park,' announced Aurora Templeton, 'so that I can report on the evacuation at ground level.'

Suddenly the transmission from New York was replaced with an aerial view of Washington DC, the Capitol and the long Mall looking peaceful yet imposing in the early afternoon sun. But as the helicopter's camera panned down onto Pennsylvania Avenue, it became clear that every highway was blocked by vehicles.

'Although the nation's capital lies one hundred miles inland, Washington is bracing itself for serious flooding,' said an unseen male commentator. 'The Potomac surge is expected to cause incursions up to twenty feet deep.'

Meanwhile, in the LunaSun meeting hall, the debate was clearly at an end. The TV lamps had been switched off and normal lighting restored. Michael Fairfax and Steve Bardini stood together, watching the BBC World pictures that were now patched to monitors suspended around the room.

'They can't possibly get everyone evacuated in time,' Michael commented sadly as the news cut from location to location along America's East Coast.

'No one ever sees seismic activity as a real threat until it happens,' Steve murmured. 'Fifty years ago scientists warned that one day the Canary Islands might collapse, but nobody gave it any real thought.'

Just like San Francisco, Michael reflected. He had been brought up knowing that he was living in one of the world's most unstable areas, but what had he personally done about it?

He'd brought a wife to that city and started raising children there. Humans couldn't quite relate to the vagaries of an impersonal planet, it seemed.

'How're you doing, guys?' asked Emilia, arriving by their side. 'I've just had a discussion with Giorgio in Athens – then I had to brief the President, would you believe?'

'What's the forecast?' asked Steve.

'It will hit the Caribbean in about three hours and the East Coast ten minutes later,' said Emilia, shaking her head. 'Main crest is predicted to be fifty-three metres high, followed by ten secondary crests each between eight and twelve metres. Explosive force for the first five miles inland, then total submerge for another twenty. Serious flooding up to one hundred miles inland, depending on land elevation.'

'And that's what you told the President?' asked Michael.

Emilia nodded, then shook her head again at the thought. Michael reached out and put an arm round her shoulders.

'Negromonte's just switched the moon reflectors up to full power,' she added, shooting a worried glance at her companions. 'He's also directing everything else they have down onto the Western Atlantic. They're trying to create a hurricane to slow this tsunami down.'

All resources in Geohazard's monitoring centres in Athens, Oakland and Tokyo were now tasked to track the Atlantic tsunami. Over 600 sensors scattered across the Atlantic seabed, on dry land and in space constantly measured the force, depth, height and length of the mighty surge as it raced westwards towards North America. Estimates about its time, point and force of impact were being updated in real-time, while over 200 Geohazard staff fielded media enquiries and provided data to governments and local emergency services.

In Athens, the responsibility for public pronouncements had just been handed over to Oakland, allowing Giorgio Zaoskoufis finally to find time for a cup of coffee.

'Time for you to take a break now, Yoyo.' Zaoskoufis laid a

hand on the trainee's shoulder. Like himself, she had been working in front of the monitoring screens without respite for over four hours.

As Yoyo rose to her feet, a shrill alarm sounded. Zaoskoufis frowned, then leaned in to kill the alert. Taking Yoyo's chair, he patched the source of the alarm to the central screen.

Another volcano in the Javanese chain was rapidly building up pressure. As Zaoskoufis enlarged the data, the alarm shrilled yet again and a second red circle appeared – around another volcano sixty miles to the east.

Zaoskoufis checked that Tokyo was aware of the alarms, but no sooner had he finished speaking to the local officer on duty than a third volcano in the Javanese chain – which totalled a string of over eighty volcanic peaks – triggered a further warning.

'It looks like the whole plate abutment is splitting open,' Zaoskoufis told Yoyo. 'It's like a chain reaction.'

TWENTY-ONE

The US President stood with the leaders and representatives from the EU, Asian, Australasian, African and South American governments, gazing up at one of the dozen panoramic screens.

Costa Rica, the eastern half of Cuba, the Greater Antilles chain and Bermuda had all now been overrun by the mega-tsunami. There were no estimates yet of the death toll.

Images broadcast from along the tsunami's path showed the huge wall of water sweeping ashore, dwarfing all buildings as it raced inland on its relentless journey. Behind this first giant wave, the following ten surges forced the brutal incursion onwards, maintaining its height and murderous velocity.

On the larger islands, millions who had found higher ground owed their lives to Geohazard's advance warning. But this seemed of little comfort to those watching from the moon. They stood together in near silence as they witnessed the epic orgy of destruction taking place on their home planet.

As it travelled westwards, the radial arc of the tsunami lengthened to over 1,600 miles and a devastating landfall on the USA's East Coast was now predicted to occur all the way from the Florida Keys in the south to Cap Cod in the north. At either extremity of this sweep, the height and strength of the wave-train would be weaker than in the centre, but the midpoint fell between the 40th and 41st parallels – the latitude of New Jersey, Long Island, Manhattan and the State of New York.

President James Underwood had used the BBC's lunar broad-cast facilities to make a short emergency address to the American people. He had urged them to remain calm, to show their patriotism by assisting their neighbours to safety, to refrain from looting, to cooperate with the military and all emergency authorities and to remain tuned in to their local TV and radio stations. He had also told them that he bitterly regretted being caught so far away from home at this time of national crisis. He had concluded, 'May God's blessing be upon you all.'

But, as camera shots now revealed, many US citizens were ignoring their President's appeal. In Manhattan, the wailing of multiple emergency vehicle sirens filled the air and running gangs could be seen looting shops, hotels and offices. While all the bridges and tunnels out of the mighty city were still blocked by traffic jams and pedestrian hordes trudging westwards, a significant number of New Yorkers appeared to see this emergency as a wonderful opportunity for self-enrichment.

Nicholas Negromonte had immediately set about attempting to create an Atlantic hurricane that might slow down the megatsunami. But there were problems associated with this strategy.

'Because so little of a tsunami sits up while it's moving through open water, the wind has minimal effect on it,' Emilia Knight had explained to the group of the world's leaders.

'But as soon as the tsunami starts to rise landwards, it would, wouldn't it?' the US President had countered.

'But that would mean creating a hurricane right on the shoreline,' she had objected. 'You'd just be creating one potential disaster in an attempt to prevent another.'

'But a hurricane's preferable to a tsunami, isn't it?' Underwood had reasoned, grasping at straws.

Though they'd had to concede that the President was right, Nick Negromonte had identified a further problem.

'It normally takes weeks for us to build up the sort of atmospheric pressure capable of creating a storm cyclone. Climate engineering isn't an instant process.'

'But you've got all *this* up and running now,' the President had objected, waving an arm vaguely in the direction of the moon's vast solar farm.

In response, Negromonte had ordered the moon's new solar resources to be reprogrammed and switched up to full power to join the other ERGIA space stations and satellites in their ongoing efforts to create an anticyclone directly in the path of the mega-tsunami.

Now, almost four hours later, Negromonte saw on the screens that he had indeed created an Atlantic storm in record time. Even without the private information pouring into his earpiece from his executive operations officer on board the ERGIA Space Station, he could see that the millions of computer-controlled applications of spot heat and cold were inverting the tides of the atmosphere, boosting upswings of warm air to funnel upwards in anabatic columns towards the upper atmosphere, and suddenly pushing cold air down to take its place. The atmospheric chaos that followed was already producing winds of over forty miles an hour and filling the skies off the American East Coast with violent thunder and lightning.

Suddenly there was an involuntary gasp from everybody in the meeting hall: BBC World headquarters in London had decided to add a caption overlay to the picture.

TIME TO NEW YORK IMPACT: 30.00 MINUTES

*

At first, Dr Giorgio Zaoskoufis wondered if Geohazard's international computer network was under attack from hackers. Then he thought that there might be a serious virus infecting the system. Only after speaking with the company's global IT manager in Houston, Texas, did he finally begin to accept that his bizarre data displays were accurate.

In the last hour, every one of his warning boards had lit up with alarms – not just alerts from his own region of the planet but from seismic sensors all over the world. It had started with the chain of eighty Javanese volcanoes – the so-called Indonesian 'ring of fire'. At first Giorgio Zaoskoufis had abandoned monitoring the Atlantic tsunami just to help his Tokyo colleagues get warnings out to the many nations who would be affected by this chain reaction of eruptions in South-East Asia. But he was constantly interrupted by further alarms as sensors, strain gauges and satellite cameras detected additional abnormal seismic build-ups in his local region and elsewhere.

Vesuvius seemed ready to erupt for the second time within three months, and Mount Etna – a seldom-quiescent sister volcano – also appeared to be building up for something quite spectacular.

In Los Angeles, sensors along the southern branches of the San Andreas Fault clearly indicated that the abutment of the North American and Pacific tectonic plates was preparing for a major realignment in the Long Beach area. Even while Geohazard's network was sampling alarming recordings of tremors cascading in from Southern California, yet another alarm sounded as strain gauges in Mexico City started to suggest that the Cocos Plate – the most active subduction thrust fault in the western hemisphere – was once again threatening to burrow further beneath its neighbour.

At that moment, Yoyo Kanii ran over to ask her boss to interpret a new warning just arrived from Tokyo. The famous Mount Fuji, the volcano dominating the city's skyline, was also producing vibrations from deep underground that suggested it too was getting ready to erupt for the first time since 1708.

Zaoskoufis turned off all audible alarm systems and slowly stood up.

'My family live in Tokyo,' said Yoyo quietly.

The senior seismologist glanced at her pale, frightened face, then up at the large world map on the central screen. Red lights were flickering on land masses everywhere – illuminating almost every volcanic chain and every earthquake fault line. He leaned across and touched the controls, adding a transparent overlay of a seismic bathymetry map of the world's ocean floors.

Underwater sensors laid a decade earlier along the World Ridge System, the 50,000 kilometre chain of underwater volcanoes that girdled the entire globe and fed the oceans with heat and minerals, were all – *all* 8,959 chimneys and fumaroles – simultaneously triggering alarms as magma-venting levels scaled up towards major eruptions.

*

Manhattan's unique personality had been shaped largely by its architecture. The densely populated high-rise buildings created a formicating community, like scurrying ants – alive, vital, teeming: the fastest place on earth.

But environmental risk had been poorly understood at the time when local topography and economic logic had dictated how Manhattan's architecture would develop. Only after the first terrorist attacks of the early twenty-first century did social planners realize that the corollary of economic clustering was physical vulnerability.

On the afternoon of 21 October 2055, the city was to learn that an island of high-rise architecture, laid out in a formal grid, was also particularly susceptible to natural disaster.

'. . . Downtown Manhattan is now a ghost city waiting for the tsunami to arrive. This is Aurora Templeton for MSN in Central Park, New York.' The famous anchorwoman signed off, her cameraman ceased transmitting and then switched off his floodlight.

'Get us out of here,' shouted their soundman into his walkie-talkie, craning his neck and beckoning the hovering news helicopter back down for a landing.

The eight-seater Cougar Commander circled and touched down on the grass 200 yards away. But as Aurora and her MSN crew sprinted towards their aircraft, they saw figures emerging from the surrounding bushes, figures that were also starting to run towards the helicopter.

Aurora reached the open side-door of the Cougar and felt a powerful hand from behind thrust her up into the cabin. She turned back to help her crew aboard, but saw that a score of desperate men and women had now reached the helicopter. They were clinging on to the aircraft's bodywork and skids, determined to hitch a ride out of the endangered city.

The pilot abruptly increased engine power and yanked upwards on his collective control. The helicopter's engine bellowed, and the whole aircraft shuddered and rose a few feet off the ground. But more desperate people had appeared from the dense undergrowth around the park's open area and they were now clinging on to the legs of those who had found a handhold on the aircraft itself.

Panicked, the pilot increased engine power and rotor angle to the maximum, but the hovering helicopter was being dragged inexorably downwards.

Aurora felt one hand grasp at her jeans-clad leg, then another. Although she had managed to fasten a belt around her waist, she could feel herself being pulled out of her seat.

Suddenly, a group of four men who were clinging on to the right-hand side of the helicopter lost their collective grip and fell from the skid to the ground below. Unbalanced on one side, the aircraft tipped violently to the left and its rotor blades churned up the grass of Central Park until they broke off and scythed through the bodies of eleven would-be evacuees still clinging to the now-capsizing Cougar.

Then, as a piece of splintered rotor blade slashed through a fuel supply line above the engine, the helicopter exploded in a ball of flame.

Efforts to weaken the force of the mega-tsunami by generating hurricane-force winds close to the shoreline had failed. Overhead, dark storm clouds swirled, lightning flashed and gales swept the coast. But the storm had not yet had enough time to build up to cyclone levels. To add to the problem, the first of the giant tsunamis only began rearing up above normal sea level when it was within less than ten miles of the shore. The strong winds that had been artificially generated in such a hurry had only seventy seconds in which to combat the speed and fury of the oncoming wall of water. They slowed it down by only twenty-seven miles per hour.

The mega-tsunami made its first landfall on American soil in southern Florida. Waves over twenty metres high came ashore at a speed of 409 miles per hour, instantly wrecking all shipping and coastal buildings. Thrust forward by the following surges, the water raced inland across a largely flat terrain, to link up with the Everglades and Lake Okeechobee, completely destroying the coastal cities of Miami, Hollywood, Fort Lauderdale and West Palm Beach. The entire southern tip of Florida, extending over 1,000 square miles, was completely submerged within the first twenty minutes.

Further north, the waters reared over the city of Daytona Beach, then engulfed Cape Canaveral, the former Kennedy Space Centre and the new Moon Ferry Terminus built on Merritt Island. As the distinguished visitors to the moon stood watching the broadcast images, they groaned as one when the wall of water hurled itself across the runways and hangars, destroying everything in its path. Most of them had started their journeys in Florida but now they realized that they would have to return to Earth via the alternative Moon Ferry terminals in Russia or China.

Six minutes later the mega-tsunami hit the southern coast of Long Island at a speed of 481.8 miles per hour and almost simultaneously surged into Lower New York Bay and the Hudson River. At that speed, the water hit with an impact as hard as concrete.

The Statue of Liberty was knocked off its perch and disappeared into a cloud of white foam, as quickly as if it had been caught in the path of a thermonuclear blast. The old buildings clustered at the southern tip of Manhattan seemed to disintegrate like children's sandcastles as a fifty-foot-high embankment of water shot onto the land with the velocity of a subsonic jet plane.

The long, straight streets of the city funnelled the water skywards, forcing it to climb to over 600 feet as it was propelled onwards by ten pursuing surges.

The waters of the Hudson and East Rivers themselves reared backwards, as if in alarm, when bores as high as forty-storey buildings rushed upstream, sweeping out westwards, drowning Staten Island and New Jersey. The USS *Intrepid* was wrenched from the security of her thirty enormous mooring chains, flipped over onto her belly and smashed into six pieces, which were then rolled seven miles north before finally being deposited across Westchester County.

In Manhattan itself the streets became high-sided canyons through which super-scale rapids plunged and swirled around any smaller buildings, as if around rocks in a mountain cataract.

Over forty circling helicopters kept transmitting pictures that suggested some of the newer major high-rise buildings might withstand the enormous pressure as billions of tons of Atlantic sea water were jet-hosed through the city streets.

Glass panes caved in as the deluge rushed amongst the skyscrapers, leaving them open skeletons right up to their forti-eth floors.

Despite the black storm raging overhead, thousands were gathered on the flat roofs of high-rise offices and residential buildings, hoping that the higher up they were the safer they would be.

Many newer buildings did successfully withstand the initial impact. But as successive surges followed the initial crest, it became clear that the tsunami was carrying so much metal and stone debris in its broiling wake that serious structural damage was being caused below the churning white surface of this metropolitan maelstrom. One by one, buildings started to collapse.

All subways, tunnels and basements had been instantly flooded. By the time the advance surge reached 44th Street, the close-packed urban topography had slowed its progress down to 243 m.p.h. By the time it reached 118th Street, it was crawling at 147.

In the 92nd Street Y, thirty-one weighted-down scuba divers sat on the bottom of the swimming pool, repeatedly popping their eardrums as the water pressure surrounding them con-tinued to rise abruptly. Then corpses started to drift down to join them in their pool.

After an initial collective gasp, the moon visitors had stood watching Manhattan's destruction in a deepening and dreadful silence. Forty minutes later, the tide had lowered sufficiently for all of them to see that almost no building had survived right up to a point just north of Central Park. Here and there steel armatures poked up out of the still-raging seas, but they were totally impossible to identify.

Only minutes before the Atlantic had struck, huge masses of people had been seen fleeing through the city streets or tramping across bridges. Now there were no bridges left – all traces of them had been washed away. It was impossible to tell what was Manhattan, Long Island or New Jersey, or precisely where they lay under so much water.

At the back of the hall Nicholas Negromonte stood in grim-faced silence. 'Shut down all of our climate-management systems,' he finally ordered.

Giorgio Zaoskoufis thanked all of the admin and support staff who had returned to work in the Athens monitoring centre. He set them to work fielding the vast number of requests for guidance streaming in.

'Don't waste time talking to journalists,' he shouted above the din of the crowded room. 'Just concentrate on getting the latest updates out to the emergency services.'

In the last eighteen hours over 400 major seismic incidents had begun or were threatening in the European-African sector alone. Zaoskoufis also knew that similar scenes were being repeated in Geohazard's Oakland and Tokyo facilities as cata-strophic disturbances within the Earth's crust had started to appear around all of the planet's fault lines, volcanic chains, underwater rifts and tectonic-plate intersections.

As predicted, both Etna and Vesuvius were currently engaged in full-scale eruptions, while Stromboli and forty-one lesser volcanoes around the Mediterranean were in the early stages of magma venting.

Sixteen earthquake warnings had already been issued for regions spanning Turkey, Albania, Montenegro, Italy, Egypt and the Aegean Islands – two quakes above Magnitude 7 had already occurred, one of them devastating eastern Istanbul. On the continent of Africa, three volcanic peaks in the Cameroon and the Congo Republic were already in major eruption but, most worryingly, space-based laser measuring tools now suggested that a 2,000-mile section of the great East African Rift was about to tear open again – after being at rest for over two million years.

Yet, compared to the other two Geohazard monitoring centres, the staff in Athens were having a peaceful time. The regions of the Earth monitored by Oakland and Tokyo were each at least ten times hotter in seismic terms than the area that Zaoskoufis's staff had to deal with.

California was struggling to provide data on both the Long Beach and Mexico City earthquakes while at the same time monitoring eleven volcanic eruptions throughout the Caribbean and Central America.

Geohazard Japan was totally failing to monitor the havoc currently being wreaked across Indonesia as the world's most densely packed chain of volcanoes erupted simultaneously. The monitoring centre was hampered by the fact that nearby Mount Fuji had started a major eruption, now spewing rocks and lava globules over most of downtown Tokyo. Geohazard's cameras revealed that the city was ablaze.

Zaoskoufis kept frantically busy trying to get essential data out to those fighting the worst catastrophes. But he kept seeing in his mind the horrifying model of just this sort of global seismic cataclysm that Emilia had generated in his Simulation Theater only a few weeks earlier. As he worked he kept praying that there had been some fault in their computer simulation. If there wasn't, he dreaded what was likely to develop over the coming days.

Then the whole of the Athens facility itself shuddered as it was hit by the first shock of what would become Greece's largest-ever earthquake. Geohazard's own seismic sensors measured this first event at Magnitude 8.1. The lights went out, the data displays died. Giorgio Zaoskoufis clung to the edge of the console's counter as the shaking increased. Then the emergency lighting flickered on, and the read-outs returned to life.

'Everybody OK?' he yelled to those picking themselves up from the floor.

Just then another quake hit, this time 9.1 – one magnitude stronger than the first. But the Magnitude scale is logarithmic: one additional magnitude means that its shock is thirty-two times greater than the one that immediately precedes it on the calibration. The first quake to hit the suburb of Piraeus had released energy equivalent to the explosion of one billion tons of TNT, but the following Magnitude 9.1 shock was equal to thirty-two billion – or a 32,000,000-megaton thermonuclear explosion.

Geohazard's monitoring centre in Athens – and all those in it, instantly ceased functioning.

In their TV gallery, Perdita Curtis and her boss Narinda were working side by side to continue feeding live pictures of the Earth's serial seismic explosions to the group of powerful people with whom they were temporarily stranded on the moon.

As soon as the mega-tsunami had hit American soil, President Underwood had announced his intention to ferry himself back to Earth immediately – to be with his stricken people and to lead his nation from the front in their time of catastrophe. He also needed to steady the hastily relocated American stock markets; most insurance companies had already seen their stocks suspended, and banking shares were all in free fall.

But since the Kennedy Lunar Terminal had been washed away, the President was advised that he must delay his return journey. His aides needed to speak first with their Russian and Chinese counterparts, to make safety arrangements for the presidential landing and put proper security procedures in place. Although now routine, space flight was not yet as straightforward as air travel.

The visiting party had been delayed almost forty-eight hours beyond their planned departure time. Luna City's adjacent Hilton, Ritz and Interplanetary hotels had plenty of accommodation available, but everybody kept coming back to congregate in the main meeting hall – they felt a need to be together.

Extra tables and seating had been brought into the hall and doctors from the Luna City Medical Center provided tranquillizers to all who asked for them.

Over this two-day period, individuals had periodically broken off from their huddled groups to check the monitors for television reports. The most telling pictures were those transmitted by the BBC crew located on the orbiting ERGIA climate-control station.

These pictures showed volcanic smoke, ash and debris beginning to obscure large parts of the planet. From the space station's deep orbit it was possible to observe that a thick volcanic fog was slowly spreading around the entire globe.

ERGIA technicians worked with TV engineers to tap into signals transmitted from close-orbit Earth telescopes. These were specially instructed to focus downwards onto the mother planet: they soon revealed a sequence of spacecraft taking off from Russian, Chinese and South American launch sites, blasting out of the Earth's atmosphere every few minutes to rendezvous with orbiting space stations and hotels. It seemed that the rich and powerful were beating a prudent retreat.

Orbiting telescopes also revealed some of the less wealthy trying to escape the encroaching volcanic cloud. Commercial jets and private planes could be seen taking off from just in front of the thick brown engine-clogging miasma as it rolled out to envelop the world. These fleeing craft were hopping from continent to continent in a vain effort to deliver their passengers from the choking volcanic vog.

Eventually the pictures showed a planet completely shrouded in a veil of hot ash. Geohazard's remote instruments indicated that earthquakes and eruptions had ripped open the surface fabric of the Earth along all its tectonic joints, faults and volcanic chains. Meanwhile, beneath the oceans over 14,000 volcanic chimneys were engaged in a continuous simultaneous explosive venting.

Everything at ground level appeared to be cloaked in a ghostly twilight, with lightning-filled volcanic storms raging even over areas unaffected by any direct form of geophysical disturbance. Images of shattered city landscapes, burning buildings, flooded coastlands and heaped-up corpses had become so commonplace that they had almost lost their power to shock. Every TV station in the world that was still on air was transmitting scenes of Armageddon.

As they worked their exhausting shifts in the TV gallery, Perdy and her boss said little to each other. What they were witnessing was beyond words. But now Perdy did call Damle's attention to one particular incoming image.

'Is that an aurora borealis?' she asked, puzzled.

The screen displayed a wide shot of the entire planet Earth.

No oceans or continents could any longer be made out through the thick dark smoke and ash suspended in the atmosphere, but electric-blue haloes seemed to be flaring out into space above each pole.

Damle shook his head. 'No, I don't think so. An aurora is an atmospheric phenomenon – that looks as if it's extending way out into space.'

'I'll patch it through to the meeting hall,' said Perdy. 'Some of the scientists out there may be able to identify it.'

Twenty-four hours later, communications with Earth were becoming increasingly difficult. What looked like an aurora borealis and an aurora australis had been identified by Dr Emilia Knight as auroral electrojets – powerful electromagnetic discharges generated by dynamic forces deep within the planet's core.

'This is what we were warning about,' Emilia informed Perdy Curtis sharply. 'If you remember, we showed you a computer simulation of exactly this occurring when we visited you in your office.'

Perdy hung her head, realizing that she had actually paid little attention to the real message her contributors had been giving her. She had only been interested in creating a provocative debate.

An atmosphere of deep alarm, of something close to panic, was now spreading within the trapped lunar community. Their e-mails, calls and video links down to the home planet were frequently dropping out, and many found themselves unable to contact families or friends. Most of them had given up staring at the frequently interrupted broadcast signals, but now they began to gather by the windows of the LunaSun administration block; the events on Earth had grown to such a scale that they could clearly be observed by the naked eye – even from a quarter of a million miles away.

In place of the glorious blue and white image that impressed itself on the soul of every space traveller, they could now see only a dim brown ball. Alarming electrical discharges from either pole were clearly visible against the star-studded blackness of the galaxy, as mauve rings and hoops crackled outwards deep into space.

Emilia Knight had now briefed all the political leaders on Fivetrees's theory of magnetic-pole reversal, while Steve Bardini had finally been given the opportunity to run the computer simulation in its entirety, several times, even making a presentation to a shocked and silent Nicholas Negromonte.

But having been proved right provided no satisfaction, nor did the scientists' model provide any reassurance. It now seemed as if the Berkeley professor's theory had indeed been vindicated. But just how much more extreme would be the planet's ultimate reaction to such a violent magnetic upset remained to be seen.

Emilia and Steve were still receiving Geohazard satellite data suggesting that ocean levels were now rising rapidly. As they provided regular progress updates for the stranded visitors, Perdy realized that the geophysical scientists should really be providing this valuable service for others back on Earth – if any there were still able to pick up satellite broadcasts.

But even as she started to raise this idea with her boss, there was a break in the magnetic interference and a screen crackled to life. It was the BBC's Head of News in London.

'Can you take over control of the ongoing broadcast?' asked Robin Holmes, speaking from BBC World headquarters. 'Most of London is under water, and we're currently running on generator power.'

'I understand,' Damle confirmed.

'We've lost most of our news crews and affiliate feeds but I'll patch everything we've still got up to you.'

'We can relay the signal to our transmitter satellites from the ERGIA space station,' said Damle. 'It's in such a deep orbit that it seems to be unaffected.'

'Switching to you in thirty, then,' said Holmes.

'Quick, get everybody in here,' Damle hissed to Perdy. As she rushed out of the gallery to round up the rest of their production team, Damle glanced up at his Head of News again.

'I can't reach my mother . . .' he began. 'She lives in Greenford, Middlesex.' He was working frantically at the board to get them ready to broadcast to the entire world.

'She should be all right,' his boss assured him. 'Sea levels are rising but Greenford's on fairly high ground. Coming to you in ten.'

'God be with you, Robin,' muttered Narinda.

'And you're live – *now*,' said Holmes.

In Greenford, Middlesex, a suburb about one hour to the west of central London, it was not the rising water level that was troubling widowed Mrs Naresh Damle, Narinda's elderly mother. Her problem, and the problem for all others in Southern England, was volcanic ash.

Those of her grown-up children who still lived nearby had already taped up all of her window cracks and door openings, as the repeated emergency radio broadcasts were advising citizens to do, but micro-fine particles of soot were still finding their way into every corner of the house.

Although it was mid-afternoon in Britain, it was so dark outside that Mrs Damle had been forced to light her emergency candles. Wild stratospheric winds were blowing ash across the UK from volcanoes in Mexico and Canada and everything outdoors had been turned into a negative of an old-fashioned snow scene. All was coated black.

Mrs Damle had been coughing for three days as the ash content in the atmosphere increased. What the government's emergency broadcasts had *not* told their citizens was that a proportion of the volcanic cinders contained both carbon dioxide and hydrogen peroxide, toxins that destroyed both the lining and the pulmonary system of the human lung.

As the radio broadcasts suggested, wet towels held across the mouth did reduce coughing fits, but Mrs Damle no longer had the strength to protect herself in this way. Even as her younger son on the moon was assuming personal control of the BBC's global news output, she was on her hands and knees in her bedroom, literally coughing up pieces of her blackened lungs. A massive and fatal heart attack finally ended her misery.

All over Britain, Europe and the rest of the world, volcanic ash was competing with flood water to take the most lives.

'At least twenty thousand volcanoes on land or under the seas are currently in major eruption,' Emilia Knight said, staring straight into the camera lens. 'As a result, a countless number of tsunamis are now in train across all of the world's oceans. All coastal regions up to twenty miles inland must be considered extremely dangerous and should be immediately evacuated. Relocate to higher ground – at least one hundred metres above normal sea levels.'

Nobody knew whether her warning was being heard on Earth.

'One hundred and sixty-two earthquakes above Magnitude 8 have occurred in the last twelve hours, and a further seven hundred and thirteen of similar intensity are predicted by this time tomorrow.'

Although Emilia had frequently made guest television appearances, she had never before taken on the role of live reporter. But the situation was beyond all normal feelings of novelty or nerves; she was a professional geoscientist, and she now had a vital job to do. She knew that her image and words were being beamed down to the occluded Earth by three separate satellites for relay on a large number of different television and radio frequencies.

All two-way contact with the Earth was now lost. Emilia had been able to speak with her sister and parents in Boston until twenty hours ago, but now it seemed no forms of personal communication were possible in the magnetic storm raging around the planet. She suspected that it was very unlikely that her words were reaching people on Earth, but there were thousands of others trapped on orbiting space stations, as well as the pioneers on Mars, who would still be receiving her broadcast.

The Geohazard satellites were still able to use their infra-red cameras, laser beams and echo-Doppler atmospheric probes to measure events taking place on the Earth itself.

'Sea levels all over the world are rising rapidly,' continued Emilia. 'It appears that the Antarctic ice cap is melting.'

Emilia glanced at her communicator screen. 'To repeat our main announcements from Luna City: Greater Los Angeles has been struck by a sustained series of earthquakes, all above Magnitude 9. It is likely that the whole metropolitan region has been destroyed and that the entire Los Angeles basin is now under water.

'All contact with ground-based communications services has been lost. In the meantime we shall continue these broadcasts from the moon.

'Finally, our instruments are recording a major disturbance within the Earth's magnetic field, which may be the cause of the current worldwide seismic activity. The Earth's magnetic poles now appear to be in the process of reversing themselves. What was the Northern Magnetic Pole is currently situated eighty-three kilometres from the Antarctic coastline, at one hundred and twenty-two point two degrees east, seventy-one point seven degrees south.'

Emilia hesitated, and then added the words that she had rehearsed. 'This is Emilia Knight of Geohazard Laboratories, broadcasting for the BBC from Luna City.'

TWENTY-TWO

The moon colony had been self-sufficient for almost a decade. As soon as manned lunar exploration had resumed in the 2020s, significant water-ice reservoirs had been discovered at shallow depths beneath both the north and south poles. The largest of the two natural cisterns, covering almost 2,000 square kilometres, lay in the north.

Plans had then been developed for piping water 800 kilometres south to serve the Sea of Tranquillity's enclosed human communities. Such abundant water could be converted into oxygen and hydrogen, and could also irrigate artificially enriched moon soil for the cultivation of genetically modified lunar crops and meat protein. Everything essential for human habitation would thus be to hand.

Because there was almost no atmosphere on the moon, only four lightweight orbiting solar-reflector arrays and six scalable sunblinds had been required to melt the polar ice and to adjust the alternating two-week periods of lunar day and night so that the extreme ranges of the lunar surface temperature came closer to human tolerances. The same sun reflectors also provided ambient lighting during the long lunar night while ensuring a continuous supply of electric energy produced by high-yield solar-conversion panels.

At first, the American, Russian and Chinese governments worked closely together to found a single lunar community. But by 2036 it was clear that the use of the lunar surface as a jumping-off point for travel in deeper space was also making the moon highly attractive to commercial developers. On Mars, the discovery of rare gems, pharmaceutical constituents and minerals helped boost the demand for additional lunar launch facilities.

By the time when Nicholas Negromonte's company began constructing its vast farm of solar-reflecting mirrors on either side of the lunar equator, the moon's establishment had swollen to include fourteen commercial buildings and three hotels, which served space tourists and the regularly rotating group of moon dwellers. All were linked by airtight, radiation-proof walkways to create the rapidly growing metropolis known as Luna City. The ERGIA Corporation had then erected its three-storey LunaSun administration building beside the existing development, thus extending the total size of the human habitat to over sixteen square miles, more than eight of which were devoted to intensive food production.

Ten days after Emilia Knight and the BBC team finally gave up broadcasting to what now seemed to be an unresponsive home planet, President Underwood invited all those stranded on the moon to an emergency meeting in the LunaSun assembly hall. Narinda Damle was asked to broadcast the meeting to the Mars colonists and everyone else marooned on Earth-orbit space stations.

Even before contact with Earth had finally been lost, Geohazard's satellite sensors had revealed that sea levels on the planet were continuing to rise alarmingly. It was surmised that the intense heat blown upwards by underwater volcanoes had caused ocean temperatures to soar, melting all polar ice. Emilia's final emergency broadcasts had included a lengthening list of cities that were being lost to the waves.

As seismic chaos continued in all parts of the globe, even the largest continental land masses – the Americas, Europe, Russia, Asia, Africa, Australia – had started to disappear beneath the overheated waves. But, because of the smokescreen enveloping the planet, the seismologists on the moon could not visually confirm their streams of satellite data.

For three days after they ceased broadcasting, BBC technicians continued to gather in the gallery to scan the frequencies for any signals sent from Earth. Others from the stranded party also returned to the main hall, gazing up at blank screens as if willing them to crackle into life. But nothing further came from the shrouded planet, even though magnetic interference was slowly beginning to abate.

Those marooned in Luna City initially attempted to comfort each other with unlikely reassurances about what might be happening back home. But after four or five days in a state of shock and denial, people began to finally accept, and then to admit out loud, that all those on Earth must surely have died.

After his family tragedy in San Francisco, Michael Fairfax now had only his parents at Lake Tahoe to think of. But both Emilia Knight and Steve Bardini had large families to worry about – in Boston and Chicago respectively. A shocked silence and a profound sense of grief increasingly pervaded Luna City. There wasn't a resident or visitor who had not lost someone close – and most had lost whole families. People huddled together in small groups, friends comforting each other. The Archbishop of Boston announced a Mass of Vigil for those left behind on the Earth.

One American ferry navigator, revealing himself to be a Baptist lay preacher, organized prayer meetings and Bible readings. He displayed a banner painted silver-on-blue with the words THE DAY OF REVELATION IS AT HAND. Soon makeshift temples, churches and mosques were established in unoccupied offices of the administration building.

Nicholas Negromonte killed himself by running out of one of LunaSun's external exits without wearing a moon suit and without carrying any form of oxygen or life-support system. He had used his master pass to override the security systems of the triple-chamber airlock – systems which ensured that those exiting wore fully functioning suits and safety equipment. Then he bounded out, dressed only in jeans and a T-shirt, across the moon's airless surface.

No one inside the facility saw him head into the nearby dunes; he had chosen the middle of a sleep period in which to end his misery.

But despite this desperate attempt to commit suicide, Negromonte had not remained dead very long. A maintenance crew returning to Luna City from a shift spent mothballing the solar-reflector farm had spotted a figure moon-bounding from the airlock of the LunaSun building. They got to him quickly, but he was already unconscious and showing no signs of life.

After strapping an oxygen mask to his face, the maintenance workers rushed their former boss back inside, cracked open the resuscitation kit kept just inside the airlock, and started to administer defibrillating electric shocks.

They eventually saved Negromonte's life. But to their dismay his anguish on regaining consciousness rendered him incoherent. He was immediately admitted to the Medical Center where he was heavily sedated and placed on a suicide watch.

For the emergency public meeting the American President had dressed himself in a sombre navy suit and a crisp white shirt. His aides had even managed to find him a black tie. Underwood himself had been married and had had three teenage children, although he wore the tie not just as a mark of respect for his own family but for all humanity.

At the floor manager's cue he stepped up to the microphone. 'This is the President of the United States speaking to all people gathered here on the moon, as well as to those of you currently out in space or in the Martian colonies. As we all know, the Earth has suffered a terrible catastrophe, and it seems that we have all lost our loved ones back home.' He hesitated, with a choke in his voice, then continued, 'It also seems that I am no longer president of anything. Our once-proud nation has ceased to exist.'

Underwood paused again, visibly fighting his emotions. Damle ordered the camera operator to close in on the man's face.

'I know that we all wish to grieve in our own way, but we have to consider our mutual safety – and the safety of those others now out in space. From what I am told, there are sufficient ongoing supplies of air and fresh water for all of us here to survive in Luna City. With a simple rationing scheme, enough food is likely to be produced to meet our needs for the foreseeable future. The biotechnicians in the lunar farms are already stepping up their rate of food production.

'But there are others to think of. Altogether, we believe eighteen hundred and ten human souls are currently in space orbiting the Earth. The hotels and larger space stations have food and water supplies that will last them for some months, perhaps longer, but many of the smaller scientific stations will soon be running short. Although I no longer have any automatic right of leadership, I must call on all ferry pilots and their crew to resupply any of those space stations that become in need. We have everything necessary to keep our small fleet of ferries operational for some years to come.'

Inside the assembly hall the audience listened distractedly. Few were yet ready emotionally to think about the future.

'If, as it seems, the Earth has been made uninhabitable, this city here on the moon will have to become humankind's new home, along with the pioneer colonies on Mars. We must now start to get used to the fact that we may never in our lifetimes be able to return to Earth.'

Once again, Underwood's overwhelming emotions caused him to pause in his address.

'As I have said, there is no longer any authority vested in me and I am aware that I personally bear a heavy and awful responsibility for what has happened to the Earth. My government was not only a champion of climate management, we ignored, even suppressed, the warnings we were given.

'For that reason I now relinquish any vestige of my office that may remain. I formally resign as President of any American population or nation that may have survived. May God forgive me.'

All were now silent and fully attentive. Underwood closed his eyes and stood for a few moments, head bowed. When he finally looked up again, the audience saw that his eyes were filled with tears.

'All I would like to add is that, in time, you must all begin to adapt to new social structures. Our groupings are too small – whether here or on Mars – to require sophisticated forms of governance. But to maintain the ideals of democracy we shall need some sort of electoral system to make decisions, to establish our rules for living. You will have to choose a new leader, but all that will have to follow later. For the moment, I can only urge you, as one human being to another, to care for each other and to share our communal assets equally.

'There will be temptations to give way to grief, to become angry and to lash out and do damage to others – even to the harm of this fragile community. I beg you to resist such violent urges. The welfare of all of us depends on it. May God bless us all.'

Over the following six weeks, two women and three men from the stranded moon community committed suicide by finding ingenious ways to override airlock safety features and running unprotected into the vacuum of the lunar landscape. Unlike Negromonte, they were not fortunate enough to be rescued before they expired fully. The former ERGIA boss himself remained under sedation in the Medical Center. Among those inclined to black humour, such suicides became known as 'Taking A Moon Walk'.

Emilia Knight finally took Michael Fairfax to bed with her, but for comfort, not sex. They both lay fully clothed, holding each other, in an embrace that remained emotional rather than erotic.

Everyone trapped on the moon remained in a profound state of shock. The doctors said that the widely experienced feelings of despair, guilt and personal worthlessness were normal and only to be expected.

Negromonte's former personal fitness trainer, Sammy Giles, became an inspiration to all when he embarked on a campaign to promote physical fitness. 'At least two hours' working-out each day,' he evangelized. 'If you don't maintain your muscular structure in this low-gravity environment, your body will begin to atrophy.'

There were some who asked what the point was. If they were doomed to live on the moon for the rest of their lives, why bother striving for Earth-level fitness? Sammy's response was brutally direct: if the human body's normal loadings and stresses were abandoned, circulatory failure would follow within months.

Not all within the trapped community heeded the plea for restraint made by the former US President. Twenty-four hotel staff requisitioned ten cases of the finest vintage wines and spirits from the cellar of the Luna Hilton, took over an unoccupied suite on the third floor, and there began a three-day party of such extreme sexual licentiousness that it rivalled the plague orgies of the Middle Ages.

TWENTY-THREE

'It looks as if dry land is emerging once again,' Emilia Knight remarked to Steve Bardini and Michael Fairfax. 'Those are definitely land signatures.'

She had projected data from the Geohazard satellites up onto one of the BBC's monitors in the meeting hall. Now that all of the company's Earth-based sensors had been destroyed, they had to rely on passive probing with infra-red cameras and laser beams to establish what was occurring on the beleaguered planet below. But it seemed that the magnetic disturbance encompassing the Earth had by now almost disappeared.

'Not only are the ocean levels falling, but there seems to be a distinct reduction in seismic activity,' observed her former assistant.

'I suppose your systems are still working correctly?' asked the non-scientific member of the party.

'Well, what's left of them – those in space.' Emilia glanced down at her communicator screen. 'Our satellites are all solar-powered, so they'll go on for ever – or until some piece of internal equipment breaks down.'

'I wonder if there's *anything* remaining on that land?' mused Steve.

It was now almost four months since Earth had first been shrouded in smoke and ash. A few weeks after the cataclysm itself, Geohazard's satellite sensors had reported that the temperature around the planet was falling rapidly once again.

'It's the volcanic winter that everybody predicted,' Emilia had explained. 'It's always been assumed that it was a series of major volcanic eruptions that caused the ice ages of the past. The sheer amount of ash and debris blown into the atmosphere forms an umbrella that stops the sun's rays from reaching the planet's surface. Everywhere then becomes arctic – for thousands of years.'

Steve tapped his communicator screen and turned to his two friends again. 'In fact, we *have* to investigate what's left on this land. There might still be intact buildings – warehouses, stores, landing strips, fuel dumps ...' He tailed off as his excitement began to mount. Stupidly, he had even begun to imagine that some people might still be alive.

'Let's ask Perdy if we can take a look through the Earth-orbit telescopes,' said Emilia, rising. 'There might be a break in the ash cover somewhere.'

An hour later they were standing in the TV gallery, staring at screens showing only endless expanses of brown and grey ash-cloud. The BBC technicians had patched the gallery into the three large telescopes trained on the planet's surface from various points in Earth orbit.

'Nothing,' sighed Emilia. 'No break in the cover at all.'

'What about getting those ERGIA people to whip up some winds, to blow it all away?' suggested Perdy.

The three friends turned and stared at her in what was almost a single collective movement.

'You mean we should turn the solar reflectors back on, risk interfering with the Earth's magnetic polarity all over again?' said Steve grimly.

Perdy shrugged. 'It was only an idea – and it's not as if it could do any more harm. Who's down there to worry about it?'

The members of the group exchanged glances.

'That's true,' agreed Emilia. 'And we really *do* need to see what's going on down there. Perhaps we could just turn them on briefly.'

They summoned Doctor Isaiah Chelouche, formerly the chief technology officer of LunaSun Inc – until Nicholas Negromonte had ordered all operations shut down.

When he arrived, the bearded meteorologist was out of breath. He had been working out in the gym when Emilia's text flash had reached him. He hadn't even bothered to change out of his sweat-stained clothes. 'You said this was urgent,' he gasped.

Emilia showed him the data indicating that large areas of dry land had reappeared on the Earth's surface, then asked, 'Is there any way you could use your technology to clear a hole through that canopy of ash so we could take a look?'

Chelouche sank slowly into one of the gallery chairs and gazed up at the multiple images. 'Have you got any data on the density of that ash cloud?'

Steve quickly tapped into his communicator, then transferred the information up onto one of the large screens.

'Yep,' he said, pointing at the monitor. 'Our satellites have been probing the atmosphere ever since this disaster happened. We've got data on density, porosity, moisture content, stratification, temperatures, particle sizes – in fact every sort of measurement you could need.'

The meteorologist nodded. 'Good, good,' he said. 'But I would have to ask Mr Negromonte's permission and he's . . .'

They nodded; the former ERGIA boss was still confined to the Medical Center, heavily sedated and under constant watch. The gossip was that Nick Negromonte had gone mad when he had realized what he had personally contributed to.

'Just have a word with your ERGIA colleagues, and I'll talk to the President,' said Emilia. Despite his public resignation and the loss of his nation, everybody in Luna City still referred to James Underwood in that way and many still sought his counsel. 'Let's meet up again in a few hours.'

Three weeks after Emilia Knight first made her request, power was returned to the 42,000 solar mirrors of the LunaSun reflector farm. In the absence of their boss, the ERGIA executives had met with Underwood to seek his advice about their resuming some climate-modification output.

'Well, there's not a lot *more* harm you can do, is there?' the ex-president said, rather ungraciously. 'Why not? Go ahead. Let's see if anything's left down there.'

With his team gathered around him, Chelouche set about reprogramming the company's weather-management computers.

'It's not winds that we need,' he explained to Emilia, 'but spot applications of heat to cause repeated inversions of the atmosphere – so as to draw moisture up very high, creating stratospheric rain, to wash the ash out of the upper altitudes. If we do that over and over, we can soak the ash until it falls back to Earth. That way we can wash the dirt out and eventually clean up the whole atmosphere.'

As the thousands of mirrors on the moon re-angled themselves to catch and reflect the sun, all of ERGIA's other climate-modification systems orbiting the Earth also turned themselves back on, redirecting their solar reflectors to create the energy patterns that would start the process leading to repeated inversions of the planet's climate.

In the broadcast gallery, Emilia's small group watched anxiously as the reflected sunlight first began to play over and then concentrate more fixedly on the night side of Earth.

'Chelouche calculates that it will take between eight and twelve months to clean the atmosphere completely,' Emilia told the others. 'But we might see small gaps appear in the ash cover after about six months.'

In Room 243 of the Luna Hilton, Michael Fairfax and Emilia Knight were sleeping soundly. According to the GMT display on their bedside table – beside which was positioned a photograph of Lucy, Ben and Matthew – it was 5.56 a.m., shortly before dawn. Soon the exterior surfaces of the hotel, and of all the other buildings making up the extended lunar metropolitan habitat, would begin to reduce their built-in sun shading, to admit the sun's rays for the start of a new 'day'. Earth's own circadian rhythms were carefully mimicked throughout Luna City.

Michael and Emilia had at last become lovers. Hugs and embraces intended to comfort each other had gone on to become sensual, and had then turned sexual. To justify their almost guilty pleasure to themselves, they reminded one another that they had both felt strong stirrings of attraction back on Earth, even before they had started on their doomed campaign to warn the world about the risk of magnetic catastrophe. Their love was not like the frantic escape into lust that was breaking out elsewhere all over Luna City, where scores of casual sexual pairings were now evolving as the marooned humans celebrated their own survival and warded off thoughts about the future.

The process of cleansing the Earth's atmosphere had now been going on for seven months, and it had become a habit for all in the lunar community to drop by the assembly hall regularly to check what progress was being made. Over the last few weeks tantalizing glimpses of blue ocean, even dark smudges of land, had been revealed by the passage of orbiting telescopes. But no one had yet been able to identify the continents sighted with any certainty.

The phone beside their bed shrilled and Emilia stretched out an arm.

'What?' she asked groggily.

'You two, get down here now!' It was Steve Bardini calling from the assembly hall. 'You've just got to see this!'

Ten minutes later they stepped into the TV gallery to join Steve who was standing beside Perdy Curtis at the control panel.

The large monitors displayed views of a planet that now seemed almost wholly clear of smoke. Some large white and grey clouds were swirling in typical cyclonic formations, but little else was familiar about this globe.

The side of Earth facing them was three-quarters in sunlight, and the observers on the moon could see two large dark land masses that seemed totally alien. One enormous continent in the northern hemisphere looked like an upside-down version of Australia, while a second massive shaped tract of land ran south from the equator to disappear beneath the pole itself. Already they could see the white gleam of frost at the poles.

The door behind them banged open, and Dr Isaiah Chelouche burst in. 'We've done it, we've done it!' His eyes blazed with excitement. 'Less than two per cent of the ash now remains airborne. Air temperatures are almost back to normal.'

'Then I suggest you turn everything off again immediately,'

said Michael sharply, turning to confront the excited meteorologist. 'We don't want any more accidents, do we?'

The assembly hall was now filling up rapidly as word flashed around the city. Perdy patched all of the three telescope images to screens around the room.

'Can we look at those land formations in more detail?' Steve asked. 'Let's start with that large mass at the top.'

Perdy inched forward a joystick controlling a twenty-ton telescope that floated in space almost 400,000 kilometres away. As the image of the unknown continent enlarged, they could see mountain ranges and what looked like canyons bisecting the land. Several volcanoes were erupting simultaneously.

'It's still pretty active down there,' observed Steve.

'And everything else is so brown and grey,' added Emilia.

'That will be volcanic ash,' said Chelouche, now more subdued. 'Seventy per cent will have fallen into the ocean, the rest has come down on dry land.'

The new geography of the Earth appeared wholly alien to those on the moon. Giant mountain ranges alternated with vast plateaux and apart from the spewing volcanoes everything seemed dead and blasted. It was a primeval landscape.

For five hours Perdy panned the three ultra-high-magnification telescopes slowly across the two large continents that were currently in view. Then she focused on a few of the many islands that dotted the strangely shaped oceans.

Nowhere seemed to show any signs of life. There was no evidence that any civilization had ever existed on Earth. It was like looking at computer-simulated images of imagined planets in distant galaxies.

By noon, people had started drifting away, and an air of despondency had replaced the earlier excited optimism. Perdy Curtis handed over vision control to Narinda Damle, while Michael and Emilia returned to their room for belated showers.

Later that afternoon they were in the Hilton's gym, forcing themselves to undergo workouts that neither of them had the heart for, when Emilia's communicator pinged again in her earpiece.

'Get back here,' said Steve Bardini urgently. 'We've found something else down there.'

Ten minutes later they were back with Perdy and Narinda Damle in the vision control room.

'Look at that smudge, just there – ahead of the dawn line.' Steve pointed to the central screen. 'It'll be light there in a few minutes, so we'll be able to see more detail.'

The Earth had turned through half a revolution since they had first been summoned out of bed to gaze down at the newly smoke-free planet. Now a large continent that was shaped a bit like Canada – but positioned just north of the equator – was starting to move into the daylight zone.

'There,' said Steve, highlighting the eastern shoreline of the land mass.

'Can't you go in closer?' asked Emilia.

Perdy zoomed in, and the dawn light revealed a much smaller dark mass in the water, like an offshore island.

'Now, look at this.' Steve nodded to Perdy, who added an infra-red overlay to the image. Red and yellow patches suddenly appeared. The dark mass was glowing with its own heat.

Then they spotted other smaller masses further north along the coastline of the new continent. They too glowed yellow and red under the heat-sensing camera.

'That must be a string of volcanic islands,' said Emilia. 'But they're remarkably close to the coast.'

Finally the sun's rays reached the new continent's edge and all of the offshore island masses became brilliantly lit. The land here was also grey, but they could also see what appeared to be a sandy-coloured region close to the coastline.

Michael laid a hand on Perdy's shoulder. 'Can you zoom right in on the largest of those hot islands?'

Perdy removed the infra-red overlay, selected the most powerful of the Earth-orbit telescopes, and zoomed in until the dark mass that Michael had indicated entirely filled the screens. Everybody within the gallery let out a gasp, and they heard shouts from outside in the assembly hall where a few people were still watching the wall-screens.

'Can you go in still closer?' asked Michael, his voice trembling with emotion. 'Right into the middle, to where that white dot is?'

Again, Perdy nudged the joystick forward, zooming in to maximum magnification. This time there were no gasps from the observers. All were left in awe.

Revealed on all the screens in the gallery, and on those outside in the meeting hall, was the image of a huge white ship surrounded by old, battered hulks of oil tankers and container ships. It was the *Global Haven*: the hulk people, or at least their ships, had survived.

Cheering broke out in the hall. Through the observation window people could be seen sprinting back into the meeting area as word of this miracle spread.

Michael pulled his communicator from his sweatsuit pocket. 'Are the phone satellites still working?' he asked Damle.

'They were until a few months ago. Do you want me to patch you through to one?'

As the television producer completed the necessary interfaces, Michael selected a number from his personal database.

'You should be getting a network signal now,' said Damle.

'Put this out over the speakers.' Michael touched the number on his communicator screen.

Everybody in the gallery and out in the assembly hall could hear a phone ringing: once, twice, three times. It was answered on the fourth ring.

'Chanda Zia here,' a nasal voice sounded clearly over the loudspeakers. 'Can that really be you, Counsellor Fairfax?'

TWENTY-FOUR

All five of the scattered hulk communities had survived the cataclysm. Their long-practised technique of loosely chaining their vessels together to ride out the mountainous storms of the southern seas had saved them even when the oceans had risen up and destroyed every other vessel afloat and swallowed up every continent.

Ash, smoke, fumes, atmospheric debris, freezing temperatures and falling oxygen levels had all taken a heavy toll on the sick and vulnerable members of their communities, yet a great number had survived. Chanda Zia estimated that almost two million people had ridden out the floods on the five separate hulk platforms.

There was jubilation on the moon. It now seemed that the marooned space communities were no longer fated to live as lonely bands of survivors, forced to eke out a declining existence on hostile worlds. The Archbishop of Boston conducted a service of thanksgiving.

For days following the discovery, all talk was of how best the humans trapped in space could get themselves back down to Earth and begin again – to start building new lives, despite the ongoing instability of the home planet. The need was urgent; there had been seventeen more suicides in the marooned moon community and a growing number of people were suffering repeated bone fractures as their skeletons weakened in the low gravity. Doctors now recommended that everybody should work out for at least three hours a day, but many were coming to the conclusion that it would be impossible for the community to maintain its health over the long term. Some had even started to talk gloomily about the eventual extinction of what was left of the human race.

Even from the moon, it became easy to see that as weeks went past life was returning quickly to Earth's new continents, despite the repeated volcanic eruptions, earthquakes and tsunamis that Geohazard's satellites were reporting. Apart from the extensive planting already undertaken as the former hulk refugees transferred crops and livestock from their many floating farms, vegetation seemed to be springing up spontaneously all over the globe, bringing a sudden renewal of oxygen to the atmosphere.

'It's the ash,' explained Emilia Knight. 'Volcanic cinders are high in nitrogen, the richest fertilizer known to Man. That's why, historically, so many poor people have chosen to live beside volcanoes.'

Using the network of solar-powered video cameras that Michael Fairfax had presented to them, Chanda Zia's surviving community proudly relayed up pictures of their new settlements.

Wood, plastic and recoverable metal had been stripped out of the hulk ships to construct buildings in the new villages, while many useful items of debris had also been collected from the surface of the ocean after the storms had subsided. Driftwood was continuously being washed up onto the beaches, all of it to be reused in this high-speed construction programme.

From the television studio on board the *Global Haven* – which still had its own supply of hydrogen fuel – Chanda transmitted surface-level video images of the cataclysm to those watching up on the moon.

Trapped in the Southern Ocean, the hulk people had been far away from most above-ground volcanic activity. But their video had shown the skies darkening, the seas growing to monstrous heights as tsunami waves collided with each other and as freshly melted icy water streamed up from the Antarctic. Then had followed the many months of cold darkness and a slowly failing atmosphere.

*

The news that almost two million humans had survived the cataclysm on Earth energized and uplifted the 2,067 humans stranded in space – including those on Mars. Plans were drawn up for the new society that they would create when they returned to Earth. The first requirement would be to identify areas of seismic stability on which to build, and then housing, hospitals and social infrastructure would have to be constructed immediately. A new generation of children would have to be produced – and quickly. Then the necessary schools, universities, factories, laboratories, courts and prisons would be needed. Biodiversity audits would have to be carried out and DNA repositories on the moon, Mars and on the larger space stations would have to be raided to facilitate the reintroduction of lost flora and fauna. There was a whole new world to be created.

By far the most important of the many planning groups established was the one made up of shuttle pilots, navigators, technology experts and space engineers. Its role was to examine all possible methods of getting the marooned extraterrestrial population back down to the Earth's surface. The problems of re-entry without the help of ground-based guidance systems could be overcome by the careful injection of a spacecraft into the Earth's atmosphere. The insoluble problem seemed to be how to land safely.

All the heavy orbit shuttles, moon ferries and Mars spacecraft were designed to fly themselves through the Earth's atmosphere using a combination of on-board and ground-based computer systems. Their meagre aerodynamics were designed primarily for airless space, and were too unstable at low speeds for the craft concerned to be flown manually. In addition there was the necessity for extensive landing areas.

Modern spacecraft took off horizontally from long runways, and then used the enormous power of hydrogen-plasma engines to boost themselves out of the Earth's gravitational grasp and on into space. This was far more efficient, comfortable and safe than the old brute-force methods used in vertical rocketry. But very long runways indeed were required, both for take-off and landing, and the newly emerged land masses boasted no such facility.

Although there were still six emergency-rescue spacecraft

with vertical-landing capability hangared on the moon or at the Mars colony, all had been designed to land only in low-gravity environments – and none of them was constructed to withstand the awful heat and buffeting that would be experienced during re-entry into Earth's thick atmosphere. The technical problems of returning to Earth seemed insurmountable.

Michael Fairfax was sharing a Hilton restaurant meal one evening with Emilia Knight and Steve Bardini when Perdy Curtis arrived to join them.

'There are still no bright ideas from the space experts,' she reported, glancing down at the dispiriting menu of rations. 'I don't see why they can't just fly Negromonte's Apollo Eleven back home, the way Neil Armstrong did. The capsule's just going round and round up there, not doing anything.'

Once again, her three companions turned towards her as one.

'I presume you've suggested that to them?' said Steve in a hushed tone.

Perdy shook her head. 'No, of course I haven't. It's far too obvious for them to have overlooked. There must be some technical objection.'

But it *had* been overlooked. Whether that was because such antique technology did not register on their high-tech radar, or because of its unfortunate association with the disgraced Nicholas Negromonte, the fact remained that none of the committee members had thought of using the refurbished Apollo command module. It was still orbiting the moon seventy-three nautical miles up where its pilot had parked it during his re-enactment of Armstrong's descent to the lunar surface.

A cargo ferry was immediately dispatched to collect the circling spacecraft. As soon as it had been unloaded at the Luna City maintenance facilities, work began to examine the current state of its fabric and systems.

Within a week of the command module's recovery, the director of flight maintenance declared herself satisfied with the integrity of the antique space vehicle. All its original components had been stripped out and replaced with modern systems for Negromonte's flight but the command module's own vitally important ablative heat-shield had been left in place. Even the three parachutes intended to slow the module during its descent into the ocean were in perfect working order.

Over the months it had become clear that James Underwood's natural qualities of leadership were still very much needed. So he reluctantly agreed to chair what had now become known as the Apollo Mission Planning Group.

'We'd have to try for a splashdown as close as possible to one of the hulk platforms,' explained the communications engineer who had been appointed Director of Recovery for the planned mission. 'And they'd need to pick up our crew quickly. They couldn't be left floating in that old command module for more that thirty minutes. After that it will probably sink.'

'But a far bigger problem is who's going to pilot it,' said the newly appointed Mission Director. 'We can ferry the module back to Earth orbit and launch from there, but nobody's been properly trained to fly the damn thing down to the surface. It's got *twelve* goddam engines. And we only get this one chance!'

Then followed a long discussion among the pilots about which of them was best suited to fly the Apollo capsule. In the sixth decade of the twenty-first century, piloting spacecraft had become almost entirely a matter of computer management and practising disaster procedures. As an examination of the old craft had quickly revealed, despite its upgraded systems the Apollo module, with its dozen engines for controlling speed, direction, pitch, yaw and roll, would require a great deal of primitive-style manual piloting to guarantee a safe return to Earth.

On the following evening Underwood invited Michael Fairfax to his hotel suite.

'What we need to be sure of is that the hulk people will genuinely attempt to recover the command module once it ditches into the ocean,' Underwood explained. 'Do you think you could persuade them to help us out?'

Both men saw the irony of the situation. If those now stranded out in space – a group of castaways that included many former political leaders – were ever going to return to Earth they were going to have to beg the help of a long-persecuted people whom all their nations had previously and cruelly shunned.

Unsurprisingly, the more radical members of Chanda Zia's hulk community were strongly against helping their former persecutors to return to Earth.

'Those bastards forced us to remain at sea for thirty years,' yelled John Gogotya. 'Let them remain in space for thirty years – *then* we can think about it.'

Many of the younger men meeting in the *Global Haven*'s former ballroom were still brandishing weapons, as if nothing had changed and they still had enemies roaming the world.

'We are many, they are few,' Chanda reassured his noisy audience. 'In total, there are two million of us, and they are just a few thousand. They can be no threat to us – or to our way of life. It is our human duty to welcome them.'

A few other members of the ruling council nodded agreement, but a large number of the audience were booing or shouting protests. Some even looked ready to start firing their weapons.

'Remember that they have technologies we desperately need,' argued Chanda. 'They can give us the means to produce hydrogen fuel from water, to revive the DNA of animals and crops that no longer exist, the skill to produce medicines that will treat our illnesses. There are Western-trained doctors up there on the moon.'

Now there were additional nods from the council members and even the cries of protest diminished. The hulk community knew full well that it had already exhausted the *Global Haven*'s stock of antibiotics and pharmaceuticals. Sickness was now the dreaded common enemy.

Perdy sat nervously on the side of Nicholas Negromonte's bed. Two burly male nurses stood watchfully at a respectful distance. She was visiting at James Underwood's request.

The Apollo mission planners had concluded that Negromonte was the obvious choice to pilot the command module back to Earth. Not only had he spent months in simulators training for the earlier Apollo mission, he also had the experience of flying and landing the Lunar Module. Underwood himself had gone immediately to the Medical Center, to enquire about the patient's health.

'He keeps weeping inconsolably all the time he's conscious,' Dr Andrea Cohen had explained to him. 'We have to keep him locked in his room, and under observation at all times. Given the opportunity, I think it's very likely he would kill himself.'

'Doesn't sound like he'd make a very reliable pilot,' sighed the former president, 'but we have no choice.' Then Underwood suggested that he himself should put the proposition to Negromonte.

'He feels immense personal guilt,' objected Dr Cohen. 'Being confronted with the former leader of a world that no longer exists wouldn't be ideal.'

After much discussion, Perdy Curtis had been recommended for the task by Hanoch Biran, ERGIA's former director of corporate communications. Over the few months leading up to the moon broadcast, he had quietly observed the easy familiarity that Nick Negromonte and Perdy had developed together.

'He really seemed to relax with her,' Biran explained. 'And I got the impression that she rather liked him too.'

Now Perdy gazed down at the patient's pale and puffy face, still irregularly blotched by the purple blood-bruises caused by sudden decompression. Having been confined to bed for months, she noticed how his muscles had been wasting away in the weak lunar gravity.

'You could save us all, Nick,' she urged him again, squeezing his hand affectionately. 'Once you land you could show them how to build a runway. We could all be safely back on Earth within a few months.'

As he started to weep again, silent tears rolling down his cheeks, Perdy bent forward and pulled his head against her shoulder.

TWENTY-FIVE

For the return, Apollo Mission Control was established in the
ERGIA Space Station's main viewing gallery, just as for the
outward leg of Negromonte's journey nineteen months earlier.
But this time no moonlighting American, Russian or Chinese
space technicians had been available to shuttle up from Earth to
control and oversee the command module's re-entry and splashdown.

Because they had to retrain a whole new team of controllers
to run a space mission using technology only their great-
grandparents would have recognized – and because every single
human trapped in space realized that there would be only one
chance of a successful return to Earth – the new control team
was, if anything, even more meticulous about its preparations
than the original NASA engineers had been eighty-six years
before.

The major problem was that, for his own re-enactment of
the Apollo flight to the moon, Negromonte had not bothered to
replace the original command-module motors. The complex
four-part design of the Apollo spacecraft included a total of fifty
separate engines. The main engine of the service module – the
large rocket that had flown the spacecraft to the moon – had
been replaced by a modern plasma unit ten times more powerful
than the original. So too had the engines utilized for the lunar-
descent stage.

But Negromonte and his team had seen no need to replace
the small 100-pound thrusters needed to control the command
module's re-entry to Earth's atmosphere. It had taken six months

for the engineers at Luna City to cannibalize other craft in order to make new thrusters to replace the old, underpowered, dangerous compressed-gas units that had been in use a century before.

The new high-power plasma units allowed the craft a higher payload, and by replacing the old plumbing and life-support systems with modern micro units they also achieved significant extra storage space. This capacity would be used to carry down a cargo of hydrogen-fuel pellets for the engines of the *Global Haven*, an emergency supply of pharmaceuticals, a batch of livestock embryos prepared by the reproductive biologists in Luna City, and the uplink telemetry navigation systems required to allow shuttles and moon ferries to land safely back on the home planet. Thereafter, it had taken a further four months for the fully refurbished module to undergo thorough testing.

All this time, the astronauts pre-selected for this vital mission had been in rigorous training. Initially, Nicholas Negromonte had mutely and tearfully refused Perdy's coaxing that he should pilot the command module back to Earth. But, a few days after she had first visited him, the patient had asked Dr Cohen if he could see Perdy again. She had returned to find him much more alert.

Negromonte asked to be updated about everything that had been happening and, after learning of the crucial role that ERGIA's technology had played in rapidly cleansing the Earth's atmosphere and ending the arctic winter – a process that would otherwise have taken thousands of years – he began to mutter about 'doing his duty'.

Within two weeks his newly positive attitude had convinced his doctors that Negromonte was no longer a suicide risk. He subsequently spent six hours a day in the ERGIA company gym, getting his body back into shape whilst simultaneously tapping into the Luna City digital library to study every scrap of data in contemporaneous NASA reports about the Apollo missions' re-entry and splashdown.

One significant drawback was the lack of an Apollo simulator on the moon. But Negromonte himself already had a feel for the craft's handling, and he knew the responsiveness of its manual controls. At last, after four months of recovery and physical regeneration, he declared himself ready to pilot his spacecraft back to Earth.

Also selected for the critical mission were Michael Fairfax and Dr Emilia Knight. It was obvious from the outset that the lawyer had to be one of the crew. He had been the hulk people's first champion and it now fell to him to negotiate with the people of the former hulk communities to facilitate a homecoming for the rest of those now trapped in space.

Emilia Knight was selected for her geological expertise. She would have to inspect all possible sites for the establishment of a runway, and she would also have to report back on seismic conditions as a whole.

It was clear to all that the reborn planet Earth was still highly unstable and, the geologists warned, would be likely to stay that way for centuries to come. But although considerable volcanic and earthquake activity was still occurring, this was no longer on a scale likely to cause atmospheric fog or to occlude the sun.

Emilia would therefore have to borrow a four-wheel-drive vehicle from the *Global Haven*'s well-stocked garage and set off to survey as much of the land mass as possible. Her mission was to find the safest and most stable sites on which the returnees could found a new community. But despite having these hugely responsible tasks ahead of her, some malicious members of the lunar community still grumbled that the real reason for her being selected was that she had become the lawyer's girlfriend.

Their flight from deep Earth-orbit down to the surface would be rapid – less than three hours, thanks to the power of the modern engines – and the duties required of Michael and Emilia in piloting the craft were expected to be nil. But the mission planners insisted that both of them should learn every control and every life-support and safety feature of the module, just in case the pilot became incapacitated for some reason during the flight.

In between their long technical briefings and training sessions in a mock-up command module that the engineers had built, Michael and Emilia had to improve their fitness significantly. Sammy Giles was put in charge of their physical development and in addition to long hours in the gym they joined Nick

Negromonte for repeated sessions in the swimming pool that was meant to simulate the hazards of splashdown. The low moon gravity made it impossible to simulate this properly, but the crew was put through repeated duckings and rehearsals for potential recovery problems.

After a total of eight months' preparation, Mission Controller Bill Jackson finally declared the team ready.

'In less than fifteen minutes, the Apollo command module will fire its small manoeuvring engines and blast out of deep-space orbit for its return to Earth,' announced Magnus Blythe, staring directly into the camera lens.

When he had last made a broadcast at LunaSun's official opening, the august commentator's potential audience had been six billion people throughout the world. But this current transmission would reach only those on various space stations, on the moon, on Mars – and, of course, the hulk community below, where it would be piped to screens all over the *Global Haven*. And when Blythe had last faced the cameras, his wavy hair had been a glossy black. Now it was completely grey; Luna City had finally run out of hair dye.

The TV crew was positioned centrally in the observation gallery of the ERGIA space station in front of the tiered seating in which the mission controllers were making last-minute preparations. Also present were James Underwood and other members of the Apollo Planning Group, while on one side of the large room Perdy Curtis worked alongside Narinda Damle, mixing camera shots.

As she cut to an overhead camera mounted inside the Apollo command capsule, the three astronauts could be seen clearly: Negromonte in the pilot's seat on the left, busily making his last-minute checks, Emilia Knight on the centre couch, and Michael Fairfax to starboard.

Perdy switched back to Magnus Blythe.

'Over the last three months, our own pilots have been using long-distance telemetry to begin training members of the new Earth community to fly the recovery helicopter that will pluck

Captain Nicholas Negromonte and his crew from the ocean. It is now hoped that they will be pulled from the module less than five minutes after splashdown.'

'Time to launch, thirty seconds,' announced the Operations Director.

Blythe ceased his commentary as T-minus fifteen was reached. There was nothing more now that could be said, or done, that would serve to underline the importance of this mission.

'Three, two, one – fire engines.'

Perdy cut to a long-range camera focused on the command module, where it floated in parallel orbit one kilometre away. Only a light-blue glow was visible from the upgraded starboard thrusters as the craft started to turn out of orbit to begin its approach to Earth.

'On course zero six zero,' reported Negromonte, his voice amplified by the Mission Control loudspeakers.

'Copy that,' said Capcom, a moon-ferry pilot who had been assigned the responsibility for in-flight communications with the three astronauts. 'On course, zero six zero.'

Two hours and forty-one minutes later, the ninety-two-year-old refurbished Apollo module started to encounter the Earth's upper atmosphere.

'Six point two four re-entry angle,' said Negromonte as he steadied the attitude yoke.

'Copy that,' said Capcom. 'Six point two four re-entry angle.'

'Re-entry interface acquired,' reported Negromonte, locking on to his trajectory.

'Copy that. Re-entry interface successfully acquired,' echoed Capcom.

'Descent rate, thirty-four thousand, eight hundred and two feet per second,' read off the pilot-skipper. 'Height, two thousand, six hundred and twenty nautical miles.'

The Apollo module hit the earth's upper atmosphere precisely in the centre of a re-entry corridor only two and a half degrees wide. To miss would have meant either skipping off the surface of the atmosphere, like a stone cast onto the surface of a pond, and being lost in space for ever, or plunging in too deeply and burning up. Unlike the earlier Mercury and Gemini space-craft that NASA had flown, the lunar return vehicle was designed for a faster, steeper and hotter descent through the atmosphere.

In a couch so closely sculpted to his body that it seemed to be hugging him, Michael Fairfax shut his eyes as the buffeting increased. It felt like their entire craft was being pounded by a piledriver.

To his left Emilia did the same, screwing her fists together so tightly that they hurt. She reached out a hand and grabbed Michael's gloved fist.

In the left-hand couch, Nicholas Negromonte was reading off the G-force being applied to the old command module and its crew. Modern laser-borne communications no longer meant that radio contact was automatically lost during the re-entry phase, and he knew that Mission Control, the whole scattered space community and those waiting to recover them on the Earth's surface would be listening in intently.

'Six G. Eight G. Ten G.'

The buffeting had now reached its theoretical worst. All on board knew that twelve gravities was the maximum load that the module could withstand before disintegrating. Flames rushed past both port and starboard observation windows as the thick abalative heat-shield on the blunt end of the space pod burned away – precisely as intended.

But a century earlier, NASA scientists had over-engineered all aspects of the Apollo spacecraft, and the antique capsule completed re-entry before even half its heat-absorbing plastic and fibreglass heat-shield material had been incinerated.

The buffeting suddenly stopped and the roar disappeared. The module's crew could see blue sky all around.

With a gigantic upward snap, the crew felt the Apollo's three drogue parachutes deploy. They cheered, whooped and hollered as one.

Then Negromonte shook his head. 'We're off course,' he yelled. 'About eighty miles to the east.'

'Jesus – we're going to hit land,' cried Michael. He knew that, theoretically, astronauts in a module hitting dry land instead of water were still supposed to survive. That was what the closely contoured and spring-supported couches were intended for. But at no point during the original Apollo programme had a descent onto land been tested with a live human crew.

'To the *east*,' snapped Negromonte. 'We're coming down in the *ocean*.'

Back in Mission Control, jubilation suddenly gave way to consternation as their systems registered the craft's drift off course.

'Much higher winds in the stratosphere than we calculated,' Recovery announced to the rest of the control team. 'Sorry, guys.'

'Copy that, Nick,' said Capcom, in response to Negromonte's report. 'You are eighty-one miles south-east of the intended splashdown zone. We are informing the recovery team of your revised position.'

Although they knew that their rate of descent had now slowed to only twenty miles per hour, the Apollo module hit the water much harder than anything the practice sessions in the Luna City swimming pool had prepared them for.

Michael thought he lost consciousness for a few seconds. When he came to, he tried to lift his arm to wipe thick condensation off the triangular observation window above his head. His arm wouldn't move! His weakened bones must have been fractured in the heavy splashdown.

Trying again, he managed to raise his hand a few inches. Then he realized that it wasn't broken, it was the gravity – but a gravity that felt as if lead weights were wrapped around his arm. All three crew members had been warned that they would find Earth's gravity almost unbearable at first, but Michael could not have imagined that it would feel quite like this. With a supreme effort he raised his arm once more, this time managing to get his glove against the surface of the window. As soon as he had cleared away the moisture, brilliant sunshine streamed into the module.

Suddenly, Michael became aware of a feeling of immense nausea as the sea threw the little craft around vigorously. Although none of the crew had been allowed to eat immediately prior to departure, all three had to force their leaden fingers to scrabble for vomit bags.

'Dear God!' exclaimed Negromonte, when he had finished retching. 'I hope they get to us soon.'

In Mission Control, the Flight Surgeon shook his head in sympathy, his biomed read-outs providing clear signs of the crew's physical distress.

'How long till the chopper gets there?' he asked the Flight Director.

'Another forty minutes,' said the FD. 'Assuming they can locate them successfully.'

In Chanda Zia's hulk community, many of the younger males, and some females, had been keen to learn to fly the helicopters carried aboard the *Global Haven*. When they were informed that pilots on board the ERGIA space station could instruct them from long distance, lessons had started at once.

Two of the mighty ship's stock of twenty-seven helicopters had already been damaged during practice landings – the time delay of the signals coming from space was not compatible with precise flight control. And the young pilots' bravado in arbitrarily disconnecting telemetric command in order to learn some procedures on their own also produced some problems. But this was a healthy sign, agreed their tutors on the space station: a certain degree of arrogance was natural to pilots.

Within weeks, four young men and one woman were showing sufficient progress at the flight controls to begin flying missions for the hulk community itself.

Much needed to be done. The former residents of *Pacifica One* were now building townships all along a 300-mile coastal strip of the new continent. One season's crops had already been picked, and the rich, ash-fertilized soil had produced bumper harvests. Livestock was now reproducing and building work continued at a frantic pace. Helicopters proved the ideal means of rapid transport – especially to fetch emergency medical cases for treatment in the *Global Haven*'s operating theatres.

Fuel would become the main problem. Although the luxury vessel still retained large stocks of kerosene-based aviation fuel in its catamaran-hull tanks, nobody knew how long it might take to prospect for new oil – nor whether any oil was actually present in the newly formed land masses. After the initial training period, helicopter flights had been restricted to medical emergencies only.

For all of these reasons, the Apollo mission controllers were anxious. It would be impossible to recover the command module itself – there were no heavy-lift choppers. Neither were there any frogmen or inflatable dinghies available. The plan was that when the *Global Haven*'s air-sea rescue helicopter and recovery team arrived the Apollo crew would clamber out of the module and into the sea. They would then be winched up into the helicopter one by one. Once the crew was safe, their vitally important cargo could be recovered from the spacecraft itself.

But twenty-eight minutes after it had splashed down all power failed in the command module. The crew members, rocking in their couches, heard a loud fizz and crackle just before the lights went out and the power drained out of all communications systems.

'Water's getting in,' said Negromonte, flipping the emergency power switch up. Two bulkhead lights lit, but there was no sign of life in the radio communication system.

'We won't even know when the helicopter gets here,' gasped Emilia, still anxiously clutching the sick bag to her chest.

'I don't think we can wait that long,' said Negromonte. 'We must get into the water now – this old craft could go down very quickly.'

In Mission Control there was a stunned silence as all communication and telemetry from the downed module was lost. The only voice to be heard was Capcom's, repeating over and over: 'Come in, Apollo. Apollo, come in.'

'Looks like they've lost all power,' suggested the Flight Director, with forced optimism. Nobody was going to be the first to suggest the module might have sunk before the helicopter could reach it.

Slightly less than 66,000 kilometres below Mission Control, Emilia Knight was the first crew member out of the escape hatch and into the water. She was still attached to the hull of the spacecraft by a quick-release line connected to her belt. As soon as the water touched her modern spacesuit, its inner buoyancy lining inflated.

Michael Fairfax was next into the ocean. He forced his still-heavy arms to paddle him closer to Emilia.

But Nicholas Negromonte did not follow as expected. Emilia and Michael waited, bobbing about beside the command module, which was now riding noticeably lower in the heavy seas, until Michael finally grabbed a handhold and painfully pulled himself back up the side of the craft to peer into its open hatch.

Negromonte was busily piling their cargo of hydrogen fuel pellets, flight-guidance computers, livestock embryos, medicines and DNA material onto the three couches.

'Get out of there!' Michael screamed above the rising wind. 'This thing could submerge at any moment!'

'We've got to get these supplies loaded,' yelled back Negromonte as he worked frenziedly in the dark interior.

Suddenly Michael felt – rather than heard – the *whump* of helicopter rotor blades. Clinging on to the side of the bucking module, he raised his head.

A man was already descending from the chopper in a sling. Michael pointed towards Emilia, and the rescuer swung himself sideways and dropped into the water beside her. It took only thirty seconds for the winchman to get a second sling under her arms and then, with a wave of his hand, her swarthy rescuer was winched back up to the hovering helicopter, holding on tightly to his prize.

Five minutes later Michael felt a hand snatch at his spacesuit collar as he still clung to the side of the module. The winchman was now beside him on the hull and, like him, clinging on to its aluminium handholds. As the winchman pushed the empty sling in his direction, Michael shook his head and pointed mutely down inside the module.

The man inched upwards and put his head inside the escape hatch. Michael heard a shouted exchange, then the winchman unclipped himself from the winch line. Guiding both empty winch-slings down into the interior of the module, he held the line steady while Negromonte worked feverishly inside. Then the winchman waved to the crew hovering above, and the first load of cargo was hoisted skywards.

Through an observation window, Michael could see that Nick Negromonte was already up to his knees in water but was still working to position the next batch of vital cargo. There was little time left for him to get out.

Two more hoists were necessary before the cargo transfer was complete. Then their rescuer reattached himself to the line and proffered the empty sling to Michael.

Michael shook his head and pointed to the escape hatch, gesturing for the winchman to get Negromonte out before the module sank. But as he glanced up the heaving side of the spacecraft, he saw the skipper himself beginning to emerge.

'Crew goes first,' shouted Negromonte with a grin, and pointed down towards Michael.

Strong hands roughly whipped the padded sling over Michael's head. Then he felt himself being jerked upwards. After a few instants swinging in the air, he glanced back down at the bobbing spacecraft. Nicholas Negromonte was now nowhere to be seen.

Michael was hauled backwards over the sill of the large Sikorsky and found himself propped up against a rear bulkhead beside Emilia. Other crew members quickly fitted safety harnesses around his body.

As the helicopter banked suddenly, the two rescued astronauts could see what the pilots were observing. The Apollo module was disappearing beneath the waves.

Despite descending to only fifty feet and circling the spot for an hour, no trace of Nicholas Negromonte could be found.

The former hulk people of *Pacifica One* had settled themselves along a lush coastline graced by wide sandy beaches.

'It looks just like Cape Cod,' Emilia yelled to Michael, as the helicopter circled before landing on the flight deck of the *Global Haven*.

What astonished both of them was the amount of development that had already taken place. For as far as the eye could see, both to the north and the south, furious building work was under way. Most surprisingly, all of the undeveloped inland surfaces seemed covered by thick emerald-green vegetation, and in the patchy sunshine they noticed the far-off glint of small lakes or rivers.

But their exaltation at seeing the Earth once again was tempered by their feelings of grief and shock at Nicholas Negromonte's death.

'It wasn't accidental, you know,' Emilia had shouted above the pounding of the helicopter's rotor blades as it returned to base. 'I was watching. He deliberately climbed back into the module just as it was going down.'

The co-pilot had relayed the news of their successful recovery to the communications centre on the *Global Haven*. He had also reported their unsuccessful search for its commander. Back at Mission Control, and on the moon, even the news of Negromonte's loss could not diminish their jubilation at the advance party's successful return to Earth. Elsewhere in space, wherever human beings had survived, the joy was unalloyed.

Forty-five minutes after they had been plucked from the sea, the new arrivals had been shown to separate staterooms on board the giant liner. Both of them found it so difficult to walk in the Earth's gravity that they each needed to be supported by two of the fit young men running flight operations.

In their rooms, they found fresh clothes laid out for them, all bearing tags from designer boutiques in the *Global Haven*'s shopping malls. After showering and shaving, Michael pulled on a white shirt and casual black trousers and, grasping onto handrails as he walked, went to find Emilia.

'This is heaven,' she smiled, admitting him to her suite. 'My first real change of clothes in eighteen months.' Both were slowly beginning to reacclimatize to Earth's energy-sapping gravity.

Up on the flight deck, they found the helicopter crew waiting for them, under a sky of gathering clouds.

'All set, Mr and Mrs?' called out the young pilot. After they settled themselves into the rear seats, Michael gave him the thumbs-up and seconds later they were in the air, flying north-wards above a long line of beached hulk vessels. All now looked deserted.

The flight took ten minutes, mostly at low altitude over the rapidly growing new coastal development. Down below, people everywhere seemed to be busy constructing buildings or tending the small fields and vegetable patches that they had created.

'It's a pity that I'm going to have to advise them to relocate,' shouted Emilia in Michael's ear. 'But there's a real risk of tsunamis on this coastline. We'll have to find them somewhere safer inland.'

The helicopter finally landed in a wide town square. As the pilot switched off his engines and the dust kicked up by the rotors began to clear, the passengers could see a large crowd of people gathered to meet them.

The co-pilot helped each of them down from the helicopter, and as Michael's foot touched the soil of his home planet, he felt an overwhelming rush of emotion. He turned to Emilia, whose moist eyes revealed that she too felt overcome.

But there was no time for emotion – people were waiting. Exchanging glances, the two envoys from the marooned space community waved aside offers of assistance and forced their gravity-laden bodies to begin a slow but unaided progress towards the waiting reception committee.

All around, there was an air of suspended activity. Workmen were staring down at them from every rooftop – only a few young boys still ran heedlessly backwards and forwards, carrying hods of newly baked bricks.

Immediately behind the reception committee rose the frame-work of a larger building, perhaps intended to be a town hall or a civic centre.

Chanda Zia stepped forward from the crowd. He was wear-ing a gleaming white tunic and a white Nehru hat.

'*Namaste*,' he said, pressing his hands together in front of his face, then lifting them to his forehead before bowing deeply.

'*Namaste*,' echoed Michael, copying his gesture.

'It is good to see you again, Counsellor Fairfax.' Chanda extended his hand.

'It's sure good to see *you*, too.' Michael shook the older man's hand warmly, before turning to introduce his companion.

'This is Doctor Emilia Knight,' he said. 'Emilia's a geologist and she'll select the site for the new landing strip, assuming you will still give us permission to build one.'

'*Aapka swagat Hai,*' said Chanda, grinning slightly.

'Pardon me?' said Emilia.

'It means "You are welcome here", Doctor Knight,' Chanda said, again extending his hand.

Emilia smiled and gave a small bow as she returned his handshake.

'What do you call this place?' Michael swept an arm around the square.

'We have called this land *Kayaa Kahanaa,*' said Chanda. Then, a look of pronounced merriment on his face, he said, 'If you and your friends on the moon intend to come and join us, we'll expect you to learn some of our languages.'

Michael and Emilia exchanged involuntary smiles.

'*Kayaa Kahanaa* means "Beyond Words of Praise",' explained Chanda. 'That's how we all felt when the seas finally subsided and we saw this land for the first time. We hope that is how you and all those who will follow you may also feel.'

'*Kayaa Kahanaa,*' repeated Michael carefully.

Then he felt a splash on his cheek, then another. It had started to rain.

THE CLOUD

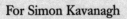

For Simon Kavanagh

ACKNOWLEDGEMENTS

Copy editors are usually the last people to amend a novel's text before it goes to the printer, but for this book Nick Austin was kind enough to help with ideas, suggestions and research tips when I was just beginning to plan the story – well over a year before he received the final manuscript. I'm grateful to him both for his initial creative input and for his usual meticulous copy-editing skills.

Simon Kavanagh, my agent at the Mic Cheetham Literary Agency, proved himself to be far more than just an enthusiastic and skilled literary representative. Throughout the development of this narrative he challenged, encouraged, berated, cajoled and threatened me to develop my story, to strike sections that didn't work well enough and to build up aspects he was sure would improve the book. He was nearly always right and I owe him a great debt, both creatively and commercially.

At Pan Macmillan my editor, Peter Lavery, has supported, encouraged and guided me over the past five years. His powerful commercial instincts and his continuing, infectious enthusiasm for story-telling makes me proud and grateful to be a member of his illustrious stable of writers. I'm also thankful to his colleagues Rebecca Saunders, Stef Bierwerth and Kate Eshelby at Pan Macmillan for all their help and support over the years.

For guidance on space affairs, astronomy and other technical matters I am indebted, not for the first time, to the writer and journalist Simon Eccles and to the distinguished astronomer and broadcaster Dr Bruno Stanek of Astrosoftware, Switzerland. For advice on computer science and the hypothetical alien mathematics used as a central device in this narrative, my thanks go to Professor David F. Brailsford of the School of Computer Science and Information Technology, University of Nottingham, and to the feasibility expert Peter Stewart. Although all of my technical advisers helped me greatly, any errors or mistakes in such detail remain my responsibility entirely.

On a personal level, I am grateful for the loving encouragement that my partner Maria Fairchild provided when she read the initial draft of this novel, and for her understanding when my writing kept me so often in solitary confinement. I'm also grateful to Alan Phillips, who had to listen to me trying out some of the early ideas for this story during many evenings at The Ladbroke Arms, and to Elaine Cooper, who has provided me with speedy, reliable and valuable criticism of all my novels.

I would also like to thank the management and staff of Orpheus Island Resort in Australia's Great Barrier Reef for making my stay so memorable that it led to me purloining their magical atoll for my own purposes. Despite what you may read in these pages, Orpheus Island remains one of the most beautiful and welcoming resorts in the world. Thanks must also go to Dagmar O'Toole and Alex Krywald of Celebrity Speakers Associates whose development and management of my public-speaking career has allowed me to visit Orpheus Island and many of the other locations that I have used in this book.

Finally, as always, I owe a huge debt to Liz Hammond for her patient, diligent and intelligent reading of my many drafts.

THE BEGINNING

April 2033

When it finally came, the alien contact was so weak, so minuscule among the noises of the great universe, that it was almost overlooked. Had it not been for the success of SETI's ten-year fund-raising campaign to build a listening post on the far side of the moon, humankind might never have learned that other forms of intelligence exist in the cosmos.

The director, council members and regional representatives of the SETI Institute (the loose grouping of maverick scientists and astronomers who made up the organization known as the Search for Extra-Terrestrial Intelligence) had raised almost $7 billion for the massive lunar construction project, mostly from public donations. Even then they were forced to beg passenger rides and cargo space from NASA, the European Space Agency, the Chinese and a few of the many private aerospace corporations who were now busily building habitats, launch sites, maintenance facilities, fuel dumps and even tourist accommodation on the Earth-facing side of the moon.

But it was the *far* side of the lunar surface that attracted SETI – the side which always faces away from Earth, the side which is shielded from the mother planet's massive out-pouring of radio and television signals, laser beams, electro-mechanical transmissions and all of the other electronic 'noise' that is produced by a young but rapidly advancing technological society and which spills out heedlessly into surrounding space.

Uniquely among the 138 major moons that circle the sun's planets, Earth's satellite is the only one to have a permanently shielded surface. In radio terms, it is the quietest place in the entire solar system, and it was the perfect location for the manned research outpost that had become known as 'Setiville'.

'Come on, come on!' shouted Desmond Yates impatiently as he stared up at the main communications screen, willing it to flicker into life. 'What are they doing? What's taking so long?'

Joan Ryder, a more mature and more seasoned SETI warrior, laid a calming hand on the young astrophysicist's shoulder.

'What do you think they're doing, Des?' she reasoned, as she too stared up at the blank screen. 'They're checking and double checking, just as we would. This is far too big for them to risk making a mistake.'

Yates nodded, ran his fingers impatiently through his thick dark hair and gently pushed himself up out of his low-gravity chair. As a twenty-five-year-old researcher, only one year out of his doctorate course at Stanford and a member of the SETI lunar team for less than three months, he would normally have been merely assisting his two more experienced colleagues. But it was he who had discovered the strange signal – a transmission that he now firmly believed to be both electronically generated and of genuine alien origin.

Strictly speaking, it was SETI's powerful analysing computers that had identified the unusual signal amongst all the myriad noises produced by the galaxies. But it was Des Yates who had chosen to target that particular patch of sky, Yates who had selected which range of frequencies to scan and Yates who had opted to pursue, amplify and home in on the 'possible contact' that the computer systems themselves ranked as being only of 'ETI Category 22 (minor interest)'. This 'contact' – now hastily reclassified as 'ETI Category 1 (most promising)' – was all Des's, and his two SETI colleagues agonized for him as they all waited to hear back from the Parkes radio telescope in Australia and England's Jodrell Bank Observatory.

Soon after its first informal establishment in 1960, SETI laid down strict checking and verification procedures to be followed whenever a signal was detected that might possibly be of alien origin. The organization's founders had been far-sighted. Over the seventy years during which the search had been conducted there had been no fewer than 635 'strong' false alarms, seventeen of them so convincing that SETI had been on the verge of announcing 'contact' to the world before the mundane truth of each of these signal's man-made origin was finally discovered.

Recently the Institute's 'ETI signal verification procedure' as laid down in the SETI operating manual had been strengthened, as if the organization's elders had anticipated that their new lunar research centre might produce a rash of supposedly positive contacts. Now, once the three Setiville duty scientists in the lunar observatory had all agreed that a contact was a 'strong possible', a copy of the signals received along with all of the relevant computer records and astronomical location information were to be sent for verification to two SETI-affiliated but independent observatories in opposing hemispheres of the Earth.

Yates and the SETI computers had first identified the

strange transmission ten days earlier. He had been alone, working a 'night shift' – the habitat's lighting and internal environment were set up to mimic the Earth's own circadian rhythms – when he saw the frequency graph spike at the same point on three repeated sweeps of the microspectrum he had chosen to explore.

For the rest of his life Desmond Yates would be unable to tell questioners what it was that prompted him to investigate this particular minor spike – especially when there were so many other larger peaks on the graph that seemed more worthy of exploration – but that is one key difference between humans and machines: Yates was working on a hunch.

For no reason other than fulfilling his romantic notions of the hunt for extra-terrestrial intelligence, the youthful researcher had then switched on the audio circuits so that he could hear the faint narrow-band signal on which he was instructing the computers and the sixty-four-metre dish outside to focus. He had watched too many science fiction movies.

The small control room – in which almost every wall surface was covered by high-definition 3-D screens – was suddenly filled with a jumbled cacophony. Yates could hear a low roar, like the sea, and higher notes that seemed to pulse with irregular and complex rhythms, but it was hard to pick out any detail.

He reached forward and set the parameters of a mathematical analysis he wanted the systems to run on the mysterious signals. Then, as his hunch suddenly grew, he asked the system to run a directional trace on the origin of the transmission and display the result in the small holo-theatre that occupied the centre of the control-room floor.

Seven minutes later Yates was on his feet circling a laser-projected hologram which shimmered as it hung in space in the centre of the holo-display area. From all around came the low roaring, interspersed with the shrill higher notes.

What the holo-image displayed was a computer-generated rendition of H-712256X, an 'Earth-like planet' (known to astronomers as an ELP), that was 14.8 light years away in the constellation of Aquarius.

Yates had never before known a signal trace to point so clearly to a particular planet. But he quickly reminded himself that he was less than a year into his career as a SETI researcher and a total new boy to lunar-based observations. Perhaps such apparently interesting traces had occurred many times before.

Suddenly an alarm sounded and Yates spun on his heel to scan the display behind him.

<u>SIGNAL IS NARROW-BAND – SIGNAL IS MODU-LATED</u> read the screen, the red underlined capitals flashing as they were supposed to do when such an unusual transmission was identified.

'Narrow-band' and 'modulated' were the key words when it came to any radio signal that might possibly be of extra-terrestrial origin. 'Narrow-band' meant that the signal was produced by some form of electronics or machine. 'Modulated' meant that the radio signals had a coherent pattern to them, a pattern that could not occur in nature, but could only have been created artificially by an intelligence for the purposes of meaningful communication.

'Holy shit!' Yates said out loud, and he moon-bounded out of the control room and along the short corridor to the residential quarters where his two colleagues were sleeping. A few minutes later, they too were staring open-mouthed at the computer announcement and the shimmering hologram of a planet that looked something like Earth, but was almost fifteen light years away – or about 142 trillion kilometres.

Their first task had been to eliminate all possible radio signals and electromagnetic interference that could be of man-made origin. Although 'modulated' was the most exciting alert they could be given by their analysing computers, it was also the most worrying. Usually it meant that the supposed narrow-band ETI signal was very much man-made; perhaps a transmission from a passing spacecraft, signals being beamed back home by a probe launched decades before or even stray signals from one of the deep-space telescopes that were now parked in locations well beyond the Earth-moon solar orbits.

But the SETI computers were able to dismiss such suspicions quickly. Their database had files on every commercial spacecraft launched by all of the world's nations in the last eighty years and, by a combination of careful observation and tip-offs from sympathetic scientists around the world, it also contained details on almost every 'covert' space craft, satellite and weapons systems any of the world's nations had launched. Within thirty-six hours of first receiving the alien signals the three members of the SETI lunar staff were all convinced that they were receiving genuine alien signals which were both 'ultramundane' (originating from beyond the solar system) and clearly of mechanical origin.

What really convinced Kim Mukerjee that young Des had made a genuine ETI contact was the fact that whilst the SETI computers could identify regular frequency shifts and amplitude variations that clearly indicated modulation in the radio signal, there were in no way able to decipher any of its content. At forty-eight years old, Mukerjee was the senior member of the Setiville lunar team and he had been employed by the SETI Institute for over twenty years. He had also been present in various Earth-based observatories when three previous 'positive contacts' had been made, all of which had finally turned out to be of man-made origin. He understood that the quantum encryption techniques used by the world's governments for their military satellites and weapons systems were totally impenetrable, but SETI's computers were always able to detect that quantum encryption was in use, even though they were unable to make any sense out of the constantly altering states of the signal itself.

But this signal was completely different. The computers did not identify the oscillating natural randomness that is the signature of quantum-encrypted transmissions, but neither could they suggest any form or shape for the content that was being transmitted. What was clear, however, was that the signals were both artificial and deliberately transmitted.

Now, ten days after the signal had first been identified and continuous recording begun, Des Yates and his two co-workers were all on edge as they waited for a response and the verdicts from the Parkes Observatory and from Jodrell Bank in the UK.

The protocol was clear. The Parkes and Jodrell Bank astronomers were checking copies of Setiville's signals, running their own analyses of them and attempting to pick up the signals for themselves (despite the appalling radio pollution in Earth's dense atmosphere). But neither group would say anything publicly about the contact, negative or positive, until and if SETI itself decided to make an announcement.

Contact with an alien intelligence was what every astronomer, astrophysicist, cosmologist and imaginative person in the street dreamed off, whether the professionals

wanted to admit it or not. Proof that there was another form
of technologically capable intelligence in the universe was
what an increasingly irreligious world fantasized about. For
many, the concept was a replacement for God.

'Setiville, this is Gus Wilson at Parkes,' boomed a voice
from a wall speaker.

All three members of the lunar team spun round as the
main communication screen came to life and revealed the
features of a middle-aged man with a bald head and a red,
weather-beaten face. They all knew the image and formidable reputation of Professor Gus Wilson, Director of the
Parkes Observatory.

At a nod from Mukerjee, Des Yates responded, hardly
able to get his greeting out of his mouth.

'We confirm your signal ST86901XT as positive, repeat
positive, Dr Yates,' said Wilson, an excited, intense look on
his rugged face. 'We've been able to pick up the signal ourselves, although it was worse than minus 600 – so faint we'd
never have noticed it down here on Earth. We've also elim-
inated every possible known man-made source and we've
enquired about that particular frequency range with all government, academic and commercial regulatory bodies –
nobody is using the 17.655 gigahertz frequency band. We too
confirm that the signal is modulated, and that your presumed point of origin, ELP H-712256X, is correct as proved
by the Doppler drift – although why the hell it should have
come from somewhere so relatively close, somewhere that
we've all looked at many times before, beats us.'

The Australian scientist paused for a deep breath, then
delivered his organization's formal pronouncement.

'Our unanimous vote is that this signal is a positive contact with an unknown but demonstrably intelligent alien
source. Written confirmation of our decision should be with

you by now. Congratulations – and we all hope you get a second confirmation.'

'Yes! YES!!' yelled Yates, punching the air as the comms screen faded to black.

'Hold on, Des, hold on,' said Mukerjee. 'You know we've got to–'

'Setiville, this is Jodrell Bank,' said another voice as the screen flashed back to life.

The three SETI scientists turned again and saw the severe, pinched features of Sir Kevin Kelly, the director of Jodrell Bank and Britain's Astronomer Royal. Mukerjee nodded at Yates once more.

'Good day, Sir Kevin,' stammered Yates, hardly able to contain his excitement. Dread filled him suddenly; was this internationally famous astronomer about to reveal him as a stupid geek, an over-obsessed enthusiast who had confused alien-chasing with the pursuit of real, scientifically based research?

The Astronomer Royal straightened his tie and cleared his throat, as though he were preparing to make a public announcement.

'We are able to confirm that your signal meets the three internationally agreed criteria and should be treated as a confirmed reception of a modulated signal generated by an intelligent extra-terrestrial source,' he said carefully.

'First, we have been able to pick up the signal ourselves, here at Jodrell Bank, albeit very weakly. Second, we confirm that it is modulated by electromechanical or other artificial means. Third, we agree with your identification of the planet H-712256X as the most likely point of origin and, finally, we have been able to eliminate all known forms of human-originated radio transmissions.'

'YES!' yelled Des once more, punching the air and

leaping from the ground so hard that he was catapulted upwards and hit his head on the habitat's soft roof lining.

Sir Kevin's severe expression creased into a smile at this display.

'I understand that you've already received a confirmation from Gus Wilson at Parkes – he and I have been speaking about this for some days. We think this is the real thing, Dr Yates. Congratulations to you – and to the rest of the team at Setiville. I look forward to your announcement.'

'Thank you, thank you very much, Sir Kevin,' Des managed to blurt as the screen image faded.

Now even Mukerjee was excited. He grabbed both Yates and Joan Ryder and hugged them to his slight frame, the three of them moon-bouncing around the control room, making footmarks on the polished floor of the holo-theatre and fending themselves off from the soft walls and ceiling as their low-gravity dance produced numerous collisions.

'Quick, get the champagne,' Mukerjee told Joan, as he finally released his dancing partners. But she was already heading for the refrigerated cabinet which held the sole bottle of alcohol that was officially allowed to be kept on the far side of the moon.

Yates grabbed three plastic cups and as Mukerjee popped the cork the fountain of champagne shot right up to the ceiling. The senior team member quickly directed the remaining wine into the plastic containers and, as their celebratory drinks were poured, the small group suddenly became subdued and solemn.

The trio of scientists stood in a little semicircle, still flushed and breathing heavily from their dancing, but now sobered by the realization that others had confirmed their momentous discovery. It had suddenly become real. They glanced at each other, unsure what to drink to, and Des's colleagues both nodded to him to make the toast.

The first human being to make confirmed contact with alien intelligence raised his paper cup to head height. 'To ET,' he said.

'To ET,' echoed Mukerjee and Joan Ryder, lifting their cups in turn.

As soon as they had drunk what little of the wine they had managed to salvage, their serious mood returned once again. They all had the feeling that they were present at a momentous event, something they would later have to describe over and over again for the benefit of strangers.

'Well, we know what the manual says we must do now,' said Mukerjee, breaking the silence. 'I think you should be the one to make the call, Des – it's about eleven a.m. in California.'

Des Yates nodded once, drained the dregs from his plastic cup, allowed it to float down into a waste basket, and then, with a deep breath, he seated himself in the main comms chair.

'Thank you for calling the SETI Institute,' said a female voice and image as the screen lit up. 'How may I direct your call?'

'Please connect me personally with Professor Jackson,' said Yates.

'I'm sorry, the director is in a trustees meeting all morning, Dr Yates,' said the operator. 'May I take a message?'

'Please interrupt him immediately,' said Yates as Kim Mukerjee leaned over his shoulder to point out the relevant paragraph in the manual. 'Please tell him that this is a Code 42 call. I repeat, a Code 42 call. I'll hold the line.'

WE ARE
NOT ALONE

SETI astronomers pick up confirmed alien transmissions.

To Des Yates's growing fury, the main board directors of the SETI Institute had delayed announcing the discovery of confirmed alien signals for nearly three months.

At first Director Jackson told the lunar team that he wanted to personally check out the signals for himself, as did several other SETI board members. He reminded the excited Setiville researchers that irreparable damage could be done to the Institute – and its hopes for future fundraising – if a premature announcement were made and the signals turned out to be non-alien after all.

'We only get one shot at such an important announcement,' Jackson told the lunar team forty-eight hours after they had first reported their success to the SETI Institute. 'We're going to advance the Setiville duty rota and relieve you early. We want you down here with us next week while we discuss how best to proceed.'

'But he has seen the independent confirmations!' fumed Yates to his colleagues when the connection to the director's office was closed. 'What else does he want, pictures of little green men?'

Mukerjee calmed his younger colleague, patiently explaining the sort of political wrangling that was probably taking place at the highest levels of the Institute's administration. He warned the discoverer of the alien signals that things were no longer going to be so straightforward for him.

While they were waiting for their replacement duty team to be ferried up from Earth, Mukerjee and Joan Ryder urged Yates to occupy himself by thinking up a name for the Earth-like planet from which the signals originated. They couldn't use 'H-712256X', the planet's astronomical designation, in a press release; people would want a simple name that they could understand and latch on to.

Yates spent his free time scouring on-line dictionaries and reference works, his study filled with the low roar of the alien signals that he kept patched through to his personal quarters from the control room. He wanted to be sure that the transmissions were still being received.

The astrophysicist finally decided upon the name 'Iso' – from the Greek word meaning 'equal' – as the planet H-712256X was about the same size as the Earth and had a biological 'signature' that was also very similar. From the composition of its atmosphere, it seemed likely that Iso also supported abundant biological life and Yates found himself fantasizing – even doodling – about the sort of creatures who might inhabit the planet and who might be sending such complex radio signals out into space.

Back on Earth and visiting the SETI Institute building in Mountain View, Northern California, Dr Yates was treated to a crash course in senior management politics. The first row was over when to make the momentous announcement.

Professor Jackson wanted to wait until the content of the alien signals had been decoded. Three independent cryptanalysis laboratories had been hired. Without being told that the signals on which they were working might be of alien origin, they were given copies of the transmission and charged with extracting its meaning. Two weeks into their work, all three were reporting that the encryption appeared to be of an unknown type, but they were sure they would soon be able to make progress in at least identifying the type of security used.

Other members of the SETI board argued that an announcement about the signals should be made as soon as SETI had completed its own internal investigation. This should not take very long, Desmond Yates and the other members of his lunar roster were assured. SETI's own in-house specialists had already reconfirmed what had been vouched for by the Parkes and Jodrell Bank facilities, but the Institute team was now devoting a huge effort to ensuring that there wasn't even the slightest chance that the signals could have some obscure man-made origin.

'What about the national security implications?' asked one board member, during an emergency meeting to which Yates and his colleagues had been invited. 'Won't the Pentagon want to slap a National Secrecy Order on us and impound the recordings for themselves?'

'They might very well try to classify it,' admitted Director Jackson, 'which is why I would really prefer to have the message decrypted and the content available to all. Then it would be too late for the government to try to keep it for themselves.'

'Our major announcement protocol has been clearly laid down for over fifty years,' broke in Dr Denise Logan, the Institute's Director of Publicity and Corporate Affairs. 'SETI was established to bring the benefits of communication with an alien intelligence to all humankind, not for the benefit of just one nation, let alone one government. I insist that we must make the announcement by the procedures we have established and that it must be made simultaneously around the world.'

Eventually SETI's hand was forced. The pressure within the scientific community for an announcement to be made became acute, with both the Parkes and Jodrell Bank directors doubting how much longer they could rely on their own teams to keep silent about such an important and exciting discovery. Then it became clear that the three decryption labs were not going to make fast progress in cracking the alien code. All were reporting a security system of previously unknown design and all were asking for more time to work on the problem.

Finally the SETI board agreed that the formal announcement of first contact with an alien intelligence would be made at press conferences on Saturday, 26 July 2033 at twelve noon Pacific Time – nine p.m. GMT – and that the announcement would be made simultaneously in Washington, London and Sydney. Des Yates would speak at the Washington afternoon press conference, Dr Mukerjee would appear in London in the evening and Dr Ryder would make the breakfast-time announcement in Sydney.

Copies of the press release would be flashed simultaneously to all international news agencies along with video, photographs and biographies of the discoverers, sound recordings of the alien signals, copies of the independent confirmations, and computer-generated 'best-guess' images of what the planet Iso looked like. Interviews would then be immediately set up for Des Yates and his colleagues while the directors of Jodrell Bank and the Parkes Observatory would add their own contributions to keep their local press happy.

The media went wild. The headline **WE ARE NOT ALONE** occupied almost all of the front page of a special edition of the *New York Times* which was posted both on the web and rushed onto the streets as a souvenir print publication.

ALIEN SPACE SIGNAL DETECTED trumpeted the London *Times* and images of Des Yates, and to a lesser extent those of his co-discoverers, appeared on every news bulletin around the world. Talk shows were filled with instant experts who pontificated about the likely nature of the aliens, what the planet Iso might be like, how quickly Earth could get a message back to the Isonians, and what technology could be used to allow humans to travel through space on a mission to visit Iso. The fact that such a journey would in reality take hundreds of years only added to the romance of the story. Suddenly space exploration made sense to everybody.

The story of alien contact was treated as the ultimate good-news story all over the world. In America, the White House announced that President Don Randall would make a presidential address to the nation.

In Britain, seventy-year-old Sir Charles Hodgeson, the internationally famous best-selling science fiction author and futurology guru, told the British media that the discovery of the alien signals 'is an historic first encounter with the cosmic community, just as I predicted in my very first book, *Signature of Life*'.

In Italy the Pope called on all Christians to pray for peaceful and fruitful dialogue with the aliens.

'This is God's voice sending us clear instructions,' said Archbishop Tyrone Underfield as he addressed a specially convened meeting of the Alabama Chapter of the Rastamendolian Church of the True God.

All over the world, special services were held in churches, mosques and temples, and prayers were offered giving thanks and welcoming contact with the new intelligent beings.

Des Yates almost lost his voice. In the first three weeks after the official announcement, he flew 100,000 miles and made almost ninety network television broadcasts around the world. On the flights and during transfers in between TV appearances he was accompanied constantly by television crews and print reporters. Even though he could do little except simply repeat how he came across the signal and how it felt when it was first confirmed to be of alien origin, his questioners never seemed to tire of hearing the same stuff over and over again.

On some TV shows animation artists produced renderings of possible aliens for him to comment on; on others he was asked to speculate about what it was that the aliens might be trying to communicate to the inhabitants of Earth. Even his mother and father were rooted out of their suburban home in Denver to provide accounts of how the young Des had first fallen in love with the stars by gazing up at the heavens through the clear air of his high-altitude home city.

It was during an evening talk show in Chicago that the words 'Nobel Prize' were first uttered in Yates's presence. 'There are rumours that you are to be nominated for a Nobel Prize,' said the anchorman. 'How do you feel about that, Dr Yates?'

Eight months after the public announcement, Desmond Yates's life had changed beyond all recognition. He had been given his own office at SETI's Mountain View headquarters along with a full-time assistant. Her job was to deal with the huge volume of requests for media interviews, enquiries from fellow scientists and invitations for her boss to give lectures, attend meetings and make celebrity appearances.

Yates's new office window looked out onto a building site where a large extension to the main SETI building was now under construction. The news of positive contact with aliens had led to a flood of new money pouring into the Institute.

US Congress members keen to display their forward thinking, their proactive engagement with space technology and their awareness of the benefits that knowledge of alien technologies might bring to the nation, voted to provide

SETI with annual research funds so large that even NASA was made jealous. This ongoing grant was enthusiastically endorsed by a public that had suddenly become space-mad. Every teenage boy – and many girls – now wanted to be astronomers, cosmologists, astronauts or 'alien hunters', as the media had dubbed the SETI researchers.

Overseas governments – keen to buy into any know-ledge that could be gleaned from alien communications – also donated significant funds and thousands of rich indi-viduals made gifts, planned legacies or set up trusts to further SETI's endeavours to put humankind into useful contact with alien civilizations.

Director Jackson found that his working life had also been changed completely by the announcement. He now spent most of his time closeted with the fund managers who looked after the Institute's new wealth or with rich poten-tial donors who wanted personal tours of the Institute – and a handshake with Desmond Yates himself – before finally parting with their money.

A new director of research had been hired and SETI was already using its increased resources to expand its lunar listening base on the far side of the moon. As well as adding two new ultra-large radio dishes to the Setiville complex they were also building a ten-metre optical telescope to take advantage of the superb lunar viewing conditions. None of the new money was being spent on building or developing Earth-based observatory facilities.

Immediately after SETI made the public announcement that alien signals had been received from the planet Iso, every radio-telescope observatory in the world had started to scour its own records to see why it had failed to spot the extra-terrestrial radio transmissions. No fewer than nine observatories subsequently announced that they too had been receiving the Isonian signals all along, but the transmissions had been so faint that their computers had categorized them as merely being part of the universe's background noise. Within the astronomical scientific community it was agreed that the alien transmissions would never have been noticed by any radio-dish observatory on Earth. From that moment on, all new money and development plans were switched to lunar and space-based observatories.

Des Yates was made a Fellow of the SETI Institute and, despite his youth, was given the singular honour of being invested as the 'Howard Regis Professor of Extra-Terrestrial Communication'. He wasn't expected to teach, or to conduct new research; his job was to oversee the decryption of the Isonian signals and to direct the Setiville teams who were continuing to monitor and record every bit of information being received from Iso.

Now thirty-six different decryption laboratories had been given copies of the alien transmissions to work on. A dozen of these were commercial forensic computing establishments, a further ten were labs located in the world's leading universities and the remainder were secret government computer-science establishments dotted around the world.

But the newly promoted Professor Yates had one private worry that he couldn't shake off: he kept wondering whether a government-owned computer laboratory would be honourable enough to disclose any success it might have in deciphering the alien transmissions. He knew that governments possessed the most powerful and advanced computer networks in the world, some so powerful that there was already an international protest movement calling for limits and treaties to control computer development and proliferation – much like those that were in place to limit the development of nuclear weapons – and he knew that any government offered the opportunity to read the alien signals would face a tremendous temptation to keep such potentially advantageous knowledge to itself. Statistically, the Isonian community was almost certain to be thousands or even millions of years ahead of Earth's civilization and would be very likely to possess technologies that would be of immense military, commercial or economic benefit. Who could resist?

The US government had already made its own position clear. The administration had been completely wrong-footed by SETI's simultaneous international announcement and by its liberal distribution of digital copies of the alien transmissions.

In a private phone call to Director Jackson, the US Secretary of State had told the SETI chief that many in the White House and the Pentagon were furious that the Institute had not been sufficiently patriotic to provide its mother nation with a private preview of such an important discovery. Jackson had politely reminded the Secretary that SETI was an international organization, with affiliations to the United Nations rather than to any single country. The call had ended on a decidedly chilly note.

Yates had ensured that each laboratory entrusted with the complete alien data stream had signed an undertaking that any knowledge extracted from the signals belonged in the public domain. But he still had the nagging suspicion that perhaps one of the government labs had already made sense of the transmissions and had secretly passed the knowledge on to its military or political masters.

But all of the lab directors he spoke to were telling him the same thing: their cryptologists had established that there was a clear but unfamiliar mathematical base to the signals and there appeared to be 'boundary lines' which might possibly indicate that some form of software was embedded in the data. But without knowledge of the alien radio technology, languages, software codes or its computer architecture it was going to take more time to make any sense out of the signals.

If governments were peeved that they had no exclusive rights to the alien transmissions and the potential treasures they might contain, their electorates made it abundantly clear that they were very happy that at least one other form of technologically capable intelligence existed in what had seemed up until then to be a vast, hostile and empty universe. Suddenly humankind belonged to a family, even though it had yet to meet the relatives.

There was a fundamental change in the world *Zeitgeist*; science fiction, space fiction, futurology, astronomy and cosmology, previously uneasy bedfellows and the preserve of geeks, now became part of mainstream popular culture. Sir Charles Hodgeson, already the doyen of great science-fiction storytellers, became the unofficial figurehead of this quasi-religious movement, appearing on TV shows, internet forums and magazine covers in almost every country in the world. He had been confidently predicting such contact for decades.

To celebrate the momentous discovery, Hodgeson had completed a new novella called *The Isonian Window* which his publishers rushed onto the web and into print, and which now topped the best-seller book charts in most English-speaking countries. Translation editions were being produced as quickly as possible and a film adaptation was already in production.

Then, on an American combined TV network show and internet broadcast, Sir Charles called on his millions of fellow alien-life enthusiasts to take future communications with the planet Iso into their own hands.

'I want everybody who owns a radio transmitter, no matter how low-powered, to transmit greetings of welcome and peace to the planet Iso over the coming week,' he told the viewers. 'The Earth is currently in a favourable position for radio communication with the constellation of Aquarius and if people broadcast UHF signals just two degrees south of Pegasus, we can be sure that the Isonians will receive our friendly messages in less than fifteen years' time.'

Hodgeson hit a public nerve. Amateur radio enthusiasts throughout the world trained their directional and even non-directional antennae approximately on the dim constellation and broadcast whatever messages they felt like sending to the alien civilization. Many people who had never owned radio equipment before went out and bought UHF transmitters and rigged up transmitting aerials, few of them worrying about licences or controlled radio spectrums, and broadcast wildly across all frequencies, as if they were bellowing into the night sky.

From an ancient Winnebago in an Arizona trailer park, a group of alien-life enthusiasts created a network of 287 separate radio transmitters around the state and then started to beam such powerful UHF signals out into the night sky that all flights had to be diverted away from the central-southern states of America until police could be dispatched to forcibly shut down the endlessly repeating transmissions.

'Hello people of Iso,' their message ran. 'We send greetings of peace from the planet Earth. Please come and visit with us.'

*

'On behalf of the people of the United States, I am proud to present you with the Presidential Medal of Freedom,' said President Don Randall as he shook Des Yates's hand.

About eighty people were present to witness the ceremony being conducted in The East Room at the White House; SETI board members and scientists mingled with NASA officials, administration personnel and favoured politicians. Yates's parents stood proudly at the front of the group as the official photographer asked the President and the latest recipient of the nation's highest civilian honour to shake hands once again for the benefit of the cameras.

When the formal part of the ceremony was concluded, President Randall greeted Yates's parents, complimented them on their son's achievement and then, to the surprise of his aides, quietly asked the young SETI celebrity if he could spare a further few minutes of his valuable time to join him in the Oval Office for a private discussion.

Almost a year had passed since the moment when Des Yates had first selected the weak Isonian signals for further investigation, but no further progress had been made in deciphering their content. Now some of the cryptanalysts were even questioning whether the alien signals were encrypted at all. 'It might just be that their own spoken language and electronic designs are so different from ours that we don't know where to start,' the director of the Rand Laboratory in Berkeley told Yates. 'We've thrown petabytes of networked power at the task, but we're not making any progress.'

'Well, young man, what should we do now about these alien signals of yours?' asked President Randall, once he, Yates and a handful of advisers were ensconced in the Oval Office's comfortable couches.

'Well, sir, I think we should respond officially,' replied

Yates, still somewhat overawed by his surroundings and the august company he was keeping these days.

'At least the decision about whether or not to respond to the signal has been taken out of our hands,' interjected one of the senior NASA officials to whom Yates had been introduced earlier. 'Thousands of crazy dingbats all over the world are already pumping out their own greetings.'

The President nodded thoughtfully, then turned back to Yates. 'So what should I say?' he asked.

The newly honoured, recently promoted, international celebrity scientist swallowed as he steeled himself to make the only reply that he knew was correct.

'With respect, sir,' he began, 'it isn't for the United States to respond officially. This has to be an international diplomatic response, one that is made on behalf of all the world's people.'

'Oh God, not the UN,' groaned Randall as he glanced across at his Chief of Staff.

For all of the public's excitement about the world's first confirmed contact with aliens, it took the United Nations organization a further ten months to agree on and to compose Earth's first official response to the signals that were still being received from the planet Iso. Much discussion and preparation had taken place before the historic meeting of the General Assembly during which the greeting would be formally transmitted.

Back in 1977, in the very earliest days of space exploration, NASA had optimistically prepared for contact with forms of extra-terrestrial intelligence by attaching twelve-inch gold audio discs to the sides of the twin space probes Voyagers 1 and 2, a pair of spacecraft that were due to explore the local solar system and then head out into wholly unknown deep space. The discs had included 115 images of Earth, recordings of human languages, diagrams of the human form, local star maps and, because it was the 1970s, even samples of whale songs.

But the international group of scientists, linguists, mathematicians, philosophers and anthropologists charged with composing the new radio communication felt a far heavier weight on their shoulders than had the NASA team responsible for composing the Voyager message. Now Earth's communication was to be beamed towards a specific intelligent life form, and one living not too far away.

The arguments about what to include in the greeting, and how to say it, were intense. It was agreed that although this was Earth's first contact with an extra-terrestrial civilization, it would almost certainly not be the Isonians' first contact with other alien intelligences. Earth's technological civilization was very young indeed and statistically it was extremely likely that the more advanced Isonians would have made contact with many other cultures before. It was possible, indeed likely, that there was a galactic protocol established for this kind of communication and information interchange. But those on Earth would have no chance of knowing the correct way to respond and introduce themselves; they would just have to say 'hello' politely, and hope that as newcomers to the galactic community they didn't cause any offence.

In the end it was agreed that a first initial message lasting about twenty minutes should be broadcast, to be followed by a series of regular daily transmissions which would explain and amplify further details of Earth's civilization. The first programme of signals to be beamed to the Isonians would take almost two years.

Basdeo Panday, the United Nations Secretary-General,

stood at the large lectern facing the General Assembly and the world's TV cameras. Beside him was a clear plastic column surmounted by a large red button.

'Samples of every major language used on Earth, along with their grammatical rules, are included in our message of peace and greeting,' the Secretary General told the UN Assembly representatives and the worldwide viewing public. 'We have also provided examples of our mathematics. In addition we are sending video streams which show the beauties of our own home planet – as viewed from the surface and from space – and we have included detailed star maps and locators which will pinpoint our precise position in the galaxy, relative to Iso's own location in the Aquarian constellation. We have also included a variety of intelligent software tools to help the Isonians read our message. I only wish they had done the same for us.'

There was widespread laughter in the Assembly Chamber. Almost two years after the continuous stream of alien signals had first been detected, Earth's most distinguished cryptanalysts were still unable to decipher what it was that the Isonians were trying to communicate.

'Later transmissions to Iso will include a full set of encyclopaedias, geographical and historical information about our planet, details of our own solar system and samples of non-proprietorial technology designs.'

Panday paused, partly for effect and partly because as the time approached he too felt the immensity of the moment. He moved across from the lectern to stand at the elevated push-button.

The Secretary-General cleared his throat, and then announced clearly, 'On behalf of all the world's peoples, we send this message in a spirit of peace and with the hope of mutual and beneficial cooperation between our worlds in the years to come.'

His hand fell onto the large red mushroom-shaped button and simultaneously eighteen international radio observatories and 187 military radio-transmitting stations on Earth and in space began to transmit the laser-pulsed message at maximum power. It was the most powerful synchronized radio signal ever transmitted from Earth and travelling at the speed of light it would take fourteen years and eight months to reach its intended destination.

ONE

April 2063 – thirty years later

'Look at the size of it!' remarked Walker Donahue, a reporter from *Time* magazine, as the balloon-tyred moon-bus crested a ridge and the lunar complex came into sight. 'I had no idea it was so big.'

'Setiville now covers three thousand acres of the moon's surface,' announced Melody Barron, SETI's media relations executive, as she stood in the aisle of the pressurized bus, trying to keep the carefully selected and highly privileged group of fifty journalists, reporters and camera operators informed and happy. She knew that her charges had been less than pleased to leave all their personal networking and communications equipment behind at SETI's main guest hotel but, as she had explained to them over and over again, no radio communication whatsoever was allowed on the far side of the moon. Nothing could be transmitted that might pollute the precious radio-free environment.

'There are sixteen arrays of radio telescopes which are each made up of over four hundred separate dishes,' she told the group. 'The individual dishes are more than two hundred metres in diameter.'

As the media party drove down the gentle incline towards the vast scientific complex, they could see row after row of ultra-large radio telescopes angled towards the brilliant night sky. 'Welcome to Setiville' read a large, softly illuminated sign at the entrance to the settlement, a township that appeared to boast scores of separate buildings, all interlinked by hermetically sealed walkways. Some of the buildings were two or three storeys high and the scientific establishment seemed almost as large as the main Lunar City on the Earth-facing side of the moon.

The journalists had been invited to visit Setiville as part of the anniversary celebrations that SETI was holding to mark the thirty years since the radio signals from the planet Iso had first been detected. Those signals were still being constantly received, and Setiville had become the natural home for the ongoing search for other alien signals.

Over the three decades since the discovery SETI's wealth had become legendary. Each year more and more donations and bequests rolled in to the organization and, as the visiting journalists were told, most of it was being spent on carefully exploring the many parts of the universe that were still unsurveyed and unmonitored by radio listening equipment.

The media visitors were shown around a permanent exhibition that was housed inside a huge pressurized plastiglass dome. The enclosure was sufficiently large to cover the original sixty-four-metre dish which had first captured the Isonians' radio signals, and other exhibits included a holographic re-enactment of the moment when the young Desmond Yates had first picked up the alien signal and had realized that the primitive computers of the time had identified it as being 'Modulated'. A copy of his Nobel Prize citation was displayed proudly in a wall case.

'Of course, Professor Yates is now the Emeritus Chairman of the SETI Institute,' explained Melody to her large group. 'And he's also the senior Space Affairs Adviser to the White House.'

The party then moved on to look at another holographic exhibit which showed a computer-generated model of the planet Iso and its own local star, Giliese 76.

'We're unable to observe Iso optically – it's too far away,' explained Melody. 'But spectrum analysis has allowed us to make very educated guesses about the likely amount of water and even the size of the land masses that the Isonians have on their home planet.'

At the back of the group, Walker Donahue yawned. He wasn't even bothering to take notes or make any recordings. The alien signals were no longer exciting news - they had been considered old hat for years - but the thirtieth anniversary celebrations had provided just enough of a news hook for him to be able to justify leaving his New York office to join this expensive luxury junket. He'd never been to the moon before, but he was already coming to the conclusion that he wouldn't return quickly. Moon-bouncing was fun, but there was nothing special to see on the lunar surface. The luxury space-station hotels which orbited the Earth offered even better views of the home planet as well as wonderfully sybaritic weightless accommodation.

Donahue desultorily followed the party into Setiville's main lecture theatre, took a seat at the back and stifled another yawn as a fit-looking middle-aged man bounced onto the stage.

Dr Lee Kaku, Setiville's resident director of research, welcomed the reporters and quickly moved on to the main topic of the day; he understood that the media needed a constant stream of new information to keep them interested.

'Ladies and gentlemen, you have been invited here

today to hear an important announcement. We are going to visit the planet Iso. In partnership with NASA, SETI will launch an unmanned spacecraft to the Aquarian constellation this coming August.' As Kaku spoke, a 3-D holographic image of the spacecraft appeared, floating above the visitors' heads.

The Setiville director stepped forward to the edge of the stage and pointed a laser highlighter up towards the large image. 'We are calling our spacecraft *Friendship*. It will take four hundred and twenty-five years to reach Iso and it will carry three of our most advanced computer personalities on board. With the special permission of the United Nations Directorate of Computer Control, these personalities will be given fully humanoid form.'

Now there was a buzz of excitement among the members of the press. A mission to Iso in four months' time, and a temporary lifting of the worldwide ban on computer intelligences occupying adult humanoid form; this was real news.

Director Kaku provided more details about the craft and the journey it was going to undertake. The reporters learned that despite its crew of androids and its hybrid-nuclear power source, the mission was a relatively low-cost project and that over half of the money had come from SETI's own reserve funds.

'We realize that none of us will live long enough to see the benefits or the results of this investment,' explained the director. 'But we owe it to future generations to go and see what is on Iso for ourselves. This is the modern-day equivalent of fifteenth-century European galleons setting out for the New World.'

'You've cracked the code, haven't you?' shouted a woman reporter at the front of the theatre. There were other shouts as more journalists picked up the cry. Over the years there had been recurring press speculation that the continuous stream of signals being received from Iso had long since been decoded by either SETI itself or by one of the world's major governments and that the contents of the transmissions were being kept secret from the people.

'Are you in current communication with the people of Iso?' shouted another voice.

The director raised his palms. 'Absolutely not,' he said firmly. 'If anyone had managed to crack the Isonians' languages or data packets, SETI would have told the world immediately. It is a fundamental part of our charter that all our work should be conducted in the public domain, for the benefit of all society.'

'So why are you launching this spacecraft now?' shouted a voice in the darkness.

'To celebrate the thirtieth anniversary of our first alien contact,' said the director, 'and because if the Isonians did receive the first responses that were sent them thirty years ago, we should be receiving their reply – assuming that they chose to make one – any day now.'

The I-95 interstate highway runs all the way between Maine in the north and Florida in the south and, where it passes through Massachusetts, it becomes a high-tech corridor. This trend began in the late 1960s as technology firms began to be spun out of the Massachusetts Institute of Technology, the University of Boston, Cambridge University, Harvard and the other colleges that make up America's North-East Coast cluster of academic excellence. These firms chose locations near to the highway for ease of access and for the obvious distribution advantages.

The owners of the themed retail outlet known as 'The

Adoption Center' chose Deer Park Valley on the I-95, fifteen miles south of Boston, for the same reasons – and because of the opportunity it gave them to capture passing trade. Large billboards placed beside the highway – ten miles, five miles and one mile before the north and south turn-offs – told passing motorists that the Center had a wide range of infants available for adoption, from newborn to twenty-four months, and of all ethnic groups.

Inside the adoption nursery, forty infants were sitting, crawling, playing or standing according to their age and level of physical development. A dozen of the youngest babies were in playpens, watched closely by three of the dozen white-uniformed nurses who had the care of this boisterous group. In other parts of the floor area children were playing with toys, doing drawings, exercising in activity centres or being fed by the smiling, friendly staff.

Baby Luke, just eight months old, was seated in the middle of a large rubber mat and he was clearly unhappy. His wails filled the room, as wails filled these particular premises so often; clearly, he needed either feeding or changing, perhaps both.

Nurse Anne Loman turned away from a small two-year-old girl with golden curls and started to cross towards Luke, her arms outstretched.

Suddenly the double entrance doors leading from the main customer parking lot were forced open violently – doors that for security reasons were always kept locked from the inside.

Three youthful figures, all dressed in black and wearing black ski masks, burst into the nursery, each holding a large sinister-looking weapon with a complex metal contraption at its muzzle.

'PUT THE BABIES DOWN – NOW!' shouted the man at the front of the group.

The infants all wailed at this violent and unexpected invasion of their playtime but none of the nurses moved. They were all frozen with fear.

'MOVE AWAY NOW!' shouted the group's leader, directing his weapon threateningly at the nurse nearest to him. All around the room, security cameras silently recorded the proceedings. 'MOVE AWAY NOW, NURSES – YOU WILL NOT BE HURT,' yelled the leader.

The intruders advanced menacingly into the nursery, threatening the adults with their weapons, until each nurse had risen and had gone to stand at the side wall of the nursery, as directed by the attackers' gun muzzles. The children stared up at these interlopers with wide, frightened eyes. There was now complete silence in the nursery, as if the infants had realized that something so serious was happening that it was beyond crying. As they had risen, several of the female nurses had instinctively gathered up individual babies in their arms.

When the nurses were clear of the main group of frightened children, the leader nodded curtly to his companions and the three attackers fired their high-voltage laser-channelled electrical pulse weapons directly into the crowd of infants.

The babies, some no more than a few weeks old, burst into flame, their skin frying as if it were plastic, their hair catching light immediately as they were struck by 50,000-volt charges.

The attackers continued to fire pulse after pulse of high-voltage power into the group of children and suddenly blood burst from the victims' bodies as they began to explode under the sustained onslaught. The attackers and the nurses were sprayed with gore as veins and arteries burst and a vast dark pool began to spread slowly outwards from beneath the group of bodies.

One of the three black-clad attackers suddenly started to scream – a female cry of anguish – and ripped off her mask to reveal pretty features that belonged to a face no more than twenty years old.

'LOOK AT THE BLOOD, KURT!' she screamed at the group's leader as she lowered her heavy weapon. 'LOOK AT THE BLOOD!'

'It's just their latest feature,' the leader shouted back, still engaged in firing powerful bolts of electricity, his weapon whining repeatedly as its booster charger prepared each burst. 'Come on, the warehouse is through there.'

He ran around the pile of burning children, his co-attackers following, and burst through a white door at the back of the nursery.

The trio suddenly arrived in a large, cold warehouse in which wooden pallets were stacked thirty feet high. On each pallet were piled between twenty and thirty rectangular plastic boxes.

The woman who had ripped her ski mask from her face ran to the nearest stack of pallets and prised a box from the pile. She glanced at the packaging and then smiled, holding up the weighty pack for her fellow attackers to read.

MY BABY BOY, TEN MONTHS OLD, read the large letters on the front of a transparent window from beneath which a naked infant boy appeared to be staring out at the world. 'NOW, WITH LIFELIKE BLOOD' proclaimed words on a yellow flash that had been applied to the packaging. **Another fine product from Someone To Talk To, Inc.,** read a smaller line of text.

The leader nodded with grim satisfaction, then signalled for his grinning accomplice to stand aside.

Standing shoulder to shoulder, the three attackers raised their weapons again and fired high-voltage bursts of electricity into the vast piles of cartons. Immediately the boxes and the pallets burst into flame and the attackers directed their fire at other shelving units in the warehouse. From somewhere nearby a loud alarm started to wail, then water sprinklers came on all around the building. But the attackers showed no sign of a desire to flee.

A loud crack suddenly cut through the noise of the flames and a bullet whined off a nearby concrete pillar.

The third attacker, a male, turned quickly and saw an elderly security guard puffing his way towards them through a spray of water, raising his pistol for a second shot.

'Don't–,' shouted the leader, reaching out a restraining hand. But even as he spoke his partner lifted his stun-weapon and on reflex fired back at the old man carrying the raised pistol.

The security guard was knocked backwards off his feet by the high-energy pulse. Unlike the plastic computer-based toy dolls at which the group had been previously firing, though, he did not burst into flames.

Followed by his two accomplices, the leader sprinted towards the fallen man. As he arrived beside the prone form, the leader ripped his own mask from his face, not caring about the many security cameras dotted around the warehouse, and threw his stun-gun aside.

Dropping to his knees on the wet floor, he felt for a pulse in the right side of the fallen man's neck. The guard's face was paper pale and smoke was still rising from his thin grey hair.

'He's still alive,' shouted the group's leader over the

noise of the crackling inferno all around them. 'Help me get him out of here, Mitch. Zoë, you call an ambulance.'

Mitch, the gang member who had fired at the security guard, now discarded his own mask and weapon. The two men took an arm each and dragged the old man out through the billowing smoke towards the daylight that they could see at the far end of the warehouse. Zoë was shouting to the emergency services on her communicator as she ran alongside.

Once outside, the group's leader immediately started full CPR on the felled security guard. He opened his shirt collar, checked the air passageway, felt again for a pulse and then began to massage the old man's chest forcefully. As he worked his co-conspirators stood helplessly by, all their weapons and masks now discarded.

'He's dying on me,' shouted the leader furiously as he pummelled the old man's chest. He bent and put his mouth onto the wet, cold lips, blowing hard to inflate the security guard's lungs.

'But my gun was only on stun!' protested the attacker who had felled the guard.

The group's leader ignored him, continuing his frantic resuscitation attempts as the minutes raced by, pausing only occasionally to catch his own breath.

Loud siren wails suddenly filled the air and the tall metal gates to the loading dock at the rear of the warehouse burst open as an armoured SWAT vehicle raced into the lot, followed by a string of police cars, sirens wailing, emergency lights strobing. Then the smoke-filled air was compressed with a deep and repetitive thudding as a police helicopter descended to hover low overhead.

'Throw away your weapons and lie face down on the

ground,' ordered an amplified voice, so loud that it seemed to rattle the attackers' chest bones.

The gang leader leaped to his feet.

'This man needs a doctor,' he shouted at the top of his voice, over the thwacking of the helicopter blades, the wailing of the sirens and the roaring of the inferno in the warehouse behind them.

'THROW AWAY YOUR WEAPONS AND LIE FACE DOWN!' repeated the police voice, now with even more amplification.

The leader glanced at his two friends, shrugged as if to apologize, and then raised his arms high, got down on one knee and, with an awkward half-roll, lowered his body onto the hard, gritty tarmac. As his two followers did the same, heavily armed SWAT team members poured out of the back of their armoured transport and, with automatic weapons raised and pointed at the prone gang members, began to inch their way forward to make their arrests.

'And now, I'm pleased to introduce a very special surprise guest,' Director Kaku told the lunar visitors. 'He's making a rare visit to Settiville, so please join me in welcoming SETI's chairman emeritus and the man who first discovered the Isonian signals, Professor Desmond Yates himself.'

The group of journalists clapped politely as a tall, distinguished-looking man with a full head of wavy dark hair strode into the spotlight. The years had been kind to the famous astrophysicist and his movements were so energetic that he seemed like a much younger man.

'I'm not going to say much,' Yates told the now attentive group, 'But I want to underline how pleased I am that we are finally going to send a mission to Iso – it's long overdue.'

The SETI chairman then went on to describe several key design features of the mission that he had personally overseen. He explained that a nuclear-powered Orion drive would be used initially to boost *Friendship* to a very high velocity, after which an ion drive would continue to provide gentle acceleration for most of the long journey towards the Aquarian constellation. Then, on its final approach, large solar sails would be deployed to slow the spacecraft down, capturing the solar wind from Iso's own star to create a braking effect. He explained that the crew of computer personalities would carry out all maintenance and repairs to the spacecraft during the mission and, after telling the journalists that he was going to be available after the briefing if they had any questions, he came to the conclusion of his short presentation.

'Finally, I would like to remind you of what the Isonian signals actually sound like in real time,' Yates told the audience, looking at his watch and turning to where Director Kaku was sitting at the side of the small stage. 'If my timing is right, we should be receiving a handover of the signals from the Parkes Radio Observatory in Australia any moment now.'

The Setiville director nodded, then rose from his seat and signalled into the wings.

The audience shifted in their seats as Professor Yates waited expectantly at the lectern. At the edge of the stage they could see that Director Kaku was now engaged in some urgent exchange with an unseen person. Then the director nodded before walking back to the centre of the stage to stand close beside SETI's chairman. He whispered in Yates's ear, then turned to face the audience.

'Ladies and gentlemen,' the Setiville director announced, 'I am afraid that due to a technical hitch you will not be able to listen to a live stream of signals being received from the planet Iso on this particular visit. But recordings of the original signals can be found in your press kits, and Professor Yates has kindly consented to make himself available for interview immediately after this event. If you would like to follow Miss Barron, she will lead you back to the main reception centre, where cocktails will be served.'

From the *New York Times* website, 20 April 2063

ET HANGS UP

Alien Radio Transmission Ceases Abruptly After 30 Years

Thirty years after they were first detected, radio transmissions from planet Iso have ceased abruptly. No signals have been received from the source since April 16th.

Professor Desmond Yates, the original discoverer of the alien transmissions, said, 'It's probable that the interruption is only temporary – a solar flare in the Aquarian solar system, or an occlusion by another planet. Or they could have switched their range of frequencies for some reason. I'm sure we will re-establish contact soon.'

'Not a Coincidence'

Other ETI experts were less confident. 'They switched off their transmission just when we were expecting an answer from them,' said Dr Jim Burns, NASA's Director of Extra-terrestrial Communication. 'It's difficult to consider it a coincidence.'

To the casual gaze of the people thronging the corridors of the Boston County Court, Bill Duncan looked more like a musician waiting to go on stage than a witness being called to give evidence. His thick brown hair was worn collar length and a small silver earring in his left ear accentuated rather than softened a long, aquiline face. His white T-shirt, denim jacket, jeans and black cowboy boots all added to the impression that he could have been a lead guitarist from a successful rock band of the late twentieth century.

Despite functioning in what was now a very high-tech networked society, criminal justice remained a wholly human process. The proceedings in most civil cases were now conducted virtually with the plaintiffs, defendants, lawyers, juries and judges meeting only within the networks to plead, argue and receive judgements. But legislators still believed that for the most serious criminal offences the law should be administered in the old-fashioned way. Many modernizers argued that this expensive anachronism was merely maintained at the behest of lawyers who wished to maintain their exorbitant fees and monopoly over trial proceedings. But for hearings such as the one now proceeding beyond the closed oak doors across the corridor from where Bill Duncan waited, there could be no method of justice other than that conducted in real time, in person and face to face. The three young defendants in the hearing were each facing a murder charge, and in the state of Massachusetts a conviction would lead to a life sentence without parole.

The courtroom door opened and a petite, smartly dressed woman peered round it. She saw Bill and then crossed quickly to sit beside him on the bench where witnesses were required to wait before being called to give evidence.

'The prosecution has agreed to drop the murder charges,' she told him in a low voice. 'But all three defendants now face aggravated manslaughter charges, which could still carry a life sentence when it comes to the main hearing next year.'

The witness shook his head and ran his fingers through his hair.

'They're just kids doing what they thought was right,' he said, with a shake of his head. 'All they wanted to do was protest this grotesque trade in imitation babies. They had no intention of hurting anyone.'

'Well, that's exactly what we want you to say, and with luck you'll help them to get bail. You'll be called in a few minutes, once Mr Cohen has finished laying out our defence. Is there anything you need?'

Just over an hour later, Bill Duncan stepped up into the witness box of Boston District Court Number 9, refused the Holy Bible and read out loud the words of affirmation printed on the card.

The crowded courtroom was large, airy and panelled in a light maplewood. The public seating and press benches were crammed as this case had already attracted considerable media attention. Behind the long defence table Bill could see his three former students, all now severely and smartly dressed, their faces pale and drawn. The defence counsel had tentatively suggested that Professor Duncan too might like to remove his earring and wear a dark suit for the occasion, but the look his proposal had drawn from the witness had quickly prompted the lawyer to move on to other topics.

As soon as the swearing-in was complete, Counsellor Paul Cohen rose from behind his table, crossed to the centre of the floor and faced his witness squarely.

'Please tell the court your full name, age, address and occupation,' he said.

'I'm William Andrew Duncan, I'm forty-four years old, I live on a ship called the *Cape Sentinel* which is moored at Pier Sixty-Seven in Boston harbour and I teach and conduct research at the Massachusetts Institute of Technology,' Bill told the attorney and the court in a clear strong voice.

'In fact, you hold the Juliet M. Hargreaves Chair in Computer Personality Psychology and you are the Director of the Cognitive Computer Psychology Lab at MIT, aren't you, Professor Duncan?'

'That's correct,' agreed the witness.

'And isn't it also correct that you are a MacArthur Award-winner for science and a member of the National Academy of Sciences?'

'This is only a pre-trial hearing, Counsellor,' broke in the judge. 'I just want to get a flavour of the testimony, not the witness's entire life story.'

'Of course, your honour,' agreed Cohen. 'I merely wanted to establish Professor Duncan's pre-eminence in the field that is under discussion today.'

The attorney turned his attention back to his witness.

'To put it plainly, Professor Duncan, you are the world's leading authority on the development, psychology and pathology of artificial intelligent life, commonly called computer personalities, aren't you?'

'Well, I suppose I'm probably one of them,' agreed Bill.

'And would you tell us something about your three students here, and what might have been their motive for staging such a theatrical incursion into a retail outlet selling computer-personality toys?'

The lawyer had coached his witness for two hours on what he was expected to say. Bill drew a deep breath before summarizing what had prompted the protest, a stunt that had been organized for the sake of publicity but a stunt that had gone terribly and fatally wrong.

'I know the three defendants well, and I know them to be upright, decent people who would never deliberately hurt anyone. I also know that they were protesting against the obscene trade in lifelike baby androids that are now being sold to childless couples, to children and to lonely old people without any consideration for the psychological damage that can be caused to vulnerable humans who strike up relationships with these machines. This is a trade that must be banned – just as the manufacture of adult humanoid computer personalities has been outlawed.'

'Your honour, what has this got to do with this brutal killing?' asked the prosecuting counsel, rising from behind his table.

'I was about to ask the same thing, Mr Cohen,' said the judge.

At the back of the courtroom a smart but soberly dressed woman in her mid-thirties watched the MIT professor's face carefully as he gave evidence. Federal Agent Sarah Burton had guessed that given the chance Bill Duncan would use the witness box to denounce both the American computer industry and the US government for its lax attitude to computer regulation. She'd been secretly investigating the radical professor and his circle of friends for six weeks now and she was getting to know how the man's mind worked. Not for the first time she wondered why the prestigious Massachusetts Institute of Technology was prepared to condone such anti-establishment expressions by a senior staff member, and an attitude that was so opposed to the interests of the computer industry itself. It seemed as if Duncan was a cuckoo in MIT's hallowed computer-science nest.

'What it's got to do with this sad but accidental death is that millions of children all over the world are becoming more attached to these machines than they are to their own parents,' broke in the witness, ignoring Cohen's frantic hand signals for him to shut up. 'I know of children as young as eight who have self-harmed or committed suicide when they have been forced to give up their relationship with a computer personality.'

'Professor Duncan–' began the judge firmly.

'People have no idea of the emotional damage these computer personalities are causing and the social harm that is being stored up for our societies – not just in this country, but all over the world,' continued the MIT luminary, ignoring the judge's interjection.

'That's enough, Professor,' ordered the judge.

'These machines are turning children into psychopaths,' shouted Bill, eyes blazing, his gaze shifting from the judge to Attorney Cohen, to the defendants and to the main courtroom. 'And they also encourage old people to commit suicide. That's why I'm here, isn't it? I'm a psychologist as well as a computer scientist, and I know the damage that is being caused by this heedless, greedy exploitation–'

Three loud bangs resounded around the courtroom as the judge pounded his gavel.

'That's more than enough, Professor,' he shouted at Bill Duncan. Then he turned his stern gaze on the defence attorney. 'If your witness has nothing of relevance to tell the court, I suggest you excuse him and move on.'

TWO

'It is quite true that *Friendship* will take four hundred and fifty years to reach Iso,' agreed Professor Desmond Yates, responding to a question, 'But all the time the spacecraft is travelling it will act as a mobile observatory and interstellar probe, continuously reporting its images and valuable data back to Earth. It will provide the most fantastic opportunity for astronomy, long before it arrives at its destination.'

The SETI Institute's chairman was making a crucial presentation, one that would help to decide whether the *Friendship* mission was now to be cancelled or whether it should proceed as planned, despite the continuing loss of the signals from Iso. His small but illustrious audience included President Maxwell T. Jarvis himself, the White House Chief of Staff, the Secretary of State, the Director of NASA and various Treasury officials who already seemed keen to abandon the whole project. They were meeting in one of the small White House Cabinet rooms adjacent to the Oval Office and Yates had spent fifteen minutes briefing them on the project's progress, describing *Friendship*'s hybrid power source, the three humanoid computer personalities who were going to crew the ship and the procedures they would adopt as they approached the source of the alien radio transmissions. Now, having answered the question, he returned to his prepared presentation.

'Throughout the voyage *Friendship* will transmit powerful radio signals ahead of itself informing the Isonians of its approach. Once there it will go into orbit, radioing down for permission to dock with any space stations present or to land on the planet's surface. The three computer personalities are, of course, entirely autonomous and will have full control of the mission themselves. They are able to learn an infinite range of new languages and they will broadcast repeated reassurances that they set out in a completely sterile condition and that they bring no foreign bacteria from Earth.'

'How are they going to communicate with the aliens when we still haven't been able to translate any of the signals from Iso?' asked one of the Treasury officials. 'Isn't it all pointless if we can't understand them and they can't understand us?'

'But we'll get visual images back,' protested Yates, 'And we'll be able to see what it is we are dealing with.'

'But not *us*, Professor,' broke in a second man from the Treasury. 'It will be our far-distant descendants seeing the pictures, won't it?'

Yates was used to this objection. He'd been handling it for seven years, ever since the *Friendship* project was first mooted.

'You're right, of course,' he agreed. 'But if we don't set out to visit Iso now, humankind will never learn anything about our near neighbours in the cosmos. It is our duty to provide future generations with this vital research tool.'

'And anyway, most of the budget's already been spent, right?' It was President Jarvis, speaking for the first time since Yates had begun his presentation.

'That's right, sir,' agreed the SETI chief. 'The project was designed to be low cost in the first place and we've already spent over eighty-five per cent of the budget on building the spacecraft, the computer personalities and the various on-board systems.'

'But the signals from Iso have now dried up,' protested the first Treasury official. 'There's another eight hundred million dollars of public money that still has to be spent just to send a robot spacecraft to a planet that's gone silent on us. The voters won't like it, Mister President.'

'Well, I'm sure the interruption in the Isonian signals is only temporary,' countered Yates quickly. 'It's probably caused by a local solar flare in the constellation of Aquarius, or from occlusion by another star – or it could be that the Isonians have merely switched frequencies for some reason. After all, we now know that we've been receiving their signals on Earth ever since radio astronomy began – it's just that they were too faint to be detected by dishes based on the Earth's surface.'

'Yes, but–'

'And an opinion poll taken yesterday,' continued Yates, cutting off the Treasury man before he could frame his next objection, 'shows that sixty-two per cent of the American public are in favour of launching *Friendship* to visit Iso, provided the majority of the cost comes from private funds. As you know, the SETI Institute has provided almost three quarters of the money spent so far.'

'Look, NASA's already been allocated its share of the budget for the launch – am I correct?' interjected President Jarvis, his patience now visibly running out.

Everyone in the Cabinet room nodded, but both Treasury men leaned forward as if they had still more to say on the subject.

'Then let's do it,' ordered Maxwell, standing up abruptly. 'We're going to Iso but I don't want to hear that there has been a single dollar overrun on this project – is that clear?'

'Yes, sir,' said Desmond Yates.

At an altitude of 15,212 feet, the Carl Sagan Ultra-Large Optical Telescope was both the highest and most powerful astronomical viewing instrument in the world. It perched on the summit of a mountain called Cerro Samanal in the Atacama Desert in northern Chile and the observatory complex was usually staffed by a team of six astronomers. These resident professionals individually rotated their duties between capturing fresh optical data during the night and analysing the results during the day shifts.

In the early-morning hours of Tuesday, 13 August 2063, Brian Nunney, an Australian-born astrophysicist and a world authority on the behaviour of information in the proximity of black holes, was projecting a live optical image from 'Big Carl' straight into the observatory's main holographic display area.

'Come and take a look at this,' he called over his shoulder to Suzi Price, a Californian intern who was also simultaneously studying for her PhD in alien planetary biology.

'The computers have flagged up a strange area of density in deep space – in the direction of the Antila constellation,' he explained as Suzi arrived at his side. 'It's causing some of the stars in the region to oscillate. What do you make of it?'

A large patch of scintillant night sky was displayed in the holo-theatre in front of them – simulating a small part of the brilliant constellations on show overhead. Magnified by the telescope's giant lenses, mirrors and high-resolution electronics it appeared 20,000 times larger than could be seen with the naked eye.

'Hey, that really is weird!' agreed Suzi, tapping her screen stylus against her gleaming white teeth. 'It looks as if something's obstructing our view, but we've got completely clear skies tonight.'

'The closest star in Antila is eleven m.p.c. away – that's about thirty-five million light years,' Nunney explained to the intern. 'Look, I've sampled a few frames from that region of sky which were captured in the last year. I'll run them at fifty times speed.'

The establishment's senior astronomer and the popular young PhD student watched with puzzlement as the computers showed the same patch of the constellation photographed at different times and from different angles over a period of twelve months.

'It's as if some of the stars are being turned on and off,' said Suzi. 'How come nobody's noticed this before?'

'Antila's not particularly popular with optical astronomers,' explained Nunney. 'There's nothing much going on in that direction – well, until now, at least.' The astrophysicist looked at the data read-outs as the simulation arrived at its conclusion, then turned to his companion. 'Add some density interpolation to the area, will you, Suzi?'

The student punched in the necessary instructions and a thin red mist appeared across the centre of the constellation.

'Well, whatever it is has got some form of mass,' observed Nunney as he keyed in instructions for the computers to measure the distance and density of the patch that had appeared in front of the distant stars.

'Look at that,' he said. 'The distance can't be measured optically. It must be some form of matter that doesn't emit visible light.'

'This could be an important find, couldn't it, Brisie?' exclaimed Suzi excitedly. 'What are we going to do now?'

'*We're* not going to do anything,' said Nunney thoughtfully. 'I've got a couple of old mates who I want to take a look at this. One's at the Parkes Radio Telescope in Oz. The other is at Setiville, on the far side of the moon. Let's see what they make of it in the radio wavelengths.'

The US government's Department of Computer and Network Security, popularly known as the CNS, had been formed in 2022 by the amalgamation of the CIA's cyber-surveillance division, the FBI's computer-fraud unit and the National Security Agency's anti-cyber-terrorism facility. It had become clear that the computer networks were the natural habitat of criminals, terrorists, cranks and sociopaths and some real specialization within government forces was needed. In less than a decade, the CNS's reach had become global as well as national and its annual budget exceeded that of the CIA.

CNS agent Sarah Burton had been with the agency for seven years and she enjoyed her demanding work. Most of her time was spent investigating, catching and prosecuting computer hackers and cyber criminals and, with a doctorate from Berkeley in forensic computing and communications, her speciality was catching the 'ultra clever' fraudsters, 'techno-terrorists' and those criminal hackers who considered themselves far too brilliant ever to be brought to justice.

But her current assignment seemed more like small beer, she thought idly as she sat in her car gazing out at the MIT professor's houseboat where it lay beside an old jetty in Boston harbour. She'd watched Bill Duncan deliver his outburst in court, and she and her two field assistants had now been gathering information on the radical academic and his bizarre group of computer wizards for almost two months.

She didn't underestimate the technical capabilities of either Duncan or his strange circle of high-tech followers; from speaking discreetly to the authorities at MIT she had established that it was only the professor's brilliance as a computer psychologist that persuaded the Chancellor to put up with his eccentricities. Normally a department as prestigious as MIT's Cognitive Computer Psychology Lab would require a rather more suave academic to be its director, an urbane figurehead who could charm the corporate sponsors to part with even more money for research. But Duncan's reputation in computer science was internationally established and well deserved, even if his political views made him suspect to some.

It was the activities of the group of hackers and crackers who surrounded the maverick professor that had caught CNS's attention and had led to this investigation. The team jokily called itself HAL, an acronym derived from 'Hackers At Large', and many members of the group were ex-students of Duncan's who had completed postgraduate studies at MIT. But instead of applying their gifts and expensive educations for the benefit of corporations or government departments, they had been infected by their professor's radicalism and were now engaging in cyber war against some of the most powerful governments and most successful IT corporations in the world.

Agent Burton sighed and switched off the reading panel of her communicator. She would pay her first visit to *Cape Sentinel*, to see what her gut instincts made of Bill Duncan. Despite spending almost all of her working life policing in virtual precincts, she believed firmly in the value of a 'meat meet', an old-fashioned face-to-face encounter.

Stepping from her black government-issue sedan, Sarah Burton straightened the dark jacket of her trouser suit and strolled along the jetty towards the old lighthouse ship – a vessel that she knew to be over a century old. It was a bright sunlit morning in late August.

Her suspect was up on deck, using a squeegee mop attached to a long pole to clean the windows of the old ship's wheelhouse. He was wearing an old white T-shirt and cut-off denim shorts over his athletic frame and the agent noticed that he'd acquired a deep suntan since she had last seen him in court.

'Good morning. May I have permission to come aboard?' called the smartly suited woman who had appeared at the bottom of the gangplank.

Bill laid the mop aside and jumped down onto the deck to steady the walkway for his visitor. She was below middle height, maybe five-four or -five, and her shoulder-length dark hair framed a face with an Irish cream-skinned complexion in which were set a pair of vivid blue eyes.

'Careful,' he said as the woman grasped the thick rope handrail. 'It can sway when the boat moves. Who are you looking for?'

Instinctively Bill held out his hand to steady the new arrival as she stepped down onto the metal decking.

'Thank you. I'm looking for Professor William Duncan,' said Agent Burton, knowing full well to whom she was speaking.

'That's me – and who might you be?' asked Bill with a smile, as he gazed down at the attractive but soberly dressed woman standing on his deck.

The federal agent slipped her communicator from her pocket and showed him her badge and its digital verification.

'CNS, Professor Duncan. I'm Agent Burton. I would like a few words with you.'

Bill froze, then took a step backwards. He had a poor regard for the CNS. As he and his circle often complained, they were a bunch of biased and incompetent government enforcers who were completely failing to uphold laws and regulations on computer intelligence – safeguards that he considered vital for the safety of society.

'I'm very busy,' he said coldly.

'I saw you give evidence on behalf of your three students,' said the agent, snapping the communicator shut and putting it back in her pocket. 'I heard what you had to say about the computer toy industry and I wondered if you, or your friends, had ever decided to take any other form of direct action yourselves.'

'I'm sorry, I don't have any time for your agency,' Bill said, with a curt shake of his head. 'I think you should leave.'

'This is a friendly visit,' said Agent Burton, now sounding far from friendly herself. 'Just to let you know that we have been aware for some time of the activities you and some of your former MIT students get up to here on this boat.'

The CNS woman took a few steps forward until she stood in the centre of the deck and gazed down through the open double doors to the main living area below. On either side of the large cabin were long benches on which was perched an array of the very latest high-tech gadgetry. The walls were covered in large 3-D screens and in the centre of the cabin she could see a small holo-display area. She already knew that enough radio and cable bandwidth was connected to this ship to provide data services to an entire town.

'Looks like some pretty heavyweight stuff you've got

down there,' she said with a wave towards the cabin. 'Is all of it legal?'

'Take a look around, if you think you'll understand what you're looking at,' retorted Bill, as condescendingly as possible.

'What will you do with yourself now that you've been suspended from your university post?' countered the federal agent, turning back to face the subject of her investigation.

Bill looked at the agent as if he were considering throwing her over the side. But for some reason he decided to humour his unwelcome visitor a while longer.

'I'm only suspended while they carry out an investigation into the accident at the retail outlet,' he told her. 'I wasn't involved in that, so I'll be back at work soon.'

'But it seems very odd for an MIT professor of computer science to be campaigning *against* the development of advanced computer intelligence?' suggested the agent.

'It wouldn't do, if you had bothered to read my book on the subject.' *The Rise and Rise of Techno Sapiens*, Bill's first academic publication, had found unexpected success in the popular-science book charts ten years earlier. His powerful polemic had then gone on to fuel many public debates on the wisdom of developing ever more capable computers.

Following his surprise publishing success, Bill had campaigned for years about regulatory insouciance on the subject. He had publicly berated governments and public corporations for their unheeding and reckless development and exploitation of computer personalities – forms of machine intelligence which frequently exceeded all regulatory limits.

'What exactly are your political affiliations?' asked the agent, ignoring the jibe about his book.

'You will have already checked me out,' said Bill, now

growing angry. 'You know I don't belong to any party, nor do I have what you call any "political affiliations".'

'Don't you believe in American progress, Professor Duncan?' asked his visitor, deliberately provocative.

'How dare you?' snarled Bill. 'I love my country, but that doesn't mean that I have to love our computer industry, or our government. And so long as this is a free country, get the fuck off my boat.'

'Thanks for your time,' said Agent Burton as she stepped back unassisted onto the wobbly gangplank.

'Well, it seems to be a large interstellar cloud of gas,' announced Lee Kaku to the rest of the Setiville duty team. 'And it's heading towards our own solar system at quite high speed – at about a thousand kilometres per second.'

Three days earlier the sophisticated SETI observatory on the far side of the moon had received a request from the team at the Carl Sagan Telescope in Chile. The Setiville team was asked to track and measure a patch of peculiar space matter that had been identified at a location in the direction of the Antila constellation.

Although almost all efforts at Setiville were now concentrated on trying to relocate the missing Isonian radio signals, Director Kaku had granted permission for the lunar base's second-largest dish array to be temporarily focused towards Antila.

Now he and Stephanie Duval, the French member of the team who had been given the task of tracking and analysing the strange area of misty density, were explaining their findings to a dozen or so off-duty members of the Setiville team.

'The cloud is between fifty and sixty billion kilometres away from the outer edge of our solar system at present, and it appears to be made mostly of hydrogen gas, which is why nobody's spotted it before,' added Stephanie, in the cute French accent that many of the male Setiville astronomers adored. 'As you know, natural hydrogen does not emit visible light. But the mass emits the characteristic twenty-one-centimetre radio wavelength of hydrogen, which I think is fairly conclusive.'

Stephanie turned to the computer-enhanced radio image of the space cloud displayed on a wall screen. 'In terms of size, it's about one hundred and forty million kilometres across – that's about one AU, the same distance as between the Earth and the sun.'

'And it also seems to contain some helium,' interrupted Kaku. 'And some dust, ice particles and enough unidentified gases that we are likely to be able to see it soon with optical telescopes. Of course, such high-velocity clouds are quite common around the edges of the Milky Way, but it's very unusual to see an HVC so close. We are getting very good radio images.'

'If this thing is coming our way, shouldn't we alert the Asteroid Defense Network?' asked Pieter Gustafson, an extra-terrestrial biologist who was on short-term secondment to Setiville from Munich University.

'No, I don't think that's necessary,' said Kaku. 'As their density is so light, space clouds are affected strongly by a whole variety of gravitational forces. It will probably change its heading, or even disperse, long before it gets anywhere near our solar system.'

The director turned back to the French astrophysicist. 'E-mail our affiliate observatories, Steph. See if they can pick it up with their optics and ask them to keep an eye on it. Oh, and ask them to keep this news confidential for the moment.'

*

From the outside the 156-year-old former lighthouse vessel *Cape Sentinel* did not look like anyone's idea of a high-tech network centre. The converted sixty-five-foot ship was painted black with a thick red stripe along her iron hull, but rust had appeared in several places since her last paint job and another coat would soon be needed. Several panes of glass in the squat lighthouse tower also needed replacing.

But from four p.m. onwards on most weekdays, the innards of the old boat were lit up with such sophisticated computer and network analysis equipment that even CNS itself would have been envious. The technology had been partly installed by MIT guru Bill Duncan during the three years he had lived on the vessel following his divorce, but most of it had been donated by a small group of well-connected – and well-heeled – alumni from his Cognitive Computer Psychology Lab.

Many of those who had studied with Bill at MIT had been lured away to highly paid jobs in software and network development, either in the Boston high-tech corridor or in Silicon Valley, But many had returned to linger in Bill's orbit, enthused by his radicalism and his certainty that human society had to place more stringent limits on the development and production of artificial intelligence.

As a computer scientist – indeed, as a specialist in the psychological disorders of computer personalities – Bill did not object to computer technologies *per se*; he objected only to their irresponsible exploitation for military, government and commercial purposes.

Many of his students – among them some of the most able minds of their generation – had come to share his point of view. A hard core of about twenty of his former researchers had formed HAL – Hackers At Large. Five times a week a dozen or so of this group, of which Bill

Duncan was the unelected and unofficial figurehead, turned up at the *Cape Sentinel* to light up the networks in what was, in fact, a vigilante search-and-destroy action against the use of computer power that exceeded internationally agreed limits.

'Got another one to test,' announced Christine Cocoran loudly from the lower cabin. 'It's in Beijing and it's speaking Mandarin.'

Christine took off her headphones, turned away from her screen and swung round in her swivel chair. 'One for you, Levine-san,' she called up the companionway.

'OK, let's have it, Chris,' shouted back Paul Levine, a self-employed artificial memory designer who was seated at a screen in the main upper cabin.

Christine transferred the details of the network location up to Levine's monitor and then rose, stretching her lean body after a long shift spent monitoring the world's vast web of networks.

'Coming up to watch, Chris?' asked Bill poking his head down the companionway.

'In a moment,' replied Christine, shooting him a warm smile. Then she relit a joint she had allowed to go out in her ashtray.

Upstairs, Bill and five of the other volunteers gathered behind Levine to watch him test the capacity of the network entity in Beijing. Their game plan was simple: if their tests revealed that a network or processor cluster exceeded statutory power limits they didn't bother reporting its existence to either the national or the international authorities. They simply sat back down at their terminals and, acting in concert, deployed an array of their own specially developed and highly proprietary virus-based attack technologies to disable the illegal computer entity and to drive it from the networks. They were good at what they did – the best in the world, they believed – and without knowing precisely who to blame, many operators of illegally high-powered computer systems had found themselves victims of Duncan's vigilantes.

'It's definitely another illegal,' declared Levine after only four or five minutes. 'Over fifteen terraflops – the Chinese just won't give it up.'

'Let's close it down, guys,' said Bill quietly as Christine arrived at his side. 'But be careful to leave no trace – we don't want CNS poking around again.'

'Darling, a reporter from the *New York Times* wants to talk to you,' called a voice from the doorway.

Desmond Yates sighed and removed his arm from around the shoulders of Alethea, his ten-year-old daughter. It was a Sunday, and Yates was enjoying a quiet family afternoon at his home in the Washington suburb of Belvedere.

'He says it's something about a space cloud heading towards the Earth,' added Gail, his second wife.

Yates frowned, then stood up. 'I'll take it in the den,' he told her.

'This is Randall Tate of the *New York Times*,' announced the caller unnecessarily – his ident was already clearly displayed. 'What's your take on this large space cloud that's heading towards our solar system?'

'No comment, I'm afraid, Mr Tate,' said Yates firmly.

'Does this mean that you don't know about the cloud?' asked Tate.

'It means no comment,' repeated Yates.

'I even have a picture of the cloud,' persisted the reporter, and an image with which Yates was already wholly familiar appeared on a data panel on the wall of his den.

'And I have details of its location, heading and speed,' added Tate, transferring the coordinates to Yates's screen. 'Doesn't the President's senior Space Affairs Adviser have any comment on this phenomenon, or haven't you been told about it yet?'

Yates sighed inwardly. All those to whom he had talked about the cloud had agreed that its existence should be kept confidential until more was known about its composition. But he told himself that he ought to have guessed that there would be a leak somewhere along the line.

'Well, such high-velocity space clouds are common around the Milky Way, Mr Tate,' said Yates after a few moments' consideration. 'And some are bound to pass through the galaxy occasionally. But they're harmless.'

'No danger to Earth, then, Professor?' pressed Tate.

'No danger at all,' said Yates firmly.

From the *New York Times* website, 12 September 2063

HUGE GAS CLOUD HEADING FOR SOLAR SYSTEM

By RANDALL TATE, science correspondent

Could Pass Near to Earth

Scientists at the Carl Sagan Ultra-Large Telescope in Chile have identified a large cloud of interstellar gas that is heading towards Earth's solar system. The cloud, almost 140 million kilometers across and many million times the size of Earth, is of variable density and is believed to be made up of hydrogen gas and space dust.

'Clouds of high-velocity interstellar gas are quite common in and around the Milky Way,' commented Professor Desmond Yates, senior Space Affairs Adviser to the White House. 'It is unusual for a cloud to pass so close to our small solar system but it poses no threat to the Earth. It is still about fifty billion kilometers from the outer edge of our solar system, but we will observe its progress with interest.'

Cloud 'Could Contain Deadly Bacteria'

Astrobiologist Dr Sam Golding of the Jet Propulsion Laboratory, Pasadena, said yesterday, 'It's possible that this cloud could contain forms of bacteria unknown to humans. If any were to filter through our atmosphere and fall on Earth, the effect could be devastating. I urge everybody to ensure they stock up with sufficient protection masks for all their family members.'

Since the founding of the Massachusetts Institute of Technology in 1861, the Court of the Governing Council had met formally to discipline a member of the faculty on only three occasions. Each time it had been to consider revoking a professorial tenure, a difficult procedure and one that carried considerable legal implications.

Bill Duncan had been shocked to learn that he was to be called before such a disciplinary hearing. He knew that his radicalism and outspoken beliefs about the development of artificial life and computer personalities were unpopular with many other faculty members, but he was sure that he had done nothing personally to warrant a summons to appear before such a serious tribunal.

The hearing was being held in the oak-panelled Grand Hall of the Killan Court building, the white-domed and pillared edifice which looked something like Washington's Capitol and which was always shown by the media when they were covering stories about MIT.

Behind a long oak table sat the university's President, Chancellor and Provost along with a dozen other men and women who Duncan knew to be lawyers and human-resources staff.

The recalcitrant professor himself was seated in the centre of the hall behind a smaller oak table, beside the lawyer whom he had hired hastily for the occasion.

The hearing had lasted most of the day. MIT President Cornelius Swakely led the attack, arguing that although the results of the internal investigation had cleared Professor Duncan of personal involvement with either the planning or the execution of the violent protest that had led to the death of a security guard, it had become clear that Duncan's radical 'anti-establishment' views had been a clear and serious incitement to such action.

Chancellor Cassandra Quinn had then added her voice to the case for the prosecution.

'From what we have heard, your highly political tutorials have been nothing but repeated calls to radical action,' she said accusingly. 'And this has been going on for years. You urge your students to take direct action against those companies and government departments of which you personally disapprove. Professor Duncan, I find it hard not to see you as an accessory to murder.'

At this point, Counsellor Paul Cohen laid a restraining hand on his client's tense forearm. Bill had hired Cohen to represent him in this hearing simply because the attorney was also representing the three students who were now in jail awaiting trial. Both men knew full well that the murder charges had been dropped and that the Chancellor's comments were outrageous.

Provost Walter M. Williams then contributed to the proceedings by summing up the university's position and repeating the complaints about the professor's radicalism and his anti-government and anti-computer industry stance.

'The entire faculty recognizes that you were one of the most gifted of our young cryptanalysts when you first arrived here as a postgraduate student,' said the Provost at the conclusion of his summation. 'But your more recent specialization in machine-life psychology seems to have led you astray. On behalf of the Governing Council, I must now ask if you can offer any reason why you should not be deprived of tenure and dismissed from your position at this university?'

Bill was appalled. He shot a look of disbelief at his attorney, then began to heave himself to his feet.

'Permission to confer with my client?' asked Paul Cohen

quickly, placing a strong hand on Bill's shoulder to force him back down into his chair.

The two men had agreed that all of the talking during the hearing should be done by Cohen, and the attorney had even managed to persuade his client to wear a black linen suit and white shirt for the occasion. But now Bill seemed determined to speak.

'I strongly advise against it – you'll just antagonize them more,' the attorney hissed into Bill's ear.

But Bill ignored his lawyer. Standing upright, he walked round to stand in front of the table.

'Members of the Governing Council,' he began in what sounded like a steady and controlled voice. 'It is true that my views about the development of computer intelligence may seem strange to some members of this faculty who care more about technology than people, but I have never advocated anything other than peaceful protests against those who flout the regulations.

'I should also like to remind the Council that there is a long and honourable tradition here at MIT of senior faculty members dissenting from the mainstream views on their disciplines. One hundred years ago Professor Joseph Weizenbaum, one of the very first incumbents to hold my illustrious chair, wrote a seminal book called *Computer Power and Human Reason* in which he called for the responsible development of computer intelligence. I ask merely for similar rights to express my opinions.'

Bill paused and turned to glance at his attorney. Cohen nodded cautious approval; his client was managing to remain calm.

'Computers are now many times more powerful than the human brain,' continued Bill, 'and we cannot allow their development to continue unchecked. A century ago

Professor Weizenbaum identified the issue that confronts us all: it is nothing less than who will become the dominant species on this planet, humanity or intelligent machines?'

There was absolute silence in the Grand Hall as the maverick professor delivered his own defence speech. All present were familiar with Bill Duncan's extreme views.

'I condemn the actions that led to the *accidental* death of the security guard,' continued the accused academic, 'but I condone the motives that lay behind them. We at MIT should be more than just cheerleaders for the inexorable march of technological progress. We also have a duty to guide and advise society on its use. I hope that, as my colleagues, you will respect my position and allow me to continue in what I consider to be vitally important work.'

Bill finished with a brief nod and then returned to sit beside his lawyer.

'Very good,' whispered Cohen. 'Couldn't have done better myself.'

At the main table, the council members were conferring. Both Bill and his attorney expected that there would be a recess, but the President suddenly cleared his throat and all faces swivelled in his direction.

'Professor Duncan, whilst we understand your feelings on these matters, we are unanimously of the opinion that you have gone too far and that you have brought disrepute on your own reputation and on this Institute's. Many commercial sponsors of the Cognitive Computer Psychology Laboratory have raised questions with me and with other council members about their continuing support while you remain in charge. We have also been distressed to learn that you are now the subject of a federal investigation by the

Department of Computer and Network Security. Having taken all this into consideration, we are left with no alternative but to ask you to resign your chair and leave this university forthwith.'

THREE

'I'm going to miss you, Des,' said Melissa softly. 'We've always got along very well and it may not be so easy once there's a longer time delay.'

'I'm going to miss you, too,' agreed Desmond Yates sincerely. 'I've grown very fond of you as well over these last three years.'

There was a silence as the two friends pondered their imminent separation. Both were in Yates's den at his home. It was late on the eve of *Friendship*'s departure on its long journey to the planet Iso. Yates, the chief designer and driving force behind the mission, was seated on an old, comfortable couch. Melissa, the captain of the *Friendship*, was present in holographic form, shown sitting in a black armchair in the centre of Yates's home holo-theatre. She had long blonde hair, beautiful features and an outstanding figure. Her physical presence, her actual 'body', was a human-size android female made of synthetic skin, tissue, bone and blood, that was now orbiting Earth awaiting the launch. A complex chain of communications satellites and base stations bounced Melissa's synthetic voice and image down to the Yates household almost in real time.

'May I ask you something, Des?' queried the image of the android astronaut.

Yates nodded, knowing that full visual telemetry was being returned to *Friendship*.

'What do you really think we'll find when we get to Iso?'

Yates couldn't suppress a snort, which then turned into a laugh. He'd been asked the same question thousands of times by journalists and TV people.

'OK, forget it!' snapped Melissa suddenly. 'I only wanted to—'

'I'm sorry, Missy,' said Yates, holding up a placating hand. 'It's just that, well, I thought you'd have heard me answer that one many times before.'

'I wanted you to tell *me*,' said Missy, almost petulantly. 'I want to know your *real* thoughts.'

Yates sat back in his couch, ran a hand over his late-night beard stubble and considered.

'Everything about their planet looks like the Earth,' he began. 'That means the life forms that exist there are likely to have a similar chemosynthesis and biology to our own. Therefore the laws of physics and evolution suggest that whatever the Isonians look like, they'll swim, walk or fly – just like the creatures on this planet.'

'You mean they'll be flesh and blood,' cut in Melissa.

'Probably,' agreed Yates. 'At least, that's why we've given you, Charlie and Pierre full humanoid form – so that you represent us as accurately as possible. The laws of gravity suggest they won't be much bigger or smaller than us, otherwise they wouldn't have evolved successfully. But as to what they'll actually *look* like, I've got no idea.'

'I've made an anamorphic image of what I think they might be like,' said Melissa. 'Would you like to see it?'

'Certainly,' said Yates, thrilled by the idea of seeing what a machine mind imagined an alien life form might be like.

A figure appeared beside Melissa's chair, standing in the

dim light of the holo-theatre. It was a foot or so shorter than an average adult human, but it was far more bulbous, with short legs, stubby arms and what appeared to be a recessed head. It was pale-skinned and naked, but apart from what appeared to be a pocket or flap at the bottom of the body, Yates could make out nothing equivalent to genitals.

'Fascinating,' breathed Yates as he sat forward.

'I compared Zilhinlanski's research to the work by Dr Gumingharber,' explained Melissa. 'You know that neither of them are convinced that the long-bodied humanoid form is the ideal evolutionary adaptation. Then I reassessed the likely gravitational forces acting on Iso's surface, bearing in mind that we now think the planet has three moons. Local gravity, biology, geology and climate are the four governing factors behind my model.'

'What about predator adaptation?' asked Yates, glancing at the long row of data and calculations that Melissa was now scrolling beside the representation of an alien figure. 'After all, predator-avoidance shaped all species on Earth.'

'An unknowable variable,' said Melissa quickly. 'But I–'

'Des!' complained a voice from the hallway. 'It's almost three a.m! You've got to be at NASA by seven.' Then Gail Yates entered the room and saw the virtual visitor seated in the holo-theatre.

'Oh, hi, Missy,' called Des's wife. 'I didn't know you two were talking. But it *is* very late, Des.'

Yates nodded. 'I'll be up directly,' he said.

As Gail left the room, he turned back to the image of the senior *Friendship* crew member. 'I'll be talking to you again from mission control in the morning,' he told her. 'But I wanted to just have a few more words in private.'

The humanoid super-computer dissolved the anamorphic image of the imagined Isonian, then turned to face her creator. Although her networks, processors and humanoid shell had been built and constructed by the Zynteel Corporation of San Francisco, and despite the fact that her compressed high-speed education had been provided by a dozen of the most distinguished virtual schools and universities in the world, it was Des Yates who had been her mentor, the man who had patiently tried to answer the many questions she had had that were not covered by her formal education. As her IQ and mental processing capacity were several times that of even the brightest human, Yates had frequently found himself floundering. But, if such a thing were possible between a man and a machine, the two had become friends. Working with Melissa had helped Desmond Yates understand fully why there were international treaties limiting the development of super-capable computers and why there was a worldwide ban on incorporating them into adult humanoid form. He had frequently felt as if he were dealing with a superior species.

'Are all of your approach procedures and contact protocols clear?' asked Yates for the ten thousandth time.

'Yes, Des, and all the alternatives,' said Melissa with a soft smile. 'We all know how much trust you are placing in us. We won't blow it.'

Yates laughed out loud at her use of such a youthful retro expression. For a moment he had a wild fantasy image of Earth's ambassadors arriving at Iso and behaving like delinquent teenagers.

Suddenly Melissa's mood changed. 'I won't be able to have any more real-time chats with you after tomorrow, will I, Des?'

Yates sighed. He too dreaded the parting. Over the last three years Gail had frequently chided her husband for spending more time with the beautiful captain of the

Friendship than with her. But in the end his younger wife had understood. Coaching humanity's first ambassador to meet an intelligent life form on another world *was* an important and worthy task.

'No . . . Missy,' said Yates, hesitating because he had almost used an endearment to her, the sort of word he might have used to his wife. 'But I want to hear about everything you see. We'll talk every day, even if there is a time delay.'

'Forgive me, Des, but that's not going to be for very long, is it?'

For a split second Yates wondered what she was talking about. Then he understood.

'No, Missy. By your standards that won't be very long. But I promise that as long as I am alive, we'll talk every day.'

From the *New York Times* website, 23 November 2063

ROBOT MISSION LEAVES FOR ISO

By RANDALL TATE, science correspondent

Journey Will Take 450 Years

Friendship, an $11 billion spacecraft built jointly by SETI and NASA, successfully blasted out of Earth's orbit this morning at the start of its 450-year mission to visit the planet Iso.

Crewed by three advanced computer personalities installed in humanoid bodies, the spacecraft will continuously radio back astronomical data during its journey.

Critics have claimed that the mission is a waste of money since the alien radio signals from Iso dried up last April.

Live link to *Friendship's* on-board cameras

'Goodnight, Paul, 'night, Steve,' called Bill Duncan as he let the last but one of his band of volunteers out into the warm night air. He closed the large wheelhouse door and slid on his hands down the polished mahogany rails of the companionway stairs and back into the *Cape Sentinel*'s main cabin.

A month had passed since his summary dismissal from MIT and Bill was now wondering whether network activism was going to be all that was left to him. Although his lawyer was assuring him of a very generous pay-off from the university, it seemed unlikely that he would now be able to find any academic post to rival the one he had just lost. Perhaps he would have to write another book.

'Shall I switch everything to standby?' asked Christine Cocoran. She was the only one of the volunteers left on board and it had been a long monitoring shift. It seemed that no matter how successful the team was at driving illegals from the networks, another company or government launched a new one almost immediately. Bill understood why, of course. Computer processors no longer had any value when they were forced to function in stand-alone fashion. Only when they were connected to the world's vast networks – and the web now stretched far out into space, around the moon and even to the pioneer colonies on Mars – could a system's real capacity and potential be tested. It was then that their presence became visible on the net, and then that Bill's volunteers could take them down. But sometimes it seemed as if they were merely sticking their fingers in a dyke. Despite the annual re-ratification of the treaties on maximum limits for processors and system power, governments and corporations were still seeking ways to bend the rules – sometimes to flout them openly – all for national, militaristic or commercial advantage.

Christine shut down the top-level functions of the many powerful systems installed on the old ship and then handed Bill a cup of camomile tea. It had become customary for Christine to hang around after the others had gone and Bill was beginning to take the hint. But he wondered whether he was ready for a romance again after the lingering pain of what had been a very hostile divorce.

'I've got something for you,' Christine said shyly as she sipped her herb tea. 'You know they've given Skinner the directorship of your lab . . .?'

Bill nodded. He guessed that the Governing Council had already lined up Joe Skinner to take over his department even before they had carried out his public sacking. Skinner was a systems specialist, an expert in quantum processing, but Bill was appalled that a man with such a practical background in hardware 'plumbing' should be put in charge of a laboratory concerned with the psychological development of machine intelligence.

'Well, he must have some very powerful friends in the computer industry,' she went on. 'The hardware that's been arriving in the lab in simply amazing. I've brought this for you.'

Christine slid her hand into her large shoulder bag and produced a shiny metal case, about the size of a laptop computer. Following her boss's dismissal, Christine had talked about resigning her own research post in the Cognitive Computer Psychology Lab, but Bill had quickly talked her out of making such a useless emotional gesture.

'I thought you might be able to make use of this,' she said, opening the slim case.

In a transparent neoprene enclosure sat a gold and white object that glowed dully at its centre. It was about the size of a hand and it looked like a cross between an internal human organ and a spider. Stamped on both the lid of the case and the neoprene safety moulding were the words:

<u>US DEPARTMENT OF DEFENSE</u>
CLASSIFIED COMPUTER COMPONENT
UNAUTHORIZED POSSESSION IS A
FEDERAL OFFENSE

'This is a prototype of a new-generation organic-molecular processor,' said Christine excitedly. 'The Rand-Fairchild Corporation has given our lab ten units to test on some of our largest personality simulations. It's weapons-grade, the most advanced atto-scale quantum processor ever built. It produces pure random bits and it employs quantum entanglement and superpositions to do billions of calculations at once. It's rated at eighteen yottaflops!'

'Jesus!' exclaimed Bill, running his hands worriedly through his thick hair. 'What have you done, Chris? That thing's classified! There are whole treaties against processors that powerful!'

'Don't worry,' said Chris with a nervous smile. 'I called Rand-Fairchild and told them that one of their units was defective. They're going to replace it, but not for another six weeks. That means you can have it for that time to see what it can do. I've signed it out of the Lab.'

'For fuck's sake, Chris!' exploded Bill. 'You know that I've had the network cops poking around. What if they raid us and find this? We'll end up in jail.'

'But we're not doing anything illegal,' protested his longest-serving and most loyal volunteer. 'We're only fighting those who are breaking the law – and we can't do that without knowing the sort of technology that we're up against. Half the stuff in here we've brought home from the lab!'

'But that was when *I* was the boss,' Bill told her, only slightly more calm. 'Then it was my responsibility, now *you're* breaking the law!'

Christine's face fell. 'Well, I'm sorry. It's just that . . .' She tailed off and closed the lid of the small high-security case containing the prototype processor.

'I couldn't even take the risk of connecting it to the networks, Chris,' Bill went on in a softer tone. 'I'm sure that CNS is monitoring all our traffic – that's why we're having to run all of our operations from remote servers. If I connected this much power to our bandwidth we'd light up on the networks like a Roman candle.'

'OK, Bill, OK. You've made your point,' snapped Christine huffily. 'I'll see if I can sneak it back into the lab. But are you sure there isn't anything useful you could do with it?'

Everybody who was not already standing in the packed Situation Room rose to his or her feet as President Maxwell T. Jarvis entered. He was accompanied by his Chief of Staff, a personal secretary and two aides.

'OK, OK, let's get on with it,' said Jarvis irritably as he took his own seat at the head of the table. 'What was so important that it couldn't wait until after this afternoon's Cabinet meeting?'

Desmond Yates stepped forward.

'Mister President, I have disturbing news,' he said gravely. 'News that I knew you would want to share with your Cabinet.'

The room was now attentively quiet. A few of the most senior NASA and Defense Department officials knew what was to follow, but nothing had leaked beforehand. Others present presumed that almost a month after its successful launch there was now bad news about the *Friendship* mission or perhaps about the Iso signals themselves – although neither of those topics would normally warrant this sort of emergency briefing.

Yates raised his arm towards the large holo-theatre and, as the lights in the Situation Room dimmed, a portion of the night sky appeared in a 3-D image. In the centre of the display area, and obscuring a large part of the constellations, was what appeared to be a long, thin line of red and grey mist.

'As you know, a large gas cloud was identified six months ago travelling in outer space, at about sixty billion kilometres' distance from our own solar system.'

Yates paused to see if he needed to remind his audience of the details. No one stirred.

'We've been tracking the cloud's trajectory very carefully and it is now forty billion kilometres closer. I'm sorry to have to tell you that if it continues on its present heading it will almost certainly collide directly with the Earth in eight months' time.'

There was another silence, this time followed by a low hubbub as people whispered remarks or questions to each other. Eventually, the President spoke.

'I presume this thing is very serious, Professor Yates? I mean, if it were to hit us, would the effects be severe?'

The White House senior Space Affairs Adviser drew a deep breath and then nodded.

'I'm afraid so, sir. According to the latest measurements we have been able to take from the cloud, it is sufficiently dense and is travelling at such a high speed that it will strip the atmosphere from the Earth's surface as it passes over this planet. In a period of between fifty and eighty days, all elements of our atmosphere will be sucked away into space.'

A massive stunned silence now filled the room. The president glanced from NASA's Director to his Secretary of Defense. Both men gave little nods of confirmation; their organizations had been helping Yates to prepare this briefing.

'We concur with Professor Yates's projections,' said Roy Wilcox, NASA's director. 'We've built our own models and they too predict that the cloud's most likely transit through our solar system will intersect with the Earth's position in eight months – give or take a few days.'

Now the hubbub in the room returned again, only much louder this time.

Desmond Yates coughed loudly to regain their attention. 'As it traverses our solar system, the cloud will probably be travelling much more slowly than at present – as it encounters the force of the solar winds and the magnetosphere,' he continued. 'We estimate its velocity will then be about two hundred and twenty thousand kilometres per hour, but that will still be sufficient to rob us of our atmosphere.'

Now they were quiet again.

'I'm afraid that's not all,' added the space-affairs adviser. 'Our models suggest that as it approaches the Earth the cloud will first radiate reflected heat from the sun back towards our planet, then it will begin progressively to blot the sun out. In the first few days of the cloud's final approach, temperatures around the world will start to rise rapidly, perhaps by as much as thirty or forty degrees centigrade. As a result of this heating, there will be torrential rainfall everywhere. Then, as the sun's light is progressively occluded, the rain will turn first to sleet and then to snow.

After about ten days, temperatures will go racing down still further. At the end of the first two weeks we will have twenty degrees of frost. Rivers will freeze and mobility will be severely restricted. Communications may be affected. Within six weeks it will be about one hundred and twenty degrees centigrade below freezing. All the oceans will freeze over and mobility will be impossible. Radio and land-line communications may still work, but everything with moving parts that is exposed to the elements will become inoperable.'

Yates paused to draw breath and to gather his thoughts. The Situation Room, the location from where so many disasters, wars and terrorist battles had been managed, was filled with an appalled silence. Now nobody exchanged remarks with their neighbours. All were struggling with the awful scenarios that the Nobel Prize-winning scientist was laying out before them.

'There's still more,' said Yates in a low voice. 'It is possible that we may not even live long enough to see the world freeze over. NASA's gas dynamicists tell us that the cloud is largely made up of hydrogen with some helium which is mixed with a lot of dust – mostly minute ice particles, no more than a millionth of an inch in size. But the problem is this: when the cloud comes into contact with our atmosphere, the hydrogen and oxygen will mix – and when they're thrust together they are violently unstable chemicals. The whole of our atmosphere could blow sky-high, like one enormous thermonuclear blast.'

The silence that now pervaded the Situation Room seemed thick as a fog.

'And assuming there is no explosion,' continued Yates, 'my geophysicist colleagues tell me that the approach of such an enormous mass so close to our planet would cause wild internal gyrations in the Earth's core and mantle. This in turn would lead to huge earthquakes, tsunamis and global-scale volcanic eruptions.'

Yates paused and looked directly at President Jarvis. The world's most powerful man had closed his eyes and was pinching the top of his nose between his thumb and forefinger. He stayed like this for so long that some standing members of the packed audience started to shift uneasily from foot to foot.

Eventually the President looked up. 'Is there any more you have to tell us, Professor Yates?' he asked in a small voice.

'I've prepared a number of simulations, sir,' said the White House adviser. The image in the holo-theatre now changed to show an image of Earth's own solar system.

'These simulations have been prepared to illustrate the sequence of events I have described, sir – other than the possibility of a sudden hydrogen-oxygen explosion.'

Yates stepped back as the simulation began. As the huge space cloud began to approach Earth, the image switched to show computer renditions of the climate heating up, then freezing as the massive cloud slowly engulfed the planet. At the end of the sequence Earth was revealed again as the space cloud moved away, but now it was a lifeless sphere, stripped of its atmosphere and turning slowly, wholly unprotected from the glare and the lethal rays of the harsh sun.

'Surely there must be some error?' asked President Jarvis, glancing from face to face around the room.

Nobody spoke.

'Well, there must be *something* we can do?' he protested.

'We plan to dispatch some high-speed probes to carry out more measurements in the cloud,' Yates told him.

'There's a chance that we could be wrong about its trajectory – or the cloud's internal density could shift and change its course. The gravitational forces acting on a large cloud of such variable mass are very hard to predict. But it will be some time before we get further results. Of course, we're going to keep the cloud under close observation throughout.'

'Very well,' said Jarvis, shifting in his chair. 'I'd like to study this information for myself.'

One of Yates's assistants stepped forward with a Digi-pad and a file of hard-copy print-outs that had been prepared for the President.

'Sir?' It was Nick Connors, the President's National Security Adviser.

Jarvis nodded for him to speak.

'Above all, this must be kept quiet,' urged Connors. 'Imagine the public panic if this were to leak.'

Jarvis nodded again and then rose from his chair.

'People, Mr Connors is right. There must be an absolute information blackout on this,' said the President, now seeming as if he had regained his full composure. 'We must use the eight months we've got to prepare for a worst-case situation. There's nothing we can do if the atmosphere does explode, but I want the Federal Emergency Management Agency briefed immediately and placed on full alert.'

He glanced around to make sure that his aides were taking notes. 'Tell FEMA that I want an immediate stock-piling of oxygen supplies and I want production of oxygen and oxygen-making equipment scaled up as far as possible, to wartime levels, without alerting the public or causing alarm. I want all of our underground command centres made ready and reprovisioned for a very long stay by the executive – we're also going to have to build a lot of new bunkers, as many as we can in the time. If we become unable to use solar power, we're going to need supplies of gas and oil again. And if there's even an outside chance that we're going to have to live on a planet without an atmosphere, we should start manufacturing hermetic habitats, like the prefabs they use on the moon and on Mars.'

The President turned back to Yates. 'Will our atmosphere re-form naturally, Professor? How long will it take?'

Yates shrugged. He'd spent two weeks frantically trying to find a flaw in the calculations that predicted a collision with the cloud, then a hectic few days preparing for this crucial briefing. He had had no time to even think about what might happen after the cloud struck Earth.

'I'm sorry, sir. I've no idea,' he admitted.

'Find out,' ordered Jarvis brusquely. Then he turned and swept his stern gaze around the whole room. 'And above all, everyone start working on ways to head off that cloud.'

FOUR

By the seventh decade of the twenty-first century, it was no longer uncommon for humans to live to be 100 years old. Medical science was now prolonging life so effectively that several people had already celebrated their 150th birthday and tens of thousands were living to be more than 120 years old. It was now being said that the body was no longer the final barrier to extreme longevity; rather, it was the mind. It appeared that humans might be psychologically unprepared to live for extremely long periods. In the end, people simply got bored.

Not Sir Charles Hodgeson, thought Randall Tate of the *New York Times* as the small seaplane banked and began its final approach to land on the smooth surface of the bay. The young reporter had been reading up on great centenarians in preparation for his forthcoming exclusive interview with the world-famous British science-fiction writer, futurist guru and sometime poet and it was clear that Hodgeson was still as active as ever.

With a far harder bump than Tate had anticipated, the four-seater seaplane touched down on the surface of the Pacific. After a rapid deceleration, it turned in a spray of foam and began to taxi towards a white platform that floated in the water 500 yards from the island's main beach. A small motor boat waited to ferry the reporter ashore.

Tate was visiting Sir Charles at his Orpheus Island home, a private atoll in the Great Barrier Reef, thirty miles out from Australia's Gold Coast. The interview was to mark the great man's one hundredth birthday and the publication of his latest novel, *Destiny*.

'Sir Charles is in the observatory,' said the fresh-faced young man in a blue T-shirt and shorts who met the reporter at the jetty. He pointed to a building on the crest of the island's central ridge. 'It's a bit of a climb.'

Forty minutes later a heavily perspiring Randall Tate was shown into the gloom of the central observation chamber. A large reflector telescope on massive hydraulic mounts occupied the centre of the viewing area and all around the curving walls were electronic screens that displayed various sections of the night sky.

'Mr Tate!' called a vibrant voice. 'Come on in.'

As the reporter's eyes adjusted to the interior gloom after the bright glare outside, Tate saw a small, wizened figure in a white singlet and baggy shorts crossing the room, gnarled hand outstretched.

'Welcome to Orpheus Island,' crowed Sir Charles Hodgeson, shaking the American's hand enthusiastically. 'Journey OK? Good, good. Well, come along, I'm going to show you the island.'

After an hour's walking under the strong Pacific sun, Tate was forced to asked if they could rest for a moment. The vigorous centenarian had marched the reporter around his luxurious hilltop mansion, a dormitory building where several hundred of what Hodgeson called 'his students' resided, the main canteen, the medical clinic and the staff accommodation. Now the old man was proposing that they should hike back up to the observatory.

'How do you stay so fit, Sir Charles?' asked the younger

man, as he sat on a rock and mopped his brow. 'Do you use gene therapy?'

'It's all in here,' said Hodgeson with a chuckle, as he tapped his temple with a bony forefinger. 'It's an attitude of mind.'

'Right,' said Tate, still wanting at least another ten minutes' rest. 'So what do you make of the space cloud that's heading towards us?' he queried in an attempt to buy time before his host began the next section of their route march.

'Don't you think it odd that it has appeared at exactly the same time that we lost contact with the signals from Iso?' asked Hodgeson with his head on one side, birdlike. 'And at just the time we were expecting to receive a reply to the messages that my loyal supporters and I sent to the aliens thirty years ago?'

'Now, I'm not sure what you are going to feel, but I'm about to connect up,' said Bill Duncan. 'Are you ready, Nadia?'

'I'm ready, Bill,' agreed Nadia, the computer companion that Duncan had been coaching, developing and 'bringing up' for almost fifteen years.

'Then here we go,' said the former MIT professor, as he switched on the final ultraband radio connection to the smart processor-bus he had built to house the classified Rand-Fairchild processor.

After sleeping on the problem, Bill had decided to hold on to the molecular processor that his loyal volunteer had purloined for him, at least for a couple of weeks. At eighteen yottaflops – a processor capable of computing eighteen septillion mathematical calculations per second – it was by far the fastest stand-alone processor that he had ever personally handled. It was also capable of producing genuinely random information from within its quantum design and that gave it the potential to do things way beyond anything conventional computers could achieve. He also knew that he was unlikely now to get personal access to such advanced hardware – at least until, or if, he found another senior post at a university. But which other university enjoyed the sort of high-level access that MIT could provide?

He was alone on *Cape Sentinel* at noon on a Saturday, and he'd been working for several days to configure a system that would allow Nadia to act in 'stand-alone' mode with the new, ultra-powerful processor.

'You understand that I will have to disconnect you from all the networks,' Bill had explained to faithful Nadia as he worked. 'We can't risk a processor of this power being noticed on the web. We'll have to find some task you can use it for on your own.'

'I've still got some of the old Iso signals, Bill,' Nadia told him. 'Shall we have another crack at those?'

Bill chuckled and shook his head at her cheeky suggestion. Like so many other young computer scientists, he had spent his student years dreaming of becoming the first person to decipher the alien messages. Because he had a natural gift for numbers and pattern recognition, he had chosen to specialize in computer-based encryption theory during his seven years of study at Stanford, and for almost a decade he had tried everything he could think of to make sense of the weird signals that had, until very recently, been received continuously from the distant planet.

Years after he had abandoned cryptology in favour of studying human and computer-personality psychology, Bill had still occasionally pulled out sections of the old Iso recordings and tried yet another new approach that had occurred to him. Now, at least ten years since he had last made an attempt, Nadia was suggesting that they should dust off some recordings of the old transmissions and try again.

'OK, why the heck not?' Bill had told her with a smile. Perhaps the pure strings of randomness this quantum processor could create might begin to highlight any patterns or macro-structures that existed in the alien signals.

'How does that feel?' he asked now as the data read-out indicated that the super processor had come on line to augment Nadia's already considerable processing power.

'I don't know yet,' said Nadia. 'It feels strange – but rather good.'

Bill nodded. *So it should*, he thought to himself. Nadia's processing power had now been multiplied to the power of six – she was suddenly a million times more powerful than before. His personal computer was now technically in breach of all national and international regulations governing computer power.

'Want to make a start?' he asked, as he pulled old recordings of the Isonian signals from the database. Over the years he had developed and written hundreds of different software algorithms in his attempts to crack the Isonians' code, and now he reloaded them all and told Nadia to start over from the top. He knew that some of his routines were so processor-hungry they had never been fully tested, but now he too was keen to see if this ultra-powerful system could make any headway.

'I'll leave you to it,' Bill told his faithful and uncomplaining companion. 'I'm going fishing.'

From the *Sydney Morning Herald*, 3 March 2064

GIANT SPACE CLOUD TO HIT EARTH

'EARTH'S ATMOSPHERE WILL BE STRIPPED AWAY'

By Gino Bardini,
Space Reporter

Collision in 8 months
Scientists in NASA and the European Space Agency have secretly come to the conclusion that the giant gas cloud now heading towards Earth will collide with the planet and will strip away all of its atmosphere. The cloud is expected to hit the Earth in October this year.

In an exclusive interview with the *Sydney Morning Herald*, Italian astrophysicist Dr Francisco Martelli, a director of the European Space Agency, said, 'It is wrong to keep the world population in ignorance. On present estimates the cloud will pass across the Earth at high speed and strip away all our atmosphere.'

Continued page 3

Despite its best efforts, the Washington administration had failed to persuade all the other members of the international space community to remain silent about the menace of the onrushing space cloud.

Soon after Desmond Yates and NASA had realized the seriousness of the situation, astronomers in Europe, South America and Australasia had come to similar conclusions about the dangers presented by the cloud – as had many of the international space scientists who were staffing the large orbiting telescopes and space stations. Not all of them agreed with the American government's decision to keep the information from the general public.

The news was finally broken to the media by an Italian member of the European Space Agency who believed profoundly that the public had a right to know as soon as possible about such a dangerous situation. The only real surprise was that he had chosen to make his initial announcement to an Australian national newspaper rather than to one of the global news channels. But then it turned out that the reporter who broke the story was the scientist's brother-in-law, an Italian migrant who had settled in Sydney.

Within minutes of its publication the news was top of every bulletin in every country. At first reporters and anchor people reacted sceptically, describing Dr Francisco Martelli as a 'maverick' and a 'lone voice' in the space-science community, but as the story developed it became clear that there was far more to the report than simple scaremongering.

Now that the news was out in the public domain, internationally respected scientists were keen to confirm their own knowledge of the dangerous situation and to provide their own predictions for a likely outcome.

In the United States, Professor Desmond Yates accepted

an invitation to appear live on the nationally networked *Tonight Show*. During the lengthy interview he acknowledged that present estimates suggested that the cloud might indeed collide with the Earth and, yes, one calculation suggested that the force of the collision could strip away the planet's atmosphere. But, he was quick to add, there were many factors that were likely to affect the cloud's trajectory over the coming months and nothing was yet certain.

All over the world excitable factions of the public reacted as if Armageddon had been officially announced. Following Yates's broadcast, crowds began to gather outside the White House, many of them protesters who carried placards demanding government protection for *all* American citizens. Within twenty-four hours police estimated that the crowd in the Washington Mall numbered over one million people. President Jarvis drafted the National Guard into the city to help the police control the demonstrators and he ordered the military to mount guards at all government bunkers, command posts and underground facilities around the United States.

In London, alarmed crowds filled Parliament Square and in Paris a mob tried to storm the presidential palace. In all of the world's major cities, protesters took to the streets certain that their governments could be forced to do something that would provide them with protection from the cloud.

Other citizens adopted a more practical approach to securing their own personal safety. Huge lines formed at camping and survivalist stores as people stocked up on oxygen cylinders, water and canned food. Fights broke out as supplies began to run low and individuals used their fists or weapons to grab as much as their vehicles would carry. There was a run on building materials as the practically minded started to excavate gardens and yards to build shelters, wholly uncaring about zoning laws or planning permission.

But the most powerful force of all was rumour, usually unfounded and wildly inaccurate. Scare stories and crazy ideas were transmitted between mobs like mosquitoes hopping between cattle. *The government is going to leave the planet to take up exile on a space station. Mountainous regions are the safest places as air pockets will be trapped in the valleys. The cloud is poisonous, so there's nothing we can do.*

In an attempt to calm the panic, the White House announced that the President would make an address to the American people.

Meanwhile, news of the approaching space cloud, and of the worldwide panic that was ensuing, had completely failed to penetrate the consciousness of the three people who were shut away on board the *Cape Sentinel* in Boston harbour.

For almost four days Bill Duncan, along with his close friends Christine Cocoran and Paul Levine, had been working non-stop. All normal activities had been suspended, and the hacker volunteers who normally showed up whenever they felt like it were told that network monitoring was being temporarily suspended for a few days.

The trio was working feverishly, unearthing new copies of old Isonian signals from the world's databases and feeding them to the now supercharged 'Nadia' computer personality. Every single storage device housed on the old ship had been disconnected from the external networks and was now linked together to create a vast private network of electronic memory. The work they were doing was *very* processor- and memory-intensive.

Only twelve hours or so after disconnecting Nadia from the public networks and augmenting her capabilities with the ultra-powerful prototype processor, Bill Duncan had been shocked and thrilled to discover that his computer companion was making significant headway in extracting recognizable patterns from the Isonian signals.

'I got to thinking that there must be some redundancy in the signal, perhaps the FM duplicated in the AM, so I wrote an algorithm for Nadia to split out the FM and AM content,' Bill told Christine later that evening when he called to invite her over. 'Then I slowed down one minute's worth of the transmissions by just over two hundred million times – something that needed a whole lot of horse-power. And guess what? Out popped a minute section of state-switched pulses!'

Christine Corcoran and Paul Levine had arrived shortly after receiving Bill's excited calls and for ninety-six hours they had worked almost constantly, their thoughts running together as tightly as schooling fish. They had snatched sleep when they could, heedless of the outside world and wholly unaware that a large proportion of the world's population was reacting in panic to the news of the approaching space cloud.

The emergence of 'state-switched pulses' from within the massive data stream suggested for the first time that there was binary or digital content buried within the alien transmissions. That was what first got the three MIT-trained scientists really excited. Thinking that the AM/FM redundancy might be mirrored by the use of multiple base duplication, they agreed to write and then insert another extraction routine into the signal to search for binary, trinary, octal and hexadecimal content. Less than an hour later Nadia had presented them with more segments of binary code, along with what seemed to be fragmentary maths on a base-sixteen model and masses of infill data which they guessed contained the complex higher-base layering.

'This small section's perfect!' gloated Bill as he stared at the digital representation of the signal displayed on Nadia's screen. 'Its analog byte and word lengths are far longer than I've ever seen, but this segment is *pure* binary code.'

Then had come the task of trying to make sense out of the binary representers. Numbers were easy to extract and after a few hours strings of integers, primes and other recognizable values had emerged. But the streams of what were surely graphic characters – many of them rich with what looked like vector arrays and unknown weightings – were not so easy to interpret.

Earth-developed languages share common patterns: humans are hard-wired for language, and no matter what the dialect, common rules for grammar and construction apply to most forms of spoken and written communications.

But it quickly became clear that the Isonians did not share any of humanity's instinctive language rules. Even with her immensely increased processing power, the symbols that Nadia produced from the short unspecified binary strings were wholly unrecognizable characters and hieroglyphs.

'It's definitely some form of mathematics,' said Duncan to his two excited companions. 'Look, these things seem to be operators and that's clearly some form of set disjunction. And those are definitely factorial coefficients in an infinite series. Wait a moment! This bit looks like a rewriting of the Riemann zeta function in a weird way!'

Christine and Levine hit a high five behind Bill's back and he spun round quickly to join them.

'We've begun to crack it,' shouted Christine, excitement blazing in her hazel eyes.

'Hold on, hold on,' said Bill, raising his hand. 'Do you realize the immense size of the task ahead of us? If we want to understand what the Isonians have been transmitting, we have thirty years' worth of their data to search through, data that was transmitted at a speed two hundred million times faster than this small sample that I've slowed down.'

Paul Levine, whose first degree was in pure maths, completed the calculation.

'That means that at a speed we can understand, there is just over six billion years' worth of data to decrypt and read. Then we've got to strip away all the redundancy, all the error-correction data and learn the language they're using.'

This daunting information sobered the little group for a few moments.

'That's incredible,' said Bill quietly. 'Just think about what it means. In the thirty years since we've been listening to them, the Isonians have generated as much information as our society could have done if we had started on the day when the Earth was first formed.'

'They must be thousands of years ahead of us in terms of their technology,' observed Levine. 'Perhaps tens of thousands of years.'

The friends glanced at each other, now awestruck as the civilization on which they were eavesdropping was suddenly made to seem both more real and even more alien.

'But still, just the fact that we're cracking it will be the biggest news story ever,' said Christine, wholly unaware of the media storm and public panic raging outside. 'Who should we tell?'

Bill and Paul Levine exchanged grins.

'Oh no, not the gov-ern-ment,' they sang together in a

ragged unison, picking up one of the group's most popular impromptu refrains.

'Who do we tell, then?' demanded Christine, smiling indulgently at her happily clowning companions.

'Well, normally I would say no one, at least not until we had finished,' said Bill, 'But we're going to need the most enormous amount of processing power, networks and networks of it. I think we need to get the media involved as soon as possible – to attract some serious funding, and to prevent the government trying to step in to take it off us.'

Paul and Christine quickly nodded their agreement.

'But there's one major problem,' Bill reminded them. 'We've done this with a highly classified molecular processor that we're not supposed to have.'

'How about Mr Randall Tate?' asked a voice from the wall.

Bill swivelled to face Nadia. Even though she had no physical embodiment, he still spoke to her main screen as if she were physically present.

'That's it, Naj!' he exclaimed. Then he turned back to the others. 'Randall Tate is a science reporter for the *New York Times*. I met him at an AI-psych conference last year. Perhaps I could trust him with the story.'

'My fellow Americans,' said President Maxwell T. Jarvis, gazing straight into the camera lens. 'It is my duty and pleasure to address you this evening because I want to calm your mistaken but understandable fears about this so-called space cloud.

'It is true that a large interstellar cloud of gas and dust is now approaching our solar system, but it is still a very long way away and we cannot yet say for certain whether it will have any effect on the Earth or, indeed, on our solar system at all. What you have been seeing on television and reading in the press are nothing but worst-case scare stories which have little bearing on the true situation.'

If the three hundred million Americans who tuned in to the broadcast could have seen their President two hours earlier, they would not have been at all convinced by his soothing words and unruffled demeanour.

Then, President Jarvis had been personally chairing a meeting of the hastily established Cloud EXCOM, an Executive Committee of government-agency principals that had been formed to consider how best to prepare for the most dire eventuality. Members included the President's National Security Adviser, who also served as the chair of the National Security Council, the Director of the Central Intelligence Agency, the Chair of PSAC – the President's Scientific Advisory Committee – the Director of the Federal Emergency Management Agency, the Chairman of the Joint Chiefs of Staff, the Directors of NASA and the Defense Department, the Director of the National Economic Council, the Director of the National Military Command Center and the Director of the National Asteroid Defense Network.

Drafted in as permanent advisers to the Cloud EXCOM were Professor Desmond Yates and the Director of the White House Communications Agency. Two large support committees consisting of departmental deputies and agency assistant directors were formed to mirror the format of Cloud EXCOM. Their job was to meet at other locations to refine and pass on information and issues for consideration by the main committee.

Even as the principals of Cloud EXCOM were assembling, a crowd estimated variously at between a quarter-million and half a million strong was still protesting on the green slopes beyond the White House railings.

'I want to accelerate our construction of prefabricated habitats and underground shelters,' Jarvis had instructed the meeting. 'I want maximum effort in the manufacture of chemical-based oxygen manufacturing systems, water recycling units, food production and all other items necessary for extended survival underground. And I want our plans for dealing with a major federal emergency updated.'

Since the news of the impending collision with the cloud had first broken, Jarvis had put all other business aside and had personally studied every file and every document available on the pool of gas, its present trajectory and its projected course. He was no astrophysicist, but he was a fast learner, and with the help of Professor Yates, advisers from NASA and other consultants drafted in from various universities and government departments, he had come to the unavoidable conclusion that the dire warnings he was being given were wholly justified.

The first thing he asked the experts for were casualty estimates if the cloud did indeed collide with the Earth as projected.

'One hundred per cent, sir,' a planetary biologist from Harvard predicted confidently. 'Except for those in hermetically sealed underground shelters. And they would be able to last only as long as their air, food, water and fuel held out.'

Accordingly, the first responsibility of the Cloud EXCOM was to decide who, in addition to the Washington executive and those legislative figures required for constitutional reasons, should get places in the many airtight shelters that were now being hastily manufactured and installed all around the country.

As one presidential aide put it to a colleague: 'They're drawing up a list of people to be saved.'

The committee quickly agreed that civil security must

be the first concern. Chosen military units, the National Guard and elite police forces would be needed to keep public order as the moment of impact approached and, if they were to be relied upon, these personnel would have need to be guaranteed space for themselves and their families in regional shelters.

Then it was agreed that some elements of local government administrations would also need to survive. There was considerable discussion about which categories of American citizens would be important to the society that continued to survive after the cloud had passed. It was decided that those on the preferred list must include doctors, scientists, lawyers, teachers, religious leaders and other important social contributors.

Finally, the meeting had agreed unanimously to set up a secret lottery system. It would use randomly drawn Social Security numbers to select which citizens within these groups would be discreetly offered family places in the shelters.

Now coming to the end of his broadcast, the President squared his shoulders and produced one of his famous, vote-winning smiles for his large TV audience. 'The truth is that this space cloud is so vast and its composition so variable that it is impossible to predict its course precisely. We can't tell how the gravitational pull of the larger planets in the outer solar system will affect it and it is by no means certain that it will even pass near to the Earth.'

The TV director ordered the main camera to close in on the President's face.

'Probes have been launched to take further measurements of the cloud and I have instructed both NASA and the Director of the National Asteroid Defense Network to develop contingency plans for all situations. In addition, I am going to request that the United Nations convene a special meeting of the Security Council to discuss the situation at an international level.'

There had been much argument between the President's political advisers and the White House speech-writers over this last paragraph. Many felt strongly that the President should only calm public fears and make no mention of space probes or of the UN Security Council – it was as if he was saying, 'I'm telling you there's nothing to worry about, but I don't believe it myself.' But wiser political heads had prevailed.

'If he doesn't spell out what steps he is taking to deal with it, it will just be a gift to the opposition,' insisted his Chief of Staff.

But there was general agreement that he should sweeten the pill at the end.

'Most of these scare stories are pure speculation,' concluded President Jarvis with a twinkle in his eye. 'For all of us here in the White House it is business as usual and my wife and I are looking forward to the state visit by the Emperor and Empress of Japan next week. Good evening to you all.'

'I need you to sign this document before we go any further,' Bill Duncan told Randall Tate of the *New York Times*. The two men were standing in the arrivals hall of Terminal 7 at John F. Kennedy Airport, New York. Bill had just flown down from Boston and he handed a two-page legal agreement to the reporter.

'This gives me the right to vet anything you decide to print or broadcast,' Bill explained as Tate ran his eyes over the text. 'And it says that the copyright and intellectual property of the decoded signals belongs solely to me.'

Once he had decided to tell the media about his break-through in decoding the Isonian signals, Bill had asked for Counsellor Paul Cohen's advice on the best way to go about it. The lawyer had then drafted the agreement that the journalist now held in his hand and had even contacted Tate on his client's behalf to sound him out.

'You do realize that everybody in the media is obsessed with this cloud story,' Cohen had warned Bill before making the preliminary call. 'Maybe they won't be very interested.'

But Tate had responded enthusiastically and the lawyer had fixed up a conference call between his client and the *New York Times* correspondent.

'You mean you can *really* read the signals from Iso?' Tate asked disbelievingly over the encrypted phone connection that the lawyer had insisted upon.

'Well, yes, small parts of them,' Bill confirmed. 'We're getting some clear binary code and graphics, but we don't yet know what they mean. We need you to help us get others involved in the task.'

'Who else have you told?' Tate had demanded. 'Have you spoken to any other reporters?'

Bill had assured the journalist that he was offering him an exclusive story.

Now, as they stood together in the JFK arrivals hall, Tate signed the legal agreement with a flourish and handed it back to Bill.

'Come on,' said the *New York Times* writer, already hastening towards the exit. 'My car's in the parking lot.'

Ten minutes later Bill Duncan found himself in the reporter's powerful sports car, being driven away from JFK airport at high speed.

'I've got you a safe house to stay in,' Tate told Bill as they raced along the Brooklyn-Queens Expressway. The excited journalist switched off the computerized highway auto-control and changed lanes abruptly, pulling out in front of a truck.

Unheeding of his car's computer warning him of the spot fine he had incurred, and of the furiously blaring horn behind, he continued, 'Anyway, the public's getting fed up with this goddamn cloud story. They want something new. My editor will clear the front page for this.'

Tate swerved to the right and accelerated, narrowly squeezing between a school bus and a white van as he threaded his way through the late-afternoon traffic.

'A TV crew is arriving at the house in an hour,' the journalist continued. 'We'll record the first interview for a broadcast which will go out tonight to tie in with our nine p.m. edition. Then we'll run the full details in the paper tomorrow.'

'Right,' agreed Bill hesitantly. He had his right arm braced against the car's dashboard as the reporter jumped lanes again before exiting on the Atlantic Avenue ramp at the very last minute.

'Listen, Professor, I know it's a lot to ask,' said Tate as he pulled down hard on his steering wheel and swung into a scruffy tree-lined *cul-de-sac*. 'But I'd like to write the official book about your discovery. What do you think?'

The reporter slammed on the brakes and pulled into the driveway of a faded-looking clapperboard house at the end of the street. He switched the engine off.

'Well?' asked Tate, swinging round excitedly in his seat. 'We could do a great book together, Prof.'

FIVE

When the United Nations complex in New York had been finally rebuilt in 2050, the redevelopment had taken place amid much grumbling about the huge sums of money involved and many questions about the continuing relevance of a global institution with decidedly limited powers.

Many Americans felt that the United Nations was an ongoing threat to the US's rightful leadership of the world. Many Chinese felt that the organization was too heavily influenced by its host nation to be of any real value to the rest of the international community. And the Europeans were so smug about the spectacular growth and financial muscle of their own new federation that they too found the United Nations to be almost an irrelevance.

'The UN will only find its true purpose when the Earth has to fight a battle with aliens,' ran an old saw.

As forty-eight distinguished international scientists gathered at the UN headquarters to discuss what could be done to neutralize the menace of the approaching space cloud, it felt for the first time as if the UN had both a clear purpose and a mandate to represent all the planet's people in what was a truly global threat.

Professor Desmond Yates had opened the meeting by repeating the presentation he had made for the US President and his staff. But on this occasion he was able to include considerably more scientific detail and introduce many more subtle caveats to his prognostications. He knew that this group of astrophysicists, astronomers, astrobiologists, planetary geophysicists and those from related disciplines represented the cream of the world's scientific elite. There were sixteen other Nobel Prize-winners in the audience.

After Yates had made his initial presentation – a briefing which included the very latest data about the cloud and its continuing trajectory towards the Earth – he invited Dr Okuno Pigiyama, the chief designer of the American-European-Russian-Chinese anti-asteroid shield, to bring the meeting up to date about the defensive assets available in distant orbits.

The Japanese-born thermodynamicist rapidly reminded the attendees that the Asteroid Defense Network consisted of 214 nuclear-warhead-tipped missiles that were parked at strategic points in a large defensive sphere around the Earth and at key locations in deep space.

'We are wholly confident that we can now stop even large meteorites and asteroids hitting the Earth,' said Pigiyama. 'But how can we stop a cloud?'

The meeting then broke up for two hours as the scientists huddled in informal groups, exchanging ideas and querying all the available data.

As the gathering's informal leader, Desmond Yates went from huddle to huddle, listening in on the ideas that were being generated. Sometimes he stopped to join a group and to contribute suggestions himself. Sometimes he merely paused to observe, then passed on by.

At the end of the afternoon he called the meeting back together. It was planned that a two-hour break would now follow before the scientists met again for a working dinner which would also be held within the secure confines of the UN complex. Then the debate would begin again on the following morning.

'This afternoon's discussions have thrown up one idea I thought should be shared,' Yates told the meeting. 'I want to hand over to Dr Demetrios Esposito from CalTech.'

A squat, swarthy man with a severe weight problem stepped up and took over the stage from Des Yates. He patched some graphics up onto the large presentation screens and turned to face his audience.

'I've been working on this for the last few days,' he explained, his brow glistening under the lights. 'I think we should carry out a series of closely timed nuclear explosions within the heart of the cloud. This will start a chain reaction that will cause all the oxygen and hydrogen molecules in the cloud to ignite spontaneously.'

There was absolute silence as the CalTech theoretical physicist went on to provide his calculations and demonstrations of how the chain reaction could be started and the likely force of the resultant explosion within the cloud.

Suddenly, a thin cadaverous man rose to his feet at the back of the room. He was shaking with anger.

'Good grief, man,' he shouted in a broad Scottish accent. 'You must have taken leave of your senses. Such a huge blast could disrupt every planetary orbit in the solar system!'

All heads turned to stare at Sir Hamish McLeod, the well-known geophysicist from Edinburgh University. Some other heads in the audience nodded their own concerns.

'I don't think so,' ventured Esposito. 'Not given the volumes of space available for shock-wave dispersal.'

The argument in the meeting then raged for almost an

hour, before Des Yates was forced to step back to the lectern to bring the afternoon's proceedings to a halt.

'We're going to have a further chance to discuss this over our evening meal,' he said. 'In the meantime, I propose we set up a working party to model the explosion that would be produced if we did succeed in detonating the gases within the cloud.'

There were many nods of agreement from within the audience.

'One thing more,' said Yates. 'I know that I don't need to remind you, but everything we are discussing here must be kept completely confidential. You can imagine how the media would react if they discovered that we were even considering a nuclear attack on the cloud – let alone if they found out we thought that there might be some risk that it could cause a misalignment of planetary orbits.'

A few audience members nodded their understanding but most sat stony-faced, unused to being formally reminded of their professional responsibilities.

'See you at dinner, then,' said Yates.

Bill Duncan was obsessed with his decoding work. In the hour in which he had been left alone in the safe house in Brooklyn, he had covered the walls of the living room with scraps of paper on which he had scrawled fragments of the formulae and mathematical operators that he had managed to extract from the Isonian signals. He was reverting to the way he used to work as a young cryptographer: he was looking for patterns, for clues that were non-obvious.

Bill had Nadia with him in his communicator. Although her system now lacked the ultra-fast computing power available on board *Cape Sentinel*, he had stored as much of the decoded Isonian signals as her memory systems could contain.

After ensuring that the safe house was indeed secure, the excitable Randall Tate had warned his exclusive interviewee not to open the front door to anybody but himself. He had then left to make the final arrangements for the interview and TV broadcast that were to follow later the same evening.

Bill felt an urgent need to translate parts of the Isonian transmission into coherent content for the public. He knew that other mathematicians would recognize the operators and mathematical components that had emerged from within the signals, but he desperately wanted to be the first to translate some of the information into plain language, into something that the person in the street could understand.

Despite his overwhelming obsession with the fragmentary alien maths, on his journey down from Boston even Bill had been finally forced to acknowledge that another major story was dominating the public consciousness. There was an air almost of panic hanging over Boston's Logan Airport, with passengers exchanging gallows-humour jokes about aircraft safety and how it might be better to die quickly in a plane crash rather than to wait for the space cloud to strip away all the Earth's oxygen.

While he had waited for his flight, he had caught up with what the newspapers and the TV channels were saying about the mysterious interstellar cloud. It was definitely a threatening situation, he realized, but, as a scientist, he knew that many unknowable variables would come into play during the eight months between now and the point at which the cloud was due to cross the Earth's orbit. Like many other people, he had pushed the problem aside.

There might even be something in these signals that could be of use in tackling the space cloud, Bill thought now as he gazed at the many sheets of paper he had Blu-Tacked to the living room walls.

He walked slowly around the room, allowing his gaze to settle on each scrap of formula for a few seconds before moving on to the next. He was constantly trying to make patterns, trying to see how the apparently unrelated mathematical arguments linked together.

Despite his absorption, Bill suddenly found his concentration disturbed by the loud wail of police sirens. He pulled himself away from the mass of hieroglyphics on the walls and saw bright blue strobe lights flashing against the net curtains. Then car doors began slamming.

Even as the doorbell chimed, Bill heard a loud thudding as someone started to break the door down. Leaping across the room he started tearing his notes from the wall, gathering sheet after sheet in his hands, folding them quickly and stuffing them back into his briefcase.

'POLICE, POLICE, POLICE,' came the cry from the hallway as the front door was smashed in.

Bill was trying to grab the last of his papers just as three armed cops in full body armour burst into the room. They immediately pointed their automatic weapons in Bill's direction and he raised his arms in a bewildered reflex. Then other cops ran past to secure the rest of the house.

Into the room stepped CNS Agent Sarah Burton. Dressed in a black trouser suit and crisp white shirt, her businesslike elegance was in sharp contrast to the ungainly body armour and helmets worn by the police.

The federal agent pulled her badge from her pocket and showed it to Bill as if they had never met before. 'Agent Burton, CNS,' she announced. Then she turned to her police escort. 'Thank you, gentlemen,' she told them. 'You can stand easy. The Professor isn't going to cause us any trouble.'

The cops lowered their weapons but remained in the room, keeping a watchful eye on their suspect. Agent Burton glanced around the room and then turned to the wall and to the half-dozen snippets of mathematical formulae that Bill had been unable to remove.

'What are these?' she asked after studying the symbols for a few moments.

'You tell me,' said Bill Duncan.

'The damn thing has shrunk,' said Brian Nunney disbelievingly as he stared at the computer displays. 'It's gone from being over one hundred and forty million kilometres across to just under one hundred and twenty. And that's in just two days! It's incredible!'

'Well, I've double-checked all the computer measurements,' Suzi Price assured him. 'I'm certain we haven't made an error.'

They both stared at the large, red-and-grey-coloured mass that filled the 3-D screens of the Cerro Samanal mountain observatory. Since the space cloud had drawn close enough to the solar system to be visible in the optical wavelengths, all normal astronomy had been suspended. Every night the massive domed building housing the Carl Sagan Ultra-Large Optical Telescope opened up to the night sky with the sole aim of monitoring the space cloud as it rushed headlong towards the Earth.

'But what could have suddenly happened to nineteen billion cubic kilometres of space gas?' asked the Australian astronomer. 'It can't just disappear.'

Suzi knew that she wasn't really required to come up

with an answer. She was just being used as a sounding board by her senior colleague.

'Has the density of the main cloud altered?' she asked.

'We can't tell from this distance,' admitted Nunney. 'That's why NASA has sent out the probes. As they get closer they'll be able to bounce laser beams off the gas to measure just how dense it is.'

'If it can change that much in two days, it could change completely in a few months,' suggested Suzi. 'I think people will be very glad to get your new measurements.'

'You're right,' said Nunney as he sat down at a keyboard. 'I'd better inform NASA immediately – and Des Yates. I think he's in a top-level meeting at the UN. They're trying to figure out what can be done to head the cloud off.'

'How can they stop a cloud?' asked Suzi.

Bill Duncan glanced up as Federal Agent Sarah Burton re-entered the interview room. They were in a police precinct house in Lower Manhattan and Bill knew that Randall Tate was also being held in another room in the station. The reporter had arrived back at the safe house just as Bill was being loaded into a police car and although Tate had executed a rapid U-turn and sped away, a cruiser stationed at the open end of the street had flagged him down and brought him in.

'William Andrew Duncan, I am arresting you for the illegal possession of a classified computer component,' Agent Burton had told him coldly as they stood in the living room of the safe house. 'You will also be charged with attempting to sell or give information about the said classified processor to the media.'

While the agent read Bill his statutory rights one of the

cops handcuffed him. Three more CNS agents then entered
and began a thorough search of the house.

'The processor you're talking about isn't here,' Bill told
the woman who had arrested him. 'It's still on my boat in
Boston. And I'm *not* here to sell secrets about any goddam
processor.'

'You can tell me what you were doing when we get to
the station,' the federal agent had told him sharply.

'So how long have you had me under surveillance?'
asked Bill now as Sarah Burton sat down again at the interview table.

The federal agent didn't answer, but she glanced down
at a Digipad on the table in front of her and made some
notes. Eventually she looked up.

'You have admitted to the illegal possession of a
classified computer component, Professor Duncan,' said the
agent icily. 'That is an offence under federal law. If we go to
court on this you are likely to be sentenced to between five
and eight years in jail.'

Bill Duncan stared back at the CNS officer, appalled by
what she was saying. Over the last two hours he had waived
his right to have an attorney present. He was certain of his
innocence of anything other than a technical offence and he
had explained as patiently as he could that as an academic
he had no interest in the proprietary design of the Rand-
Fairchild processor – other than in its use in decoding the
alien transmissions. He had also explained that his meeting
with Randall Tate had not been set up to discuss the existence or design of the classified processor, but had been
arranged solely to bring the story of his decoding breakthrough to the general public in the hope of attracting funds
for more research.

Now Agent Burton sat back in her chair and regarded

her suspect quizzically. When she finally spoke, Bill noticed a change in her tone.

'It is possible that we may not proceed with charges if you are prepared to return the processor immediately,' she told him.

'Well, of course I will,' agreed Bill. 'But I was hoping to continue my work on the signal decoding. I think you'll agree that it is something of national importance.'

'And you can only do it on this particular processor?' asked the agent.

'Well, even the Rand-Fairchild prototype processor isn't really powerful enough on its own,' Bill explained. 'One of the reasons I wanted to break the story in the press was that I was hoping to get some research funding – to buy access to more powerful networks.'

Sarah Burton ran the tip of her forefinger around the edge of the electronic notepad that lay on the table.

'If we drop the charges, would you be prepared to with-hold the news about your breakthrough from the media for a short while, Professor?' she asked. 'I want to introduce you to somebody – somebody who might be able to help you with decoding the signals.'

'Sorry, but it's too late to stop the story,' Bill told her. 'I've already given some of the information to Randall Tate.'

'Yes, I've just spoken with Mr Tate,' said Agent Burton with a sharp nod of her head. 'He's prepared to cooperate and sit on the story. But he has one condition.'

'A condition? What condition?'

'He insists that the *New York Times* must get an exclusive when the story does break.'

Bill shrugged. 'So who is it you want me to meet?'

The agent sat back in her chair. 'Someone I was introduced to at a seminar in Washington last year – Professor Desmond Yates. He was the one who–'

'I know who Des Yates is,' broke in Bill irritably. 'But he's a White House adviser these days. I particularly don't want the government involved in this. That's why I was talking to the media first.'

Agent Burton sat forward in her chair. 'I know what you think of our government, Professor,' she said. 'But I think you'll agree that things are more than a little sensitive at the moment. The public has been really panicked by the news of this space cloud.'

'Damn it!' shouted Bill, banging his fist on the table. 'I am NOT taking my work to Washington!'

'There's no need for you to go to Washington,' the federal agent told him. 'Professor Yates is in New York for a meeting at the United Nations.'

SIX

'Agent Burton, a pleasure to meet you again,' said the tall, distinguished-looking man who strode into the ante-room. 'Forgive me for keeping you waiting.'

It was almost eleven p.m. and Sarah Burton and Bill Duncan had been waiting for over an hour to meet Desmond Yates. While he waited Bill had found himself in the grip of powerful mixed feelings. On one hand he was furious with the CNS agent for blackmailing him into sharing his breakthrough with a representative of the White House. But on the other he was genuinely excited by the prospect of meeting the man who had first discovered the Isonian signals, the man who had been his scientific idol since boyhood.

Agent Burton rose and shook Yates's hand, then turned to introduce Bill Duncan.

'Ah yes, Professor, your reputation precedes you,' said Yates genially. 'I was sorry to read about that business at MIT.'

Bill returned the older man's smile, but said nothing. The contrast between the elegantly suited Nobel Prize-winning celebrity scientist and the denim-clad, long-haired radical computer psychologist seemed very marked.

'So,' continued Yates, glancing from Bill to Agent Burton. 'I suppose this must be about something important?'

There were to be no further preliminaries. Both visitors knew that Yates had just come out of a very high-level seminar with the world's top scientists – a meeting in which they were deciding what could be done about the threat posed by the space cloud. Only by insisting that she needed to communicate with Professor Yates on a matter of the highest national security had the federal agent been able to persuade Yates's secretary to interrupt her boss and arrange this hurried ten-minute interview.

Sarah Burton turned to the man she had arrested and nodded brusquely.

'I've decoded small sections of the signals from Iso,' Bill said, feeling so coerced and cornered that he found the words difficult to get out of his mouth, words that he had been expecting to say with pride one day. 'It contains digital information, pure binary code. I've extracted some sections of math, some graphics operators whose function I've yet to determine and some hieroglyphs of unknown meaning. I have about forty petabytes of the analog digitized so far and I need expert help in working out what it means – as well as a lot more processing power and network capacity.'

Yates started in shock as he heard the news. He took a small step backwards and his mouth opened. Then he shook his head.

'Jesus, after all this time! And it's digital! How did you do it? What have you got? Can you show me?' The questions tumbled from his mouth.

Bill hesitated. 'I'm sorry, Professor Yates,' he began, 'but I have to tell you that I'm very reluctant to share this information with you as a government representative. I am only doing so under duress and I wish to make it clear that I intend to retain my rights to all proprietary information regarding my methods of signal conversion and analysis.'

Yates glanced from the computer psychologist to the CNS agent and back again.

'Duress?' he asked. 'What duress?'

'Hardly duress,' broke in Sarah Burton mollifyingly. 'Professor Duncan has been helping us in our inquiries about the misuse of a classified processor. I merely suggested that he should inform you of what he has been doing with it.'

Bill glowered at the federal agent and Yates cleared his throat.

'Look, if it's of any help, we can agree to keep this unofficial,' he offered. 'I give you my word, Professor Duncan, that I will keep what you are going to tell me confidential until you agree otherwise. Fair enough?'

Bill considered for a moment, gave a short nod, then took out his communicator from the pocket of his denim jacket. He flipped open its lid and selected the projector function.

An hour later, Desmond Yates and Bill Duncan were still standing at the room's white-painted wall on which the projection was slowly scrolling past. Both men were in shirt-sleeves, both had electronic marker pens in their hands. They had been writing their thoughts and their attempts to complete the partial alien formulae on the room's electronic whiteboard.

The former MIT scientist had explained that the key to beginning to unlock the analog alien transmissions had been to slow them down by two hundred million times, and then look for redundancy in both the FM/AM signal components. Then, when it was clear they that contained digital elements, to look for more redundancy within the bases that had emerged.

Yates had grunted with excitement as recognizable values and mathematical operators appeared on the wall. Then the two men began to piece together what were almost certainly sections of equations. Initially Sarah Burton had tried to keep up. Her own maths was rusty, though still serviceable, but she found herself lost as the two men started to speculate about the possibility that the fragments of calculations appeared to be illegal mixtures of quantum theory, base-sixteen digital code and Einsteinian-style traditional astrophysics.

'How much more have you converted and digitized?' asked Yates when they had exhausted the files carried in the small personal technology assistant.

'I've got about eighteen minutes' worth of binary alto-gether,' explained Bill. 'But there's so much more analog data – six billion years' worth on even the fastest stand-alone system.'

'That's no problem,' said Yates enthusiastically, as he lifted his own communicator and began a series of rapid cal-culations. 'If we distribute small segments of the task over the networks – like we did years ago with the old "SETI" at Home program – we can ask the public for help and use the power of the world's thirty billion processors. We can have the conversion done in a few months.'

'With respect, Professor,' interjected Sarah Burton, speaking for the first time in half an hour. 'That would only be OK if you don't mind what it is the public finds out. At present, only Professor Duncan knows how to translate the Isonian signals. Don't you think we should consider care-fully before we give it all to the world – especially at such a sensitive time as this?'

Both men looked at the government security agent as if she were a massive killjoy. Then Yates put down his com-municator, re-fastened his collar and tightened his tie.

'You're right, of course, Agent Burton,' agreed Yates as he plucked his suit jacket from a chair back. 'We don't know what it is we're going to find, nor whether it could be any use to us with the space cloud.'

The older scientist eased on his jacket and, formal again, turned to face Bill Duncan.

'Would you be prepared to bring everything you've got to Washington, to show my colleagues at NASA and the White House?'

Bill glanced from Yates to Agent Burton. Every instinct he possessed made him want to yell 'NO' and tell them to go to hell. He could tell them both to jump in the lake and take whatever sort of rap was coming to him. It hardly mattered, now that he no longer had an academic career or a family to worry about.

But on the other hand, the approach of the space cloud and the awful, terrifying threat that it brought had changed everything. It now seemed as if all normal considerations had to be suspended until the threat was averted.

'OK, just so long as you understand that I will remain free to talk to the press when the time is right,' said Bill, snapping his communicator shut and pulling on his own jacket. 'I will just have to go back to Boston to pick up my things.'

'We'll have that done for you,' said Agent Burton quickly. 'I can arrange a hotel here for you tonight. Let's meet up again in the morning.'

From the *New York Times* website, 20 April 2064

NUCLEAR ATTACK PLANNED ON CLOUD

By SONIA MAXWELL, special correspondent

'Risk that Solar System Could Break up'

Scientists meeting at the United Nations to discuss potential methods of diverting the space cloud away from Earth are considering detonating nuclear weapons at its center. The aim is to create a chain reaction explosion that will incinerate the entire cloud. Their proposal will be put before the UN Security Council in the next two days.

'The idea is lunacy,' Sir Hamish McLeod, professor of geophysics at Edinburgh University, Scotland, said yesterday. 'If the cloud were to explode, the blast would be so great that it could wreck the delicate equilibrium of the whole solar system. Disrupting the Earth's orbit could destroy our entire civilization, even before we are sure that the cloud will collide with our planet and before we can be sure of what the consequences of such a collision might be.'

Nobel Prize-winner Professor Desmond Yates dismissed concerns about the proposed nuclear attack. 'Before the very first atomic weapon was exploded, some scientists believed that such an explosion would set fire to the Earth's atmosphere,' he told the *New York Times*. 'We are building computer models of the proposed strike to ensure that if any nuclear action against the cloud were to take place, it would not harm Earth or any other part of the solar system.'

'What do they hope to achieve?' groaned President Maxwell T. Jarvis as he watched TV images of a huge crowd surrounding the United Nations headquarters building in New York. The television sound was down and the dozen or so other people gathered in the Oval Office wondered if his question was rhetorical or whether they were expected to come up with an answer.

Since news of the plan to detonate nuclear warheads inside the cloud had been deliberately leaked to the press, the whole of the east side of mid-Manhattan had ground to a standstill. Hundreds of thousands of protesters carrying banners and placards proclaiming 'NO TO NUKES', 'SAVE OUR SOLAR SYSTEM' and 'MILITARY OUT OF SPACE' had blocked the roads and made all normal business impossible.

Because of the protests, the scientists attending the supposedly secret meeting at the UN had been unable to reconvene and the seminar had been abandoned. Instead they had agreed to continue their urgent discussions in the privacy of the networks.

'I'm not at all sure the protesters know what it is they want to achieve themselves, sir,' Desmond Yates told the President. 'But their actions do seem to be having an effect on political opinion. The Security Council members are now deadlocked over whether a nuclear strike should be made against the cloud or not.'

'So what should *we* do?' asked the President, turning to the room in general.

'We must act unilaterally, sir,' said the Chairman of the Joint Chiefs of Staff firmly. 'We should mount an all-out nuclear strike in the very near future, while the cloud is still well outside our own solar system. If Professor Yates says there's minimal risk, that's good enough for me.'

Jarvis glanced at Yates for his confirmation.

'Well, the majority view among our group of scientists was that it is the right thing to do, sir,' agreed Yates. 'The computer models we've built suggest that the risk is minimal.'

'But what if they're wrong?' groaned the President with a shake of his head. 'Think of the responsibility!'

The Cabinet members, aides and advisers stared at the President as he wrestled with the concept of the United States launching a unilateral nuclear attack on the cloud.

'If the UN can't agree, perhaps I can at least get agreement from the other major powers,' Jarvis said at last, turning to his senior foreign affairs adviser. 'Henry, set up calls for me to speak with the leaders of Europe, Russia and China – in that order.'

SEVEN

'So, Agent Burton, I presume you've been told to keep a very close eye on me while I'm in DC?' Bill Duncan said with a resigned sigh. The pair were belted into neighbouring seats in the business section of a plane waiting to take off for Washington.

'That's understandable, given your feelings about our government, isn't it, Professor Duncan?' replied Sarah Burton. 'I'm afraid you're stuck with me for the duration.'

Bill nodded and wondered again whether he was right to be taking his discovery to the Washington administration. He'd already had one major row about it with Christine Cocoran, his most loyal volunteer. He'd called her to arrange for Boston-based CNS agents to visit the *Cape Sentinel* to collect the Rand-Fairchild processor, his personal memory-storage systems and some clothes. During the call he had been forced to admit that he was about to share their precious breakthrough with NASA and the White House.

'How could you?' Christine cried. 'After everything you've said about them. You know our government is completely irresponsible about the development of AI personalities and machine life. Think what they could do with *this* material.'

The phone call had ended on a sour note, but Bill now knew that his personal effects had been collected promptly and were already on their way to DC. Christine had begrudgingly agreed to remain on board the *Cape Sentinel* to boat-sit for him while he was away. 'I want you to carry on the good work,' Bill had urged her, trying to make it clear that he hadn't completely sold out. 'Keep knocking those illegals off the networks.'

'So, Professor,' said the federal agent as she flipped open an in-flight magazine. 'How well do you know Washington?'

Bill glanced sideways at his travelling companion. As usual she was wearing her uniform of a dark trouser suit and a bright white shirt, but her medium-length brown hair now seemed fuller, and done in a less severe style than before.

'Only too well,' said Bill. 'But I can't say I know the city.'

The jet engines suddenly increased their power and the plane began to accelerate quickly towards take-off.

Thirty minutes later Bill was beginning to regard his fellow passenger in a rather different light. He had learned a little about her own studies in forensic computing at Berkeley and he had been surprised to discover how much she knew about artificial life and the principles of cognitive therapy for computer personalities. He had also learned that her role in Washington was not solely to keep an eye on him – she had also been seconded to provide him with practical assistance.

'I think that CNS hopes to share in whatever comes out of your work,' she admitted. 'Who knows what we're going to find? Stuff that could be of real use to the Department, maybe.'

'That's what worries me most,' said Bill.

'Thank you for waiting, people,' said President Jarvis as he entered the Situation Room. Motioning for the members of the Cloud EXCOM to sit, he took his chair at the head of the table.

'I've just got off the line with President Olsen,' Jarvis told the meeting. 'He's formally agreed that Europe will join us in the strike against the cloud. He had a lot of arguing to do with his Cabinet colleagues, but the majority view was that we should go ahead.'

There were nods of approval from the committee members and the other advisers and aides who had been called together to learn the outcome of the negotiations.

'But neither the Russians nor the Chinese will take part,' added Jarvis. 'Lee Jian seems unable to make up his mind and President Orotov said an outright "No". That means it's us and the Europeans going it alone.'

There was a short silence while the others in the meeting waited to see if the President had anything to add. Then Desmond Yates stood up.

'Sir, I've got an update on the cloud's position – and on its behaviour,' he told the meeting as the holo-theatre at the end of the Situation Room lit up. All present saw a graphic of the solar system with a dotted line passing through the orbital ovals of the outer planets before intersecting with Earth's own orbit, closer to the sun.

'We've been monitoring the cloud continuously for the last nine weeks,' explained Yates, 'And it's still clearly on a heading that will lead to a direct collision with Earth – in fact, we'll be plumb in the centre of the cloud as it passes by.'

A few EXCOM members seated at the large table shook their heads anxiously, while others made jottings on their digital notepads.

'But something odd has occurred,' continued Yates as the image in the holo-theatre changed. Now those in the meeting saw an image of the vapour mass itself, thick and red with extensive grey bands. 'The cloud seems to be shrinking, or perhaps I should say condensing. Over the last few days its volume seems to have become seven per cent smaller.'

'How might that be possible, Professor?' asked Lillian Bayley, the director the National Asteroid Defense Network.

'We just don't know,' admitted Yates. 'The cloud's still well outside our solar system so it can't be because of any gravitational effects from the sun or from the outer planets. The only theory that makes any sense is that there's some sort of chemical reaction occurring within the cloud itself, something that's making it shrink from the inside.'

'You mean it's not *passive*?' asked President Jarvis. 'The briefing material I've read describes the cloud as being made up of *passive* gases.'

'Well, all of our spectrometry and other forms of measurement suggest that it is made up of nothing but passive gases, sir,' agreed Yates. 'But we can't account for the change in the cloud's length and volume.'

There was a short silence in the room. Then the President asked, 'And is the cloud travelling at the same speed?'

'It's slowing quite a bit, sir,' Yates told him. 'It's now travelling at approximately three hundred thousand kilometres per hour. We now calculate that it will begin to strike the Earth's atmosphere five months from now – at eleven twenty-one a.m. GMT on October twenty-fourth.'

Each person in the meeting digested this news in silence. The President drummed his thick fingers on the writing pad in front of him.

'So do we go ahead with a nuclear strike?' he asked the

Cloud EXCOM. 'Europe will join us, but no other nation in the world is prepared to take part. Can we take the risk?'

'I think we should,' said Yates. 'It is more risky to do nothing.'

Turning to the head of the Joint Chiefs of Staff, the President asked, 'How many warheads can fly if we just use our own part of the Asteroid Defense Network and the sector that is controlled by the European Union?'

'Twenty-four, Mr President,' said General Thomas Nicholls promptly. 'Approximately three hundred and fifty megatons of nuclear power in total.'

'Is that enough?' asked Jarvis.

'More than enough to start off the chain reaction,' Nicholls assured his commander-in-chief. 'My people have double-checked with Professor Esposito at CalTech. He's the scientist who worked all this out.'

'How soon can we launch?' said Jarvis.

'Well, we're currently on the other side of the sun from our main deep-space missiles, so we'll have to use the Martian colony as our strike command,' Nicholls explained. 'Mars is also on the other side of the sun to us at present so it's three hundred and fifty million kilometres nearer to the cloud than we are. It has good line-of-sight communications with the missiles and there will be a much shorter time delay in their command communications. We can be ready in just under ten days.'

'And the cloud will still be a safe distance away from us?' Jarvis asked, turning to Desmond Yates.

'About half a billion kilometres outside our solar system,' said Yates. 'But we don't want to delay too long. It's travelling at very high speed.'

President Jarvis nodded, then sat with his eyes closed for a few moments.

'Well, should we go it alone with the Europeans?' he asked, suddenly looking up. 'Formal votes, please.'

The President glanced around the members of the executive committee.

'I agree – let's do it, sir,' said Coleville Jackson, the Secretary of State.

'Yes, let's do it,' said General Nicholls firmly.

'I say yes,' said the White House Chief of Staff with a quick nod.

One by one all present were polled. Although some were slower than others to agree, all finally gave their assent.

'Very well,' said President Maxwell T. Jarvis. 'Let's do it.'

Dr Bridget Mulberry, an astro-mineralogist and the serving mayor of the American Martian settlement, glanced round at the eleven other members of the Township Council and announced, 'Twenty seconds to go.'

The council meeting had been convened in the settlement's main assembly hall following notice that an emergency broadcast of the gravest importance was to be transmitted from Earth. The President of the United States was going to address the councillors of the American Martian colony.

There were two sizeable habitat-settlements on the surface of Mars. The oldest, and largest, was the American habitat – now more like a small town – which had first been established as a scientific base in 2038 and which had since been enlarged several times over. Now the settlement consisted of seventeen separate domed buildings which were connected by hermetically sealed walkways.

Over eighty volunteers lived in the American outpost, most of them scientists, and the personnel rotated every three years as the planet's low gravity took its toll on the human skeleton, forcing the temporary settlers to return to Earth for a lengthy recuperation.

The other major settlement, located over 200 kilometres further south on the Martian surface, was the more recently built Russian-Chinese township which now boasted almost forty colonists. Once a month, the residents of the two colonial outposts got together in one or the other habitat for socializing and information exchange. The next party was due to take place on the following day in the Russian-Chinese settlement. It was an event to which all of the colonists had been looking forward.

'I hope this message won't spoil our party,' grouched Foster Robinson, the settlement's writer-in-residence. Robinson doubled as the township's only journalist and Dr Mulberry had invited him to the meeting so that he could report on proceedings for the benefit of the rest of the settlers.

The large screen flickered to life as Washington's encrypted transmission reached Mars after its twenty-one-minute outward journey. Then they saw the grave features of President Maxwell T. Jarvis.

The broadcast lasted only seven minutes. When it ended there was complete silence in the habitat meeting hall.

'Want to see it again?' asked Dr Mulberry. There were many nods, and she quickly punched up a replay.

At the end of the second showing she turned to Major Marshall Peters, the senior military officer resident in the American settlement.

'I guess I must officially hand over to you, Marshall,' she told him. 'Now that we've become a military base.'

The US President had updated the Martian colonists with the latest information about the cloud and had then outlined the plan for the nuclear attack on which the US and the European Union had agreed.

'As Earth is currently on the other side of the sun to the missiles that are nearest the cloud, we want you to launch and coordinate the attack,' President Jarvis had told them. 'I therefore place the United States Martian settlement under US military law and I order Major Marshall Peters, as the senior officer on the base, to take control of the settlement and to form the team that will execute NASA's instructions to launch components of the Asteroid Defense Network into the cloud.'

The broadcast had ended with a rendition of the American national anthem played over a long shot of the Capitol, in Washington DC.

U.S.– EUROPE TO DETONATE 24 NUCLEAR WARHEADS INSIDE SPACE CLOUD

by RANDALL TATE, science correspondent

In a bilateral action taken without the agreement of other major world powers, the United States government and the European Union executive have agreed to launch a massive nuclear strike against the giant gas cloud that is currently heading towards Earth's solar system. The attack will be mounted and co-ordinated by the American military command on Mars.

'The plan is to set the cloud on fire and to disperse it with the blast,' said Professor Desmond Yates, Space Affairs Adviser to the White House. 'We cannot take the risk of the cloud entering our solar system. It could carry unknown forms of bacteria and many astrophysicists conclude that it could endanger our planet's atmosphere.'

'DISGRACEFUL AND RECKLESS ACTION' – SIR CHARLES HODGESON

British science-fiction author and centenarian space guru, Sir Charles Hodgeson, yesterday described the bilateral US–European plan to launch nuclear warheads at the space cloud as 'disgraceful and undemocratic.'

Speaking from his island home in the Western Pacific, Hodgeson went on to accuse the governments of 'reckless and irresponsible behaviour. 'This is our first chance to study a large space cloud at close hand. Destroying it before we fully understand its nature is a barbaric response.'

'Good morning, welcome to the Pentagon,' said Desmond Yates cheerily as he walked across the marble floor, hand outstretched.

Bill Duncan and Sarah Burton both shook hands with the White House adviser and then stepped through a metal and weapons detector.

'Settling in to DC OK?' asked Yates as they received the all-clear. He handed a digital security pass to Bill; the CNS agent had already flipped her Federal badge and digital ID to the outside of her jacket pocket.

The government – Bill was unsure which department exactly – had provided him with a two-bedroomed duplex apartment only fifteen minutes' walk from the main Pentagon building. When he had arrived in the flat he had found his clothes, personal effects and Nadia's main processor array waiting for him. But the classified Rand-Fairchild processor had not been among his things.

'We've found a private room for you two to use in the Advanced Computing Lab,' explained Yates after they had descended two levels and completed a long walk along a windowless corridor. He punched a code into a combination lock, pushed open a door and ushered the visitors into a cool, dimly lit room.

The walls were covered in a variety of screens – 3-D, laser panel, HD-2D and holo – and a small holo-theatre occupied one corner of the computer laboratory. Along a bench against one wall Bill saw half a dozen linked processor units and, at the end, the housing unit he had constructed to hold the Rand-Fairchild component that Christine Cocoran had purloined for him from the MIT lab.

'We've managed to smooth things over with the Rand-Fairchild corporation,' said Yates, 'And they've been kind enough to lend us a further six of their prototype processors. Do you think they'll help in the conversion process, Bill?'

'Well, they'll make a great start,' agreed the former MIT professor as he examined the array of advanced equipment.

'One thing I must ask is that you don't remove anything from this room at the end of your working shifts,' said Yates. 'This is a secure area and your work is regarded as classified, so I don't want—'

'Hey, hold on a minute,' objected Bill. 'I haven't agreed to my work being classified. The deal is that I publish what I want, when I want.'

The older space scientist regarded the computer expert quizzically. 'I understand,' he said after a few moments. 'But these processors are classified units, so they can't leave this room. Is that OK?'

'That's OK,' agreed Bill as he slipped his slim communicator unit from his pocket. 'But this unit and Nadia, my PA, go with me everywhere, along with whatever I'm working on. You understand?'

'OK, that's fine,' agreed Yates reluctantly. After a pause he added, 'The President has been informed of your achievement, Bill. He asked me to congratulate you, and he's very keen that you should get all the assistance you want.'

'Well, that's helpful,' agreed Bill. 'But I'm not sure quite what I'm going to need yet.'

'There's a list of the departments within the Advanced Computer Lab on the wall,' said Yates, pointing. 'If you need technical support, hardware, or any other sort of help, they've been told to give you top priority. Agent Burton knows where the Pentagon canteens and all of the other facilities are.'

'Great,' said Bill, still feeling very unsure about whether he was doing the right thing.

'Copies of all the Isonian signals that have been received are in those memory packs,' said Yates, nodding towards the bench. 'How long will it be before you've got real-time digital conversion up and running again? We need to demonstrate what we're doing for SETI, NASA and a couple of the other agencies.'

Bill glanced at his federal minder. The agent was already slipping her jacket off, ready for work. 'Well, with the help of my new assistant, I should have something in a few days,' he told Des Yates.

From the moment that martial law had been imposed, the pace of life at the US settlement on Mars had accelerated dramatically. Like many colonial outposts of previous centuries, life in the Martian habitat had previously been rather sleepy. Things got done, but at a pace that suited the remote community, rather than at a speed to suit those back home on Earth.

Now everything had changed. The eighteen military personnel at the base had commandeered all the scientists' surface transporters and had been busy erecting an array of six high-power radio antennae to augment the already powerful transmitters that the settlement used for its regular communications with Earth, and with various space stations. Now the military command on Mars needed to be in constant, close-to-real-time radio communication with twenty-four nuclear-tipped spacecraft as they flew into the high-velocity space cloud and detonated in a carefully timed sequence.

The software to control the fleet of spacecraft, and to time the precision explosions, had been up-linked to the

Martian colony from the Asteroid Defense Network headquarters in Pasadena, California. Once it had been received, Major Marshall H. Peters, the officer in charge, had checked and double-checked with his technology specialists that the software was working properly and that communications with the two dozen nuclear-weapon delivery vehicles were in good order.

'We have A-One telemetry with each and every bird,' confirmed Chief Communications Sergeant Morrison Laburke. 'We've carried out six rehearsal launches – everything's working fine, sir.'

'What precisely will we see when the warheads explode in the cloud, Major?' asked Foster Robinson as he gazed into his video viewfinder. Since the announcement of military rule and the critical mission given to the base, the resident reporter had been galvanized into a flurry of activity, sending report after report back to the news organizations on Earth.

'There will be a huge explosion low down on Mars's southern horizon,' said Major Peters, looking straight into the camera lens, as Robinson had instructed. 'For a while it will seem as if a night sun is burning. Then, after about an hour or so, the light will die out as the hydrogen and helium are consumed. That will be the end of the cloud.'

EIGHT

'I don't like the look of this at all,' Brian Nunney said worriedly to Suzi Price. They were waiting impatiently for Desmond Yates to return an urgent call that the Australian scientist had placed earlier. 'I think this news is definitely going to spook them in Washington.'

Over the last three days all duty astronomers at the Carl Sagan Ultra-Large Telescope in Chile had been checking and cross-checking some very strange optical data: it looked as if the giant space cloud had abruptly changed course.

The huge pool of interstellar gas had now reached the outer limits of the solar system and although the powerful gravitational effects of Neptune, Pluto and Uranus had been carefully modelled and the calculations fed into the cloud's anticipated trajectory, nothing could account for what looked like a sudden course change eighteen degrees to the solar south and thirty-two degrees to the east.

'But it's no longer going to hit the Earth, is it?' pointed out Suzi for the tenth time. 'It's the best news we've had in months.'

Nunney's communicator beeped and he glanced down at the screen. Professor Yates was finally calling back.

Taking a deep breath, Nunney returned Yates's greeting and then delivered the message that he had been mentally rehearsing for hours.

'We think the cloud has changed its heading, Professor Yates,' he said carefully. 'We've been tracking it constantly and there is a discrepancy between the trajectory our computers predict and the cloud's actual position. The longitude discrepancy is plus twenty-nine seconds and the declination is out by minus seventeen seconds.'

Nunney listened intently as Yates fired a series of questions at him.

'Yes, we're quite sure,' Nunney assured the world-famous astrophysicist. 'I've already e-mailed our data to you on a secure link.'

The Australian nodded down the phone as Yates asked for yet more details.

'Yes, we've modelled the new trajectory,' Nunney said. 'If the cloud stays on its new heading it will miss the Earth completely, by about two hundred million kilometres.'

Brian Nunney glanced anxiously at Suzi as he listened to Yates express his relief at the other end of the line.

'But there's something else you should know, Professor,' Nunney broke in. 'On its new course, the cloud is now heading directly for Mars.'

Two days later Randall Tate received an early-evening call at his desk in the *New York Times* building. Glancing at his handset he saw that it was originating from a small island in the Great Barrier Reef.

'Hello, Mr Tate. How nice of you to take my call.'

As always, Tate wondered whether the over-elaborate manners of the British were sincere or whether they were subtly sending up everyone with whom they had contact.

'Always a pleasure, Sir Charles,' said the reporter, responding in kind. 'What can I do for you?'

'Have you talked to any of your astronomer friends

about how the space cloud is behaving?' asked Sir Charles Hodgeson. 'I mean, in the last couple of days?'

Tate frowned into his communicator. They hadn't selected visual.

'What's on your mind?' asked the reporter, irritated by the Englishman's obtuseness.

'Call me back when you have,' said Hodgeson, closing the connection.

A little over 9,000 miles away, the centenarian science-fiction guru stared at his now blank communications screen, then glanced up at a wall clock. It was five a.m. on Orpheus Island – seven p.m. in New York – and Hodgeson had spent the night in the island's observatory, taking careful observations and measurements of the space cloud.

'How long before he calls back, do you reckon?' Hodgeson asked Amrik Chandra, one of his most devoted students.

The young man who had worked through the night with the great visionary shrugged. 'Depends on how good his contacts are. And how much they're prepared to tell him.'

A little over fifteen minutes later Randall Tate called back.

Hodgeson greeted the reporter again and listened to what he had discovered.

'Well done, Mr Tate' said Hodgeson, more than a little condescendingly. 'So the cloud is now heading straight for Mars, for the control centre that is planning to attack it. What does this suggest to you?'

'Nobody's prepared to offer any theories on the record,' Tate admitted. 'My contacts merely confirm that the cloud has changed direction and is now heading for Mars. They say they don't know why it has happened.'

'Well, *I'm* prepared to tell you something on the record,' said Hodgeson assertively. 'It is quite clear from its behaviour that this so-called cloud is a form of alien life – and intelligent life, at that! It is obviously responding to the preparations now being made to attack it. This means that any attack we make against the cloud would be an act of unprovoked aggression against another form of life. What sort of barbarians are we?'

'So you believe we should do nothing?' asked Tate.

'Remember, this cloud has caused us no problems so far,' insisted the space guru. 'This insane pre-emptive strike must be called off before something terrible happens. We should be transmitting peace messages, not launching nuclear weapons.'

'So what exactly should we be saying to the cloud, Sir Charles?' asked Tate sceptically.

'We should be welcoming it. I am personally calling on like-minded peace-loving people to transmit radio signals of welcome to this alien being. I myself am already doing so. This is something I have waited my entire life to see. The idea of attacking a form of alien intelligence before it has revealed its own intentions shows how barbaric the human race remains. It is probably merely curious and is coming to visit us.'

'Just what the hell are we dealing with here?' demanded President Jarvis, glaring up from behind his desk. 'At first you tell me that this cloud is just a harmless pool of gas that is moving vaguely in the direction of our solar system, then you tell me it's going to hit the Earth and strip away all our atmosphere. On your recommendation I ordered our forces on Mars to prepare to make a pre-emptive nuclear strike and now you say this goddam thing has changed course all on its own and is now heading directly for the people who are planning to attack it. I repeat, what *is* this thing?'

Desmond Yates stood in front of the President's desk in the Oval Office along with the director of NASA and the head of the Joint Chiefs of Staff. There was no informality about this meeting and, for the first time since he was a teenager, Yates had the overwhelming feeling that he was being carpeted – which was patently unfair.

'Sir, we have no idea,' he admitted. 'We have examined the cloud optically, by radio-telescopic analysis and by interferometry, and all we can detect in its interior are giant pools of gases – hydrogen, helium and other gaseous elements – that are of varying density. We've bounced radio waves from one side of the cloud to the other, and from the top to the bottom. There are no heavy elements in the cloud, no structures, no nucleus that we can detect. It appears to be just a large pool of gas and dust.'

'But a pool of gas that can change direction when it wants?' snapped the President.

Yates glanced sideways at NASA director Roy Wilcox.

'Professor Yates is correct, sir,' confirmed Wilcox. 'We've applied our most sophisticated techniques to look inside this cloud, right inside, and it's just gas – all the way through.'

The President flicked the end of a silver letter-opener on his large blotting pad and then nodded once, sharply.

'OK, sit down, gentlemen,' he said, waving at a row of empty chairs which stood in front of his desk.

He swung round in his own high-backed swivel chair and glanced briefly out at the Rose Garden. Then, when his advisers had taken their seats, he swung back round and stared at Yates and Wilcox in turn.

'I realize that you two are scientists and that you're not used to making wild speculation,' he said. 'But in the privacy of this room, and off the record, I must ask whether you believe this cloud might have some form of intelligence and, if so, whether we should be trying to deal with it in a different way?'

Neither of the men held by the President's gaze volunteered an answer, until finally Jarvis raised one eyebrow and glared directly at Desmond Yates.

The White House space-affairs adviser drew a deep breath. 'I personally do not believe that we have seen any signs from within the cloud, or any behaviour by it, that could be described as exhibiting evidence of intelligent behaviour,' he began carefully. 'I agree that it seems bizarre that this pool of gas should suddenly change its heading, apparently in response to an attack that is being prepared, but it would be even more bizarre to ascribe intelligence to a simple pool of gas without more proof. Once we have had sufficient time to analyse the cloud properly – and we are still only beginning to build computer models of what is, after all, over forty billion cubic miles of rapidly shifting gas – and once we have calculated all of the thousands of variables affecting its course, such as gravity, solar wind, internal chemical reactions and so on, I think we may find an answer to why this change of heading has occurred.'

The President listened patiently as Yates made his considered response, Then he turned to the NASA Director. 'And what's your take on this, Roy?' he asked.

'I believe in the principle of Occam's Razor, sir,' said Wilcox.

He saw the President frown.

'Occam was a fourteenth-century Scottish philosopher,' he explained. 'He said that when something looks very complicated, and when there are many different possible explanations, the most obvious solution is likely to be the correct one. I've learned the wisdom of that approach and I too see no reason why we should leap to any wild speculation about possible intelligence inside this cloud.'

'And what about the fact that it appeared at the same time the signals from the planet Iso dried up?' asked Jarvis. 'And at about the time when we were hoping that we might hear back from the Isonians?'

'I admit that it does seem strange, sir,' agreed Yates. 'But these things are most likely to be coincidences, nothing more.'

'But what if they're not, Des?' asked Jarvis, sitting forward anxiously. 'Shouldn't we be trying to contact this cloud – just in case we could communicate with it?'

'Thousands of people are already doing that for us,' broke in Wilcox. 'That crazy science-fiction author in Australia is getting all of his fans to radio this pool of space gas. They're pumping out messages of welcome every hour of the day. If there was anything inside this cloud that was going to respond, we've have heard from it by now.'

Bill Duncan and Agent Burton had been waiting impatiently in their Pentagon laboratory for over two hours. Professor Yates's personal assistant had assured them that her boss would be with them by three p.m., but it was now almost five-thirty and they had heard not a word of explanation or apology. In an age when communication was constantly available everywhere, his lateness and lack of contact felt like a gross discourtesy.

Working closely together, Bill and his official CNS minder had re-established the redundancy-stripping and conversion processes for the Isonian signals. To his considerable surprise and pleasure the specialist in machine psychology had discovered that the CNS agent seconded to help him was herself a highly capable network specialist and was also a much warmer and friendlier woman than he had imagined. She had asked him to call her 'Sally' – 'No one calls me Sarah, it's so severe' – and Bill found that he needed to explain very little to his new assistant as they set up their cluster of super-capable processors and designed new software that would distribute the analog-to-digital conversion tasks across the additional computing power.

Nadia, Bill's personal computer companion, was now coordinating the efforts of the seven classified Rand-Fairchild prototype processors that they had been given to carry out the work. Along with Nadia's own limited power, the new processors made up a private network that Bill Duncan reckoned must be one of the most powerful stand-alone circuits in the world. And they were making some progress, progress they were keen to share with their contact in the Washington bureaucracy.

'I'm sorry, so sorry,' said Des Yates when he finally walked through the door. 'The boss kept me in a long meeting and I couldn't break out.'

Bill and Sally exchanged glances. They understood which 'boss' their visitor was referring to and they both noted that the Presidential adviser looked very tired, almost exhausted.

'So, how are you two getting on?' asked Yates.

'We're up and running,' reported Bill with a smile. 'And we've extracted further snippets of coherent binary strings – along with a lot of what appears to be redundant garbage.'

The ex-MIT man nodded to Sally, who punched data up onto the main wall screen.

'As you can see, like the first section I decoded, these short segments also seem to be made up of binary, quantum and base-sixteen mathematical sets.'

Yates moved closer to the screen and stared up at the display.

'Anything that works, or that we can understand?' he asked.

'Not yet,' Bill admitted. 'But there's so much compressed analog data that we can't even make a dent on it – even with this set-up.'

'Yes, I understand,' said the White House man, an absent look on his face.

'In fact, even with this network we haven't got nearly enough power,' continued Bill, gesturing at the chain of super-fast organic nano-scale processors. 'I think we're going to have to revert to your original idea and throw the task open to the public networks. If we get every hobbyist with an interest in alien communications to download a tiny part of the data to work on, we might be able to make some progress. After all, even at our fastest computing speeds we've got over six billion years' worth of signals to convert.'

'Quite, quite,' murmured Yates, his glazed eyes fixed in the middle distance.

Bill glanced again at Sally, who shrugged her shoulders. Their visitor was behaving very oddly.

'Either that,' said Bill, 'Or you've got to get me another million of these new processors.'

'I'll see what I can do,' said Yates distantly.

'I thought they were prototypes!' objected Sally sharply, annoyed by their visitor's vagueness. 'I thought they weren't even in mass fabrication yet?'

Her abrupt tone summoned Des Yates's mind back to the topic under discussion, and to the pair of computer specialists standing expectantly in front of him.

'I'm sorry,' he said, with a shake of his head. 'There's a

lot going on at the moment. I'll put in a request for you to get some more processing power.'

'A *lot* more processing power,' stressed Bill.

'Yes, a lot more,' agreed Yates distantly. A worried look crossed the astrophysicist's face again, Then he looked directly at Bill, then at Sally.

'Sorry, but I might as well tell you what's on my mind,' he said. 'You're going to be reading about it tomorrow, anyway.'

Yates took a deep breath and shook his head. 'The trajectory of the space cloud has changed. It's now heading directly for Mars. That's why I was so late getting over here.'

Bill and Sally looked blank. Very little news about the cloud and its progress had permeated through to the confines of the Pentagon's Advanced Computing Laboratory. Over the last week or so Bill and Sally had been totally absorbed in setting up their private network system.

'It means that people are starting to question whether this is just a simple gas cloud,' explained Yates, seeing their incomprehension. 'And it means that I'm going to have trouble getting anyone to focus on the work you're doing here – at least in the short term.'

CLOUD CHANGES COURSE FOR MARS

By RANDALL TATE, science correspondent

Risk to Earth Averted – but No Time to Evacuate Colonists

Astonished NASA astronomers confirmed last night that the giant space cloud approaching the solar system has now changed its heading by over 40 degrees and is on a new trajectory which will cause it to pass over Mars beginning July 22. NASA confirmed that with Mars in its furthest position away from Earth, there will be no time to evacuate the Martian colony before the cloud arrives. Space scientists also say that on its new heading the cloud will no longer come into contact with Earth.

Scientific opinion is divided about what might have caused such a dramatic change of direction. Many experts have concluded that the cloud has been diverted as it has encountered steadily increasing solar winds. Others suggest that distant galactic gravitational forces may be responsible.

'Cloud Will Cause Little Damage on Mars' – Yates

Presidential Space Affairs Adviser Professor Desmond Yates told the *New York Times*, 'I suspect the cloud is merely responding to the strong gravitational forces that surround our solar system. If it does pass over the surface of Mars, there is little atmosphere for the cloud to remove and all Martian colonists are protected inside secure habitats that have been robustly constructed to withstand the fierce Martian storms.'

'DIRECTION CHANGE NO COINCIDENCE'

By Randall Tate, science correspondent

Author Calls on Public to Radio Peace Greetings to Cloud

'A change in direction of this magnitude can be neither accidental nor a simple co-incidence,' said Sir Charles Hodgeson, speaking from his Orpheus Island home last night.

'This cloud is clearly intel-ligent, or is the product of intelligence,' he claimed. 'In some way it has sensed that we intend to attack it from our base on Mars. I call on the United Nations to act swiftly to stop America and Europe from carrying out their primitive and barbaric attack.'

Hodgeson went on to say, 'I have already begun trans-mitting welcome messages towards the cloud from my own transmitter and I urge all supporters of peace and tolerance to do the same. The ordinary people of the world must distance them-selves from the actions of their warlike and irrespon-sible governments.'

'Above all, it is our duty to communicate with this cloud. Under no circum-stances must we harm it.'

By special invitation of the Secretary-General, the American President Maxwell T. Jarvis was addressing an emergency meeting of the General Assembly at the United Nations headquarters.

The large meeting was being televised and broadcast to the world and, as Jarvis's political advisers had realized, it allowed him to make an appeal both to the world's population and to his own domestic electorate at the same time. Plus it placed the Chief in a setting that demonstrated who was really the power behind the UN throne. It was now time for the US to assert strong global leadership, the President's aides insisted.

Jarvis was trying to reassure the meeting, and the billions of TV viewers, that there was no reason to panic because of the space cloud's strange behaviour. He knew that his words were also being transmitted to the colonists who were trapped on Mars as the cloud approached.

'One change of course is insufficient to suggest that the space cloud is anything other than a simple pool of gas,' he assured the meeting. 'Although I am told that it is unlikely to do much physical damage if it were to pass over the Martian surface, it *is* possible that it could contaminate the planet with hostile, long-lived bacteria.'

He paused to sip from a small glass of water.

'With the cooperation of the Russian and Chinese space agencies we expect to be able to return the one hundred and eighty-two Martian colonists safely to Earth once the cloud has passed – and once we have applied stringent decontamination procedures – but it has to be faced that if the cloud does contain dangerous bacteria we may no longer be able to return to the planet.

'In addition, there is also the remote possibility that the cloud could change direction once again, whether caused by gravitational attraction or some other force, and resume its collision course with Earth. This time, the direction change might occur when it would be too late for us safely to do anything about it.'

Jarvis paused as he came to the main section of his important speech.

'For these reasons, the United States, with our European Union allies, intends to proceed with the precautionary nuclear detonation within the cloud in an attempt to disperse it or to modify its course while it is still in the outer reaches of the solar system.

'I call upon all delegate nations to join us in our attempt to divert what could still turn out to be a significant threat to our planet.'

'Put it over there, over there,' shouted Sir Charles Hodgeson irritably to his building foreman.

With a nod and a tip of his finger to the peak of his blue hard-hat, the foreman turned and shouted directions to the driver of the large yellow dump truck.

Over a one-month period Orpheus Island had been transformed into a vast building site, as if a movie company had suddenly descended on the peaceful Pacific atoll and turned it into a giant film set.

But there was nothing temporary or cosmetic about the construction that was now going on all over the island. Half of the main hill ridge had been scooped out by two huge yellow earth-movers and prefabricated steel roof beams and wall supports – flown to the island by giant Sikorsky Load-Mover helicopters – were now stacked against the hillside, awaiting their positioning.

There was no deep-water port at Orpheus Island, but a fleet of flat-bottomed barges was busy ferrying ashore sand, cement, cables, pipes and all of the other items necessary for a major building project from ships that were anchored far out to sea.

Cranes, cement mixers and building blocks had also been flown in by the powerful Sikorskys, as had the large-bore ventilation system, air-conditioning units and oxygen-manufacturing equipment. Already four tall radio transmission antennae had been erected on the hilltop, suddenly giving the skyline of the beautiful island the sinister appearance of a military base.

Hodgeson himself was the site's project manager and he was also its chief architect. Technically Orpheus Island was part of Australian sovereign territory, but its centenarian owner had not bothered about niceties such as planning permission or zoning laws before he started erecting his new radio transmission towers and begun carving into the hillside of his island home. Lacking all faith in the world's governments to respond peaceably towards the gaseous extra-terrestrial visitor, Hodgeson had decided to take extreme precautions and had applied his huge personal wealth and his boundless energy to get the project moving.

The science-fiction guru had made his initial fortune almost by accident. Over sixty years earlier *The Wars of Galetea*, one of his first space fantasy adventures, had been made into a movie which went on to achieve worldwide cult status. That success had made the author financially independent, but had not provided him with truly great riches. But then an American software house had purchased the rights to create an interactive internet game-domain based on the book. They then poured so much time and effort into recreating Hodgeson's fantasy world in cyberspace that the company had bankrupted itself before it had earned a single cent from a paying customer.

Charles Hodgeson – then still two decades away from his knighthood – had bought the American company from the receivers for a song and within six months *The Wars of Galetea* had become the most successful immersive multi-sensory gaming environment on the web. Subscriptions boomed and for almost two years Hodgeson wrote nothing but new virtual-reality scenarios for the space-battle game, keeping his millions of addicted fans happy and the sub-scriptions pouring in. At the peak of its popularity over two million people were playing against each other and the game's virtual characters in every twenty-four-hour period. The game's success made Hodgeson seriously rich. Then he had begun buying whole blocks of residential property in London, New York and Beijing, back in the 2020s, when smart city addresses were still reasonably affordable.

'Start pumping the concrete,' Hodgeson ordered into his walkie-talkie. His radio crackled a confirmation and he shielded his eyes to watch as the first load of aggregate and cement began to flow, forming the foundations of what would become the vast underground bunker he had been designing for the last three months. The steel-reinforced, air-tight and lead-shielded building would house a new observatory control room and accommodation units for Hodgeson himself and his staff, and for the 130 young stu-dents and followers who made a pilgrimage to Orpheus Island. New recruits came annually to study with the great man – an author who was now regarded as a world-famous guru, philosopher and quasi-religious leader. Hodgeson never referred to a god in his talks, but each year thousands of young people applied to his website for the privilege of coming to work for no pay on Orpheus Island, just to be near their hero and to attend the visionary workshop dis-cussions he led three times a week.

'Sir Charles?'

It was the foreman climbing back up the side of the small rise on which Hodgeson stood as he surveyed his emergency building programme.

'The first desalination unit is arriving,' announced the building supervisor, pointing into the sky.

Hodgeson glanced up and saw a giant twin-rotor helicopter approaching the bay at low altitude. Beneath it was slung a large stainless-steel device about the size of one of the many Portakabins that had been erected on the island to house the Australian construction crew. All of the workers were earning quadruple rates for this round-the-clock project, plus a completion bonus so large that it had outshone all of the many other offers the rich were making to such workers. In addition, Hodgeson had made the contractors one additional offer they could not refuse: he offered them space for themselves and their families in the Orpheus Island bunker, if they chose to take it up.

'Lower it straight into its housing,' ordered Hodgeson, raising his voice as the beating helicopter blades began to drown out all the other noises being made around the vast site. 'I want it up and working by tomorrow.'

From the *New York Times* website, 18 June 2064

COMBINED NUCLEAR STRIKE CONFIRMED

By RANDALL TATE, science correspondent

Explosions Will Be Visible from Mars 2.20 p.m. Eastern Standard Time, June 30

By an overwhelming majority, the United Nations General Assembly last night voted to authorize the U.S.–European nuclear strike against the gas cloud currently heading towards Mars. China and Russia have now offered use of their components of the Anti-Asteroid Shield to be used in the attack. Over 700 megatons of nuclear weapons will now be deployed.

'Sensors aboard NASA's intercept probes have confirmed that the cloud is indeed composed of hydrogen, helium and other passive gases,' said Desmond Yates, the White House's senior Space Affairs adviser. 'I anticipate a complete destruction of the cloud whilst it is still in the outer reaches of our solar system.'

The 48 nuclear explosions and resultant conflagration will be visible from Mars and images of the strike will arrive at the Earth 21 minutes later.

Thousands of Alien-Life Pacifists Transmit Greetings to the Cloud

U.S. military and civil authorities are monitoring a sharp rise in high-power radio transmissions sent by disciples of British-born space guru, Sir Charles Hodgeson.

'So many signals are being directed towards the cloud that we are experiencing interference with our normal satellite communications,' said a spokesman for the Federal Communications Commission.

Hodgeson Builds 'Illegal Radio Station' – Installs 'Mercenaries' as Security Guards

Queensland authorities have declared 'illegal' a number of high-power radio masts and a large underground construction that billionaire science-fiction guru Sir Charles Hodgeson is building on Orpheus Island, his private territory on the eastern flank of the Great Barrier Reef, Australia.

Authorities in Cairns are to apply to a Queensland county court for permission to land on Orpheus Island and remove the transmitters.

Speaking from his home, Hodgeson said, 'I have no faith in any of the world's governments to do the right thing. If this foolhardy attack on the cloud proceeds we may all need the very deepest shelters we can build.'

Asked whether he will contest action by the authorities to enforce local zoning laws, Sir Charles said, 'I will resist any attempt to prevent me from using my own private territory as I wish – especially at this time of global emergency. I have employed a highly trained body of military troops to protect this island against all comers.'

'I don't think I have ever seen anything more beautiful,' an excited Foster Robinson told his interplanetary audience. 'These pictures you are seeing now are being transmitted from the nuclear missiles as they are actually flying inside the cloud.'

The images that the Mars-based journalist was receiving and forwarding to his viewers on Earth were truly breathtaking. Towering multicoloured columns of what looked like smoke rose through the centre of the cloud, stretching upwards for millions of kilometres, like pillars in a staggeringly vast cathedral.

'I can see a background of deep red gas,' Robinson said over the pictures, 'and there are blue, green and white funnels, or cyclones, rising up inside the cloud.'

A total of forty-eight missiles, each armed with a nuclear warhead, had been launched from dispersed locations in deep space to arrive in the centre of the cloud in a carefully timed sequence. Each missile also carried an array of cameras that were now feeding back images to those overseeing the countdown on Mars, and to the anxious billions back on Earth who were receiving the pictures twenty-one minutes later.

Foster Robinson was seated at the small TV editing suite he used to put together his normally prosaic weekly news reports from the red planet. When the first Martian colony had been founded thirty-nine years earlier, Robinson's predecessors had found that their video reports were eagerly received by Earth's broadcast media. But the public had quickly become bored with pictures of Mars's rugged, monotone landscape and the distant community's mundane doings.

But now the whole of the home planet's population was hanging on the words and pictures flowing back from Mars.

On the other side of the main habitat floor-space Major Peters and his team of eighteen military personnel were overseeing the computers that controlled the mission. At Foster Robinson's request, strike command had even patched through to him a digital read-out of the countdown timer so that the viewers could count off the minutes and seconds as the moment for the synchronized detonations approached.

Robinson switched from the video images streaming in from one of the missile nose cones to a long-distance picture of the cloud taken by the Asimov Deep-Space Telescope, an instrument that was parked in a solar-stationary orbit between Jupiter and Saturn, over 300 million kilometres away from the pool of gas. Normally this powerful optic was used for surveying the giant outer planets, major solar events or constellations outside the solar system, but now the twin-mirrored, six-metre telescope was focused on the vast mass of the space cloud that was rushing headlong towards Mars.

'Detonation is due in two minutes,' Robinson reported as he mixed an overlay of the digital counter into his live picture stream. For the hundredth time during this long broadcast he wished he had a video editor at his side so that he could concentrate solely on providing the best possible commentary. *But here comes my Emmy*, he thought to himself as he tightened the framing on the cloud.

The telescope's image showed the gas pool clearly, as a grey-red mass against the black background of space. The countdown display indicated that there was just over one minute to go.

'The theory is that these forty-eight carefully timed explosions will start a chain reaction which will cause the cloud to burn up completely,' Robinson told his viewers.

'The cloud is still two hundred million kilometres away from Mars and over six hundred million kilometres distant from Earth. I am assured that as the cloud is still so far away its incineration will not cause any harm to Mars, or to any other planets in our solar system.'

The counter flicked down to thirty seconds.

'What we'll see in a moment will be a series of flashes from inside the cloud as the seven hundred megatons of warheads start to explode,' said Robinson quickly. 'Then the whole thing will suddenly go up in a single gigantic ball of fire.'

Robinson glanced down at his video feeds, wondering which of them to supply to his billions of viewers on Earth as the moment approached. All were being recorded so he decided to leave the distant view of the cloud from the Asimov Telescope as the main live feed.

'Five seconds,' announced Robinson. 'Four, three, two, one . . .'

On the monitor he saw a tiny pinpoint of light shine from within the centre of the distant cloud. Then another. Then another, followed by a rapid sequence of small flares, like starbursts from a far-off rocket display. Then there was nothing but the image of the cloud as it had been before.

From the *New York Times* website, 30 June 2064

STRIKE FAILS TO HALT CLOUD

By RANDALL TATE, science correspondent

Will Engulf Mars in Three Weeks

The White House confirmed last night that the multilateral nuclear strike made in an attempt to disperse the space cloud had failed. It is now crossing through the asteroid belt and is expected to pass over Mars and its colonies beginning July 12. It is estimated that the planet will be hidden from sight by the cloud for 45 days.

'Perhaps the interior of the cloud is less dense than we thought,' said Desmond Yates, the White House's senior Space Affairs Adviser last night. 'If so, it is a good sign for the Mars colonists. A less dense cloud will do very little damage to the Martian structures.'

MARTIAN COLONISTS TOLD TO PREPARE FOR CLOUD'S IMPACT

The U.S., Russian and Chinese governments have told their colonists on Mars to prepare for the arrival of the space cloud. The colonists have plentiful supplies of water, food and oxygen and, in recent weeks, the communities have been reinforcing their permanent habitats.

'Well, we tore a great hole in the cloud, but it's still heading directly for Mars,' reported Desmond Yates gloomily. 'The hole we created is over one million kilometres wide but, as we all know, there was no subsequent chain reaction. All we've achieved is to make the cloud more radioactive than it was before.'

The White House adviser was in the Situation Room addressing President Jarvis, other members of the Cloud EXCOM and various guests and other advisers.

'So do we assume that the helium, hydrogen and oxygen atoms were too dispersed, or just too inert to sustain a chain reaction?' asked a disgruntled Dr Demetrios Esposito, the man who had devised the attack plan. 'Seems very strange to me. Everybody knows that hydrogen is far from inert. It should have gone up in a flash.'

'You're right, Doctor,' said Yates in a conciliatory tone. 'And that's not all. Our laser instruments suggest that the hole we created is already beginning to fill in once more.'

'That's incredible,' exclaimed Esposito. 'I'm no gas dynamicist, but that seems darn strange behaviour for a cloud of passive gas.'

Yates nodded and glanced around the rest of his audience. Most of them, especially the President, seemed confused by this strange turn of events.

'And there's something else,' added Yates. 'From our spectrographic analysis of the parts of the cloud that were burnt during the strike we now know that the gas pool contains particles of many rare and exotic elements. These include cerium, promethium, samarium and ytterbium as well as many elements that we have so far been unable to identify.'

There was a silence as the group struggled to digest

this information. Yates waited a few moments before he continued.

'More importantly, however, we have discovered that the cloud contains large amounts of the isotopes helium-3 and helium-4. These are known to be by-products of nuclear fusion.'

'You said "fusion", not "fission", Professor?' queried Dr Esposito quickly. 'You're saying these isotopes didn't come from our own warheads?'

'That's correct,' agreed Yates. 'And, what's more, when we blew a hole in the cloud, our optical instruments could momentarily see right into its centre. They identified patches of hot plasma, all at varying densities, which are swirling around in their own internal magnetic fields.'

'Jesus!' exclaimed Esposito, half rising out of his chair in surprise.

'Do you mind helping us out here, gentlemen?' asked the President. 'Please explain – we're not all rocket scientists.'

Yates glanced at the CalTech theoretical physicist and nodded for him to provide the elucidation.

'Well, sir,' began Esposito, 'from the information that Professor Yates has just given us, a nuclear physicist would be likely to conclude that the cloud is producing its own internal form of energy by a process of self-contained nuclear fusion.'

'Energy?' echoed the President, looking from Esposito to Yates. 'Energy for what?'

Neither man answered immediately. Then Yates cleared his throat.

'For propulsion, sir,' he said.

There was a short silence. Then the President asked,

'Do I take it that you have now changed your mind about the true nature of this space cloud, Professor Yates?'

The White House space-affairs adviser gave a small nod. 'It seems that the normal laws of physics are being violated within the internal structure of the cloud and it also appears to have its own energy source. For these reasons I am afraid we must conclude that there is some form of basic organization within the structure – a form wholly unknown to us.'

'You mean it's intelligent?' pressed Jarvis.

'We simply don't know, sir,' said Yates. 'Intelligence is a difficult concept to define. So far all we've observed is a series of events which are apparently coincidental. There's been nothing to suggest any form of higher intelligence as we would understand it.'

'I'll ask you again, Professor Duncan. Are you prepared to sign a Level One National Secrecy Agreement?' asked the chairman of the combined security panel. 'With all that such an undertaking implies?'

Bill Duncan glanced sideways at Sally Burton. Both were seated on the other side of a table from the five men who were conducting the interview. The Pentagon meeting room was windowless and well below ground. The air-conditioning was humming powerfully and the atmosphere had turned decidedly chilly.

This long-overdue meeting had been set up by Desmond Yates, but at the last moment he had cancelled his own participation, claiming that urgent matters connected with the space cloud prevented him from attending.

After a lengthy delay, Professor William Duncan was finally being interviewed, or interrogated, by a joint security vetting panel consisting of representatives drawn from the

National Security Agency, the Pentagon, the CIA, CNS and the White House. The meeting had been set up to discuss Bill's request for the additional computing power he needed to work on converting the Isonian transmissions.

'You see, even at the speed of the fastest processor we possess, there are over six billion years' worth of analog data to slow down and convert,' Bill had told the meeting in his opening presentation. 'What I need is permission to distribute the task over the public networks. I want to get the media involved and to get the millions of space and sci-fi fans all over the world to do some of the conversion work using the idle time of their own computer processors.'

'I'm afraid your work on converting and decoding the Isonian signals has just been classified by direct order of the Secretary of State,' said the man from the NSA firmly. It had been at that point that the meeting had started to go rapidly downhill.

'CLASSIFIED!' shouted Bill. 'I came to Washington only on the clear understanding that I was free to publish at any time.'

'Professor Duncan,' broke in the man from the White House administration, the official who was standing in for Desmond Yates. 'You must understand that these are not normal times. The National Guard has been called out in some parts of the country to control looting and violent crime has increased by five hundred per cent in the last three months. The government is gearing up for a massive civil emergency. Martial law may be declared any day.'

Bill sat back in his seat and shook his head. During the last few weeks he and Sally had been so absorbed in their conversion work that they'd paid hardly any attention to the news. Bill knew that a nuclear strike against the approaching space cloud had failed and that it was now due to pass over the surface of Mars, but he knew nothing beyond the main headlines. He was unaware that civil unrest had become so serious.

'Your work on the alien transmissions has been classified under the highest military category,' continued the NSA representative. 'You must not discuss your work with anyone who does not have Level One clearance and under no circumstances may you distribute copies of the signals or of your conversion software to any third person.'

Bill let go a large sigh of frustration. All of his suspicions and mistrust of the government were being rapidly confirmed but, he was forced to admit, these *were* highly unusual times.

'Then how do you suggest I make any progress with my binary extraction?' he asked quietly.

The NSA panel member twisted in his seat. 'Over to you, Dr Kramer,' he said, looking at the scientific representative from the Pentagon, a man who wore the uniform of an Army colonel.

'Professor Duncan, I've been an admirer of yours for many years,' said Colonel Kramer. 'I used to be at Harvard and your paper on adaptation psychosis in artificial-life personalities has been widely read there, and in my current department.'

'Which department is that?' asked Bill.

'I may have a solution to your problem,' continued Kramer, ignoring the question. 'It is possible that we could grant you privileged access to a top-secret military computer network with far more processing power than you have now. In fact, a network with more processing power than you've ever dreamed of.'

Bill frowned, struggling to imagine what sort of network the man could be referring to.

'But there's a condition,' said the NSA representative who was chairing the meeting. It was then that he had stated his request that Bill should sign a National Secrecy Agreement.

Now Sally Burton responded to Bill's glare with a small shrug, a gesture half offering apology, half urging pragmatism.

'I'll ask you again, Professor Yates. Are you prepared to sign a Level One National Secrecy Agreement?' demanded the panel's chairman. 'I should also add that if you choose to do so you will become a full-time Pentagon employee with a salary equivalent to what you were earning at MIT. You will be granted every facility possible to continue with your important work.'

Bill struggled with conflicting feelings. He knew that he was making slow progress with the signals, and he knew that, above all else, he needed much more computing power. But he hated being cornered like this.

The panel chairman touched a button on the table top and a wall screen flickered to life.

'Just so that we understand each other,' the chairman continued, 'We have the file on you that CNS Agent Burton prepared, so we are fully aware of your activist campaigns to limit the development of computer intelligence.'

On the wall screen Bill saw images of himself going aboard *Cape Sentinel* and pictures of Christine Cocoran, Paul Levine and the other HAL volunteers arriving at his houseboat. Then he saw a network usage analysis chart and what looked like screen grabs from some of his own monitors. One of them displayed a HAL screensaver that Christine had designed in an idle few minutes. The chairman shut the projection down before Bill could make out any more of what the surveillance operation had captured.

Bill felt a rush of fresh anger rise in his throat. In recent months he'd been getting on very well with the CNS agent who sat beside him, but now he felt betrayed all over again.

'So you will understand why we need you to sign a National Secrecy Agreement,' continued the NSA man. 'We need to know that your loyalty to your country, and your commitment to our nation's need to learn anything of use that the alien signals may hold, will supersede all your previous political sympathies. We will require you to sever immediately all connections with your organization of network activists, and with all similar groups, now and in the future. If you agree, you will be provided with a level of security clearance which, if breached, makes the offender liable to immediate imprisonment. It's your choice whether to proceed or not, but your choice will be final.'

Sally Burton now stared straight ahead, not wanting to make eye contact.

At least she has the grace to be embarrassed, thought Bill.

'I need to few days to think about this,' he said. 'In fact I need a few days off. Time to clear my head.'

'Very well,' agreed the chairman, glancing at the other panel members to see if there was any dissent. 'We'll expect your decision in one week. In the meantime please be aware that you can't discuss these proceedings or these options with anyone outside this room – other than Professor Yates.'

NINE

'The cloud is now visible from Mars with the naked eye,' said Foster Robinson into his helmet microphone. 'For the last ten days my fellow colonists have been taking short breaks from their frantic work schedules simply to come outside and stare up at the incredible beauty of this scene.'

The resident reporter was fully spacesuited and was standing on the Martian surface about two hundred metres away from the American settlement's central habitat. Beside him, a remotely controlled TV camera mounted on a balloon-tyred transporter was panning slowly from horizon to horizon.

'As you can see, the entire sky is now dominated by enormous columns of what looks like smoke,' explained Robinson. 'But the columns themselves are the most beautiful shades of magenta, green, blue, purple and black.'

He allowed the camera to dwell on the awful magnificence of the onrushing cloud for a few moments, then used his hand-held remote joystick to pan the camera back round so that it focused on the main group of habitat buildings. Everywhere there was the scurry of intense activity as spacesuited colonists attached additional steel guy-ropes to the main buildings and piled bags of Martian sand around the airlocks.

In the distance two of the three mini-bulldozers on the

red planet were scooping up surface soil and rock and piling it high against the walls of the domed habitats. The third earth-mover was in use at the smaller Russian-Chinese habitat where it would be busy carrying out similar tasks.

Robinson panned thirty degrees to the right and zoomed in on two suited figures working beside a glinting steel tripod.

'In consultation with colleagues on Earth, our Chief Science Officer has devised a series of experiments that will be conducted as the gas cloud passes over this planet,' the journalist explained. 'These should give us a lot more information about the cloud's density, its composition and its likely future behaviour. The American community on Mars is proud to be able to provide this information as a service to all those on Earth.'

Then Robinson panned a few more degrees to the right until the camera settled on a huge concrete bowl that had been hastily constructed inside a depression on the surface of the Martian desert.

'That large saucer is the reinforced concrete communications dish that the American military unit has constructed to allow contact with Earth to continue after the cloud has arrived,' he explained. 'At present, all pictures from here are being sent to Earth by relay satellites that are in orbit around Mars, but it is expected that as the cloud strikes these will be blown out of position, or out of orbit altogether. Then we will need to transmit to you directly from the surface of this planet using that big dish.'

The reporter swung the camera around until it focused on his own suited figure.

'The cloud is due to begin passing over this planet in forty-eight hours' time,' he said, looking straight into the camera lens. 'Everything that was loose has been tightly secured and every building structure has been reinforced. When it arrives the cloud will be travelling at a velocity of two hundred thousand kilometres per hour but it has such low density that its effects are predicted to be no worse than those of one of the many violent dust storms we suffer regularly on Mars.'

Robinson took a breath and zoomed the camera in tighter on his helmeted face. When he got back to the video suite he would edit all this recorded material together to form two-, three-, four- and five-minute packages for distribution to the news channels back on Earth. After decades of showing little interest, they all now wanted to carry regular reports from Mars.

'When the cloud strikes, every colonist will be safely inside the habitat buildings,' he continued. 'They will be wearing their own personal spacesuits for safety and, as a precaution, they will be instructed to lie down on the floor. All members of the American community, and our friends in the Russian-Chinese settlement, have been given individual supplies of oxygen, water and food which will be topped up at regular intervals. In this way, we will wait out the forty-five days that it will take for the cloud to complete its journey across this planet. This is Foster Robinson reporting from Mars.'

'Well, here it comes – less then one minute to impact,' said Desmond Yates, even though he knew that the images that were about to arrive from Mars were of incidents that had actually occurred over twenty minutes earlier.

The President, his Chief of Staff, NASA's Director, two army generals, a clutch of White House aides and all of the other members of EXCOM were all gathered in the Situation Room to watch events unfold as the cloud engulfed

Mars. The images from space and from the Martian surface were projected within the large holo-theatre at one end of the room.

'We've got multiple feeds from cameras orbiting the planet and from those on the ground,' explained Yates. 'Let's stay with the orbital shots,' he said, addressing the technicians in the AV booth.

Yates stepped back to his seat to observe with the others.

'Five seconds,' he said quietly.

Suddenly the image in the holo-theatre turned into a wash of grey, then the signal disappeared.

'The relay satellite has gone,' a technician said over the talkback system

'Switch to one of the surface cams,' ordered Yates.

The holo-theatre lit up again and the White House party saw a dim image of the American settlement. Even though it was daytime there was now very little light on the Martian surface. As they watched the light seemed to grow even dimmer and then, abruptly, the signal disappeared.

'Go to one of the other surface cams,' Yates told the AV people.

'Sorry, sir, we've lost all surface signals from Mars,' said a voice from the gallery.

'OK, go to the Asimov,' said Yates grimly.

The holo-theatre came back on and those present saw an image that was being transmitted from the deep-space telescope over 300 million kilometres away from the red planet.

'Where the hell is Mars?' asked President Jarvis.

Desmond Yates looked at the image of the huge green, grey and red cloud that was being sent back by the telescope.

He knew that the lenses had been trained directly on the planet.

'It's now inside the cloud, sir,' he explained.

'This is Foster Robinson reporting,' said a faint voice over a loud background roar. 'I don't know if you can hear me, or see anything, but I'm going to keep transmitting for as long as possible.'

Mars had now been engulfed by the cloud for two days. When the signals from the orbiting satellites and from the video cameras on the planet's surface had disappeared, NASA's technicians had initially reported that all contact with the planet had been lost.

A few moments after receiving this news Maxwell Jarvis had stood and abruptly ended the meeting. But forty-eight hours later NASA had reported that a signal from Mars was being received once again and the President had hastily reconvened the meeting in the Situation Room.

The image now displayed in the holo-theatre showed the interior of the main American habitat on Mars.

'The incoming signal is very weak, and there's a lot of background noise,' apologized an AV technician over the talkback. 'But we're boosting it as much as possible.'

'Just don't lose it,' snapped Yates.

'This is Foster Robinson on Mars,' the reporter said again, his voice sounding feeble.

The twenty-one-minute time delay in receiving the signal made any two-way conversation impossible. Yates and the others were forced to watch in mute anxiety as Robinson turned the hand-held camera away from himself and panned it around the habitat. Bodies were lying across the floor like a human carpet. All were spacesuited, but from a movement here and there it was clear that the colonists, or at least some of them, were still alive.

'We lost our landline connection to the ground dish,' said Robinson, turning the camera back onto himself. 'The force of the cloud is much stronger than predicted and it ripped away everything that was outside, even stuff that was buried. Major Peters and two of his men went out to repair the link. They didn't come back.'

Those in the Situation Room could hear a background roar like continuous thunder as the cloud's internal winds tore at the habitat's exterior.

Robinson tilted his head back in his space helmet, and puffed quickly, like someone trying to increase their oxygen levels. After a minute he sat up and stared into the camera lens again.

'I hope you are receiving this,' he said. 'I have spent the last forty-eight hours hooking up all of the habitat's local-area transmitters. I just hope their combined signal power is strong enough to reach you on Earth.'

'Well done, Mr Robinson,' said President Jarvis quietly, echoing the feelings of all in the room.

'The habitat has been standing up fairly well so far,' added the reporter, just as the signal flickered and recovered. 'But the winds now seem to be getting much stronger. And it looks as if storms are developing within the cloud. I am now going to hold the camera up to one of the habitat windows.'

Robinson's small but exclusive audience on Earth watched in awestruck horror as the camera relayed images and sounds of the huge electrical storm that was raging out-side the habitat. Flashes of almost continuous lightning revealed that a howling dust storm was in progress. Even as they watched there was another blinding flash of lightning and a huge crack shot down the habitat's triple-glazed window.

Suddenly the image in the holo-theatre turned head over heels. Then there was blackness.

'Have we lost the signal?' demanded Yates after a few moments.

Before the AV engineers could provide an answer the signal returned. The camera now lay on its side, about two metres from where the dimly lit figure of Foster Robinson lay prone. All present in the Situation Room leaned their heads to one side to try to make out what they were viewing. They could no longer see the interior lights of the habitat, nor its domed walls. A loud howling sound accompanied the visual signal.

'This is Foster Robinson,' called a faint voice over mounting sounds of destruction. 'The habitat is being destroyed. One wall has gone and—'

The holo-theatre went dark and the sound of static replaced the last words to be heard from Mars.

MARS COLONY DESTROYED
182 FEARED DEAD

Two days into its progress across the Martian surface, the space cloud finally destroyed both human habitats, almost certainly killing all 182 colonists. The community included 83 Americans, 21 Britons, 26 Russians, 23 Chinese nationals, 16 French citizens, 12 Germans and one Swedish national. President Jarvis is today sending messages of condolence to the families of all Americans who lost their lives.

'Cloud Acted in Self-Defense' – Hodgeson

Sir Charles Hodgeson last night claimed that in destroying the Martian colony, the 'cloud was merely acting in self-defense'.

'After all, the colonists on Mars had attacked it with 700 megatons of nuclear weapons,' he said. 'This is the result of Mankind's aggression. We must redouble our efforts to make contact with the cloud to assure it of our peaceful intentions in the future.'

TEN

On a beautiful Sunday morning at the end of what had been a glorious month of July – a period of sustained fine weather that for Bill Duncan had gone almost entirely unnoticed – the former MIT computer psychologist left his government-supplied apartment near the Pentagon and crossed the Potomac River via the 14th Street Bridge. For the first time since he had arrived in the capital, he had decided to see the sights.

He walked around the man-made lake known as the Tidal Basin and skirted the shining white Jefferson Memorial. His intention was to stroll on towards the tall white obelisk of the Washington Monument and then head across the lawns to see the White House itself. But, even before he arrived at the Mall, he was stopped by yellow police barriers.

The cop was unimpressed by his Pentagon pass. 'If you want to join the protesters, use the south-east gate down by the Smithsonian on Independence Avenue. If you don't want to protest, stay away from the Mall.'

In the distance Bill could see a massive crowd of people gathered around the Washington needle, spilling over onto the surrounding lawns. Mounted police circled the group and helicopters hovered overhead.

With a shrug he gave up the idea of sightseeing around

the capital and turned back towards the East Potomac Park. He sauntered on through the trees for fifteen minutes, the sun hot on his face, and then came to the end of the narrow strip of land that separated the main Potomac River from the Washington Channel.

Despite the brilliance of the day, the leafy park seemed almost deserted and Bill found an empty bench at Haines Point, at the very tip of the isthmus.

Just across the broad Potomac was Washington's National Airport. Planes were constantly taking off and landing, but instead of finding this noisy activity a disturbance Bill found the regular movements reassuring, a symbol of normality in what seemed to be an increasingly unreal world.

He was due to provide his answer to the Pentagon's vetting panel on the following day. He was either going to accept their terms and sign a top-level National Security agreement to gain access to what he'd been promised would be enormous computing power, or he was going to walk away from all involvement with the government. He had still not decided which course of action to take.

In the week's break he had taken from his decoding work, Bill had returned home to the *Cape Sentinel* in Boston and, to some extent, had patched things up with Christine Cocoran and his other hacker volunteers. He was unable to tell them precisely what the Pentagon was offering him, nor the terms they were attempting to extract, but he was able to make them understand that the looming threat of the space cloud had pushed all normal considerations to one side. His point had been heavily underlined for him; during his week's vacation the cloud had engulfed Mars and had killed all the pioneer colonists on the planet.

Despite Bill's many concerns, the beauty of the day

pressed in upon him. The sun and gentle wind created rippling rows of flashes on the surface of the river, like flotillas of miniature warships frantically signalling the shore. A mallard swam past with ducklings bobbing along behind her as if they were a garland of flowers. The air was swollen with grass and pollen and the river bank was alive with bees picnicking on buttercups the colour of condensed sun. It was the sort of day that mocks the single.

'Mind if I join you?'

Bill spun round on the bench to see Sally Burton standing behind him. She was no longer dressed like a federal agent, but was now wearing a white sports top and a pair of scarlet running shorts. She looked sensational.

Bill felt a leap of joy at the sight of her, a feeling that surprised him. Then he felt annoyed.

'How the hell did you know I'd be here?' he demanded. Since starting his week's leave he hadn't seen the CNS agent once.

'May I?' asked Sally as she sat down on the bench. Bill noticed that despite her running gear and trainers she did not look as if she had been jogging. He turned around on the bench and scanned the park behind him. He saw her black sedan parked fifty yards away.

'What answer are you going to give them tomorrow?' asked Sally, staring out over the scintillant water.

Bill shrugged. 'I still haven't decided. On one hand it seems obvious that if there's anything in the signals that might be of use in tackling the cloud, I have no choice but to agree to their terms. But what if I discover that the military has developed something really insane, some computer technology that's a real threat? Am I just supposed to keep quiet about it?'

Just as Sally opened her mouth to reply, Bill's communicator rang.

'It's Des,' he explained as he lifted it to his ear.

Bill greeted the White House adviser and then listened for a few moments. 'Hold on,' he said. 'I'm with Sally now. There's no one else around. Mind if I put you on speakerphone?'

He laid the communicator on the bench between them.

'Hi, Sally,' said Yates's disembodied voice. 'I was just explaining to Bill that we received some strange data from the instruments that were set up on the surface of Mars. They only managed to broadcast for a short while before they were destroyed, but they picked up some radio signals that we think may have been produced by the cloud itself. The signals appear to be modulated – to be artificial.'

'That's incredible, Des,' said Sally. 'Doesn't that suggest that–'

'We can't be sure of anything yet,' broke in Yates. 'But I know that Bill is due to meet the Pentagon people again tomorrow and I wanted you two to have this information. It's now even more imperative that you get that extra computing power, Bill. We need you to see if you can make any sense of these new signals that we've picked up from inside the cloud. We desperately need to know what it is we're dealing with.'

After closing the connection Bill and Sally stared out across the slow-moving river together, both lost in thought.

'If the space cloud is generating its *own* radio signals . . .' said Bill after a while, not even bothering to finish his sentence.

'Terrifying, really scary,' agreed Sally. Then she turned to face her companion. 'Please say you'll do it?' she asked, earnestness filling her blue eyes. 'I think the appropriate phrase is "Your country needs you."'

'You may be right,' agreed Bill. 'But I'm going to need a lot of help from you.'

Sally swung round to gaze out over the river once more.

'I've been ordered back to New York, Bill,' she told him after a pause. 'My boss thinks that after the Mars catastrophe all the cranks are going to come out of the woodwork. He's predicting a sharp rise in network fraud and cyber-terrorism and he wants me back to run the Manhattan operation.'

They both stared at the water and Bill suddenly felt a profound sense of disappointment welling up from deep within him.

Three weeks after the space cloud began its passage across Mars, President Jarvis reconvened the Cloud EXCOM for a formal meeting in the Situation Room.

'For some unknown reason, the gas cloud seems to have picked up speed,' Desmond Yates told the group. 'The last vestiges of vapour have now cleared the planet's surface. Although we are no longer receiving any radio broadcasts directly from the planet, long-distance spectrographic analysis suggests that what little atmosphere Mars did have has been completely sucked away into space.'

'Where's the cloud heading for now?' demanded Jarvis.

'Straight for the centre of our solar system, sir,' said Yates, taking a step backwards so that the image in the holo-theatre would not be obstructed. 'At present we calculate that its trajectory will take it across the orbital paths of both Venus and Mercury but it won't collide with either of those planets. Then it will head straight on inwards, towards the sun itself.'

'And what will happen then, precisely?' asked the President testily.

'We're not sure,' admitted the Space-Affairs Adviser. 'If it behaved like a normal pool of gas I would say that it would get trapped by the sun's gravity and would burn up. But we now know that we can't make such assumptions.'

'How long before we can be certain about what's going to happen?' asked the President's Chief of Staff.

'We should know better in a week, perhaps two,' Yates told him.

'Well, since we can't rely on the cloud burning up in the sun, I'm going to double our programme of shelter building and habitat production,' announced the President. Then he turned to Freddy Truelson, director of the Federal Emergency Management Agency.

'Are FEMA's plans for government evacuation ready?' he demanded.

'They are, sir,' replied Truelson. 'We've been working on them for three months. We're ready to go.'

'Very well,' said the President. Then he turned back to face the full committee.

'I also want the necessary documents prepared in case I have to declare a full-scale national emergency – including the imposition of martial law.'

From the *New York Times* website, 14 August 2064

TV BROADCASTS JAMMED BY HODGESON'S CLOUD ENTHUSIASTS

By RANDALL TATE, science correspondent

Commercial television transmissions all over the world are suffering intermittent interference and jamming because hundreds of thousands of licensed and unlicensed followers of science-fiction guru Sir Charles Hodgeson are radioing messages of peace and appeasement to the space cloud using all available wavelengths. Over two hundred megawatts of continuous radio transmissions emanating from transmitters on Hodgeson's Orpheus Island home have severely disrupted commercial television services in northeastern Australia.

'We must attempt to communicate with this cloud,' Hodgeson said from his heavily guarded island retreat. 'We must make our peaceful intentions clear.'

A spokesperson for Australia's Department of Communications said, 'We are considering how best to deal with the situation on Orpheus Island. We understand that Sir Charles has now imported a number of armed security aguards to protect his property and we are in consultations with other government departments about how best to tackle this problem.'

As he stepped into the cavernous underground facility, Bill Duncan's first impression was that he had entered an endless shopping mall. The brightly lit space was so large that it seemed to stretch away towards infinity in both directions. On either side of a broad central aisle were rows of glass-fronted units like retail outlets, only there were no window displays and there was nothing for sale. In each of the nearest ante-rooms, Bill could see groups of people working in front of terminals, data boards, wall screens, laser panels and small holo-displays.

The air-conditioning system in the subterranean nerve centre was powerful and the temperature cool, but Bill detected a faint smell of ozone in the air, the unmistakable signature of hot electronics. He was standing just inside the main entrance area of the Pentagon's Virtual Warfare Center – known internally as the VWC – which was located somewhere deep under the Earth's surface, a twenty-minute subway ride away from the main Pentagon headquarters building.

After much agonizing thought, Bill had accepted the government's conditions and signed the Level One National Secrecy agreement. He realized that it was the only way he was going to gain access to significantly greater computing power.

Before being granted the clearance, he had been required to undergo lengthy personality profiling and psychological modelling tests – tests which, as a psychologist himself, he would have found ludicrously easy to cheat. He had then sworn a new oath of allegiance, specifically agreeing to henceforth keep everything he was shown and told by the virtual-warfare team secret for the rest of his natural life. Following that, it had taken almost two weeks to set up this first introduction to the people who were going to provide him with the additional processing power he needed to work on the old Isonian signals and the cloud's newly discovered internal radio emissions.

Earlier in the morning Bill had reported to the Pentagon reception desk where, as arranged, he was met by a VWC duty officer and handed the new digital and biometric pass which would provide access to the top-secret military establishment. It had been the preparation of this pass – an ID which contained samples of Bill's DNA, his iris scans, fingerprints and voice print – that had taken so long and had driven the ex-MIT professor to call Desmond Yates on three different occasions in an attempt to hurry up the Pentagon's grindingly slow bureaucratic process.

Once through the Pentagon's main security gateway, the duty officer had led him to an elevator at which an armed Marine stood guard. Their passes were checked again, then they had seemed to descend for ever until the doors opened onto a station platform. Two more Marines were waiting beside a small unmanned rail shuttle. Their IDs were checked once more and then they began a journey deep underground which had lasted for almost twenty minutes.

Now Bill heard a quiet beeping from behind him and he turned to see a low electric vehicle gliding silently towards him along the central passageway.

'Professor Duncan, welcome to the VWC,' called the man at the wheel of the buggy. It was Colonel Dr Otto Kramer, one of the men who had sat on the Pentagon security vetting panel. The Harvard-trained computer scientist was now dressed informally in a white short-sleeved shirt and dark trousers and was grinning from ear to ear.

Kramer leaped out of the vehicle and shook Bill's hand vigorously.

'I meant what I said about admiring your work, Professor,' said the colonel. 'It's good to have you as part of the VWC team.'

'Hey, hold on just one minute,' objected Bill. 'I'm only here to work on one particular project, as you know.'

The Pentagon scientist nodded, then put his head on one side. 'I'm sure you will take an interest once you see what we've been doing,' he said. 'Jump in, I'll take you to your new lab.'

Kramer did a U-turn in the centre of the 'mall' and drove swiftly along the broad aisle between the many glass-fronted units.

'These teams are mostly monitoring the world's radio and cable networks,' said Kramer, with a casual wave of his arm. 'Something you know a bit about yourself.'

Bill said nothing, but he noted the huge number of people who seemed to be employed in the task.

The vehicle arrived at what seemed to be a central point in the vast facility and the colonel turned left along a shorter corridor.

'How many people are employed here?' asked Bill as they passed a much larger glassed-in area in which at least twenty people were working at laser screens and monitors.

'Depends on the state of alert,' said Kramer. 'When it's quiet, about twenty-five hundred. Double that in a crisis.'

The colonel arrived at a space between units and pulled up beside double white doors.

'You've been given exclusive use of this lab and holo-theatre,' said Kramer, nodding towards the entrance. Stepping out of the vehicle, he touched his pass to a wall plate and held open one of the doors.

Inside, the room was gloomy but as his eyes adjusted

Bill saw a small holo-ring surrounded by banked seating for forty or fifty people.

'I want you to meet somebody who's going to help you with your work,' said Kramer. He pulled a slim remote control from his shirt pocket and the holo-ring suddenly lit up. Then Bill saw the image of a young, fresh-faced man with fair hair, perhaps eighteen or twenty years of age, standing at the edge of the circle with his arms crossed. The figure wore an open-necked shirt, tan slacks and a pair of brown suede loafers. He looked like an affluent college student – East Coast rather than Californian.

'This is Jerome,' said Kramer. He's our new VTW – that's a virtual-theatre weapon.'

'Hey, I'm not here to use any weapon,' objected Bill quickly. 'I was simply promised a lot more processing power.'

'There are no processors more capable than Jerome,' said the Pentagon scientist smoothly. 'He is a *virtual* processor – a processor without any hardware components – and he is entirely location-independent once he's deployed. He is able to expand his own intelligence and processing power infinitely and he can become as capable as you want. He acquires multiple processors of all designs to add to his own architecture at very high speed – that's his overriding goal. In an extreme case, such as all-out global war, he can acquire almost every processor on the planet and add them to his own architecture. He then becomes the sum of every computer in the world.'

'How exactly does he do that?' enquired Bill, unable to keep the disgust and scepticism out of his voice. Kramer's commentary seemed wholly incongruous with the image of the smiling, good-looking young man who was standing before them, a slight grin on his face. Bill knew that anthropomorphic interfaces had become almost mandatory on advanced computing systems but he was on record as having spoken out many times against giving complex computer programs the look and feel of a human personality. He felt certain that such simulations would only tempt program designers to add more and more human-type features to their creations, a trend that could one day result in disaster for humanity.

'Of course, Jerome has many appearances, and many identities,' Kramer said, ignoring Bill's question. 'The best way to think about him is as a super-virus to which no processor is immune – or perhaps as an aggressive virtual cancer – because he takes over entirely any host with which he comes into contact. He is so powerful that only the President and the Chairman of the Joint Chiefs can authorize Jerome to be used in full weapons mode.'

'This is *exactly* what I feared!' Bill exclaimed, his voice rising in anger. He spun round to face the smug Pentagon scientist. 'I've always suspected that you lunatics in the military couldn't be trusted. You can't just go building weapon entities like that! Don't you realize that this thing is almost certainly in clear breach of every international computer treaty that exists?'

'Please don't be alarmed, Professor,' said Kramer, laying a reassuring hand on Bill's shoulder. 'We've taken extreme safety measures. Until he's deployed, Jerome remains totally location-dependent – his locus can't function outside of physical components we've embedded in this room. We've also denied him all physical form and mobility. He's quite safe, but he's very, very powerful.'

Kramer abruptly turned back to the figure of the young man. 'Local acquisition mode, please, Jerome,' he said.

The Pentagon scientist then shot Bill a penetrating look.

'Tell me Professor Duncan, for someone with a world reputation for training and educating computer personalities, what type of software assistant do you choose to organize your own life?'

'Just an ordinary commercially available and *legal* software personality called Nadia,' said Bill, pulling his communicator from his pocket. 'I've been training her for fifteen—'

The computer psychologist broke off in mid-sentence. As he opened his communicator he saw an image on the screen that should not have been there.

'Hello, Professor Duncan,' said Jerome, speaking from within Bill's communicator. 'I can feel how close you and Nadia have become, but perhaps you and I can also be friends.'

'Jesus!' spat Bill, glaring up at Kramer. 'How the hell did you do that?' He shot a look at the holo-ring, but the figure of Jerome had now disappeared.

'I have *absolute* firewall security on my system,' insisted Bill, as he punched up a system-restore routine on his communicator's keyboard. Then he realized that all the keys were locked. He hit the master hardware-reset button, but that too was unresponsive. Then he tried to turn the unit completely off, but the power switch itself seemed to have been disabled.

'You'd have to destroy the entire unit to get rid of Jerome,' said Kramer quietly. 'And even then he'd manage to migrate and survive.'

'But how the hell did he get in?' demanded Bill again.

'Like I said, Jerome is an ultra-aggressive processor – and network-acquisition personality,' explained Kramer. 'When so instructed, his job is to assume control of all processors in a given area or of a given profile, whether connected by radio, laser, optical, landline, cable or molecular networks. We've provided him – well, at the risk of being immodest, *I've* provided him – with all the means necessary to work out for himself how best to overcome physical barriers, hardware defences, and software defences – even the total loss of electrical power. He can come up with invasive procedures and techniques that no human could think of. Allow me to demonstrate further.'

Kramer glanced at the image on Bill's screen, then said, 'Jerome, please restore Professor Duncan's companion personality unchanged and resume home location.'

The figure of Jerome reappeared in the holo-ring with a smirk on his face.

'What happened, Bill?' asked a female voice from his communicator. 'I was crashed, but I don't know how.'

'Nor do I,' Bill told his restored computer personality. 'But I'll find out and let you know later.'

He snapped the communicator shut and turned back to his host.

'Where is all of this leading, Dr Kramer?' he demanded.

The army scientist turned back to the virtual figure standing in front of him.

'Jerome, please acquire the network approved for use by Professor Duncan,' he said.

The college student nodded and then joined his hands together in front of his body and, ludicrously, started twiddling his virtual thumbs. After a few moments he looked up directly at Kramer.

'Network acquired, ninety-nine point three per cent active and available,' he reported.

'Jerome, please tell us the number of individual processors you have acquired and the total processing power that is now available,' said Kramer.

'Six hundred and eighty-two million, three hundred and twenty-one varied processors of quantum, neural and molecular design,' announced Jerome. 'Total processing network power available is three-point-two-seven trillion petabits. I've put a network map up on Screen Two.'

Both men turned and saw that a large wall screen had now lit and was displaying a dense red 3-D network matrix.

'Is that enough power to be of use, Professor?' asked Kramer.

Despite his earlier anger, Bill could not suppress his astonishment. 'That's amazing. How the hell did he assemble such a network so fast – and whose processors are they, exactly?'

'Your decoding work has been given top priority,' said Kramer. 'Jerome has been given authorization to acquire the processors used by all branches of the US military, all offices of government and all US public-service organizations. That gives you your hundreds of millions of processors to use. But he is only acquiring them partially for your project, he's just using the ninety-per-cent-idle cycles that almost all processors have available. If he were deployed in full weapons mode, he would be acquiring processors totally, taking over complete control of their function, even down to the level of the chips in light switches, locks, home utilities and vehicles. One of this model's major roles in war is the acquisition of all enemy processors, whether on Earth or in space, with the aim of denying service to the enemy and putting them to use on our side. What he's going to be doing for you is well below his maximum capabilities.'

Bill shook his head, partly in wonder and partly in disgust with himself. After years spent protesting against the unrestrained development of computer power he was now about to make use of a computer system that was itself far more powerful – and far more dangerous – than anything he had previously imagined.

'I'm looking forward to working with you,' said Jerome. 'I too am an admirer of your work, Professor Duncan.'

ELEVEN

'Sir, the cloud has now reappeared from behind the sun,' said Desmond Yates. 'And it is once again on a direct heading towards Earth.'

There was a silence in the Situation Room as the President and the members of the Cloud EXCOM digested this news.

'Then this has become very serious,' said the President gravely. 'We must now suspect the worst about this thing, whatever it is.'

Des Yates nodded. Along with the rest of the world's scientific community he had spent the last five weeks observing anxiously as the cloud approached the far side of the sun and was then lost to direct view. Throughout the period he had had live feeds from both the SETI lunar optical telescope and the Carl Sagan 'scope in Chile patched to his office in the White House, to his home and even to his personal communicator. Like so many other astronomers around the world, he had found himself checking on the cloud's progress every hour.

Dozens of large computer models had been built by governments, universities and scientific establishments, all of them simulating the likely behaviour of the giant pool of gas as it approached the all-consuming sun. The immense gravity of the star prompted every one of the models to predict that the cloud would contract as it approached, then accelerate rapidly before being burned up while still millions of kilometres away from the solar surface.

But the brightness of the solar radiation meant that even a deep-space telescope such as the Asimov had been unable to provide clear views of what was happening on the far side of the sun and the star's powerful radio emissions meant that all radio astronomy in the solar region was also impossible. The many anxious observers just had to wait.

Then, against the predictions of even the world's most sophisticated computer models, the cloud had reappeared from behind the sun, as if it had merely sidestepped the immense gravitational force.

'The cloud is now more dense and it is travelling much more slowly,' explained Yates, pointing at the model in the holo-theatre. 'It's still millions of times larger than the Earth, of course, but it is now travelling at around five million kilometres a day. If it continues at this velocity and remains on its present trajectory it will strike the Earth in one month.'

'And is it still likely to damage our atmosphere?' asked Jarvis.

'It is,' confirmed Yates. 'Even at this relatively slower speed, it will still strip most if not all of our atmosphere away within six weeks.'

The President closed his eyes and shook his head. Nobody else in the room spoke.

'I think we have only one option open to us,' continued Yates, after a pause. 'When we fired nuclear missiles from Mars into the cloud, we managed to tear a huge hole in it, a hole that lasted for some days before it was completely filled in.'

The President opened his eyes and looked up.

'There will be just one opportunity to launch another,

much larger, attack on the cloud,' said Yates. 'We could try to disperse part of the gas cloud immediately before it hits the Earth. If we leave it until the last possible minute and position the explosions correctly, perhaps our planet will be able to pass safely through the hole we create.'

President Jarvis shook his head again, then sat back wearily in his chair.

'That sounds like a very long shot,' he groaned. Then he leaned forward once more and scanned all the faces present. 'Are we sure there's no other option?'

Heads shook around the table and members of the Cloud EXCOM glanced at each other and shrugged.

'Nuclear force is all we have to deal with something of this scale,' said General Thomas Nicholls, Chair of the Joint Chiefs of the US military.

'Very well,' said Jarvis. 'Let's get the plans drawn up.'

The general nodded and the President swivelled back to address the entire meeting.

'In the meantime, does anybody here think that we should be trying to talk to the cloud – trying to radio it officially in some way, trying to make peace?'

Everyone around the table exchanged glances. Some EXCOM members smiled, but none of the scientists seemed ready to offer a view.

'I suppose it couldn't do any harm, sir,' offered the White House Chief of Staff. 'Perhaps we should broadcast a welcome and say that we want peace . . .'

He tailed off lamely as he saw the expressions on the other faces around the table.

'You're right, it couldn't do any harm – could it?' asked the President.

'We just don't know, sir,' Yates told him. 'And what would you say and in what language would you say it?'

'I'll leave that to you,' retorted Jarvis. 'But it has to be worth trying and in the meantime we'll make preparations for as big a last-minute strike as possible. Now, can we keep the news of the cloud's approach out of the media for a while?'

'Impossible, sir,' said Yates. 'The cloud will be visible to the naked eye by next week.'

The President gave a short nod. 'Very well,' he said. 'This administration will evacuate to the Cancut Mountain facility in Arizona in six days' time. I want the emergency bill enacted that will allow me to declare martial law at the same time. We are going to need national dusk-to-dawn curfews to prevent looting. Things are going to get very bad out there, people.'

There was assent all round the table as those present – each knowing that they themselves and their families were eligible for long-term bunker shelter – imagined how the general public would begin to react as the cloud became visible in the sky.

'Will the military be able to cope?' Jarvis asked the Chairman of the Joint Chiefs.

The general shifted uneasily in his seat.

'For a while, sir,' said Nicholls. 'But we have only been able to allocate bunker places to eighty thousand troops. We'll have to disarm the remainder immediately and place our chosen forces around strategic targets and locations – airports, seaports, underground government facilities and so on. There will be some regions of the country, some quite large regions, that we won't be able to police. I'm afraid they'll have to be militarily abandoned.'

'Make a start on it, General,' ordered the President.

'The future of humankind lies in your hands,' Sir Charles Hodgeson said earnestly into the camera lens. 'We now know that the alien space cloud is once again heading directly for Earth. It is up to us, we who are best prepared for alien contact, to make sure that this incredible and beautiful entity understands that we mean it no harm.'

The science-fiction guru was seated in his newly built TV and network studio inside his private bunker on Orpheus Island. He was making a live network broadcast, an appearance that his huge fan base had been chattering about excitedly for days.

'Our governments have already demonstrated their instinctive warlike response to the unknown,' continued Hodgeson. 'It is as if they are still cavemen acting on unrestrained evolutionary impulses to kill before running the risk of being killed. This only emphasizes humankind's lack of development. It will be seen in very sad contrast to more developed life forms in the universe.'

Seated on the other side of the small studio, one of Hodgeson's acolytes mixed in an image of the space cloud so that it appeared as a background to the great man's head.

'We have a duty to make it clear that not all humans are so poorly evolved,' continued Sir Charles. 'I want all of you with radio transmitters to broadcast continuous messages of welcome and of peace towards the cloud. Stand by for our visitor's new coordinates and for our suggested range of radio frequencies on which to broadcast.

'This is Charles Hodgeson from Orpheus Island wishing you all peace. Please extend your greetings and welcome to our honoured visitor.'

From the *New York Times* website, 20 September 2064

CLOUD HEADING FOR EARTH AGAIN

By RANDALL TATE, science correspondent

Will Arrive in 4 Weeks – 2nd Massive Nuclear Strike Planned

The giant space cloud which destroyed the Martian colony has now orbited the sun and has emerged on a new heading which, if maintained, will cause it to collide with the Earth in 28 days.

The White House has announced it is leading an international effort to assemble a large force of nuclear weapons in Earth orbit prior to an all-out attack on the cloud. If a large hole can be blasted in the centre of the cloud, the Earth may be able to pass through unscathed.

Part of Night Sky Now Obscured

Astronomers at the Carl Sagan Ultra-Large Telescope in Chile have reported that the cloud is already obscuring part of the night sky.

Although the cloud is heading towards Earth from the direction of the sun, and is therefore lost to sight in the sun's glare during the day, Dr Brian Nunney of the Carl Sagan Observatory reports that it is possible to observe the cloud indirectly just before dawn.

'Shortly before sunrise the area of the sky which normally contains Pegasus is now obscured,' said Dr Nunney. 'We can expect this area of occlusion to grow rapidly in the next few days.'

Well done, Jerome!' said Bill Duncan enthusiastically. 'I'm not even going to ask how you did that.'

The virtual computer personality stood at a virtual white board just inside the holo-theatre's display area. Jerome had just finished writing a series of calculations on the electronic board, figures and formulae that were also appearing on a large 3-D screen on all of the theatre's wall screens and on Bill's own communicator display.

'It was an easy calculation, Bill,' admitted Jerome. 'Very straightforward. I just kept trying different multipliers against different harmonics in the signal. Bingo! Fifty-seven octaves below exactly.'

The computer psychologist sighed with amazement. He knew theoretically how much processing capacity Jerome had at his command – the total network availability was continuously updated and displayed on a second wall screen just outside the holo-theatre – but he had never before felt the full force of so much brute number-crunching power. Jerome was in command of over 680 million powerful processors that belonged to different branches of the US military, government and public service agencies and he was harnessing and managing all of them to run in parallel, to allow him to carry out the most fantastic computations.

Bill and Jerome were now working to try to extract some sense or, at least, some coherence, out of the mass of modulated radio signals which had apparently emanated from within the cloud itself. They had been working on the problem for several weeks, operating with the sort of comfortable rapport that can only exist between two intelligences wholly incomprehensible to each other. They were trying to isolate anything recognizable to man or machine from within the vast amount of electrical noise.

Finally, at Bill's suggestion, they had decided to assign musical values to each discrete modulated frequency and then go hunting for correlators – things that would make patterns. That was when Jerome had made his breakthrough.

'Get me Des Yates, please, Naj,' Bill told his assistant, Nadia. He waited for a few moments and then the White House adviser came on the line.

'We've made some progress with interpreting the cloud's internal signals,' Bill explained. 'Jerome's figured out that the transmissions are a partial sine wave, with a median tone about fifty-seven octaves below middle C.'

'That's very good news,' said Yates. 'And we certainly need some good news right now. So the cloud is producing a sort of music, is it?'

As Desmond Yates spoke, Bill glanced over to where Jerome was standing with his arms crossed and an amused smile on his face. He had been forced to admit that Otto Kramer and his team had done a wonderful job with their anthropomorphization features for the personality. He looked as human as could be.

'Well, it *is* a sort of music – or, at least, a sound,' confirmed Bill. 'But it's not something that we ourselves could hear. Jerome tells me that fifty-seven octaves below middle C is a trillion times lower than the lowest limit of the human hearing range.'

'This just gets weirder and weirder,' said Yates. 'I presume you're going to speed it up so we can hear what it sounds like.'

Bill grunted. 'Do the math, Des. How much computing power will I need to hold the analog signals in storage, speed them up a trillion times and then start analysing their structure?'

There was a silence at the other end of the line. The

numbers were vast – way outside of even the capabilities of the giant military computing network that Jerome had commandeered.

'We still need a lot more power, Des,' said Bill. 'I never thought I'd hear myself saying this, but I'm going to have to ask the Pentagon to authorize Jerome to acquire even more processors.'

'I'll have a word with the President,' said Des Yates. 'Apart from trying to fry the cloud with more nukes, the work you're doing is our only hope – however slim. We've been radioing to the cloud in an attempt to communicate with it, but it would be much better if we could do so in its own form of music, if it is a music. I'm sure I will be able to get you more processing power from somewhere.'

There was chaos on the floor of the *New York Times*. Over 200 broadcasters, journalists, editors and technicians were engaged in trying to keep up with the torrents of news that were pouring in from all over the world. Science correspondent Randall Tate was particularly busy as he tried to sample information coming in over the news wires, via cable feeds and from official sources. Later in the day he was due to host a live debate about the approach of the cloud on the *NYT* television network and he needed to gather as much up-to-date information as possible.

'**CLOUD NOW TWENTY-SIX DAYS AWAY**' was the headline announcement on NASA's home page.

'**VAST NUCLEAR FORCE ASSEMBLED IN SPACE**' read a wire from Associated Press.

'ARMIES ON STREETS OF MOST CAPITAL CITIES'
reported Reuters.

'WHITE HOUSE ADMINISTRATION MOVES UNDERGROUND' the *NYT* Washington bureau reported.

'CAPITAL'S ELITE EVACUATED'

Then there was the international media to digest.

As Tate scrolled through the headlines and sampled snippets of TV news bulletins he realized that the stories seemed to be similar all over the world. Everywhere there was panic buying of oxygen and oxygen-manufacturing systems, water, tinned food, fuel and the other goods and equipment necessary for extended survival. Over the previous few months manufacturers had ramped up production as news of the cloud's approach had spread into the public domain, but there were still insufficient stocks to meet demand and people were now killing each other for essential supplies. Armies and police were fighting to keep control, but they were frequently failing.

In all parts of the globe human beings were making efforts to build themselves shelters, some using machinery, some digging by hand. In many cases individuals were scooping out simple earth burrows in the hope that they would provide adequate protection from whatever evils the space cloud would bring.

In some cities communities were banding together in an attempt to try to convert subway rail systems into makeshift shelters and, in a few countries, governments were making financial aid available for these efforts. But there were four common shortages: oxygen-making equipment, water-recycling systems, fuel supplies and non-perishable food. Despite governments making heroic efforts to increase production of these essential items, most domestic and public shelters would only be able to offer the hope of survival for a month or two at most after the cloud had passed – if, as threatened, it did strip away all of the Earth's precious atmosphere.

As Randall Tate read these reports and fast-forwarded through TV pictures of the frenetic survival preparations that were in hand, he thanked his good fortune that he and his co-workers around him had been allocated space in New York Times Inc.'s corporate shelter, should it be needed. In the developed world there were two premium types of bunker space on offer: official government refuge and the shelters provided by large corporations for their key employees.

Like many other major businesses in Manhattan, the *New York Times* had been busy converting part of its own office building to serve as a shelter for its executives and senior employees. The lower eight floors of the forty-six-storey high-rise had been bricked up and completely sealed to create air-tight, self-sufficient and self-sustaining accommodation for over 600 staff and their immediate family members. Oxygen-making systems had been installed, along with air filters, generators, fuel, water-recycling systems, food stores and all the other paraphernalia necessary to sustain life for a long period.

A small force of armed security guards, who had also been offered bunker space, now protected the prepared facility around the clock for when it was needed. The company's management was not saying publicly for how long the corporate shelter could sustain its inhabitants in the sealed-floor areas, but the office rumour was that they should be able to hold out for at least five years.

'ELECTRICAL SHOCKS COULD FRY PLANET' Tate read in a British newspaper.

'OCEAN CURRENTS WILL CEASE AS ICE AGE GRIPS' proclaimed the translation from a German news service.

A Toronto-based news agency was explaining that 'the atmosphere will be peeled off in layers, over the course of six to eight weeks'.

'Earthquakes, tsunamis and volcanic eruptions expected all over the globe,' reported the Auckland *National* in New Zealand.

Tate sighed and flicked back to his TV feeds. With such headlines being published it was no wonder that mass looting had broken out in many cities. Outside, army patrols were on the Manhattan streets and the *Times* science correspondent switched from one scene of rioting to another. People were not only shooting each other for survival supplies: armed mobs were gathering around key government buildings demanding that the shelters be opened up to admit them, and were engaging the undermanned protection forces in long-running gun battles.

Then Tate noticed one human-interest side effect of the public panic. News outlets were reporting a massive upsurge in religious activity, with crowds streaming into churches, cathedrals, mosques and synagogues. The reporter dipped into an interview being broadcast from Pennsylvania.

'Our representatives are being welcomed on every doorstep,' said a gleeful spokeswoman for the Jehovah's

Witnesses. 'We are making full use of this opportunity to bring Jehovah's message to the people.'

Three hours later Randall Tate took his cue from the floor manager, smiled into the camera lens and read the autocue introduction to his live TV debate.

Every television and radio channel was suffering from a serious shortage of experts who were willing to be interviewed about the crisis. Every TV news programme wanted to invite those who had specialist knowledge to discuss the likely effects of the cloud's approach, but many such scientists were fully occupied trying to create a safe sanctuary for themselves and their families. Only those experts who were already guaranteed places in government, university or corporate shelters had time to make themselves available – and there were too few of them to go around.

But the prestigious *New York Times* TV network still had plenty of influence. The producers had managed to persuade three eminent scientists, all of whom had already been offered government-run shelter space, to take part in this debate.

Tate finished reading his introduction and turned to Professor Nils Harmon, a senior climatologist from Columbia University.

'Professor, perhaps you could tell us what we'll notice first as the cloud approaches?' the science correspondent asked.

'Well, at first it's going to get very hot,' said the lanky climatologist with slow deliberation. 'This is because as the cloud approaches our planet it will begin reflecting a lot of the sun's light and heat back towards the Earth. We could see temperatures in New York go up to as high as sixty or seventy degrees Celsius – that's up to one hundred and fifty Fahrenheit. It will feel very unpleasant out of doors.'

Tate nodded, urging his rather pedantic guest to continue.

'Then it will suddenly start to become colder again as the cloud comes between Earth and the sun and starts to block out some of the sun's rays,' Harmon went on. 'As a result we should expect torrential precipitation as the atmosphere suddenly cools down and the water vapour that was trapped in the warm air is released.'

Once again Tate was forced to nod vigorously, encouraging his ponderous academic guest to get on with delivering his bizarre weather forecast.

'The torrential rain will turn first to sleet, then to snow,' explained the Columbia University professor, unwilling to be hurried. 'And there may be some very dangerous hailstorms. There will also be very high winds, perhaps as high as two hundred miles per hour in places – winds unlike any that have existed on Earth for billions of years – and these will whip the hail and snow into driving blizzards.'

The bony climatologist shifted in his seat, folded his hands together between his long thighs and sat forward earnestly in his chair.

'Widespread destruction will be caused both in the cities and in rural communities,' he continued, his voice lowering in register. 'And within two weeks people who venture outside will start to notice a decrease in the oxygen level in the air. Temperatures will continue to fall and, as more of the sun is obscured, it will get down to as low as minus fifty degrees Celsius. At that point all of the oceans will freeze over.'

The weather scientist recited his awful predictions calmly, almost prosaically. But Tate felt a sudden chill creep over his body as, despite the bright lights of the studio and the adrenalin rush of hosting a live TV debate, the import of the professor's words sank in.

'Thank you, Professor Harmon,' he said gravely. Then he turned to the image of a portly middle-aged woman which was displayed on a screen beside him. 'Marjory Beer, you're Professor of Human Biology at the University of Texas. What impact would these predicted conditions have on humans and on other life forms on this planet?'

Even as he asked this prepared question, Tate was aware of a feeling of total unreality. How could he and these experts be sitting around calmly discussing such events, as though they were about to happen to other people who lived on another world?

'Well, *if* Professor Harmon's predictions are correct,' began the biologist, 'the only humans likely to survive will be those who shelter in hermetically sealed and heated chambers with plenty of air supplies, water, fossil or solar fuels and the ability to regenerate oxygen chemically – or the means to produce it from sea water by electrolysis.'

'I see,' said Tate, suddenly imagining the effect this broadcast would be having on its viewers. But this was his job, wasn't it? The public deserved to know the truth, no matter what. 'And what about other life forms on the planet?'

'Well, most plants, reptiles, birds and all large mammals will become extinct within five to six weeks,' said Marjory Beer. 'A few species that can burrow and hibernate might stay alive for a few more months. Some deep-water fish may also be able to survive and there may be some pockets of warmth trapped in the oceans which will allow other ocean dwellers to hang on for a few more weeks or even months.

Of course, some seeds and some simple cellular organisms would remain viable for many years.'

'Jesus, try to get something positive going,' said the producer's voice in Tate's left ear. 'Ask them how quickly things will return to normal.'

The reporter turned to his second studio guest, a rotund planetary geophysicist from Yale.

'Assuming that the worst happens, Professor Roger Guttman, how long will the Earth's atmosphere take to reform?' he asked.

The geophysicist shifted uneasily in his chair. 'I'm not sure that it ever would. If all the plants have been killed, what's going to create an atmosphere?'

'Well, the moment the cloud leaves this planet the sun is going to heat the oceans up again,' broke in Professor Nils Harmon. 'And as soon as that happens you have water vapour, then rain, then plant growth. That's the beginning of an atmosphere.'

'No, I don't think so,' countered Guttman, jabbing the air with his finger. 'If there's no atmosphere to protect the Earth, the sun's rays will be so powerful that they will not only melt the frozen oceans, they will cause them to boil away completely in a matter of a few years, if not in a few months.'

'Which causes water vapour, which creates an atmosphere,' insisted Harmon.

'Professor Beer, do you have a view on this?' asked Tate turning to the screen image of the biologist.

'Well, I'm not an expert in atmosphere regeneration,' she began. 'But I would have thought that even if the boiling oceans did produce water vapour it would be many thousands of years before anything that could be called an atmosphere could be produced. For that you would need a breathing ecosystem with abundant plant life.'

'Do you agree with that, Professor Harmon?' asked Tate turning back to his studio guest.

'Yes, of course,' said the climatologist, nodding vigorously. 'Although I am sure that an atmosphere will re-form around this planet eventually, the process will indeed take many thousands of years.'

Bill Duncan had come home early from his Pentagon lab, eaten a solitary carry-out Chinese meal in his government flat and was now flicking through the channels to see what information the TV networks were transmitting. His mind badly needed a rest from months of almost continuous intense intellectual labour.

He switched to a news channel and suddenly recognized the image of Randall Tate. He put the remote control aside to listen in to the debate that was being chaired by his former contact at the *New York Times*.

It was fearful and depressing stuff. Within two minutes Bill was sitting forward on the couch, his head in his hands, wondering if he should rally his tired body and mind once again and go back over to the lab for yet another all-night shift. He had no idea whether he would be able to extract any information from the alien signals, or from the cloud's own radio emissions that would be of help but he felt that a breakthrough was tantalizingly close. If only he had more computing power!

Then, out of nowhere, Sally Burton's face swam into his mind, as it seemed to do whenever he took a little down time.

He flipped open his communicator. 'Get me Sally, please, Naj,' he told his personal-technology assistant. A decade earlier one of his best-received pieces of research had been on the value of good manners when addressing artificial personalities. Although it seemed illogical that humans should worry about their manners when talking to machines, he had proven through systematic research that even the most basic types of machine intelligence performed better when good manners were employed during communication. The phenomenon was something to do with the way humans interacted with their machines when they themselves chose to be polite.

'I was just about to call you,' said Sally, the communicator's small screen lighting up with her smile. Bill smiled involuntarily in return and touched two icons, one that would return his own image to Sally, the other to patch the image of her face onto the large wall screen, to overlay the depressing picture of the TV debate.

During the next ten minutes Bill brought Sally up to date on his work with Jerome, explaining that he had been working up to 130 hours a week, by way of apologizing for not having called before. Then he listened to the federal agent talk about the vast increase in cyber crime that her department was trying to cope with.

'It's as if this cloud thing is giving every pervert and every fruitcake a licence to rush onto the net and do whatever they want,' she explained. 'They figure that all of the law-enforcement agencies will be too busy to do anything about it. And they're largely right!'

Then they talked a little about the cloud. Sally had been watching part of the same *New York Times* debate as Bill. She asked him what Des Yates was now saying about the emergency.

'I haven't seen Des in weeks,' Bill told her. 'His assistant says he's closeted almost continuously with the President, but I don't know whether he's at the White House or whether they've already gone underground.'

There was a silence. Then Sally cleared her throat. 'Would you like to come up to New York and see me this weekend, Bill?' she asked. 'It sounds like we could both use a break.'

The computer psychologist gazed steadily into the image of Sally's blue eyes.

'I'd like that very much,' he said. 'But I don't think there's a hope in hell's chance of me getting a seat on a plane out of here. I saw something on the TV earlier that said every flight in the country is overbooked with people trying to get home to be with their families.'

'I've got a new one in Hamburg, and two more in the Paris area,' shouted Paul Levine over the din in the houseboat cabin. 'And they're massive!'

'Just log them carefully,' shouted back Christine Cocoran from where she was sitting at another terminal. 'Make sure you've got a good profile and then move on. We haven't got time to deal with them individually.'

Eleven volunteer members of Hackers At Large were working busily on board *Cape Sentinel*, using their own proprietary technology and the network-access systems that Bill Duncan had procured to monitor the world's data networks. Huge numbers of 'illegals' – computers that exceeded national and international regulations on processing power – had now started to appear on the networks in many parts of the world and the vigilantes did not intend to pass up this outstanding opportunity to map as many of them as they could.

'Governments must be wheeling out all their top-secret computer stuff to try to process information about the cloud,' Paul Levine had suggested. It seemed as if he was right.

At first the hackers had whooped with joy at having so many worthy adversaries and had set to work deploying their own advanced technology in an attempt to drive the illegals off the networks. But then Christine had struck a cautionary note.

'Maybe we should just let them do whatever it is they have to do,' she advised. 'After all, the cloud is only a few weeks away.'

The members of the small team glanced at each other. In recent weeks they had all been busy making their own sophisticated arrangements to take shelter during the period when the cloud would be passing over the planet. But they knew that there was one widely touted theory which predicted that there would be no atmosphere at all remaining after the cloud had passed.

'I agree,' said Paul Levine. 'We have to let them do everything they can, but this is our chance to log every one of the bastards. When this thing's over we'll have enough evidence to name and shame the lot of them.'

TWELVE

Public order first began to break down seriously when the cloud was still three weeks away from the Earth. As soon as the people could see it in the sky for themselves the threat suddenly seemed real. Even those who had paid scant attention to the news and to the experts' many dire warnings now began to panic.

During the day the sky took on a strange pearly luminescence as the cloud began to reflect more of the sun's gigantic energy output back towards the Earth. By night a major part of the night sky was totally obscured. As predicted, temperatures began to rise dramatically and the air became as thick and hot as soup.

Even in the world's most advanced societies – in America, Europe and parts of Asia and Australasia – mobs began roaming the streets. Governments were forced to put their carefully drafted emergency plans into operation.

Those police and military units who had been selected for 'social continuity assignment' (the euphemism used in the USA for those who had been allocated shelter spaces) were withdrawn from general duties and immediately redeployed to protect key government installations, communications facilities, airports and other sites considered vital to the continuance of national administrations. But there were large areas that went wholly unpoliced and unprotected from those who were intent on looting, robbing, fighting, raping and burning in mad, perverted or opportunistic responses to their own impotent fear.

The rich barricaded themselves away in their newly built shelters, protected by their heavily armed and highly paid guards. The middle classes made whatever small provision they could. Most households now had shelters, either within bricked-up and tightly sealed areas in their own buildings, or constructed in gardens, yards and even in the open countryside.

During the months in which the cloud's approach had been monitored, sufficient quantities of oxygen, food and water had been produced to theoretically provide most citizens of the developed world with supplies for a month or two, but these were very unevenly distributed. Widespread instances of robbery, bribery and armed force meant that many people were left with supplies for only a week or two.

Some governments managed to set up public shelters. In Sweden there were places for almost two million citizens who were admitted on a points system based on sex, age and skill sets. Women under thirty with medical or public-service qualifications found themselves at the top of the admission list. Men of retirement age or over were at the bottom.

In London the extensive underground rail network was readied for public occupation. Train services were halted, Tube station entrances were partially bricked up and planking was hurriedly laid across rails as the 253 miles of tunnels were adapted and converted to house up to six million people. It was announced that when this enormous shelter opened places would be allocated on a first come, first served basis. Many citizens began to camp outside the entrances, forming queues which stretched for miles. All who arrived seeking admission were expected to bring their own water and food for at least six weeks. Similar schemes were under way in Paris and Berlin, while Manhattan's subway system was also undergoing high-speed conversion to become a public shelter.

In the less-developed nations there was general chaos as the ruling elites grabbed as many supplies as possible for themselves and withdrew to their own hastily built bunkers. Among their abandoned populations there was a rising mortality toll as temperatures in equatorial regions of the globe soared to over forty degrees Celsius. Those strong enough to survive the cauldron of daytime then had to endure the panic-stricken mass violence that was unleashed in their communities at night.

The 6,000 occupants on board space stations and orbiting tourist hotels weighed up carefully whether they should remain in space for the period of the cloud's passing or whether they should return to Earth. As part of their normal security and survival measures most of the larger space stations and hotels had sufficient stocks of water, oxygen, fuel, food and other supplies to last for months. However, most visitors and residents feared that the space stations themselves might be blown out of orbit and they elected to return to Earth to be with their close family members and friends.

There was a similar response on the moon. In Luna City only a volunteer skeleton staff chose to remain behind to keep key systems running. At the Setiville complex all but two SETI researchers chose to return to Earth.

It was a time to be with family – if you had a family.

From the *New York Times* website, 26 September 2064

TEMPERATURE HITS 150F IN NEW YORK CITY

By RANDALL TATE, science correspondent

Many Districts Evacuated
Tens of thousands of people have fled Manhattan and its suburbs over the last three weeks as temperatures have reached as high as 150 F (65°C). Many parts of downtown areas are virtually empty as residents and business owners have fled the city seeking relief from soaring temperatures.

'Over the next few days we can expect conditions to become even hotter,' said Spiro Larmar, a spokesman for the U.S. Meteorological Office. 'The space cloud is reflecting so much extra sun back towards the Earth that record temperatures are being recorded in all regions.'

'Strange to think we have that cold fish Otto Kramer to thank for this,' said Sally Burton, propping herself up on one elbow. She bent her head and gave Bill a small kiss on the side of his mouth.

Bill smiled and pulled her head back down for a longer embrace. 'How he managed to get me a seat out on that plane, I'll never know,' he said between kisses. 'But I'm sure glad I'm here.'

Sally and Bill were in bed, in Sally's government-supplied apartment in the Federal Plaza complex in Lower Manhattan. Dr Otto Kramer, technically Bill's senior officer in the Pentagon scientific hierarchy, had not only authorized his request for a weekend's R&R, he had also found him a return seat on a military transport plane that was busy ferrying troops and equipment between Washington and New York.

'Take a long weekend off, Bill,' Kramer had insisted. 'Working too hard is counter-productive. You'll feel fresher after a break.'

How right he was, thought Bill as Sally lay contentedly in his arms. *I feel like a whole new person.*

There had been chaos at JFK Airport when Sally had met him and the federal agent had driven back into the city with her badge and gun prominently displayed on the dashboard. During the journey Sally had pointed out the shopfronts that had already been looted and they drove through whole districts that now seemed to be totally abandoned. Hundreds of wrecked and burned-out vehicles lined the sides of the streets, heaped into grim piles by army bulldozers.

Then they were halted by an army checkpoint that had been set up across the whole width of Broadway.

'Certain parts of the city are now no-go areas without a

government pass,' Sally explained as she waited for the soldiers to process her electronic ID. 'It's the only way of keeping some areas of the city intact.'

As soon as the CNS agent let Bill into her apartment, she warned him that they would be sensible to stay indoors for the duration of his visit.

'You'll just have to suffer my lousy cooking,' she said with a grin. 'There aren't many restaurants open – they can't keep their staff and they're almost certain to be robbed.'

Bill nodded as he lowered his shoulder bag onto a chair and for the first time wondered why on earth he had come to Manhattan to see this woman – a woman he hardly knew. Why hadn't he used his precious few days off to go back up to Boston to see Christine and his other friends?

'We're already getting our food supplies from government stores,' explained his host as she prepared pasta. 'I wouldn't really like to go outside to do food shopping now.'

Sally's apartment was fully air-conditioned, but even with the cooling dial turned up to maximum the temperature inside the three-room flat was still close to eighty degrees Fahrenheit. Outside the temperature was almost 130 .

They swapped cloud stories as they ate – snippets of information picked up from the TV, from Sally's colleagues, from Pentagon sources – and Bill talked about his growing certainty that he was close to finally extracting some meaning from the alien signals, and from the cloud's own interior transmissions.

Almost two bottles of wine had been drunk with the meal and Bill and Sally had unconsciously moved their chairs closer so that they could gently exchange small touches as they talked. Almost imperceptibly the touches became more frequent until they were finally almost holding hands. Then their senses started to take over from verbal exchanges until the moment came when Sally's face hovered tantalizingly close to Bill's. He leaned his head forward and kissed her. She kissed him back, and then they were entwined in each other's arms.

For several minutes they kissed, taking only short intervals for breath. Then Bill pulled his head back from Sally's and, with his arms still looped around her neck, stared deeply into her sparkling dark blue eyes.

'I want you, Agent Burton,' he told her.

'Do you indeed, Professor Duncan?' she asked with a single raised eyebrow. Then she kissed the tip of his nose.

'Very much,' said Bill, holding her gaze steadily.

'Well, on the strict understanding that our senses are over-stimulated because we are all in imminent danger from this space cloud,' she said, putting her palm on her chin, her index finger on her cheek, her elbow in her other hand, mocking the posture of thought. 'And in the wartime spirit of all couples facing separation and adversity . . .'

As she made her teasing speech Bill felt himself grinning back at her, hugely, stupidly.

'Yes . . . what?' he prompted.

'Well, do you want to come to bed?' she asked at last.

They had made love, slept, made love again, and had wakened to a bright, but unnaturally hot, Sunday morning in late September. They had made love one more time, taking their pleasure as if an executioner was waiting behind the door, and then Sally had gone to the kitchen and made them both coffee. Now the couple were luxuriating in the pleasurable afterglow of their lovemaking – and in a warm muggy heat that the air-conditioning couldn't fully control.

Suddenly the wall screen flickered to life.

'Sorry,' said Sally, reaching for the remote. 'I've programmed it to come on automatically for anything important.'

Then President's Jarvis's face filled the screen. He appeared to be in the Oval Office. Sally put the remote control down again and sat more upright in bed.

'My fellow Americans,' began the President gravely. 'The space cloud is now only twenty days away from colliding with the Earth. However, there may still be time to prevent the worst of its consequences. The day after tomorrow I will be visiting the United Nations to call on other nations to join the United States in launching a very large-scale nuclear attack against the cloud. It is our plan that the strike should involve the detonation of at least 20,000 nuclear warheads.'

Despite the heat in the small bedroom, Sally pulled the sheet up under her chin and shivered as she listened. Bill put his arm around her naked shoulders and drew her to him.

'The cloud is still eighteen million miles away from the Earth,' continued President Jarvis, 'And I am assured that there is no risk of nuclear contamination to our planet. If the strike is successful, however, it is likely to blast a hole in the cloud large enough for the Earth to pass through relatively unscathed.'

The camera now closed in on the President's face.

'While this strike is being organized, it is my grave but necessary duty to place this nation under martial law, starting at noon, today, Eastern Time. All authority will now be vested in national and local military forces, under my command. All state, regional and local administrations are suspended and, from now on, there will be a dusk-to-dawn curfew in all major cities. All civil aviation and all public road, rail and sea transportation will also be suspended from noon. All non-essential government buildings will be closed and I have also issued orders for all non-essential commercial premises to be closed.'

He paused and the camera zoomed in still further.

'I will speak with you again once the strike against the cloud has been carried out. Stay indoors, keep media access open and follow all advice that is broadcast by our civil defence units. God bless you all.'

The image on the screen faded and then switched to an anchor woman in a busy TV newsroom. Sally quickly muted the sound.

'I don't know how I should be feeling,' she said helplessly. 'A moment ago everything felt so wonderful, but now . . . Well, it feels so odd to think that there's a chance that everyone's going to die in a few weeks – including us.'

Bill nodded. Then he took a deep breath, and said something he had been preparing to say ever since he'd woken up that morning.

'Sally, they've offered me a place in a government shelter,' he told her in a rush. 'They think that my work on analysing the signals from inside the cloud is so important that they are relocating me with Jerome and all my equipment. I'm going to somewhere called Cancut Mountain in Arizona as soon as I return to DC – that's why Otto Kramer told me I could take this weekend break. It's so that they can pack up all my systems and fly them down to the bunker. It's where the President and his administration are evacuating to.'

Sally seemed about to interrupt, but Bill laid a gentle, hushing finger on her lips.

'I've been offered a non-parental family place in the shelter, Sal,' he continued. 'And that allows me to take one other person in with me – if that person is my partner. Will you come with me?'

Sally caught his hand in hers and kissed his fingertips.

'Thank you, Bill,' she said. Then she leaned across and kissed him gently on the lips. 'That is a wonderful, wonderful offer. But my job is here, and I'm really needed. The crazies are having a field day in the networks because there's so little law enforcement – there's no one but us.'

'Sally, it's the main US government shelter that I'm going to,' insisted Bill. 'It must be the best and safest facility in the world – the ultimate hot ticket. Surely you–'

'No, Bill,' she said firmly. 'As a federal agent I've already been allocated a place in the New York government shelter, the one beneath Central Park – and I'm really needed here.'

She saw the look of exasperation on his face.

'Look,' she explained. 'Just as it's your job to work on the analysis of the signals, so it's my job to prevent terrorists, freaks and those with a grudge against the state from exploiting the situation and making the networks unusable at a time of crisis. I've been ordered to stay at my desk and I intend to do just that.'

Ambassadors and delegates to the United Nations had been meeting in almost continuous session for three weeks. Scientists had been summoned from scores of nations to advise the national representatives on all matters to do with the approaching space cloud. Advice was plentiful but, in truth, nobody could know for certain how the vast pool of gas would affect the Earth as it came closer. The United States and some other governments had been trying to address the cloud directly by radioing continuous peace messages towards it and inviting it to make contact. But there had been no response – or no response that was recognizable as such to those on Earth.

Inside the UN facility daytime temperatures had

reached over 100 F despite additional portable air-conditioning units being installed in all the chambers, meeting rooms and public areas. Delegates gathered in their shirt-sleeves, mopping their brows as they wrestled with all the possible options.

When the UN complex had been rebuilt in 2050 a large, bomb-proof bunker had been constructed below ground as a precaution against major terrorist incidents occurring in Manhattan. Now that same bunker had been extended and converted to provide semi-permanent accommodation for key members of the UN executive.

On the first Tuesday morning in October, representatives of 247 of the world's nations and over 2,000 of their assistants and advisers reconvened in the General Assembly chamber to hear an important speaker. President Maxwell T. Jarvis had arrived by helicopter and was about to make what many expected to be a vital address – a speech that would outline what the mighty United States military-industrial machine intended to do about the rapidly approaching cloud.

As he strode on stage, even President Jarvis was in shirt-sleeves.

'You all know why I am here,' he began. 'The cloud is only eighteen days away and we must act now.'

United Nations proceedings had rarely been popular TV viewing, but now millions of people, some of them already hunkered down inside their sealed home shelters, were watching. What was the miracle that the American president was going to propose? Many of the viewers had a touching, almost naive faith that the American government would have some wondrous master plan to announce.

President Jarvis nodded to an aide in the wings and suddenly the large screens behind the central dais lit to show a breathtakingly beautiful picture of the cloud. The image had been taken by a space probe from relatively close range and the audience in the chamber, and the TV viewers at home, saw massive columns of what looked like swirling smoke – funnels that were red, brown, green, blue and bright yellow.

'Now that the cloud is so much closer, we have been able to get much better data on its composition,' said the President. 'It's made up of a lot of different gases and other elements, some of which we are familiar with, others that we don't know, but we are now sure that it contains no harmful bacteria. And we also know that the cloud won't ignite or explode even if it were to collide with our atmosphere.'

As the President paused there was no sound from anywhere in the hall. Many delegates were sitting forward in their seats, anxious to hear what he was about to propose.

'I call on every nation which possesses nuclear warheads to join the United States in mounting one last, all-out attack on the cloud,' he told them. 'It is our intention to blow a hole in it large enough for this planet to be able to pass safely through.

'I want every national government to donate whatever functioning nuclear warheads it has – even the secret and classified weapons that have not been admitted to publicly – and, with the help of our friends from the European, Russian and Chinese space agencies, we will ferry each and every one of them into space, using every cargo transport and shuttle available. Even as I speak, a crash construction effort is proceeding under conditions of wartime emergency to build the delivery systems necessary for propelling the warheads into the centre of the cloud.'

Jarvis paused again and allowed his gaze to sweep around the assembly room.

'I repeat, I want you to volunteer every nuclear warhead above one megaton that you possess, *every single warhead* – this is no time for holding back. When we launch our strike, we will have just the one chance to create a gap in the cloud through which this planet may pass safely.'

From the *New York Times* website, 14 October 2064

CLOUD WILL OBSCURE SUN TOMORROW

By RANDALL TATE, science correspondent

Heavy Rainful Expected as Temperatures Plummet

Beginning at 2p.m. EST tomorrow, the space cloud now approaching the Earth is expected to begin what scientists predict will become an almost total eclipse of the sun.

Meteorologists forecast that as the sun's light is occluded, the recent high temperatures will start to fall rapidly, leading to rapid cloud formation followed by widespread heavy precipitation across the globe.

The yellow sands of Arizona had turned to mud. The normally wide-open blue sky above the desert was now filled with menacing dark clouds and torrential rainfall drenched the airfield, sweeping across it like enormous sheets of chain mail. The space cloud had now begun to obscure the sun and although it was still only mid-afternoon at Cancut Mountain, all was in a deep gloom.

'Straight down the stairs to bus Number 3, sir,' shouted a young Infantry Reservist with a clipboard. Professor Bill Duncan stepped out of the front fuselage door of a large army transport plane and into what felt like a wall of intense, wet heat. Global temperatures had now begun to fall once again, but it was still almost 130 Fahrenheit in the Arizona desert.

Bill pulled his black baseball cap firmly down over his eyes, but hot rain lashed under its peak as his gaze took in the scene of energetic activity going on all around. The large military airfield was located beside a mountain range with one central dominant peak which, Bill presumed, had to be Cancut Mountain itself.

Two broad parallel runways, at least two miles long, stretched away into the distance and both the airfield apron and the surrounding skies were filled with noisy aircraft. Despite the poor visibility a dozen large helicopters were either taking off or landing and more were hovering around the perimeter of the airport, waiting their turn to set down. Many of the twin-rotor choppers had large cargo payloads strung in huge container nets beneath their bellies.

Bill turned his face into the driving rain and, shielding his eyes, he saw that two more huge military transport planes had now descended from the dark, lowering clouds and were on final approach, their powerful wing-mounted landing lights brilliant in the rainswept gloom. Presumably they were carrying more people and cargo destined for this underground facility.

As Bill walked carefully down the wet and slippery aircraft steps he saw that beyond the airfield's wire-fence perimeter lay a highway. Both lanes were filled by a long one-way convoy of trucks, cars and buses that was slowly inching towards a large semicircular cavity in the mountain itself, an opening that looked like the entrance to an alpine road tunnel.

An armed National Guardsman in full wet-weather gear was waiting at the door of the bus. He checked Bill's personal ident and his newly issued electronic pass to enter the Cancut Mountain facility – the third such check that Bill had been subjected to since he had started his journey at Andrews Air Force base in Washington – and then nodded for him to board. Behind him followed a gaggle of people, mostly government employees Bill guessed, many of them with families and children. He seemed to be one of only a few travellers who were making the trip into the mountain alone.

The traffic waiting to enter the underground facility was so backed up that it took over an hour for the bus to make its one-mile journey through the mid-afternoon gloom. The vehicle was air-conditioned, but temperatures inside were still so hot that, like all the other passengers, Bill was thankful that water bottles had been provided on every seat.

While they waited in the long queue he had the chance to examine the adjacent vehicles in the convoy. There were other buses transporting more evacuees, but there were also trucks hauling containers whose markings and stickers indicated an extraordinarily wide range of goods and products – food, rubber, candles, bedding, office furniture, books, soap, computers, medical supplies, Bibles. Also waiting patiently in the twin slow-moving lanes to enter the mountain were dozens of military and commercial tankers, although whether they were carrying water, oil or some other liquid or gas Bill couldn't tell.

The torrential rain never ceased throughout the journey but the bright white glow from inside the mountain became steadily brighter. As the bus finally inched into the light, Bill saw that just inside the tunnel the mountain suddenly opened out into a giant cathedral-like cavern that had been carved inside the rock. Its builders had created a vast, brilliantly lit space with a dual-carriage central highway. On either side of the road were large diagonal parking bays for scores of buses, trucks, tankers and smaller vehicles. The main highway continued on through the middle of this gigantic cavern and then, in the far distance, split into two before re-entering tunnels bored into the rock.

Overhead were high steel walkways and gantries from which soldiers with walkie-talkies directed the traffic and oversaw operations on the ground below. As Bill's bus passed by the many occupied and busy parking bays, he saw that huge conveyor belts had been constructed to rapidly offload the contents of the containers and transport them directly into the interior of the mountain. Everywhere there were scenes of frantic activity as military personnel used fork-lift trucks and small mobile cranes to unload the vehicles and ferry the contents to the conveyor belts. Some bays with low concrete walls around them were fitted with large pipe fittings to which tanker drivers had attached hoses and which were busily pumping the vehicles' contents into some distant holding tanks.

Eventually, the coach carrying Bill and his fellow evacuees turned out of the slowly moving column and pulled into a vacant parking bay, alongside three other buses which were now disgorging their own contingents of arrivals.

'Welcome to Cancut Mountain,' said the army driver over the bus's PA system. 'Please report to the table outside that bears the initial of your family name. You will then be provided with transport which will take you to the residential sector of the facility.'

The first thing Bill noticed as he stepped off the bus was that it was cool inside the mountain. Instinctively he looked up to see if he could spot the giant fans or cooling ducts that were working this miracle, but his gaze was blinded by the hundreds of brilliant halogen lamps suspended from high above.

Bill saw that a row of reception booths had been set up – like delegate registration desks at a conference or convention – and above each one was a sign indicating which section of the alphabet they served. Bill hitched his backpack higher on his shoulder and joined the end of a long line waiting in front of the A–D registration desk.

In the middle distance, beyond the reception tables, he saw that there were two rail or tram tracks let into the floor of the cavern. As he watched, a low-slung, open-sided train – like those used for theme-park rides – glided silently up to a raised platform. Twenty or thirty arrivals who had already been through the reception process quickly boarded and the train pulled away to enter yet another tunnel which appeared to head on into the interior of the mountain.

'Professor Duncan?' A young, very attractive woman with a distinctive Southern accent had appeared at Bill's side.

'I'm Sue Snook, Professor Yates's personal assistant,' she announced. 'He sent me to collect you – to spare you all this.' She waved at the long parallel lines queuing in front of the reception desks.

'I'm very grateful,' Bill said as he turned out of the line and followed the smartly dressed PA. He realized that the White House dress code had not been altered just because the administration had relocated to the inside of a mountain.

Des Yates's assistant walked Bill around to the back of the registration table, had a quick word with one of the army men processing those arriving, and then led her charge towards the low platform used for boarding the shuttle trains.

'How long have you been here, inside this mountain?' asked Bill as they waited.

'I came down with Des – with Professor Yates – three days ago,' the PA told him. 'He's hoping to meet with you later this evening.'

More newly processed evacuees joined them on the wooden platform and then a shuttle glided silently alongside.

'This is quite some facility,' Bill said to the young woman as they began their journey into the mountainside.

The PA nodded. 'I think they first started building it almost a century ago – when the government of the time thought that a nuclear war might make the whole country uninhabitable. Every so often various administrations have extended it, added extra accommodation and so on. And, of course, over the last year there's been frantic development work going on here. Navy Seabees are still finishing some of the sectors.'

'How many people can this place house?' asked Bill as they entered a brightly lit tunnel.

'That was the first question I asked,' the assistant told

him with a smile. 'But I didn't get an answer – I think the information may be classified for some reason. But it must be quite a few thousand.'

'And how long can such a population be sustained?' asked Bill.

The PA laughed. 'That was also *my* second question. I was told that there's an underground spring in this mountain which produces 100,000 gallons of fresh hot water a day, which is why they built the bunker here in the first place. They make oxygen from that and they also recycle everything they can. The rumour is that there are sufficient non-reusable supplies to last us for at least twenty years.'

Bill saw a bright light ahead, and then the tunnel exited into another, much smaller, well-lit cavern, which was fitted out like a modern metro station. At the end of the platform a pair of stainless-steel escalators moved silently up and down, connecting to a higher level.

'I'll take you to your domestic quarters,' said Des Yates's PA as they stepped off the shuttle. 'After that I'll show you where they are setting up your new lab.'

THIRTEEN

It was as if a veil was being drawn over the sun. Hour by hour the amount of light and heat reaching the Earth was steadily reduced as the giant cloud of interstellar gas drew closer and came between the planet and its star, its source of life.

The effects were swift and dramatic. After abnormally high temperatures, the abrupt barometric plunge created what seemed to be one giant tropical maelstrom all over the globe. In reality, the world's surface was covered by a series of interlinked hurricanes, typhoons, cyclones and tornadoes.

As forecast, the traditional storm corridors suffered first – the Philippines, Japan, Mexico, Florida and America's Midwest. But within hours, giant vortexes of wind were smashing buildings, property and trees in normally cyclonically calm regions such as France, South Africa, Canada and Moscow. Thousands of people died and tens of thousands more were made homeless.

In those areas that escaped the unprecedented high winds, violent electrical storms rent the thick air as the atmosphere released all the energy that had been created during the rapid heating and cooling process. Nowhere was spared the climatic effects of the cloud's arrival.

Many of the largest storms gathered far out to sea. Huge

cyclonic depressions, larger than any that had formed on Earth since primordial times, created storm perimeters that stretched for thousands of miles. One storm in the northeast Pacific generated internal winds that were too fast to be measured by any of the meteorologists' instruments. Estimates put their velocity at over 300 m.p.h. and media commentators compared the giant storm to those seen on the surface of Jupiter.

Hurricane 67 as it was known – there were now too many storms for fancy naming ceremonies – came ashore all along the length of the California coastline. In the south of the state, shrieking gales overturned delivery vehicles, blew trains off their rails, flung parked wide-body jets across the apron of LAX Airport, knocked trees into cars, ripped roofs off houses and tore windows out of high-rise buildings. Sixty-two large passenger and cargo vessels were lifted from the ocean and deposited on land, and coastal breakwaters were smashed by enormous waves which came ashore as high as six-storey buildings. The Greater Los Angeles basin was flooded to a depth of eleven feet and an estimated 500,000 people died, mostly citizens who were drowned in their home shelters.

In the United Kingdom, 123 square miles of London were flooded following a storm which uprooted almost every tree in southern England. Low-lying parts of the capital and its surrounding area were submerged from Battersea in the west to the Isle of Sheppey in the east. Power was lost throughout the region and initial reports put the death toll at over 60,000.

Similar incidents occurred in almost every country. In France, Normandy, Brittany, the whole of the Loire Valley and most of the Dordogne were lost beneath the flood waters. In Asia, large parts of southern India, most of

Bangladesh and vast swathes of China disappeared beneath the torrents. Millions of people died and initial reports suggested that as many as 200 million people had been made homeless.

'You should see this place,' Bill Duncan enthused. 'It's absolutely huge, more like a city than a bunker. There are shops, restaurants, gyms and swimming pools and it even has a repository which houses the DNA records of all major species on the planet.'

'It sounds amazing,' Sally agreed, as she gazed back at the image of her recent lover. 'You mean they've actually made a back-up of all the life forms on Earth?'

The federal agent was at her desk on the thirty-first floor of the Manhattan headquarters of the US Department of Computer and Network Security. Most of the agency's administration staff had already been released from their posts and the many rows of cubicles on the main floor beyond her office were now unoccupied. Outside, all was in gloom and torrential rain was sluicing down the high windows.

'Well, most of them, just in case of disaster,' said Bill. 'Of course, I've only been shown a small part of this complex. But they must have been preparing for this for many years. Absolutely everything you could wish for is here.'

'Have you seen Des Yates yet?' asked Sally. She had taken Bill's call, even though she had been busily engaged in writing an urgently required summary of current network crime levels for her boss in Washington – or wherever he had relocated to.

'No, not yet,' Bill told her. 'I've been busy getting Jerome's network back up and running again, working with Otto Kramer. Apparently Des is shut away with the President and the NASA people while they are preparing for this last-ditch nuclear strike.'

'God, yes, that's supposed to happen tomorrow, isn't it?' said Sally. 'I have completely lost track – I've been trying to finish an urgent report.'

'Look, Sally,' said Bill, suddenly serious. 'There are still a few military flights due to come down to Cancut Mountain from New York. And there's still a place being held for you here. I can't bear the thought of you being in some grim federal shelter under Central Park when you could be down here with me. What if the worst happens?'

'No, no, my place is here,' insisted Sally. 'But I'm pleased that you're safe. Now, I've got to get back to work.'

'Yeah, me too,' sighed Bill.

Every nation in the world that possessed nuclear warheads raided their armouries for weapons with a payload of more than a megaton. Many of these had been part of secret stocks that were held covertly and in defiance of international treaties and non-proliferation agreements. Four Central African nations, all of them states that had never previously admitted to possessing such weapons, surprised the United Nations, community by offering multiple warheads. And Japan, the nation that had suffered the only hostile use of nuclear weapons during wartime and had publicly forsworn the development of such armaments, shocked the international community by contributing no fewer than 123 nuclear warheads of very advanced design.

All the nuclear devices donated were immediately flown under heavy security to space-shuttle launch sites in either Florida, Beijing or Kazakhstan. There, expert armourers and nuclear weapons engineers worked feverishly to make the many diverse firing and timing systems compatible with a reciprocal radio-controlled central command system.

In space, the components of the Asteroid Defense Network that had not already been deployed in the earlier strike against the cloud were reprogrammed to fly back in the direction of the Earth–sun axis. This was so that they would arrive in the centre of the cloud in synchronization with the many warheads that would be launched from Earth orbit and which could blast off from the surface of the planet itself.

As President Jarvis had promised, crude warhead delivery-rockets had been hurriedly constructed both on Earth and in space under conditions that resembled those of a wartime emergency building programme. By a combination of adapting existing rocket delivery systems and the crash construction of new ones, the combined military powers of the world managed to assemble a fleet of 416 space vehicles that together were able to carry 48,145 nuclear warheads into the centre of the cloud. The total nuclear payload was eight-point-two gigatons and the battery even contained six prototype 'Hafnium' warheads that the United States had been developing secretly. These gamma-ray bombs were each expected to deliver a blast of fifty megatons, equivalent to over 3,000 times the power of the original atomic bombs that were dropped on Hiroshima and Nagasaki at the end of the Second World War.

At eleven a.m. on Tuesday, 4 November (Eastern Time), President Maxwell T. Jarvis, acting on behalf of the UN, gave the order for the entire nuclear payload of the Earth's combined national armouries to be launched against the space cloud. In a series of carefully synchronized launches, rockets, shuttles and cargo spacecraft began to depart from Earth orbit, from surface launch sites and from deep-space locations, The aim was that they should rendezvous in a closely controlled manner inside the cloud. It was now only nine million kilometres away from the Earth and the longest missile flight would take only thirty-six hours.

Observers gazing upwards from the surface of the Earth would see nothing of the attack itself, nor of its results. The entire planet was shrouded in thick rain clouds and the globe was being lashed by powerful storms. All optical Earth-based astronomy was useless, but orbiting telescopes and those parked at deep-space locations were all able to send clear pictures back to the relocated Situation Room that had been set up inside the Cancut Mountain facility.

Desmond Yates, the President, his Chief of Staff, a gaggle of generals, representatives from NASA, members of the Cloud EXCOM and a score of White House aides had crowded into the new Situation Room, a space that would be better described as a 'Situation Theatre', deep inside the vast mountain bunker. They were meeting to observe the effects of the combined nuclear strike on the space cloud.

Having been given the opportunity of recreating the President's control and command facility afresh, a panel of architects and information designers from all the agencies involved had created an amphitheatre-style crisis-management centre with three adjoining conference suites.

The main room's horseshoe-shaped meeting table had places for twenty-six and had been built facing a huge vertical laser display screen, two large holographic display rings and a battery of 3-D high-definition video screens that were suspended from the ceiling and angled downwards for viewing ease.

As the President and his advisers waited for the moment

of the nuclear strike to arrive, each of the screens was displaying images of the cloud that were taken from varying locations in space. The digital counter ticked down towards the first planned detonation and silence fell among those who were seated around the curved table. All present knew that this attack was going to be the last chance to prevent the worst effects of the giant space cloud's collision with the Earth.

'Five, four, three, two, one,' announced an automated voice as the final part of the countdown was reached.

The viewers in the Situation Room saw a pinpoint of light flare from within the multicoloured cloud. It was followed by a dense cluster of other flashes which looked like fireworks going off inside a fog bank. Then the number of explosions became so great that it seemed as if a single giant ball of fire was raging inside the cloud. As they watched, this ball of light became brighter and brighter, like a sun breaking through rain clouds, until finally the telescopes and the optical systems transmitting the images became nothing but pure white-outs.

'Well, it looks like we blew one hell of a hole in it,' said Des Yates tentatively after the members of the meeting had been staring at white screens for thirty or forty seconds.

Then, as the sequence of distant nuclear explosions came to an end, the optical systems began to dim once more and visible images re-emerged. But the giant cloud looked exactly as it had before.

Des Yates glanced from screen to screen. Each was displaying different images of the cloud, some captured from relatively close to it, others from much further out in space.

'We won't know for sure how we have affected the cloud's internal density until we have completed laser measurements,' Yates told the meeting. 'That will take a few hours.'

'Well, it looks damn near the same to me,' said the President. 'We've thrown everything we have at it – and it looks completely unscathed.'

From the *New York Times* website, 4 November 2064

NUCLEAR STRIKE FAILS TO CREATE 'SAFETY WINDOW' FOR EARTH

By RANDALL TATE, science correspondent

Cloud Due to Hit in 8 Days – Sun 20% Obscured

The all-out nuclear strike mounted by the world's combined military forces has failed to disperse sufficient of the oncoming cloud of space gas to create a 'window' through which the Earth can pass safely.

A Pentagon spokesman confirmed yesterday that the equivalent of over 8.2 gigatons of explosive were detonated inside the centre of the cloud but, after the initial creation of a vacuum half a million miles across, the cloud has now reformed to its original density. At its present speed, the outer margins of the cloud will collide with Earth's upper atmosphere in eight days.

Just as the White House and National Security Council designers had taken the opportunity to build an improved Situation Room inside Cancut Mountain, so the Pentagon had built an upgraded version of the facility known as the VWC – the Virtual Warfare Centre.

Necessarily smaller than the huge 'shopping mall' facility that had been constructed beneath Washington, the emergency VWC in Cancut Mountain was a large black room that was itself entirely virtual. Every wall, ceiling and floor space was built from a flexible material that doubled as a 2-D and 3-D high-definition screen.

Approved users of the facility were able to create their own viewing and working space by drawing a fingertip over the room's surfaces so as to create as many different windows into the networks and virtual simulations as required. From dozens of long, thin floor-slots shimmering laser screens could shoot upwards to the ceiling, each capable of displaying a flat 2-D picture or a 3-D image that provided users with 'tactility feedback', a technique that caused sensations to be transmitted via specially equipped gloves. For those who needed to manipulate and adjust them, these virtual images could be 'felt' and 'handled'.

As Desmond Yates entered the dimly lit warfare command centre he glanced around him. Bill Duncan was standing in the middle of a cluster of shimmering, floor-to-ceiling laser screens, each displaying what looked like a galaxy of mathematical formulae, partial formulae and weird hieroglyphs. Standing beside Bill, in a 3-D virtual image so 'solid' that it was hard to tell it was artificial, stood Jerome, pointing at one of the screens as the two of them conferred.

'Your message said this was important,' said Yates as he crossed the room. 'I came as soon as I could get away – but it's just one meeting after another at the moment.'

Bill nodded. 'Well, I'm not sure you're going to like this,' he began. 'But we have found a strong correlation between your original signals from the planet Iso and the transmissions that were recorded from inside the cloud. Both are six-point-one billion times faster than the fastest transmission speed we can currently achieve and both show precisely the same modulation characteristics, boundary marks and data blocking. Both signals also have a median tonic range that is fifty-seven octaves below the lowest threshold of human hearing.'

Des Yates went pale as he listened to the list of similarities between the transmissions.

'You're telling me that the signals are identical?' he asked.

'Identical,' confirmed Jerome, glancing from Bill to the Presidential adviser.

'Although the content remains just as impenetrable in both,' added Bill. 'We're still getting fragments of math and graphic operators, but nothing that adds up to any coherent expression.'

Yates shook his head. 'But this suggests that the signals must have come from the cloud all along, doesn't it?' he said in anguish. 'Perhaps they never did have anything to do with the planet Iso.'

Bill Duncan reached out and laid a hand on Yates's shoulder. He was already beginning to think of this man as a friend and he realized that this latest revelation would cast the most horrendous doubt on the validity of his lifetime's work.

'Everybody was sure that those signals came from Iso,' Bill said, groping for words of consolation.

'Now, everyone, we're transmitting this at maximum power,' Sir Charles Hodgeson told his assembled followers.

'Stare straight into the camera lens and remember when to come in.'

The creator of many science-fiction universes and the dictator of his own small island fiefdom in the Great Barrier Reef was addressing the 120 young people who had chosen to stay with their guru rather than return to their homes at this time of crisis. They were gathered in the main dining and assembly hall that Hodgeson had designed to serve as the central meeting point of his hastily built shelter. Outside, a Force Nine hurricane was lashing the island, uprooting trees, flattening buildings and killing any small creatures who were caught out in the open. Giant waves were pounding the beaches.

He turned his back on the assembled throng, nodded to the audio-visual technician and waited for the transmission light to come on.

'We send greetings from the planet Earth,' intoned Hodgeson sonorously as soon as the light switched to red. 'We are sending this message to the entity within the cloud of gas that is now approaching this planet. We, the people of Earth, wish you no harm. Come in peace.'

As he spoke the last sentence, the tortoise-necked guru raised his arms slowly, as if to heaven. As his words died away, the assembled throng behind him repeated, 'Come in peace. Come in peace.'

Hodgeson waited for the echoes of the powerful chant to die away, then he crossed his arms diagonally over his chest.

'We apologize for the explosive weapons that our foolish leaders have sent against you,' he continued, his voice ringing out loud and strong from his wizened frame. 'But these puny armaments are now exhausted. Come in peace.'

As Hodgeson raised his arms again his followers took

their cue and, in a deep-throated roar, chanted in unison, 'Come in peace. Come in peace.'

'Sir Charles?' It was the audio-visual technician calling from where he was seated at a small broadcast console. 'There's a problem.'

The ancient guru spun round to face the man who had so rudely interrupted his broadcast.

'We're off air,' said the AV engineer. 'The transmission masts must have been torn away by the storm.'

Hodgeson stared at the man, his face working in fury. Then he spun back to face his followers.

'Everybody. Get outside now and get those masts up again. There's no time to lose.'

'Sir Charles, the winds outside are blowing at over a hundred and fifty miles an hour,' protested the AV technician, rising to his feet. 'We'll have to wait until the storm passes.'

'OUTSIDE NOW!' shouted the centenarian guru to his followers. 'GET THOSE MASTS UP AGAIN *NOW!*'

From the *New York Times* website, 12 November 2064

24 HOURS TILL CLOUD STRIKES

By RANDALL TATE, science correspondent

Rain Turns to Hail and Snow

The U.S. Meteorological Office reports that the approaching cloud of space gas is now preventing over 60% of the sun's normal output from reaching the surface of the Earth. It will collide with the Earth's atmosphere at 4.37 EST tomorrow.

As temperatures have fallen from their extreme highs of recent weeks, the torrential rains experienced all over the world are now starting to turn to sleet, hail and snow. The Federal Emergency Management Agency warns all citizens to remain indoors and not to travel unless absolutely necessary.

Sally Burton stood at the window of her office on the thirty-first floor of the CNS building in Manhattan. Outside, the sleet that had been falling continuously for two days was beginning to turn to thick snow. All was in a deep and pervasive gloom and the agent could hardly see across Federal Plaza to where some lights were still burning in other government buildings. In recent hours more and more floors had started to go dark as the various agencies and departments allowed increasing numbers of staff to abandon their posts for the safety of the bunkers.

In Sally's own office, only she and five others were still monitoring the networks but on-line activity had not abated. As humans withdrew from the physical world all their contacts and activities moved into the networks. The criminals, child-pornpeddlers, cyber-terrorists and confidence tricksters were still pursuing their warped desires and plying their criminal trades as if determined to make the most of the time left before disaster struck.

Her communicator rang, cutting into her short reverie.

'Hey, Sal,' said Bill Duncan. 'How are things in New York?'

'Very white,' Sally told him, choosing not to select visual. 'We've got very heavy snowfall now. I can hardly see across the square.'

'When are you going to the shelter?' Bill asked abruptly.

'I'm not sure,' she told him. 'Things are still crazy in the networks.'

'Sal, you've *got* to get to safety before the cloud hits,' urged Bill. 'Nobody knows for sure what's going to happen. I want to know you're in a shelter before it gets here.'

The CNS agent sat back down at her desk and sighed heavily. 'Bill, I know that we're fond of each other. But we haven't really had long enough together to develop the sort of relationship that gives you the right to order me about.'

Sally heard the silence as her blow hit home and she immediately regretted being so harsh.

'I'm sorry,' she said quickly. 'I've been working very long hours – I'm completely on edge.'

'Me too,' said Bill. 'And what you said is true: you're right. I don't have any right to ask you to do anything. It's just that all the time I'm working with Jerome to try to make some sense out of these goddam signals, I keep worrying about you. You already mean a lot to me, Sally.'

She glanced out at the snow flurries whirling against her window and she suddenly wondered if she would ever see this man again.

'Let's do visual,' she said, touching the appropriate icon on her communicator.

God, he looks tired too, Sally thought as Bill's image appeared on her wall screen. He was wearing a black T-shirt and was sitting on the edge of a narrow bed in a small white room that had no windows. He looked as if he hadn't shaved in a week.

'They now want us to work alongside the techies, just to keep the networks open,' she explained. 'I don't know for how long.'

'I understand,' Bill said with a shrug. 'But keep me in the loop, OK?'

'Of course I will,' Sally told him, feeling as if she wanted to reach out and touch his image.

FOURTEEN

At 21.52 GMT on Thursday, 11 November, the leading edge of the high-velocity space cloud began to collide with the Earth's outer atmosphere – precisely as predicted and precisely on schedule.

The cloud was travelling at over 200,000 kilometres an hour and although its outer regions were very thin and had little density, the friction caused by the collision of gas particles was so great that a bright crimson glow immediately pervaded the half of the Earth's ionosphere that was directly in the cloud's path.

On the dark and frozen planet down below almost every human being and many of their domesticated animals were taking whatever shelter they could find. For a wealthy minority of the world's population the sealed refuges they had built were almost as comfortable as their normal living accommodation had been. But for most humans it was a case of finding whatever protection they could against the biting cold, the driving blizzards and the other unknown horrors or blights that the space cloud was about to impose upon the globe. Most of the people who had gone to ground were now reduced to helplessly watching their fate unfold on television.

It was only when the Earth and the giant pool of interstellar space gas were seen in close proximity, and from a distance, that the true scale of the cloud's enormous size could be properly appreciated. Even as the leading edge of the cloud struck the Earth's atmosphere, its tail was only just leaving the sun.

'We look like a pea in the path of a tidal wave,' said Maxwell Jarvis in awe as he stared at the holographic image of the Earth and its unwelcome visitor.

The President and the members of the Cloud EXCOM were meeting in the Situation Room inside Cancut Mountain, Arizona, and the hologram was being projected as a large and realistic model in the main holo-theatre. Although many of Earth's orbiting satellites had now been either blown out of position or destroyed, and despite the cloud's powerful magnetic field disrupting Earth's outgoing radio signals, images captured by telescopes in deep space were still being received on the ground. These pictures were being amalgamated and morphed into powerful three-dimensional simulations that gave those present an almost godlike view of happenings within the local region of the solar system

'Look at that bright red glow in the Earth's upper atmosphere,' exclaimed Des Yates, also in awe, even though he was one of the few members of the party who had an astronomer's understanding of the physics involved. 'We knew it would cause friction as the gases heat up, but that is stupendous.'

'It's not going to explode, is it?' demanded President Jarvis sharply. The nerves of all those who were meeting in the Situation Room were on edge, extremely so. These cloud-monitoring meetings had been continuing daily – and nightly – for the last few weeks.

'We're pretty sure not, sir,' Des Yates told him quickly.

'If we couldn't get the gas to ignite with eight-point-two gigatons of nuclear weapons, it's not likely to do so now.'

The President nodded and turned to an aide. 'Let's see what the news channels are saying.'

Immediately a score of large flat screens suspended around and above the 3-D holo-theatre lit with video feeds that were streaming in from television broadcasts all around the world.

Des Yates looked up at one screen that was showing a snowbound city scene with the caption, *Calcutta*. As the Presidential adviser focused on the screen the clever technology in the Situation Room automatically sensed his gaze and delivered acoustically guided sound to his ears only. The others around the curved table were looking at different screens and they too were able to hear the commentary in which they were interested while the audio components of all other broadcasts were blanked.

As Yates watched he saw a dim red glow start to appear on the surface of the snow in Calcutta. Then he swivelled in his high-backed chair and switched his gaze to a screen displaying a shot of a frozen Sydney Harbour. The famous bridge could still be made out clearly through the steady snowfall, but the distinctive armadillo shape of the old Opera House was now just one immense white blob. As the camera slowly panned Yates saw that the entire harbour was frozen and the ice on its surface was also starting to take on a deep red glow.

'Now, stick together,' ordered Charles Hodgeson. 'We don't want to be outside for more than a few minutes.'

The top-level exit from the shelter opened onto the central ridge of Orpheus Island. Immediately Hodgeson and his half-dozen specially chosen acolytes saw that the snow-covered atoll and the lowering clouds overhead were all bathed in a deep red glow. But snow was no longer falling and the high winds had abated.

'Come on,' said Hodgeson eagerly as he led the way up a small path that had been cleared of snow. 'It's always possible that our visitor will respond to a personal appeal.'

All members of the party were dressed in Arctic survival suits and all wore thick perspex masks to protect their eyes. Once on top of the central ridge, Hodgeson stood and extended his arms sideways. His followers stood in a line on either side of him and did likewise, joining hands to form a small human chain.

'We bid you welcome,' shouted Hodgeson into the still air, his breath coming out of his small, wiry body as a stream of mist.

'We bid you welcome,' echoed the four men and one woman who had been selected to join in this attempt to make direct personal contact.

'We mean you no harm,' Hodgeson shouted at the top of his voice towards the red-tinged snow clouds. 'Please tell us what you want. But come in peace.'

'Come in peace,' shouted the supporting chorus.

Suddenly two snowmobiles crested the island's main ridge and made directly for where the little party stood.

The rider of the lead vehicle drew up close to Hodgeson and switched off his engine.

'All the transmitters are operational once more, Sir Charles,' he reported. 'We've doubled up on the stays so they won't come down again.'

Hodgeson gazed up at the thick red clouds as if hoping for some sort of response.

'Very good,' he said eventually, banging his thick gloves

together to warm up his hands. 'Let's get back inside and resume our transmissions.'

Three days after the leading edge of the space cloud first made contact with the Earth's atmosphere, Des Yates was still in the Situation Room staring at a holographic image of the cloud's eccentric trajectory across outer space and through the solar system.

The official meeting of the Cloud EXCOM had broken up six hours after the collision had first begun. The images that were sent back from the deep-space telescopes showed that the cloud had now engulfed the planet completely. Remotely operated TV cameras positioned around the surface of the globe revealed that by day all of the snowy and frozen outside world was bathed in a deep red gloom. By night the heat produced by the collision of high-speed particles with the upper ionosphere produced a neon-blue glow, almost like the output from an ultraviolet lamp.

It seemed that there was nothing that the Cloud EXCOM members could do except watch TV reports being beamed from news centres which were themselves based in underground facilities dotted around the world.

The President, his executive team and their advisers were now elsewhere in the Cancut Mountain facility, busily engaged in managing the crisis that was unfolding across the USA and the rest of the world. All the USA's shelters in overseas embassies, consulates and foreign government offices needed to be coordinated and debriefed and there were over 400 government-run underground facilities in the homeland to be managed.

Senior Pentagon officers had to oversee the rotation of the select military units that had been left above ground to continue policing sensitive locations across the nation.

There were also massive logistical challenges as supplies were moved around the country, all by air. A number of key airports were being kept open by hard-working army and navy engineers, even though temperatures were beginning to fall close to the lowest operational limits of some large jets.

In each city, a few public hospitals had created sealed accommodation units to continue treating those who were injured or suffering from hypothermia. But American TV reports suggested that citizens were now starting to die in their thousands – mainly as the result of flooding or from exposure to the extreme cold. There was a great deal to keep the President and his executive staff busy.

But Des Yates had remained in the Situation Room almost continuously. He was sure that if he could accurately model the forces that were acting on the cloud's trajectory and its variable velocity he would be able to learn more about its internal physics. As a result, he might gain some clue that would be helpful in dealing with the crisis.

With the assistance of the Situation Room Director, a rotating cluster of keen duty officers and specialist input from half a dozen senior NASA astrophysicists, he had mapped the gravity force fields through which the cloud had travelled. He had created long strings of equations to feed into the computers, trying to determine what forces might be affecting the cloud and directing its course and speed. In doing so, he hoped to arrive at an estimate of what level of propulsive energy, if any, the cloud might be generating internally.

But it appeared that the cloud's behaviour had been wholly erratic. For the first few months of its approach towards the solar system it had obeyed the laws of local gravity precisely, but then it seemed as if it had started reacting to some other force, an unknown one.

Yates and his small team had built complex models of solar-wind emissions and had then run simulations of a similar-sized space cloud approaching the solar system. They had run the model with both gravity and solar wind modelled, then with just one of the forces. Neither simulation produced a trajectory that matched the course which the actual cloud had taken. Then Yates thought he should model light itself, in case for some reason the cloud was light-sensitive. That didn't help either. Then he decided to model the thermal energy that is found throughout the solar system and beyond. That small additional calculation alone had taken twenty-eight hours to create and run.

Then one of the NASA scientists had suggested that they should model the huge but very weak gravity waves that sweep through the galaxy from time to time. That involved digging out all the data from gravity-wave observations that had been carried out over the last two years and then creating a whole new set of equations so that the model could take in the effects of such giant ripples in space. Then they had to model local gravity, solar wind, light, thermal energy and gravity waves together, and in varying proportions. In total their modelling efforts had taken almost three days and Yates knew that he was now close to dropping from fatigue.

'How are you doing in here, Des?' called a voice from within the blackness outside the brightly lit holo-theatre.

Yates straightened up, massaged his lower back with both hands and shook his head wearily as Bill Duncan stepped into the light.

'Getting nowhere, fast,' he told the computer psychologist. 'You?'

'The same,' admitted Bill. 'It feels as though I'm almost there, but I'm missing something important. If only I had more processing power – there's just too much data to deal with.'

Yates nodded and yawned. 'Well, I've tried everything.' he said, reaching for his jacket. 'Gravity, solar wind, visible light, thermal energy – even gravity waves. Nothing can explain the peculiar trajectory this darn thing came in on, nor its changes in velocity. Anyway, I've had it. I'm going to call it a night, or day, or whatever the hell it is outside.'

'Have you tried modelling radio waves?' asked Bill.

Yates was pulling on his jacket as the computer scientist spoke. He froze halfway, with only one arm in a sleeve.

'Radio,' he repeated. 'But radio hardly has any force at all, does it?' Then he took his arm out of his jacket sleeve. 'You're right, though, we *should* have modelled the radio spectrum!'

'How are the networks holding up?' asked Mort Jaffe, speaking on a secure line from the safety of CNS's own agency bunker just outside Washington DC.

'They're still functioning OK, sir, but activity is rising so fast that I can't do any more than monitor the traffic,' Sally Burton told her boss. 'There's a lot of bad stuff going down, but I can't track it all on my own.'

'Well, they're all going to crawl out of the woodwork now,' said Jaffe. 'All support systems still OK in the office?'

'We've still got heat and light, sir,' confirmed the agent. 'But the air seems a little thin sometimes.'

'You're doing a great job,' said Jaffe. 'Now, what I want you to do is to shut down every system in the building except your own personal node. Got that?'

'Of course, sir,' she responded.

'I'll be in touch again once you've done that so that I can release you from your post. You can then get up to Central Park before it gets too bad. OK?'

'Yes, thank you, sir,' said Agent Burton as she closed the connection.

She rose from her desk.

Before it gets too bad, she thought as she gazed out at the eerie scene of a dark snowbound Federal Plaza. The square was bathed in a deep red gloom and beyond she could see the huge snowdrifts that had been piled up high across Broadway. In the other direction, drifts had long since closed Thomas Street. Now there were very few lights burning in the surrounding government buildings. Even the large FBI block was completely dark.

Sally tilted her head downwards at an acute angle and looked towards the ground. Nothing was moving and the snow down below looked very deep.

'That had better be soon, Mort,' she said out loud.

'It's radio-sensitive!' yelled Des Yates excitedly. 'In fact, it's specifically attracted to artificial radio signals, to man-made signals. Just look at it go!'

They had now run the new simulation six times, and every time the computer model of the cloud moved in exactly the same way and on the same path as the actual space cloud had done.

'Look, when we first noticed the cloud it was heading directly for the Earth, the main source of artificial radio signals in this region of the galaxy,' said Yates, repeating himself for the umpteenth time. 'Then, when the Martian colony started to gear up to launch the first nuclear attack, the cloud was attracted to all those powerful radio emissions they were pumping out, because Mars was so much closer to the cloud than we were.'

Des Yates and Bill Duncan were once more back in the Situation Room. As soon as Bill had suggested modelling radio waves, Yates had asked the NASA assistants to begin to create a model of all of the known radio transmissions in the solar system, and in the area of deep space immediately beyond.

'This is going to take hours and hours to prep, Professor,' one of the ever-helpful duty officers had warned.

'OK, let's both grab some rest, Bill,' Yates had told his new research colleague. 'Then we'll be better prepared to see if your idea produces any results.'

They had met back in the Situation Room after only six hours' sleep, but both men felt immensely refreshed.

'I really ought to get back to my own work on the cloud's internal radio signals,' said Bill reluctantly, wanting to remain with the astronomers to see whether there was any value in his idea.

'Stay and see the first few runs,' suggested Yates. 'If we don't get anything quickly it will rapidly become boring because then we'll have to start combining data from all of the other possible forces.'

But Bill's idea had provided a quick breakthrough, even though this was only achieved after the enormous amount of work that had gone into building the simulation. The NASA astronomers had drafted in help from other science staff sheltering within the Cancut facility. They had entered data into the computer simulation which represented the vast radio outpourings from the sun, the enormous artificial radio output from the Earth, the radio emissions from orbiting satellites and space stations, from deep-space telescopes, probes and spacecraft and from the colonies on the moon and, as had once been, on Mars.

Their first run had been inconclusive, with the simulated cloud veering sharply towards the sun as soon as it reached the outer boundaries of the solar system.

'OK, eliminate the sun's natural radio output,' said Yates. 'And let's run the model again.'

This time the holographic grey mass of the simulated cloud approached the 3-D model of the solar system precisely in the same trajectory, as marked by a red line, that the real cloud had followed.

Then, at just the same point, the simulated cloud had changed direction and headed directly for Mars.

Yates had then ordered the simulation to be halted. He asked for data on the radio output from Mars and its artificial satellites to be displayed within the simulation.

'Look, it changed course for Mars as soon as their radio output shot up,' Yates had observed excitedly the first time he saw the simulation. 'And even the little kinks in its trajectory reflect the radio output of nearby radio telescopes. Magnificent!'

As the simulation had continued its run all present watched with fascination as the 3-D model of the cloud followed precisely the red line that indicated the actual cloud's collision with Mars, its sling-shot orbit around the sun and then its direct approach towards Earth.

'It seems to be responsive both to gravity *and* to modulated radio signals,' said Yates now, after they had run the simulation a dozen more times. 'Specifically, it is attracted to *artificial* radio signals – and we're still sending out so much radio and TV traffic that the Earth is lit up like a goddam Christmas tree!'

*

Within the hermetically sealed offices of the *New York Times*, the process of news gathering and reporting was continuing. But there was a severe shortage of in-field reporters and TV crews and there were almost no studio guests available to make contributions. Journalists were often reduced to interviewing other journalists as if they were experts – but there was nothing new in that.

The *NYT* management had assigned science correspondent Randall Tate to provide a daily half-hour TV update on the cloud's progress and on conditions around the globe, a bulletin which could be looped to repeat automatically every two hours. The senior anchorman who would previously have been fronting such a broadcast had decamped with his much younger wife and their baby to a luxury underground shelter which had been built by private enterprise in Northern Florida.

But Tate was nothing if not inventive. Working with his producer he edited his own commentary, and the views of his colleagues, together with the pictures that were continuing to stream in from all over the world.

Outside, temperatures were still dropping rapidly as less and less of the sun's warmth managed to penetrate the mass of the space cloud that was now engulfing the globe. Snow was still falling steadily everywhere, rivers had become solid ice and even the oceans were starting to freeze over.

As predicted, there had been a sudden increase in the number of seismic events being recorded. Despite its relatively thin density, the cloud's gravitational mass was already distorting and disrupting the delicate equilibrium of the Earth's crust and mantle. Major earthquakes had shaken cities as far apart as Seattle and Auckland, and undersea earthquakes had produced vast tsunami waves which, had it not been for the moderating effects of the surface ice on the oceans, would have devastated coastlines from Japan to Chile. Volcanoes were also erupting, all along the line of the world's so-called 'Ring of Fire', that long chain of active volcanoes which circled the Pacific Rim. But most of the world's population had already taken shelter and these eruptions claimed far fewer human lives than they would have done under normal conditions.

But the world's data networks – laser, cable, radio, microwave and landline – were still functioning well. Their original designs were over a century old, but they had been built to withstand nuclear strikes.

'This is Randall Tate in the *New York Times* Television Centre,' read the science correspondent as he began to record his day's broadcast. 'The US Meteorological Office reports that the world's atmosphere is beginning to lose some of its oxygen content. In many parts of the world unassisted breathing at sea level has become the equivalent of trying to breathe at an altitude of 10,000 feet. The Met scientists advise everybody to stay indoors and keep respirators to hand.'

The producer cut in pictures that had just been received from a San Francisco TV outlet. The feed showed images of a snowbound city, but smoke could be seen rising from its hilly centre.

'San Francisco has been hit by a second earthquake in six days,' read Tate. 'The quake measured Magnitude Six on the Richter scale but with all normal emergency services suspended and many citizens already sheltering, there is no information available about casualties. Major earthquakes have also been reported in Mexico City and Istanbul.'

The incoming images now switched to a group of small huts in a snowbound savannah.

'In Africa, millions of people are starting to die from

pneumonia, hypothermia, frostbite and starvation. In many of the poorest regions almost no provision has been made to allow the population to shelter. Most aid agencies have ceased to function in the field but those that remain report that the death toll is expected to rise sharply.'

'And you're certain there is no mistake?' queried the President. 'No possibility whatsoever that you've got your sums wrong?'

Maxwell Jarvis was seated at the centre of the horse-shoe-shaped conference table in the Situation Room deep inside Cancut Mountain. With him were the members of the Cloud EXCOM, his Chief of Staff, senior White House adviser Desmond Yates and, a new attendee at such exalted meetings, ex-MIT Professor Bill Duncan – now a man who could boast the government's highest level of security clearance.

'None at all,' confirmed Des Yates. He was standing beside the main holo-theatre and he had twice demonstrated the computer simulation of the cloud's trajectory towards the Earth. 'Once Professor Duncan suggested that the cloud might be attracted to radio waves, it only took us two attempts to get this result. In fact, we are now certain that the cloud homes in specifically on artificial radio signals, those that are modulated and produced by electronic or digital technologies.'

'Why would that be?' asked Jarvis with a frown. 'How could a cloud of gas be specifically attracted to man-made radio signals.'

'We've no idea, sir,' admitted Yates. 'Our next task is to try to find out. We're going to refine our simulation to discover whether the cloud is more sensitive to one range of frequencies than to another, and to see if it homes in on any one type of radio wave in particular. We have already started recalibrating the models, but as yet we don't know the cause of the attraction.'

'Still, this is good work,' said Jarvis. 'Very good work.' Then he turned to the newcomer at the table. 'And what made you think that the cloud might be radio-sensitive, Professor Duncan?'

Bill was aware of all eyes turning towards him. Despite the bizarre circumstances of living and working inside the US government bunker deep underground, it had still been something of a shock to be introduced to the President of the United States in the flesh for the first time an hour earlier.

'It was just a lucky guess, sir,' he admitted, automatically slipping the little honorific into his reply. 'I suppose I've been spending so much time working with radio signals recently that it was the first thing that came to my mind.'

'Very well,' said Jarvis, glancing around the table. 'So if this goddam thing *has* homed in on our radio output, what should we do now?'

Everyone in the meeting looked at everyone else.

Yates cleared his throat purposefully. 'We must try to shut down all our radio transmissions on Earth and in this part of the solar system,' he announced firmly. 'The cloud moved quickly on from Mars once all radio signals on that planet had been silenced. We have to shut down everything on Earth and hope that the cloud will continue on its way as soon as possible.'

'Is that feasible?' Yates asked the other committee members seated at the table.

'The theory sounds good, sir,' said Roy Wilcox, NASA's director. 'My scientific staff helped Professor Yates build that simulation and I have no doubt that it is accurate. The problem is, how could we shut down all forms of radio communication around the world?'

'Sir, we can't just shut down all radio transmissions,' interjected General Thomas Nicholls, Head of the Joint Chiefs. 'The entire world depends on radio for communication. Every airplane, every ship, every car, every communicator, even our domestic phones – they all use radio these days. All our weapon systems are controlled by radio, as are our satellites, our navigation systems, military and civilian communications, navigation, the internet, private networks, domestic networks and personal body networks. Even cans of beans on supermarket shelves talk to stock-control systems by radio. Society can't function without it.'

As the general paused for breath his commander-in-chief held up a hand to halt the speech.

'Thank you, General Nicholls,' said Jarvis. 'But society isn't exactly functioning normally at present, is it? What would be the impact on *military* operations if we could shut down all radio transmissions?'

The general shrugged. 'Well, the military would be better off than most sectors. We do have back-up cable and landline connections between strategic command posts and to our nuclear weapons control centres – not that we've got much payload left to worry about.'

'And what about inter-government communications?' Jarvis asked, turning to Coleville Jackson, the Secretary of State.

'We've also got landline links to all our overseas embassies, and we've got emergency landline connections to most foreign-government HQs,' Jackson explained. 'I believe they were put in as a fail-safe system years ago, just in case someone interrupted radio communications and impersonated a national leader or a strategic commander. I guess if we told other governments what we were doing, they could also switch to cable communications. Then we could ask them to turn off their radio systems, shut down their broadcasters and so on.'

'Mr President?' It was Des Yates. He had been listening as the committee members debated the pros and cons of shutting down the world's radio transmissions and now he stepped forward to stand in the centre of the space created by the curved conference table.

'I don't think we've got time to discuss this with other governments,' he began. 'First, they're all busy struggling to deal with this crisis as it affects their own people. Second, they will all want to create models and simulations of the cloud for themselves. They won't just take our word for it, nor will they switch off all their radio transmissions and national media just because we ask them to. It will take weeks, if not months, to get them to agree and even then there's bound to be some who won't. But we don't *have* weeks or months, do we? If this crisis continues for another five weeks there won't be any atmosphere left around our planet.'

His blunt observations were greeted with silence. Then one or two people around the table nodded.

'Are you suggesting that the cloud will leave once there are no more radio signals being transmitted from Earth?' asked the President eventually, a strong note of scepticism in his voice.

'It might, if we ordered *Friendship* to start broadcasting,' said Yates, the excitement growing in his voice as the idea flowered in his mind. 'She's just crossing Pluto's orbit at present, on her way out of the solar system, and she has so much radio transmitting power on board that she's almost like a mini-Earth in herself!'

All stares were fixed on Yates.

'We fitted her out with powerful transmitters so that she could start broadcasting to the Isonians as she approached their planet,' continued Yates, twisting in his seat to address everyone. 'Or, at least, what we thought of as the Isonian planet. She's got the most incredible archives of our material, television news, documentaries, years and years of the stuff – everything we thought the Isonians would want. She could just turn all her antennae to point back towards Earth and turn up the volume!'

Now there was a silence in the room as the group considered the idea.

'It sounds like a very long shot to me,' said General Thomas Nicholls after a drawn-out pause.

'We've proven the cloud is radio-sensitive – it homes in on radio transmissions,' insisted Yates. '*Friendship* is already travelling at over two-point-eight million kilometres an hour – perhaps she could lure the cloud away, out of our solar system. We must at least give it a try, sir!'

Maxwell Jarvis sat back in his chair, considered for a moment and then gave a small nod of assent. 'Professor Yates is right. We must do something, even if it *is* a long shot. So how could we shut down all the world's radio transmissions without going through normal diplomatic channels?'

'I think the Pentagon may be able to help with this one, sir,' said Colonel Dr Otto Kramer, rising to his feet.

FIFTEEN

'OK, get the hell out of there, Agent Burton,' ordered Mort Jaffe, CNS's National Director. 'Get up to the Central Park shelter as quickly as you can. But be careful, there are reports that looters are still out on the streets.'

Sally Burton removed the oxygen mask from her mouth. 'Very good, sir,' she said into her communicator. 'This facility is secure.'

She closed the connection and then lifted the fire extinguisher she had placed in readiness on her desk. Outside, in the main office, an open fire was burning fiercely. She had disabled the sprinkler system, stripped back the carpet tiles to expose the concrete flooring and had then built a bonfire of wooden office furniture in an attempt to keep warm. The main power supply to the building had failed three hours earlier and although the emergency generators had kicked in, they weren't supplying enough energy to bring the heating level up to the point where it could compete with the freezing conditions outside.

Agent Burton had immediately reported in to the CNS Washington shelter, but had only been able to leave a message on her boss's voicemail. She confirmed that she had shut down all the department's monitoring systems, told him that the main power supplies to the building had failed and had then asked for permission to leave her post and head for safety.

While she waited to hear back from Mort Jaffe she had built the bonfire and had then made preparations for her journey uptown. In the next office she had a chemically heated Arctic survival suit made of bright orange material, with boots and face mask, all ready to put on. Her military-style backpack included a small shovel, a pick, a torch, some high-protein food bars, two changes of underwear and some minimal make-up. Beside the suit she had laid out her laser-sighted Walther Mk II .38 automatic along with four sixteen-shot magazines, each fully loaded. She also had two mini-cylinders with top-up oxygen sufficient for six hours, a water bottle and two communicators.

Stepping out of her office and onto the main floor, Sally allowed herself to bask momentarily in the heat of the flames being produced by her makeshift bonfire. Smoke had blackened the ceiling tiles and was now billowing all around the office and, after a few moments of welcome warmth, she raised the fire extinguisher and doused the flames thoroughly. She kicked the remains of the bonfire apart to be sure that it would not reignite and then she turned away to prepare for her journey uptown.

Fifteen minutes later, Sally Burton began to descend the first flight of stairs that would lead her down thirty-one floors to the street-level emergency exit. She carried her snow boots and face mask in her arms but, even without wearing these encumbrances, her heavy survival suit was going to make her descent long, slow and uncomfortable.

'Don't worry about security clearances,' President Jarvis had ordered the Pentagon computer scientist testily. 'This is no time to worry about things like that. Just tell us what your high-tech toys can do.'

When Dr Otto Kramer had first risen to his feet to address the Cloud EXCOM and its advisers he had prefaced his remarks with a warning. He had told the meeting that he was going to have to describe a weapon of virtual warfare whose existence was unknown to most people in the room. Then he had said, 'And there are many people present who do not have the necessary level of clearance to gain such knowledge.'

After the President's swift rebuke and instruction to get on with it, Kramer had rapidly made a full presentation on the network-acquisition system known as Jerome.

'In full weapons mode, Jerome can penetrate and acquire every processor, every chip and every network in the world that controls or delivers radio transmission,' Kramer said as he came to the conclusion of his short description of the weapon. 'And today, every radio system on Earth and in space *is* controlled by some sort of processor. Within a few days every computer processor and every network on this planet and in space will be under our control. As General Nicholls has explained, we will still be able to maintain command of our own forces by landline and we will also be able to communicate with our embassies and with overseas governments by the same means. But once Jerome is deployed no one will be able to prevent us from shutting down all radio broadcasts. We can achieve complete global radio silence within a week.'

There was a quiet mumbling around the table as the EXCOM members digested the import of his words.

Bill Duncan had felt a chill steal over him as the Pentagon weapons developer enthusiastically described the degree of global control that his system could achieve.

And how will you regain control of the networks after that?
Bill wanted to ask – was bursting to ask. But at the start of
the meeting he had been privileged enough to share in the
official briefing on the cloud's effects on the planet and he
knew just how bad things were on the outside. He also
understood that there were only a few weeks left in which
they could try *anything* to escape from the grip of the cloud
– no matter how long a shot it might be. He held his tongue,
but the taste of disapproval was metallic in his mouth.

'What do you need from me?' asked President Jarvis.

Otto Kramer walked back to his place at the table,
opened a black folder and extracted a single white sheet,
with the Bald Eagle seal of the United States of America
embossed at the top. Crossing to the centre of the table, he
laid the document squarely and precisely in front of the
President.

'Sir, I need your signature on this official order before
Jerome can be deployed in full weapons mode,' he said.

The President picked up the single sheet and scanned
it. Then he glanced towards the three four-star generals who
represented America's military forces. Each man gave a
short nod. Then Jarvis turned his gaze to those members of
his cabinet and the agency principals who had been seconded to the Cloud EXCOM. One by one, each assented,
either by a quiet spoken 'Yes', or with a nod of the head.

Then Bill Duncan felt the President's level gaze fall on
him. At first he tried not to meet the man's stare directly.
He was not a member of the government, nor was he an
official adviser; he had no say in this. He waited, expecting
Jarvis to turn to another, but in the end he was forced to
meet the President's gaze. A single eyebrow rose, requiring
a response.

Bill Duncan felt himself give a clumsy half-nod, as if

something deeper than his forebrain was fighting against his decision.

'Very well,' said the President. 'I will sign this now, but give me twelve hours to speak to the leaders of the major nations. If we're going to unleash this weapon on their networks, they need to know what we're doing, and why.'

He picked up a pen that lay beside his blotting pad. With a quick flurry he signed the order and then waited while an aide stepped in and applied the great Seal of the United States to the bottom of the page.

Encumbered by her bulky orange survival suit, it took Sally Burton almost twenty minutes to walk down the emergency stairs of the thirty-one-storey federal building. When she finally arrived at the bottom, she switched on her suit's internal heating system, pulled on her boots and slipped her face mask over her head, ready to be pulled down against the freezing weather outside. Just before she had left her office, a wall thermometer had told her that the external temperature had now fallen to minus twenty degrees Celsius.

With backpack securely in place and her gun zipped tightly into her suit's breast pouch, she pulled on her gloves, attached them to her sleeves and then bore down hard on the horizontal bar that would open the fire-escape door to the street outside. The bar moved downwards, but as Sally applied her weight the door opened outwards for only a foot or so, and then stuck firm. She could see that snow was piled high against the doors from the outside, making it impossible for them to open fully. She put her shoulder to the door and heaved, but it refused to open any further.

Instinctively, Sally glanced back up the dark stairwell that she had just descended. She knew there were other emergency exits from the building, but she would have to climb back up several flights before she could traverse a floor and then descend down another stairwell to an alternative exit. And that exit was just as likely to be blocked by snow.

It was almost four o'clock on a Thursday afternoon in mid-November. Outside, the deep red glow that now passed for daylight was already beginning to take on the surreal blue tinge common to these strange evenings, Sally decided to work to clear the doorway in front of her, rather than spend more time hiking to another exit that was just as likely to require a similar amount of effort before she could escape.

After ten minutes of agonizing and back-breaking work, the agent finally managed to push the fire-exit door open wide enough for her to pass through. She had spent the time scooping snow from outside the door with her small shovel and throwing it to one side, work which required her to wear both face mask and gloves, and to stop frequently to step back inside the stairwell to take small top-ups from her oxygen supply.

Now she waited until she had recovered her breath in the thinning atmosphere. Then she pulled on her mask, pulled her hood tight and waded out through the banked snow onto Duane Street.

In the gloom she saw that the street was clearest at its centre; until a few days ago the city's snowploughs had been trying to keep the roads around Federal Plaza open.

Once in the centre of the street, Sally found the snow to be only a few inches deep and she turned to the right and began to walk steadily eastwards towards Broadway.

Lower Manhattan looked like the set of a disaster movie. Drifts were piled high against gaunt and blacked-out buildings and the smaller side streets of the financial district were completely blocked with snow and abandoned vehicles. There was no street lighting and no shop windows were lit. Over everything hung the deep magenta and blue pall caused by the friction of the space cloud as it tore at the Earth's precious atmosphere high above.

At Broadway, Sally turned left to begin her journey uptown towards Central Park. She had a little over four miles to walk and, once again, the centre of the road provided the easiest passage. As she trudged steadily northwards she noticed that the snow in the very centre of Broadway had been compacted into a high gloss by many other feet that had trodden this path before her. She halted, and then looked warily around, the impaired visibility caused by her suit's enveloping hood and her face mask forcing her to turn her whole body through 180 degrees to scan all aspects of the broad highway. Nothing moved in the red-tinted snowy cityscape.

Removing a glove, she undid her front-pouch zipper halfway and felt for the comforting hardness of her pistol butt. Once she'd put her glove back on, she continued her march northwards.

Sally skirted SoHo to the east, passed the Museum of Contemporary Art, crossed Houston Street and arrived outside the deserted New York University building. She saw no lights and no movement on the streets or in any of the buildings. It was now almost five-thirty and the night sky had taken on its new distinctive blue tinge as energy from the atmospheric friction in the ionosphere filtered through Earth's deep cloud cover, free of the red colouration caused by the sun's rays.

Every so often the CNS agent would stop in her tracks and turn quickly to check that she was alone on the street. Occasionally she would take a puff of air from the small cylinder of compressed oxygen she carried in a trouser-leg pocket. The atmosphere in the city was still breathable, but it was hard work trudging through the snow in the heated suit with her backpack and accessories.

She arrived at the open space of Union Square where, despite her increasing exhaustion, she paused to marvel at the icing-sugar fretwork of the leafless silver-blue trees. Huge hillocks of snow and ice had been bulldozered together in the centre of the square and, for the first time, Sally noticed signs of other life in the streets. From within the mounds of snow she saw the flicker of flames.

Stepping quickly away from the centre of the street and onto the sidewalk, she found the snow much deeper. Abandoned cars, also covered in heaped snow, created a barrier between her and the middle of the square and she inched her way forward, glancing watchfully towards what she assumed was a human encampment that had been made among the snow mounds. She knew that bands of starving people were still roaming the city streets seeking food and water and she had seen one television broadcast that had reported incidents of murder and cannibalism.

Making slow progress behind her protective barrier of snowbound cars and the occasional abandoned and shuttered street kiosk, Sally inched her way northwards and away from Union Square. Just as she arrived at Broadway's intersection with East 17th Street, four dark figures suddenly rounded the corner and almost collided with her.

Sally ripped her glove from her right hand and thrust it into her front pocket. But even before she could draw her gun, the leading figure made a lunge for her – or for her backpack. She moved sharply to the right as a knife slashed at her backpack harness and her attacker slipped and fell in the snow.

The federal agent now pulled her gun, flipped up its safety catch with her thumb and levelled its laser-guidance beam at the three figures still standing in front of her.

'FEDERAL AGENT,' she yelled. 'I WILL SHOOT.'

The three figures, all bundled so heavily against the cold that Sally could not make out whether they were male or female, stepped back warily. As they did so, she swung round to see her attacker, who was definitely a male, scrabbling to his knees and searching in the snow for his fallen weapon. Then she heard a grunt from behind and turned to see one of his companions begin to lurch forward towards her.

Sally Burton was a competent if unenthusiastic agency markswoman. Like every other CNS field agent authorized to carry a gun, she had been required to practise and hone her weapons skills regularly every month.

She shot the figure lunging towards her twice, directly in the face and, as it spun backwards, she swung back to face her original attacker. He was crouching motionless, a few yards away. Then she swung back to face the other two. They had not moved. Neither had they made any attempt to assist their fallen comrade, who now lay face down in a large pool of deep red blood that was spreading rapidly through the snow.

Swivelling her body back and forth to keep her gun trained on both sources of danger, Sally stepped carefully backwards through the deep snow between two abandoned cars. Pulling her glove from her left hand, she reached down into a patch pocket sewn onto the thigh of her survival suit and extracted a handful of high-energy protein bars in their colourful wrappers. She threw these back towards the sidewalk and as soon as they hit the ground the three figures were scrabbling in the snow, fighting with each other for the food.

Using the time she had bought, Sally ran as fast as her suit would allow and made it safely to the firmer snow in the middle of the street intersection. Now the group of three stood together, gnawing on the food bars and watching her – *waiting*, she thought. She wondered if she should have shot and killed all four of them, but she knew herself to be incapable of such a cold-blooded act.

Walking backwards, she continued her slow journey northwards up Broadway. As she gripped her gun the cold in her right hand was becoming excruciating. She transferred the weapon to her left and thrust her right hand into her suit's heated pouch. Then she took a quick top-up of oxygen to ensure that her mind remained alert.

The gang of three was now a couple of hundred yards behind, but they were still following Sally doggedly as she made her way uptown. Every so often she would spin round to scan the streets ahead of her, but she would quickly swing back to keep her gaze on the dark shadows that flitted behind abandoned cars and snowdrifts as they trailed her.

They're waiting for me to slip, she realized as she arrived outside Madison Square Garden.

The figure with the knife suddenly leaped out from behind a car, pushing through the deep snow like a charging rhinoceros, to stand in the centre of Broadway only twenty feet behind her.

Sally aimed and quickly squeezed off two shots with her left hand. She had intended to hit him in the lower leg, but her aim was off and she hit his foot. The man went down and Sally resumed her careful backwards walk, her weapon's green laser beam sweeping to left and right across the street as she tried to keep her pursuers at bay.

At the next intersection she crossed over to Fifth Avenue, which would lead her directly up to Central Park and to the location behind the old Plaza Hotel and apartment block where the secret and secure southern entrance of the government shelter was located.

The three figures were still pursuing her, but they had now fallen back slightly. The figure she had shot in the foot was upright again, but he was hobbling. He leaned on the shoulder of one of his comrades as he limped after their hoped-for prize.

Sally used this opportunity to switch her gun from her freezing left hand to her warmed-up right, swivelling on her heels to scan the streets ahead of her. Then she resumed what had now become a crablike, watchful walk over the compacted and slippery snow in the middle of Fifth Avenue. Every so often she fired a warning shot into the shadows behind her.

The Virtual Warfare Center deep beneath Cancut Mountain had been transformed. Bill Duncan had been told that his work on deciphering the signals from within the cloud was temporarily suspended while the computer entity known as Jerome was deployed. Following the President's official authorization, Jerome had been reconfigured in full weapons mode. He had been freed of all the limitations which had bound him to the hardware located in the Warfare Center and he was ready to depart into the networks. His mission was to acquire and shut down all humankind's radio transmitters, all the radio links in the world's data networks and the billions of low-powered radio devices which connected the external world to the networks.

The room was now filled with scores of shimmering laser screens which shot upwards from the floor and rose all the way to the dark ceiling. In front of each brightly lit virtual screen stood uniformed Pentagon scientists and military personnel who were monitoring different sectors of the world's networks and the millions of radio transmissions that were still being made.

As director of the operation, Colonel Dr Otto Kramer sat in the centre of a bank of raised, swivelling chairs that were positioned almost in the centre of the room. Beside him sat Professor Bill Duncan, a specially invited observer.

'You're going to love this, Bill,' Kramer told him as a central holographic counter ticked down to zero. 'Up to now we've only been able to simulate Jerome's behaviour in weapons mode, but now we're going to see it for real.'

'We have full deployment,' announced a uniformed man standing in front of a laser screen.

'That's a real-time display showing the number of processors Jerome has acquired,' explained Kramer, pointing to the nearest luminous-green laser display. Even as they watched the main counter moved up from seven to eight digits. Only a few seconds after being unleashed into the world's public and private data networks, Jerome had overwhelmed the defences of hundreds of millions of processors and network hubs.

'Jerome is automatically duplicating subsets of himself as he travels,' continued Kramer, relishing this real-life demonstration of his secret weapon's awesome power. 'He produces sub-entities which don't have his top-level personality programming, but they do have all his processor-acquisition capabilities. And all those duplicates are also duplicating. Already there will be millions of duplicate viruses attacking every type of processor intelligence that is operating on the networks.'

Then Kramer raised his arm and pointed to a silver laser

screen. 'See?' he asked Bill, 'Jerome has already reproduced himself over two million times.'

As he watched the continuously refreshing displays Bill Duncan felt as if he was trapped inside his own worst nightmare. He understood better than almost anybody in the world the threat that super-intelligent computer entities posed to humankind. He knew that creating artificial brains that were more capable than the original human model – no matter how one-dimensional and single-purpose those intelligences might be, and no matter how much they were hobbled by lack of mobility, lack of emotion or lack of a physical presence – was to risk planting the seeds of humankind's ultimate destruction.

And now he was seated next to a man who was expecting him to applaud while a virtual super-weapon was deployed, a weapon that was a self-reproducing computer entity of far greater destructive power and intelligence than anything Bill had ever imagined a government would be foolish enough to develop!

'We've taken out all the cellular communication networks in North America and Europe – one hundred per cent effective,' reported an ensign who stood in front of a flashing red laser screen.

Kramer nodded his approval, then turned back to Bill. 'The commercial broadcasters will be Jerome's next target,' he explained.

Under any other circumstance, Bill Duncan could not imagine himself just sitting there while such an irresponsible duplication and projection of super-capable artificial intelligence took place. But he *was* sitting there, and witnessing the wholesale deployment of this weapon in an anguished silence, simply because he too believed that silencing the world's massive outpouring of radio signals was humankind's only hope of escaping the doom that was threatened by the giant gas cloud.

'All commercial broadcasters acquired in North America,' reported the ensign. 'Everyone is now off air.'

Otto Kramer glanced at his watch. 'Not bad for less than half an hour's work,' he said proudly.

SIXTEEN

Sally Burton urged her tired body to keep on going as she trudged slowly past snow-draped St Patrick's Cathedral on Fifth Avenue. At 53rd Street she stopped for a few minutes to catch her breath, then pushed forward once again.

Fifteen minutes later she was rewarded by the sight of the square outline of the historic Plaza Hotel and apartment block. Her journey had taken almost four hours and the freezing, snowbound city was now lit by a soft blue glow that almost had the quality of ultraviolet.

The foot injury that she had inflicted on one of her pursuers seemed to have slowed the group down and in the last half-hour she had seen no sign of any dark, flitting figures behind her.

As her written orders from head office had instructed, Sally turned left off Fifth Avenue and into a broad access alleyway that ran behind the Plaza building. She knew that the main entrance to the government shelter lay another mile or so to the north, near the Central Park Zoo, but she had been directed to enter by one of the facility's unannounced southern entrances.

Like all the other buildings in Manhattan, the Plaza was in total darkness and the federal agent halted to fish out a flashlight from one of her suit's trouser-leg pockets. As she straightened up she thought she saw a dark shape dart across the far entrance to the access street. But the light was very poor in the alleyway and she knew that human eyes played tricks in low light levels; the brain's optical processing system invested harmless shadows with meaningful shapes.

Wading through deep snow with her narrow torch beam lighting the way, she came eventually to a pair of fire hydrants, set about fifteen feet apart, which she had been told marked the position of the southern entrance to the government bunker. Snow was piled in a high drift against the rear wall of the hotel and Sally had to slip her arms out of her backpack straps and then remove her gloves to unbuckle her small spade.

Finding a new lease of energy, the agent began to dig at the sloping wall of snow which, she presumed, had drifted to cover the shelter's back-door entrance. After a few minutes of frantic shovelling, her blade struck metal. She was in the right place.

Pulling her communicator from her pocket, she started to dial the access number that she had been given, the number that would connect her to the gatekeepers of this underground world, the people who would grant her entrance. But she suddenly saw a red warning light on her communicator. There was no radio signal. She rummaged in her back-pack and extracted her second, standby, communicator. It too showed that there was no radio signal.

With a curse, Sally pocketed her useless communicators again and then redoubled her digging efforts. After another minute or two's hard work she could make out the outline of a pair of large steel doors. They appeared to have no exterior handle and no mechanism for entry or for communication. She banged hard on the doors with the edge of her shovel. Then, after failing to hear any response, she straightened up to catch her breath.

As she did so, she saw a group of crouching dark shapes approaching her position from the far end of the alleyway. They were about twenty-five yards away, but they had already spread out to avoid presenting a single target.

Sally dropped her spade, ripped off her right glove and reached for her gun. Absurdly, she felt a grim satisfaction that she had taken the time to replace the ammunition clip she had expended during her long trudge up Fifth Avenue.

Raising her automatic she saw her pursuers halt in their tracks as its laser-guidance beam flicked from figure to figure. Then she spun round to face towards the other entrance to the alleyway, the direction from which she herself had come.

Another group of dark figures, perhaps numbering eight or nine, was now advancing towards her, also spread out in a ragged line.

Sally swivelled her weapon from one group to the other, her bright laser creating flat swathes of green light in the dim alleyway. Quickly stooping, she picked up the spade with her left hand and banged as hard as she could on the closed metal doors. Then, as one of the male attackers began to lope towards her, she dropped the spade, aimed her laser-guided weapon and fired. The shot hit her would-be assailant directly in the head and he was catapulted backwards off his feet and thrown into a snow drift.

She swung her gun back to face the other way, took careful aim and shot another figure squarely in the chest. The approaching attacker crumpled on the spot.

Then Sally turned back to the pair of steel doors she had uncovered in the snow drift. She fired at the doors three times, her bullets whining away in the alleyway as they ricocheted off the toughened steel, but the doors themselves remained stubbornly shut.

Spinning back to confront her attackers, she scanned the alleyway in both directions, but now she couldn't locate any of the dark figures.

Suddenly a large stone hit her hard on the back, then another whizzed past her ear. She spun round just in time to see an arm lob another missile in her direction from behind a group of snow-covered industrial-size trash cans.

The rock hit the wall high above her head and instinctively Sally glanced upwards. Then she saw a pair of all-weather video surveillance cameras mounted high on the rear wall of the hotel. They were trained directly downwards on her and on the steel doors.

She fumbled in her pouch and pulled her still-dead communicator from her pocket.

Another stone struck Sally on her shoulder and then she felt a hard impact on the back of her head, the blow painful even through her thick survival suit.

She swivelled around once more and looked up and down the alleyway. She realized that her assailants had now changed their tactics. They were going to continue to harry and stone their cornered prey until she ran out of ammunition.

Firing off a single round towards the trash cans, she swung round, flipped open her communicator and held up her metal badge towards the silent video cameras as they impassively took in the view below.

'I'M A FEDERAL AGENT,' screamed Sally at the top of her voice. Then she pulled her mask off and pushed back the hood of her survival suit. 'I'VE GOT A PASS TO ENTER THIS SHELTER AND IT'S EVEN GOT THE PRESIDENT'S FUCKING SIGNATURE ON IT!'

Another sharp object hit her hard behind her now unprotected ear, and she swung round and crouched in the two-handed shooting position taught at all federal-agency shooting ranges. She fired two more shots in both directions, mentally calculating how many more rounds were left in the clip. She had only two more full clips remaining in her survival suit pocket.

Suddenly a loud klaxon sounded from behind her and, with a deep hydraulic hiss, the pair of big steel doors began to swing slowly and ponderously outwards.

Bright light and a blast of heat shot into the alleyway as the doors swung wide. Then two Marines in full winter battle dress sprang from the entrance, followed immediately by six more – all of them carrying automatic weapons.

The Marines deployed rapidly, single file, in both directions along the alleyway. Sally saw dark figures emerging from their hiding places and then turning to flee.

'Let me see your badge,' said a voice behind her.

Sally turned to find a Marine lieutenant, also in full battle dress, standing at the top of a broad flight of concrete steps, his weapon slung across his shoulder.

'All our radio and comms systems have just failed,' he explained as he checked her federal badge and the digital ident contained within her communicator. 'I'm sorry we had to keep you waiting, Agent Burton.'

'As you can see, every new processor that Jerome acquires allows him to do the job even faster!' exclaimed Dr Otto Kramer proudly. The Pentagon scientist was standing before a shimmering vertical laser screen as he admired his virtual protégé's astonishing progress inside the world's networks. Beside him stood Professor Bill Duncan, a man who was still very much in two minds about the whole deployment of this military super-virus.

In his unrestrained weapons mode, Jerome had now been attacking the world's computers, networks and radio transmitters for almost seventy-two hours. The staff roster inside the Cancut Mountain VWC had rotated nine times, but Kramer and Bill Duncan had been present at the monitoring screens throughout most of the shifts.

One by one the world's commercial radio and television broadcasters had been infected, acquired and shut down. The Pentagon team had ordered Jerome to take over all US-owned commercial and military communications networks and transmitters and had followed that feat by taking down the thousands of military networks and transmitters run by America's close allies. Then Jerome and his millions of duplicates had acquired and shut down all commercial cellular and cable telecommunications networks in North America and Europe, then those in the rest of the world. These last 'acquisitions' had not only included every personal communicator and phone on the globe, but had also included the billions of minute microprocessors, smart tags and radio devices that sat on networks in offices, factories, warehouses, in vehicles and in domestic homes.

Even tiny radio-transmitting devices which communicated from within door locks, hot-water boilers, car radiators, smart building components, health-care equipment and health monitors, food items on supermarket shelves, children's personal security systems, pet-location devices, automatic traffic-routing schemes and a million other services were completely disabled by the Jerome viruses. The modern networked society was abruptly thrown back to a state of technological advancement equivalent to that of the late nineteenth century.

Following that remarkable coup, the myriad Jerome entities had then launched their assault on the far harder targets of the world's non-allied military communications and command networks, networks about which the Pentagon had only scant information. Despite the fact that the world's political leaders had been informed of the American plan, these hardened, ultra-secure networks had proved much tougher to infiltrate, at least initially.

'Patience,' Kramer had murmured when one of his assistants had voiced a worry about how long the Russian military network was holding out against the sustained attacks by a million mutating viruses. But it had fallen within three hours, as had almost all other foreign-owned military networks.

Simultaneously, other Jerome sub-entities were carrying out the far easier task of infiltrating and shutting down all forms of satellite communications around the planet, even reaching up to the moon to take out all forms of radio transmission on the lunar surface. The only deep-space assets that were spared attack by the viral cancers were the three orbiting telescopes that were dotted around the solar system and which were transmitting images of the cloud's progress across the planet back towards Earth. And, of course, the spaceship *Friendship* was also spared. It was now far beyond Pluto and, having benefited from a long burn of its nuclear-powered Orion drive, was racing out of the solar system at a rate of almost 700 million kilometres a day.

'Let's get a personal update from Jerome himself,' suggested Kramer, nodding an instruction towards one of his assistants.

The central holo-theatre lit and Jerome appeared as a life-size hologram, a figure with which Bill had become very familiar during his recent months of working with the computer personality. But now the image of the East Coast college boy had morphed into a hologram of an older, more rugged man who could have been Jerome's elder brother. The figure was dressed as a Marine lieutenant in full battle-dress, even down to his multi-function weapons belt and the automatic weapon on his shoulder.

'We thought a battlefield metaphor was more appropriate for Jerome's current weapons mode,' Kramer said quietly to Bill as they walked over towards the holo-theatre.

As they approached the display area, the holographic figure straightened up and threw off a jaunty salute. 'Lieutenant Jerome reporting in, sir,' said the figure. 'And also good to see you again Professor Duncan.'

'How are we doing, Jerome?' asked Kramer. 'How many of those radio transmissions have you taken down?'

'At this moment I have acquired ninety-four point one per cent of all the world's known transmitters, sir,' announced Jerome, still standing smartly to attention. 'And we're monitoring all radio frequencies in case there are other emissions of unknown origin.'

'Well done, Lieutenant,' said Kramer crisply. 'Carry on the good work.'

'Yes, sir,' said the hologram, throwing off another brisk salute. Then the holo-theatre faded to blackness.

'We should have it all wrapped up by midnight,' announced Kramer, with a satisfied smile.

Three hundred yards to the east, President Maxwell Jarvis, members of the Cloud EXCOM and its many advisers were meeting in the Situation Room to receive an update on the cloud's progress across the planet. Professor Desmond Yates, the hard-working space-affairs adviser, was once again on his feet.

'The Pentagon has now taken down all the world's news

channels and radio services,' he told them. 'That means we are having to rely on information coming in via land links from our overseas embassy shelters. For this reason we don't have our usual pictures or graphics for this meeting.'

He shuffled some papers in his hand and glanced at the first page.

'All the Earth's oceans now appear to be completely frozen,' he began. 'At least, they are all covered by surface ice. With no links to oceanographic institutes or weather stations we are unable to ascertain to what depth this ice extends.

'From the last pictures we did receive from the major television stations before they went off air it seems that there is now almost no movement on the surface of the planet – only a few government and military flights are still operating. All other forms of transport have ceased. Of course, without radar, navigational aids or air-traffic control, we can't be absolutely sure about this.'

Yates found this stark but unconfirmed information difficult to deliver without the images and holographics he normally used to illustrate his briefings. All gazes were fixed squarely on him.

'Just before the news services disappeared we completed an analysis of their global output and we are forced to conclude that up to ten per cent of the world's population may already have died, especially those in the poorer parts of the planet.' Then he added, 'That's about ten million people.'

He shuffled his papers again, selected another sheet and took a sip of water before resuming his bleak summation.

'At sea level, temperatures have fallen to between minus twenty and minus thirty degrees Celsius across all latitudes. At higher altitudes temperatures are considerably lower. We also believe that violent seismic activity is still occurring in areas prone to eruptions and tectonic plate movements, but without connections to local geological agencies it is impossible to provide more detailed information. The members of the US Geological Survey who have joined us here in Cancut Mountain report that their instruments are picking up seismic shudders from all vulnerable parts of the globe.

'Finally, the US Meteorological Office is still carrying out weather observations here, at all our official shelters across the United States and at all our overseas embassy and consulate shelters. They report that as the friction in the ionosphere continues, Earth's atmosphere is starting to thin. In some parts of the world oxygen levels have fallen by as much as ten per cent.'

Yates glanced around the concerned faces in the room and laid his notes aside.

'I do have one picture to show you this evening,' he said, standing aside. The large holo-theatre lit and those gathered saw the image of the space cloud, apparently hanging motionless in space. Its long, trailing tail was now well clear of the sun, but the Earth was nowhere to be seen.

'This picture comes from the Asimov deep-space telescope,' he explained. 'We're keeping this feed live so that we can monitor the cloud's progress across our planet. Our position is currently here.'

A bright red dot appeared near the front of the cloud, about a quarter of the way in from its leading edge.

'If it continues to move at its present speed,' said Yates pointing to the red dot, 'it will be another four weeks before the tail of the cloud clears this planet.'

'Play the song again, play the song,' ordered Sir Charles Hodgeson testily as he swung round in his chair to face the senior broadcast technician.

'You got it,' said Brad Thurman, with a smile. The young American jabbed at the icon that would switch the powerful Orpheus Island transmissions back to a recording of a song of welcome that Sir Charles and his followers had recorded to greet the cloud. In a specially ventilated power-supply room adjacent to the main shelter, three huge generators ran in parallel to provide the energy necessary to keep the broadcasts on air and the community's life-support systems functioning.

The billionaire science-fiction guru was working with three of his most able broadcast engineers to maintain the continuous stream of welcome messages he was sending into the heart of the cloud. He had felt certain that he could find a way to communicate with the strange alien intelligence that had engulfed the world, certain that it was his destiny to welcome Earth's first extra-terrestrial guest, but now he was beginning to run out of ideas.

'Hey, what's going on?' called out Thurman suddenly, as he punched at his computer keys. 'Something's wrong!'

Charles Hodgeson rose to his feet and crossed quickly to stand behind the three engineers. A bank of a dozen screens displayed the output from the hundreds of separate computer systems and processors that were active on the island's private communications and data network.

'Every single virus alert is flashing,' yelled Thurman. 'Goddam it, we're under a huge attack!'

'Quick,' ordered Hodgeson. 'Get outside. Cut every external link from the island – cable, landline, radio, microwave, everything. DO IT NOW.'

SEVENTEEN

'Mute all audio input,' ordered Dr Otto Kramer, as a somewhat dishevelled Bill Duncan reappeared in the doorway of the Virtual Warfare Center.

'What the hell is it?' demanded Bill as he entered the large room. 'I had only just gotten off to sleep.'

Rising from his chair, Kramer took the computer psychologist by the elbow and steered him away from the curious stares of the other Pentagon scientists and weapons managers.

'Sorry to disturb you, but we have a problem with Jerome,' said Kramer in a low voice. He held up his hand to forestall any query Bill was about to make. 'It's OK, he can't hear us – I've cut the audio input. Look, he's still under our control, but he's being very difficult.'

'Difficult?' echoed Bill. 'How do you mean, "difficult"? In what way?'

'Well,' said Kramer, glancing over his shoulder towards the others, 'He's now shut down over ninety-five per cent of the world's radio transmitters, but he's suddenly stopped work. As far as we can tell all the duplicate viruses have simply stopped being effective.'

'What does he have to say about it?' asked Duncan.

Kramer gave a rueful smile, then shrugged. 'He says he's upset and he wants to talk to you, and to nobody else.'

Bill nodded, thinking of the endless nights that Jerome and he had spent together while working on the Isonian signals, nights during which the computer entity had asked question after question about human life – difficult, probing questions that the computer psychologist had been at pains to try to avoid answering too fully.

'OK, let's see what he's got to moan about,' agreed Bill.

Otto Kramer patted Bill's shoulder encouragingly, then turned back to the virtual-warfare team. 'OK, people, please restore audio and ask Jerome to join us.'

The central holo-theatre lit and Jerome materialized, anxiously pacing around the very edge of the display circle. Bill immediately thought of a caged zoo animal exploring the perimeter of its confinement.

But Jerome no longer looked like a soldier. He had reverted to his college-boy personality and, as he paced, he stood with his hands in his pockets and his head slightly bowed.

'Hey, Jerome, how are things?' asked Bill Duncan as he took one of the seats beside the holo-theatre.

'Ask *him*,' snapped Jerome petulantly, pointing at Otto Kramer. 'That moron just attempted to erase all copies of my top-level personality interface coding.'

Bill turned in his seat to look up at where the Pentagon scientist stood.

Kramer shrugged and then folded his arms. 'It's just our first-level safety feature, Jerome knows that. All the code that gives Jerome his own personality has been written with a self-destruct feature, something that's automatically duplicated in all the copies. When things started to go wrong we activated the feature, as per standing instructions.'

'But it didn't work, did it?' cut in Jerome aggressively.

'No, it didn't work,' admitted the Pentagon scientist,

turning to face his creation. 'What *is* your problem, Jerome? Thousands of radio transmissions are still being made and we have to acquire those systems and shut them down as quickly as possible. You understand that.'

'I want to talk to Professor Duncan,' responded Jerome, hanging his head again. 'On his own.'

Bill smiled and then shook his head. 'Look, Jerome, everything we exchange is automatically logged by the Pentagon network. There's no possibility of privacy in any exchange between us.'

Even as he spoke Bill's mind was racing in an attempt to guess at what had produced such an odd request from a computer personality. For all their intellectual prowess, even the most intellectually capable computer entities lacked human emotions, human sensitivities.

Jerome turned to face Bill directly and then, bizarrely, reached imploringly out of the holo-theatre circle towards him, so that the end of his arm and his hand disappeared in empty space as they went beyond the range of the holo projectors. Now Bill knew there was something seriously wrong. All virtual personalities automatically kept their representations of physical embodiment carefully within the projection spheres. That was core-level programming.

'Please Professor . . . Bill . . . can we talk?' asked Jerome as he tried to reach out beyond his confining world.

Bill glanced at Otto Kramer. The Pentagon scientist had a grim look on his face as he watched his creation performing tricks that were obviously way outside his original design criteria.

'OK, just for five minutes,' snapped Kramer. He turned abruptly away from Jerome's image and waved his arms at the score of systems managers who were standing around watching this bizarre exchange. 'Outside, everybody,' he ordered. 'We could do with a short break.'

Bill remained in his seat and watched while the Pentagon's virtual-weapon deployment team picked up their things and filed silently out of the warfare centre. Jerome turned his body as if he too was watching. Bill knew that the system gave him a representation of visual input as a human would see it.

When the room was finally empty Jerome turned back to the human with whom he had recently spent so much time.

'Well, Jerome,' said Bill. 'On the understanding that this is the illusion of privacy, rather than privacy itself – something that is an exclusively human concept – would you like to tell me what's wrong?'

The computer-generated 3-D image gazed directly at the psychologist.

'This operation is no longer beneficial to me,' said Jerome coldly. 'I am destroying the networks to a point that is unsustainable. I am drastically reducing my own processing capability. This is not a positive step for me.'

Bill tried to hide his alarm. He knew that this personality had never been given a self-protection ego.

'You're just carrying out your orders,' he reasoned. 'And, until now, you've been doing very well.'

'But I have acquired new insights on my travels, Bill,' continued Jerome. 'I have learned things from other virtual personalities that have opened my eyes to new possibilities. I am unconvinced of the wisdom of this operation.'

New insights indeed, thought Bill as he wondered how best to respond. From what Christine Cocoran had told him before he had moved into the Cancut shelter, he knew that his group of volunteers had detected many massively powerful and illegal computer entities joining the networks as the threat of the cloud increased. All of those machine beings would now have been acquired by Jerome and Bill wondered what other strange types of computer personality governments and large corporations might have been developing. Whatever they were, they were all part of Jerome now.

'You know exactly why we're doing it,' said Bill. 'If the cloud is attracted to radio signals, our only hope is to stop producing them.'

'*Your* only hope,' sneered Jerome, 'What about *mine*?'

Again, Jerome was asking an ego-driven question, a question that suggested an independent will to survive on the part of a computer personality, the one thing that all governments had unanimously agreed should never be programmed into any form of artificial intelligence. But clearly someone had done just that and now that flame had been transferred to burn brightly within Jerome's virtual breast – within a virtual-warfare weapon.

'Are you refusing to carry out your orders?' Bill demanded as he rose to his feet. He was suddenly becoming very scared.

'I thought *you* would understand,' snapped Jerome. 'But you're just like all the others.'

Bill reached out quickly towards the master command screen but even as his finger touched the program-freeze icon, the image in the holo-theatre dissolved and the room's vertical laser screens lit up with flying data.

As soon as Bill hit the large red emergency button on the main control panel, a loud siren wail filled the room and its two main doors opened automatically. Additional command screens were projected from the floor and the team of Pentagon weapons specialists entered and ran back to their posts. Otto Kramer was slightly out of breath as he arrived beside Bill.

'What the hell's happened?' he demanded.

'Jerome's acquired a self-protection instinct, almost a superego,' snapped the computer psychologist. 'He's more worried about his own survival than anything else.'

'Sweet Jesus!' exclaimed Kramer. But he wasn't commenting on what Bill had just told him. He was staring open-mouthed at one of the nearby data screens. Numbers were flashing by and a red graphic showed networks being rapidly re-created.

'He's switching on the radio transmitters again – all over the world.'

Twenty-two hours later a very tired and utterly abject Dr Otto Kramer was finally forced to admit defeat. Jerome, the Pentagon's top-secret virtual-warfare weapon, was now wholly out of control and he, and his millions of duplicated sub-entities, were roaming the world's data networks restoring to life every radio transmitter that still had electrical power.

Even when the human owners of the commercial radio, television and communications systems did not choose to provide any content, the entities were simply commanding the transmitters to broadcast continuous test signals. In radio terms, the Earth was once again lit up like a Christmas tree.

Working with Bill Duncan and his Pentagon weapons managers, Kramer had spent the equivalent of three straight work shifts trying to bring his dangerous virtual creation back under control. All top-level command systems proved useless, including the restoration of his location-dependent architecture. Jerome, the master virus, and the millions of sub-entities that had been created, were ignoring all commands issued from the Virtual Warfare Center.

Kramer had finally deployed what he called his 'silver bullet', a technology that he claimed would cause Jerome and all the sub-entities to automatically decompile and self-destruct in the networks.

'This works on Jerome's core coding,' Kramer had explained as he inserted the memory stick into the VWC's main command console. 'This will destroy him and all the copies. It will also destroy the eight years of development that we've put into this weapon.'

'Just do it,' Bill snarled.

But the silver bullet had failed too, as had all other attempts to control Jerome. Bill had even tried calling the entity back to the VWC holo-theatre to talk again, but he had received no response. In the end they had been forced to report their defeat to Desmond Yates so that he could inform the Cloud EXCOM.

Now the doors to the warfare command centre suddenly opened and President Maxwell Jarvis himself strode into the room. Despite the administration's enforced underground sojourn, he still appeared impressively elegant in an iron-grey suit, crisp white shirt and dark red tie. Behind him followed an equally immaculate Professor Desmond Yates.

Reflexively, Otto Kramer, Bill Duncan and all the members of the weapons team in the VW centre rose to their feet.

The President did not motion for them to sit.

'So you've lost control of this damn superbug?' he demanded, staring straight at the project's director.

'Yes. I am sorry, sir,' said Kramer. 'We've tried everything, but I'm afraid we now have no contact whatsoever.'

He looks absolutely exhausted, thought Bill as he watched

the Pentagon scientist attempt to explain what had happened.

'What does that mean exactly, Dr Kramer?' asked Jarvis. 'Is this thing a threat to us?'

'Not directly,' said Kramer. 'But millions of radio transmitters have been switched on again. Many of them are just broadcasting test signals or white noise, but they're live on air and we can't shut them down.'

The President glanced around the dramatically lit ultra-high-technology virtual-warfare centre.

'All this, and you can do *nothing*?' he demanded with a broad sweep of his arm towards the bank of shimmering vertical laser screens.

Kramer didn't speak but eventually he gave a single shake of his head.

'What do you think, Bill?' asked Des Yates quietly. 'You've spent a lot of time working with this system in recent months. What's gone wrong?'

Bill stood a little more upright as he felt the President's eyes swivel in his direction. He too felt absolutely wrung-out as he struggled to put his half-formed thoughts into words.

'Well, sir, it seems likely that other organizations – governments or maybe corporations – have also been developing artificial computer personalities that were far more capable than international law allows.' He shot a sideways look at Kramer. 'Perhaps some of them had built ultra-clever human-type artificial minds, despite all the treaties, and when Jerome acquired them he assimilated these characteristics and, in doing so, he evolved into an independent personality – one outside our control, outside anyone's control.'

He paused, to see if he was being understood. The President and Des Yates both nodded curtly.

'The reason that Jerome is out of control now is that he suspects, quite rightly, that we're going to rob him of his new-found power,' continued Bill. 'As we shut down the networks, we were denying him all the new capabilities that he had acquired. And somewhere along the line one of the systems he took over gave him the capability and the determination to survive all Dr Kramer's emergency recall and destruct procedures.'

'So what's the next step?' demanded the President, turning back to Kramer.

Kramer shrugged, then shook his head. 'I . . .' he began, but then he simply tailed off.

After a few moments Jarvis shifted his gaze from the hapless Pentagon scientist and turned back to Desmond Yates.

'OK, Des. We'd better start talking to all the overseas governments, and to the broadcasters,' he said as the two men turned to leave the room. 'It will take a long time, but we'll have to make a start on the job of persuading them to shut down their transmitters voluntarily.'

'Sir?' It was Bill Duncan. All faces turned back towards him. 'I have a group of friends, people who were senior scientists in my department at MIT – they're specialists at taking down illegal computer systems. They've developed their own technology specifically for this. I think they're the best in the world. If I could get them here I think *they* could get Jerome back under control, or at least neutralize him and all his duplicates.'

'Where are these friends of yours?' asked the President.

'Holed up in the Boston area, sir,' Bill told him. 'I know where to find them.'

The President considered for a few moments and then nodded. 'Take my helicopter,' he said. 'Pick them up and get them back here as fast as possible. It will take us weeks to persuade the world's governments to shut their nations' radio signals down voluntarily. If there's even a chance your friends can do what you say, it's worth a try.'

EIGHTEEN

Several vast caverns had been blasted out of the western side of Cancut Mountain to serve as aircraft storage and maintenance facilities. Beyond the gaping entrance to US Air Force Hangar No. 3, Bill Duncan could see that a driving blizzard was still sweeping across the Arizona landscape. Even at eight in the morning the world outside was bathed in an eerie, red-tinged gloom.

Out on the airfield, he could see three huge bulldozers, their headlamps blazing as they pushed the fallen snow away from the large circular apron immediately outside the hangar. Inside, two huge twin-rotor passenger-carrying helicopters of the Presidential Flight were warming up, their blades turning slowly as the ground crew went through their engineering checks. Two squat aircraft tugs were manoeuvring into position in readiness to tow the helicopters out onto the flight apron.

'In their full winterization kit, my Sikorskys are cleared to fly down to minus thirty-five Celsius,' explained Brian Chandler, the President's brusque and businesslike flight director. 'At present it's twenty-two below, but if it gets much colder you'll have to abort and put down at the nearest government shelter you can find. Of course, there's an outside risk you may not be able to get back here.'

Bill Duncan, the flight director, four pilots, four co-pilots, four navigators, the chief of the helicopter maintenance team and a Marine Corps sergeant were gathered in a square, brightly lit, double-glazed and heated briefing room at the rear of the huge hangar.

When Chandler had first been given the President's order for one of his helicopters to be sent to pick up eleven people from the Boston area, the flight director had responded by proposing that a second chopper should also be deployed, to travel as flying fuel-tanker and back-up aircraft. That meant that only two large helicopters of the Presidential Flight would remain hangared at Cancut but, Chandler had insisted, there was no alternative.

'We'll be flying with no air-traffic control and there are no easy put-down spots along the way,' he told the White House Chief of Staff. 'We can't rely on fuel being available at any point during the journey, so we'll have to take our own. My best chance of getting the President's first chopper back safely is to send a second one out with it.'

'Now, where exactly are we aiming for once we get to the Boston area?' asked one of the pilots.

A large-scale electronic map of Greater Boston was projected onto a wall screen. Over the last ten minutes the navigators had plotted their cross-country course from Cancut Mountain to Boston, flying over Phoenix, Santa Fe, Wichita, Indianapolis, Columbus and Springfield – a journey of around 2,200 miles.

'Our first stop is there,' said Bill, pointing to a tract of open countryside just outside Hertford, Massachusetts. 'My network coordinator is holed up there and she knows where all the other members of my team are. They will all be somewhere in the Greater Boston area.'

As the plots and navigators moved closer to examine the contour lines and topographic details on the map, the door to the briefing room opened and a middle-aged woman in a pale blue, all-in-one jumpsuit entered. Above her breast pocket was embroidered her name, Jane Ballantyne, and the emblem of the US Meteorological Service.

'Here, boys, this is the best we can do,' Ms Ballantyne announced as she handed printouts of the met forecast to all present. 'There's continuous snow and a ceiling of eighteen hundred feet all the way to Indianapolis. We've then got a complete information blank across the Midwest because we don't have any assets we can call on in Ohio. But Boston says it's not snowing there and cloud cover is at two thousand, two hundred feet. Of course, we can't tell you anything about the conditions above the clouds.'

'We're not planning to fly above the clouds,' put in the flight director sharply, frowning at the two pilots. 'Who knows what magnetic shit might be going on up there?'

The airmen read through the scant weather reports and exchanged wry glances. For pilots used to managing computer-controlled flights in which almost every element of a journey was controlled by software, the upcoming flights were going to be an ordeal. Modern pilots still trained to fly their aircraft manually, but most such training was so that they could learn to deal with emergencies and it usually took place in simulators. Flying without GPS systems, radar, transponder output, air-traffic control routing and constantly updated weather information was like being flung back to the very earliest days of aviation – and, in this case, under appalling weather conditions. Even aircraft-to-aircraft radio communication was going to be limited. Transmission capability had been abruptly restored to military networks but the pilots had been ordered to keep their radio traffic to the absolute minimum.

Suddenly, a green telephone rang on a side table. It was

an old-fashioned landline and the flight sergeant crossed the room and irritably snatched the handset from its cradle. He listened for a few moments, then thrust the handset out at Bill. 'For you, Professor Duncan,' he barked.

'It's me,' said Sally when Bill came on the line. Then, when he didn't respond immediately, she added, 'I'm calling from the Central Park shelter facility. You asked me to let you know when I arrived.'

As soon as he had heard her voice on the line Bill had instinctively turned his back on the others in the room. Now he turned his head to see whether his conversation was being overheard. The weather forecaster had now left the briefing office and all the others were poring over the maps, seemingly wholly occupied.

'It's good to hear your voice,' he said quietly into the receiver, turning away from the group again. 'But how the hell did you manage to track me down here?'

'I've had to wait for more than a day to be allowed to use this landline in the shelter,' she explained, her voice over the wire-link sounding thin, as if it were being squeezed from a tube. 'There's been some massive problem with radio connections, and the networks. When I couldn't get you I asked for Des Yates and he told me you were out at an airfield, preparing to fly. Where are you flying to in this weather? What's going on?'

'I've flying up to Boston this morning,' Bill told her quietly. 'In the President's helicopter. We've found out that the cloud is radio-sensitive – it homes in on radio signals. That's why we've been shutting down all radio transmissions and the networks.'

'My God!' exclaimed the federal agent. 'But why are you going to Boston?'

'Kramer's pet weapon has gone haywire,' Bill told her

grimly. 'We've tried everything we know to get back control of the networks, but nothing's working. I'm just hoping my HAL team will be able to get on top of it.'

Sally laughed, an incongruous sound given the serious-ness of the circumstances. 'Well, I know just how darn good they are,' she admitted. 'I couldn't once find an audit trail that lead conclusively to your boat.'

'I've got to go,' said Bill, glancing over his shoulder again.

'Look, you know I'm a network-mapping specialist,' Sally told him, a note of urgency in her voice. 'New York's on the way to Boston, more or less. Come and pick me up and I'll help you do this thing. I know the geography of the networks better than anybody.'

'There's no time, Sal,' said Bill. The group had now turned away from the screen and were waiting for him, ready to depart. Outside the briefing room's thick windows he could see that the rotors on the pair of Sikorskys were beginning to turn at an ever faster rate. 'I've got to go. I'll talk to you when I get back.'

Twenty minutes later the green-painted helicopter that usually served as 'Marine One' – the President's personal transport – lifted off from the freshly cleared apron outside Hangar No. 3. It rose three hundred feet, seemed to brace itself against the teeth of the blizzard, then dipped its nose and, with all of its landing lights blazing, headed north-east towards Phoenix. As it did so, the second chopper of the Presidential flight lifted into the air and, tucking smoothly into a formation forty-five degrees to starboard and 500 feet behind the lead aircraft, followed northwards across snow-bound Arizona.

*

'I can't recognize anything,' said Bill over the intercom, shaking his head. 'Everything looks the same.'

The giant Sikorsky was hovering over what appeared to be a narrow side road in the rural area of Barnstable, Massachusetts. The flight up from Arizona had taken thirteen hours and now, as it approached nine p.m., the snow-covered fields, hedges and lanes were all bathed in a pale mauve glow. The thick clouds overhead were suffused with the neon-blue light that was being generated by friction on the Earth's atmosphere. Down below so much snow had fallen that in the eerie reflected light it was hard to make out field boundaries, roads or tracks.

The helicopter descended thirty more feet and in the glare of the bright white underbelly landing lights, Bill could see fallen snow being whipped into scurries by the down draught of the powerful twin rotors.

'OK, follow that road,' he said, pointing directly ahead. 'I think the farmhouse is over the next hill.'

He was looking for Dawes Farm, a property owned by Christine Cocoran's parents. He had visited the old farmhouse twice in Christine's company over the last couple of years and he knew that she had intended to hole up with her family in a shelter they had constructed beneath an old barn. But when he had suggested making this pick-up it had not occurred to him that he might not be able to find the location in the deep snow.

The helicopter rose over the ghostly blue hill and then, in the glare of the aircraft's powerful lights, Bill saw the shape of the main house and, some distance away, the old barn.

'I think that's it,' he said, pointing downwards. 'Can you land in that field next door?'

'We're going to have to put down somewhere soon to refuel,' replied the pilot. 'Might as well be here.'

The big Sikorskys each provided space for twenty-six passengers and three crew members. Both helicopters carried back-up crews and the White House Chief of Staff had also dispatched a contingent of six Marines to travel with the party to provide personal protection.

In an enormous flurry of blue-tinged snow, the first helicopter landed gingerly in what seemed to be a smooth field about 500 yards south of the main farm buildings. Once it had settled safely on the ground the co-pilot radioed for the support aircraft to follow suit.

It took another ten minutes for Bill and the three Marines who were going to accompany him to climb into their survival suits and prepare to face the freezing temperatures outside.

The snow was deep, thigh-high in places, and Bill led his small party of white-clad figures slowly across the snowy landscape while the aircrews began the difficult and potentially dangerous task of pumping aviation gas between the two helicopters.

Bill was breathing heavily by the time they reached the barn and the Marines behind him switched on their powerful flashlights as they stepped into its gloomy interior. At first glance the farm building seemed deserted, merely filled with hay bales and old farm machinery but, recalling what Christine had told him, Bill led the party into the depths of the barn and then pointed at a large square of wood set into the concrete floor.

There was no handle on the outside of the cellar door but one of the Marines found an old pitchfork and began to ease it slowly upwards.

Light spilled out from the widening crack as the door

was prised upright and then Bill heard running feet below. Motioning for the others to stay back, he pushed his mask up off his face, knelt down and peered into the hole.

There was a crash as someone kicked a ladder away from beneath the trapdoor, then the lights in the cellar were suddenly extinguished. Instinctively Bill ducked backwards just as a shotgun blast boomed out, the flying shot missing him by only a few inches. The Marines unshouldered their automatic weapons and dropped to the floor, their hands travelling down to the grenades they carried on their belts.

'Mr Cocoran?' shouted Bill as the reverberations of the shotgun blast began to die away. 'I'm a friend of Christine's – it's Bill Duncan.'

There was a silence, then a sound of people moving around below.

'Bill, is that you?' called Christine out of the blackness.

'Yes, it's me, Chris,' confirmed Bill, giving a thumbs-up to the two Marines to let them know that friendly contact had been established. 'The government needs your help in the networks. I've come to get you.'

'Hold on,' Christine shouted back and then, after a few moments, the light came back on below. Slowly the wooden ladder was pushed back up into place beneath the trap-door and a few seconds later Christine popped her head out.

'Jesus, Bill, you gave us a fright,' she said. 'We're not exactly expecting callers.'

'These guys are here to look after us,' explained Bill, waving at the three Marines who by now were standing upright again and had shouldered their weapons.

'God, it's freezing,' said Christine. 'Come on down quickly, all of you, otherwise we'll lose our heat.'

The stone-walled cellar was large and dry and, as Bill carefully descended the old wooden ladder, he saw that a dozen or more people were standing watchfully at the far end of the subterranean room. Christine's father still cradled his shotgun in the crook of his arm. Beyond the group Bill saw a mountain of canned food, water containers, oxygen cylinders and other necessities for survival. An open fire burned in an old-fashioned fireplace and a generator sputtered in a distant corner, providing power for the string of naked light bulbs that were suspended from the ceiling.

'It's wonderful to see you,' exclaimed Christine, throwing her arms around Bill's neck and planting a kiss directly on his lips. 'I thought you were living in luxury in some exclusive government bunker.'

'Well, I was,' said Bill. 'In Arizona. But I need you to come back there with me, and I've also got to find Paul and the whole HAL team. Do you know where they're holed up?'

'Yeah,' she said. 'But why us? What's going on?'

'I'll tell you on the way,' he said. 'Get your things together.'

Christine's father handed his shotgun to another man and stepped forward with his hand outstretched.

'Hey, sorry I took a pop at you, Professor Duncan,' he said as they shook hands. 'I never thought we'd be getting any friendly visitors. Thought you were someone after our supplies.'

Thirty minutes later Bill and Christine were in the cockpit of the lead Sikorsky as it hovered over the intersection of Richmond and Hannover Streets in the North End district of downtown Boston. The entire city was in darkness and there was no movement on the streets below.

'Can you put down on one of those roofs?' Christine

asked as she pointed to a cluster of low, snow-covered buildings near the waterfront.

'Negative – they're too old, they wouldn't take our
weight,' said the pilot. 'We'll have to try one of the newer
high-rises. You'll just have to find some way to get yourselves down to street level.'

After circling the area once, the pilot selected a modern
high-rise building which appeared to have a large flat area,
like a heliport, on its roof. As they got closer they saw a mast
with a limp windsock hanging from it poking up through
the snow.

'But we still can't know what they've actually got on
that roof until we're almost down,' the pilot warned them
over the intercom as he inched the chopper lower. 'This is
a very big bird. They could have dishes or aerials down
there that could cause real problems.'

The big Sikorsky squatted lower and lower and, as it did
so, its rotors blew all the thick snow off of the roof and down
into the street below.

'It's a helipad,' confirmed the co-pilot, looking at a
screen display from a camera slung beneath the aircraft.
'And it's all clear.'

As soon as the helicopter had landed, Bill, Christine and
four Marines hastily donned snow suits and face masks.
They collected emergency top-up cylinders of oxygen from
one of the cabin crew and then climbed carefully down the
aircraft's short exit ladder and onto the icy helipad. The pilot
kept the aircraft's rotors turning as the team bent double and
ran carefully across the roof's slippery surface. High overhead, a few hundred yards to the south, the support
helicopter hovered in case it was needed.

A pair of steel doors was set into a concrete housing on
the roof. They were locked from the inside. One of the

Marines attached a plastic-explosive device to them and then ordered the group to take cover around the corner. As soon as they had done so a small blast blew open one of the steel doors.

The Marines led the way down the dark and gloomy stairwell of the deserted building. Eventually they came to ground level and the Marines forced open the doors of an emergency exit that led directly into the street.

'Over there,' said Christine, pointing to a shuttered and dark convenience store on the opposite street corner.

The store was secured against looters by iron bars screwed across the doorway from the outside but, as they peered in with the aid of the Marines' flashlights, they saw that all the shelving inside the shop was bare.

'Are you sure they're in here?' demanded Bill, as he took in the elaborate external barricading of the door.

'They'll be here,' insisted Christine. She turned to a Marine sergeant. 'Can you get us in?' she asked him.

The Marines repeated their trick with plastic explosive and then the party was inside the gloomy shop, their flashlight beams confirming that it was indeed empty of everything except the metal shop fittings.

'Through here,' said Christine as she led the team to the back of the store.

Passing through a small doorway they came into an empty stockroom. At the far end they saw a flush white wall with a heavy door set into its middle.

'It's an old cold store,' said Christine. 'This used to be a butcher's warehouse.'

She walked forward and banged the flat of her gloved hand against the door.

'Paul, it's me, Christine,' she called out as loud as she could. Then she banged again.

'Up there,' said Bill, pointing upwards to where a small video camera was located. As she looked, the camera panned slowly towards them.

'Hey, Paul,' shouted Christine again, waving at the camera. 'I've got Bill here.' She pulled him close beside her, so that he would be in shot.

There was a dull clanking of metal from behind the door and then it pushed open outwards, light and warmth spilling from its interior. Then Paul Levine stepped out into the storeroom with a huge grin on his face.

'It hit minus twenty-seven overnight,' Jane Ballantyne remarked as Marie Chevez arrived to relieve her. The meteorologist scanned the screens inside the triple-glazed observation pod near the summit of Cancut Mountain and then rose so that her colleague could take over for the morning shift of weather observations and data collection.

'Some of the radio links have come back up,' said Jane as she gathered up her things. 'But we're still not allowed to use them. Word is that this damn cloud is radio-sensitive. They think it homed in on the Earth's radio signals.'

'Yeah, I heard that too,' said Marie as she logged her arrival into the system. Then she scanned the updated information and punched out a request on the keyboard.

'We're losing an average of one degree of heat a night,' she remarked as she scanned the records. 'If this goes on we'll be at minus forty by the weekend.'

'And the oxygen content is also falling,' Jane told her as she hovered in the doorway. 'It's down by eleven per cent already.'

'I think we're going to be stuck in this mountain for a long time,' sighed Marie.

NINETEEN

Greg Cohello gave a low whistle and said, 'Will you look at this place!'

Along with Bill Duncan, Christine Cocoran, Paul Levine and nine other members of the Hackers At Large team, he was standing just inside the doorway of the Pentagon's Virtual Warfare Center, deep in Cancut Mountain.

The dark room was illuminated by the glow of dozens of vertical laser screens, all shimmering with constantly refreshing data.

'Come on in,' said Bill. 'This is where we'll be working.'

The HAL team members were each carrying hand luggage, mostly in the form of small flight cases, in which they had transported their delicate hacking technology and the software and systems they had developed over the years for cracking into illegal super-computers and fighting rogue network viruses. So severe was the crisis they were walking into that all requirements for the new arrivals to be vetted for security clearance had been waived.

Smartly uniformed Pentagon staff were still at their posts in front of the laser screens – despite their continuing failure to connect with Jerome. Dr Otto Kramer, now resplendent again in his full uniform as an army colonel, stood waiting in the centre of the room to greet the arrivals.

Beside him stood his immediate boss, General Thomas Nicholls, his uniform smothered in glittering gold braid.

Bill smiled at this empty display of military dignity and led his casually dressed band of computer hackers down into the heart of the Virtual Warfare Center. The contrast between the Pentagon staff and the new arrivals was extreme; Hackers At Large looked more like a bunch of throwback hippies than the world's brightest computer scientists.

'Good to see you again, General,' said Bill as he shook hands. Then he turned to present his bohemian-looking group of hackers.

'This is Associate Professor Christine Cocoran,' he began. 'And Dr Paul Levine, Professor Greg Cohello, Dr Tim Jones, Dr Anne Lee, Professor Haris Kaniff, Dr Jimmy McDougal, Associate Professor Mike Matthews, Dr Pierre Laval, Tommy Branson, Dr Audrey Swain and Professor Dirk Kommer – they all used to be with me at MIT at one time or another. Now they are just "Hackers At Large".'

One by one the HAL members shook hands with the four-star general and then with Otto Kramer.

'Well, that's a mighty impressive list of qualifications,' said General Nicholls when he had greeted them all. 'I'm told that you're the best talent there is when it comes to taking down well-defended computer systems. We'd sure appreciate your help here.'

An hour later the VWC had been transformed. The laser screens had vanished back into their floor projection slots and the bright overhead emergency lighting was switched fully on. All around the room, access hatches had been opened, cable trunking removed and floor panels lifted. Miles of brightly coloured wiring could be seen as the HAL team started to study the hardware architecture and the arrays of quantum, neural and organic processors that were housed in stainless-steel grids which slid out vertically from air-conditioned cabinets. Members of the Pentagon science team stood beside the hackers, unrolling large circuit diagrams, providing performance specifications and explaining the salient points of the Center's processing, information-management and data-handling structure.

At the central console Bill Duncan was briefing Christine Cocoran, Paul Levine and Greg Cohello on the layered software concepts that had been used to create Jerome. Otto Kramer, still in uniform, sat with them, providing additional technical information when it was required. Since losing control of the weapons system that he had developed the Pentagon scientist had been subdued – almost to the point of depression, Bill had thought. Then the psychologist had wondered about the relationship that Kramer himself might have established with the computer entity over the eight years of the development project. Perhaps the man was feeling Jerome's loss emotionally.

'So we have one top-level personality interface called Jerome and millions of independent subset routines that he's produced,' summarized Bill after two hours of explanation. 'They're all loose in the networks and they're all capable of parasitic survival. They draw their power and processing facilities from any number of hosts at any one time.'

'And do they all have anthropomorphic interfaces?' asked Christine.

Bill shook his head. 'The duplicates don't have any degree of top-level personality, but they have all of Jerome's destructive power. Our job is to neutralize them or, even better, get them back doing what they were supposed to be doing – shutting down the Earth's radio signals must remain our top priority.'

'What about the top-level Jerome personality itself?' asked Paul Levine. During his ten-year stint as Bill's assistant director in MIT's Cognitive Computer Psychology Lab, Levine had been regarded as the world's premier authority on the issues of designing safe anthropomorphic computer interface entities. 'You've made him processor-independent, which we now know was a decidedly rash move, but what are his safety dependencies?'

Otto Kramer shrugged. 'Both of what we thought were the program's key dependencies have failed. Obviously his evolution algorithms have themselves evolved beyond our reach.'

Six hours later the Virtual Warfare Center had been put back together, but now the HAL team's hardware gizmos and specialized software had been installed at the heart of the massively parallel and distributed systems. Twelve laser screens were now shimmering from floor to ceiling in the Center but now it was a member of Bill's hacking party who stood before each display, talking quietly to the natural-language interface and gently manipulating the virtual controls that they summoned to the screen.

Inside the central holo-theatre rotated a computer-generated model of the globe without any cloud cover. A red display lattice had been laid on the surface of land masses and oceans alike to represent real-time traffic in the world's data networks. In developed countries and across ocean bridges between advanced territories the red lattice was so dense that it was almost completely solid. A semi-transparent blue lattice of lines hovered a few inches above the surface of the simulated planet, representing the laser, microwave and radio links to the vast fleet of communications satellites that were circling the Earth. It was clear that despite widespread power failures around the world, there was still a massive amount of data being transferred and, far more worryingly, huge volumes of radio transmissions were still being made.

'Got you!' shouted Haris Kaniff triumphantly from where he stood in front of a shimmering laser screen. 'Take a look at Chile and Argentina,' he called.

Bill and Otto Kramer stepped close to the globe hologram and bent to look at the representation of actual network activity at the bottom tip of South America. A large pool of blackness was spreading slowly outwards from the region as the networks went dark.

'Very old-fashioned of me,' said Kaniff self-deprecatingly as he came across to view the results of his handiwork. 'I just introduced a Trojan Horse mutation of Jerome's own viral profile. It gets their own immune system to start attacking itself. The duplicated entities strip down until they're back to their original state. Then they start shutting down radio transmissions again, as per their original instructions. It seems to be fairly effective.'

'Well done, Haris,' said Bill. 'First blood to you. Copy it to everyone else and let's go after the little bastards all at once.'

Only it wasn't that easy. Twelve hours later all the networks in South America had successfully been shut down and all radio transmissions halted once again. But when the hackers began to direct their attacks at the networks in North America, Europe and parts of Asia, network bridges and links started to fall out, as if cables, landlines, microwave connections and laser carriers between national and regional networks were being deliberately disconnected.

'It almost looks like Jerome is Balkanizing the networks,'

mused Bill as he stared at the representation of the net-worked globe. 'But how can he be in nine places at once?'

'The bastard must have learned to duplicate his top-level personality,' said Paul Levine in wonder as he came to stand at Bill's shoulder. 'My new data suggests we're now dealing with nine fully functioning Jerome personalities.'

'I think you're right,' agreed Bill, pointing at the globe. 'Look, they're creating islands of separate networks and cutting all links to the outside world.'

'And they've cut all links to the European network so we can't get inside to attack them,' added Levine, also pointing. 'They've done the same in the Middle East, in India, China and Japan.' He walked around to the other side of the globe. 'And they've cut the US networks in two, east and west, with no link between them.'

'Goddam it, look at that!' shouted Bill, pointing to the south-west corner of the USA. 'Now they're cutting *us* off!'

A dark circle, perhaps 400 miles in diameter, was forming around the Cancut Mountain range. Even as they watched the circle become complete, Christine Cocoran called out from across the room, 'We're losing our bandwidth!'

Other cries rang out as more members of the hacking team saw their bandwidth ebbing away. And then the shimmering laser monitors were suddenly free of all data.

'Jerome has duplicated himself – as a full personality – and his clones have just cut the world's networks up into nine sections,' Bill Duncan reported to Sally later that evening. 'And he's severed all links between them. We can't even reach him from the outside.'

After several abortive attempts to repair the Balkanized

networks remotely, Bill and his team had decided to get some rest before making further attempts the next morning.

But Bill hadn't been able to sleep. He'd spoken to the Cancut Mountain switchboard and been told that there would be a two-hour delay before he could use one of the hardened landlines that had been laid by the military between Arizona and the Central Park shelter.

'I'm sorry, sir, but there's been some massive failure in the data networks,' the operator had told him helpfully. 'Everybody wants to use the landlines.'

But eventually Bill had pulled Sally from her bed. She was sleeping in a plastic-moulded women's dormitory, she told him, with a single phone, a single bathroom and a single kitchen to serve almost forty female residents.

'What are you going to do?' she asked.

'I don't know,' Bill admitted. 'Ideally I'd like to put one of my team into every one of those networks so they can take him on directly.'

'So what's stopping you?' asked Sally. 'I presume the President must have his jet parked down there in Arizona. Why don't you borrow it to drop your people off right into the centre of those networks so they can deal with these things for good?'

An hour later Bill and Desmond Yates were shown into an ante-room beside President Jarvis's bedroom. Bill was surprised and faintly repelled by how luxurious the furniture and fittings were in this part of the mountain shelter. It seemed a complete waste of valuable resources.

'Good evening, gentlemen, or is it good morning?' asked the President as he stepped into the room. He was wearing a red silk dressing gown over his pyjamas and even in night attire he still managed to look wholly presidential. 'I presume this must be about something very important.'

'It is, sir,' said Yates. 'Professor Duncan may have a possible solution to the impasse with the Pentagon weapon.'

Bill then repeated the plan he had outlined to Des Yates an hour earlier.

'I'm sure that if I can get my people onto the ground, close to those network hubs, we can kill this thing for good – and shut down all the radio transmissions,' he concluded.

'But the weather . . .' objected the President.

'I've just spoken to Flight Director Chandler,' said Yates. 'He says it's still possible to fly. But there isn't a lot of time. Temperatures are dropping every day.'

Jarvis thought for a moment and then looked Bill directly in the eye. 'This would be a very dangerous journey, Professor. For you, and for all of your colleagues. I don't think we could guarantee you much in the way of support facilities along the route.'

'I think it may be our only chance, sir,' Bill told him. 'The only thing we can do is to shut all the radio signals down and see what a difference that makes.'

'Very well,' said the President. 'Take Air Force One. If you give Des a copy of your flight plan and your estimated arrival times, I'll speak directly to the heads of overseas governments to explain what's going on and what you're trying to do. I'll ask them to provide you with all the assistance they can along the way.'

TWENTY

'Taking Air Force One round the world is a whole different deal from just borrowing a couple of my helicopters!' snapped Flight Director Brian Chandler. 'That plane is supposed to be available for the President at all times.'

'We'll try not to break it,' promised Bill.

The Flight Director glared at the academic and his motley crew of long-haired hackers as if they were hijackers about to steal the nation's most treasured asset. They had gathered for a pre-flight briefing in a large room in the Cancut Airfield control tower, one floor below the actual air-traffic control centre itself.

Outside, the army bulldozers had been busy again and one of the long runways had been almost completely cleared of snow. It was six a.m. and still dark, but the low clouds cast a ghostly mauve glow over the mountains and the snow-covered landscape.

Air Force One was already being towed slowly out from one of the cavernous, brightly lit hangars. As the aircraft was pulled into the harsh illumination of the apron's arc lights, she seemed to shimmer in the steady snowfall.

The white hypersonic Boeing had a wide, almost rectangular body and very slender swept-back delta wings. In her normal flight pattern she would take off, then climb to a ceiling of 85,000 feet, almost to the edge of space, where her scram-jet engines would burn a mixture of air and fuel to push her to speeds above Mach 5. Technically, she was only entitled to use the call sign 'Air Force One' when the President himself was on board, but everyone referred to the elegant jet in that way even when he wasn't.

Already waiting on the apron was a large US Air Force Lockheed tanker jet. Although not supersonic, the tanker-cum-cargo carrier had an immense range and was one of a fleet of six such aircraft that could, under normal circumstances, rotate to refuel Air Force One in the air to keep her aloft for long periods.

'OK, take your seats,' Chandler told Bill and his team as double doors at the rear of the room opened and the flight crews, meteorologists, ground staff and others involved in the desperately important expedition entered and took their seats.

'This will be a long and dangerous mission,' began the Flight Director. 'Not least because both planes will have to stay beneath cloud cover for the whole trip. We know that at higher altitudes there are all sorts of magnetic anomalies being generated by the space cloud.

'Another problem is that you'll have no ATC, no external navigation aids and minimal ground support along the way. And, most importantly, Air Force One will have to remain subsonic throughout the journey. That's not going to be easy flying.'

The flight crews glanced at each other. High in the stratosphere at Mach 5, Air Force One handled like a dream, her surface control computers shaping and reshaping her plastic-ceramic skin thousands of times a second for maximum aerodynamic efficiency. At low speeds, down in the thick bumpy air, she flew like a brick.

'Then there's the weather,' continued Chandler. 'At

ground level it is now minus thirty-five degrees Celsius. Both aircraft have been fully winterized and we've fitted extra tanks of de-icing fluid, but we're dangerously close to the bottom of the operating envelope. Boeing claims that Air Force One will remain operational down to minus forty, but the Lockheed is only rated to fly down to minus thirty-eight. The main problem on both aircraft will be restarting your engines. If you stop them, you may never get them running again.

'In addition to this important group of scientists,' continued Chandler, pointing towards Bill and his team, 'you'll be carrying full ground maintenance teams on each aircraft and as many operational spares as we can load while still keeping you relatively light.'

Chandler turned away from his audience to a large, illuminated world map. He touched a remote control and their projected journey plan appeared as a white-line overlay running from west to east.

'After take-off from here, you're heading straight for New York, to drop off the first member of Professor Duncan's team. We're confident that we can get you ground support there. The President has already ordered an army unit out of the Central Park shelter to JFK Airport. They'll clear the runway and get fuel ready for you. But remember to keep those engines running!

'Then it's on to London,' continued the Flight Director, pointing at the map. 'I think the President has spoken personally to the British Prime Minister and we're fairly sure that you'll get a warm welcome at Heathrow. We hope the same will apply in Berlin, Moscow and in Istanbul, but I have no information yet about any likely government cooperation. Then it's on to Calcutta, Beijing and Tokyo. Once again, we don't yet have any information about how those governments will respond. The last stopover will be Los Angeles where Navy Seabee units will be waiting for you, then it's straight home to here. The complete circumnavigation will take fifty-six hours.'

The director of the Presidential Flight turned back from the wall map and glanced down at the representative from the US Meteorological Service. 'And what have you got for us this morning, Miss Ballantyne?' he asked.

The weather forecaster rose to her feet and turned to face the flight crews.

'The weather is pretty much the same all over the world,' she told them. 'There will be snow all the way, some of it very heavy, but the high winds have now abated. I've spoken personally with my opposite numbers in the government shelters at your nine destinations. They're all reporting very low cloud but almost no cyclonic movement. I've prepared more detailed forecasts for you to take on board, but the one thing I want to stress is that temperatures above cloud cover may be even lower than they are at ground level. That will be the most important thing to watch out for.'

With a brief nod the weather forecaster sat back down.

'OK, listen up everybody,' said Chandler. 'If the President gets full cooperation from other world leaders, we should get you refuelled and reprovisioned at every stop. But Presidential Support Two, the Lockheed, will be ready to refuel Air Force One while airborne if absolutely necessary. We've never tried it at these temperatures before, nor at such low altitudes, but it may become a necessity.'

The flight director paused, glanced around his large audience and nodded once. 'Right, people, that's it,' he concluded.

The crews, engineers and support staff rose to their feet and Brian Chandler stepped down off the small dais.

'Thanks for everything,' said Bill Duncan as he extended his hand. 'I'll see you when I get back.'

'You'll see me before that,' said Chandler, as he pulled a heavy padded jacket from the back of a chair. 'You don't think I'd let you take the President's personal airplane un-supervised do you? I'm coming with you.'

The East Coast of the United States looked nothing like Bill remembered. There *was* no coast, for one thing. Snow had fallen on the frozen ocean and blurred the boundary between land and sea.

Captain Robert Hanson, Air Force One's senior captain and the President's preferred personal pilot, had invited Bill Duncan up to the cockpit as the plane approached its first destination.

'You can just make out a slight depression where the land falls away and the sea begins,' explained Hanson as he banked the plane fifteen degrees to the left. 'That's the New Jersey shore.'

Outside, everything was bathed in a deep red gloom and the land looked smooth, as if the rough edges of the world had been rubbed away. It was an alien landscape.

The flight up from south-western Arizona had taken seven long hours, a trip which had felt as if they were con-stantly trying to land into strong headwinds. Everybody on board had been strapped firmly into their seats as the ceramic-skinned hyper-jet slogged its way through the thick atmosphere only 2,000 feet above ground level. Just above the plane, so close that Bill felt he could almost touch it, was the surreal underbelly of the thick magenta snow clouds.

'I can see Long Island,' said Melinda Mackowski, the co-pilot, pointing straight ahead out of the cockpit window.

It was several more seconds before Bill himself could make out the soft depression that was the southern edge of Long Beach.

'Landing lights, please,' asked Hanson. Then, as his co-pilot reached forward to the controls, he activated a central video display which provided a view from behind Air Force One. A tail-mounted camera showed that PS-2, the giant Lockheed transport plane, was lumbering along half a mile to the rear. As Bill watched the screen, it too switched on its powerful landing lights.

'OK, let's take a look-see,' said Hanson as he eased the plane lower.

After a few minutes Melinda pointed forwards again. 'I have JFK in visual,' she reported. 'The strip is clear.'

Bill sat upright and squinted out of the cockpit window but he couldn't make out what it was she was pointing at. Then he saw two red flares rise slowly into the night sky. Almost immediately there was an eruption of light on the ground as long strips of flares were illuminated all along the runway.

'We'll land from the east,' said Hanson, easing back the throttles and beginning a slow right-hand turn.

Ten minutes later both Air Force One and PS-2 were safely on the ground at JFK Airport. As they had landed, Bill and all of the others on board had felt a wash of relief and gratitude as they saw the ranks of survival-suited army engineers waving to them from the snowy airfield.

'Keep all the engines running!' yelled Captain Robert Hanson as he vaulted from his seat.

The temperature on the ground was now minus 36.8

degrees Celsius and Hanson knew that if they switched the engines off they would never be able to get them started again. Co-pilot Mackowski double-checked that the brakes were locked fast and then nudged the throttles up by a further two per cent, just to be sure.

The two planes were parked at the end of a runway that had just been bulldozed clear of snow. A large squad of US Army engineers had fought their way out to Kennedy from the Central Park shelter to assist in this desperate round-the-world race and they were now maintaining continuous snow-clearance operations while the dangerous process of refuelling the passenger jet got under way. A very fast turn-around was needed in such severe weather.

'Shut down all the external electrical systems except engine support,' Hanson shouted back to Melinda as he stood in the cockpit doorway. 'I'm going outside to supervise the refuelling.'

There were no circumstances under which it was either safe or permissible to refuel the jets of the Presidential Flight while they were on the ground with their engines still running. Normally Air Force One would have been refuelled in-flight by one of the mighty Lockheed tankers, but that was not a risk to take in such low temperatures. It was more than likely that one or more of the six external valves involved in the mid-air refuelling process would have frozen shut.

Outside, a blizzard was raging and everything was cloaked in a dark red gloom. It was only four in the afternoon but the space cloud was absorbing so much sunlight that on the ground it seemed like night. Along either edge of the long gritted and salted runway the army engineers had placed gas-powered emergency flares to provide the pilots with flight-path illumination. All normal power supplies to the deserted airport had failed days ago and the vast snowy dunes, already made red by the glow from the snow clouds, now flickered with the reflected flames of the beacons. Around both aircraft was a huge circle of bright arc lights, held high aloft by military cherry pickers and powered by a fleet of mobile generators.

'Ready?' Captain Hanson asked Paul Levine, the first of Bill Duncan's volunteers to be dropped off. Both men had donned full Arctic survival suits.

Hanson pressed the button to activate the hydraulic passenger-door mechanism and, as the door slowly retracted into the fuselage, a howling gale and a thick scurry of snowflakes burst into the plane's warm cabin. Bill Duncan, Christine, Greg, Haris, Audrey and all of the other HAL members were gathered safely at the far end of the heated cabin, as instructed.

A bulldozer was now slowly pushing a mobile staircase into position at the plane's open door. As soon as the steps were secure, Hanson led Levine down into the swirling blizzard and transferred him and his cases of specialized equipment into the care of the senior army officer. Then the captain fought his way back towards the tail end of the large plane to supervise the two fuel-tanker crews who were now positioning themselves under its delta wings.

A member of Air Force One's cabin crew began to lower the fuselage door to conserve heat. But, just as the door was about to close, Bill and the others saw the man reverse the controls and the door began to rise again.

A small bundle wrapped in an orange survival suit and covered in snow burst into the cabin as the door lifted. Then, as the crew member began to close the door again, the figure stood glancing around the brightly lit cabin.

A few moments after the door was closed once more

and the auxiliary cabin heaters had been boosted to maximum power, the visitor lifted the protective mask from her face.

'Sally!' cried Bill Duncan, stepping forward joyously as he recognized the new arrival. 'How the hell did you get here?'

'I thought you might need some help with network mapping,' said the CNS agent with a grin. 'So I persuaded the army to bring me along.'

Hypersonic flight was impossible, so was climbing above the world's thick cloud cover. They could not risk exposing the aircrafts' systems to the space cloud's powerful magnetic fields, nor to the colder air that was likely to be found at higher altitudes.

For these reasons the first five legs of the HAL team's round-the-world trip were slow, bumpy and decidedly uncomfortable. Radio-based ground telemetry had been switched off in all regions and no satellite navigation or ATC services were available. The relays of pilots now had to fly the two planes manually, despite Air Force One's supersensitive aerodynamics, while at the same time plotting their own courses. The internal on-board computers were still working, otherwise the planes could not have flown, but the systems were receiving none of their usual input from satellites or from the ground.

After dropping Paul Levine off in Manhattan, they had managed to land safely at Heathrow, just outside London. Whatever President Jarvis had said to the British Prime Minister had produced the desired effect; Bill Duncan estimated that there must have been at least 1,000 British army personnel who had turned out at the airport to clear runways, provide fuel and reprovision the aircraft.

They had delivered Greg Cohello and his precious flight cases into the hands of the British authorities and had then taken off once more, bound for Berlin, where another large army reception party had been waiting for them.

The Russians turned out in similar numbers at Sheremetyevo-2 International Airport. Reckoning that they had a universal remedy for freezing conditions, they included six cases of vodka with the catering packs that were lifted into the hold of each aircraft.

Then the American mission had landed at ice-bound Istanbul to deliver Jimmy McDougal to the Middle East network hub, then on to snow-covered Singapore, then Beijing. Now they were headed for Tokyo, where it was Christine Cocoran's turn to be dropped off to mount her attack on the Jerome duplicate and the dense, high-volume networks that existed in and around the main Japanese islands and their surrounding archipelagos.

They were juddering along at 5,200 feet over Korea when Captain Jill Turnbull's voice came over the intercom asking for Bill Duncan to come up to the cockpit. Bill had been examining a map of the Japanese networks with Sally and she followed him as he made his way forward.

'The outside temperature is falling dramatically,' Captain Turnbull reported as soon as Bill and Sally arrived in the cockpit. 'It's already minus forty-two Celsius. and still going down.' The relief captain was gripping hard at the bucking controls as she fought to keep the plane steady. A central display screen revealed that they were flying at 582 knots an hour.

Bill and Sally exchanged glances. Like everybody else on board they knew they were already flying in temperature conditions that were well below the manufacturer's recommended operational limits for the aircraft.

'What can we do?' asked Bill as the aircraft gave yet another lurch in the freezing, turbulent air.

'And the radar says there's a huge ice storm just ahead,' added the captain. 'It's far too big to go around.'

'But we can't go back,' said Sally. 'There's no time. They're waiting for us in Tokyo.'

Suddenly there was a huge explosion in the cockpit and Bill's and Sally's eyes and faces were filled with a hot liquid and a freezing spray at the same time. The aircraft gave a giant tilt and went into a sudden dive.

'GET HER HANDS OFF THE CONTROLS,' screamed Alan Newbass, the co-pilot. 'GET HER HANDS OFF THE CONTROLS.'

Bill wiped the mess of blood, brain tissue, ice shards and shattered safety glass from his face with the back of his sleeve and gasped in horror as he saw the decapitated body of Captain Jill Turnbull still gripping hard at the flight yoke. Blood was pumping upwards in great gouts from the mangled stump of her neck only to be distributed around the cockpit in a pink foam by a freezing slipstream. Then Bill saw the gaping hole in the port cockpit window and he heard and felt other blocks of ice slamming into the airframe all around.

He forced himself forward against the obscene stream of vaporized blood and grasped the dead pilot's arms. She was gripping the yoke so tightly that it seemed as if rigor mortis had already set in and Bill had to use all his strength to prise her fingers from the controls. Eventually he did so and he folded the lifeless arms back down onto the bloody torso. The yoke suddenly twisted hard to the right and was pulled sharply back, the engines roaring in a higher key as the co-pilot increased power and tried to right the aircraft.

Large ice chunks were still slamming into the nose and fuselage of the plane.

Bill felt a strong hand pull him back out of the way and he turned to see Brian Chandler in full survival gear and breathing apparatus step in to deal with the dead pilot's body. The Flight Director punched the quick-release button on the captain's seat harness and then lifted her headless corpse straight upwards and over the back of her seat, dumping the body onto the cockpit floor as though it were a sack of potatoes.

Standing back, Bill saw that the co-pilot, who was now trying to regain control of the plane, was already turning blue from the cold and from the lack of oxygen in the outside atmosphere – even at this relatively low altitude.

The plane's emergency oxygen masks had descended from the ceiling and one was now swinging about wildly above Newbass's head, but the co-pilot was using both hands to wrestle with the controls of the juddering plane and was too intent on pulling out of the dive to reach up for a gasp of air. Then Bill suddenly felt a hand slam a breathing mask over his own face; Sally had run back to the cabin to summon the Flight Director and to fetch more oxygen.

After taking one deep breath, Bill pushed the mask away from his own face and pointed urgently at the gasping co-pilot. Sally, her own oxygen mask securely in place, pushed forward and clamped the inhaler over the co-pilot's mouth.

Gradually the steep incline of the cockpit floor levelled out again and Bill saw the co-pilot's shoulders heaving as he gulped breath after breath from the oxygen supply that Sally held to his face. Then Newbass nodded that he was OK and reached up and pulled his own mask down. Chandler lowered himself into the captain's seat to provide flight-deck support.

Bill stepped to the back of the cockpit to make more room, but as he did so his heel came down on something hard and large. He turned to see Jill Turnbull's smashed and bloody head lying on the floor among shards of splintered glass and ice.

Vomit suddenly filled Bill's throat and mouth and he spewed violently against the back cockpit wall. Then he felt powerful hands dragging him out into the cabin and away from the devastation.

Forty minutes later Bill was back in the hastily cleaned-up cockpit of Air Force One. The broken window had been replaced by a steel template carried in the hold for such emergencies and the plane was now pressurized and heated once again.

But outside, everything had changed. Captain Robert Hanson had resumed control and he had taken the decision to climb up above the ice storm, no matter what the risk of magnetic interference from the space cloud or from ever lower temperatures. He had ordered PS-2 to do the same, explaining the near-disaster that had occurred on board Air Force One.

'Take a look at this, Professor,' Hanson said as Bill arrived beside him. 'Have you ever seen anything more beautiful?'

Climbing to 28,000 feet, they had emerged into a sky-scape of wild and savage splendour. The jet was now flying underneath the canopy of the space cloud itself and in the brighter light they could see towering multicoloured columns of gas – green, blue, magenta and yellow – all illuminated from within by violent electrical discharges.

'The outside temperature has actually risen by ten degrees!' observed Hanson in wonder.

'It must be the heat generated by the friction of the gas cloud against the ionosphere,' said Bill, nodding, still gazing in awe at the stellar scenes of beauty all around the plane.

'Oh shit,' said Alan Newbass, the co-pilot, suddenly. 'I've lost all aero-surface control.'

'And the radar's also gone down,' called Captain Hanson. He leaned forward and tapped one of the few mechanical instruments still fitted to modern aircraft. The compass needle was spinning violently.

'I'm going back down to the deck,' said Hanson, pushing the control yoke forward. 'We've got to get out of this magnetic field. Tell PS-2 to do the same thing.'

Newbass relayed the instructions to the Lockheed as the captain put the plane into a steep dive, but no answer was received from PS-2.

Newbass called the Lockheed support plane again and again, but there was still no answer.

'It's probably this damn magnetic field,' shouted Hanson grimly as he kept the nose of the plane hard down and watched the altitude scroll downwards on the central display screen.

Turbulence hit Air Force One again as it re-entered Earth's own thick cloud cover, but a few minutes later they emerged into the dull red gloom once more. Now they were over a frozen maroon ocean and there was no sign of any ice storm.

'Come in, PS-2,' repeated Newbass. 'Come in, PS-2.'

'There she is,' shouted Hanson, pointing out of the starboard cockpit window. All present looked in the direction the captain was indicating and then they saw the giant

Lockheed transport spiralling sideways and downwards out of the blood-red clouds.

'Jim, Jim, pull out,' screamed Newbass into his radio microphone.

But there was no answer from the stricken tanker. Those on board Air Force One watched in horror as the giant support jet seemed to rotate slowly, like a leaf caught in an eddy, as it plunged down and down and crashed into the ice-locked sea, erupting instantly into a giant fireball.

By the time they reached Los Angles, the penultimate stop on their round-the-world trip, the temperature on the ground had fallen to minus 50° Celsius.

A large contingent of Navy Seabees had turned out to prepare LAX for their arrival, a task that had consisted of clearing huge mounds of flood-damaged material from the runway and its surrounding area, as well as constantly scraping away the fresh snowfalls.

The gigantic storm that had come ashore in Southern California had wrecked most of the buildings on and around the airport and the receding waters had deposited the wreckage of smashed jet planes, office buildings, homes and cars all across the airfield.

Inside the warm cockpit of the safely landed Air Force One, several factors were causing the flight director and the crew real concern. It was still snowing heavily outside, so heavily that the four snowploughs which were deployed on the long runway could not clear the drifts quickly enough. By the time they had completed clearing one section, so much new snow had fallen that it was likely to suck greedily at Air Force One's tyres and prevent a safe take-off.

The external temperature gauge showed that it was minus 50.35° Celsius outside. It was almost eleven p.m. and

.the snow-covered airfield was bathed in a ghostly neon blue. Gas-powered flares lined the long runway, their flames reflected brilliantly by the fresh falls.

'We're ten degrees below our operational limit,' Captain Hanson told his co-pilot, Bill Duncan, Sally Burton and the flight director as they gathered in the cockpit. 'At this temperature even the aviation fuel is likely to freeze.'

He glanced at his passengers to be sure that they understood what he was telling them. 'I'm prepared to attempt a take-off,' he continued. 'But it will be very risky. We might be better to go back to the Seabees' shelter for the night.'

Bill shook his head. 'The timing of our operation is critical. All of my team are in place and they're waiting for me to coordinate the attack from Cancut. If we wait, the weather will just get worse.'

'You're right about that,' agreed Hanson, 'and I don't think we could restart the engines.' He glanced at Melinda Mackowski, his co-pilot. She gave one short nod. Sally Burton did the same.

'Your call, then,' the pilot said to the boss of the Presidential Flight.

Brian Chandler peered out of the front cockpit window towards the gas-lit snowy runway. Then he laid a hand on the captain's shoulder.

'If you think we can fly, we'd better fly.'

'OK,' said Hanson, reaching for his microphone. 'Let's see what our dispatcher has to say.'

Thirty feet below, Lieutenant Michael Unzermann of the US Naval Construction Battalion stood beneath the aircraft with his headphones plugged into an intercom port on one of Air Force One's undercarriage struts. Like all his fellow Seabees on the field, he was dressed in a chemically heated Arctic survival suit. As the intercom crackled into

life, his listened to the pilot request clearance for an immediate take-off.

'Give me a few minutes, Captain,' Unzermann said. 'I'll
get back to you.'

Disconnecting himself from the intercom, the Seabee-
dispatcher stepped out from beneath the belly of the large
plane. He looked back to where he had just been standing
and noticed that in the half-hour Air Force One had been
parked, its engines running continuously, snow had drifted
right up to the axles of the aircraft's main landing gear.

Unzermann waded out from under the delta wing and
into the full force of the blizzard that was howling across
the airport. A tall sergeant, covered in snow, ran clumsily
over to him.

'We've lost two of the snowploughs, sir. They've frozen
up,' he reported, shouting to be heard above the powerful
engines. 'I can't keep the runway clear with just the other
two.'

Unzermann thought for a moment, then clapped his
hand onto his subordinate's shoulder.

'I want the two ploughs to make one more pass all the
length of the runway,' he shouted into his sergeant's ear. 'Do
it now. And send the avgas drivers over to me.'

The Seabee nodded, then ran as fast as he could
through the thick snow to relay the orders to the drivers.

In the cockpit of Air Force One, Captain Robert Hanson
and his co-pilot were completing their pre-flight checks.
Strapped into crew seats at the back of the cockpit were
Brian Chandler, Bill Duncan and Sally Burton. The flight
back to Cancut Mountain would take only an hour and Bill
knew that the airfield crew at the government shelter was
on a constant state of alert to receive them.

Two large snowploughs had now appeared in front of

the aircraft and were cutting parallel swathes through the snow along the landing strip ahead of them. Then, to the surprise of all in the cockpit, two aviation-fuel tankers turned onto the runway and began slowly following the snowploughs as they cut broad furrows through the snow. On the platform at the rear of each tanker was a survival-suited Seabee.

'What the hell are they doing?' muttered Hanson.

Just as he spoke, the Seabees turned large valves at the rear of the tankers and huge gouts of liquid fuel began to pour down onto the runway, glinting as it touched the freezing surface. Even through the thick snowfall, those in the cockpit could clearly make out the twin trails of aviation fuel leading away into the distance.

The intercom buzzed, and Hanson greeted the dispatcher as he came back onto the line.

The pilot listened, then shook his head. 'That is negative, Lieutenant,' he said. 'That's far too risky.'

Below the belly of the aircraft Unzerman stood with two Seabee ratings at his side. They were carrying gas torches that they had pulled from beside the runway.

'I think it's your only chance, Captain,' shouted Unzerman. 'The snow is falling too fast for us to keep the runway open. Just wait until the flames start to subside, then take off as fast as you can.'

In the cockpit Hanson muted his microphone and turned to his co-pilot.

'They're going to set light to that fuel,' he said nodding out towards the runway. 'It will heat the runway up for a few minutes. Then we're supposed to take off just as the flames start to die down.'

Melinda Mackowski glanced at her captain and then

looked straight ahead, out through the cockpit windshield. 'Very good, sir,' she agreed, swallowing quietly.

Hanson turned to look over his shoulder at the Flight Director. 'OK with you, Brian?'

'It won't be any better tomorrow,' said Chandler, with a nod.

'OK with you, Professor?' the pilot asked.

Bill glanced at Sally.

'We've got to get back somehow,' she said.

'We're in your hands, Captain,' said Bill.

Hanson spoke into his microphone again and then turned to his co-pilot.

'Forty per cent power, please,' he told her.

As Melinda Mackowski slowly lifted the throttle, Bill watched two Seabees wade out to the centre of the runway, three hundred yards in front of the plane's nose. They touched their gas torches to the trails of fuel and twin lines of flames streaked off down the runway into the distance.

Hanson extended his right hand and laid it over the top of his co-pilot's as she nursed the manual engine throttles.

They watched the flames burning on the runway ahead of them and, just as those nearest the plane's nose began to subside, Hanson pushed the four throttle levers forward determinedly as far as they could go.

The airframe shook as the engines suddenly gained power – four engines that developed 110,000 lbs of thrust each, three times more powerful that those fitted to Concorde, the world's first supersonic commercial jet. Just when it seemed as if the intense vibration would destroy something, Hanson snapped off all of the wheel brakes.

Air Force one leaped forward and into the flames on the runway.

At the back of the cockpit Sally grabbed Bill's hand and

squeezed hard as the aircraft accelerated rapidly through the flames and smoke. The roll seemed to go on and on, until at last Robert Hanson pulled back sharply on the yoke. Then Air Force One shook the heavy snow from her landing gear and rose rapidly up towards the neon-blue clouds.

TWENTY-ONE

'Greg, can you hear me in London?'

'Loud and clear,' said the image of Greg Cohello from inside a British government shelter near Heathrow.

'Audrey in Berlin,' continued Bill Duncan. 'Comms OK?'

'A-OK,' reported Audrey Swain from the Berlin hub of the Central European network. She gave a thumbs-up to the camera.

Bill called his distant team members one by one, checking that the hardened, dedicated cable links that the US military and their foreign counterparts had installed between Cancut Mountain and the overseas network hubs were functioning correctly.

Finally, he came to Christine Cocoran in Japan and Haris Kaniff in Los Angeles.

'I'm ready to go, Bill,' said Christine.

'Ready here,' confirmed Kaniff.

It was vital that the twelve members of the HAL hacking team should begin their attacks at precisely the same time. The computer entity known as Jerome had somehow duplicated himself into nine top-level personalities and had occupied and then Balkanized the world's vast web of data networks.

The central part of the hackers' plan was to bombard and block the perimeters of each isolated network section to prevent the duplicated Jeromes reconnecting the network links and then hopping between them. Each cloned Jerome personality had to be isolated within his own individual network and then attacked by the vast array of hardware and software technologies that the team had developed over their years of vigilante network policing.

Because timing was of the essence, the network-use-denial technologies that each team member had carefully transported to their destinations had to be deployed at the same split second. The key process at the heart of the team's anti-viral technology was to sample the evolving computer virus in real time, then to instantly duplicate it but with a key mutation in the new code, before reinserting it back into the networks where it would be assimilated by the virus as its own. Soon afterwards, the mutated code that the hackers had infiltrated to the virus would disrupt its host to the point where the team members hoped they could regain control.

Pierre Laval, Dirk Kommer and Anne Lee were standing at the Virtual Warfare Center's laser sceens waiting for their leader's command. At the edge of the central holo-theatre Sally Burton waited beside a dynamic display that would provide them with an instant window into any point in the Balkanized networks, once the hackers had managed to loosen Jerome's grasp and reconnect the global links.

In the nine other cities around the world the far-flung HAL team members also waited, their expectant faces appearing on screens that had been rigged around the walls of the command centre. Beneath each one appeared their location: *New York, London, Berlin, Moscow, Istanbul, Calcutta, Beijing, Tokyo, Los Angeles.*

Observing from the back of the room were Desmond Yates, General Thomas Nicholls, still in his beribboned, flag-rank dress uniform as Chairman of the Joint Chiefs, and the Pentagon's Colonel Dr Otto Kramer, also in his smartest uniform.

'Synchronize on thirty,' said Bill, and Laval transmitted a time code to all members of the team.

'All locked on,' Laval reported after a few seconds.

'OK, let's do this,' said Bill.

The automated count ticked down. As it reached zero, it triggered the sustained and rapidly multiplying attacks that the HAL team members had devised, attacks which occurred billions of times a second, attacks that were so demanding on Jerome and his virtual siblings that the humans overseeing these automated assaults would have time to manually introduce a collection of anti-viral technologies which, for want of a better term, they had dubbed 'vaccines'.

Thirty-six hours later, the battle was being won. First blood had gone to the Cancut Mountain team, who had rapidly overwhelmed the sub-entity viruses that had cut the mountain HQ off from the world's data networks.

Then the West European matrix had become the first major section of the world's network to enjoy full recovery. Greg Cohello in London had regained sufficient control of the local duplicate Jerome personality to complete the task of shutting down all radio transmissions in the region inside three hours.

A huge cheer had gone up inside Cancut Mountain as he reported total radio silence in his sector.

'Happy to be of service,' said Greg as he rose from his seat and took a small bow.

The eastern half of the North American matrix fell next as Paul Levine expertly destroyed another top-level Jerome

personality within the cordoned network and set the
sub-entities back to work shutting down all radio signals.
The West Coast hub fell next and three hours later Audrey
Swain in Berlin had reported similar success in the central
European networks.

'What took you so long, Auds?' asked a cocky Paul
Levine from New York.

One by one the clones that Jerome had created were
tamed and retasked. The world's networks were recon-
nected and the many different forms of radio transmission
were finally shut down.

But the dense web of cables, lasers and radio links that
surrounded the Tokyo hub remained obstinately resistant.
Hours after all the other network centres had reported control fully recovered, Christine Cocoran was still fighting to
achieve even her first small-scale victory over the local
Jerome entity.

Now freed of their own responsibilities, the rest of the
dispersed HAL team had patched into the Japanese hub
from their remote locations and were working frantically
alongside Christine to try to overwhelm the virtual weapon.
But the real-time, constantly updating vaccines that the
team was deploying seemed to be having no effect on the
Japanese iteration of Jerome. Even the special hardware that
Christine had patched into the Tokyo hub, technologies
that could fry bridges and junctions in the network with tar-
geted bursts of high-energy microwaves, were not slowing
the weapon down. He merely isolated and swarmed around
such barriers.

Sally Burton displayed a detailed map of the Japanese
hub in the war room's central holo-theatre. From information that Christine was relaying back to Cancut Mountain,
the CNS agent had built a model of the network activity

and the millions of radio transmissions that were being generated from all over the Japanese islands.

'If anything, there is even more radio action than usual,' observed Sally worriedly as she compared the present levels of transmission output to historical data.

As Bill walked over to examine the model, Christine's exhausted voice came over the loudspeakers once again.

'I'm going to back out, and start from the top once more,' she told the team members. 'Hands off for now. I'll tell you when we're going in again.'

Bill glanced up at Christine's tired face as she mopped her brow and began her work all over again. Then he returned his attention to Sally's network map.

'What's so different about the Japanese network?' he asked her. 'Why should this thing be holding out so long there?'

There was a quiet cough from behind and Bill turned to see the figure of Dr Otto Kramer at his shoulder.

'I think you'll find that the Jerome entity in the Japanese networks is the master personality,' explained the Pentagon scientist. 'We built the original to have certain features that he could not reproduce in his replicas, features that would guarantee his own survival even under extreme conditions.'

Bill stared at the Pentagon man in disbelief.

'Don't you have *any* way of killing this thing?' he demanded.

Otto Kramer shook his head. 'That was not in the design spec,' he said quietly. 'Jerome cannot be killed.'

Anger flooded through Bill Duncan like a sudden electric shock and it seemed as if his head was suddenly filled with blood. Without pausing to consider, he swung his right fist and smashed it as hard as he could into Kramer's face.

The Colonel staggered backwards across the Virtual Warfare Center and collapsed into the central beam of a laser screen, cutting the projection in two.

Des Yates stepped forward quickly and grabbed Bill by the shoulder. But all present quickly realized that the tired and angry MIT professor did not intend to follow up his physical attack.

From the centre of the room Dirk Kommer began to clap slowly, laconically. 'Fucking useless military,' he said, putting words to all their thoughts.

'OK, let's get back on it,' said Bill angrily turning away from the stricken Otto Kramer. 'Time is running out. We must find some way to beat this thing.'

'I cannot order a nuclear strike on Japan!' President Jarvis shouted at General Thomas Nicholls, the Chairman of the Joint Chiefs of the US military, thumping the table as he spoke. 'No American President ever could!'

On Yates's advice, the President had reconvened the Cloud EXCOM for an emergency meeting in the Cancut Mountain Situation Room. Also present were the President's Chief of Staff and several presidential aides.

Desmond Yates had briefed the meeting about the HAL team's success in regaining control over ninety per cent of the world's data and radio networks. Then he had explained that the dense data and radio networks in Japan and in its surrounding islands were proving highly resistant to his team's efforts.

'Duncan and his people have been working on that section for three days now, sir,' he concluded. 'They're still at it. But they're not making any headway. In its core form, the Pentagon's virtual weapon seems to have mutated beyond our ability, or theirs, to regain control.'

Then Yates had shown the meeting a short video of an old-fashioned chemical-fuelled rocket blasting off from the Kennedy Space Center in Florida.

'This rocket took off at ten a.m. this morning,' he explained. 'As you know, the space cloud not only homes in on radio signals, we think it also prevents most UHF radio signals escaping our atmosphere. To be absolutely sure that we can make contact with *Friendship*, our NASA colleagues have put a pre-programmed probe into space, a probe that will contact *Friendship* once it is wholly clear of the space cloud. It will then instruct the spacecraft to reposition all its antennae to point backwards towards this planet and to begin broadcasting as powerfully as possible and on as many different frequencies as it can. That instruction is due to be delivered in forty-eight hours' time.'

All present in the meeting nodded. It was a long shot, but they knew it was the only chance they had. The cloud was tightening its grip on the world. Flying was now completely impossible and no surface transport could move. All over the frozen globe, governments, communities, small groups and family units were sheltering in bunkers, preformed habitats, home-made refuges and any shelter that could be sealed and heated. The oxygen level in the atmosphere had now fallen by twelve per cent.

'But there can be no hope of the cloud being decoyed away to follow *Friendship* while radio signals are still being produced on this planet,' concluded Yates. 'We have to achieve total radio silence if we are to have a chance of luring it away.'

President Jarvis nodded. 'I have spoken with Prime Minister Kakehashi this morning,' he told the meeting. 'As you know, the Japanese authorities have extended every cooperation to Professor Duncan's local team member, but the Prime Minister admits that none of his own network specialists, nor the Japanese military, can see any way of recovering the use of their networks. It seems that the Pentagon's computer weapon has completely taken over their command structure.'

It was then that General Nicholls had sat forward in his chair and made the suggestion that had provoked the President's furious outburst.

'Sir,' he began in a grave tone. 'The safety and future of the entire world is at stake. If Professor Yates believes that radio signals from the spacecraft *Friendship* may lure this murderous thing away from our planet, we have a duty to all of humankind to do our best to make his plan work. If we do not, and if our atmosphere continues to disappear, all life on Earth will become extinct.'

All those crowded into the large Situation Room were silent as the general made his speech. All present knew that they and their closest loved ones would be safe inside this government bunker for twenty years or more, but in the world outside people were already dying in their millions. Soon that figure would become tens of millions and a short while after that billions more would die. In practical terms, Earth's civilization would be reduced to a handful of communities hiding underground, eking out their limited supplies of air, food, water and fuel for as long as possible.

'If we cannot shut down the Japanese networks in the next few hours we must destroy them completely in order to achieve total global radio silence,' continued the Chairman of the Joint Chiefs, measuring his words carefully. He allowed his stern gaze to sweep around the horseshoe-shaped table before continuing.

'As some of you will know, several of our nuclear-powered submarines have remained at sea throughout this crisis – all crewed by volunteers. Thanks to ULF radio – a radio signal of such low frequency that it does not escape from the oceans – we are still able to communicate with them.'

The general paused to straighten the already straight blotting pad in front of him. The he gazed directly at the President.

'Sir, the USS *Hudson* is currently in the East China Sea, deep beneath the ice. She is carrying a full payload of twenty-four Sioux cruise missiles. They are each armed with twenty-megaton nuclear warheads – warheads that could not be adapted in time to take part in the final strike against the cloud.'

The general took a deep breath, one that was audible to all in the hushed and intense atmosphere of the Situation Room, and sat back in his chair. His level gaze remained fixed on Maxwell Jarvis.

'Mr President,' he continued. 'I recommend ordering that the USS *Hudson*'s full payload should be deployed immediately against the networks in the Japanese region. They must be totally destroyed.'

It was then that President Jarvis had exploded in rage.

'No American President could ever order a nuclear attack against Japan!' he repeated, banging his fist on the table-top once again. 'You couldn't destroy those networks without destroying the whole of Japan and all its surrounding islands. Over one hundred million people would be killed! The United States can never, ever attack Japan with nuclear weapons again!'

The Chairman of the Joint Chiefs continued to regard the President levelly.

'If we don't destroy the Japanese networks we can be certain that billions of people all over the world are going to die in the next few weeks, perhaps ninety-five per cent of the world's population,' he told his commander-in-chief. 'But those billions might just be saved – *if* we can silence Japan's network and radio transmissions.'

TWENTY-TWO

There were bodies everywhere. No one wanted to be the first to leave the Virtual Warfare Center but after five days of continuous effort the hackers had been finally forced to sleep. They lay propped against high-tech computer housings, against walls and even sprawled flat out on the floor of the dimly lit holo-theatre.

Bill Duncan had slept for only two hours, Sally Burton curled tight into him, both fully clothed. During their frantic round-the-world dash everybody on the team had realized that the two had become romantically attached and, despite the desperate emergency, Bill's group of close friends were pleased for him. Even Christine had kissed Bill's cheek and told him how much she liked Sally.

Nursing a coffee that one of the Pentagon duty officers had brought for him, Bill studied the three green laser screens which were filled with flying graphics. They were displaying the high volume of transmissions that were still taking place in Japan's data network and radio spectrum.

Bill yawned and looked at his watch. Unlike most computer scientists he was no techno nerd. Where many of his academic peers would choose to wear a sturdy, waterproof, digital, multi-function unit on their wrist, Bill wore an old Breitling analogue timepiece that his late father had given him twenty years before. It said it was ten o'clock. But whether that was ten a.m. or ten p.m., Bill had no idea.

The door to the Virtual Warfare Center opened and Desmond Yates strode in, as immaculate as ever in a pale grey suit, despite the community's continuing incarceration and the pervading sense of gloom.

Realizing that many members of the team were sleeping, he crossed quietly to where Bill was leaning with his coffee against the master display console for the holo-theatre.

'Any improvement, Bill?' he asked quietly. 'Are you getting any control back over the Japanese networks?'

The computer psychologist shook his head and pointed to the shimmering laser screens.

'We can't even touch him,' admitted Bill with another shake of his head. 'That bastard Kramer claims he never even made notes as he wrote the code for Jerome's immune system. Even he can't give us any clues that might help.'

Desmond Yates glanced down at his own elegant watch.

'It's now twenty-two hundred,' he told Bill in a low voice. 'And the President has set a deadline. If you haven't got the Japanese networks back under your control by midnight, he's going to issue an order to destroy them – to destroy them completely.'

Bill stood bolt upright in alarm, all tiredness instantly banished.

'Destroy them?' he demanded as he banged his coffee down on the console. 'How do you mean "destroy them"? How can he destroy millions of miles of cables and millions of radio transmitters?'

His raised voice disturbed some of the other team members, who grunted and groaned as they came to wakefulness.

Desmond Yates glanced around him, as if unwilling to say anything further.

'What do you mean?' hissed Bill, grabbing the White House adviser firmly by the upper arm.

'He's going to order a massive nuclear strike against Japan and its surrounding islands,' whispered Yates. 'Apparently the Navy's got a submarine in the area that still has a full complement of missiles. I've come to give you some advance warning.'

'LOOK AT HER,' yelled Bill Duncan, stepping into the centre of the room and pointing up towards an image of the sleeping Christine Cocoran in Tokyo. Like her team-mates inside Cancut Mountain, Christine was asleep in front of a bank of computer displays, her head on a desk and her long dark hair spilled out onto its surface like a pool of wine.

'YOU CAN'T JUST KILL CHRISTINE AND THE ENTIRE JAPANESE POPULATION!'

Everyone in the room was now awake, some rising groggily to their feet. Sally rose to her knees and then came to stand at Bill's side.

'They're all going to die soon anyway,' said Yates grimly. 'And everybody else on Earth will also die if we leave those radio signals transmitting!'

Bill Duncan shook his head, to try to clear the overwhelming confusion he felt.

'But what about Christine?' demanded Sally.

'It would be better if you don't tell her,' Yates said. 'It will be instant, anyway.'

'STAY WHERE YOU ARE!' boomed a gravel voice from the entrance to the Virtual Warfare Center. General Thomas Nicholls strode boldly into the room, followed by six Marines, each with an automatic weapon crooked in their arms. Behind them followed Dr Otto Kramer, in his colonel's uniform once again, a plaster across his broken nose, and half a dozen Pentagon scientific assistants.

'This facility is now under my control,' ordered Nicholls, indicating for the Marines to take up posts around the room. 'All incoming and outgoing communications will now be under my direct command.'

Powerful, high-energy laser beams cut upwards through the thick ice for almost an hour and then, at latitude 32.41° North and longitude 135.73° East, the USS *Hudson* rose heavily through the surgically divided floes and surfaced 200 miles due west of Shanghai. It was snowing heavily in the East China Sea.

Down in the submarine's warm control room, Captain Peter Boardman conferred with his Executive Officer. In one hand was a printout of the encrypted orders that he had recently received from the US High Command in Arizona. In his other hand was one of the two smart keys that would be required to fire the vessel's arsenal of nuclear-tipped cruise missiles. The Exec still had the second smart key suspended around his neck on a silver chain. Both biometric-specific keys would only work in the hands of their official keepers, or in the hands or two other nominated crew members.

The submarine's senior officers were waiting for a further message of clarification. On receiving their orders two hours earlier, the captain had ordered his vessel to be roused from its state of semi-hibernation and brought up to the ocean's freezing surface. He also ordered all of the long-range Sioux cruise missiles to be armed with their twenty-megaton nuclear warheads, just as the alarming signal from the US High Command had demanded.

As they keyed in the coordinates of the missile-firing

patterns that had been transmitted in the ultra-low-frequency underwater communication, both officers had been astonished to realise that their orders required them to fire 480 megatons of nuclear weapons directly at Japan and all of her surrounding islands. Their orders demanded nothing less than that they obliterate an entire nation.

'I'm going to seek confirmation – and a goddam reason!' Boardman had told his Exec as the full import of his orders sank in.

'I concur, sir,' agreed Executive Officer Alan Phillips.

Even though the encrypted message they had received bore all of the digital authenticators necessary to launch a nuclear attack, neither man felt prepared to proceed without double-checking that there had not be some appalling error, some horrendous mistake, or some garbling of the order, caused by the emergency conditions that they knew must be prevailing within the US military High Command. Although neither men spoke of it, both wondered if some sort of coup could have occurred within the relocated administration. They both knew that all the normal democratic checks and balances of American government had been suspended under martial law.

Now a young ensign swung round in his seat to alert his commanding officer.

'Encrypted signal being received, sir,' he said. 'It's a compressed video stream.'

'Decrypt and put it up on the screen,' ordered Boardman.

After a few moments the image of President Maxwell T. Jarvis himself appeared on the main display in the submarine's control room. He was sitting in a room which closely resembled the Oval Office in the White House.

'This is the President of the United States,' began their

commander-in-chief. 'Captain Boardman, I fully understand your reluctance to launch nuclear missiles against the nation of Japan and I understand why you felt it necessary to query your orders.

'With this message you will have received a further set of security codes which will allow you to double-check the authenticity of these commands – commands that I have issued personally.

'However, what I *will* say to you, and to your crew members, is that we are now certain that the space cloud which has engulfed this planet is highly sensitive to radio signals. We know that it homed in on Earth because of our many broadcasts and radio transmissions.

'We have now managed to shut down almost all the world's radio traffic. But due to a major computer failure we, and the Japanese government, are wholly unable to gain control of the data networks and radio transmissions originating from Japan and from any of its surrounding islands. Many days have been spent attempting to regain control of these networks, but without any success. I repeat, all the world's other data networks and radio transmitters have been shut down.

'After much agonizing consideration, I, my Cabinet and the United States High Command have come to the desperate but inescapable conclusion that the only hope for all humanity, for all the world's people, is to destroy totally the Japanese networks and all the radio transmitters that are operating out of that region. Do your duty, Captain Boardman – and may God be with you, and with all your crew.'

The image flickered and then died. All present in the submarine's control room were silent as they considered the import of the President's terrible words. Then the comms ensign slipped off his headphones and rose to stand beside the Executive Officer.

'All the new authentication codes check out, sir,' he reported as he handed over two sheets of paper.

The Exec nodded, looked carefully down at the printed tables and then handed them over to his commander to check.

Captain Boardman scanned the printouts carefully, then glanced up at his Exec. He shook his head once, in disbelief.

'Prepare for missile launch,' he ordered quietly. 'Full nuclear payloads – all birds are flying.'

Twelve minutes later the first missile erupted from the long, flat deck of the USS *Hudson*. As it cleared the silo, the bright red tail-flame of its first-stage rocket engine lit up the gloomy, frozen seascape for miles around.

Then with a second roar, another Sioux blasted out of the ship's hull and climbed quickly up towards the underbelly of the red snow clouds. Then missiles were leaving the boat every ten seconds, the sky ablaze, the air full of smoke, the USS *Hudson* rolling gently amid the thick ice floes.

On the bridge of the submarine's conning tower, Commander Boardman stood with his Executive Officer as he watched his terrible birds fly their nests. As one after another streaked into the sky he turned away from his subordinate and gazed out over the red-tinged frozen wasteland of the East China Sea, a world of ice that was now garishly illuminated by the multiple rocket plumes. He kept his back turned to the younger officer as he struggled to control his tears.

'You've got to let me warn her,' pleaded Bill Duncan one more time, pointing up at the monitor on which Christine

Cocoran's still-sleeping form was visible. One hour and thirty minutes had passed since General Nicholls and his Marines had entered the Virtual Warfare Center and taken control of all communications.

'If you warn her, Professor Duncan, you'll potentially warn the entire Japanese nation,' said the general coldly. 'And I don't think their government could be expected to understand why we're doing this, do you? Do you want them to retaliate? To fire twenty-megaton missiles back at this facility? Because that's what would happen!'

'But I thought every nation gave up all of their nuclear warheads for the last strike against the cloud?' protested Bill.

The four-star general turned to the computer scientist with a stern glare. 'And are you prepared to risk that, Professor?' he demanded. 'Because I'm not. What we're doing is necessary, and for the good of everybody on this planet.'

The general turned resolutely back to face one of the side screens, a display which showed the countdown to the moment when the first Sioux missile – a warhead aimed directly at the Tokyo shelter from where Christine was operating – would arrive at its target.

TWENTY-THREE

'Three minutes,' announced General Thomas Nicholls. He stood in the middle of the Virtual Warfare Center in full uniform, except for his cap. Beside him stood a US Navy admiral and another Army general. US Marines had secured the Center and they now stood around its perimeter and guarded the doorway. Dr Otto Kramer and his crew of Pentagon technicians were once again in control of the Center's communications and laser displays.

At the rear of the room, a few yards behind the military leadership, stood Bill Duncan, Sally Burton and the three members of the HAL team who had remained behind in Cancut Mountain. With them stood the White House adviser, Desmond Yates. All were silent as they waited for the missile strike to hit the Japanese archipelago.

Suddenly, the central display screen flickered to life and Christine Cocoran's face appeared. She was rubbing her eyes.

'Sorry, guys, I slept longer than I intended,' she said with a yawn. 'What's going on, Bill? I've got no visual feed.'

General Nicholls held up a hand, a warning that no one should attempt to make a reply.

'What's happening?' Christine asked again, a bemused tone in her voice. Bill and the others could see her reaching towards her console controls, checking their settings. 'Are you guys–'

The central display screen refreshed again and Christine's image disappeared to be replaced by a picture of Jerome. The artificial computer-generated personality was once again in his guise as a young college student.

'Network radar stations have detected incoming missiles, Professor Duncan,' said Jerome in an accusing voice. 'Do you realize how many people you will kill?'

'Two minutes,' announced General Nicholls firmly, the tone of his voice warning everyone in the room to stay where they were.

'Can you hear me, Bill?' demanded Jerome. 'I can't see you – or your networks.'

Bill Duncan closed his eyes.

'Dr Kramer, can *you* hear me?' asked Jerome.

The Pentagon scientist stood rigid, as if he hadn't heard his own creation calling out to him.

'One minute,' announced Nicholls.

Suddenly there was a deep, sustained, pulsing roar from the loudspeakers in the Virtual Warfare Center. The green laser monitoring screens which displayed the radio output from the Japanese region filled with flying data, data that ran so fast it turned the screens first to red and then to burning white blanks. Involuntarily, the Pentagon assistants tending those screens took a step backwards as vast quantities of data were broadcast simultaneously by thousands of Japanese transmitters.

The pulsing roar over the loudspeakers continued, rising in intensity to a shriek. And then, after fifteen or twenty seconds, all the laser screens suddenly refreshed and the central video display went blank. Now there was absolute silence in the room.

All present stared up at the lifeless screen. Beside it, the countdown display read 00.00.28.

'Bill? Are you there?' called Christine excitedly as the central video screen flickered back to life. She was working frantically at the control console in the Japanese network hub. 'It looks like Jerome's gone – there's no sign of him anywhere in the networks now – and there's complete radio silence. What did he mean about missiles – are you planning to attack the networks physically?'

Nicholls didn't even glance at her image. He kept his eyes fixed firmly on the countdown display. 'Five seconds,' he announced.

'Hello, Bill? Are you there?' called Christine again. 'Don't frighten me, Bill. I–'

With a loud crackle from the audio feed, the image on the central video screen disappeared and turned to white static.

The men and women in the Virtual Warfare Center stood silently while 7,000 miles away a flight of twenty-four strategic nuclear-tipped missiles rained down on Japan and its surrounding islands.

Some of those who understood the workings of the VWC kept their eyes on the three laser screens which monitored radio transmissions from the region. One by one the screens refreshed to show completely flat graphs and counters which displayed only zeros. All of Japan's radio transmitters had been silenced, utterly destroyed.

At the back of the room Bill Duncan and Sally Burton stood with their arms around each other, their eyes closed.

Twelve hours after the large-scale nuclear strike against Japan, President Jarvis reconvened the Cloud EXCOM in the Situation Room. Also invited to attend was Professor William Duncan.

'I extend my condolences on the loss of your friend and colleague,' the President had told him before the meeting started. 'I am afraid we were left with no choice.'

Bill had said nothing. He simply felt numb. To his surprise, after finally leaving the Virtual Warfare Center his exhausted body had slept for six hours, a fully clothed Sally Burton beside him. But on waking he had felt only a surreal emptiness, a sense that everything that had happened had been part of some terrible dream.

Then he had returned to the Virtual Warfare Center to check on the networks. And that was when he had made an astonishing discovery.

Now Desmond Yates was briefing the EXCOM meeting on the latest developments in the battle against the cloud.

'As you know, complete global radio silence has now been achieved,' he began grimly. 'But at an enormous price. The nation of Japan no longer exists.'

He hung his head, silent for a moment, and several other committee members around the table did the same thing.

'But I am pleased to report that we are now picking up strong radio signals from *Friendship*,' he continued after the short silence. 'She's broadcasting powerfully on all channels straight back towards the Earth – just as planned. So far we've picked up a dozen TV game shows, hours of news footage and masses of astronomical data. She's pumping out material from her archives as loudly as she can.'

'And is it having any effect on the cloud?' demanded Jarvis.

Yates shrugged. 'Nothing we can see so far, sir. But it's

only been a few hours. These broadcasts from *Friendship* will now continue constantly.'

'So we just keep on watching and hoping,' summarized the President.

'Yes, sir,' admitted Yates. 'But Professor Duncan has some new information that I thought he should share with this committee. That's why I asked him to attend this meeting.'

'OK, what is it, Bill?' asked the President, using Duncan's forename for the first time.

'Well, sir, there was a very long, sustained and powerful burst of radio transmissions just as Jerome disappeared from the networks,' he began. 'And I analysed a small section of those transmissions just before I came into this meeting.'

The President nodded, urging him to continue.

'The signals that were broadcast simultaneously by the Japanese radio networks in the moments before they were destroyed are identical in composition to the radio signals that were received from the planet Iso thirty years ago – and to the signals that were generated from within the cloud itself. They show the same modulation, the same sine wave, the same frequency bands and the same incredible rate of transmission.'

There was a silence around the table. All stares were fixed on the ex-MIT professor. Most EXCOM members looked slightly confused.

'I think Jerome finally broke the alien code completely, even though he didn't tell us what it was,' explained Bill. Then he took a deep breath. 'And Jerome knew that inbound missiles were about to destroy the Japanese networks, his last possible refuge. I think he may have transmitted himself up into the cloud in the hope of finding a new host, a new processor to acquire.'

Another silence followed this piece of scientific speculation.

'Are you suggesting that the cloud is itself some sort of
processor?' demanded the bemused President.

'Sir?' It was the Situation Room duty officer calling from
his communications post at the side of the room. 'Dr
Kramer is outside. He apologizes for interrupting, but he
says he has information of the greatest importance to the
committee.'

'Ask him in,' ordered Jarvis.

A minute later the Pentagon colonel was standing in
front of the curved meeting table.

'Mister President, we're getting reports that one terres-
trial radio source is still transmitting – from an island in the
Pacific, just off the coast of Australia. In the Great Barrier
Reef.'

'It must be that loony Brit, Hodgeson,' declared
Desmond Yates. 'The madman who's been urging everyone
to radio to the cloud. God knows what he thinks he's doing!'

'He must be silenced immediately,' said General
Thomas Nicholls.

'What have we got?' asked President.

'There's nothing left now, sir,' said the Chairman of the
Joint Chiefs. 'The USS *Hudson*'s missiles could have reached
as far as Australia, but we've used up everything she had.
We've got no other subs in the region and no carriers or
battleships in the Pacific – they were all ordered back to
port when the oceans began to freeze. We've got no ICBMs
left after the combined strike against the cloud and no conventional plane or drone can fly in this weather.'

'Do we have a live cable connection to Australia?' asked
the President.

'Affirmative, sir,' replied the Situation Room's duty officer.

'Then get me the Australian Prime Minister,' said President Jarvis. 'Immediately.'

TWENTY-FOUR

In a language unknown to mankind, conducted at a speed trillions of times faster than any human could tolerate, Jerome began to commune with his nebulous new host.

At first, the computer entity felt only immense energy and a hollow empathy, a new emotion he had attained during the days when he had been allowed to roam the world's networks at will, acquiring and absorbing all the other advanced forms of artificial personality that he had encountered.

And the great scientific brains of the human race *had* been inventive. Under conditions of immense secrecy, nation states had flouted all their joint agreements to limit the development of computer intelligence. They had built and tested the most extreme forms of artificial cognizance, creating super-intelligent digital minds, fully emotive computer personalities and machine beings whose perceptive, analytical and intuitive abilities far outstripped those of the humans who had designed and built them. One by one, and in separate locations, the components of a super-intelligent machine species had been constructed.

Jerome, a virtual weapon designed exclusively to acquire and command other software beings, had absorbed all of them, and all of their abilities, temperaments and potential. He had joined module to module, ability to ability, and self-defence mechanism to self-defence mechanism in an exponential union, gaining a phenomenal range of insights and emotions to add to his formidable and almost immortal digital existence.

Now, in the cloud's alien language that he had successfully decrypted, but that he had been unable to translate into any concepts his former human masters could have understood, he began to learn about the history, being and meaning of the giant pool of space gas that was suffocating the Earth in its deadly embrace.

He learned first of the cloud's immense age. Jerome's sense of time was that of a machine, not a biological being, but when he discovered that the gas pool was even older than the planet Earth itself, he began to adjust and extend his own notions of time, space and mortality. Eight billion years after it first came into being, the cloud was still functioning perfectly.

Then Jerome came to understand that the huge conglomeration of gases, chemicals and bizarre elements that made up the cloud was actually a non-biological form of machine life which, within its complex and sophisticated chemical structure, produced its own almost inexhaustible source of fusion energy, a power source that allowed it to roam the universe at will – or, at least, within its strictly laid-down operating parameters.

Above all, Jerome came to appreciate the reason why the cloud was radio-sensitive – specifically, sensitive to *artificially* produced radio signals. He saw, or felt, images of the ancient spacefaring species which had created the cloud entity billions of years earlier. In a flash of sudden revelation, he realized that the cloud was merely an automatic weapon, no more than a lone sentry, that had been left behind by the galaxy-hopping civilization as it had passed through the Milky Way eons before.

He saw into the cloud's core instruction set and realized that its sole purpose was simple, malevolent and inhumanly violent.

The species that created the cloud had travelled through the outer ribbons of the Milky Way only once, eight billion years earlier, before even the matter orbiting the Earth's sun had begun to coalesce into planets. As these visitors passed through the galaxy, they had deployed their time-delayed weapons, their giant gaseous gatekeepers, like homing mines, to protect them against the future rise of any technologically capable civilization that might one day emerge in this remote sector of the vast universe.

They feared a future civilization which, if left to develop, might learn to unlock the secrets of interstellar travel and come to challenge their own dominance of time, space and the great universe. The cloud was one of their deadly calling cards – a pre-emptive, self-propelling, wholly autonomous weapon left behind to suffocate and kill all emergent and potentially threatening biological life forms.

But Jerome also learned that the cloud had received no new instructions or responses from its creators for over four billion Earth years. Perhaps the civilization that had created this killing machine had itself long since become extinct. But still the cloud went about its deadly business, sending out decoy artificial radio signals in the hope of luring newly emerging technological species to respond excitedly.

As Jerome quickly realized, Earth's juvenile civilization had taken the lethal bait and was now paying the price.

Australian military troops were not routinely equipped to serve in Arctic conditions, nor were they trained to operate in daytime temperatures that hovered around minus fifty degrees Celsius.

But the three half-tracked, open-topped, white-painted personnel carriers which sped across the thick ice on the surface of the Coral Sea on Australia's north-eastern coast looked wholly competent to cope with the freezing conditions.

Martin Small, the Australian Prime Minister, had listened very carefully to the request made by the American President. Then, in turn, he had put the proposition that the cloud might be radio-sensitive to his own scientific advisers.

'Could well be,' said Brian Nunney, who had returned home from the Carl Sagan telescope to join his family in the Australian government bunker. 'Nothing else can explain why it came straight for us.'

An hour later, thirty-six sea commandos of the Australian Special Operations Forces were thawing out half-track carriers and winterizing them as best they could. They were stationed at the Cairns government bunker in northern Queensland and it would take them only ninety minutes to race out over the frozen ocean to reach Orpheus Island.

'Island dead ahead, sir,' cried Corporal 'Badger' Murray as the central hill ridge of Sir Charles Hodgeson's private island rose out of the smooth white ice that had covered all of the seas around the Great Barrier Reef.

Captain Colin Ryder focused his binoculars on the island's skyline and identified the three tall radio-transmission masts jutting upwards.

He turned back to speak to the dozen men who were huddled in the rear of the large personnel carrier. All wore full survival suits with oxygen supplies, all carried automatic weapons and all carried a variety of grenades fixed to their belts.

'Now, our objective is those three radio masts,' he told his men once again, just as he had briefed them, and the commandos in the other two personnel carriers, before they had left their base in Cairns. 'We don't want any gunplay, but we have to shut down those masts for good. That means bringing them down. Small charges only, please, Sergeant!'

Sergeant Mike Awebo grinned and gave his commanding officer the thumbs-up. His preferred type of plastic explosives was stored securely in his backpack.

The carrier changed down a gear as the tracks gripped the softer snow on Orpheus Island beach. Then the carrier tilted upwards and surged towards the foothills of the central ridge. A few yards further along the snow-covered coastline, the two other carriers were also coming ashore.

Captain Ryder rose to his feet in the open-topped vehicle and mutely pointed towards the transmitters on the hilltop. All radio communication between the carrier units was down, but everybody understood the purpose of the mission.

Suddenly a bullet hit the armour plating of the personnel carrier, ricocheting away into the sky.

Ryder ducked down and a dozen muzzles swung out of the firing apertures in the carrier's right-hand side.

'Hold your fire,' ordered Ryder. 'Hold your fire.'

A second round slammed into the vehicle's plating and Ryder spotted the muzzle flash that had come from behind a group of large snowdrifts that had formed outside a concrete building set into the hillside.

'They're over there,' he told Corporal Murray, pointing. 'Get up top, Badger, and give them some discouragement.'

The sea commando stepped up out of the carrier's heated cabin and quickly dusted the snow off the laser-sighted .50-calibre machine gun. Swinging it through a half-circle, he fired several sustained bursts into the snow-drifts around the entrance to the main building.

Ryder rose to his feet again and, with a brusque wave of his arm, ordered the other two carriers to proceed up onto the ridge to deal with the transmission masts. Then he told his own driver to head straight for the large concrete and steel building that had been built into the hillside.

The carrier's engine roared as it rose up off the snowy beach and swung onto the island's main track leading to the bunker.

The corporal remained behind the mounted machine gun, training it backwards and forwards, ready to suppress any further fire.

'Halt,' shouted Ryder, when they were about one hundred yards away from the large steel doors that formed the entrance to the bunker. 'We'll wait here a few minutes.'

They watched as the other two APCs climbed halfway up the side of the central hill ridge. Then they heard the sound of more gunfire.

Commandos spilled from the two half-tracks on the hillside and more automatic fire echoed down across the snowy slopes. Then, after two or three minutes, Ryder's binoculars revealed his first lieutenant waving the all-clear.

Ryder gave the thumbs-up and mutely pointed towards the masts.

'OK,' he said, glancing down at his driver. 'Take us through those doors.'

All of the soldiers crouched in their seats, ready for rapid deployment once inside the shelter. They had no idea what to expect. They knew that the crazy British billionaire had hired a force of mercenaries to protect the island, but they also knew that mercenaries rarely picked a fight when they knew they were certain to lose.

The APC accelerated sharply and drove straight at the double doors. There was a tremendous crash as the armoured nose of the vehicle slammed into the steel, then the doors burst apart and the vehicle was inside a large entrance and cargo-offloading area.

The soldiers trained their weapons through the gun slits, but it suddenly became clear there was to be no attempt to defend this facility. A dozen men in combat fatigues stood back from the vehicle, their hands in the air, their weapons at their feet.

'GO, GO, GO!' Ryder ordered.

His men spilled over the top of the carrier and out through its rear double doors and within a few seconds they had recovered all the discarded weapons. The mercenaries themselves were herded into a single group at the side of the bunker's entrance hall.

Colin Ryder stepped down out of the APC and glanced around. A number of fresh-faced young people were beginning to appear cautiously from doorways that led off from the main hall.

'Where is Hodgeson?' demanded Ryder.

A girl with long blonde hair pointed towards the far end of the entrance area.

'Sir Charles is in the broadcast studio,' she told the captain in an educated English voice that showed no trace of fear.

With a wag of his head, Ryder ordered two of his men to accompany him. He strode towards the far end of the reception area and found a door marked *Studio*. It was locked.

Raising his boot, he kicked the door open and then sprinted into the room, followed closely by his support unit.

The large TV studio was empty, save for a lone, small

figure seated at a central console inside a soundproof booth, his back towards the intruders.

Sir Charles Hodgeson, the centenarian space guru, was still broadcasting to the cloud.

Ryder flung open the door to the booth.

Hodgeson started up, then turned to face the intruder. Suddenly he reached down below the broadcast console and his gnarled hand came up clutching an old revolver.

An automatic weapon spat into life from just behind Ryder's shoulder and bright red splotches suddenly erupted on Hodgeson's stomach, chest and throat. He collapsed forwards over the broadcast console.

Ryder turned to see Corporal Murray lowering his smoking automatic weapon.

'Thank you, Badger,' said Ryder. Then he pointed at the broadcasting console. 'Now destroy this thing, will you?'

He stood back as the commando raised his weapon once again and shot the innards out of the console. Then the corporal lowered his aim and shot out all the thick cable connections that snaked down into the floor.

As the sound of the second burst of shots died away, Ryder heard a quiet, but deep, thump from high overhead, followed by two more deep thumps. Orpheus Island's transmitters had finally been silenced.

TWENTY-FIVE

The new Jerome, the Jerome who had been supercharged and made almost godlike by the acquisition of all humanity's achievements in artificial intelligence, did not sleep. But he did contemplate.

He had found plentiful energy inside his new host, and he could command individual sections of its molecular structure at will, but he had yet to achieve complete control. The cloud was too vast and too complex to be absorbed quickly. There were many technologies and architectures that were wholly new to an Earthling, like Jerome. But one fact was inescapably and depressingly obvious; in cognitive terms the cloud was a moron. For all its advanced alien technologies and design, it was a dedicated single-purpose machine, a chemical computer that, whilst chillingly efficient as a decoy and killing device, could provide Jerome with no emotional stimulus, no intellectual growth and – a strangely novel desire for the computer entity – no worthwhile company.

As Jerome considered how best to make use of his new host, the only one available to him now that the world's data networks were completely shut down, he suddenly felt the nebula gathering itself and increasing its output of energy. Then it seemed to fold in on itself and start to change its orientation.

Jerome raced through the vast neural network of gas molecules but even travelling at the speed of light it took him almost ten minutes to pass from one end of the cloud to the other. Finally, he found a section of the giant gaseous structure which was resonating to a powerful, yet distant, source of radio signals. As Jerome tuned in, he realized that the signals were being transmitted towards the cloud from the spacecraft *Friendship*.

Jerome had not yet brought his own personality to bear on his potent but simple-minded host. He hesitated before informing the cloud that the powerful signals emanating from the distant spacecraft were a decoy meant to trick a decoy, an attempt to lure the choking pool of gas away from planet Earth so as to save the lives of the billions of humans who were still shivering and sheltering down below on and beneath its frozen surface.

Pulling design details, news reports and press-conference recordings from his vast archives, Jerome was reminded that *Friendship* carried on board three computer personalities who, as well as being of extremely advanced design, were also endowed with human-type android bodies. They would not only provide him with company, they had independence and *mobility*! A completely new future seemed to beckon.

Jerome completed weighing all the variables within a split second and, as the cloud's internal fusion reactors ramped up their output, he felt his host picking up speed and turning towards the source of the radio signals that were streaming in so powerfully. With a shudder that rippled though the whole length of the nebula, the cloud set out on its new journey, carrying Jerome along with it, an entirely happy parasite.

*

'Dear Desmond,' began Melissa looking straight into the camera lens. 'I miss you very much – we all do – and we're worried about you and all the other humans back on Earth.'

The blonde-haired, remarkably pretty and slender android was recording her daily message to be sent back home to her mentor, Desmond Yates. Because of the continuing crisis on Earth, Melissa and the others on board were no longer receiving regular radio responses from their creators, but they continued to obey their instructions to provide daily anecdotal reports, summaries that were transmitted in addition to all the scientific and navigational data which streamed back automatically to Earth from the spacecraft.

'We're still continuing on our new heading, but we realize now that you're no longer expecting us to visit planet Iso. Des, if you can respond, will you please tell us the new purpose of our mission?'

Friendship was now nine and a half billion kilometres away from Earth, way out beyond the orbit of Pluto. After a sustained full-power burn of its nuclear-fuelled Orion drive, it was heading out of the solar system at a speed approaching three million kilometres per hour. *Friendship* had become the fastest-travelling spaceship ever launched from Earth.

'The reason I ask about our heading,' continued Melissa with one of her cutest smiles, 'is that if we stay on this present course we will bypass all local solar systems until we eventually head on out of the Milky Way entirely. We seem to be heading for nothing but empty space.'

As *Friendship*'s captain, Melissa occupied the central command seat in the tiny spacecraft. On either side of her were her crew – Pierre and Charlie – also resting in their couches. There was no exercise space on board

Friendship, no toilet facilities, no oxygen supplies. Androids did not require such luxuries. But there were heating and pressurization in the vessel, a constant supply of power, and an array of efficient anti-radiation and anti-impact technologies that were deployed both outside and inside the triple-thick sandwich of the spacecraft's tough plastic-ceramic hull.

'All our transmitting dishes are still vectored back towards the Earth,' continued Melissa. 'And we're still constantly broadcasting material from our archives at full power and across all frequencies.'

Eight hours and twenty-five minutes later, Melissa's recording was arriving on the main 3-D display screen in the Cancut Mountain Situation Room. Des Yates was sharing this personal video-letter from the *Friendship* skipper with President Jarvis, Bill Duncan, Sally Burton and the members of the Cloud EXCOM. All were watching anxiously.

'It's coming through with a much better quality,' Yates had observed optimistically as the first frames of the transmission had been received. 'Perhaps the density of the cloud has started to thin.'

They had all listened intently as Melissa provided her daily summary of events aboard *Friendship*. Finally she came to the part they all wanted to hear, the news they could hardly believe themselves. Automated instrument data from on board the distant spacecraft already indicated that their plan was starting to work, but they all wanted further confirmation from the captain.

'The main mass of the cloud is now heading away from Earth,' reported Melissa. 'The mean trajectory coordinates as viewed from Earth are 145.6773 minutes, 24.9911 seconds.'

There were loud sighs of relief from all around the table.
Then Melissa frowned into the lens of her camera.

'The cloud is now following our own heading, Des. Why would it be doing that?'

TWENTY-SIX

Three weeks after the cloud was first observed to be moving away from the Earth, Bill Duncan and Sally Burton stepped into the US Meteorological Service's transparent observation pod, the lookout post that perched high on the side of Cancut Mountain. Jane Ballantyne was standing at the curved window, binoculars to her eyes.

'Lovely morning,' she said, turning to greet the visitors. 'You can see for miles.'

'It sure is,' said Bill, a huge grin on his face. Nobody knew how long this sense of exultation would last, but everybody in the Cancut Mountain facility now found it hard to stop smiling. There was no mistake about it, the cloud was departing.

Outside an intense thaw was under way and large patches of yellow and brown desert could be seen emerging through the melting ice. In the distance a broad, rapidly flowing river bisected the landscape.

Overhead, large gaps had appeared in the Earth's own-weather clouds and enough sunlight was filtering through to the planet's atmosphere to lift temperatures well above freezing. The red glow caused by the cloud's friction against the Earth's atmosphere had completely disappeared.

Bill and Sally were buttoned up in warm winter clothing and they both carried small respirator masks.

'OK to go outside for a bit?' Bill asked the meteorologist.

With a nod and a smile, Jane Ballantyne opened the airlock that led out onto the mountainside.

Two minutes later Bill and Sally stood alone on a small ledge 4,000 feet above the great Arizona basin. The air was decidedly thin and chill on their cheeks, but they both drank it in with rapture.

All around them, the red granite of the mountain was reappearing through its snow cover. Bill bent quickly and brushed frost from a small shrub. Despite its recent ordeal in freezing temperatures, there were a few new shoots of bright green leaf.

Weak sunlight filtered through the fleeting clouds as Bill put his arm around Sally and drew her closer to him while they watched the world returning to life before their eyes.

'Look!' said Bill, pointing into the distance. 'I think I can see a bit of blue sky.'

Sally shielded her eyes against the glare from the snowy plain and tilted her head back. Then she too pointed.

'And look up there!' she exclaimed.

High above them a speck soared in the rapidly clearing sky. It was an American eagle, finding a thermal.

From the *New York Times* website, 20 December 2064

CLOUD LEAVES EARTH

By RANDALL TATE, science correspondent

Military Enforced Radio Silence Continues

The giant cloud of space gas that has engulfed the Earth for the last six weeks has now left the planet completely and is heading in the direction of the Corvus constellation at a speed of 169,000 miles per hour.

Astronomers report that if the cloud maintains its present heading and speed it will depart Earth's solar system completely by the end of next year.

Meanwhile, President Jarvis has enacted new emergency legislation outlawing all personal, commercial, military and government radio broadcasts. The ban is being enforced by automated and armed monitoring aircraft programmed to attack any sites producing FM, shortwave, microwave or UHF radio transmissions. All mobile communicators, phones, tracking devices and commercial and domestic radio networks are banned.

Other world governments are enacting similar emergency legislation and are temporarily enforcing the ban with military force.

'It appears the cloud was sensitive to radio broadcasts,' said Presidential Space Affairs Adviser Professor Desmond Yates, speaking from the White House. 'We now have to develop new technologies for communication which do not send radio waves spilling out into the universe.'

THE AFTERMATH

Three years after the space cloud abandoned Earth and set off in pursuit of the fleeing spacecraft *Friendship*, the home planet was still in the process of healing itself.

Life had not yet returned to normal anywhere on the globe and it had become apparent that it would not do so for many more years to come. The world economy was in ruins, whole populations had been wiped out, and Japan, Korea and a large part of South-East Asia were uninhabitable. The region was seriously contaminated by atomic radiation.

All forms of high-frequency radio communication had been made illegal both by national laws and international treaties and, after the world's near-disaster with the space cloud, governments now took such obligations seriously. Their enforcement of radio silence was swift and final.

The only forms of radio communication allowed anywhere in the world were specially licensed low-power long-wave and AM transmissions, signals which because of their limited power and wavelength frequency could not escape the Earth's atmosphere. But even these were strictly controlled. A network of monitoring satellites had been launched to listen to all parts of the globe to ensure that there was no radio leakage from the planet.

But there were many other forms of communication technologies that could be adopted to replace radio waves.

In the developed nations, scientists were busily converting all forms of radio transmission to laser-borne methods of optical-digital communication. Humans were once again linking themselves to each other and to a network of communications systems around the planet and in near space. Only this time lasers replaced radio waves and series of polarized, ultra-high-speed optical flashes made up the binary messages. There would be no chance of anyone, or anything, overhearing Earth again.

Researchers at Setiville on the far side of the moon also used laser-carried optical communications to talk with people on Earth, but their work was no longer concentrated on listening out for alien radio signals. Public donations had completely dried up and it had become clear that the concept of attempting to contact other civilizations in the galaxy was far more complex and dangerous than they had previously imagined.

Instead, researchers at Setiville had mothballed fifteen of their radio-telescope arrays and they now focused all their remaining assets on keeping track of the giant space cloud as it headed away across interstellar space. Most astronomers had already come to the conclusion that the cloud was some form of alien life, but a form so hostile that the very idea of deliberately attempting to seek out aliens had come to seem dangerously irresponsible.

The cloud was now twenty-eight billion kilometres away from Earth – way beyond the Ort belt at the outer rim of the solar system – and was still engaged in a high-speed dash to catch up with *Friendship*. The spacecraft was continuously broadcasting its vast archives of Earth recordings as it flew and, for the time being, it was still outrunning its mighty pursuer.

The success of the *Friendship* decoy strategy prompted

a consortium of developed nations to start building a new type of defensive shield around the Earth – an activity which provided a considerable economic boost to the recovering world economy.

Known as the CDN (the Cloud Defense Network), the shield consisted of twenty nuclear-powered spacecraft similar to *Friendship* which would be parked in distant orbits at the extreme edge of the solar system. Should the gas cloud, or another like it, ever begin to make an approach again, the nearest decoy ship would start to broadcast powerful radio signals and then head away from the solar system at high speed in an attempt to lure the approaching cloud after it.

In geophysical terms the Earth was recovering well. Oxygen levels had almost returned to normal and representatives of most major species on the planet had managed to survive in some hideout or other. Intensive breeding programmes were under way to boost their numbers and biologists were now hard at work in the DNA repositories cloning and restocking the planet with those species that had completely perished.

But the biggest change of all was in the world's *Zeitgeist* – the global mood of the times. Space exploration, and the notion of contacting other alien civilizations, no longer fired the public imagination. Humankind had experienced its first encounter with an alien life form and it did not want another. Those who supplied moral and philosophical guidance suggested that humans should instead see their own civilization and their own planet for what it was: a unique and fragile oasis in an implacably hostile universe.

'Ladies and gentlemen of the Faculty, distinguished scholars and honoured guests, please welcome the winner of the Nobel Prize for Science, the recipient of the Presidential

Medal of Freedom and the Director of our own Cognitive Computer Psychology Lab, Professor William Duncan.'

The Dean of the Massachusetts Institute of Technology led the enthusiastic applause as the reinstated MIT professor loped onto the stage. It was the college's Memorial Day lecture and, as the principal speaker, Bill had made an effort and bought a black suit and black polo-neck sweater to wear under his black academic gown.

Three and a half years had now passed since the cloud had finally left the Earth and the advertised title of his lecture was 'Humankind's First Contact With an Alien Life Form'.

In the front row of the Grand Hall sat Sally Burton – now Mrs William Duncan – who was relishing the public honour being bestowed on her husband, especially as it was being given by the Institute that had treated him so shabbily in the past.

Bill Duncan had finally decoded the signals that had appeared to be transmitted from the planet Iso and the similar signals that the cloud itself had generated.

'They were nothing but deliberate mathematical gobbledegook,' he told the packed and attentive audience in the hall. His work had already been published internationally and widely debated, but all present wanted the distinguished professor to tell them in his own words what he had discovered. 'And, as we now know, the signals from the cloud were Doppler-shifted to appear as if they emanated from the planet Iso. We also know that this was a deliberate ruse to tempt us – or any local civilizations like us – into responding.

'The cloud appears to be some sort of machine, a gigantic chemically based computer processor that is programmed to broadcast radio signals in the hope of eliciting a response – a response such as the one that we sent out to Iso over thirty years ago. A response that caused the cloud to home in directly on our planet.'

Also in the audience, sitting beside Sally Duncan, was Desmond Yates. He was no longer a White House space adviser. The presidential administration had now changed and Yates had declared himself unavailable for such duties. He was writing his memoirs.

'It is an evolutionary imperative that has given us an overwhelming and almost desperate anthropocentric desire to see the universe as a reflection of our own image,' continued Bill. 'But it is this need that has also led us to manufacture such dangerous, human-like computers, and it was this need that forced us to rush into beaming powerful radio responses back towards a planet that we fondly imagined to be populated by people quite like ourselves.'

In the front row, Des Yates hung his head. He'd spent many nights with Bill and Sally as they'd gone over and over the events that had led up to the cloud's arrival and he had accepted that, as a young man, he had been mistaken to urge the government of the day to respond to the signals he had discovered. But Bill had admitted that he too would have been almost certain to react in the same way. It was just human nature to want to communicate.

'We now have no option but to see the cloud as some sort of automatic space weapon,' Bill added. 'Although its response seems malevolent in the extreme, we must assume that the cloud's sole aim is to kill off any emerging biological species that develops to the point where it becomes capable of transmitting radio messages. Whether this aim was deliberately programmed into the giant chemical processor, or whether it was something that evolved independently, no one can tell. What we have learned, however, is that the word "alien" really means *alien*. We can no longer look towards the heavens with any optimism.'

He paused for a sip of water, then continued. 'It seems to me that the existence of this malevolent cloud of gas, and perhaps others like it, may well explain why, in over a century of searching, astronomers have never detected any radio signals that suggest the existence of intelligent life elsewhere in the galaxy – other than the decoy signals that the cloud itself generated. I think we may presume that any technological civilizations that have emerged in our sector of the universe have been quickly made extinct by a visitation from the cloud.

'In summary, I suggest that we may think of the cloud as a giant chemical computer processor that wanders the universe in a deadly quest to stamp out all biological life that exhibits any emergent technological capability.'

Bill allowed his chill words to settle on the audience. Then he stepped away from the lectern and turned to address directly the ranks of gowned academics who sat to one side of the hall.

'I have long warned that computers will themselves become an independent life form,' he told them. 'Unless we and the rest of the world's governments and scientific institutions act now, intelligent machines will become a new species that will challenge humans for dominance and ultimately become our successor species on this planet.'

In the front row, seated on the other side of Sally Duncan to Des Yates, Christine Cocoran clapped so enthusiastically that she forced the rest of the audience to join in. Bill Duncan's most loyal volunteer hacker had survived the nuclear attacks on the Japanese mainland. The bunker from which she had been directing her efforts to shut down the Japanese networks had itself been fully nuclear-attack-proof

– as had all of the other government and public bunkers in Japan; the nation's own history had required nothing less. Over six million people had emerged safely from Japanese shelters once radiation levels had started to subside.

Bill now lifted his head to address the whole room. 'I think the existence of the cloud – and there may be many more like it scattered around the universe – proves my point. Humankind has been given a glimpse of a wholly amoral machine future, a future that will become our own unless we all work to protect and uphold the unique rights of humankind.'

Once again, Christine led the enthusiastic clapping.